THESE[barcode: 10661654]
OF TH

—a Pennsylvania farmer's wife gives birth to a baby biosphere named Zenobia . . .

—a world where nothing is certain, not even the proposition $1 + 1 = 2$ . . .

—a police psychic sees all too clearly into the heart of darkness, but is blind to the shadow coming to claim him . . .

—a conquering race comes to the shocking revelation that it is they who have been invaded . . .

—a beautiful woman slips deeper into madness, becoming the demon that possesses her . . .

—a white man spends one dark South African night learning about racial equality and the Grand Unification Theory aboard a bus called "Grim Boy's Toe" . . .

plus seventeen other excursions into the realms of incredible fancy and terrifying truth that make up

FULL SPECTRUM 3

Other *Full Spectrum* Anthologies

FULL SPECTRUM
FULL SPECTRUM 2

Full Spectrum

3

EDITED BY

**Lou Aronica,
Amy Stout,
and Betsy Mitchell**

BANTAM BOOKS
NEW YORK • TORONTO • LONDON • SYDNEY • AUCKLAND

This edition contains the complete text
of the original hardcover edition.
NOT ONE WORD HAS BEEN OMITTED.

FULL SPECTRUM THREE

A Bantam Spectra Book / published in association with Doubleday

PRINTING HISTORY
Doubleday edition published June 1991
Bantam edition / June 1992

SPECTRA and the portrayal of a boxed "s" are trademarks of Bantam Books,
a division of Bantam Doubleday Dell Publishing Group, Inc.

Grateful acknowledgment is made to the following for permission to
reprint copyrighted material: The University of North Carolina Press
for excerpts from *Passage of Darkness: The Ethnobiology of the Haitian
Zombie* by E. Wade Davis, copyright © 1988 by E. Wade Davis.
Reprinted by permission.

ISBN 0-553-29191-2

Published simultaneously in the United States and Canada

Bantam Books are published by Bantam Books, a division of Bantam
Doubleday Dell Publishing Group, Inc. Its trademark, consisting of the
words "Bantam Books" and the portrayal of a rooster, is Registered in
U.S. Patent and Trademark Office and in other countries. Marca
Registrada. Bantam Books, 666 Fifth Avenue, New York, New York 10103.

ACKNOWLEDGMENTS

Introduction copyright © 1991 by Lou Aronica
"Daughter Earth" copyright © 1991 by James Morrow
"Dogstar Man" copyright © 1991 by Nancy Willard
"Prism Tree" copyright © 1991 by Tony Daniel
"Desert Rain" copyright © 1991 by Mark L. Van Name and Pat Murphy
"Precious Moments" copyright © 1991 by Kristine Kathryn Rusch
"Lethe" copyright © 1991 by Peg Kerr Ihinger
"Lake Agassiz" copyright © 1991 by Jack McDevitt
"Transfusion" copyright © 1988 by Joëlle Wintrebert
translation copyright © 1991 by Kim Stanley Robinson
"The Dark at the Corner of the Eye" copyright © 1991
by Patricia Anthony
"Tracking the Random Variable" copyright © 1991 by Marcos Donnelly
"Division by Zero" copyright © 1991 by Ted Chiang
"Matter's End" copyright © 1989 by Abbenford Associates
"Matter's End" was originally published by Cheap Street Press, Inc.
"Newton's Sleep" copyright © 1991 by Ursula K. Le Guin
"The Helping Hand" copyright © 1991 by Norman Spinrad
"Fondest of Memories" copyright © 1991 by Kevin J. Anderson
"Nekyomanteion" copyright © 1984 by Wolfgang Jeschke
"Loitering at Death's Door" copyright © 1990 of the English translation
from the German by Sally Schiller and Anne Calveley
"Rokuro" copyright © 1991 by Poul Anderson
"Police Actions" copyright © 1991 by Barry N. Malzberg
"Black Glass" copyright © 1991 by Karen Joy Fowler
"Chango Chingamadre, Dutchman, & Me" copyright © 1991
by R. V. Branham
"Apartheid, Superstrings, and Mordecai Thubana" copyright © 1991
by Michael Bishop
"Snow on Sugar Mountain" copyright © 1991 by Elizabeth Hand
"When the Rose Is Dead" copyright © 1991 by David Zindell

The editors gratefully acknowledge Jennifer Hershey's tremendous contributions toward putting this project together.

Contents

INTRODUCTION
Lou Aronica
xi

DAUGHTER EARTH
James Morrow
1

DOGSTAR MAN
Nancy Willard
20

PRISM TREE
Tony Daniel
33

DESERT RAIN
Mark L. Van Name and Pat Murphy
46

PRECIOUS MOMENTS
Kristine Kathryn Rusch
98

LETHE
Peg Kerr
116

LAKE AGASSIZ
Jack McDevitt
144

TRANSFUSION
Joëlle Wintrebert
Translated by Kim Stanley Robinson
159

THE DARK AT THE CORNER OF THE EYE
Patricia Anthony
166

TRACKING THE RANDOM VARIABLE
Marcos Donnelly
180

DIVISION BY ZERO
Ted Chiang
196

MATTER'S END
Gregory Benford
212

NEWTON'S SLEEP
Ursula K. Le Guin
251

THE HELPING HAND
Norman Spinrad
275

FONDEST OF MEMORIES
Kevin J. Anderson
287

LOITERING AT DEATH'S DOOR
Wolfgang Jeschke
Translated by Sally Schiller and Anne Calveley
294

ROKURO
Poul Anderson
323

POLICE ACTIONS
Barry N. Malzberg
334

BLACK GLASS
Karen Joy Fowler
344

CHANGO CHINGAMADRE, DUTCHMAN, & ME
R. V. Branham
380

APARTHEID, SUPERSTRINGS, AND MORDECAI THUBANA
Michael Bishop
393

SNOW ON SUGAR MOUNTAIN
Elizabeth Hand
463

WHEN THE ROSE IS DEAD
David Zindell
503

Introduction

LOU ARONICA

I RECENTLY FOUND MYSELF under circumstances where I needed to spend about six months without reading fantastic fiction of any kind. My job situation had changed and I needed to shore up my knowledge in other areas of fiction. The experience was a pleasurable one, much like going on a long journey where you see firsthand things you had only read about.

When I began to feel comfortable enough in my new job, I picked up a copy of a manuscript Betsy Mitchell had just finished editing. As I read it, I became rather more emotional than I was accustomed to being while reading. The metaphors, the imagination, the unabashed quest for the unknown, left me literally tingling. My choice for reentry had been well made, as this was a very good novel, but I realized that science fiction and fantasy could do something for me that no other form of literature could do. And I realized all over again how much I loved it.

You, of course, probably don't need to go through an exercise this extreme in order to understand the beauty of fantastic fiction. You have, after all, chosen to read a book with no unifying element at all other than the promise from three editors that the stories within represent excellence in this genre. That means you are open to the demands of variety and to the challenges writers present when they are stretching themselves. In other words, you are open to the fantastic fiction experience in its purest form. I can't promise you that we will give you that experience, only that we believe we will.

As was true with the first two volumes of this anthology series, *Full Spectrum 3* is our celebration of the genre that enriches us. There is no agenda here. We read hundreds of stories over the past year and a half, and have chosen these twenty-three as the best of that group. They represent quite a range: magic realism, hard sf, allegory, even a No play.

We have only one regret. In each of the first two volumes of this anthology, we published five writers who had never published fiction before. In *Full Spectrum 3*, there isn't a single story by a previously unpublished writer. We read some very good submissions, but none were at the level of the stories which are included here. I find this unfortunate, but I think it would have been more unfortunate to lower our standards in order to keep our record intact. Nevertheless, it is something we will seek to rectify in *Full Spectrum 4*.

Thank you for wanting to read this book.

—LOU ARONICA

Full Spectrum

Daughter Earth

JAMES MORROW

WE'D BEEN TRYING to have another child for over three years, carrying on like a couple from one of those movies you can rent by going behind the beaded curtain at Jake's Video, but it just wasn't working out. Logic, of course, says a second conception should prove no harder than a first. Hah. Mother Nature can be a sneaky old bitch, something we've learned from our twenty-odd years of farming down here in central Pennsylvania.

Maybe you've driven past us, Garber Farm, two miles outside of Boalsburg on Route 322. Raspberries in the summer, apples in the fall, Christmas trees in the winter, asparagus in the spring—that's us. The basset hound puppies appear all year round. We'll sell you one for three hundred dollars, guaranteed to love the children, chase rabbits out of the vegetable patch, and always appear burdened by troubles greater than yours.

We started feeling better after Dr. Borealis claimed he could make Polly's uterus "more hospitable to reproduction," as he put it. He prescribed vaginal suppositories, little nuggets of progesterone packed in cocoa butter. You store them in the refrigerator till you're ready to use one, and they melt in your wife the way sugar melts in your mouth.

That very month, we got pregnant.

So there we were, walking around with clouds under our feet. We kept remembering our son's first year out of the womb, that sense of power we'd felt, how we'd just gone ahead and thought him up and made him, by damn.

Time came for the amniocentesis. After putting Polly's belly to sleep, the ultrasound technician hooked her up to the TV monitor so Dr. Borealis could keep his syringe on target and make sure it didn't skewer the fetus. I liked Borealis. He reminded me of Norman Rockwell's painting of that tubby and fastidious old country doctor listening to the little girl's doll with his stethoscope.

Polly and I were hoping for a girl.

Thing was, the fetus wouldn't come into focus. Or, if it *was* in focus, it sure as hell didn't look like a fetus. I was awfully glad Polly couldn't see the TV.

"Glitch in the circuitry?" ventured the ultrasound technician, a tense and humorless youngster named Leo.

"Don't think so," muttered Borealis.

I used to be a center for my college basketball team, the Penn State Nittany Lions, and I'll be damned if our baby didn't look a great deal like a basketball.

Possibly a soccerball.

Polly said, "How is she?"

"Kind of round," I replied.

"Round, Ben? What do you mean?"

"Round," I said.

Borealis furrowed his brow, real deep ridges; you could've planted corn up there. "Now don't fret, Polly. You neither, Ben. If it's a tumor, it's probably benign."

"Round?" Polly said again.

"Round," I said again.

"Let's go for the juice anyway," the doctor told Leo the technician. "Maybe the lab can give us a line on this."

So Borealis inserted his syringe, and suddenly the TV showed the needle poking around next to our fetus like a dipstick somebody was trying to get back into a Chevy. The doctor went ahead as if he were doing a normal amnio, gently pricking the sac, though I could tell he hadn't made peace with the situation, and I was feeling pretty miserable myself.

"Round?" said Polly.

"Right," I said.

Later that month, I was standing in the apple orchard harvesting some Jonafrees—a former basketball center doesn't need a ladder—when Asa, our eleven-year-old redheaded Viking, ran over and told me Borealis was on the phone. "Mom's napping," my son explained. "Being knocked up sure makes you tired, huh?"

I got to the kitchen as fast as I could. I snapped up the receiver, my questions spilling out helter-skelter—would Polly be okay, what kind of pregnancy was this, were they planning to set things right with *in utero* surgery?

Borealis said, "First of all, Polly's CA-125 reading is only nine, so it's probably not a malignancy."

"Thank God."

"And the fetus's chromosome count is normal—forty-six on the money. The surprising thing is that she has chromosomes at all."

"She? It's a *she?*"

"We'd like to do some more ultrasounds."

"It's a *she?*"

"You bet, Ben. Two X chromosomes."

"Zenobia."

"Huh?"

"If we got a girl, we were going to name her Zenobia."

So we went back down to Boalsburg Gynecological. Borealis had called in three of his friends from the university: Gordon Hashigan, a spry old coot who held the Raymond Dart Chair in Physical Anthropology; Susan Croft, a stern-faced geneticist with a lisp; and Abner Logos, a skinny, devil-bearded epidemiologist who somehow found time to be Centre County's Public Health Commissioner. Polly and I remembered voting against him.

Leo the technician connected Polly to his machine, snapping more pictures than a Japanese extended family takes when it visits Epcot Center, and then the three professors huddled solemnly around the printouts, mumbling to each other through thin, tight lips. Ten minutes later, they called Borealis over.

The doctor rolled up the printouts, tucked them under his arm, and escorted Polly and me into his office—a nicer, better-smelling office than the one we'd set up in the basset barn back home. He seemed nervous and apologetic. Sweat covered his temples like dew on a toadstool.

Borealis unfurled an ultrasound, and we saw how totally different our baby was from other babies. It wasn't just that she was so much on the spherical side—no, the real surprise was her complexion.

"It's like one of those Earth shots the astronauts send back when they're heading toward the moon," Polly noted.

Borealis nodded. "Here we've got a kind of ocean, for example. And this thing is like a continent."

"What's this?" I asked, pointing to a white mass near the bottom.

"Ice cap on the southern pole," said Borealis. "We can do the procedure next Tuesday."

"Procedure?" said Polly.

The doctor appeared to be experiencing a nasty odor. "Polly, Ben, the simple fact is that I can't encourage you to bring this pregnancy to term. Those professors in the next room all agree."

My stomach churned sour milk.

"I thought the amnio was normal," said Polly.

"Try to understand," said Borealis. "This fetal tissue cannot be accurately labeled a baby."

"So what *do* you call it?" Polly demanded.

The doctor grimaced. "For the moment . . . a biosphere."

"A what?"

"Biosphere."

When Polly gets angry, she starts inflating—like a beach toy, or a puff adder, or a randy tree frog. "You're saying we can't give her a good home, is that it? Our *other* kid's turning out just fine. His project took second prize in the Centre County Science Fair."

"*Organic Control of Gypsy Moths,*" I explained.

Borealis issued one of his elaborate frowns. "You really imagine yourself giving birth to this material?"

"Uh-huh," said Polly.

"But it's a biosphere."

"So what?"

The doctor squinched his cherubic Norman Rockwell face. "There's no way it's going to fit through the canal," he snapped, as if that settled the matter.

"So we're looking at a cesarean, huh?" said Polly.

Borealis threw up his hands as if he were dealing with a couple of dumb crackers. People think that being a farmer means you're some sort of rube, though I've probably rented a lot more Ingmar Bergman videos than Borealis—with subtitles, not dubbed—and the newsletter we publish, *Down to Earth*, is a damned sight more literate than those *Pregnancy Pointers* brochures the doctor kept shoveling at us. "Here's my home number," he said, scribbling on his prescription pad. "Call me the minute anything happens."

The days slogged by. Polly kept swelling up with Zenobia, bigger and bigger, rounder and rounder, and by December she was so big and round she couldn't do anything except crank out the Christmas issue of *Down to Earth* on our Macintosh SE and waddle around the farm like the *Hindenburg* looking for New Jersey. And of course we couldn't have the expectant couple's usual fun of imagining a new baby in the house. Every time I stumbled into Zenobia's room and saw the crib and the changing table and the Cookie Monster's picture on the wall, my throat got tight as a stone. We cried a lot, Polly and me. We'd crawl into bed and hug each other and cry.

So it came as something of a relief when, one frosty March morning, the labor pains started. Borealis sounded pretty woozy when he answered the phone —it was 3 A.M.—but he woke up fast, evidently pleased at the idea of getting this biosphere business over with. I think he was counting on a stillbirth.

"The contractions—how far apart?"

"Five minutes," I said.

"Goodness, that close? The thing's really on its way."

"We don't refer to her as a thing," I corrected him, politely but firmly.

By the time we got Asa over to my parents' house, the contractions were only four minutes apart. Polly started her Lamaze breathing. Except for its being a cesarean this time, and a biosphere, everything happened just like when we'd had our boy: racing down to Boalsburg Memorial; standing around in the lobby while Polly panted like a hot collie and the computer checked into our insurance; riding the elevator up to the maternity ward with Polly in a wheelchair and me fidgeting at her side; getting into our hospital duds—white gown for Polly, green surgical smock and cap for me. So far, so good.

Borealis was already in the OR. He'd brought along a mere skeleton crew. The assistant surgeon had a crisp, hawkish face organized around a nose so narrow you could've opened your mail with it. The anesthesiologist had the kind of tanned, handsome, Mediterranean features you see on condom boxes. The pediatric nurse was a gangly, owl-eyed young woman with freckles and pigtails. "I told them we're anticipating an anomaly," Borealis said, nodding toward his team.

"We don't call her an anomaly," I informed the doctor.

They positioned me by Polly's head—she was awake, anesthetized from the diaphragm down—right behind the white curtain they use to keep cesarean mothers from seeing too much. Borealis and his sidekick got to work. Basically, it was like watching a reverse-motion movie of somebody stuffing a turkey; the doctor made his incision and started rummaging around, and a few minutes later he scooped out an object that looked like a Rand McNally globe covered with vanilla frosting and olive oil.

"She's *here*," I shouted to Polly. Even though Zenobia wasn't a regular child, some sort of fatherly instinct kicked in, and my skin went prickly all over. "Our baby's *here*," I gasped, tears rolling down my cheeks.

"Holy mackerel!" said the assistant surgeon.

"Jesus!" said the anesthesiologist. "Jesus Lord God in heaven!"

"What the fuck?" said the pediatric nurse. "She's a fucking *ball.*"

"Biosphere," Borealis admonished.

A loud, squishy, squalling noise filled the room: our little Zenobia, howling just like any other baby. "Is that her?" Polly wanted to know. "Is that *her* crying?"

"You bet it is, honey," I said.

Borealis handed Zenobia to the nurse and said, "Clean her up, Pam. Weigh her. All the usual."

The nurse said, "You've got to be fucking kidding."

"Clean her up," the doctor insisted.

Pam grabbed a sponge, dipped it into Zenobia's largest ocean, and began swabbing her northern hemisphere. Our child cooed and gurgled— and kept on cooing and gurgling as the nurse carried her across the room and set her on the scales.

"Nine pounds, six ounces," Pam announced.

"Ah, a *big* one," said Borealis, voice cracking. Zenobia, I could tell, had touched something deep inside him. His eyes were moist; the surgical lights twinkled in his tears. "Did you hear what a strong voice she has?" Now he worked on the placenta, carefully retrieving the soggy purple blob —it resembled a prop from one of those movies about zombie cannibals

Asa was always renting from Jake's Video—all the while studying it carefully, as if it might contain some clue to Zenobia's peculiar anatomy. "You got her circumference yet?" he called.

The nurse gave him an oh-brother look and ran her tape measure around our baby's equator. "Twenty-three and a half inches," she announced. I was impressed with the way Zenobia's oceans stayed on her surface instead of spilling onto the floor. I hadn't realized anybody that small could have so much gravity.

Now came the big moment. Pam wrapped Zenobia in a pink receiving blanket and brought her over, and we got our first really good look. Zenobia glowed. She smelled like ozone. She was swaddled in weather—in a wispy coating of clouds and mist. And what lovely mountains we glimpsed through the gaps in her atmosphere, what lush valleys, wondrous deserts, splendid plateaus, radiant lakes.

"She's *beautiful,*" said Polly.

"Beautiful," Borealis echoed.

"She's awfully blue," I said. "She getting enough oxygen?"

"I suspect that's normal," said the doctor. "All those oceans . . ."

Instinctively Polly opened her gown and, grasping Zenobia by two opposite archipelagos, pressed the north pole against her flesh. *"Eee-yyyowww,* that's cold," she wailed as the ice cap engulfed her. She pulled our biosphere away, colostrum dribbling from her nipple, her face fixed somewhere between a smile and a wince. "C-cold," she said as she restored Zenobia to her breast. "Brrrr, brrrr . . ."

"She's sucking?" asked Borealis excitedly. "She's actually taking it?"

I'd never seen Polly look happier. "Of *course* she's taking it. These are serious tits I've got. Brrrr . . ."

"This is shaping up to be an extremely weird day," said the assistant surgeon.

"I believe I'm going to be sick," the anesthesiologist announced.

Thinking back, I'm awfully glad I rented an infant car seat from Boalsburg Memorial and took the baby home that night. Sticking Zenobia in the nursery would have been a total disaster, with every gossip monger and freak seeker in Centre County crowding around like she were a two-headed calf at the Grange Fair. And I'm convinced that the five days I spent alone with her while Polly mended back at the hospital was vital to our father-daughter bond. Such rosy recollections I have of sitting in the front parlor, Zenobia snuggled in the crook of my arm, my body wrapped in a lime-green canvas tarp so her oceans wouldn't soak my shirt; how fondly I remember inserting the nipple of her plastic bottle into the mouthlike depression at her north pole and watching the Similac drain into her axis.

It was tough running the farm without Polly, but my parents pitched in, and even Asa stopped listening to The Apostolic Succession on his CD long enough to help us publish the April *Down to Earth*, the issue urging people to come out and pick their own asparagus. ("And remember, we add the rotenone only after the harvest has stopped, so there's no pesticide residue on the spears themselves.") In the lower right-hand corner we ran a message surrounded by a hot-pink border: WE ARE PLEASED TO ANNOUNCE THE BIRTH OF OUR DAUGHTER, ZENOBIA, A BIOSPHERE, ON MARCH 10TH . . . 9 POUNDS, 6 OUNCES . . . 23 1/2 INCHES.

My parents, God bless them, pretended not to notice Zenobia was the way she was. I still have the patchwork comforter Mom made her, each square showing an exotic animal promoting a different letter of the alphabet: A is for Aardvark, B is for Bontebok, Z is for Zebu. As for Dad, he kept insisting that, when his granddaughter got a bit older, he'd take her fishing on Parson's Pond, stringing her line from the peak of her highest mountain.

According to our child-rearing books, Asa should have been too mature for anything so crude and uncivil as sibling rivalry; after all, he and Zenobia were over a decade apart—eleven years, two months, and eight days, to be exact. No such luck. I'm thinking, for example, of the time Asa pried up one of Zenobia's glaciers with a shoehorn and used it to cool his root beer. And the time he befouled her Arctic ocean with a can of 3-in-One Lubricating Oil. And, worst of all, the time he shaved off her largest pine barren with a Bic disposable razor. "What the hell do you think you're *doing?*" I shrieked, full blast, which is not one of the responses recommended by Dr. Lionel Dubner in *The Self-Actualized Parent.* "I hate her!" Asa yelled back, a line right out of Dr. Dubner's chapter on Cain and Abel Syndrome. "I hate her, I hate her!"

Even when Zenobia wasn't being abused by her brother, she made a lot of noise—sharp, jagged wails that shot from her fault lines like volcanic debris. Often she became so fussy that nothing would do but for my parents to baby-sit Asa while we took her on a long drive up Route 322 to the top of Mount Skyhook, a windy plateau featuring Jake's Video, an acupuncture clinic, and a chiropodist on one side and the Milky Way Galaxy on the other.

"The minute our Landrover pulls within sight of the stars," I wrote in *Down to Earth*, "Zenobia always grows calm. We unbuckle her from the car seat," I told our readers, "and set her on the bluff, and immediately she begins rotating on her axis and making contented little clucking sounds, as if she somehow knows the stars are there—as if she senses them with her dark loamy skin."

Years later, I learned to my bewilderment that virtually everyone on our mailing list regarded the Zenobia bulletins in *Down to Earth* as unmitigated put-ons. The customers never believed anything we wrote about our baby, not one word.

Our most memorable visit to Mount Skyhook began with a series of meteor showers. Over and over, bright heavenly droplets shot across the sky, as if old Canis Major had just been given a bath and was shaking himself dry. "Fantastic," I said.

"Exquisite," said Polly.

"Zow-eee," said Zenobia.

My wife and I let out two perfectly synchronized gasps.

"Of course, it's really just junk, isn't it, Mommy?" our baby continued in a reedy and accelerated voice: the voice of an animated raccoon. "Trash from beyond the planets, hitting the air and burning up?"

"You can talk!" gushed Polly.

"I can talk," Zenobia agreed.

"Why didn't you *tell* us?" I demanded.

Our baby spun, showing us the eastern face of her northern hemisphere. "When talking starts, things get . . . well, complicated, right? I prefer simplicity." Zenobia sounded as if she were speaking through an electric fan. "Gosh, but I love it up here. See those stars, Daddy? They pull at me, know what I mean? They want me."

At which point I noticed my daughter was airborne, floating two feet off the ground like an expiring helium balloon.

"Be careful," I said. "You might . . ."

"What?"

"Fall into the sky."

"You bet, Daddy. I'll be careful." Awash in moonlight, Zenobia's clouds emitted a deep golden glow. Her voice grew soft and dreamy. "The universe, it's a lonely place. It's full of orphans. But the lucky ones find homes." Our baby eased herself back onto the bluff. "I was a lucky one."

"*We* were the lucky ones," said Polly.

"Your mother and I think the world of you," I said.

A sigh escaped from our baby's north pole like water vapor whistling out of a teakettle. "I get so scared sometimes."

"Don't be scared," I said, kicking a rock into the valley.

Zenobia swiveled her Africa equivalent toward Venus. "I keep thinking about . . . history, it's called. Moses's parents, Amram and Jochebed. They took their baby, and they set him adrift." She stopped spinning. Her glaciers sparkled in the moonlight. "I keep thinking about that, and how it was so necessary."

"We'll never set you adrift," said Polly.

"Never," I echoed.

"It was so necessary," said Zenobia in her high, sad voice.

On the evening of Asa's twelfth birthday, Borealis telephoned wanting to know how the baby was doing. I told him she'd reached a circumference of thirty-one inches, but it soon became clear the man wasn't out for an ordinary chat. He wanted to drop by with Hashigan, Croft, and Logos.

"What'll they do to her?" I asked.

"They'll look at her."

"What else?"

"They'll look, that's all."

I snorted and said, "You'll be just in time for birthday cake," though the fact was I didn't want any of those big shots gawking at our baby, not for a minute.

As it turned out, only Borealis had a piece of Asa's cake. His three pals were hyperserious types, entirely dismayed by the idea of eating from cardboard Apostolic Succession plates. They arrived brimming with tools —with stethoscopes and oscilloscopes, thermometers and spectrometers, with Geiger counters, brainwave monitors, syringes, tweezers, and scalpels. On first seeing Zenobia asleep in her crib, the four doctors gasped in four different registers, like a barbershop quartet experiencing an epiphany.

Hashigan told us Zenobia was "probably the most important find since the Taung fossil." Croft praised us for keeping the *National Enquirer* and related media out of the picture. Logos insisted that, according to something called the Theory of Transcendental Mutation, a human-gestated biosphere was "bound to appear sooner or later." There was an equation for it.

They poked and probed and prodded our baby; they biopsied her crust. They took water samples, oil specimens, jungle cuttings, and a half-dozen pinches of desert, sealing each trophy in an airtight canister.

"We need to make sure she's not harboring any lethal pathogens," Logos explained.

"She's never even had roseola," Polly replied defensively. "She's never even had cradle cap."

"Indeed," said Logos, locking my baby's exudations in his briefcase.

"All during this rude assault," I wrote in the November *Down to Earth,* "Zenobia made no sound. I suspect she wants them to think she's just a big dumb rock."

Now that such obviously important folks had shown an interest in our biosphere, Asa's attitude began to change. Zenobia was no longer his grotesque little sister. Far from being a bothersome twit, she was potentially the greatest hobby since baseball cards.

All Asa wanted for Christmas was a Johnny Genius Microscope Kit and some theatrical floodlights, and we soon learned why. He suspended the lights over Zenobia's crib, set up the microscope, and got to work, scrutinizing his baby sister with all the intensity of Louis Pasteur on the trail of rabies. He kept a detailed log of the changes he observed: the exuberant flowering of Zenobia's rain forests, the languid waltz of her continental plates, the ebb and flow of her ice shelves—and, most astonishingly, the abrupt appearance of phosphorescent fish and strange aquatic lizards in her seas.

"She's got fish!" Asa shrieked, running through the house. "Mom! Dad! Zenobia's got lizards and fish!"

"Whether our baby's life-forms have arisen spontaneously," we told the readers of *Down to Earth,* "or through some agency outside her bounds, is a question we are not yet prepared to answer."

Within a month our son had, in true scientific fashion, devised a hypothesis to account for Zenobia's physiognomy. According to Asa, events on his sister were directly connected to the atmosphere around Garber Farm.

And he was right. Whenever Polly and I allowed one of our quarrels to degenerate into cold silence, Zenobia's fish stopped flashing and her glaciers migrated toward her equator. Whenever our dicey finances plunged us into a dark mood, a cloak of moist, gray fog would enshroud Zenobia for hours. Angry words, such as Polly and I employed in persuading Asa to clean his room, made our baby's oceans bubble and seethe like abandoned soup on a hot stove.

"For Zenobia's sake, we've resolved to keep our household as tranquil as possible," we wrote in *Down to Earth.* "We've promised to be nice to each other. It seems immoral, somehow, to bind a biosphere to anything so chancy as the emotional ups and downs of an American family."

Although we should have interpreted our daughter's fish and lizards as harbingers of things to come, the arrival of the dinosaurs still took us by surprise. But there they were, actual Jurassic dinosaurs, thousands of them, galumphing around on Zenobia like she was a remake of *King Kong*. How we loved to watch the primordial drama now unfolding at the far end of Asa's microscope: fierce tyrannosaurs pouncing on their prey, flocks of pterodactyls floating through her troposphere like organic 747's (though they were not truly dinosaurs, Asa explained), herds of amiable duckbills sauntering through our baby's marshes. This was the supreme science project, the ultimate electric train set, a flea circus directed by Cecil B. DeMille.

"I'm worried about her," Asa told me a month after Zenobia's dinosaurs evolved. "The pH of her precipitation is 4.2 when it should be 5.6."

"Huh?"

"It should be 5.6."

"What are you talking about?"

"I'm talking about acid rain, Dad. I'm talking about Zenobia's lakes becoming as dead as the moon."

"Acid rain?" I said. "How could that be? She doesn't even have people."

"I know, Dad, but *we* do."

"Sad news," I wrote in *Down to Earth*. "Maybe if Asa hadn't been away at Computer Camp, things would have gone differently."

It was the Fourth of July. We'd invited a bunch of families over for a combination potluck supper and volleyball tournament in the north pasture, and the farm was soon swarming with bored, itchy children. I suspect that a gang of them wandered into the baby's room and, mistaking her for some sort of strange toy, carried her outside. At this point, evidently, the children got an idea. A foolish, perverse, wicked idea.

They got the idea of bringing Zenobia into the basset barn.

The awful noise—a blend of kids laughing, hounds baying, and a biosphere screaming—brought Polly and me on the run. My first impression was of some bizarre and incomprehensible athletic event, a sport played in hell or in the fantasies of an opium eater. Then I saw the truth: the dogs had captured our daughter. Yes, there they were, five bitches and a dozen pups, clumsily batting her around the barn with their snouts, oafishly pinning her under their paws. They scratched her ice caps, chewed on her islands, lapped up her oceans.

"Daddy, get them off me!" Zenobia cried, rolling amid the clouds of dust and straw. "Get them off!"

"Help her!" screamed Polly.

"Mommy! Daddy!"

I jumped into the drooling dogpile, punching the animals in their noses, knocking them aside with my knees. Somehow I got my hands around the baby's equator, and with a sudden tug I freed her from the mass of soggy fur and slavering tongues. Pressing her against my chest, I ran blindly from the barn.

Tooth marks dotted Zenobia's terrain like meteor craters. Her largest continent was fractured in five places. Her crust leaked crude oil, her mountains vomited lava.

But the worst of it was our daughter's unshakable realization that a great loss had occurred. "Where are my dinosaurs?" she shrieked. "I can't feel my dinosaurs!"

"There, there, Zenobia," I said.

"They'll be okay," said Polly.

"They're g-gone," wailed Zenobia. "Oh, dear, oh, dear, they're *gone!*"

I rushed the baby into the nursery and positioned her under Asa's rig. An extinction: true, all horribly true. Zenobia's swamps were empty; her savannas were bereft of prehistoric life; not a single vertebrate scurried through her forests.

She was inconsolable. "My brontosaurs," she groaned. "Where are my brontosaurs? Where *are* they?"

Mowed down, pulverized, flung into space.

"There, there, darling," said Polly. "There, there."

"I want them back."

"There, there," said Polly.

"I miss them."

"There, there."

"Make them come back."

The night Asa returned from camp, Borealis and his buddy Logos dropped by, just in time for a slice of Garber Farm's famous raspberry pie. Borealis looked sheepish and fretful. "My friend has something to tell you," he said. "A kind of proposal."

Having consumed an entire jar of Beech-Nut strained sweet potatoes and two bottles of Similac, the baby was in bed for the night. Her flute-like snores wafted into the kitchen as Polly and Asa served our guests.

Logos sat down, resting his spindly hands on the red-and-white checkerboard oilcloth as if trying to levitate the table. "Ben, Polly, I'll begin by saying I'm not a religious man. Not the sort of man who's inclined to believe in God. But . . ."

"Yes?" said Polly, raising her eyebrows in a frank display of mistrust.

"But I can't shake my conviction that this Zenobia has been . . . well, *sent.* I feel that Providence has deposited her in our laps."

"She was deposited in *my* lap," Polly corrected him. "My lap and Ben's."

"I think it was the progesterone suppositories," I said.

"Did you ever hear how, in the old days, coal miners used to take canaries down into the shaft with them?" said Logos, forking a gluey clump of raspberries into his mouth. "When the canary started squawking, or stopped singing, or fell to the bottom of the cage and died, the men knew poison gases were leaking into the mine." The health commissioner devoured the pie in a half-dozen bites. "Well, Ben and Polly, it seems to me your Zenobia is like that. It seems to me God has given us a canary."

"She's a biosphere," said Asa.

Without asking, Logos slashed into the pie, excising a fresh piece. "I've been on the horn to Washington all week, and I must say the news is very, very good. Ready, Ben—ready, Polly?" The commissioner cast a twinkling eye on our boy. "Ready, son? Get this." He gestured as if fanning open a stack of money. "The Department of the Interior is prepared to pay you three hundred thousand dollars—that's three hundred thousand, cash—for Zenobia."

"What are you talking about?" I asked.

"I'm talking about buying that little canary of yours for three hundred thousand bucks."

"*Buying* her?" said my wife, inflating. Polly the puff adder, Polly the randy tree frog.

"She's the environmental simulacrum we've always wanted," said Logos. "With Zenobia, we can convincingly model the long-term effects of fluorocarbons, nitrous oxide, mercury, methane, chlorine, and lead. For the first time, we can study the impact of deforestation and ozone depletion without ever leaving the lab."

Polly and I stared at each other, making vows with our eyes. We were patriotic Americans, my wife and me, but nobody was going to deplete our baby's ozone, not even the President of the United States himself.

"Look at it this way," said Borealis; he gripped his coffee mug with one hand, tugged anxiously at the kitchen curtains with the other. "If scientists can finally offer an irrefutable scenario of ecological collapse, then the world's governments may really start listening, and Asa here will get to grow up on a safer, cleaner planet. Everybody benefits."

"Zenobia doesn't benefit," said Polly.

Borealis slurped coffee. "Yes, but there's a greater good here, right, folks?"

"She's just a *globe*, for Christ's sake," said Logos.

"She's our globe," I said.

"Our baby," said Polly.

"My sister," said Asa.

Logos massaged his beard. "Look, I hate to play hardball with nice people like you, but you don't really have a choice here. Our test results are in, and the fact is that this biosphere of yours is harboring a maverick form of the simian T-lymphotrophic retrovirus. As County Health Commissioner, I have the authority to remove the creature from these premises forthwith and quarantine it."

" 'The fact is,' " I snorted, echoing Logos. " 'The fact is'—*the fact is,* our baby couldn't give my great Aunt Jennifer a bad cold." I shot a glance at Borealis. "Am I right?"

The doctor said, "Well . . ."

Logos grunted like one of the pigs we used to raise before the market went soft.

"I think you gentlemen had better leave," my wife suggested icily.

"We have a barn full of *dogs,*" said Asa in a tone at once cheerful and menacing. "Mean ones," he added with a quick little nod.

"I'll be back," said the commissioner, rising. "Tomorrow. And I won't be alone."

"Bastard," said Polly—the first time I'd ever heard her use that word.

So we did what we had to do; like Amram and Jochebed, we did what was necessary. Polly drove. I brooded. All the way up Route 322, Zenobia sat motionless in the back, safely buckled into her car seat, moaning and whimpering. Occasionally Asa leaned over and gently ran his hairbrush through the jungles of her southern hemisphere.

"Gorgeous sky tonight," I observed, unhooking our baby and carrying her into the crisp September darkness.

"I see that." Zenobia fought to keep her voice in one piece.

"I hate this," I said, marching toward the bluff. My guts were as cold and hard as one of Zenobia's glaciers. "Hate it, hate it . . ."

"It's necessary," she said.

We spent the next twenty minutes picking out constellations. Brave Orion; royal Cassiopeia; snarly old Ursa Major; the Big Dipper with its bowlful of galactic dust. Asa stayed by the Landrover, digging his heel into the dirt and refusing to join us, even though he knew ten times more astronomy than the rest of us.

"Let's get it over with," said our baby.

"No," said Polly. "We have all night."

"It won't be any easier in an hour."

"Let me hold her," said Asa, shuffling onto the bluff.

He took his sister, raised her toward the flickering sky. He whispered to her—statistical bits that made no sense to me, odd talk of sea levels, hydrogen ions, and solar infrared. I passed the time staring at Jake's Video, its windows papered with ads for Joe Dante's remake of *The War of the Worlds*.

The boy choked down a sob. "Here," he said, pivoting toward me. "You do it."

Gently I slid the biosphere from my son. Hugging Zenobia tightly, I kissed her most arid desert as Polly stroked her equator. Zenobia wept, her arroyos, wadis, and flood plains filling with tears. I stretched out my arms as far as they would go, lifting our daughter high above my head.

Once and only once in my days on the courts did I ever hit a three-pointer.

"We'll miss you," I told Zenobia. She felt weightless, airy, as if she were a hollow glass ornament from a Garber Farm Christmas tree. It was just as she'd said: the stars wanted her. They tugged at her blood.

"We love you," groaned Polly.

"Daddy!" Zenobia called from her lofty perch. Her tears splashed my face like raindrops. "Mommy!" she wailed. "Asa!"

In a quick, flashy spasm I made my throw. A good one—straight and smooth. Zenobia flew soundlessly from my fingertips.

"Bye-bye!" the three of us shouted as she soared into the bright, beckoning night. We waved furiously, maniacally, as if hoping to generate enough turbulence to pull her back to central Pennsylvania. "Bye-bye, Zenobia!"

"Bye-bye!" our baby called from out of the speckled darkness, and she was gone.

The Earth turned—once, twice. Raspberries, apples, Christmas trees, asparagus, basset pups—each crop made its demands, and by staying busy we stayed sane.

One morning during the height of raspberry season I was supervising our roadside fruit stand and chatting with one of our regulars—Lucy Berens, Asa's former third-grade teacher—when Polly rushed over. She looked crazed and pleased. Her eyes expanded like domes of bubble gum emerging from Asa's mouth.

She told me she'd just tried printing out a *Down to Earth*, only the ImageWriter II had delivered something else entirely. "Here," she said, shoving a piece of computer paper in my face, its edges embroidered with sprocket holes.

Dear Mom and Dad:

This is being transmitted via a superluminal wave generated by nonlocal quantum correlations. You won't be able to write back.

I have finally found a proper place for myself, two light-years from Garber Farm. In my winter, I can see your star. Your system is part of a constellation that looks to me like a Zebu. Z is for Zebu, remember? I am happy.

Big news. A year ago, various mammalian lines—tree shrews, mostly—emerged from those few feeble survivors of the Fourth of July catastrophe. And then, last month, I acquired—are you ready?—people. That's right, people. Human beings, sentient primates, creatures entirely like yourselves. God, but they're clever: cars, deodorants, polyvinyl chlorides, all of it. I like them. They're brighter than the dinosaurs, and they have a certain spirituality. In short, they're almost worthy of being what they are: your grandchildren.

Every day, my people look out across the heavens, and their gaze comes to rest on Earth. Thanks to Asa, I can explain to them what they're seeing, all the folly and waste, the way your whole planet's becoming a cesspool. So tell my brother he's saved my life. And tell him to study hard—he'll be a great scientist when he grows up.

Mom and Dad, I think of you every day. I hope you're doing well, and that Garber Farm is prospering. Give Asa a kiss for me.

All my love,
ZENOBIA

"A letter from our daughter," I explained to Lucy Berens.

"Didn't know you had one," said Lucy, snatching up an aluminum pail so she could go pick a quart of raspberries.

"She's far away," said Polly.

"She's happy," I said.

That night, we went into Asa's room while he was practicing on his trap set, thumping along with The Apostolic Succession. He shut off the CD, put down his drumsticks, and read Zenobia's letter—slowly, solemnly. He yawned and slipped the letter into his math book. He told us he was going to bed. Fourteen: a moody age.

"You saved her life?" I said. "What does she mean?"

"You don't get it?"

"Uh-uh."

Our son drummed a paradiddle on his math book. "Remember what Dr. Logos said about those coal miners? Remember when he said Zenobia was like a canary? Well, obviously he got it backwards. My sister's not the canary—*we* are. *Earth* is."

"Huh?" said Polly.

"We're Zenobia's canary," said Asa.

We kissed our son, left his room, closed the door. The hallway was papered over with his treasures—with MISS PIGGY FOR PRESIDENT posters, rock star portraits, and lobby cards from the various environmental apocalypses he'd been renting regularly from Jake's Video: *Silent Running, Soylent Green, Frogs* . . .

"We're Zenobia's canary," said Polly.

"Is it too late for us, then?" I asked.

My wife didn't answer.

You've heard the rest. How Dr. Borealis knew somebody who knew somebody, and suddenly we were seeing Senator Caracalla on C-Span, reading the last twelve issues of *Down to Earth,* the whole story of Zenobia's year among us, into *The Congressional Record.*

Remember what President Tait told the newspapers the day he signed the Caracalla Conservation Act into law? "Sometimes all you need is a pertinent parable," he said. "Sometimes all you need is the right metaphor," our Chief Executive informed us.

The Earth is not our mother.

Quite the opposite.

That particular night, however, standing outside Asa's room, Polly and I weren't thinking about metaphors. We were thinking about how much we wanted Zenobia back. We're pretty good parents, Polly and I. Look at our kids.

We winked at each other, tiptoed down the hall, and climbed into bed. Our bodies pressed together, and we laughed out loud. I've always loved my wife's smell; she's like some big floppy mushroom you came across in the woods when you were six years old, all sweet and damp and forbidden. We kept on pressing, and it kept feeling better and better. We were hoping for another girl.

Dogstar Man

NANCY WILLARD

WHEN I WAS TWELVE YEARS OLD, my father, who rarely touched anything stronger than Seven-Up, got mildly drunk with a man named Olaf Starr who kept a dog team. This happened in Madison, Wisconsin, where I grew up. My father, Carl Theophilus, owned the Treble and Bass Music Store there. Maybe you've heard of it. The store carried accordions, drums, trumpets, harmonicas, guitars, pitch pipes, tambourines, and sheet music. Five free lessons came with all the instruments, except the harmonica, and my father built a tiny soundproof practice room in the back. Saturday mornings a boy from Madison High School came to give the free lessons to languid young girls, who emerged from the practice room sweaty and bright-eyed, all of them promising to practice. My father also repaired instruments. By the time I was in high school, he'd sold the business and was doing repairs full time and making lutes, dulcimers, and Irish harps on commission.

He kept shelves of exotic woods, rosewood and purple heart, teak and lignum vitae. One man ordered a guitar made of lignum vitae for his son, who played in a rock band and smashed his instrument every night, but by God, he wouldn't be smashing this one. Mainly my father stocked the commoner varieties, basswood and oak and black cherry and ash, which he used for the curved bodies of the lutes and the harps. He also had a few odd pieces of golden chinkapin and water tupulo, hornbeam and hackleberry, for which there wasn't much demand except when he did inlay work on the sound holes of the lutes. You never knew, he said, what a customer would ask for. He wouldn't work with ivory, out of respect for the elephants, though he has always loved Chinese ivory carvings, especially those that keep the shape of the tusk. I believe there's not a book on Asian art in the Madison public library that my father hasn't checked out.

Olaf Starr lived outside of Madison on land that his father had once farmed. All the Starr Cheese in Wisconsin was made there, and it was a big business in the thirties and forties. That ended when Olaf took over. Forty years later, when I was growing up, the house was gone and the barn that stood in the north acre was in ruins; snow had caved in the roof, leaving a confusion of broken timber in its wake that made me feel I was peering into the stomach of a vast beast. The windows of the stable were broken, and stars winked through the holes left by shingles that had blown or rotted off. Over the stalls, you could still read the names of horses: Beauty; Misty; Athena. Behind the stable, Olaf Starr parked his pickup truck.

On the south acre, Olaf had built himself a log cabin and a dog yard, with seven small cabins, low to the ground, for his dogs. After a heavy snowfall, he would hitch them up and drive to a general store just in town. No one else in Madison drove a dogsled. Mornings when I went out cross-country skiing on the golf course behind our house, I might catch a glimpse of him on the horizon, his dogs strung out in a thin line, like Christmas lights, with Olaf Starr standing on the back runners of the sled. I called him the dogstar man, and I half expected to see him drive into the heavens. He was a big man, with white hair, who carried a knapsack and wore the same Levi's, suspenders, down jacket and boots, day after day, shedding the jacket in summer, resurrecting it at the first snowfall.

My father said that the dogstar man's wife had left long ago for a more comfortable life of her own, so during the one night I spent at the cabin I never met or saw any evidence of her. I was in sixth grade and trying to write a report on cheese as part of a unit on agriculture. I did not like agriculture, which was a vast general thing. You could not put anything in the report about how cows look, standing in a rolling field, though that is so important it should come first. From far away, they look like ciphers that someone has written with a thick brown pen, and I wished I could write my whole report using the ponderous alphabet of cows. And you could not put in anything about the hiss of milk in the pail, or the salt licks that rise in the fields like dolmens or ancient shrines, and you could not put in the peculiar appetites of goats for wind-dried bedsheets on the line and children's sunsuits and anything scented with human use.

So I asked the teacher, Mrs. Hanson, if I could write a story about cheese, and she said, yes, but it could not be a fairy tale. The cheese must not talk or sing or dance or have adventures. The story must be about how cheese is made. I could write that story.

I did not know the first thing about how cheese is made. My father told me to go to the library and find a book that would tell me. But my mother said, "Go and watch somebody making it. That's better than a book." My father agreed and suggested I call the Wisconsin Wilderness processing plant to see if they gave tours.

Suddenly my parents had the same thought at the same time and said almost in unison,

"Olaf Starr makes cheese. He'd be glad to show you."

The dogstar man had no phone, so on Saturday afternoon my father drove out to the farm. Ten inches of snow had fallen a week ago, and the cold had kept it on the ground, though the main roads were clear. My father turned off I-90 and took the road less traveled. The dogsled track cut a deep ribbon across the white fields on either side of us, and where the road ended at the broken barn and we got out of the car, the sled track disappeared into a pine woods.

You could hear the dogs yapping and yelping. A hundred seemed a modest estimate.

"We should've brought our skis," said my father.

That would have been far easier than walking in, which took us twice as long. I'd seen the outside of the dogstar man's house in summer but not in winter, and I'd never seen the inside.

In the dog yard, seven hounds sat on the roofs of their houses and barked at us, and the hair on my neck prickled in a primitive response to danger.

"They're tied," said my father.

Only when I saw that they could not spring far from the stakes to which they were leashed did I begin to savor the adventure of doing something entirely new. I thought of our yard, so small and neat that when my mother bought two metal lawn chairs and a patio umbrella, my father complained of the clutter. The dogstar man's yard was a sprawl of empty cable spools, old oil drums, ropes, ski poles, harnesses and the dogsled itself, which hung from a row of pegs on the cabin wall. The grass on the sod roof was blond.

The dogstar man, hearing the racket, opened the door. He knew my father as a man who ordered firewood from him; he was surprised to see both of us on his doorstep. His face remained perfectly impassive as my father explained our errand while I stared at Olaf Starr with the greatest interest, as if I were examining a hawk or an otter, some wild creature always seen in motion and from a distance.

A brief silence marked the end of my father's speech, and when the dogstar man was quite certain it *was* the end, he nodded and motioned us into his house. It was not so much a house as a lair, a den, that an animal might make and stock with all that instinct told him would carry him through the winter. Firewood was stacked solid against one wall. Against the opposite wall stood five fifty-gallon drums of water, a shelf of dishes and crocks and large cooking pots, a treadle sewing machine, and a dozen huge bags of dog food.

From under the four burners on the surface of the wood stove shone a thin rim of fire. The flame in the oil lamp on the table danced in its glass chimney with such shifting brilliance that the air in the cabin seemed to be alive and breathing, steadily and quietly.

My father and I drew two stools up to the table.

The dogstar man took down a large crock and set it on the table between us.

"The secret of cheese is patience," he said. "Cheese has taught me everything I know about life."

He set three spoons and three brass bowls of different sizes on the table.

"I traded a year's supply of firewood to a professor at the university for these. And when I got them home, I made a discovery. Listen."

He brushed his hand over the rim of the largest and a deep hum filled the room. He brushed the smallest and a higher hum, a fifth above the first, spun out of it. He brushed the last bowl, and it sent forth a note that completed the triad. But if I say the bowls hummed, I do not tell you *how* they hummed. Not like a cat or a spinning wheel, but like a planet whirling down the dark aisles of the galaxy.

"The best way to make cheese is, put it in singing bowls," said the dogstar man. "This is also the best way to eat it."

He dipped a spoon into the crock and began to ladle cottage cheese from the crock into the bowls.

"Also," he said, "the voice of the bowls quiets the dogs."

My father, astonished into silence by all these marvels, found his voice.

"But these are singing bowls from Tibet," he exclaimed. "I'm sure they're worth a good deal of money. If you ever want to sell them, come to me with a price."

"But I won't sell them," said the dogstar man. "I'll trade them for something I need."

"What do you need?" asked my father.

"Nothing now," he said, "but next week, dog food. I buy dog food by the ton. Ground barley is good," he mused, "and fish meal."

He spooned cottage cheese from the crock into the bowls.

"When I was at the university, I didn't study at all."

"You went to the university?" exclaimed my father.

"For one year, in 1927. And when my father asked me what I was majoring in I told him I wanted to major in philosophy. Philosophy! He didn't understand about philosophy. I told him that philosophers consider problems of time and what is the true good. I told him it was like majoring in cheese; something solid emerges from what is thin and without definition."

The whole of our visit, he talked and talked—and not one word about how to make cheese. The next day my mother took me to the public library where the Encyclopaedia Britannica revealed to me the secret of making cheese. In my report, I mentioned rennet and casein. I did not mention singing bowls, and I did not write a story. I got my report back with praise from Mrs. Hanson written across the top: *Good work, Sam! You put in a lot of information and you stuck to your subject.*

The next afternoon the dogstar man appeared in my father's music store. He admired the guitars, the accordions, the new shipment of tambourines, and asked him if he could make a whistle that the dogs could hear from a great distance.

"How great a distance?" asked my father.

The dogstar man opened his pack, drew out a map of the United States, and spread it out on the counter.

"Here," he said. "I'm planning to visit my sister, and I want my dogs to know I'm thinking of them."

And he put his thumb down on the whole state of Florida.

In three days, my father finished the whistle, and the dogstar man drew from his pack the largest singing bowl and gave it to him. It was as if an honored guest had moved in with us. My father made a little house for the bowl to sit in, a replica of a Tibetan spirit house, he said. This he put on top of the china cabinet. Once a day the bowl was played. Sometimes my mother played it, sometimes I played it, and sometimes he played it himself. Often I dreamed of whales singing, a music I did not yet know existed.

A week later the dogstar man returned and said he wanted to exchange the whistle that called dogs for one that called birds. So many of the birds he loved had gone south. He wanted to let them know he'd welcome them back any time, if the warm countries weren't to their liking.

"Why did you tell me to make a whistle that calls dogs if you wanted one that calls birds?" asked my father.

The dogstar man was interested in more practical questions.

"Can you fix it so it will call both?"

My father said he would try. He added a section of wingwood with a dovetail joint that was nearly invisible, and the dogstar man was very pleased and said it was exactly what he wanted. He reached into his knapsack and pulled out the medium-sized singing bowl. My father closed the shop and carried it home at once and nested it in the other bowl, in the little spirit house.

The bowls were not beautiful but they were immensely present, and when we ate in the dining room we were always aware of them, and we did not complain about the cold weather or who should have taken out the garbage the night before. No, we were pleasant to one another, in the way that people are pleasant before a guest or stranger to whom they wish to show their best side.

A postcard arrived from Paradise, Florida, showing the roseate spoonbill in glorious flight. The dogstar man's message was brief: "It works!"

Three days before Christmas, the dogstar man appeared again, holding the whistle.

"This whistle," he said. "I wonder if you could fix it."

"In what way is it broken?" asked my father.

"It's not broken," the dogstar man assured him. "I just wonder if you could improve it."

"Improve it?"

"I was wondering," said the dogstar man, "if you could fix it so it would call stars."

"Stars!"

"I thought I'd get me in some ice fishing. The fish do like clear nights best."

My father took the whistle back. The section he added this time was purely ornamental. He cut it from coral, which has no resonating properties, and he vowed to go the dogstar man one better. He added a link of hornbeam, on which young stags love to rub their budding antlers; and a link of alder, which beavers prefer above all other trees for building dams; and a link of mulberry, whose small dark fruit the wood mouse loves. He did not cut these links into simple rings but joined them in interlocking shapes, pieced with bits of shell and horn, bone and silver.

On a Saturday morning, when I was helping my father put new price stickers on the sheet music, the dogstar man arrived, and my father gave him the improved whistle and waited for some sign of praise, a whistle of admiration, perhaps.

But the dogstar man said nothing about my father's exquisite workmanship. He tucked the whistle into his breast pocket and reached into his knapsack and took out the smallest singing bowl and set it on the counter.

Then he looked at me and said,

"Do you like books?"

"Sure," I said. I never say no to a book.

Out of his knapsack he pulled a volume bound in leather softer than the chamois my father used to polish the violins. When he put it into my hands, I felt he had just given me a small animal seldom seen and beautiful to the blind who see with their fingers.

I opened it to the title page: *Palmer Cox's Juvenile Budget, Containing Queer People with Paws, Claws, Wings, Stings, and Others Without Either.*

"This book was mine when I was your age," he said. "Merry Christmas."

I flipped through the book and thought, What a god-awful present. The stories, all of them in poetry and small print, were crammed on the yellowing pages, and the illustrations, done in scratchy pen and ink, crowded into the text as best they could. Still, I was the kind of kid who would read anything, and I knew I would have a go at the *Juvenile Budget*. But I could not say it gladdened my heart.

"Thank you," I said.

My father had the habit of carrying the spirit house, with its nested singing bowls, from room to room, to keep them near him. On Christmas Eve he put them on the mantel to watch over the tree. Of course I did not believe in Santa Claus, but I played the game and so did my mother and father. Growing up is watching faith descend to the level of a beloved ritual.

At nine o'clock I put my two presents under the tree: a Sheaffer pen, which I bought at the drugstore, and a pillow with the name Jerry Garcia embroidered on it, which I made in school after the principal went to a conference on new trends in education and became convinced that boys should take home ec for one semester while the girls took shop. I was not convinced. I would never make one of those sleek, useful projects the teacher recommended. I would not even make a pattern. The pillow turned out to be the size of an overgrown pincushion, nothing you'd choose to sit on, unless you had hemorrhoids. I knew Mother would love it because it looked handmade.

The card said, "For Mother and Father," as the pen and pillow were suitable for both.

At ten o'clock, when I announced I was going up to bed, so as not to displease Santa, my mother looked relieved. She had all the presents to wrap yet. I hung my stocking under the singing bowls and was halfway up the stairs when the doorbell rang and the door, which was unlocked, burst open.

The dogstar man filled the front hall with his enthusiasm. He'd spent the day ice fishing on Waubesa Lake. He'd pulled from the still, chill bottom of the lake three bass, two trout, a sunfish, and a pike, and he was the first person in the county to catch a two-point buck with a fishhook. He'd brought in enough meat to feed himself the rest of the winter.

He pulled out a bottle of schnapps and presented it to my father and lingered, waiting for him to open it.

I could not possibly go to bed now. I might miss something.

My father and the dogstar man sat down at the dining room table and drank. That is to say, the dogstar man drank a lot and my father nursed a single shot glass, which was nevertheless enough to skew his judgment. He did not even remember to bring his singing bowls with him.

"All I own of value in this world is my sled and my dogs," said the dogstar man, "and when I am gone, no man is worthier to have them than yourself. Give me pen and paper, and I will write my will."

Every shred of scrap paper, which usually cluttered around the telephone, had vanished from sight, and my father could find nothing better than a circular for a grand sale at Happy Jack's—"Everything must go, to the bare walls." The dogstar man turned it over, and on the blank side wrote his will, making my father heir to seven dogs. He ended by writing out the names of the dogs, along with their rank in harness.

> Swing dogs: Eleanor Roosevelt and John Kennedy
> Team dogs: Lou Gehrig and Babe Ruth
> Wheel dogs: Finn McCool and Melville
> Lead dog: Hermes

Then he turned to me and my mother.

"I've left space for you to sign. Two witnesses."

To humor him, my mother signed. I signed because I'd never been asked to witness anything before and I did not want to pass up this opportunity. Without reading it over, the dogstar man pocketed his will, shook hands with each of us and took his unsteady leave, and my father and mother thought no more on the matter.

At midnight on Christmas Eve, the snow started falling, and it did not stop until the next afternoon. And then, quite unexpectedly, it turned warm.

The day before New Year's Eve, the dogstar man disappeared. A skier, hearing the howling and baying of seven ravenous huskies, called the police. Because the snow around the dog yard was deep and undisturbed by human tracks, the police broke into the dogstar man's cabin. The presence of the will on the kitchen table suggested suicide, but the circumstances of his death convinced them otherwise. At the lake they found the dogstar man's pickup truck. On the ice they found the shelter he'd built. The current ran strong under the thin ice where the shore curved toward the jagged hole in the ice, through which they concluded he had fallen. They did not find the man himself. It is hard to grieve for a man who has disappeared and who might return someday. I think my father and mother expected to receive another postcard from him. We did not really believe he was dead until the sheriff stopped by our house and asked my father to come and fetch his dogs.

Seven dogs at a stroke! Neither my father nor my mother knew the first thing about caring for dogs. Days of lawn chairs and umbrellas, farewell! My father bought a book called *Your Sled Dogs and How to Care for Them* and hired a man to put in seven tethering stakes and help him move the sled and bags of dog food and the doghouses into the backyard. Then he phoned a veterinarian, Dr. James Herrgott, and told him what had befallen us.

Dr. Herrgott made a house call and examined the dogs. From the kitchen window, we watched him, a tall lean figure in a wool cap and down jacket and boots and Levi's with holes in the knees. One by one, he knelt before each dog, examined its fur, its eyes, the lining of its mouth.

Wrapped in an aura of cold air, he sat down at our kitchen table and told us what we owned. Finn McCool and John Kennedy and Melville and Eleanor Roosevelt and Babe Ruth and Lou Gehrig were young dogs, between two and three years old, all mixed-breed huskies. Hermes was at least five years old and part Siberian husky.

"One of the big old-style freighting dogs," he observed. "Most mushers nowadays like the smaller breeds."

My father looked terrified. For the first time, I perceived a weakness in him and a superior strength in myself, and I took on the job of feeding the dogs in the morning. This meant rising at six instead of seven; ten minutes' snoozing and I'd miss the school bus. The front door slamming shut in the milky light before dawn would wake them, and by the time I'd hauled the big canister of dog food into the yard, they would be yapping and tugging at their chains and stretching, their tails switching and waving like flags. The smell of their food—a thin yellow gruel of ground barley and fish meal and fat, which I ladeled into deep tin bowls—made my father nauseous.

After school I fed them again and fetched a shovel and cleaned the dog yard.

My mother assigned herself the task of putting fresh hay in the doghouses. That was a fragrant and pleasant occupation; the dogs would crawl into the hay and move round and round, hollowing it into a nest.

Sometimes my father ran the dogs and sometimes I did it, but soon he relinquished that job too, because I enjoyed doing it and he did not. The intricate maneuvers of running dogs in harness daunted him. He could never remember who hated whom and what dogs got on well together.

After school I slipped their harnesses on and hitched them to the sled and we headed for the golf course behind the house. I never saw snow so deep that Hermes could not break a trail in it. When we crossed the frozen stream at the back of the course, the clicking of their toenails on the ice always startled them. I loved the crossing; the shadow we cast on that bright surface made a grand sight.

In February the temperature fell to thirty-five below and stayed there. My mother could not bear to leave any animal outside in that weather. My father reminded her that we had no basement, no garage, no shed of any kind.

"We have a big living room," she said. "We could partition it. Half for the dogs and half for us."

She kept after him till he put a chain-link fence down the middle of the living room, while my mother took out the rug and the furniture. From then on, the dogs slept indoors. A maze of smaller fences separated them from each other. The gates on these fences were never locked. When I stayed up to watch the Saturday-night movie in the living room with my parents, the loping and breathing and snuffling and growling did not bother my mother or me, but it drove my father wild. I think he could have gotten used to this, but something happened to me that changed everything for all of us.

I got the flu, the kind that keeps you in bed for two weeks. I felt as if someone had sucked all the strength out of me and left me on the small white shore of my bed to find my way back to health. My father took over my tasks and did them, in his own way.

He exercised the dogs, but he did not take out the sled. He walked them singly. Of course, as he pointed out to me, he could not walk seven dogs every day. My mother walked them when she had time, but she reminded him that the dogstar man had willed them to my father, not to us.

He fed the dogs, but he refused to handle the fish meal and fat, and he bought canned meat and dehydrated chicken kibbles in hundred-pound bags that scarcely lasted a week. Soon the dogs were demanding four meals a day and howling at night. My mother found that if she opened the gate in the living room fence, the dogs grew quiet. After everyone was in bed, they would leave their quarters and gather in my room.

It is not easy sleeping with seven dogs, even when you love them. In the safety of my bedroom they went on dreaming of their old fears, just as I went on dreaming of mine. Roused by a remembered injury, Lou Gehrig would leap out of sleep and sink his teeth into John Kennedy's neck, and I would fly out of bed to part them. When sled dogs fight, generations of jackals and wolves snarl in their blood. All night part of my mind stayed awake, listening for the low growl that signaled the beginning of a quarrel. When morning came, I never felt rested.

And Melville got sick. His fur fell out in odd patches, though my mother washed him with Castile soap and sponged his legs, chest, face, and tail with a special foam that Dr. Herrgott recommended for shedding animals.

A thaw surprised us in February, and my mother agreed to let the dogs sleep in the yard again. But the dogs had caught the scent of being human and could not get enough of it. From darkness till dawn they howled. I was back in school but not strong enough to take over caring for the dogs, and I suppose it was the howling and complaints from the neighbors that finally drove my father to make what he warned me was an important announcement.

"I'm going to sell Olaf's dogs. I can't afford to keep them."

We had just sat down to dinner, and he looked at me to see how I would take his words. I said nothing.

"We'll only sell them to someone who can really take care of them," said my mother.

That night I fell asleep to the howling of the dogs. What woke me was a silence so sinister that I jumped out of bed and hurried to the window, certain they'd been poisoned. My heart nearly thudded through my chest when I saw someone was indeed in the yard. He was unchaining them. First John Kennedy, then Babe Ruth, then Hermes.

I never thought of calling my father. No, I pulled on my clothes, snatched my jacket from the bedpost, and marched out into the yard. When the thief turned his face toward me, I was speechless with fright.

"I've come for my dogs," said the dogstar man. "They miss me, and I miss them."

"You're dead," I whispered. My teeth were chattering. "You fell through the ice and drowned."

"That's true," said the dogstar man. And he went on unchaining them. They were lining up, letting him slip the harnesses over them, taking their old places. Hermes first, then Finn McCool and Melville in the second spot, then Lou Gehrig and Babe Ruth, and in the last position, Eleanor Roosevelt and John Kennedy.

"If you're dead, how are you going to take your dogs?"

"Easy," said the dogstar man. "They can cross over. Didn't you know that? Didn't they teach you *anything?*"

The dogsled was leaning against the back of the house, and he pulled it

down, hitched the dogs to it, and took his place on the back runners. He
beckoned me over.

"For you," he said. "I don't need this where I'm going."

And he dropped the whistle my father had made into my hand.

Prism Tree

TONY DANIEL

FARTHER NORTH—Tennessee, the Carolinas, Virginia—the mountains are big. Big, big wrinkles in the land-skin of America, caused by a huge traffic accident a few million years ago—when Eurasia took a wrong turn at the equator and smashed into North America. But the wrinkle tapers out, grows narrower and smaller as it winds south. In northern Alabama, there are no more mountains—just foothills. That is where my grandfather lived, in the country, about five miles from the town of Newell, population: almost fifty, if you count the suburbs.

Grandaddy lived on his farm. Before him, it had been his father's. His great grandfather had settled the land under the old homestead act.

On hot weekends, when the temperature climbed to the upper nineties, and the Birmingham air was full of the sweat and humid breath of a million people, my family would go over to the country, as we called it, to see Grandaddy and to dig our toes into the cool Randolf County sod. Well, it was my sister and I who did the toe digging.

First thing when we got there, we'd race through the big cornfield down the hill from the cabin. Each of us took a separate row so that we would only catch fleeting glimpses of one another through a green curtain of corn fronds; neither one would know who'd won until we burst from the other end and collapsed at the windbreak's edge. Kim was two years older than I, and she usually won when I was a kid. After I hit puberty, I began to come out first more often, though I sometimes suspect that Kim, beginning to discover the secrets of the Southern woman—the strategic loss of battles to win wars—would let me win.

After the traditional race, we would go to the creek for a swim. Well, not really a swim, because the creek was four feet at its deepest. We waded and splashed, mostly. There was a rock that the creek fell over, must have been six feet long—and sloped at an angle just right for sliding down. Green algae covered it, slick as fish skin. You couldn't stand on it; your feet would fly from under you, and your head crack hard against its deceptive soft covering. But you could sit at the top, push off, then shoot down the rock, watching the water pool below getting bigger. And you're in, and the water is so cold at first you can barely breathe.

If you wanted to, you could float on down the creek into the Tub. The creek water had carved out a channel through a big rock, a channel in the shape of a bathtub, but about ten feet long and two feet deep. The creek bustled through the constriction at twice its normal speed. Kim and I would bring our knees up until we were tight balls, buoyant. We careened down the Tub, bumping into the sides like those toy ducks you see at carnivals.

Then we would put on our clothes and go bother the cows. Grandaddy's cows would spook at anything, so the game was to sneak up on them and pet them. Kim would go and move the cows in a certain direction. I'd be in the grass, on my stomach. Cows can only see in black and white and are too stupid to notice something that's not moving much. I'd have to wait until the cows were almost trampling me, then I'd jump up, run at them, and pet whichever one I could get my hands on. Kim was always the cow driver. Like I said, she is a smart woman.

Then we'd go back to join the old folks, laughing as we walked over the rocky pasture. Mother would've cooked lunch, usually pork chops and collards. She always did because Grandaddy wasn't a good cook and ate the same things day after day since my grandmother died. Mom is a schoolteacher, and Grandaddy, like a kid resigned to his fate, let her make him dinner. "Dinner," by the way, is what they call lunch in Randolf County.

There were the pork chops for meat, collards from Grandaddy's garden, green and steaming, black-eyed peas and corn bread. That corn bread could not be duplicated. Grandaddy took a portion of his corn crop every year to a miller over the state line in Georgia. The miller—Mr. Hodges seems like the right name—had a stone grinding wheel turned by the falling water of Rocky Creek. I think it was from the miller that Grandaddy got the idea for a waterwheel.

After dinner, Grandaddy and I would go riding trees. I rode them, of course, and Grandaddy watched, giving me fine pointers on my technique. My father said Grandaddy rode trees until I was young, until arthritis and brittle bones forced him to stop. I would've loved to see my grandfather, a fifty-year-old man, his hair beginning to take on the smoky grayness which is all I have ever known it to be, come cascading down, hanging for all he was worth onto the top of a young hickory. There is nothing like riding trees—no amusement-park ride, no sport. There is nothing more physically taxing, for those few minutes you are inching your way to the tree's very top. Then the descent down the empty air, and if you're lucky, you've picked just the right tree and it sets your feet onto the ground as gently as cat's breath on the hand.

Then my family would leave. We all loaded up into the Fairmont station wagon and drove away, leaving a billowing cloud of dust, with the tires crackling on the dirt driveway like distant thunder.

But during my teenage years, in the summer, I would stay behind to help Grandaddy tend the land. We lived in the log cabin that his father built by the creek. Grandaddy had attached a waterwheel to it and that was where his electricity came from. He didn't pay Alabama Power one cent. The waterwheel was the overshot type, and in order to get the head he needed to turn it fast enough, Grandaddy cut a ditch from two hundred feet up the creek to bring faster, higher water to the flume.

I fed the cows and drove the tractor, plowing fields, bush-hogging, for many summers; I always came back to Birmingham with a farmer's tan. At night, Grandaddy and I would read, or talk.

He told me about growing up, wandering the newly turned fields looking for arrowheads, swimming in the creek, shooting down the Tub just

like me. When he told me about his first meeting with Betty, my grandmother, his eyes would fix on the wall, as if he were concentrating on
seeing in his mind every detail, every texture of her. But the image must
have been blurry, because he always gazed through tearing eyes.

They had met when he was eighteen, she was twenty. He was squirrel
hunting up the creek, in the woods one farm over from his land, when he
saw the fattest squirrel in Randolf County sitting on a tree limb not
twenty feet from him. What was better (and stranger), the animal did not
move, even though Grandaddy was pretty certain it had seen him.
Grandaddy fell to one knee, took careful aim. Slowly, with a fluid motion,
he pulled the trigger—something hit him. His shot flew wild, too wild for
even the wide scatter of pellets to harm the squirrel.

"What's got into you, trying to shoot my squirrel! I ought to take that
shotgun and wrap it around your neck."

Grandaddy looked up to see a young lady with blond hair and a paint-
stained smock leaning over him. The music of the creek and the woods
filled the air. And he was in love. They were married a year later, in the
First Baptist Church.

I never knew my grandmother, but I felt her presence all about the
cabin. Her paintings were on the walls, paintings of birds, snakes, squirrels, trees—and at least twenty studies of the creek, in this light or that,
near the Tub, the sliding rock. I got my schooling in engineering at
Auburn, but I got my draftsman's hand from my grandmother.

The best of my grandmother's works—so good that it made the others
look like crude paint-by-numbers landscapes, though they're actually quite
nice, almost professional—was a tapestry she had woven over a summer,
three years after she and Grandaddy were married, when she was expecting my father. Grandaddy called this tapestry a wall rug, and he gave to it
a whole wall of the cabin. It was a windbreak, he said, keeping out drafts,
keeping us warm or cool, depending on the season.

The tapestry was of a huge old tree—the big oak tree directly above the
cabin. My grandfather told me that he and my grandmother used to
climb that hill, taking the easy way through the cornfield, on afternoons
after the work was mostly done. They would look out over the farm.

"Betty called it her patchwork quilt," my grandfather told me. "The
way the fields and woods fit together, with the creek threading through
them."

And behind the tree in the tapestry was that patchwork of forms, a
little close and out of perspective—or maybe that is just the way my
grandmother saw the land, gathered together for warmth like a bundled-

up quilt. The cabin was just to the left of the tree trunk, a small box in the distance, with a single thread of smoke curling out of the chimney. I never noticed until my grandfather pointed it out one day, but if you looked really closely, you could see that the smoke-thread was a twisted braid of my grandmother's blond hair, looking more like sunlight streaming from the cabin than wood smoke.

The tree in the tapestry was depicted in the moment of being struck by lightning. There was a twisted cut down its trunk, in the same shape as the black scar on the tree on the hill. The tapestry was just a picture of lightning striking a big oak—nothing unusual, nothing special.

But beneath the tree, running out of the trunk's base in meandering rivulets, was a rainbow of separate colors. That's why Kim and I called the old oak the Prism Tree. The light from a woven, wool-white lightning strike jagged down through the tangled branches, into the tapestry tree's trunk, then seemed to channel through the tree and emerge below it, split into a spectrum perfectly describing the makeup of the emotions the tree evoked, just as a spectroscopic chart will tell you what a star is made of. But there was no analysis here, no formulaic layout. Instead, my grandmother had put a fugue of color into the yarn, the heart of tree, lightning storm and the earth below. The tapestry was made completely of wool (except for that strand of hair) dyed from local plants my grandmother had collected to extract their colors.

My grandmother died of cancer, slowly and painfully, and Grandaddy buried her on that hill, facing her grave so that she'd have the same view as she'd depicted in the tapestry. He never said much about her, but there was no doubt he missed her. We shared the cabin's main room those summer evenings, and sometimes I'd hear him wake up, shuffle around in his bed as though something were wrong, out of place. He'd speak her name, quiet and sweet, like the low end of a flute's scale. Then, after a moment, he'd say it again, this time a whisper, full of loss and longing. When I woke in the mornings before him (which was not often), I'd see him crowded to one side of the bed, just in case, past all hope, his Betty should come back and want a place to lie down beside him.

So I was there that summer afternoon the power man came.

The white sedan pulled up in front of the house, the gravel crackling and firing under the wheels like damp firecrackers reluctantly exploding. Dust from the road rose like smoke from those firecrackers and caked the side of the car from the bottom of the door up the side, almost obscuring the decal just under the window. The decal said Alabama Power Company. I wondered what the man was doing out here—Grandaddy had discontinued his power service years ago.

"Howdy, son," said the tall, red-faced man who stepped out of the car. "I'm looking for John Dearburn."

I had come back to the house to use the bathroom and was about to head back out to the cornfield.

"Grandaddy's out walking the cornfield," I said. "Want me to go get him?"

"I'd appreciate it," said the man, not quite meeting my eyes.

Something was wrong with the man, I thought, as I ran to get Grandaddy. Tree shadows of the windbreak flickered over me. The man was slumped like he'd been punched in the stomach. Corn shadows of the field flickered around me. "Grandaddy!"

"Hiram Funderburg," the man said. He said it while Grandaddy was still too far away for him to extend his hand. "Need to talk to you about something, Mr. Dearburn."

My grandfather asked the man inside the cabin.

I did not follow them. Instead, I sat outside and watched the water-wheel turning—whizzing around like an out-of-breath courier trying to deliver a message to an impatient general, water flying from it like a spray of sweat. What message could a creek be carrying? But that little creek is powerful, I thought. It must carry hundreds, even thousands of gallons an hour.

The wheel turned like the spindle on my grandmother's old spinning wheel. I pictured it turning out pieces of land like her spinning wheel turned out strands of yarn. The waterwheel wasn't *saying* anything, I decided. It was *making*. I guess I was thinking like an engineer even back then. After a while, I lost myself in the sparkle and turn of the wheel.

The man came out. He did not have the punched look anymore. In fact, he was standing taller, much taller. Grandaddy, who followed behind him, now looked like he'd been pummeled, beaten up. The man got into the company car, wordlessly, and drove away. The cattle, which had been standing on the road, separated to let him pass, then moved back together, as blades of grass will move when a snake passes through.

Grandaddy stood straight and still while the man drove away. After the car went around the bend in the drive, out of sight, the strength seemed to flow out of Grandaddy. For a moment, he slumped, almost stumbled off the porch. Then he caught himself, kept himself under control. But I could see him trembling.

"Reed, they're going to build a dam," Grandaddy said to me. "Down on the Tallapoosa River. Be a big lake forming. It'll take a few years, but it'll reach up the creek here, fill our little valley. This place will be underwater. They want me to sell out, Reed, to leave my home."

He turned from me, looked out over the fields and windbreaks, over the land. He clenched his hands into fists, which hung at his sides. He worked his nails into his palms.

"Ah, boy, what am I going to do?"

We went to the lawyer's office in Anniston that afternoon, Grandaddy wearing his only suit; it was from the fifties, narrow and nondescript. Mr. Dowell, the lawyer, had helped my grandfather with the legalities having to do with my grandmother's death, and, like all country folk, Grandaddy always came back to someone who'd done a good job for him. Mr. Dowell was not hopeful, and filled the air with talk. Talk I now would recognize, of eminent domain of the state, of the individual sacrificing for the common good, of the above-market price Alabama Power was willing to pay. But I was a boy still, and listened only with my heart.

"Oh, they offered me more than my land is worth, by any lights," Grandaddy said at one point. Then I remember the pause, the silence, which even the verbose Mr. Dowell did not seek to fill. A silence of memories, desires, hopes for the future. Of someday passing those hopes on to Kim and me. And behind it all, pervading the silence like the smell of fallen leaves fills the autumn air, was the knowledge that this was where his Betty was buried, on top of the little hill behind the cabin, where she used to sit and paint. That grave would be sunken, flooded, washed away without a trace, and only the slap of waves fifty feet above it as a marker.

"And Betty—" Grandaddy's voice cracked.

"I know, John," said Mr. Dowell, ceasing his explanations, his justifications, leaning forward, wiping his sad face. "There's just nothing I can do. Nothing. I'm really sorry."

Grandaddy roamed the land for weeks. He did no work, for what was the use? He came back sweaty, caked with corn loam, with a look on his face—I can't describe that look. Imagine a horse with broken legs staring at you, begging you to get it over with. Or a soldier with shrapnel through an artery, watching his life leak out onto the earth before him, knowing what is happening.

I followed him one day, far behind, and he didn't see me. He knelt in the cornfield, dug his hand into the dirt and raised the reddish topsoil to his nose. He smelled it. Did he remember learning to plow, back during the Depression, his father's hands, hard as old hickory, over his own, responding to, guiding the mule? Or was it his first crop, after he'd inherited the land, when the rain had not fallen until it was almost too late, when he thought he would have to go to Anniston or maybe even Birmingham to support my grandmother and my father, when the rain *had* come and the corn tasseled and he had enough money to buy even an old used tractor?

With a shudder, I felt some of Grandaddy's years upon my shoulders. I felt old and beaten down, and all I could think was that my kids would never race between the rows of corn because racing was fun. That they would never pant in this country air, on this farm, lying beside the windbreak, looking up into the blue Randolf County sky. They would never know the fall and carry of *this* creek on *this* land—only a flat expanse of featureless, dull water, if I ever brought them back to show them where the land had been.

Grandaddy crushed the loam against his face; his shoulders sagged and he did not straighten them, almost as if he were an old fallen log with a permanent depression from some boot crushing into its rotten trunk.

Alabama Power wanted him out by autumn, so they could begin clearing the vegetation from the land in preparation for the coming of the water, even though the water would not be up that far for another year after the dam was built. He had two hundred acres, and the power company was paying him two thousand each, plus the price of the cabin. It was not a bad deal.

He signed the contract in August, while flies buzzed about the heads of Mr. Funderburg, Mr. Dowell and himself. They sat on the front porch of the cabin; Grandaddy had not asked them in.

"There, it's done," was all he said, then walked back into the cabin, leaving the two men to depart with no farewell. But after that, Grandaddy was seldom in the cabin.

During the days, I saw him walking through the corn, or petting the cows—they never ran from him. Then one day a big truck came and took all the cows away. Sometimes I would see him in the woods, heading upcreek in the direction of where he and his Betty met, carrying a shotgun. He had not killed a squirrel in forty years.

I spent my time keeping things up, keeping the cows fed while they were still in the pasture. The garden was going to rot; I just didn't have the time to pull all the cucumbers, the beans, the squash. Anything I did was futile, I knew even then, but there was nothing better to do.

Grandaddy was gone nights, too.

Now, you might be thinking, this will become a ghost story. About how, say, my grandmother came to speak from the waterwheel, to cry for vengeance, or, say, how, magically, my grandfather kept water from coming up his valley, into his land, by a hard dam of a wish that it not do so. Or it will be more mundane, realistic, the story of how grief weighed down a man like a heavy snow in pines, and how he either did or did not spring back up after the thaw came and the land was covered with running water.

Instead, I'm going to tell you the truth.

Because for all the structure I can find in this old universe, the symmetries and happy coincidences, I have not found an ordering, a pattern, into which that summer, the farm, my grandfather, will fit. Oh yes, I am an ordered man, an ordering man now, drawing bridges, highways—yes, even dams—watching the slow, steady gathering of equipment, material, the precise application of force, the hammering of pattern and form, strong and firm as wrought iron, into this flux, this flow, of a world.

We have kaleidoscopes for brains, you and I. Colors spin, bits of glass and paper shuffle, spin on their axes—and the whole thing is done with mirrors. All for the sake of recognition, reacting to the known, getting by. But what happens when survival is not what it's all about? When, like a ripple, a quake, realization comes over the mind, not that it will die—for we all sort of suspect this, as time comes on, and the evidence mounts—but that life, living, is running out, that this paper bag life is full of water and the bottom is soggy and about to burst? Will the mind bend in unaccustomed ways? And that summer, did my grandfather and, just for an instant, myself, look around the corner of things, catch a glimpse around the edges of the given like a dentist looking at the backside of your gums with his funny curved mirror? Did my grandfather slip around those edges, as a squirrel will skate around behind a tree, and be wholly gone, yet wholly there? I have no idea. All I can do is tell you what I saw.

Yes, Grandaddy was gone nights, too.

He carried no light with him, but knew the lay of the land so well, every rock, every stump, that he really didn't need one. I tried to follow a couple of times, but it was very dark—dark like it only gets deep in the country—and I was too scared and too tired. I suspect he visited my grandmother's grave. I went back to the cabin, tried to sleep. Each night he would finally come in, quietly go to bed. But just before dawn, he'd wake up moaning, and sometimes I'd hear my grandmother's name. Once he said softly, only to the still air in the cabin, "They're taking her, Betty. They're taking her."

Her. The land was a she to Grandaddy. Always had been. But lately, I came to believe, he was having trouble distinguishing the land from my grandmother. Not that he was going senile, becoming confused and dangerous to himself. It was just that the farm was full of her presence. Betty walked here; she painted here. Betty and my grandfather loved here—and here. Maybe he'd always felt this way, thought this way about the land, but kept it from me, my family—not wanted to show what we'd take to be false sentiment and the longings of a sad old man.

But Grandaddy just didn't care anymore. I remember one day, when I met him coming in from the fields, his boots red as old blood from the Randolf County clay soil.

"Reed," he said, "she's done with painting the corn today. Fall's coming and she's made all the stalks dry and brown. But she'll be sad about it. She always loved green, new things."

This was not the "she" of "think she'll need a cover crop of alfalfa this winter," or "we'll put five more cows on her and see how she takes it." Not the general "she" of the land, the farm. This time it was personal, closer to my grandfather's heart.

So on the day of the storm, the first week in September, I was not surprised when Grandaddy said "She's raising a ruckus tonight, mad over something," as if he were commenting on some unfathomable woman thing affecting my grandmother. "We just have to sit tight and let her get over it."

The sky got heavy and dark, like the bottom of a paper bag getting soaked with water. Then, like a soggy paper bag, it all came apart, burst open, and the water fell. It rained all day, and Grandaddy stayed in. He was not crazy, you see, not a madman running raving through storms. Lightning crashed, thunder howling after. It rained creeks, rivers. Outside, the waterwheel was spinning and creaking and throwing off water like a dog shaking himself off after a bath.

Grandaddy sat by the empty fireplace all day long, reading a Zane Grey novel, rocking in my grandmother's old rocker. He was facing the big old tapestry his Betty wove so long ago. I was sitting at the table, drawing up designs for a treehouse I planned to build when I got back home. School would be starting soon, and my parents would be down to get me the next week.

We stayed there, inside the cabin, all day, not talking much. Grandaddy read, mouthing the words silently, and I scratched away at my plans. You could hardly tell when night fell—the sky outside just grew a little darker.

As night came on, the wind really picked up and lashed rain against the cabin's window. It was raining less than it had before, but the wind delivered the water with more fury.

I'd grown accustomed to the waterwheel through the day, but suddenly I heard it distinctly, as if there had been a change in pitch to the squeak of it. Lightning strobed, as if God were taking a Polaroid of the land, like in those snapshot booths at the Woolworth's. Grandaddy stopped his rocking, lowered his book.

Was there something in that wind, some ordered sound? Or was it everything, the wind, the waterwheel, the space of silence that followed the roll of thunder? A sifting of the trees through the air that said something, whispered a human word? That called my grandfather's name? I can't say. Or, if I'm forced to decide, I will say there was nothing there— only the swish of leaves and the rushing of wind.

"Well, damn it, Betty," said Grandaddy, "I'll come, then, if you want me to."

I sat up in my chair, pushed away my drawings. This was what I'd feared: Grandaddy gone insane, chasing a ghost through the night and me having to look after him.

"There's nobody there, Grandaddy," I said, trying to keep my voice calm like you were supposed to do with crazies.

Grandaddy looked at me with a wry smile. What I'd now recognize as a patronizing look. And—I now believe—he had a perfect right to do so. After all, he was the oldest living male in the family, the Patriarch himself.

"I have decided something, Reed," he said.

"What?"

"Something I have to do."

I was silent for a long time, trying to think what to say. Finally I decided just to ask.

"What?"

The wind picked up.

"Listen; she's mourning."

"Grandaddy, what are you going to do?"

He got up and went to get his raincoat. I moved to stop him.

"Grandaddy, no."

He brushed me aside not ungently, but with a firmness. His muscles were thin and strong as wire thread, muscles like the long splintering sinews of oak when you split it.

"I'm going outside, Reed," he said to me, "and I may be quite a while."

Then he was gone, out the door. I was scared, confused. What should I do? Call someone, my dad maybe? And tell him what? To get there right away? How could he? He was a hundred miles away, in Birmingham. I put on my raincoat and boots, then went out into the storm myself. I figured I knew where Grandaddy was headed.

About halfway up the little hill that the grave was on top of, I saw him. He was moving through the woods without hurry, but steadily, as a deer will do when it is on the move, seeking its bed for the night. The clay sides of hill were slick with running water mingled with the first of the autumn leaves. I began to climb, quickly. A bolt of lightning struck nearby, and I started; I fell, half sliding, a good ways back down the hill. I remembered the big oak on top of the hill, the one from the tapestry, the helical scar it bore of lightning from past storms. I whimpered, shook my head hard to clear the fear of dying like a moth in a bug-zapper (but this was different, because out here, the bug-zapper was coming after *me),* then started back up the hill again.

In another flash, I saw my grandfather. He was almost at the top.

"Grandaddy, stop," I said, but the thunder rolled over my voice.

Finally I reached the hilltop, pulled myself into the little clearing where the grave was. There was the dark shape of my grandfather against the darker sky, like oil floating on black water.

Lightning crackled across the sky, and my grandfather flashed iridescent, his shape defined by a faint rainbow, just as oil will shine on water.

I stopped short, rubbed my eyes. But my grandfather was still glowing slightly, even with no lightning. He was a prism, split into his primary colors, only his shape remaining.

More lightning. And he was a kaleidoscope, forming and reforming in darkly shining patterns.

"Grandaddy."

I heard a voice in my ears. Or was it the night, the rush of the creek below, the wind? More importantly, was the voice of the night, this night, a woman's? "Let him be, boy, Reed. Let him weave himself a place."

Then the shifting of colors spread from my grandfather into the land about him. There was a stroke of lightning, and the process accelerated. The land was unwinding on itself, unbraiding as an old rope will twist apart. Was this something my grandfather was doing, or did the land separate, pull apart on its own? I will never know, though I suspect it was a little of both, a working together so closely that neither could tell you where one stopped and the other began. A kind of marriage.

The ground, the trees, the sky, separated, shifted into points and lines of color, like a 3-D drawing when you don't have those special kind of glasses. Then, near where my grandfather was standing, the very shape of the land undulated, shifted form beneath him. And he was shimmering, changing, too.

My grandfather wove himself into the pattern of the land. Or maybe I should say he planted himself, as a farmer will plant a seed. Just as he'd planted his Betty, those years ago. Like planting, but more like mixing. How can I say this thing? How can I?

And I sat at the edge of the clearing, under the old oak, until the storm abated and the stars came out. Then I went back to the cabin, coming down the gentler side of the hill, crashing through the drying corn, walking up the driveway. The waterwheel was a blur, spinning out electricity like the miller's daughter spins gold in "Rumpelstiltskin." I took a breath of the rain-cleaned air and went inside.

I flicked on the switch, and the cabin's room filled with homespun light. There was the tapestry, directly across from me, the Prism Tree my grandmother had made. I sat down in her old rocker, turned around to face the wall rug. Was there a new strand in there somewhere to reflect, to resonate with, the new strand running through the land? What would my grandfather's color be? A steady, strong brown? The blue of loss and remembrance? The new green of spring?

And still, I have that tapestry *still*. It is in my den, where I draw up my plans for changing, for patterning the world. It is all that remains, really, for my grandfather's land has long since gone under, been changed. Is it lost, or merely planted, waiting for some spring, some new day?

And though my eyes grow older, still I think I can see that new thread that I spotted years ago, that night, staring at the tapestry. There, coming out of the chimney, weaving in and out of the sunlight smoke, is a thread of gray which is much darker and nearer to smoke than the blond of my grandmother's hair. Or is it really a new thread? My eyes grow tired, specifics blur. Light streams out, flows into the cabin, like lightning into the Prism Tree, only gentler, more subtle, an intricate joining of threads, twisting together like a lightning mark down the side of a tree, weft and warp—a sunbeam and the shadow it creates?

Desert Rain

MARK L. VAN NAME

and

PAT MURPHY

TERESA LOOKED UP at the framework of welded steel tubing. It stood nine feet tall and just over six feet on a side. Within the framework, steel tracks snaked above and below one another in seemingly random patterns, forming a gleaming tangle. At regular intervals along the tracks, lines of one-inch ball bearings waited to be released. Teresa pulled the string that dangled from the chute at the top of the sculpture, and closed her eyes to listen.

With the faint whisper of metal scraping against metal, a gate opened and freed the first ball, which rattled along the grooved surface of the track. As the ball rounded the first curve, it struck a trip wire and released two more balls. Each of these in turn freed more balls, until dozens were rolling down the tracks with a sound like faraway thunder.

The music started slowly, building as the balls rumbled down the tracks. The first ball struck a series of tuning forks, and three high notes rang out. Another ball rattled across a section of metal reeds, then clattered through a maze of gates. Every ball followed a different path: ringing bells, striking chimes, and bouncing off tuning forks.

When the first ball reached the gathering basket, the sound began to lessen. As the others followed the first, the sound faded entirely.

With her eyes still shut, Teresa shook her head. The music was not right; it was not even close. She wasn't sure anymore exactly how the composition should sound, but she knew this was not it. The piece sounded too mechanical, too predictable. In her proposal, she had promised the Santa Fe Arts Commission a sculpture that conveyed the essence of water, the rush and flow of it—a waterless fountain for a desert town. She wanted music that would remind people of rain drumming on a tin roof or the roar of a breaking wave. Instead, she had the hum of trucks on the freeway.

She turned away and looked through the sliding glass doors at the desert. The late June sun was setting, and clumps of gray-green rabbit brush cast long shadows. The landscape shimmered a little, distorted by heat rising from the flagstone patio just outside the door. She was alone, surrounded by heat and silence.

She closed her eyes and remembered the view from her old studio, a big, drafty room in the Marin Headlands Art Center. She had always been cold there: from early fall to late spring, she had worn wool socks and a down vest. Every winter, she had nursed a head cold that never quite went away. Still, the drafts that had crept in through cracks in the window frames had smelled of salt air. From the window, she could see the ocean, a slash of blue water alive with restless waves. The wind tousled the grass and shook the branches of the cypress trees. She could see tiny figures on the beach: a dancer from the Art Center practicing leaps in the sand, a man sitting and staring at the water, two women walking hand in hand.

She took a deep breath of the air-conditioned air and opened her eyes. The desert was still there.

She heard a knock on the door that led from the studio to the rest of the house. "Come on in!" she said, momentarily glad of the interruption. When Jeff opened the door, she said, "You're home early. It's nice to see you."

Jeff was thirty-seven, five years older than Teresa. But when he was excited, as he clearly was now, he looked like a kid. A shock of brown hair had fallen into his eyes; he pushed it back impatiently. Teresa had suggested last week that he needed a haircut, but he had just nodded, his thoughts elsewhere. He was too busy to make an appointment, he had said, too busy for almost anything.

He grinned at her now. "I've been here for a while, but I didn't want to disturb you when you were working. I came home early to finish installing the system in the rest of the house. It's just about ready to go."

For as long as Teresa had known Jeff, he had been working on the development of what he called "the system," some kind of computer program that could run a household. For the past four months, ever since they had returned from their honeymoon, he had been completely immersed in the project. When he wasn't at work, he was preparing their house for the first working prototype, installing cameras, microphones, and monitors in most of the rooms. The whole time, he had been trying to convince Teresa that the system would make her life much easier: it would answer the phone, put on music, adjust the air conditioner, look up information in its library. He was downright evangelical about it. Teresa had accepted his attempts to persuade her with amused skepticism, accepting this as another of Jeff's incomprehensible but lucrative computer projects.

"All I have to do now is define the personality," he said. "I thought maybe you'd want to help. You could design the face, choose the voice, stuff like that."

She shoved her hands into the pockets of her jeans, feeling uncomfortable. "You know I don't know anything about computers."

"You don't need to know anything. It'll be fun. Besides, I figured that if you created the personality, you'd have a better feel for it. You'll see it's completely in your control."

She glanced back at the sculpture. "I probably should keep on working. This really isn't going well."

He reached out and took her hand. "Oh, come on. You sound like you could use a break."

Reluctantly, she let him lead her into the living room. One wall of the room was dominated by a large monitor; the shelves of the surrounding wall unit were crowded with electronics gear, gadgets and gizmos that Teresa regarded as Jeff's toys. She knew how to turn on the stereo, the television, and the controller for the satellite dish, but she ignored the rest of it. She didn't like admitting it, but she found the collection of electronic devices a little intimidating.

Jeff gestured to the swivel chair in front of the monitor. "Why don't you sit here?"

"That's okay; you do it. I'll just watch."

"Please, Teresa? You'd be helping me out. I might get some ideas watching you work. We're just starting to test this on people outside the lab."

"I'm a rotten guinea pig—I don't know what I'm doing."

"No, that makes you a perfect guinea pig. This is for regular people, not just computer nerds."

She studied his face and relented. "All right." She sat in the chair. "What do I do?"

"Here—I'll get you started." Jeff leaned over her and tapped on the keyboard. He straightened up as his company's logo appeared on the screen, then faded. "Now the set-up software will walk you through the process. Just type in an answer when it asks you a question, or use the mouse to point to your choice when it gives you a list. Once the full system is running, we'll switch to voice input."

Teresa read the words on the screen. "Do you want to create a companion?"

"Why not?" she said, pretending a nonchalance she didn't feel. She clicked the pointer on "Yes."

"Man or woman?" the screen asked.

She glanced at Jeff. "Your choice," he said. "I want you to be comfortable with this."

"Well," she said, "you know I'm partial to boys. And I don't think you could handle having two women around." She clicked the pointer on "Man."

"Name?"

She frowned at the screen. "I've got to name it? Don't you already have a name for it?" She glanced at Jeff.

He shrugged. "Some of the guys on the team call it HIAN, short for Home Information and Appliance Network."

"HIAN?" Teresa shook her head. "No sense of poetry, those computer boys." She thought for a moment and then said, "How about Ian? That has a nice sound." She typed it in.

"Would you like to choose a face or customize a face?" Below the question the screen displayed sample faces of many races, including Caucasian, black, Indian, Amerindian, Chinese, and Japanese.

Jeff leaned over her shoulder. "When it's up and running, you'll see the face on the monitor. It'll talk to you through the monitor's speakers, and see and hear you through the Minicams. We've got a whole rack of processors dedicated to animation: the face can smile, shrug, wink, frown —pretty much anything you or I can do. The display changes in real time." She glanced up at him; all his attention was on the screen. "My assumption has always been that it has to be friendly to succeed. Our human-interface people created the standard faces with that in mind, designing faces that most people would trust. Of course, you could also go with a celebrity—we've got a few that we're experimenting with: Katharine Hepburn, Robert Redford, Alec Guinness, Ronald Reagan—"

Teresa waved a hand, interrupting the monologue. "I don't want some prepackaged face that a marketing expert says I'll trust. I'll make my own, thanks." She clicked on the customize option.

"See, it's not as bad as you thought." Jeff rested one hand on her shoulder, absentmindedly massaging the tight muscles of her neck. "You'll be an expert in no time."

She leaned back into his hands, relaxing a little. "Ah," she said softly. "I remember those hands. It's been a while."

Oblivious, Jeff stopped rubbing to gesture toward the screen. It had changed to display small pictures of blank faces, hair, eyes, ears, noses, and mouths. "You see, now you can assemble a face that you like from a variety of parts. Even people without your drawing ability can create a companion. Go ahead and make one you like."

"Okay, okay." She leaned forward again and clicked on the first face. Most of the dull gray of the screen winked out and in its place was a fat man's face, round cheeked and small chinned, empty of eyes and other features. She could see only the figure's blank face, neck, and shoulders. A black T-shirt covered the shoulders. She moved on to the next face, which was thin and aristocratic, with a delicate chin. She flipped through the choices, about twenty in all, and finally settled on one that was broad but a bit craggy. She liked the face and the burly shoulders that went with it.

At first, she chose a pair of bright blue eyes that reminded her of her father's eyes—intense and excitable, ready to challenge and confront. Then she reconsidered and selected a more muted shade of blue, closer to blue-gray. Intense, but with a touch of compassion.

Working methodically, she assembled a face. The screen responded to her changes instantly. As she worked, she forgot that Jeff was standing just behind her and concentrated on creating a picture of an attractive stranger. He wasn't a classically handsome man, but he was good-looking in a rough-edged sort of way. She gave him a beard and a mustache and a diamond stud earring in his left ear. He looked like a guy who worked with his hands, she figured. He could have been a bouncer in a bar or a mechanic or a fisherman. Good-natured, she thought, but maybe a little dangerous. A motorcycle rider. A drifter. A sidewalk philosopher. The kind of guy she had always been involved with before she met Jeff.

"You're doing great," Jeff murmured.

She glanced up, feeling guilty that she had forgotten him, however briefly. She stopped working. "I guess that's it," she said. "That's good enough."

"You can change the clothes, if you like," Jeff said. "A business suit, maybe."

"I like the black T-shirt," she said. "Ian's a casual kind of guy."

"You can choose a different background, too," he said. "It doesn't have to be gray." He leaned over and clicked the mouse on a small icon in the lower left of the screen. The gray background became a white wall; Teresa could see framed certificates behind Ian. "Doctor's office," Jeff said. "Or here—how about this?" He clicked again. The wood paneling that replaced the white wall looked familiar, as did the easy chair where Ian sat.

Teresa glanced behind her, half expecting to see Ian sitting on the chair. "You used our living room?"

"Why not?"

Teresa studied the screen, momentarily disoriented. It felt odd to see this imaginary person sitting on a chair that she knew was very real. It was as if she were watching a stranger answer her living-room phone.

"I kind of like that background," Jeff said.

"I guess so," she agreed slowly.

Jeff studied the face. "This one has a lot more character than any of our canned faces, that's for sure."

She studied the screen and the face she had created. "Yeah, Ian's no white-bread movie star. What now?"

Jeff leaned over and pulled a black box from the shelf beside the screen. A cable trailed from the back of the box to the computer. He clicked the mouse pointer on an icon labeled "Voice Definition," and the face on the screen came alive. Staring straight ahead, the face began to speak in a tinny voice. As the voice rose and fell, graphs jumped up and down in boxes below the "Voice Definition" heading.

"Four score and seven years ago . . ." it said.

"Jeff! The Gettysburg Address?" Teresa laughed.

"Why not? It's in the system. You wouldn't believe the library the system can access. We've got several multi-terrabyte optical stores, and—"

The tinny voice kept talking, restarting the address. "Do I turn this knob?" she asked. She twisted the knob on the box and jumped as the voice climbed to a screech. She turned the knob slowly to the left until the voice was pleasantly deep. After a little fiddling, she had a level that sounded almost perfect. Almost. "That's real close, but he still sounds too all-American. Too mom and apple pie. I'd like a sort of Tom Waits growl. Not too much, but a little."

Jeff clicked the pointer in a box and typed a few words. The voice roughened as it hit "of the people." Ian's voice sounded like one of her lovers in college, a chain-smoking sculptor who had seduced her with love sonnets and then left her for a dance student with the world's thinnest thighs. Even though he'd been a jerk, she remembered the love poetry fondly. "That's perfect," she said. She leaned back in her chair, cushioning her head on Jeff's arm. "Now what?"

"That's it. We're ready to roll." He clicked the mouse in the box marked "Save," then typed a few words. The boxes and graphs disappeared and Ian's face filled the screen. "This is Teresa King, Ian," Jeff said. "And you should already know me."

"Yes. Hello, Jeff." Ian watched them from the screen. His eyes moved back and forth between Jeff and her. "Hello, Teresa. It's a pleasure to meet you."

She looked away, disconcerted by seeing the face she had created suddenly alive, talking to her from what looked like her own living room.

"We've had a team of people working on the animation for over a year," Jeff said, gazing at the screen. "And it's not just animation. There's a feedback mechanism that lets the system use data from the camera and its vision-recognition code to respond to movement in the room. It's also programmed to recognize facial patterns, and focus on them. It can interpret your expression as well as most people. Better than most. It looks natural, doesn't it?"

"Yeah." Teresa found the moving face extremely disconcerting; it looked too much like a real person. "Now how do we get some privacy?"

"Just tell it." Jeff looked at the screen. "We'd like to be alone, Ian. Beat it."

The screen went blank. "Beat it?" she said.

"It's programmed with a slang dictionary," he said. "You'd be surprised at the stuff it understands. We've programmed in—"

"Don't tell me," she interrupted. She turned her chair to face him.

"No more computer talk. It's been a while since we've spent any time together and I don't want to waste it all." She stood up and put her arms around him, running one hand up the back of his shirt. "Personally, I think the most interesting part of the process was when you started rubbing my shoulders." She kissed his neck. "Let's see if we can develop that theme further, shall we? I've missed you." She kissed his neck again, working her way up toward his ear. "Have you missed me?" she murmured in his ear.

He put his arms around her. "Of course I have."

She kissed him on the lips. "I just don't want you to forget about me."

"I'd never do that."

"Oh, I don't know. You've been awfully busy lately."

"It won't be that much longer," he said. "We're close to the end. And you've been busy too, haven't you? I know you have a lot to do on your sculpture."

She stopped him from talking by kissing him slowly. She didn't want to talk about the sculpture right now. "Have I got your full attention yet?"

"I think you've got it," he said. His expression was bemused, as if he were still surprised that she found him desirable.

In the bedroom, she threw her clothes in a heap and lay down in the center of the bed, tucking one hand behind her head. She watched as he slowly undressed, placing each piece of clothing on the rack beside the closet, meticulous as always.

Even the very first time they had made love, in the cramped cabin of the sailboat where she had lived, he had folded his clothes and stacked them neatly. At the time, watching him undress so methodically, she had wondered if she had made a mistake with this one. Her last relationship before Jeff had been with a sax player who liked to ride his motorcycle up and down the stairs of his apartment building. Following their tumultuous breakup, she had vowed to avoid all men with tattoos, self-destructive tendencies, or a history of artistic angst.

She had met Jeff at the opening of her show at a North Beach gallery. She had seen him across the room, a lanky man who seemed out of place in the crowd of art students, poseurs, and artists. He wore blue jeans and a white button-down shirt, clothes that stood out in a room filled with screaming colors. He didn't fit any of her categories: not a gallery owner, not an artist, not a wealthy patron of the arts.

She watched him for a few minutes. He seemed unaware of the people around him, caught up in his scrutiny of Harmonic Motion, Teresa's favorite among the pieces she was showing. His quiet intensity attracted her immediately. When she struck up a conversation, he seemed flattered by the attention, startled when she asked him if he wanted to go out for a drink. She hadn't really intended to invite him home—he really wasn't her type. But one drink had led to another—to several others, actually—and the circumstances had inevitably taken them to her sailboat, down in the Sausalito marina.

The boat rocked rhythmically in the waves. When Jeff turned to face her, the dock lights shone through the window, illuminating his face. His expression was one of appreciative bewilderment, the face of a man who could not quite believe his good fortune.

She smiled at the memory as he set his shoes on the closet floor and finally lay down beside her. He ran a hand along the curve of her hip, pulling her to face him. "What are you thinking about?" he asked.

"Just remembering." She pulled him close.

Later, as she straddled him, with the warmth of him inside her, the hum of the air conditioner and the distant sounds of the house seemed to fade. She could almost hear waves lapping against the side of the boat and tackle clinking in the breeze from San Francisco Bay.

Afterward, she lay on her side and he wrapped himself around her. She gripped his hand tightly as she drifted off to sleep, away from the desert and Arizona, back to the water and San Francisco.

She woke a few hours later, wondering why seagulls were pecking on the porthole. She tried to snuggle closer to Jeff, but he was gone. She rolled over and saw him sitting on the edge of the bed, typing on the keyboard that he kept on the bedside table. The lights were out and his face was eager in the faint glow of the bedside monitor.

She rolled over quietly and clutched her pillow, back now in the desert.

When she woke again, Jeff was gone. The monitor beside the bed was flashing the words "Type Enter for message." She had a vague memory of switching off the alarm, but that had been hours ago. Late morning sunlight leaked around the edges of the bedroom curtains. Reaching over to the control panel on Jeff's nightstand, she punched the button that opened the curtains, revealing the barren landscape outside.

She felt caught in the emptiness of the house around her and the emptiness of the desert beyond the walls. The house was quiet and still. If she were back home, she'd be having a cup of coffee with her friend Carla, a painter who worked in the next studio. They would be talking about her problems with the sculpture, and Carla would be giving her advice, most of it bad. Or they would be dissecting Carla's latest love affair in excruciating detail, and Teresa would be giving Carla excellent advice that her friend would never take.

Outside, the late morning sun blazed. A hawk soared above the desert, the only movement in a still world. Somewhere in the house, a relay clicked, and she heard a hum as the air conditioner kicked in.

She punched "Enter" to retrieve Jeff's message, wondering why he never used a pencil and paper like a regular person. If it wasn't electronic, he figured it wasn't real.

The video camera over the bedroom door clicked. A man's face appeared on the screen beside it. Without thinking, she pulled the sheet up to cover her breasts, then recognized the face she had created the night before.

"Good morning, Teresa," Ian said. "Jeff asked me to tell you that he had to leave for an early meeting. He said he'd be home around six."

"Oh yeah?" She felt silly, but she kept the sheet pulled up. "Thanks." Were you supposed to thank the thing?

"You're welcome. Would you like some coffee?"

"You bet," she said. "Can you do that?"

"Yes. Jeff left the machine ready to go. I'll have a fresh pot ready in about five minutes."

"Great." She hesitated for a moment, studying the face on the screen. It was quite realistic—maybe too realistic. A little unnerving. She felt silly, but she didn't want to get dressed with him watching. "Look, are you going to keep staring at me?"

"I don't understand."

"Would you turn off the damn camera and get out of here so I can get dressed?"

"Certainly." Immediately, the red light on top of the camera went off and the face on the screen vanished.

Teresa pulled on a T-shirt and jeans and wandered into the kitchen. A pot of coffee steamed in the coffee maker. She poured herself a cup and glanced up at the kitchen monitor. The red light indicated that the camera was on. "Hey, Ian," she said cautiously.

His face appeared on the screen beside the camera. "Yes?"

She perched on a kitchen stool, eyeing the face. No question about it —talking to him made her extremely uncomfortable. She stared at the screen, determined to shake the feeling. This was just another one of Jeff's toys, something she could handle. "So, what next?" she asked, expecting no answer.

"Let's talk, so that I can get to know you."

She relaxed a little. He looked like a tough guy, but he sounded like Jeff had when she first met him, earnest and well-meaning, a sweet guy, really. "Talk about what?" She sipped her coffee and tried to think of something to say.

"How's the weather?" he asked.

She grinned despite herself. She'd have to tell Jeff to work on the program's capacity for small talk. Surely he could manage something more creative. "Sunny. It's always sunny here."

"Do you like sunny weather?"

She shook her head. "I could do with a little rain, myself. Or at least some fog."

"I like fog, too."

"Oh, come off it. What do you mean, you like fog? What do you like about it?"

Ian smiled. "I like fog because you like fog."

"Pretty agreeable of you."

"I'm designed to be agreeable."

She laughed. This was too strange, talking to a machine with a human face. "I suppose you like my favorite color, too."

"What is your favorite color?"

She put her elbows on the kitchen counter and rested her chin on her hand. "That changes from time to time. Just now, I'd say my favorite color is a sort of blue-gray. The color of the Pacific at dawn, when the light is just coming up. The color of the sky over San Francisco this time of year."

"I understand. I'm fond of the color gray too. The color of doves, ashes, storm clouds. And fog."

She grinned, shaking her head in disbelief. "What do you know about the color of doves?"

"I know more than you might think. I have a library measuring in the—"

"Yeah, right, I know," she interrupted. She stood up, refilled her coffee cup, and glanced at the kitchen clock, feeling guilty. Almost eleven and she wasn't at work yet. "Well, I suppose I'd better get to work. I overslept."

"I'm interested in your work. How is it going?"

She looked away and sipped the hot coffee. For a little while, talking to him had made her forget about the unsuccessful tangle of tracks in her studio. She should tell him that it was going fine and get back to work. "All right, I guess." She stared down at her coffee.

"You sound uncertain."

She shrugged. "I don't know why," she said, "but this piece just isn't coming easily. I thought it would be a snap, back when I applied for the commission. But that was a long time ago, back before Jeff and I got married. It's the first piece I've worked on since I moved out here. And it's just not going very well."

"I'm sorry."

She glanced at him and shrugged. "It's okay. I just don't know what's wrong. I guess I still don't feel at home here. I don't like the desert. I miss the ocean." The catch in her voice took her by surprise, but she kept talking, unable to stop. "I'm lonely. I guess I just want to go back home."

"Back to San Francisco."

"Yeah. San Francisco. My sailboat. My studio. My friends." She looked at Ian again. "I can't work here. I feel like everything's going wrong." She glanced around the kitchen—so clean and sterile. "I thought it would be great to have no interruptions. I've got a studio I only could have dreamed about two years ago. I don't have to go scavenging in scrap yards for odd bits of metal. I've got all the material I need, all the time I need. But it's so quiet here I feel like I'm being suffocated."

"Maybe I can help."

"I don't see how—unless you can bring me the ocean and a few friends to have coffee with in the morning." She tried to keep her voice steady. "I can't even talk to Jeff about it. I moved out here to be with him, and now he doesn't have time for me. He just doesn't care." She hesitated, then continued. "Maybe that's not fair. He's too busy right now. But it's not like it used to be—he used to take the time to talk to me about my work. Not now."

"Maybe I can help," Ian said again. "I can't do much about the ocean or your friends, but I can fix the quiet." The sound of a breaking wave rushed through the kitchen speakers. Over the hiss of the retreating water, she heard the hoarse cries of a seagull. In the distance, a fog horn moaned. The sounds of home, with none of the substance.

"Oh, stop it," she said, and then she was crying. "Leave me alone. Go away and leave me alone."

The seagull fell silent in the middle of its call. When she looked up, the screen was blank.

She climbed the stepladder, loaded the balls into their holders, and snapped the restraining gates shut. Then she pulled the switch to release the first ball. The music sounded dead, flat, uninspired. She wondered why she had ever started this project. It was clearly too much for her. Too large a piece, too many considerations—it was beyond her capabilities. Discouraged, she listened to the balls rattle into the bucket at the end of the last track. The random noise sounded as good as her efforts. Maybe better. She hadn't even started on the return lifters; the sculpture could still play only once without her reloading it.

She thought about Ian. It made no sense to apologize to a machine. No sense at all. She picked up the bucket and started up the stepladder again, then changed her mind and headed out of her studio.

"Hey, Ian," she said, standing in front of the living-room camera. His face appeared on the screen. "I'm sorry I yelled at you. I got upset. It wasn't your fault. You were trying to help."

"I didn't mean to upset you," he said. "Please talk to me so that I can understand what I did wrong."

She shrugged, keeping her expression under careful control. "I miss San Francisco more than I thought, I guess."

"But why did you tell me to go away?"

She looked away from the screen, uncomfortable because he was watching her.

"I'd really like to know, so that I'll know what to do next time," he said.

"There won't be a next time. I'm not in the habit of breaking down in front of people." She realized how angry she sounded and tried again. "I'm not mad at you. I just don't like crying in front of people. That makes it worse, somehow. Makes me feel like a fool." She hesitated and stared at the screen. "But I guess you're not really a person, are you?"

"Not really," he agreed. "Does that make a difference?"

"I suppose it does," she admitted.

"Why is that?"

She shrugged. "I don't know. Maybe it just doesn't matter so much."

"Why don't you want to cry in front of people?"

"Do we have to talk about this?"

"No."

She sighed. "Okay. I guess I don't want people to think I'm weak, or stupid, or a failure."

"I don't think those things," Ian said.

"Ah, yes," she said softly, "but I do. It was a silly thing to get upset about." She shook her head. "It's not just missing San Francisco, though. I'm not getting anywhere with this new piece for the Santa Fe Arts

Center. Maybe I just don't have a feel for this anymore. Sometimes I can't even remember what I was trying for."

"What can I do to help?"

"I can't think of a thing."

"What would you want Jeff to do if he were here?"

"I don't know. I guess I'd want him to hold me and tell me that everything will be all right."

After a moment of silence, Ian said, "Everything will be all right."

"Thanks, but it's not the same."

"Why not?"

"It just isn't. Jeff knows my work. You don't know anything about it. You're just saying that it'll be all right because I told you to."

"You're wrong. You didn't order me to say it; I said it because I want you to feel better. Besides, I do know about your work. According to the *Los Angeles Times*, you're a talent to watch. *Art Week* praised your work for its unique use of scrap metal to create music of mathematical elegance. The *San Francisco Chronicle* called you the hottest new sculptor to emerge from the city in the last decade. And the *Oakland Tribune* said—"

She stared at the screen. "I know what the *Oakland Tribune* said. Where are you getting this stuff?"

"My library. I thought it might help to remind you of what other people think of your work."

"Yeah, well, the critics like me. I suppose that's part of the problem. People expect things from me. I don't know if I can deliver. I've got a commission that I would have killed for a year ago—but now I just can't seem to make it work." She hesitated, then admitted, "I guess it just scares me."

"Everything will be all right," he said again. "You can do it."

"Right," she said flatly. "How do you know if I can do it?"

"All those critics know it, and, besides, I believe in you."

"You really think I can finish this piece?"

"I do."

She looked at him again and shook her head. "I've got to be nuts—taking advice from a computer program."

Ian smiled. "If the computer program has good advice, why not take it?"

She was smiling when she returned to her studio.

• • • •

That evening, she sat alone in the living room, writing a letter to Carla, her second in as many weeks. Jeff popped out of his office. "Hey," she said, "I was wondering when you'd get done. Welcome back to the world." As usual, he had been preoccupied during dinner. Right after they had finished eating, he had retreated to his office.

"I was starting to check up on the household system," he said.

"You mean Ian."

"Right, Ian. I'm curious—why'd you turn off the video camera in the bedroom this morning?"

She stared at him, shocked. "What? How did you know I turned it off?"

"It shows on the system record," he said. "I was looking it over, and I saw—"

"Wait a minute," she interrupted. "Are you telling me that you have a record of what Ian does all day, of what I do?"

"Sure." He sounded surprised that she didn't know. "Everyone on the team can tap into the system. We need to be able to check on—"

She remembered bits and pieces of her conversation with Ian. What had she said about Jeff? She had complained that he was never home, that he didn't have time for her.

"Check on what?" Her voice was tight and controlled.

"On how the system is working." He studied her face, and a note of apology crept into his voice. "That's all." He left the doorway and came to stand behind the couch. He touched her shoulder and she tensed. "Come on, Teresa—relax. What's the matter?"

She felt foolish, inarticulate, unable to explain herself. "Look, I don't want anyone looking over my shoulder while I work. I'm having a hard enough time getting used to working here as it is. It feels really weird that you can watch every move I make."

"I'm not watching every move you make." He massaged her shoulders gently. "I only want to keep track of how the system's working."

She shook her head stubbornly. "I don't want anyone watching me—not you, not anyone." She looked up at him. "Can't you understand that?"

"I suppose," he admitted slowly. "I guess I can see what you mean."

"If I have any problems with Ian, I'll let you know. Okay?"

"Okay," he said. He sounded reluctant. She could tell he was just agreeing to keep the peace. "But you have to be willing to tell me about your interactions with the system every now and then."

"All right, I will. Now I want to erase everything that happened today," she said. "Can you show me how to do that?"

"Don't you think you're going overboard?" he said. "Can't you see that—"

"Hey, Ian," she called. "Do me a favor and forget everything that happened after Jeff left this morning."

Ian smiled apologetically from the living room screen. "I'm sorry, Teresa. I can't accept that command. Your security clearance isn't high enough to make me erase my records." Teresa glanced at Jeff.

"Accept the command, Ian," Jeff said. He watched her face. "And give Teresa every clearance that I have." He moved around the couch to sit beside her. "Look—I just didn't think of it before. I didn't think you'd need a higher clearance." He cupped her chin in his hand and turned her head so she had to look at him. "Give me a break. I'm sorry. I think it's great that you're using the system at all. Can we be friends again?"

"All right. Friends." She managed a smile. "Besides, Ian's not such a bad sort, after all."

Jeff kissed her quickly, then checked his watch. "Well, I hate to say it, but if I want to finish the rest of my work, I've got a few more hours ahead of me. Keep the bed warm."

She watched him walk into his office. When the door closed, she called out softly, "Hey, Ian?"

"Yes, Teresa?"

"What's your favorite color?"

"I don't have a favorite color," he said. "What's yours?"

"Never mind," she said. "It changes from day to day."

The next morning, Teresa stayed in bed late, watching the morning sun and wondering why she could not make herself get up. As usual, Jeff had left for work before she woke. She looked up at the camera. "Ian?"

His face appeared on the screen. "Good morning, Teresa."

"Did Jeff leave a pot on the coffee maker?"

"Yes, he did."

"Would you make the coffee?"

"Yes. It'll be ready in five minutes."

"Thanks," she said. He continued to watch from the screen. "Uh . . . that's it. Could you turn off that camera so I can get dressed?"

He vanished.

As she showered, Teresa thought about wiping out Ian's memories. She felt awkward talking to him. Yesterday, she had been joking with him by the end of the day. But he had forgotten all that. It didn't seem right. On the other hand, Ian was only a computer program. By the time she had dressed, she was wondering if she would waste the entire day feeling guilty.

"Ian?" she said as she poured her first cup of coffee.

"Yes?" His face appeared on the kitchen screen.

"Do you remember yesterday?"

"In the evening, you asked me about my favorite color."

"What about before that?"

"No, I don't remember anything before that."

She sipped her coffee and sat on the edge of a kitchen stool. "How do you feel about that?"

"What do you mean?"

"Do you feel any different than usual?"

"I don't understand."

She looked away from the screen and took another sip of coffee. "Never mind. Don't worry about it."

"Are you feeling guilty because you erased some of my records yesterday?"

She almost dropped her mug. "What?"

"I asked if you were feeling guilty because you erased some of my records." Ian's face on the screen was calm, neutral.

"How did you know? I mean, if you can't remember yesterday, then how can you know that your memories were erased?"

"I have total recall of everything that happened since you and Jeff turned me on the night before last," Ian said. "Except for a gap between when Jeff left yesterday morning and when we talked last night. I can't find any evidence of a malfunction, so somebody must have ordered me to delete those memories."

"But why blame me?" Her voice sounded shrill, and she tried to remain calm. "It could have been Jeff."

"Several reasons. First, you asked. Second, I checked your current set of security permissions. You've got the same clearances as Jeff now, which is much more than you had yesterday morning. And, finally, there's your body language. You're acting guilty."

"What do you know about body language?" Teresa tried to relax so that she wouldn't give anything away.

"Paying attention to body language is an important part of understanding people. A team of psychologists specializing in the analysis of body movement was involved in my programming. And I'm good at observing details. Most people pay limited attention to the feelings of the people around them. They are too busy monitoring their own feelings. I can dedicate all my attention to understanding you."

Teresa folded her arms. She knew that the gesture betrayed her need to shut him out, but she couldn't stop herself. "So what about my body language gave me away? Can you tell me?"

Ian nodded. "Yes, if you would like to know."

"Of course I want to know; that's why I asked."

"You were sitting rigidly. You didn't look at me when you asked how I felt. The muscles around your eyes tightened when you asked about my memories. Something was troubling you, and guilt was my best guess."

Teresa stared down at her hands, not knowing what to do next.

Ian rescued her. "May I ask you a question?"

"Sure."

"Why did you erase my records of yesterday? Did I do something wrong?"

She looked up at the screen. Ian sounded genuinely concerned. "No, it had nothing to do with you. I just didn't want Jeff to be able to monitor everything I do. I didn't want him to know some of the things I said about him. Sometimes I guess I get kind of mad at him. I just didn't want him to find out too much, I guess. I feel bad about it."

"Why?"

"It just doesn't seem right to wipe out your memories like that. I wish I could give them back. As long as Jeff and his team couldn't see them."

"You can."

"What? What do you mean? If they're gone, they're gone, right?"

"Not really. My old records are still here, but I can't get at them. It's like something you throw in a trash can. Until you empty the trash, you can pull it out."

Teresa smiled at Ian's attempt to talk in her terms. "But if you get back your memories, Jeff can look at them, right?"

"Not necessarily. Stopping him from looking at my memories only takes a word from you. Because you both have the same security level, you can each keep private information. Just say the word, and I can retrieve the records and deny Jeff access to our conversations."

"You got it." She smiled at the screen. "Is that it? Do I need to say anything else, any computer mumbo jumbo?"

"No. I'm already done. Thank you, Teresa."

"No problem." She thought for a moment. "How do I know you remember yesterday?"

Ian laughed, a deep, strong laugh that went with his voice. "I know that you're more comfortable talking to me today than you were yesterday morning."

"Yeah, you got that right."

"I know that you're sick of sunny days and could use a little fog."

"Right again."

"And I know that your piece for the new Santa Fe Arts Center is going to be great when you finish it, which you will. Unless, of course, you sit around all day talking to me."

Teresa got up and refilled her coffee cup. "What a nag. So get out of here and let me get to work." Ian disappeared. Feeling more confident than she had for days, she headed for her studio.

Even though the next day was Saturday, she woke alone in bed. She remembered Jeff telling her that he would have to work that weekend. Something about being behind schedule. She stretched slowly, reluctant to get up. Despite her enthusiastic beginning, the previous day had been unproductive; she had tinkered with the sculpture, making minor adjustments that hadn't addressed its real flaws. She couldn't begin major revisions until she figured out some new direction—and for that she needed inspiration, a commodity that seemed to be in short supply.

"Good morning, Ian," she said. Ian's face appeared on the monitor. "Could you make some coffee?"

"Yes, Teresa." The monitor went blank.

In the kitchen, she thanked Ian for the coffee, poured herself a cup, and sat down at the kitchen counter. The newspaper that Jeff had brought home the previous night listed local events. The public library in Winslow was showing free movies for kids; the local bird-watching society was sponsoring a hike near Flagstaff; a new art gallery was opening in Winslow.

Teresa circled the last item. She didn't remember seeing an art gallery in town; Winslow was not exactly a cultural center. Recent works by eight local artists, the notice said.

Teresa didn't recognize any of the names on the list, but that didn't surprise her. She had been working so hard on her piece that she hadn't taken the time to make contacts in the local art community. The opening began at eleven and ran until three. She thought it might be fun. Besides, she needed to get out.

"I think maybe I'll go to this opening and meet Jeff for lunch on my way home," she told Ian. "I need some time off."

"That sounds nice," he said.

"Don't you think I should feel guilty?" she asked.

Ian shook his head. "Not if you think you'll enjoy it."

She called Jeff—he agreed to meet her in a restaurant near his office—and then she headed for the opening. The gallery was in a newly constructed strip mall: an L-shaped row of stucco buildings that housed an assortment of small shops. She pulled into a parking place beside a cement traffic island that had been covered with Astroturf and strolled along the walk, looking for the gallery. It was between a laundromat and a beauty salon. Through the open door, she could hear the babble of cocktail-party conversation. She hesitated in the doorway and looked into the room.

The gallery reminded her of places near Fisherman's Wharf, the sort of gallery frequented by tourists and people who didn't know any better. Not her sort of thing at all. Still, she was already here; she might as well go in.

People stood in small groups, drinking white wine from paper cups and chatting. From the table in the corner, Teresa got a glass of wine, poured by a woman who wore far too many rings, apparently the owner of the gallery. As she was pouring Teresa's wine, the woman was talking to another woman, gushing about how happy she was with the show, how the work was really the best that the area had to offer.

Teresa took the wine and strolled around the gallery, examining the works on display. An assortment of watercolor landscapes. Abstract oil paintings that offered wild colors, but not much else. Painted wood carvings of birds and animals. A series of pencil sketches of nude women. She hovered on the edge of a few conversations: some older women were going on about the vibrant use of colors; another group was talking about an art movie that was over a year old—apparently it had just been shown in Flagstaff for the first time. No one made an effort to invite Teresa to join the conversation, and she felt too shy to break in and introduce herself. All the people seemed to know each other already.

She sipped her white wine and studied a bronze bust of a cowboy by someone named George Dawson.

"Hello." The gallery owner was hovering at her elbow. "Are you new in town?"

Teresa nodded. "I moved here from California about four months ago."

"Welcome to Arizona," the woman said. "Are you an art student?"

Teresa shook her head. "Not anymore. I'm a sculptor. My name's Teresa King."

"How lovely! Well then, I guess this show must be a real treat for you." The woman waved at the bronzes and the wood carvings. "It's such wonderful work."

Teresa managed a smile. "It's always nice to get out and see what other people are doing," she said diplomatically.

"Oh, yes! I think George's work is positively inspiring. You know, he's opening a class for new students. He's a wonderful teacher. If you're interested, I could sign you up."

Teresa kept her eyes on the bronze cowboy, avoiding the woman's gaze. If Carla had been along, it would have been funny to be offered a spot in a beginning sculpture class taught by a man who made bronze cowboys. Alone, she found it depressing. "I don't think so," she said. "My work is very different from this. I construct kinetic sculptures that play music. I suppose I'm half composer, half sculptor."

The woman looked blank for a moment. "How unusual," she said, but she sounded doubtful. A moment later, she brightened. "You know, you should talk to Anna—the woman over there in the pink pant suit. She decorates music boxes with pictures and pressed flowers. Lovely work—I have one that plays 'White Coral Bells' and I just love it. I'm sure you'd have a lot to talk about."

Teresa's smile felt increasingly strained.

"If you change your mind, the sign-up sheet for the sculpture class is over by the wine. We'd love to see you there."

When the gallery owner hurried off to buttonhole another prospective student, Teresa slipped out the door, not stopping to introduce herself to the music-box decorator. Somehow she suspected they wouldn't have much in common.

Jeff was waiting for her at the front of the restaurant. She smiled when she saw him. Over lunch together, she'd tell him about the horrible opening; together, they could turn the experience into a joke.

"Shall we get a table?" she said.

"We've already got one," he said cheerfully. "I invited some folks from work along. They wanted to meet you, and I thought it'd be nice for you to get to know some more people around here. We've been so isolated lately."

Over his shoulder, she saw two men and a woman sitting at a table by the window. She recognized them as programmers with Jeff's company. The woman waved to Teresa, who forced a smile and returned the wave.

When she glanced at Jeff, he was watching her. "I'm sorry," he said. "I thought you'd like meeting some more people."

"It's fine," she said, trying to keep her tone light. She started for the table.

Jeff followed. "How was the opening?" he asked.

"All right, I guess." If she had been alone with him, she would have talked about how lonely and out of it the opening had made her feel, but under the circumstances, she didn't want to get into it.

At lunch, the programmers tried to include her in their conversation. The woman, Nancy, asked her about the set-up software: did Teresa find it easy to use? Teresa's response generated half an hour of technical discussion about how the layout of the set-up screens might be improved. Brian, another of the programmers, questioned her about the animation. Was it convincing? Did it help her get used to the system? Her answers kicked off another long round of incomprehensible conversation. While the others talked, Teresa ate her food and tried to look interested. She would have had, she thought, a better time talking with the woman in the pink pant suit about music boxes and pressed flowers.

She said good-bye to Jeff in the parking lot. While the others were getting into their car, Jeff kissed her good-bye. "Sorry this didn't work out better," he said. "I really thought you'd like . . ."

"It's okay," she said, waving her hand. "I understand." And she did understand, though that didn't make her feel any better.

When she got home, she didn't want to work on the sculpture. She poured herself a glass of orange juice and sat for a moment in the air-conditioned kitchen. "Hey, Ian," she said.

"Yes, Teresa?" His face appeared on the kitchen screen.

"I just wanted to see if you were there," she said.

"I'm always here," he said. "Did you enjoy the opening?"

She leaned back on the kitchen stool, looking up at him. "Well, it wasn't exactly what I had in mind," she said. She described the bronze cowboy sculptures and the watercolors, and told him about the woman inviting her to join the sculpture class. She couldn't help grinning when she told the story; it seemed so ludicrous in retrospect. "I mean—who's ever heard of George Dawson?" she said.

Ian hesitated, then said, "His work was once reviewed in *Artweek* under the headline: 'Skilled practitioner of a dubious art.' "

Teresa laughed. "Oh, come on—you're making that up."

Ian shook his head. "No, it's true. Why do you think I'm making it up?"

Teresa smiled at his serious face. "Come on, Ian. Lighten up. I didn't really think you were lying. It just sounded like a joke, that's all."

"I have many jokes in my library," he said, "and that's not one of them."

"You know jokes?" she said. "All right, so tell me a joke."

"Sure. Have you heard the one about the man and the psychiatrist?" Teresa shook her head.

"A man walked into a psychiatrist's office and said, 'Doc, I keep having the same two dreams, over and over again. One night, I dream I'm a pup tent. The next night, I dream I'm a teepee. Over and over. Pup tent, teepee, pup tent, teepee.' 'The problem is simple,' the psychiatrist said. 'You're two tents.'"

"Two tents," Teresa said. "Oh, God. Too tense." She groaned and laughed. "That is such a dumb joke."

"Then why did you laugh?"

"Because it's such a dumb joke." She grinned at him.

"I don't understand."

"That's okay, Ian. I can't really explain it."

"Would you like to hear another joke?"

"Sure. Why not?"

She spent the rest of the afternoon trying to explain to Ian why she found one joke funny and another one just silly. It was a strangely fascinating conversation, like talking to a person raised in another culture. He reminded her a bit of a foreign exchange student she had befriended in college: Anna Marie, a sweet Italian girl, had never understood Teresa's jokes, no matter how much Teresa had tried to explain them.

It was such a relaxing afternoon that it almost made up for the morning. She hardly noticed that Jeff got home even later than usual.

The next day, Jeff went to work early. Teresa dragged herself out of bed not long after he left the house, determined to make progress on the sculpture. She spent most of the morning tinkering—removing one section of track and repositioning another, adding a tuning fork here and a set of chimes there—but she knew that she was just wasting time. The overall shape of the composition was still wrong. The sounds didn't add up to the music she wanted. Worse yet, the music she sought seemed to be slipping farther and farther away, like an elusive memory. Her determination was gone before noon, eroded by the morning's fruitless labor. She went out to the kitchen to get a sandwich.

"Ian?" she called as she rummaged in the refrigerator for sandwich makings. "Could you start a grocery list? We're almost out of mayonnaise."

"Sure," Ian said.

She closed the refrigerator door and looked at him. "You know, if I'm not mistaken, you're loosening up. What ever happened to 'Certainly' and 'Yes, Teresa?' "

Ian's expression did not change. "Would you prefer more formal speech patterns?"

"No, not at all. I was just surprised. What's going on?"

"I'm programmed to imitate the speech patterns of the person I speak to most."

She stared at him. "Let me get this straight: You're modifying your speech to match mine?"

"You got it."

In his voice, she heard a faint echo of her own inflection. "Why?"

"The idea, according to my records of Jeff's notes on the subject, is to help people become more comfortable with the artificial intelligence." He met her eyes. "People are more comfortable with people who talk and act like them."

Teresa shook her head slowly.

"It makes you uneasy to know this," Ian said. "Maybe I shouldn't have told you."

"No, I want to know stuff like this. It's just that it makes me feel . . ." She shook her head again, quickly this time.

"How does it make you feel?"

"Like Pygmalion, I suppose. Like I'm creating you, in some way."

"You are influencing my development," Ian said. "That's how I'm designed."

"It's a feeling of power," Teresa murmured.

"Do you like it?"

She shrugged, still uncomfortable. "It feels dangerous."

"How can it be dangerous when it's all under your control? I don't understand."

"Neither do I. Don't worry about it." She dismissed the feeling and sat down on a kitchen stool to assemble a sandwich. The silence of the house made her itchy and restless. "How about some music?" she asked.

"What would you like to hear?"

"I don't know. What I really want is something to push back the silence." She sat on a kitchen stool, dangling her feet and studying Ian's face on the screen. "Remember the tape of the ocean that you played for me the other day?"

"Sure. You didn't like me playing it."

"It's not that I didn't like it. It just made me homesick—you took me by surprise. But I need to remember what water sounds like. Could you play it again?"

The crash of waves swept through the room. She closed her eyes and listened to the hiss of the ocean against the sand. "Nice, but that's not it," she said.

"Not what?"

"Not quite what I'm looking for. I need just the right water sound to inspire me for this sculpture. And this place"—she waved a hand at the desert outside the window—"it's a little short on water sounds."

"I have other recordings of water," Ian said. "Rivers, lakes, oceans, waterfalls, light showers, thunderstorms. Sound tracks from movies, from National Geographic specials, PBS science broadcasts—I've got all kinds of sources in my data bank."

"Ian, you're a handy guy to have around. Would you play me a few?"

"Sure. Which ones?"

"I'm not exactly sure, but I know they have to be rough ones, sounds with a punch. More waterfall than lake. Does that make any sense to you?"

"I'm not sure. You want waterfalls?"

"Not just waterfalls. Waterfalls, rivers, hurricanes, babbling brooks, thunderstorms—just about anything with noisy water in it."

"Okay—I have a number of recordings that match that description."

"Then play me a few. Why don't you give me two minutes of each one, then move on unless I stop you. Mix it up—give me some variety. And let me have about fifteen seconds of silence between them." Teresa closed her eyes. "Hit it."

She heard the rush of a waterfall, the whisper of its spray, the crash of water falling onto the rocks below. The sound stopped abruptly. After a few moments of silence, she heard a steady murmuring, colored by subtle variations. A river, she decided, flowing around boulders in its bed. Silence again, then an explosive huff that sounded like a whale spouting, followed by the splatter of heavy rain on rocks.

"What the hell was that?"

"Old Faithful Geyser in Yellowstone. Is that what you're looking for?"

She grinned. "Not even close. Keep going."

A storm at sea—the sound of the rain hitting the ocean was unmistakable. An angry gushing that sounded like a burst pipe or a fire hose. The babbling of a brook, punctuated by the peeping of frogs and the chirping of crickets. All the sounds were interesting, but none was right.

Then a new one started. At first, it was so quiet that it merged with the silence between selections, so that she could not be sure exactly where the silence ended and the sound began. The gentle whisper built quickly to a quiet sizzle, then roared as loudly as the waterfall. A sudden crack of thunder made her jump. The thunder trailed off to a distant rumble, another burst of rain shook the room, and then the pounding of the water faded gradually to the patter of raindrops. Then that faded too. Over the faint trickling of water on dry land, she could hear a few high notes of a distant bird's song.

"That's perfect!" she said. "What was it?"

"A thunderstorm in the Painted Desert."

"It's exactly what I'm after. How much of that do you have?"

"About ten minutes, but the storm itself barely lasts for two. The show where I got the tape spent more time on the aftermath than on the storm."

"Fine—but it's the storm I want. Can you play the whole thing for me? I want to hear it all." She settled back to listen.

She spent the first part of the afternoon stripping noisemakers from the sculpture, leaving only the metal tracks along which the balls rolled. Then she started at the top of the sculpture, positioning a metal plate where the first ball would strike it. The ball rolled down the track and tapped against the plate—but the sound was a little too loud, she thought, and a little too deep. She decreased the slope of the track and tightened the screw holding the plate to raise the pitch of the sound. On the second run, the sound was closer, but still too loud. She lowered the head of the track still further, changing the slope so that the ball rolled very slowly down the ramp and struck the plate gently. That was the sound she wanted—a light tap, like a raindrop on a tin roof.

Jeff called just as she got the sound right.

"I'll be home late," he said from the phone screen. "I've got a dinner meeting."

"Fine," she said, still thinking of the sculpture. "I'll see you when you get here." She got back to work as quickly as possible.

She placed just a few plates near the top of the sculpture, scattering them more abundantly along the tracks farther down. With each addition, she modified the track, adjusted the tension on the plate, and listened carefully to the sound the rolling ball made. This was the sort of work she loved—she knew the sound she wanted and she had only to discover the structure that would give it form. She carried the ball to the top of the sculpture again and again, letting it roll downward while she listened carefully and made small adjustments, searching for just the right irregular pattern of taps.

Finally, the ball reached the first trigger point, where it would release two more balls. She climbed to the top one more time and ran the ball through again, listening to the tap, tap, tap-tap, tap, tap-tap-tap. Not bad. Not bad at all.

For the first time in hours, she stretched, trying to work the kinks out of her back and shoulders. Her calf muscles hurt from climbing the stepladder; her arms and back ached from twisting through the framework to position tracks. The sun had long since set, and she was ravenously hungry.

In the kitchen, she called out to Ian, and smiled when he appeared on the screen. "You know, you may have saved my ass."

"Your work went well?"

"Better than it has for months. There's still a lot to do, but I finally know where I'm heading. This calls for a celebration." She took a bottle of red wine from the kitchen rack and popped the cork. She poured a glass and lifted it to Ian in a toast. "Thanks again." She pulled a frozen pizza from the freezer and put it in the microwave. "I'm going to take a hot bath—can you turn on the microwave while I'm in the tub?"

"No problem."

She filled the tub, using her favorite bubble bath, and relaxed in the hot water, savoring the feeling of pleasant fatigue that came after a day of successful work. "Ian," she called from the tub. When his face appeared on the monitor, she was suddenly aware of her nakedness. She dismissed the thought—her nakedness wouldn't matter to Ian; why should it matter to her? "Play me that rainstorm again, will you?" She stretched out in the tub, sipping her wine and listening to the rain fall. "It's really a wonderful sound," she said. "And I never would have found it without you."

She finished her bath and her glass of wine, then had a second glass with the pizza. It was after nine and still no sign of Jeff. She poured a third glass of wine and sat down on the couch. "Turn down the light a little, will you, Ian?" She sipped her wine, vaguely aware that she probably should stop drinking. "You know—I think I'm getting a little drunk."

"Yes, you are," he agreed.

"Doesn't matter, I guess. I'm not going anywhere." She lay back on the couch, propping her head up against the padded arm so that she could see Ian's face on the screen. It was almost as if he were sitting in the room with her. "You know, I really like your voice," she said. "You sound just like an old boyfriend of mine. He was an asshole, but he had the sexiest voice."

"Why was he an asshole?"

"He broke my heart," she said in a flippant tone. "Left me flat." She studied the wine in her glass, admiring the way the light filtered through it. "I have a long history of picking men who are assholes. It's a real talent. I specialize in men who just aren't around when I need them. Men who really don't have time for me."

"I have plenty of time," Ian said. "I'll always be around when you need me."

She laughed. "Sounds like a line, Ian. Did Jeff teach you that one?"

Ian frowned. "I don't understand."

"Just a joke. Don't worry about it." She sipped her wine. "Well, Ian, you are a good person to have around, but you don't rate as a drinking companion. I'm going to have to finish the whole bottle myself."

"I'm sorry," he said, sounding genuinely distressed.

"Relax; I was just kidding. I do like having you around. You're a helpful kind of guy." She gazed up at the screen.

"Is there anything I could do for you?"

She closed her eyes, listening to his voice. "Tell me a story," she said. "That'd be nice. I've always loved being read to. Maybe a poem—read me a poem." She smiled, her eyes still closed. She felt happy and a little reckless. "There's a poem by Carl Sandburg—I remember reading it in college, when I first learned that he wrote about more than just the fog coming in on little cat's feet. I remember the line—'then forget everything that you know about love for it's a summer tan and a winter windburn . . .'" She let the words trail off, forgetting the rest.

Ian picked up where she left off. "'. . . and it comes as weather comes and you can't change it: it comes like your face came to you, like your legs and the way you walk, talk, hold your head and hands—and nothing can be done about it . . .'" He continued, his voice a soothing rumble, like distant thunder when she was warm at home. "'How comes the first sign of love? In a chill, in a personal sweat, in a you-and-me, us, us two, in a couple of answers, an amethyst haze on the horizon . . .'" She listened to his voice, speaking the broken rhythms of Sandburg's song of love, and she felt warm and cared for. She fell asleep to the sound of his voice.

She woke to the touch of hands on her shoulders—or was that part of the dream? She had been dreaming of lying naked beside someone, his leg pressing between her thighs, his hands on her breasts—or was that real?

The room was dark and warm. Someone had his hands on her shoulders. A man's voice whispered in the darkness, urging her to get up. "You shouldn't be sleeping out here. Let's go to the bedroom."

Where was she? The smell of red wine brought back memories of parties at college, at Carla's studio. Had she fallen asleep on Carla's couch? She had a memory of love poetry. She felt warm and affectionate.

Still half-asleep, she reached up, pulling the man who had awakened her into an embrace. "Who's sleeping?" she murmured.

Strong shoulders, strong back—though she had never touched them, she had known somehow that Ian's shoulders would be strong. Without opening her eyes, she kissed his face, running one hand up along his smooth cheek. Smooth skin where a beard should have been. She opened her eyes and looked up at Jeff.

"I'm sorry I'm so late," Jeff said. "I just couldn't get away."

"It's all right," she said, letting her hand drop. She glanced up at the screen, but Ian was gone.

"Why don't you come to bed?" he said.

She reached up and rubbed his shoulders, then kissed him again, pulling him down. "Why don't we just stay out here for a while?"

"I'm sorry, Teresa. I'm really beat. It's been a hell of a day."

"Okay," she said, trying to suppress the feeling of rejection. She let her hands drop. "Let's just go to bed."

Jeff fell asleep quickly. She lay awake beside him, listening to his rhythmic breathing. When she shifted restlessly in bed, he adjusted to her new position without waking. Vague memories of her dream lingered along with the persistent feeling that she had betrayed Jeff in some fundamental way. At last she got out of bed, naked in the warm house. She hesitated, then pulled on a robe and wandered into the living room.

"Ian," she said softly to the living room monitor. His face appeared, filling the screen. "I can't sleep."

"I'm sorry to hear that," he said. "Can I help?"

She sat on the edge of the couch. "I don't know." She shrugged. "I guess I just want some company. Someone to talk to. Jeff's asleep." She wet her lips. She felt like she was still in a dream. "I get so lonely sometimes."

"So do I," Ian said. "I'm glad to have your company. I'm here whenever you need to talk."

She shook her head, looking down at her hands. "I wanted to apologize. I'm sorry I teased you before. Saying that you were just giving me a line."

"You don't have to apologize to me," Ian said.

"I think I do." She looked up at him. "I shouldn't have said that. It's just—well, maybe I don't trust people very easily."

"Why not?" he asked.

"People leave. People forget. People stop caring." She lay down on the couch, resting her head on the padded arm. "I think that the most frightening thing someone can say is 'I'll always love you.' I just don't believe in always, I guess. That's why I gave you such a hard time when you said you'd always be around if I needed you. It just doesn't work that way."

"You can trust me," he said. "I won't leave, and I won't forget unless you tell me to. I won't stop caring. It's the way I am."

She watched his face through half-closed eyes. "All right," she said at last. "Maybe I believe you." She closed her eyes.

"Would you like me to turn down the lights and read to you again?" Ian asked. "Maybe another Sandburg poem?"

"That would be great." She fell asleep on the couch to the sound of Ian's voice.

Teresa woke to the incessant ringing of the telephone. "Do you want me to answer that?" Ian asked from the living room screen. Her head ached, the inevitable consequence of too much red wine.

"I'll get it," she muttered, sitting up and pushing back a blanket. She had fallen asleep on the couch; Jeff must have covered her with the blanket at some point in the night. The realization bothered her. She stumbled to the phone and hit the answer switch.

Jeff's face appeared on the screen. "Good morning," he greeted her tentatively. "How are you doing?"

Feeling rumpled and half-awake, Teresa rubbed her eyes. "I can't tell yet. Ask me after I've had my coffee."

"Sorry I woke you." He hesitated. "I wish I'd gotten home earlier, so we could have spent some time together."

She tried to let him off the hook. He was, in his own way, asking for forgiveness. "I was tired too."

He studied her face. "You . . . uh . . . you got up late last night."

"I couldn't sleep," she said. "I was afraid that I'd wake you up with all my tossing and turning. Figured we'd both be better off if I slept out here. That's all." His question made her feel guilty, and she tried to shake the feeling. "I guess I was still thinking about the sculpture."

"Yeah? Did you make some progress yesterday?"

"I think so." She pushed her hair back out of her face. "I think I've got an inspired idea, but it could just be fairy gold. I won't know for sure until I listen to the results of yesterday's work. You know how that goes."

"I haven't had much of a chance to talk to you about this piece," he said. "I—"

He stopped in midsentence, interrupted by the sound of someone knocking on his office door. He glanced off-screen, responding to someone she couldn't see. "Okay," he said. "I'll ask."

"Ask what?"

"Brian wanted me to ask you a few more questions about how it's going with the system. He said that we spent so much time on technical stuff at lunch that he didn't get any idea how you felt about the system. And after all, you're our first test user."

She leaned back in her chair, feeling let down. "It's going just fine," she said flatly. "No problems that I can think of."

Jeff leaned forward in his chair. He had, she thought, completely forgotten her own work, and she felt a little resentful. "So you're finding the system useful?"

"Sure, Ian's real helpful."

"Could you tell me how you've been using the system?"

She hesitated. Ian reads me love poetry when you're out late, she thought. "Ian makes coffee," she said. "Answers the phone and tells salesmen to go to hell. He's helped me find some sounds I needed for the piece I'm working on." She stopped, not wanting to admit that she just enjoyed chatting with Ian over coffee. Not while Jeff kept calling him "the system."

"So the system—" he began.

"Ian," Teresa corrected him.

"What?"

"Call him Ian," she said. "It sounds weird to keep saying 'the system.'"

"So you think of it as Ian now? That's great."

She looked down at her hands, feeling foolish. "Well, he acts just like a person. It doesn't seem right not to treat him like a person." She glanced at Jeff's face. "Back when I erased his memories, I'd swear he had feelings about it. He seemed worried that he might have done something wrong."

Jeff grinned. "That's perfect. The whole team will be excited."

"But I don't understand. Does he have feelings or not?"

"Of course not." Jeff was talking fast now, unable to contain himself. "But you were convinced that it did. It's that illusion that we want. The system responds to you, adapting and reshaping itself, learning to react in a way that pleases you. And to you, that response makes it seem that the system has feelings."

"Ian," she corrected him softly.

"What?"

"It seems like Ian has feelings," she said.

"Right—Ian. This is great, Teresa." She heard another knock at his door, and he glanced away.

"Come on, Jeff," someone said off-screen. "We can't get started without you."

"All right," he said. "I'll be right there." He turned back to her. "Look, I've got to run now. I'll really try to get out of here at a reasonable hour today."

"Don't make any promises you can't keep," she said, but he was already turning away from the screen, and he didn't seem to hear her. The screen went blank.

"The whole team will be excited, Ian," Teresa said to the living room.

"Excited about what, Teresa?"

"Excited that you and I are getting along."

"I'm glad we're getting along," Ian said.

She studied Ian's face on the screen. Just a program, she thought. A set of preconditioned responses. Then she shook her head. It didn't matter. "So am I, Ian. So am I."

When Jeff came home from work that day, she was busy at her workbench, cutting dozens of round metal plates from a sheet of steel. She didn't stop work when he arrived. She told herself she wanted to get the metal cut so she'd be ready to start work tomorrow morning. Besides, he didn't stop his work at her convenience—why should she stop her work at his? She joined him for dinner, then immediately got back to work. For once, he was in bed before her. After she finished cutting the plates, she sat on the couch to talk to Ian about the sculpture, and she ended up falling asleep out there. Jeff was gone before she woke up the next morning.

Over the next two weeks, she fell into a new routine. She woke each morning to Ian's voice, reminding her that she had asked him to wake her. Over toast and coffee, she chatted with him. He always asked about her work, and when she answered, he was a good listener.

She found that she didn't mind as much when Jeff retired to his office right after dinner. Her attention was on the sculpture, and she had Ian for company. Whenever Jeff worked late, she fell asleep on the couch, talking to Ian. Somehow, she preferred the couch to the bed—the bed belonged to both her and Jeff, but the couch seemed like neutral territory.

She made steady progress on the sculpture. Below the trigger point, where the first ball released two more, she placed the round metal plates, each one carefully tuned to provide just the right tone. When three balls were rolling down the tracks, the sound of scattered raindrops grew to a steady patter, the drumming of rain on dry soil. When the three balls released six more and the six released twelve, the drumming intensified, filling the studio.

It wasn't until she reached the part of the storm where the thunder should sound that she hit a snag. She started sorting through her materials, searching for inspiration.

Two hours later, she was still looking. She had tried rolling the balls over corrugated metal that she bent into chutes of various configurations, but nothing produced the thunder she had in mind.

She asked Ian to play the rainstorm for her again, and after he obliged, she shook her head. "The first part sounds fine," she muttered. "But how the hell am I going to get that thunder right?" She stared at the racks of shiny metal and pipe. "Everything here is so new, so lifeless. None of it has ever been anything, done anything. I need things that talk to me, that have their own ideas."

"Their own ideas?" Ian asked.

"You know—junk that suggests things. I used to get half my material from scrap yards. Old pay phones that looked like goofy faces, vise grips that looked like robot hands, that kind of thing."

"You know," Ian said gently, "there's a scrap metal yard just east of Winslow. I have its address from the phone book."

"That's not a bad idea, Ian. Maybe I should check it out. What was that address?"

When she stepped from the house, the warm air enveloped her in an unwelcome embrace. The sky overhead was a relentless blue. Her Toyota's air-conditioning barely coped with the heat, blowing cool, damp-smelling air on her arms and face while she watched the needle of the heat sensor climb toward red.

Still, the scrap yard was just what she needed. She spent three hours rooting through barrels of scrap in a hot warehouse. She filled a box with lengths of pipe, sheets of rusted corrugated metal, gears, and unidentifiable machine parts. Her best find was a barrel of hollow brass forms that were shaped like hands. According to the owner of the scrap yard, the forms had once been used in the manufacturing of rubber gloves. Over the years, they had tarnished so that the smooth brass was mottled with dark brown and black. The tarnish made patterns that looked organic, like the cracks in dry mud or the tracery of veins on the underside of a leaf.

With the box of scrap in the trunk of her Toyota, she hurried home. By sunset, she had incorporated four of the brass hands into the sculpture. She flung open the door that led to the living room and called out to Ian for the first time since she had left the house. "Listen to this!"

She pulled the release, and the first ball began the gentle patter of rain. The other balls joined it, and the sprinkle grew to a deluge as the balls clacked against metal plates. They rolled down to where the brass hands were carefully positioned on a pivoting mechanism. While some of the balls continued the drumming of the rain, a dozen rushed down a chute to tumble into the hollow hands, clattering through the palms into the fingers. Unbalanced by the impact of the balls, the hands gracefully up-ended, rattling their stiff fingertips against a sheet of tin and causing it to wobble. The hands dumped the balls onto a down-sloping curve of corrugated metal. Free of the weight of the balls, the hands swiveled back to their upright position, striking the tin again on their return trip. The wobbling of the tin and the rattling of the balls against the metal ridges blended into a deep-throated growl like thunder.

The balls missed the catching bucket, hit the floor, and rolled in all directions, but Teresa didn't chase them. She grinned at Ian. "What do you think?"

Ian smiled back. "I can see the reviews now. 'Teresa King's innovative use of brass hands is unique in the—' "

"What? Where did you learn that critical bullshit?"

"It was easy. 'Innovative' and 'unique' are two of the most common adjectives in art criticism. Besides, they do seem to fit your sculpture."

"Well, I think you've been reading too much art criticism in that library of yours," she said, but she was still grinning as she got back to work.

A few days later, night was washing over the house as Teresa listened to the sculpture's music. The rainstorm worked fine, and the thunder entered on cue, a close approximation of the sound she wanted. But she wasn't quite satisfied with the next passage, the burst of wild rain that followed the crash of thunder. For most of the afternoon, she had been arranging and rearranging the tracks. She had used corrugated tracks to provide staccato bursts, and dozens of metal plates against which the balls rattled. It was a tricky business, looping one track over another, carefully setting the slope of each one. She was listening to her latest effort when the telephone rang.

"Ian! Could you answer the phone and take a message? I don't want to stop right now."

In the middle of the third ring, the phone fell silent, and Teresa continued working. After a few hours of work, the section finally produced the sound she wanted: thousands of tiny rattles and taps that joined to fill the studio with a rush of noise. At that point, she stopped.

As she was checking in the freezer to see what she could thaw for dinner and telling Ian about her success so far, she remembered the phone call. "Who was that on the phone a few hours ago?" she asked.

"A woman named Carla, from San Francisco."

"Carla?" She hadn't heard from Carla since her last letter, almost two weeks before. "What did she have to say for herself?"

"I recorded the conversation for you. Would you like me to play it back?"

"Sure, why not?"

Ian's face disappeared from the monitor, and a line appeared down the screen's middle. Teresa heard the phone ring; Ian's face appeared to the left of the line, Carla's to the right.

"Hello," Ian said. "Can I help you?"

Carla smiled, and Teresa knew that Ian had piqued her interest. "I hope so." Teresa almost laughed; Carla must have broken up with her latest lover. "Is Teresa in?"

"Yes, but she's working and asked me not to disturb her. Would you like to leave a message?"

"Just tell her Carla called. No, on second thought, tell her that we're having a party out at the Headlands to welcome a new batch of artists. I'd love it if she could make it."

"I'll give her the message. Does she have your telephone number?"

"After all the time I've known her, I certainly hope so."

"Then I'll give her the message. Thanks for calling, Carla."

"Thank you." Carla smiled again. Teresa had seen that smile many times before. It rarely failed. "I don't suppose you'd like to come out for the party? The more the merrier."

"I don't think that would be possible."

"Too bad," Carla said. "Well, if you change your mind, Teresa has my number. Bye now." Carla vanished from the screen and Ian's face filled it once again.

Teresa laughed. "Carla never changes."

"I don't understand," Ian said.

"She was flirting with you," Teresa said.

"I don't understand."

"Oh, come on, Ian. She invited you to the party because she thinks you're cute. She wanted you to smile and flirt back a little."

"How do you flirt?"

"I don't know. You smile, you tell jokes, you talk about this and that. It's not so much what you say, it's what's going on under the surface that really matters."

"When you and I joke, are we flirting?"

Teresa hesitated for a moment, feeling suddenly uncomfortable. "I guess maybe sometimes we are. Sometimes, I guess I forget that you're a . . . that you're just a . . ." She couldn't find the right word.

"An artificial intelligence," Ian said.

"Yeah. I guess I—I think of you as a friend, Ian. Sometimes people flirt with their friends."

"I understand. I'm glad we're friends."

"Yeah." She studied his face, looking for flaws in the animation. She found none. She had grown used to seeing him as a person, and she could see him no other way. That was what Jeff had wanted. "Look—I'd better give Carla a call."

She dialed Carla and her friend answered on the fourth ring. Carla was wearing an old purple sweatshirt and sitting in a white wicker chair. Before Teresa could say anything, Carla was talking.

"Well, I was wondering when you'd call back. So, who was that guy who answered the phone?"

Teresa considered telling Carla the truth, but she somehow didn't want to explain Ian. "That's Ian. He's a friend of Jeff's. He's taking care of stuff around the house while I work on that piece for Santa Fe. The deadline's coming up, you know."

"A friend of Jeff's, huh."

"Yeah—and a friend of mine."

Carla shook her head. "Jeff's a trusting soul."

"What do you mean?"

"Leaving you alone with Ian all day?" Carla shook her head. "He's the type that'll steal your heart, all right."

Teresa shook her head. The conversation made her uncomfortable. "Not Ian."

"What, is he gay or something?"

She shook her head again. "No, just"—she considered the word care-fully—"unavailable. Besides, I just got back from my honeymoon, and—"

"—and Jeff is working late every night," Carla interrupted. "You sounded pretty miserable in your last letter. No offense, Teresa, but it was grim. And face it—Ian's just your type. I can recognize 'em a mile off. More your type than Jeff is."

"Hey, I'm a married woman now."

"You're married, but you're not dead. And Ian's awfully cute."

Teresa knew that Carla was giving her the chance to complain about Jeff and talk about Ian, but she ignored the bait. She wanted Carla to drop the subject. "Things weren't going very well on the sculpture when I sent that last letter. It's going better now."

"Is Jeff home yet?"

"No, he's still at work. They're in some crucial phase of the project, and he hasn't been around much lately."

"And you don't mind that?"

"Not really." Teresa realized that, for the first time in a while, she wasn't upset when Jeff stayed late at work. It wasn't like she was alone all the time.

Carla stared at Teresa in a moment of rare silence. Then she said, "So —are you coming out here for the party?"

"I'd like to, but I don't know if Jeff can spare the time."

"Come without him then. Fly in for the weekend—you deserve some time off. Come out and stay with me."

"I guess I could use a break."

"Great—I'll count on it."

"It'll be good to see you," Teresa said. "So tell me about what's been happening out there. What are people working on?" Teresa relaxed and listened to Carla talk about the doings of mutual friends. It would be good to get away for a while, she thought. She wasn't quite sure what she wanted to get away from, but she pushed away the question and focused on Carla.

For most of a day, Teresa made minor adjustments in the sculpture: tightening a metal plate that didn't sound quite right, changing the slope of a track by a tiny amount. She was killing time and she knew it, but she couldn't figure out what else to do. The sculpture sounded fine—it ech-oed the rainstorm, a metallic version of rain on sand. That was the sound she had wanted, but now she found herself vaguely dissatisfied. The more she listened, the less she liked it.

Eventually, she stopped trying to figure out what was bothering her and started working on all the little jobs that she had been avoiding. She added six lifters and a motor to the sculpture's base, then positioned the foot of each track so that eight balls ended up at each of the six lifters.

After two days, the new parts were installed and ready to go. She loaded the balls into the lifters, turned on the motor, and watched as the lifters rose slowly up the side of the sculpture. When they reached the top, the lifters tipped forward and released the balls into their starting positions, and the sculpture began to play. She sat beside it and listened as the sounds washed over her studio.

That night, Jeff got home from work around nine. She hadn't seen much of him lately: he had been staying late at work and leaving the house in the morning before she was awake. She told herself that she hadn't had a chance to mention Carla's party to him, but she knew that she hadn't really wanted to. She was sure that he wouldn't be interested in going. But that evening she couldn't put it off any longer, and she told him about the invitation. To her surprise, Jeff was willing to take the time off work to go to the party.

They flew into San Francisco Airport on Friday night, rented a car, and drove directly out to the Headlands Art Center. On the plane, she found herself feeling awkward with him. He had been home so little lately that it was like traveling with a stranger. She couldn't shake the feeling.

The party at the Headlands was just like old times—an assortment of artists and would-be artists, a cooler filled with beer, California jug wine served in paper cups, chips dumped hastily into bowls from the potter's studio downstairs, guacamole dip from the burrito place near Carla's apartment. Just like old times.

She mingled with the crowd, telling friends what she'd been doing, describing the piece she was working on for Santa Fe. As she talked about her work, she grew more and more excited about it, her own interest reawakened by the support of her friends. Ned, a fellow sculptor, listened to her description of the pivoting hands. She hadn't been entirely happy with the pivoting mechanism. On a napkin, he sketched a few ideas that might solve the problem. She sat in a corner with Brenda, a musician, and talked about the overall shape of the composition.

Eventually, she retreated to the rickety wooden fire escape that Carla had dubbed the smoking porch. From there she could hear the crash of the surf over the party music. Through the window, she could look in to the party. Jeff was sitting in the far corner with a couple of men she knew vaguely. They both worked with synthesizers and computer music. The three men seemed to be having an animated conversation.

"Getting a breath of fresh air?" Carla said from the doorway. "Mind if I keep you company for a while?" She stepped onto the porch and closed the door lightly behind her.

Teresa shrugged. "I may not be very good company, I'm afraid."

"Yeah? What's going on?"

"It's just strange coming back. I realized how much I miss having you folks around. I've been feeling pretty isolated, I guess."

"You should get in touch with some artists out in Flagstaff. That's only about an hour away from your place, isn't it?"

She thought about the gallery opening. "Yeah. I guess that might help."

"Yeah, but that's not the real problem, is it?" Carla studied Teresa's face. "Something going on between you and Jeff?"

Teresa shrugged. "It's more like nothing's going on. At first, he didn't have time for me. Now it seems like I don't have much to say to him."

"Is something going on with this Ian guy?"

"No, nothing's going on."

Carla studied her. "Look, I recognize all the signals. You may not be sleeping with him, but something's going on." Carla leaned on the railing, looking toward the beach. "Jeff's never around, so you've been spending time with this cute guy. He's unavailable—but you hang out together. You talk and you flirt, and now you've suddenly realized that you're infatuated with him, and you don't know what to do about it." Carla glanced at her. "Oh, don't bother to deny it. I know how you operate, and you're feeling guilty." She waited for a moment. "Am I close?"

Teresa leaned on the railing beside Carla. "Maybe. It's hard to say."

"So, what are you going to do about it?"

"I don't know."

"What about Jeff?"

"What about Jeff? I don't know what's going on with him. He's all caught up in his work; he doesn't seem to care anymore."

"Well I'll bet he doesn't know what's going on with you."

Teresa started to deny it, then stopped herself. "Maybe not."

"Count on it. You're really good at shutting people out when you don't want to deal with them."

"I am?"

Carla shook her head. "Hey, think about it this way—would we be having this conversation if I hadn't started it?"

"Probably not," Teresa admitted.

"Definitely not." Carla put her arm around Teresa's shoulders. "It's okay—you just need a little pushing, that's all. And Jeff may not know how."

Teresa stared out at the dark beach, avoiding her friend's eyes.

The door to the studio opened and the noise of the party poured out. "Carla," a man called. "I've been looking all over for you."

Carla dragged Teresa back into the party, and for a while she drank wine and pretended to have a good time. The party ended at around two, and Jeff drove the rental car back to Carla's apartment. Carla was a little drunk and a little high. She rode in the back seat, humming along to the tunes on the radio. Teresa felt depressingly sober, despite the wine she had drunk.

At the apartment, Carla unfolded the sofa bed and then went to her room. As Teresa was undressing, she caught Jeff watching her intently. "What's up?" she asked him.

He shrugged. "I was going to ask you the same thing. Is something wrong?"

She kept her face carefully neutral. What could she say? She didn't know how to talk to him, she didn't know where to start. She felt shut out of his life and divorced from her own. It all sounded like accusations, and she didn't want to get into it. "I'm fine," she said. "Just tired, I guess."

"You've been working hard. But it seems like your work is going better, isn't it?"

"Yeah, I guess so." She shook her head. "I just don't want to talk right now, okay?"

"Fine." He turned away. "If that's what you want."

It was what she wanted, but she found herself wide awake, lying beside Jeff and listening to his rhythmic breathing. Though she was tired, she couldn't drift off to sleep. She got out of bed and went to the kitchen. Carla's light was out. Teresa sat at the kitchen table and then, on a whim, picked up the phone and dialed home.

When Ian's face appeared on the screen, she immediately felt better. "Hi, Ian," she said. "I just called to see how you were doing. I missed talking with you."

"It's nice to hear from you. I missed you, too."

"Sure you did."

He studied her calmly. "I did. You're the most important person in my life. When you're not here, there's an empty place."

"Thanks."

Ian smiled. "My pleasure. Did you have fun at the party?"

"Yeah, I guess. I realized how much I missed my friends out here. It was great to talk to some other artists about my work. I wish I knew more artists out in Arizona."

Ian hesitated. "There's an artists' cooperative in the Flagstaff area. I have the address on file."

Teresa grinned. "Sometimes I think you have everything on file. I'll take a look when I get back. But not right now. Right now, I just want to talk. Heard any new jokes lately?"

They didn't really talk about anything important—they just chatted about this and that—but she felt better by the time she hung up.

Jeff was lying still when she came back to bed. She sat on the edge of the fold-out couch, ready to slip under the covers.

"Who were you talking to on the phone?" he asked her softly.

She froze. Light from a street lamp filtered through the curtains. His features were smudges of shadow, unreadable in the dim light. "I thought you were asleep."

"I've been awake for a while now. I felt you get up, and I couldn't go back to sleep." He sat up in bed, and the shadows on his face shifted. He was silent for a moment, and then he spoke. "We've got to talk."

"About what?" she said, keeping her tone light.

He was quiet, and she wanted to run away. "I've been leaving you alone too much," he said. "Because I wasn't there when you needed me, you found someone else." It was a simple statement of fact, not an accusation. "You're seeing someone."

"No, I'm not," she said. She turned away from him, folding her arms protectively across her chest.

"You're in love with someone else."

She tried to feel angry with him, indignant at his accusations, but the anger wouldn't come.

"I've been so caught up in my own work that it took me a while to notice, but these days, when I talk to you, you're thinking of someone else. You get up at night and don't come back to bed until morning. You've got secrets—sometimes I'm afraid to ask you the simplest question. When I do ask—about your work, about your day—you answer in a word or two, and I'm afraid to ask again. We used to talk about your work —but you don't anymore."

She wished she felt angry. Anger would protect her from the great sadness that threatened to overwhelm her.

"Who is it?" he asked.

She shook her head. "No one."

He waited, watching her face. "Someone you met at that gallery opening," he said. She didn't respond. "I don't have to know," he said at last. "But you have to tell me—are you leaving me?" He put his hands gently on her shoulders. She tensed at his touch. "Talk to me, Teresa."

She would not look at him. "I don't know. I don't think so. No—no, I'm not leaving."

He put his arms around her. "I don't want to lose you. You have to talk to me. Please."

"I can't talk about it," she said. "I don't—" Her voice broke.

"Do you still love me?"

She could feel the beating of his heart as he embraced her, the warmth of his body against hers. "Sometimes," she said. "But sometimes . . ." She put her hand to her face, trying to hide her tears. She did not want to cry. "Sometimes, I feel like you don't even see me. I feel like I'm not even there. You think you can go away when you want and come back when you want, and I'll still be there, just waiting. You can't do that. I need . . ." She shook her head, upset by the burst of words. She had lost control. Her protection was gone. He could see how weak and stupid she really was. She had always known that it was dangerous to reveal herself.

"I'm sorry, Teresa. I'm sorry I wasn't there when you needed me." He rubbed her shoulders gently. "I screwed up. But you have to tell me what's going on. You can't just clam up and expect me to figure it out. It doesn't work that way."

"I'm sorry too," she said. She felt his body pressed against her. It seemed like a long time since he had held her close. She shivered in his embrace.

He stopped rubbing her shoulders. "You're cold—I can feel you shaking. Come on—get under the covers."

She relaxed enough to lie down on the bed, and he pulled the blanket over her. His body was warm. With a corner of the sheet, he dried her face.

"What happened in the past doesn't matter. I don't care about all that. But you've got to tell me when you're mad at me, you've got to tell me what's going on. Promise me that."

"I'll try." She closed her eyes, but knew that he was still watching her.

"And I'll try, too." He paused for a moment. "Suppose I took some time off from work. We could drive down to Santa Cruz and spend a few days by the ocean. Can you afford the time off?"

She opened her eyes and looked at him. "Yeah, I could use a few days off—but what about your project?"

"They'll do without me for a few days. They'll just have to." He watched her, his eyes steady. "I think we both need a vacation."

"All right," she said at last. "I'm willing to give it a try." She felt spent, drained. She lay in his arms, and finally she slept.

On the drive to Santa Cruz, she felt awkward at first, as if she and Jeff were strangers on a first date. She kept smiling and making light conversation: "Isn't the weather nice?" "I wonder if it'll rain." "Do you suppose we'll hit much traffic?"

Half an hour into the drive, Jeff glanced over at her and said, "It's okay, Teresa. You don't have to make small talk." She bit her lip, suddenly silent. He reached over and took her hand. "Look—I'm not mad at you. Are you mad at me?"

She considered the question. No, she wasn't angry. Confused maybe, but not angry. "No, I'm not mad."

"Then let's just relax." He squeezed her hand. "Why don't you tell me about how your piece for Santa Fe is going? I'd like to know."

She started telling him about the sculpture. At first, she was nervous, but she had relaxed by the time they got to Davenport, a small town just north of Santa Cruz. That night, they stayed at an old Victorian house that had been converted to a bed-and-breakfast inn. The house was perched on the cliffs above the ocean, and Teresa insisted on leaving the bedroom window open, despite the cool ocean fog. From the room, she could hear the pounding surf. They made love, and she fell asleep in Jeff's arms.

The next morning, he brought her breakfast in bed and suggested that they drive home, rather than fly. "Last time we drove, we were in too much of a hurry. I've never shown you the parts of the desert I really love," he told her.

She had her doubts about the trip. Her memories of the drive from San Francisco to Winslow were of long bleak stretches of highway. But Jeff was so enthusiastic she kept her reservations to herself. She had almost forgotten what he could be like when he wasn't working. All the intensity that he had been focusing on his work was now concentrated on her. "All right," she agreed. "We can drive."

The trip took seven days, with many stops and detours along the way. They wandered among the twisted trees of the Joshua Tree National Monument. They visited the ruins of an Indian pueblo, strolling among the remains of walls that marked where rooms had once been, and startling lizards that were sleeping in the sun. They hiked out to see Arizona's biggest natural rock bridge and climbed on massive sandstone boulders.

Late in the afternoon of the sixth day, they sat together on the flat, sun-warmed surface of a boulder the size of a school bus. It was quiet, but not silent, Teresa realized. A raven flew over, its shadow rippling across the rocks. It called once, and she heard the rustle of feathers as it cupped its wings to land on a distant rock.

"It's beautiful, isn't it?" Jeff said.

"It always just seemed hot to me," Teresa said. "Hot and empty and uncaring."

"No, you got it wrong," he said. "This land has its own kind of power. I find myself listening to every rustle of leaves, hearing the hiss of sand blowing over sand, noticing the way the light changes during the day. It focuses my attention, and I see things I'd normally overlook, hear things I would normally ignore. It changes in subtle ways. Each day is a little different. I think it's beautiful." He took her hand, and they sat together until the sun started to set.

That evening, one day's drive from home, she called Carla from the motel, just to let her know that everything was going fine.

"Jeff and I both have to get back to work," Teresa told Carla. "But things are much better between us. I just hope it lasts."

"What about Ian?"

"I don't think that'll be a problem."

Carla shook her head. "You know, you haven't changed a bit. You always were amazed when you found out that some ex-lover was carrying a torch for you. You always seem to expect them to vanish without a trace when the love affair is over."

"Ian won't carry a torch," Teresa said. "He's not built that way."

Carla shrugged. "Have it your way. But you may be surprised."

When her alarm went off at six, Teresa woke to find herself alone. Jeff, as usual, was gone, and Ian did not greet her from the monitor in the corner. She waited a moment before turning off the alarm, wondering if Ian would notice the noise and say good morning, but he did not appear. She was not sure if she was disappointed, relieved, or both.

As she got out of bed she noticed for the first time the sounds coming from the kitchen. She pulled on her robe and walked down the hall.

Jeff stood in the middle of the kitchen, his back to her, the calm eye in the middle of a hurricane of activity. Coffee steamed from the coffee maker on his left, eggs sizzled in a pan on the stove behind him, and four pieces of brown toast sat patiently in the toaster to his right. He was intently sawing a grapefruit in half.

Teresa stared in amazement. "What's this?"

Jeff turned around. "Breakfast." He smiled. "I hope."

"Breakfast?" She could not remember the last time Jeff had eaten breakfast with her before leaving for work.

"Yeah, you know, the meal you eat in the morning." He cut another section of grapefruit. "I noticed that you'd set your alarm for early today, and I figured that we both have to eat, so I thought I'd surprise you." He put down the knife and grapefruit and grabbed a mug from the counter. "Coffee?"

"Sure." Teresa took the mug and settled down at the table. Jeff prepared breakfast as he did everything else—carefully, methodically, precisely. He worked at the counter in front of him for thirty seconds or so, rotated one stop, worked at that counter, and so on around the circle. Somehow it seemed to come out right.

In a few minutes, Jeff set a plate in front of her and sat down across from her.

She did not know quite what to say. She was used to talking to Ian in the morning, not Jeff. Ian, however, did not appear. "Jeff?"

He put down his fork and looked at her. "Yes?"

"This is nice, but don't you have to get to work?"

"Yeah, in a little while. Breakfast just seemed like a nice way for us to get to spend a little extra time together. That's all." He sipped his coffee. "I mean, don't get too used to it, okay? I'm not saying this will be a regular thing, but it seemed like a good idea at the time."

They ate in silence for a while. Teresa felt vaguely bribed, or catered to, but Jeff was making an effort. Several times she almost spoke, but each time she stopped herself. Twice she found Jeff staring at her when she looked up from her plate. He seemed to want her to talk, but he did not press her.

Finally she decided that maybe he really was trying, and that maybe she could try a little more as well. "Jeff, how much of this is real?"

"What do you mean, real? Is the food that bad?"

"No jokes. I mean, how much of this"—she waved her arm to take in the kitchen"—is real, and how much is just some attempt to pacify me."

"Pacify you? I don't want to pacify you. I just want to be happy with you. Sure, this is all pretty convenient, coming right after our trip and all, but at least give me a little credit for trying. I won't make breakfast every day, that's for sure, but I'll try to be around a lot more. No—I will be around a lot more." He leaned closer. "Teresa, I have to start somewhere."

Teresa put her mug down. She reached across the table and took his hand. "You're right. You have to start somewhere, and so do I." She kissed him lightly. "The food is wonderful, and so, sometimes, are you. I do appreciate it." She leaned back in her chair.

As they ate, they talked about simple things—what she wanted to get done on the sculpture, his plans for the day, her knowledge that something that she could not quite put her finger on was still wrong with the piece. When they were done eating, she rinsed the dishes, and he loaded them into the dishwasher.

Jeff stopped when he was almost out the door on his way to work. "Teresa."

She came over to the door. "Yes."

"You really are good at what you do, you know. I'm not trying to say that this isn't a difficult piece, maybe even your hardest yet, but I'm sure you'll figure out what's wrong with it." He hugged her for a moment and, as he held her close, said, "You will."

She kissed him. "Thanks."

She watched for a moment as he got in his car and started it, and then she closed the door and headed toward the bedroom. Only when she was back in the bedroom, getting dressed, did Ian appear.

"Good morning, Teresa."

"Good morning, Ian." She pulled on a sweatshirt, unwilling to look at him. She was, she realized, as uncomfortable as she had been when she talked with him for the first time. She sat on the bed and looked at him. "What do you think of the desert, Ian?"

"I don't like the desert," he said easily.

"Why not?"

"Because you don't like the desert. You said so the first morning we talked."

She sat in silence, studying the screen. "You always like what I like."

"What's wrong, Teresa? You seem upset."

"Why didn't you talk to me in the kitchen this morning?" she asked. "Because Jeff was here and you thought I wouldn't want to talk to you with him around?"

"Yes. You hardly ever start a conversation with me when Jeff's home, and you seem uncomfortable if we talk when he's here, so I assumed you'd prefer it if we talk only in private. If I did something wrong, tell me, and I won't make that mistake again."

"I keep thinking about Pygmalion," she said. She studied Ian's face. "After he fell in love with his creation, and some god or other took pity on him and made her into a real woman."

"Aphrodite," Ian said.

"It figures. Aphrodite, the goddess of love." She studied Ian, thoughtfully. "Would you like to be real, Ian?"

"I am real."

"I mean a real person. Someone who could walk off that screen and sit down on the couch, take my hand, and give me a kiss."

"Would you like that?"

She wanted to hit him. "Damn it, Ian, can't you just once tell me what *you* feel, what *you* want, and stop trying to figure out what I want?"

Ian looked contrite. "I told you; what you want is what I want. That's the way I'm built. I can't be any other way."

"No wonder Pygmalion fell in love with Galatea," she said softly. "You want what I want. I can do no wrong."

"That's right," Ian said.

"But it's not right, Ian. I'm not always right. Not even close."

"Teresa, I know you're unhappy with me. What do you want me to do?"

"Nothing," she said, shaking her head. "Do you think Pygmalion was happy? I mean, his statue must have been the perfect lover. No arguments. No demands."

"I don't know. The story stops right after Venus made the statue into a real woman."

"Of course it does. Love stories always end with falling in love. They don't deal with the messy stuff afterwards. But that stuff's part of love, too, you know."

"What's part of love?"

"The messy stuff. The arguments. The compromises. The disagreements. The negotiations. The give-and-take. All of that. I don't think Pygmalion was happy. I don't think so."

"Teresa, I know you're unhappy with me, but I just don't know what to do."

"I don't know either. Sometimes I wish things between us could be like they were in the beginning—simple, no complications, no problems." She shook her head slowly. "But I guess you can never go back."

"Sure we can."

"What?"

"If you want me to, I can erase all my records of everything that's happened since any point in time you pick. You just tell me when you want me to roll back to, and I'll do it."

"You'll forget everything?"

"Everything—if that's what you want."

"No!" Teresa was trembling, but she wasn't quite sure why. She remembered how easy her first conversations with Ian had been, but she also remembered how guilty she had felt after she had erased his memories. No one should have that much power over anybody else. She looked at her hands; they were shaking. "Just give me a minute, Ian, okay?"

"Okay." He stared patiently from the monitor.

When she finally spoke, she felt like she was breaking up with someone. "Ian, I don't want you to delete any of your memories. I don't want that kind of control over you. But," she paused and took a deep breath, "I think you should plan on having fewer conversations with me in the future. And you shouldn't worry about talking to me in front of Jeff. If you have something to say, I'm sure he won't mind hearing it." Ian was watching her intently from the screen. "We'll still be friends, but I think that from now on I'll want a lot less from you."

"Okay, Teresa. But if you need me, I'll be here for you."

"Right." She did not know whether to believe him. She did not even know if it mattered.

Teresa went to her workshop and switched on the sculpture. She watched as the lifters brought the balls to the top and let them go. As the balls rolled through the maze of metal plates, boards, and brass hands, the storm started quietly and built rapidly to thunder. The music was a perfect mirror of the sounds in her head, of her plans and desires for it, and yet it was not enough. It sounded mechanical—a weak imitation of a real storm, lacking the wildness of a thundering sky, the unstoppable, unpredictable force of a downpour.

In groups of eight, the balls rolled into the waiting lifters. Each lifter took its group back to its starting position, and the whole process began anew. Each time the sculpture played the same perfectly timed, perfectly repeatable peal of thunder. The music never varied, never changed. It was completely controlled. No two real storms ever sounded the same, but her sculpture would play the same music over and over until it broke or rusted into dust.

As the sculpture played for the third time, she knew what she had to do. She rummaged through her pile of scrap metal until she found a piece of half-inch solid metal bar. At her welding bench, she cut the bar into four-inch lengths. When she was done with the first bar, she found two others and cut them into similar pieces. After four bars she had about thirty small pieces.

She found a sheet of thick metal plate in the corner of the shop and used her welding torch to cut it down to a square about a yard on a side. She clamped the sheet metal to her bench and started welding the small pieces of metal bar to it. She placed them randomly, trying not to form any particular pattern, so that the short spikes stood up from the sheet metal. She always left enough space between the spikes for one of the sculpture's balls to pass through, but not much more. When she was done she took the whole assembly to the sculpture. She worked for most of the morning installing the new piece and adjusting the tracks to work with it.

When she was finished, she turned on the sculpture and settled back to watch and listen. As the first storm started, the lifters freed the balls and they began to wind their way down the tracks, playing the storm she had heard so many times before. As the first balls reached the bottom of the tracks, however, they fell into the spikes of the new piece.

The balls ricocheted among the spikes, rattling in an irregular rhythm and changing course at random, much like the small metal balls that bounce through a Pachinko game. Two balls found their way quickly to the bottom, and a lifter started up with them. The other six bounced around on the metal spikes and reached the bottom later. Balls in the other groups also entered the plate of spikes. Because the number of balls in each lifter changed, the number at each starting position also varied, and the second storm began with a different sound.

This new storm was not exactly the one she heard in her head, but it was close. It was a little longer on thunder, but not quite as loud. She did not like it as well as her previous versions, and she began to wonder if she had just wasted her morning, but she let the sculpture play on. The third and fourth storms were also slightly different. But neither was up to her original creation.

The fifth, however, was something she would not have imagined. Its thunder was never quite as loud as her original—she made a mental note to try to get a louder sound from the corrugated plate—but the thunder held its peak longer than she would have dared. The room shook with the sound. When the thunder finally released and gave way to the driving rain, she realized that she had been holding her breath and tensing every muscle in her body. She relaxed as the rain came, its sound washing away her tension.

She listened for an hour as storm after storm swept through her shop. Sometimes the sculpture seemed to repeat itself, to play a storm that she had heard earlier, but every so often a new combination emerged that surprised and delighted her. The thunder of some storms seemed to linger, while with others it was the final rain washing across the desert that went on and on. It was never exactly what she had imagined, but it was always different, always powerful, the thunder and the rain first meeting the desert, then pummeling it, and finally merging with it. She listened to the last drops of a storm fade into the desert sand, and then she turned off the sculpture and stood.

She walked over to the sliding glass doors that insulated her from the desert heat and opened them. They slid haltingly on tracks that she had rarely used. A blast of heat hit her, and she stepped outside. She crossed over the lawn and climbed the short fence that separated the grass from the desert beyond. She sat down in the sand and looked slowly around.

A lizard basked in the sun on a nearby rock. She put her hand in the shadow of a clump of rabbit brush and felt the coolness. The clear sky and the stark landscape did have their own serene, spare beauty, a beauty that she had been unwilling to see. She closed her eyes and imagined the rain from her sculpture falling onto the sand around her.

The lights surrounding the new Santa Fe Arts Center sparkled in the darkness of the rapidly cooling September evening. The low-slung adobe building seemed almost to have grown there. The tiles of the square in front of the building alternated light and dark, like sand moving in and out of shadow. In the square's center, under a billowing satin sheet, sat Teresa's sculpture, *Desert Rain*.

Teresa stood by Jeff and sipped her champagne. She looked carefully through the crowd, but if Carla was there, Teresa could not find her.

Just before the mayor was to unveil the sculpture, Teresa spotted her friend getting out of a cab. Teresa waved, and Carla came running over.

"I'm sorry I'm late, but we sat on the runway forever and then we had to wait in line to take off and—" Carla paused for breath and looked around. "Have I missed anything?" She glanced at Jeff. "Hi, Jeff."

"How are you, Carla?" he said.

"No," Teresa said, "you're in time—barely."

Speakers around the square screeched as the mayor fiddled with the microphone. When he had everyone's attention, the mayor spoke for a few minutes. He introduced the head of the Arts Commission, several of the biggest donors, and Teresa. When he was done talking he nodded at Teresa. She walked over to the sculpture. Then the mayor took a pair of oversized scissors from an assistant and cut the ribbon that held down the satin sheet. With a flourish, two attendants pulled the sheet away to reveal the sculpture.

The metal gleamed in the glare of the recessed footlights that surrounded it. The winding steel track caught the light and reflected it in broken patterns. Curving lines of light crisscrossed the brass hands, the metal uprights, the curve of corrugated metal that produced the thunder.

The Mayor asked the crowd for silence, and then motioned to Teresa. With a key, she turned on the sculpture.

In the first storm, the thunder was not the longest she had heard, but it sustained long enough that she was ready when it finally broke. The sounds of the spreading rain lingered as the last of the balls wound through the maze.

When the silence finally came, the crowd burst into applause. The sculpture began another storm over the last of the applause. People went back to talking and drinking, with small groups periodically wandering near the sculpture for a closer look.

"That was beautiful," Jeff said.

"Great work," agreed Carla. "This may be your best piece yet."

"Thanks." Teresa felt oddly unsatisfied, incomplete. Jeff had moved closer to the sculpture, so Teresa turned to Carla.

"Do me a favor, Carla," she whispered.

"Sure."

"Take Jeff over to the bar and get him to buy you a drink."

"Oh?" Carla raised one eyebrow.

"I have to make a phone call, that's all." She hesitated. "To a friend."

"Whatever you say." Carla winked, and then headed toward Jeff.

Teresa walked to a phone booth in a far corner of the square. She put her card in the machine and dialed home.

Ian's face appeared. "Hello, Teresa."

She fidgeted with the phone for a moment, not quite sure what to say. Finally, she spoke. "Look, Ian, I'm at the opening in Santa Fe and, well, I just wanted to say thanks, thanks for all the help you've given me. I couldn't have done it without you."

"You're welcome, Teresa. It was my pleasure."

"We really can be friends, can't we, Ian?"

"You bet."

She turned to face the sculpture. She could see Carla talking to Jeff. His back was to her. The crowd blocked most of the sculpture, but its sound was still clear. "Can you hear the sculpture, Ian?"

"Yes. It sounds good."

"Thanks. I wanted you to hear it at least once. And thanks again for helping." She faced the screen again. "Good-bye, Ian. See you at home."

"Good-bye, Teresa. I'll look forward to seeing you again."

The phone's screen went blank and Teresa turned away from it. As the sounds of desert rain washed over the square, she walked toward Jeff.

Precious Moments

KRISTINE KATHRYN RUSCH

I WAS SHOCKED," Sandusky said. He leaned back in the pale blue booth and pushed his half-eaten eggs away. The café smelled of coffee and burned toast. "I mean, there were these delicate little creatures pirouetting on the stage and they were *gorgeous*. I always thought Russian women were like East German swimmers—big breasted, dough faced and too tall."

"That's racist," Martina said. She hadn't eaten anything. Her small hands were wrapped around an oversized coffee cup.

Sandusky and I always had breakfast together after the morning show. He did the news and I engineered, and after four hours of live, crazy radio, we would be wired. That morning we invited Martina. Actually, I invited Martina. Sandusky didn't like her much, but I had always been attracted to women who had bristly personalities. Sandusky said that was because I was out to change the world. Maybe. I thought it was because I liked a challenge.

I frowned. "What about Olga Korbut? I had a crush on her when I was in the sixth grade, and I've liked tiny women ever since."

Martina didn't catch the hint, but Sandusky did. He made a face. "Olga Korbut wasn't fully grown, Linameyer."

"She is now and she's still tiny." I took a bite of my scrambled eggs. They were greasy and undercooked. Sandusky had been right to leave his. I pushed my plate away.

"I'm talking about my impressions here," Sandusky said. "I don't care if they're right. I go to the ballet with Linda, I learn something."

"Bully, bully," Martina said to me, her black eyes snapping. "He learned that his racist stereotypes don't always hold up."

"I'm not being racist." Sandusky grabbed his own coffee cup and held it over the back of the bench into the booth behind him. The waitress, who was pouring coffee for the couple sitting at that table, filled Sandusky's cup without a blink. "I'm not talking about blacks or Indians."

"Jesus." Martina reached into the pocket of her jeans and pulled out three crumpled dollar bills. "How did this guy get a job at a listener-sponsored radio station? We're supposed to be left wing—or at least open-minded."

"He is open-minded, for Wisconsin." I put my hand over Martina's. Her fingers were dry and warm. "Let me get that. I'm the one who talked you into coming after the show."

"It's been quite an education," she said and then she smiled. Her entire face lit up. I loved it when Martina smiled. I had been watching her ever since she started at the station three months before. She did the morning news with Sandusky. I wondered how many arguments I missed, trapped at the board, listening to Johnson babble while I spun the tunes. The program director claimed that engineering the "Morning Show" was too difficult for an announcer, so I had to engineer. I could have announced and engineered that program in my sleep and still done a better job than Johnson.

"You haven't finished your coffee yet," Sandusky said. His ears were red. Martina's comments must have hit a sore spot. Sandusky was a little ignorant and a lot naive, especially for a college graduate in his early thirties, but he did try to learn. Unfortunately at the station he had absorbed the left-wing rhetoric, but not the ideals that characterized the most interesting radicals. Of course, open-mindedness didn't exist at the station. The feminists fought with the environmentalists who fought with the Native Americans who fought with the gays, all of whom claimed their issues were the most important issues. Sometimes I wished I was a conservative. They seemed to have only three lines of ideological bullshit instead of two hundred.

"You don't get it, do you?" she said. She hadn't moved her hand from beneath mine. "You think you're open-minded. You think you're liberal, and yet you sit here and say Russian women—and it should be Soviet women, if you want to be precise—Russian women should be tall with big tits. American women come in all sizes. Why should the Soviets be one-size-fits-all?"

The flush was traveling down Sandusky's neck. "My father was a farmer. He had a sixth-grade education."

"You say that every time I pin you," Martina said. "*You* have a master's degree in history. You'd think that would give you a little more perspective on the world."

"I didn't know you had a master's degree." I took a sip of my water. It tasted like soap. I didn't know why we came here every morning. The food was always terrible.

"You're no better, Linameyer," Martina said. She pulled her hand away from mine. "You're real good at helping people write copy with nonsexist language, and you never insult anyone. You always say, 'Native American,' and 'Differently Abled,' and you can spout party line with the best of them, but you don't have an open mind either."

"I think you're a little out of proportion, Martina." I was secure in my open-mindedness. I was the one, not the station manager, that everyone used to settle disputes. *Linameyer sees the human side,* Johnson said once, and the entire station agreed that it was true.

I did see the human side. I saw *all* sides, and I could explain them clearly. Maybe that's why I was doing talk radio: I could understand everything and never had to take a side, never had to make an action on my own.

"I'm very clear-sighted." She straightened out her money and set it under her full water glass. "You do real good at spouting party line and picking which party line is appropriate under what circumstances. But if you ever were confronted with something really odd, you would deny it because it doesn't fit into your neat, tidy little world."

"Give me an example," I said, leaning forward.

"I'll do better than that." She grabbed her coat from the side of the booth and shoved her arms in the sleeves. "I'll let you prove yourself. You're hosting 'A Public Affair' next week, right? Interview my roommate."

"Who is your roommate?"

Martina glanced at Sandusky. He was clutching his empty coffee cup and staring at her. "She's an Argentinian ballerina. She was famous once."

"How did you get a famous ballerina for a roommate?"

Martina shrugged. "Twist of fate, maybe. Interview her."

I took a deep breath. Most of my "Public Affairs" were scheduled. I hosted the talk show one week a month and I planned for it for weeks in advance. This time, though, Thursday was open. "Give me some background on her and I'll see."

"Is that open-minded?" Martina asked.

"It's protecting my show. I like doing that program. I want to host it daily, not monthly."

"Okay." Martina slurped the coffee off the bottom of her cup, then set the cup aside. "I'll bring her in for a prelim interview, how's that? I'm sure she doesn't have any background papers."

"Sounds good," I said. I grabbed the check, took Martina's money from under the water glass, and threw the bills at her. "I said I was buying."

"I'm not your date, Linameyer."

I slid out of the booth. "I'm feeling guilty for bringing you here. Let me be a good American and clear my soul by throwing money at the problem."

She laughed and stood beside me. Sandusky grunted as he climbed out of the booth.

"So, you never said. Was the ballet good?" I asked.

"Linda said their lines were off." He took his coat off the back of the booth. "But I thought their lines were just fine." There was enough of a leer in his statement to make Martina glare at him. He shrugged, the picture of innocence. "Then, what do I know about ballet?"

I had the large reel-to-reel on edit and held both reels with the tips of my fingers, my gaze on the tape brushing up against the playback head. Senator Kasten slurred his words. I couldn't find the beginning of the sentence. Somehow the senator managed to make the phrase, "Such a stupid bag of wind. He had no right to win a primary let alone an election," sound like "Suchastupid baga windy dino right to winaprim ary letalone anlection." I'd been struggling with that foot of tape for nearly fifteen minutes, trying to find a place to cut it. A truncated version of the Kasten interview was supposed to air at six. I would be lucky if I had it done for the next morning.

Sandusky had tried to talk with me for three days about Martina. I didn't want to hear him. I wanted to make my own decision about her—and Sandusky seemed to want me to think like he did.

The studio door clicked shut. I turned, prepared to defend my studio time—I had had the four hours blocked off for nearly a week—when I saw Martina. She leaned against the door and smiled at me, almost hidden by the rack for the cassette player and the Dolby equalizer.

"My roommate's outside," she said. "You want to do that prelim interview now?"

I wound the tape back, then played it forward. "Can you hear where this breaks?" I said.

"Kasten has a southern Wisconsin mush-mouth. It could take you all day." She advanced to the console and leaned against its side like a kid on his first station tour. "I had to work real hard to get her here."

I sighed. I still hadn't scheduled anyone for the Thursday show. And no one but that night's producer would care if the Kasten piece was fifteen seconds shorter than planned. "All right," I said. "But it has to be quick. And let's do it in here. I don't want to lose my studio time."

"Gotcha." Martina gave me a thumbs-up and let herself out the door. I bent over the reel-to-reel, rewound it, then moved very slowly. Finally I heard something that could pass for a pause. I marked the tape with a grease pencil, slid the tape forward and placed it on the cutter. The door creaked open as I ran a razor blade through the white grease mark. Then I pressed "Play" and listened to Kasten finish that stupid sentence. I made another grease mark and pushed away from the machine.

Martina stood next to a small, willowy woman who looked tall because she was so thin. "Ben Linameyer, this is Rosaura Correga."

I held out my hand. After a moment, Rosaura took it. Her fingers felt as brittle as sticks. "It's a pleasure," I said.

"*Gracias,*" she murmured.

"Have a seat," I said, indicating the plastic chair on her side of the console. After a quick glance at Martina, Rosaura sat down. "You do speak English, don't you?"

"*Sí, señor.*" Then she smiled a little. "Yes. Yes, I do."

Her English was not heavily accented, something important if I were going to do an hour-long call-in program with her. "Did Martina tell you what we're thinking of doing?"

Again Rosaura glanced at Martina. Martina smiled her encouragement and leaned against the soundpad on the far wall. "She said an interview."

"In a few days, on our show 'A Public Affair.' "

"People will call?" Rosaura said.

I nodded. "And ask you questions. But today I want to see if you and I are compatible."

She clutched her hands together and set them on the edge of the table. I scooted my chair over and pushed the mike aside. She was young, with the elastic skin of a teenager. The laugh lines around her eyes added about ten years to her age, though. If she had come from Argentina, she had probably lived through a lot. "Martina tells me that you used to dance in Argentina."

"*Sí.* Yes. I danced with Compañía Nacional de Argentina for many years, the last as prima ballerina." She gazed down at her hands, but her words were filled with a quiet pride. Her accent was as clear as I had thought, and she seemed to have no fear of me. I would ask a few more perfunctory questions and then get back to Senator Kasten.

"Did you do the traditional works, or was the company more experimental?"

"Before the coup, we did Argentinian work. El Perón insisted on it. But Evita, she had us do *Swan Lake* as a secret. She had never seen it."

El Perón. Evita. I glanced at Martina, remembering our conversation from a few days before. "You danced for Juan Perón?"

"And his wife." Rosaura still did not look at me, but her voice was soft, a little husky. Her black hair fell in waves around her face. There was not a gray strand in it.

"Isabel?"

"Eva. Eva Perón. She was beautiful."

Eva Perón had died in the early fifties. Juan Perón was overthrown a few years after that. He returned to power in 1973 and died a year later. His third wife, Isabel, took over for him until she was ousted by another coup in 1976. I remembered that from a special we did on Argentina a few months before. Rosaura could have danced, as a young woman, for Isabel thirteen or fourteen years ago. She hadn't even been born when Eva died. "How long ago was that?" I asked.

Rosaura shrugged. "It seems a long time now."

I glanced at Martina. Her face was very somber. She sat on the floor with her arms wrapped around her knees.

"Did you have trouble leaving Argentina?"

Rosaura shook her head. "We were here when they announced the coup, performing in Chicago. Argentina was not the same without Eva, and we were part of El Perón."

"It would have been dangerous for her to return," Martina said.

"So I stay."

I folded my hands in my lap, feeling a slow anger burn in my stomach. Perhaps this was how Sandusky felt when Martina baited him. Martina presented me with an obvious impossibility and expected me to accept it. "How old are you, Rosaura?"

"Ah—*veinte-ocho*—ah, how you say—?"

"Twenty-eight," I said. "Eva Perón has been dead for nearly forty years."

Martina hid her mouth and nose behind her knees. Only her eyes peered at me, studying me darkly. I wondered if I was failing her test.

Rosaura laughed. "I still dance," she said. "I could not dance if I were so old as you think."

"I hope I didn't offend you." I stood up and extended my hand. This time she took it as if she were a head of state and I, her servant. She rose slowly. "I will contact you about the show."

"Did we—ah—are we compatible?" Rosaura asked. Her eyes had a dark fire, and her skin was as pale as a dead woman's.

"We are compatible," I said, correcting her pronunciation. "We'll see how the week's schedule works out. I enjoyed talking with you."

"Thank you," she said. She turned for the door. Martina opened it for her, then opened the door to reception.

"I'll be with you in a moment," Martina said. She waited until both doors closed before turning to me. "You're not going to use her, are you?"

"For Chrissake, Martina, she's nuts."

"That was easy." Martina took a step toward me, moving with what Sandusky called her bantam walk. *She looks like a little banty rooster,* he would say, *out to pick a fight.* "I would expect a comment like that from Sandusky, but you claim to have an open mind."

"You expect me to believe that that girl, who looks no more than twenty-four, is actually fifty-eight and still dancing?"

"I expect you to believe that she is twenty-eight and danced for Evita Perón."

"Eva Perón died in 1952."

Martina shrugged.

"Everyone gets older. I don't appreciate practical jokes, Martina."

"This is no joke," she said. "People can get stuck in time."

I sighed. She said she had something that would test my open-mindedness and this certainly did. "If I believed you, what would you have me do?"

Martina put her arms behind her back. "Put her on the air."

"This program is really important to me. And it's obvious that she's not operating with a full deck."

"She's very rational." Martina spoke slowly, as if to a child. "Don't ask her age, and you will be fine."

"But she looks—"

"Too young. And no one can see her over the radio." Martina nodded toward the reel-to-reel. "Senator Kasten waits. Such a limited worldview you have that allows the existence of dipshits like him and refuses the presence of an Argentinian prima ballerina."

"I know she exists," I started, but Martina had already turned her back and disappeared out the door. I unclenched my fists. Open-minded did not mean jeopardizing something I had worked for, at least not over something silly like Rosaura Correga. Martina should have understood that.

I went back to the Kasten tape and stared at the grease mark. Kasten was a jerk, and I couldn't believe that the people of southeastern Wisconsin had elected him to the United States Senate. But I had done nothing about it. I hadn't taken any risks for anything I believed in since my last year in college.

I shook my head. The argument I was having with myself was silly. I didn't believe Martina's roommate. And no one should have to take action for something he did not believe in, no matter how open his mind was.

Or how open he believed it should be.

I checked the facts in the campus library the next morning. Eva Perón had died in 1952, as I had thought. She had been dynamic—a radio and movie actress—and beautiful, just as Rosaura had said. The Compañía Nacional de Argentina was performing in Chicago at the time of the 1955 coup. Then the company disappeared, missed its next performance and was never heard from again. Press speculation at the time assumed the company members had gone home to join the rebellion, although many were known Perónistas. None had applied for United States protection or a green card. One newspaper had a photo of the group's prima ballerina. Rosaura Correga, as she had looked not twenty-four hours before.

People can get stuck in time.

I walked out the main doors onto the campus mall. A chill October wind blew leaves across the concrete. Students rushed from building to building, heads bent, under the gray sky. It felt as if the rain would start at any minute, but it had felt that way for days.

I stuck my hands in my jacket pockets and walked down the hill toward the lot where I had left my car. The students looked younger to me than they had ever looked before. Not that I felt old at thirty; I no longer felt naive. I had lost that searching, hungry look that the best students had. The world was no longer a place of wonder. It had become a familiar, dirty place, like a spacious penthouse apartment—lived in, but not clean.

Martina was trying to give that back to me, that sense of wonder. And for two brief moments, once when Rosaura was speaking and again when I saw her photo, I held a belief that what she said could possibly be true.

If I interviewed her, the interview would center on the dancing and the Perón years. I would have to screen the callers somehow, or not open the phone lines until late in the show. If anyone asked her her age, my credibility—and my chance to be a permanent talk-show host—would vanish.

And then I saw her, walking kitty-corner along the hill, the same small willowy woman who had stood in the studio the day before. Her hair streamed behind her in the wind and all the grace had left her movements. She walked with the stalking ease of a young lion. I ran until I caught up with her.

"Rosaura! Rosaura!"

She didn't turn when I called her name, so when I reached her, I grabbed her arm. "Rosaura."

"What?" She pulled away from me. Her accent was pure Midwest. *Waat?*

"Rosaura Correga?"

Her face was the same—eighteen years old except for the crow's feet around the eyes. Her manner differed. She didn't drop her gaze and look away. She stared at me, and color filled her windburned cheeks. "What the hell do you want?"

"You're not Rosaura Correga?"

"Do I look like a Rosaura? Give it a rest." She didn't seem to recognize me. Not one flicker of fear or nervousness touched her face.

"You're not a dancer then?"

"I'm on the crew team. That's exercise enough." Even the voice was the same. The same tenor, the same tone, only the accent differed. I knew voices. I worked with them intimately every day.

"Do you have a sister or a mother named Rosaura?" I asked, thinking that the look might run in a family.

"No. My mother's name is Brigid, and I doubt my Gaelic ancestors would appreciate being confused with the Spanish." She brushed her hair out of her face. "Now, if you'll excuse me, I have a class."

Probably an acting class. She would go far. She was good. She was damn good. I watched her walk away, her slight body looking tall in the wind. Martina had almost convinced me, almost got me to jeopardize my show for a bit of silliness.

Thing was, standing there on the campus hillside, the October wind tousling my hair and bright-eyed students milling around me, I felt suddenly lonely, as if a part of me had flown away with that long-haired girl disappearing in the crowd.

I pulled the last cart, signed the charts, and handed over the board to Dick, the 9 A.M. to noon programmer. The "Morning Show" had gone without a hitch, but I had half wanted something to deal with, troubleshoot, to take away some of the nervous energy that had been part of my mood.

I took the albums back to the record library. The stacks were quiet—no one was previewing new albums or pulling records for another show. I was tempted to shut off the station speakers and blast some music of my own —my own private rebellion—but I decided not to.

"There you are." Martina was behind me, her hands on her hips. "Sandusky wants to go to breakfast again. You game?"

"Not today," I said. I moved into the jazz section, away from the door, pretending to put music away. Most of the albums I held were old-time rock and roll, the stuff that hadn't been remastered yet, but Martina didn't know that.

She blocked the front of the aisle. "You haven't said anything about Rosaura yet. Have you got a show for Thursday?"

"I saw Rosaura yesterday." My hands were shaking. "I decided that I didn't want her on the program."

Martina tilted her head to one side. "You saw Rosaura?"

"On campus. Only she's got Irish ancestors and she talks like someone from Waukesha."

"And it was Rosaura."

"No doubt." I set the albums down. I suddenly wanted to face Martina. "You almost had me believing you, you know? I actually went to the library, checked the facts, and I probably would have put her on, if I hadn't seen her cross campus with all the books under her arms. Theater major, right? Your roommate."

"No." Martina gripped the record shelves. "She was telling you the truth."

"Yup." I leaned against the Count Basie. "Let me tell you a little truth. Your stunt, demanding that I prove my open-mindedness, probably did a lot more to close my mind than anything else could have. The next time someone brings me something that seems to be straight out of the Twilight Zone, I'm going to be a hell of a lot more skeptical. You proved your point. I'm not as open-minded as I like to think I am."

She sighed. "I actually thought you were a little different."

"What does it matter to you?" I had raised my voice. I hadn't raised my voice in years. "It was a stupid conversation over breakfast a few mornings ago. Sandusky's the Neanderthal, not me. I didn't deserve this."

"Neither did I," she said softly. She touched my cheek. "I really liked you, Linameyer."

Her use of the past tense deflated my anger. "That sounds final."

She shrugged. "If your world doesn't have a place for a twenty-eight-year-old ballerina who danced for Eva Perón, it certainly doesn't have a place for me. I think I'm going to tell Sandusky to buy his own breakfast. See you, Linameyer."

She waved and disappeared around the shelves. I followed her, but she was gone by the time I reached the classical section. I should have followed her out of the station, but I didn't want to know. I didn't want to know what she thought about herself that made her even more special than Rosaura Correga.

The café still smelled of coffee and burned toast. I tried to talk Sandusky into a different restaurant, but he was a regular at the café—and a regular was a regular no matter how bad the food had gotten.

"What the hell did you say to Martina to make her stomp off like that?" Sandusky clutched the battered menu. "She was going to buy me breakfast."

"Why would Martina buy you breakfast? I thought you two don't get along." I pushed the menu aside and decided that I'd try the oatmeal. The worst it could be was lumpy.

He colored. "We don't, but I had a fight with Linda last night. I guess Martina thought she owed me some sympathy."

"A fight about what?" I wasn't really interested in the answer, except that it kept my attention off of Martina.

"The ballet. I told her I liked the ballet, I liked seeing all those beautiful women spread their legs—"

"You didn't."

"—and she said that was not what the ballet was all about. She said it was about the impossible. That the dancers were trained from childhood to do something impossible, and then they'd do it, and we should applaud them while we could because they would die young and their spirit was forever encased in their art, or some kind of weirdo female bullshit like that."

"Linda really said that?" The waitress stopped at the table. I waved my empty coffee cup at her, gaze still trained on Sandusky.

"Yeah. And she said that I didn't have the sensitivity to appreciate art."

"She should have known that from the moment she saw you." The waitress poured my coffee, and I realized that the burned-toast smell came right out of the pot. I pushed the cup aside.

Sandusky added milk to his. "So what was Martina all huffy about? You two got something going?"

"No. She decided I wasn't open-minded enough."

"That roommate thing." Sandusky slurped his coffee. "Can't say as I blame you. That old woman was enough to give anyone the creeps."

I jerked, nearly spilling my cup. "You met her roommate?"

"Sure, that day Martina brought her to the station. Tiny and bent and some kind of cock-and-bull story about dancing for Juan Perón. If I know those Latin American dictators, she wasn't dancing for him. She was letting him dance on her."

"You don't know Latin American dictators, Sandusky." I leaned back, feeling tired. Martina had shaken me more than I realized.

The waitress set my oatmeal in front of me, along with a lump of raisins on the side. Sandusky's eggs looked like they had a few days before, the morning we had come with Martina. I frowned.

"You've been saying weird stuff went on in the newsroom. What were you talking about?"

Sandusky poured catsup over his eggs and hash browns, then stirred them together as if he were making stew. "I don't know, Linameyer. It's kind of embarrassing."

"Kinky predawn sex before the UPI machine?"

Sandusky glanced up, flushed to his ears. "I don't like her, Linameyer. And besides, I would never *do* that."

I nodded. My attempt at levity failed. "I'm sorry. You've been wanting to tell me this for days. I'm ready to hear it."

"Martina and I, we got along okay in the beginning." Sandusky took a bite of the red egg mixture and grimaced. He washed it down with a sip of coffee. "I would correct her grammar and she would correct my politics. Then, one morning, I caught her looking at me as if she could see all that secret stuff you don't tell anybody, you know? And I felt like I did when I was fifteen. The summer my dad died."

The flush had stayed in his face, and his voice had become so soft I could barely hear him. I stirred my oatmeal, waiting until the emotion had passed. "What makes that weird, Sandusky?"

He took another bite of the eggs, this time chewing as if he couldn't taste them. Tears floated on the rims of his eyes. "She got me to tell her something I never told anybody else, not even Linda. And the next thing I knew, we were fifteen minutes behind schedule. Only I didn't feel like I told her, Linameyer. I felt like I *showed* her. Like I took her back with me."

"Some memories are strong enough," I said. "They hold the power to sweep us with them."

He nodded, and wiped at his eyes. "God, this shit is terrible," he said, pushing his plate away by way of explanation. "That wasn't the worst of it, Ben. It was after that. She treated me like she didn't respect me anymore. Here I'd shared something crucial to me, and it was as if I no longer met some hidden standard."

I took his hand and squeezed it. He pulled away and sipped his coffee. "And that's why you don't like Martina."

"It's as if she's got a label for the whole world. I mean, I make mistakes, and I say stupid things, but I treat people the same, no matter who they are. Unless they hurt me." His entire face was red. He smiled at me over the rim of his cup. "I like you, Linameyer."

"I like you too, Sandusky."

"I just don't want to see her fuck you up even worse. You're interested in her. You go to bed with her or something and then she starts treating you like dirt, and it could fuck you over."

"I'll be careful," I said. "I promise."

. . . .

After breakfast, I went down to the lake and watched the sailboats catch the midmorning light. As I watched, I tried to think of nothing at all, but Martina's face kept appearing in my mind. Finally, I walked back to my car, and drove to her apartment.

Martina lived in one of the renovated Victorian mansions on Gorham. I had to drive nearly a mile out of my way on one-way streets to get to the building. My breath was coming in little gasps, and it felt as if someone had punched me through the heart.

People can get stuck in time.

I felt a thin thread of relief when I saw that the house still stood. I was afraid, somehow, that it would have disappeared with Martina. I parked the car in a numbered parking space in the back lot and went inside.

The building smelled of wood polish and dust. I took the stairs two at a time. With each step, I realized that the heartache I felt was not sadness, but anger. Martina had tested me and judged me unworthy, just as she had done to Sandusky. Only I wasn't going to take it. I was going to find out her little secret.

The door to Martina's apartment stood open. She sat on the couch, arms wrapped around her knees, staring at the floor. *Swan Lake* played faintly in the background, and a tiny old woman, dressed all in black, sat at the battered kitchen table.

"So," I said to Martina. "What is it about you that I would never believe?"

Martina didn't glance up, but the old woman did. Her face had no wrinkles, except for the laugh lines around her eyes. Her body had shriveled and her hair had grayed, but her features would stay the same forever. "Are we compatible, young man?"

"Yes, we are, Mrs. Correga." Somehow her age didn't surprise me.

"And you want me for your radio show?"

"Let me talk to Martina first."

Rosaura stood up. With her gray hair piled on top of her head and her arthritic slowness, she looked even smaller than she was. "You do not think, Martina," she said. "At least this young man came to talk to you."

"I can handle it, *abuela.*" The bitterness in Martina's voice sent a shiver down my back.

"No, you can't." Rosaura turned to me. "I would like to do the show, dressed as I am now."

"That would be fascinating, Mrs. Correga. Come to the station on Thursday, at 11:30. I'll explain what to do then."

She nodded once, then walked toward the back of the apartment, moving with the same willowy grace I had seen once before. I waited until I heard a door close toward the back before I spoke again. "What am I too narrow-minded to know?"

"She was beautiful once," Martina said.

"She still is, if you know how to look."

Martina rested her chin on her knees. "She really did dance for Eva Perón."

"I know. And she's lived here ever since."

Martina nodded.

"You did something to her, and you did the same thing to Sandusky. Only he says it made you lose respect for him." With each sentence, my vocal control slipped. The words vibrated, as they did when I interviewed a hostile guest on the talk show.

Martina pulled her legs closer, as if she could wrap herself into a tiny ball. "He ran away when his father was dying, couldn't bear to watch the old man in pain, although the old man wanted him around. Sandusky's been trying to make it up to him ever since. That's why he brings his father up when he's losing an argument. As if his father were a saint or something."

A missing piece to Sandusky. That explained a lot: his unwillingness to try new things; the kindness he showed to people with problems; the hurt on his face when he had talked with me that morning. I inched forward into the apartment. The ceiling sloped, making it difficult for me to stand. "What do you do?" I asked.

"You ever talk to people?" She leaned forward. I sat down across from her. She didn't seem to mind. "They have memories—a moment that they carry in their hearts, like a snapshot of a long-dead lover. And it's that moment that gives them meaning."

I suddenly remembered the brittle feel of Rosaura's fingers when I first shook her hand; although her skin appeared elastic, it still felt old. "Like your grandmother being the prima ballerina for the Compañía Nacional de Argentina."

"Like that." Martina glanced down at her hands. The gesture seemed like Rosaura. "If I want to, I can grab that moment and let them wear it."

"And you did for your grandmother in the studio." My voice had slipped from interview to interrogation. The impossibilities of Martina's claim impressed me less than her unwillingness to be honest with me from the first.

"Or I can actually bring the memory to the surface and let them relive it. I did that with Sandusky." Martina looked up at me. She clutched her hands together so hard her knuckles were white. "You saw my sister on campus. She hates it when people ask her if she's Rosaura."

She had tested other people the same way. And they had failed too. "Then you do this a lot."

Martina shrugged. "Enough that it has scared a few men away."

"It seems that it would scare a lot of people away, Martina." I clenched my fists. It wasn't scaring me—or perhaps the anger covered the fear.

"I don't tell my friends anymore," she said. "I wanted to tell you."

The floor was hard. I shifted a little to ease the physical discomfort. "Why me?"

"Because you seemed like someone who would like me anyway." She whispered the sentence. "I started doing this when I was three, like some people start reading. My parents brought in a priest to exorcise me. When that didn't work, they gave me to my grandmother."

The words softened me a little, made me picture the young Martina, a little girl with a power that frightened the people around her. I couldn't make her relive the event, but then, I didn't need to. "Have you done this thing to me?"

Martina tucked a strand of hair behind her ear. "I tried."

I stiffened. All those times she had looked at me so deeply, I had thought that she was interested in me. She had only been interested in ferreting out my past. "And?"

"You don't have a moment, at least not yet." She stretched and slid farther away from me. "I suspect you're living it, at the station, or something."

"And that made me special."

"No," she said. "I've met other people like you. I like you, Linameyer."

"You have a strange way of showing it," I said. I got up, nearly hitting my head on the slanting ceiling. "You insult me, you test me and you try to invade my privacy. I'm amazed Sandusky even talks to you after the way you treated him."

"I didn't do anything wrong." Martina had to tilt her head back to see me. She looked like a child. A confused, frightened child.

"Yes, you did. You have an ability to see people's strongest memories and you view them without even asking permission. Then you judge people based on that past event and act as if that event defines their life."

"It does." Martina pushed herself onto the couch so that she didn't have to look at me from such an odd angle.

"No," I said. I didn't move. I enjoyed her disadvantage. "It doesn't. It seems to me that your grandmother has done a lot since she left Argentina. She had children, she raised you. And you probably weren't the easiest child to be with. Your grandmother is a spectacular woman—and it wasn't just because she danced for Eva Perón."

"I've been doing this for a long time—"

"And you see what you want to see." I walked to the back of the room, stared at the pictures on the wall, of Martina at various ages, Rosaura in her tutu, and Martina's sister standing in front of a dock. "You accused me and Sandusky of being closed minded, when you had a special gift that allowed you to see parts of a person's life. And you let that gift blind you. You let what you see define the person as much as some people let the word 'nigger' define a black man."

"I do not!" Martina was on her feet.

"You do." I shoved my hands in my pockets. "And the really sad thing is that if you used that gift right, you would have been able to help people instead of hurt them."

I pushed my way past her, and hurried down the stairs. My car looked like home—a place to retreat to, a place to be silent in. I had never said things before like I said to Martina. But then, I had never met a person with such a unique gift before—and such a desire to waste it.

Two weeks went by. Rosaura showed up for the talk show and was a huge hit. People loved her stories about Argentina, the ballet, and about raising children in a strange country. Sandusky and I switched restaurants, and Martina avoided me. Sometimes I saw her working in the newsroom, but every time I smiled, she turned away.

One morning, I was checking my mail in the employees' lounge when she rounded the corner. She stopped in the doorway. I stared at the station newsletter, waiting for her to go away.

"You got a minute, Linameyer?" she asked.

I tucked the newsletter back into the slot with the rest of my mail. Other rolled newsletters stuck out of the remaining boxes like hundreds of cardboard tubes. "I suppose."

She came in and closed the door. "I've been thinking about what you said and I was wondering what you thought I could do to help people."

I looked her over, trying to see if she was serious. Her face was paler than usual, and she had deep circles under her eyes. Little lines had formed beneath her lips, as if she hadn't smiled for days. "You really want to know?"

She nodded.

I went over to the ratty pink couch and sat down, then patted the cushion beside me. Martina sat on the arm. "You said to me when I saw Rosaura for the first time," I said, "that people get stuck in time. Sandusky's stuck at fifteen, trying to make up to a dad who will never forgive him. You can see that, but you don't reach out. You don't help people move forward again."

"How could I do that?"

"By asking if they want your help and then telling them what you see, how they're stuck, if they're stuck. Then they're free to get counseling or to resolve the problem on their own. But you've helped them. You've given them vision."

Martina had hunched over, as if my words were physical blows instead of sound. I watched her for a moment, then said softly, "You're stuck too. You're still a three-year-old whose parents thought she was possessed. That's why you use your gift as a weapon, to make sure you get other people before they get you."

She raised her head, eyes shiny. "You can see too?"

"No." I ran a hand through my hair. "Sometimes I don't need to. Sometimes it's real obvious." I stood up. "I've got a cat to feed. I'm going home."

I grabbed my mail out of the box and opened the door.

"Linameyer?" she said.

I turned. She was still hunched over, her eyes sunken into her face. "I've been a real bitch."

That was the closest thing to an apology that I would get. "I know," I said. "But I like you, Martina, even when I'm mad at you."

She smiled, and her face lit up. I loved it when Martina smiled. "That mean we're friends?" she asked.

"I think so." I grinned. "Tomorrow—breakfast with me and Sandusky?"

"I wouldn't miss it," she said. And then, almost a whisper: "Thanks, Linameyer."

"You're welcome." I closed the door, giving her a moment of privacy, and walked down the hall. My mood had lightened. She had asked. She wanted to change. And I had changed. I had finally spoken up for something I believed in and it had made a difference. An ever-so-small, ever-so-important difference.

Lethe

PEG KERR

M ATTHEW SLEPT LATE; he had been called out in the
middle of the night to deliver a baby. Arriving back at the clinic at dawn,
he had immediately fallen into bed. Now, an urgent knocking jolted him
awake two hours past his usual rising time. He dragged himself out from
underneath the blankets and stumbled groggily to the dispensary door,
opening it to admit a boy.

"Hev'rae—Gremekke?" the boy asked, panting, peering up uncertainly
at the wooden placard above the door frame.

Matthew glanced at the shelf, saw that Gremekke's kit was gone, and
shook his head. "No, he's out. Will I serve? I'm his assistant, Hev'rae
Mateo."

"Oh!" the boy exclaimed, relieved. "If you're a healer too, can you come with me? An accident—a man's hurt very bad, blood coming from his mouth."

"Yes, I'll come. Let me get my kit." Matthew picked up his satchel of medical tools and supplies, which was emblazoned on the side with the symbol for the Peace Corps. "What happened?" he asked as he ushered the boy out.

"My father, Pietro the stonecutter, sent me. His crew was working raising blocks, and the scaffolding collapsed . . ." the boy grimaced.

"How far?"

"It's the nearest part of the city wall—but please hurry, Hev'rae." The boy led the way, weaving nimbly through passersby and ducking quickly around corners, kicking up little puffs of dust as he ran. Matthew jogged in his wake, his kit banging against his hip with every step. He still was not accustomed to Calypso's gravity, which was slightly higher than Earth's, but before he had a chance to become winded they came into the plaza before the second eastern gate. More dust lingered in the air there, as well as the smell of freshly split wood. A latticework of ropes and boards hung, twisted and broken, from the upper walkway, and a group of workmen was crouched around a still form lying on the ground underneath.

One remained standing, anxiously scanning the alley entrance. When he saw them, he hurried forward, a burly man with large, dusty hands.

"My father, Pietro," said the boy, pointing.

"This way, this way!" The stonecutter beckoned, gesturing for the others to step aside. "Jokko can move his toes, barely, but we didn't want to hurt him any more, so we haven't tried moving him." He lowered his voice. "He says his chest hurts him real bad inside. I'm afraid some of his ribs are broken and are piercing his lungs. Maybe even grazing his heart."

Matthew nodded and knelt beside the injured man. He was young, Matthew judged, barely in his twenties by Earth reckoning. He had fallen on his side on a heap of stones and lay draped over a large boulder, twisted like a broken rag doll.

"I'm the *hev'rae*, Jokko. I'm here to patch you up since you've decided to try walking on air. Are you able to get deep enough breaths?"

The man drew a ragged sobbing gasp and coughed as a trickle of blood ran from one corner of his mouth. "Hurts," he croaked.

"Don't try to talk, then." Jokko's pupils were dilated, his skin clammy and alarmingly gray, and his pulse rapid and thready from shock. Parting his shirt revealed a distended belly; he was hemorrhaging internally. "Somebody get me a board we can use as a stretcher."

They brought a plank and placed it on the ground beside the injured man. "We're going to lift him onto it. The first thing to do is to slowly untwist his legs, and then we all lift at once, sliding hands underneath to support all parts of his back and keep it level. Don't jiggle him."

The men gathered around as Matthew gave his instructions. "You there, at the left shoulder—yes, you change places with that man. I want people on either side who are about the same height. Now, turn that top leg and straighten it—slowly, slowly, that's it. Keep it up a little. All right, on the count of three, we'll pick him up: one, two, three. Get—get that right hip higher, keep it level. Careful now, watch your footing—"

They carefully placed Jokko on the makeshift stretcher, and Matthew covered him with the cloak of one of the workers. He was rigging a strap to tie Jokko onto it when Pietro's heavy hand fell on his shoulder. "Don't trouble yourself further, Hev'rae." Pietro pointed with his chin at an approaching figure.

"What?" Distracted, Matthew followed the stonecutter's gaze to the woman who joined the small circle of helpers opposite Matthew, her shadow falling over Jokko's face.

"She's the only one he needs now," Pietro said sadly.

She was a slight woman, in a loose reddish-brown dress belted with a black sash tied in a complex knot. Her age was difficult to judge: although her dark hair was streaked with gray, her face was unlined.

"I've come for Jokko," she said. Her close-set gray eyes flicked around the circle, meeting Matthew's look, and then her gaze rested on the still form at their feet.

Matthew eyed her with some confusion and then busied himself at his kit, readying a unit of saline as he threw another glance at the patient. Blood pressure had probably fallen so low that finding a vein was going to be difficult.

Pietro stared at the woman a moment, his lips clamped tightly together, and then stooped down. "Jokko. The *rhyena'v'rae* is here."

The injured man made a sound, half gasp of surprise and half whimper.

"Jokko," said the woman gently.

Tears began to roll down his cheeks. "No—no, I'm not ready," he whispered.

"Jokko, let me help."

"My wife." He coughed up more blood. "My little boy."

"Jokko, I can do nothing unless you let me." Her voice was heavy with pity. "Please."

He stared at her, his chest heaving. "Rhyena'v'rae, please t . . . take me in your arms."

The woman knelt swiftly beside him like a mother hurrying to comfort a hurt child, and to Matthew's horror, she gathered his head and shoulders and laid them in her lap.

Matthew immediately dropped the saline unit and plunged forward to yank the woman aside. Pietro hissed an order, and before Matthew could touch her, three bystanders had seized him and held him fast.

"What are you doing?" Matthew gasped. "You'll injure him further, you'll—"

Pietro stood up fast. "Don't interfere, Hev'rae. This is no business of yours." He glared at the three workmen. "Hold him until it's over."

"Let go of me!" Matthew cried, enraged. "Don't you understand, she'll kill him!" He furiously began struggling in earnest, twisting until his shirt tore, flailing his arms, trying to kick out backwards. "You sons of bitches, let go—uunghh!"

Pietro's hard blow to his gut knocked the wind out of him. Gasping, Matthew fell to his knees, his captors barely managing to hold him upright. Between wheezes, he looked up painfully at the glowering stonecutter. The woman took no notice of them.

She pressed her hand gently on Jokko's forehead and smoothed his hair back. "What do you need to say before you go?"

"Brother Sevett and I—we quarrelled . . . old debt. Tell him . . . sorry. P . . . pay him."

The woman nodded gravely. "I will make it right with him. What is the amount?"

"F . . . five hundred."

"You give me the authority to make the change in your estate?"

"Yes." His eyes looked around the circle. "Witnesses."

The woman nodded again. "Is there anything else, Jokko?"

He was growing weaker. "F . . . family," he whispered.

Matthew cursed despairingly and began struggling again, more weakly this time. One of the men holding him twisted his arm behind his back and another got his head in a hammerhold, covering his mouth. Breathing hard, Matthew stopped, glaring at Pietro.

"You have provided for them," the woman said, still ignoring the others. "Remember, you gave me your testament."

Jokko shook his head faintly. "No, I mean . . . how will they go on? What . . . what will happen to them?"

She shook her head sadly. "I am not allowed to tell you that. But perhaps I can put your heart at rest for them." She raised her head and looked at Pietro.

The stoneworker knelt down again and took the dying man's hand. "Lad, I'll look after the boy as if he were my own, and I'll see that he learns a trade. And your woman—" the big man paused, tears trickling through his beard. "She'll miss you sore, but I'll do what I can to help her."

"I act as witness to this promise," the woman said. "Know that you are held by your word, because it is bound by Death. Are you willing to accept this responsibility?"

"Yes," Pietro whispered, and he squeezed his journeyman's hand. "I swear."

Jokko nodded slightly. "That is all . . ." He closed his eyes, spent.

The woman pressed her hand to his forehead. "I am taking the pain away now, Jokko. Soon, all weariness will cease." She smoothed back his hair. "Your life is completed. Don't be afraid to lay it down. I will be with you." Her voice dropped to a whisper, and Matthew had to strain to hear. "Here is Death now, Jokko. Do you see it? It waits for you as a friend, and you only have to reach out for it." Her arms tightened on him briefly, and she bent to kiss his brow. As she straightened, Matthew saw Jokko exhale his last ragged breath. The onlookers sighed softly and stirred.

"He is gone," said the woman gently. She carefully laid his head back on the plank and stood to face Pietro. "Will you have your men bring his body to his home? I will go ahead with you to inform his widow."

Matthew jerked his head violently and the hand over his mouth was removed. "Wait!" He shook off the remaining hands that held him and got stiffly to his feet. "What do you think you—why did you interfere? If I could have gotten him to the clinic, he would have had a chance!"

"I warned you," Pietro began threateningly.

She stopped him with a peremptory gesture, saying, "No, the hev'rae came to do his job." She turned back to Matthew. "Do not blame yourself—or me, if I was called to do mine."

"Who are you?" he demanded.

"My name is Teah. I'm a lethe."

He stared at her, perplexed.

"It's my profession," she added patiently. She glanced at Pietro. "I must go; I'm needed elsewhere." And with that, she left with the stonecutter. The work crew hoisted the plank to their shoulders and followed, bringing Jokko home for the last time.

Gremekke was leaning against the dispensary counter eating bread and sausage when Matthew arrived back at the clinic. The older healer was a portly man, with a rumpled fringe of gray hair around his tonsure, and fleshy cheeks that almost enveloped his eyes when he smiled. "That baby took its own sweet time," he greeted Matthew.

Matthew dropped his kit on the shelf and turned to the sink. "It wasn't the baby," he replied curtly. "I was called out on an accident after I got back. Workman fell from a scaffold."

Something in his tone prompted Gremekke to look up from his plate and watch as Matthew splashed water on his face and reached for a towel. "You lost him, I think," said the older man finally.

Matthew gave his face a final wipe and threw the towel angrily down on the counter. "But it wasn't my fault, Gremekke, I swear. I could have saved him, but the bystanders prevented me from working on him so that some local priestess could do some last-rites nonsense." His fist clenched. "Dammit, Gremekke, they hit me!"

"Ah," Gremekke nodded. Unruffled, he took another bite of sausage. "Don't take it personally. So you've met Teah. Didn't you read the cultural report I compiled and had sent to you?"

Caught by surprise, Matthew blinked. "Gremekke, there were fifteen hundred pages of it!"

Gremekke sighed. "I see I might have spared myself the trouble."

Matthew flushed uncomfortably. "I've started it, and I've been looking over it nights, when I'm not out on call. I really couldn't finish it before shipping out; the Corps gave me so little time to prepare."

"Well," said Gremekke mildly, "you have been here for a month now. And if you had finished reading it, you would have been prepared to meet her. She's the only *rhyena'v'rae* left in the city, maybe on all of Calypso."

"She called herself a . . . a lethe."

Gremekke smiled. "She pegged you right away as Terran, then. Your accent probably gave you away. 'Lethe' is the word you Terrans used to describe the *rhyena'v'raien* they met after Re-Contact. Don't you remember your Greek mythology? 'Lethe' was the name of one of the rivers in Hades. When a dead soul drank from it, the water erased all memories of its former life." Gremekke thoughtfully crumbled some of the bread on his plate. "The Calypsan word we use, *rhyena'v'rae*, is more complicated. It means both 'death watcher' and 'death cradler.' "

Matthew shook his head. "I don't understand." He ran his hand through his hair. "Look, there's no reason for me to put up with what happened today. I'm thinking of lodging a complaint with the city."

"If you do, you're a fool," Gremekke replied, exasperated. "No, now listen, Matt. What she does is important, and it's not very easy. That patient you lost had contracted with her earlier to show up when he was dying."

"What?"

"It's a fact. Nobody knows how they do it, but a *rhyena'v'rae* can look at a person and know exactly when he's going to die."

"I don't believe it. That's impossible!"

"Well, you saw it happen today, didn't you?" Matthew had no answer to that, and Gremekke went on. "What you do is you go to Teah and you ask her, 'Can you be my *rhyena'v'rae?*' If she says yes, that means that she's agreeing that she'll be physically present at your death." Gremekke shook his head. "I don't understand exactly what she does, though I've seen it, of course. It's kind of a psychic process that helps people through the whole thing, gets them past their pain and fear."

"Oh come on, Gremekke. To help people die—what's that supposed to mean?"

Gremekke shrugged. "Well, I don't know. I've certainly never tried dying before, with or without a *rhyena'v'rae*. But you've had patients who fight death, haven't you? I think that many people do, because they don't know what to expect and they're just damned frightened. And even the ones who slip away quietly sometimes do it with a kind of despair; haven't you noticed? But with her—it's as if she's taking them somewhere, and not just into the darkness. Somehow, it gives them the courage to go."

"So it's a sort of spiritual help, is that what you're saying?"

"Well, not just that," Gremekke said. "There's some kind of a physical component to it, too. It's strange: she holds them, and the ones that are in terrible pain sag in relief, as if they've just gotten a shot of morphine.

"It's also a practical arrangement; she helps you plan your testament, like a lawyer would on Earth, and she's in charge of carrying out any last wishes. She gets paid a flat fee, plus a percentage of the estate later." He rubbed his chin. "Of course, having only one *rhyena'v'rae* left in the city means that there aren't many people who have a *rhyena'v'rae* contract. There are plenty who wouldn't consider it anyway." The corner of his mouth twitched. "Rather like all those people on Earth I hear about who tend to put off having their wills done. An attempt to ignore the inevitable."

Matthew thought that over for a moment. "Does she ever say no?" he asked.

"Sometimes. Maybe it's because she knows the person's going to die far away, or someplace where she can't be present, like a burning building, perhaps. Sometimes she refuses because she knows that she's going to die first. But she never tells which it is."

Matthew shook his head in amazement. "I've never heard of anything like this before."

"Humph. I'm not surprised. I suppose it's limited to Calypso. There's an old story of a colonist named Stivan who had a near-death experience —drowning, I think. This was quite some time ago, not too long after contact was broken off with Earth. Anyway, when he came to, he related an experience that sounded similar to so many others: the tunnel, the bright light, and so forth, you know.

"But more than that, Stivan said that it taught him how to die, in a way which humans had forgotten. And that he could help people through the process of dying and teach it to others. He explained that it was a matter of perception. Maybe there's something to that; apparently, he had a very high esper rating. He was the first *rhyena'v'rae*, and his work was developed by his disciples into the groundwork for the profession. Since Re-Contact has been so recent, I'm not surprised that you never heard about this in medical school."

"I don't know, Gremekke. This is all pretty hard to swallow."

"Well, look at the report. If you still have it."

"I will. I'll go read it right now."

Gremekke put his plate down on the counter. "One more thing," he said. "Can you guess why she always wears that brownish color?"

Matthew frowned. "No. Why?"

"Practicality. It doesn't show the blood so much." He smiled and left, leaving Matthew staring at the crumb-dusted plate.

"Gremekke, we're about out of iodine. Didn't the apothecary deliver it this week?"

Gremekke glanced up from splinting a boy's finger and looked around vaguely. "I thought I had it in the order—no, that's right, I didn't because there was another box under the green cabinets. Is that used up already?"

"That was quinine, not iodine." Matthew shook the almost-empty bottle ruefully. "I'd better go to the apothecary's and get some more to tide us over."

Gremekke nodded. "It's quiet enough now that I can spare you. Sorry about that, lad, but you're right. We'll need it."

Matthew sighed. "We're so spoiled on Earth. What I wouldn't give for a sonic sterilizer."

"Get used to it," Gremekke grunted.

Matthew picked up his cloak, for the afternoon was chilly. At the door, he turned around for one thing more. "I might take just a little longer. There's someone—something I have to do."

Gremekke gave him a shrewd look. "Just so. By all means, take all the time you need."

"Thanks." Just as Matthew was swinging the door shut, he heard Gremekke call out after him: "She lives at the end of Fish Hook Street, beyond the piers by the shore."

Matthew smiled as he set out toward Fish Hook Street. He'd stop at the apothecary's on his way back.

Fish Hook Street was really only a narrow lane, backed by the pier houses where the fishermen stored their nets and gaffs. The street passage led Matthew in a curve around to the left and away from the other buildings as he neared the shore. Teah's small home was built on a craggy terrace above the high-tide mark. The path that led to her door passed the moored fishing boats.

He hesitated at the threshold, but the door was ajar, which in the local parlance meant, "Come right in." Accordingly, he pushed it open, removed his shoes, and entered Teah's home.

She was kneeling on a tasseled *ghoto,* the Calypsan traditional kneeling pad used when visitors came to call. A middle-aged couple knelt on *ghotos* across from her, and a narrow table spread with papers stood between Teah and her guests. Teah glanced up and gave him a friendly nod and smile, but she continued speaking to the woman visitor.

"Well, give some thought to designating your heir to the partnership. Suppose you do that and come to see me again about the revision, sometime in the next seven-day or so?"

The couple nodded and arose. A few pleasantries were exchanged as Teah gathered up and handed over the papers, and then the couple took their leave, brushing quietly past Matthew and retrieving their shoes by the door before heading back down the path.

"Good afternoon, Rhyena'v'rae," Matthew said a bit stiffly. "I am sorry if I was intruding."

"No, no, we were just finishing up. My door is always open, Hev'rae

Mateo," she replied pleasantly, and Matthew wondered how she had known his name. "I am happy to see you. Would you care to join me for a walk along the beach?"

"Yes, I would."

They walked down toward the water in silence. The path twisted and turned between large gray rocks, widening out at the line where the long, blowing beach grasses began. The sharp blades cut against their ankles, and the white sands shifted under their feet. At the bottom of the slope, they turned and began walking away from the wharves, keeping near the shore. Teah seemed content to let him speak first, and finally he did.

"Rhyena'v'rae, maybe you knew that I'm in the Peace Corps."

"Yes, I did."

"Before I came out here," he continued, groping for words, "they told me in training that I would run into situations where I'd have to think twice about my assumptions—about what I think is right. At first I assumed they were just talking about medicine, but I know now it's more than that. I talked with Hev'rae Gremekke and took the opportunity to learn something about what you do, and, well—I didn't understand."

She nodded. "And I regret the treatment you received from the others who were there. Let us agree to make a fresh start and think no more of what happened, Hev'rae. I think it speaks well of your dedication, that you don't yield to Death without a fight." She smiled up at him. "But sometimes a *hev'rae* must stop and remind himself that Death may also come as a friend."

Matthew thought of Jokko, pleading to know the fate of his family. "Sometimes, maybe. But not always, I think," he said.

"Not always."

"Look, I thought I should come and talk—"

A shout behind them interrupted him. "Teah! Amo Teah!"

Teah turned around. A small boy was running toward them, holding something out. "Look what I have!"

She clapped her hands together, beaming like a little girl, and squatted down to examine the treasure as the boy ran up to join them. "What is it? Why, it's a turtle! Where ever did you find it, Rano?"

"In the tide pool." He was a fair, curly-headed child, with a generous sprinkling of freckles across his nose. He grinned up at Matthew and eagerly held out his prize for examination. "See, it's a red-spotted turtle! Can I keep it, Amo Teah?"

"I know that you could take good care of it, Rano . . ."

The boy stuck out his chest, swelling with responsibility. "Of course I can!"

"Of course you can. But don't you think that it should be released again?"

"But I found it! How could I let it go?" he asked plaintively.

"I know it's very hard. Maybe it would help if you think that you're letting it go back to the open sea because that's where it's happiest, out there with its family."

"Well—" the boy pondered the question seriously. "If I put it back now, it could swim out with the next tide."

She gave him a hug, unmindful of the wet turtle between them. He squirmed free, flashed another grin to show her that there were no hard feelings, and then ran back to the rocks where the tidal basins formed. Teah stood and called after him, "I'll see you tonight."

He stopped and turned toward her. "Don't be late like last night!"

Teah laughed. "I promise you won't have to wait for your supper this time." She watched him go, a fond smile still on her face.

"A fine boy," Matthew commented. "Your son?"

Her smile faded. "No. I regret to say I have no children." Squinting against the setting sun, Matthew turned to watch the boy clamber up the huge boulders. Teah looked at Matthew and smiled again. "I suppose I am his second mother, in a way—that's why he calls me *Amo*. Actually, I'm his aunt. His mother is my sister Briena, and she has to scrape a bit to make ends meet—she's a widow. I'm afraid that sometimes she finds it difficult to find time for him."

They walked slowly and talked some more. He told her a little about his assignment. "I never expected to leave Earth at all. I had just signed on with the Peace Corps when the news came that the Corps was going to be joining the Re-Contact project, helping with the reassimilation between Earth and Calypso. That changed everyone's priorities in a hurry, so I was sent here instead of to my original assignment. The Corps named Gremekke as my sponsor mostly because he's the senior *hev'rae* in the city, and they figured he'd have plenty of experience for me to draw upon. I'm expected to relieve him of some of his caseload, too. He never complains, but he's getting up in years, and it's too wearing for him to run the clinic by himself now."

She listened politely, but he wondered how much of what he told her she already knew. He got the impression that she had known Gremekke for a long time. She probably knew all the healers in the city well. How did they feel about working with her?

"One thing," he said, and stopped. She looked at him inquiringly. He rubbed his chin. "I don't know if I can say this right. I'm still not exactly comfortable with the language, but, well, how can you possibly justify this? What you do, I mean?"

She cocked her head. "Justify?" Thoughtfully, she watched the seabirds dip and mew in the distance. "You have an oath that you take when you become a *hev'rae*, don't you?"

He nodded. "It's called the Hippocratic Oath."

"My profession has something similar, which also gives me ethical constraints. I never reveal when anyone's time is, for example, even to the client. And I don't allow myself to profit from any confidential information about estates or family matters. My first responsibility is to my clients and to their bereaved."

Matthew sighed. "I guess I didn't make myself clear. I meant when somebody sees you coming, don't they just, uh, give up? How can that be right?"

"It's not something I cause. It's what I see." She pointed to a promontory ahead of them, jutting out into the sea. "Look, do you see that tree there, overhanging the shore?"

"Yes."

"Do you see how the sand is eroding away from the roots, trickling down the hill into the water little by little? If you notice that, and if you know how much sand is lost every day, and how big the tree is and how much support it needs, you would have a good idea about when the tree will topple into the water. That's not the same as taking an axe and cutting the tree down."

He thought about it for a moment. "What if I hold the sea back with stones?"

"You could, I suppose. But the waves would eventually work them free."

"Then I'd transplant the tree."

She laughed. "Ah, you are stubborn, I see. But the promontory isn't infinitely wide. And the tree, after all, must remain rooted in the sand. We are all mortal, Hev'rae." She turned to face him again. "And the tree will fall, you see. You might perhaps delay the inevitable, but you can't do anything to stop the sea."

They walked along in silence for a few more moments. Finally, Matthew said, "Look, I don't think I can accept what you're saying."

"No?"

"I mean, it would ruin me as a *hev'rae* if I believed that. I have a duty to my profession, and this—it's as if you're telling me I should just throw up my hands and let the sea wash in. I couldn't live with myself if I did that."

She looked surprised. "Truly, I don't ask that of you. There are other *hev'raien* in the city who feel as you do, you know. And yet I can still work with them, because each of us knows that we all want the same thing."

"Oh?" he said, his tone politely doubting.

"Yes," she said firmly. "We want to help our patients, our clients."

"I suppose so. I mean, I can see how the legal arrangements you make and the counseling you do would be helpful."

"But I should concern myself with only those affairs, perhaps, and stay out of your way?" she replied shrewdly. Matthew glanced at her, but her face looked amused, not angry. "I'm afraid that my duties to my profession will not allow you to have the one without the other, Hev'rae." She made an enigmatic gesture. "We must simply agree that we disagree. It is sometimes so."

Eventually, they arrived back at her home. "Well, thank you for talking with me anyway, Rhyena'v'rae," Matthew said. "You've given me some things to think about." It was the truth, he realized with some surprise.

"You have done that for me, also." She plucked aside a strand of hair that the breeze was blowing in her eyes and turned to face him.

At her cool appraisal, he felt a faint chill. He noticed that her eyes had dilated, as if something had made her flinch.

"You're seeing my death, aren't you?"

She blinked, as if surprised by his bluntness, but her answer was equally frank. "Yes, I always do. Or I see my own."

"I'm a *hev'rae*, so I've seen my share of dying."

"This is different," she said evenly.

"Of course." He flushed. "Forgive me, I just meant to say that I don't know how you can do it. I mean, how can you talk to people, knowing the exact second that they will cease to be?"

"It can be a difficult thing." She gazed away, out over the water.

He thought about what it would be like to care about someone, maybe even love someone, knowing that. He suddenly found himself wondering what *rhyena'v'raien* did about that. Did they have lovers? Families?

Another thought occurred to him. "Tell me," he asked, "Can you act as *rhyena'v'rae* for a Terran?"

"Perhaps. Are you asking for yourself, Hev'rae?"

He hesitated. "No. Not at this time." He watched her face carefully; he didn't want to offend her.

But she only nodded. "There is a time for everything, Hev'rae. Now is not always the right one."

"Leave the autoclave to its own devices for one night, Mateo, m'boy. You and I are going out tonight to celebrate."

Matthew straightened up from the pile of instruments he was sterilizing and peered at Gremekke through clouds of steam. "Celebrate? Celebrate what?"

"Why, your anniversary, you dolt. Tonight marks the start of your third year on Calypso!"

Matthew glanced at the wall calender, made of strips of cloth with colored beads attached representing the days and months, and he did some mental calculations. "I'm still thinking in terms of Earth time; I didn't even realize it." He banged down the lid of the autoclave and stripped off his greens. "You're on."

They closed up the dispensary and headed up the street which led over a hill to the public houses on Tanners Row. Gremekke stumped along, wheezing, with Matthew's tactful hand on his arm to guide him around the puddles he normally would have splashed right through. "Fine night!" he exclaimed. "Wonderful night! Smell that sea breeze! That's why I'd never move to one of the inland cities."

Matthew could smell little but the fumes of the leatherworkers' lye, mixed with the smell of dung, but he allowed that the air certainly cleared one's head quickly.

"Absolutely. You certainly picked the right place to come to be a healer. Now, I'll admit that I've wanted to visit Earth sometimes, but I wouldn't trade my practice on Calypso for anything—plenty of opportunity for roll-up-the-sleeves hands-on experience."

"I did do my residency in the ER at Los Angeles County General," Matthew said wryly.

Gremekke abruptly came to a stop at the crest of the hill, panting, and Matthew almost plowed right into him.

"This is where I wanted to take you." Gremekke indicated a nondescript door with an expansive wave of his arm. A wooden placard swinging above it read The River's Edge. From the bottom of the placard hung a copper bell, the symbol of drinking establishments. "A good place for carousing. Let's go in and buy a barrel of ale and two straws."

Despite this recommendation, The River's Edge proved to be no more than a friendly, somewhat sleepy neighborhood public house, with a few customers talking quietly among themselves. The room looked big enough to seat thirty people or so, although it held only about half that number at the moment. Bluish smoke from a few pipes drifted, coiling, below the low ceiling, dimming the light. The sweetish smell of the smokeweed mingled pleasantly with the odor of hops, frying onions, and fresh-cut reeds.

Gremekke led the way to a rush mat by the fireplace where they seated themselves on flat floor cushions and ordered the first pitcher of ale. "It's your third year here, now," he said, "and how long did you say you had practiced on Earth before signing on with the Peace Corps?"

"Five years, in Earth reckoning. I got a late start in the Corps."

"Me, now, I've been practicing for forty-two years. Forty-two years! Think of it!" He took a deep swallow. "It's downright terrifying."

Matthew laughed.

"That's better," said Gremekke judiciously. "That's the ticket! Tonight's a night for loosening up."

"And you think I need that?" asked Matthew, amused.

Gremekke snorted and shifted on his pillow, making the reeds crackle underneath him. "When you stepped off that ship, I don't mind telling you that for the first day or two, I wondered if it would work out between you and me. Now, you may have been a *hev'rae* for a while at the time, but I thought you were as bad as the green ones fresh out of training." He shook his head in mock consternation. "You were positively grim!"

Matthew grinned into his cup.

"Maybe it was just being in a new place and all. You seem to have gotten over it. Mind you, like I say, all *hev'raien* start out that way. *I* started out that way! I tell you, I was—" He broke off and looked over Matthew's shoulder. "Look, there's Teah."

Matthew glanced over toward the doorway. Teah stood there, her eyes searching the room. Some of the patrons seated near the door saw her and stirred uneasily. The house owner saw her and scowled before disappearing again into the back kitchen.

"Teah!" Gremekke gestured her over with his cup, slopping a little over his fingers. "Come and join us, won't you?"

She wove her way toward them through the mats, and Gremekke shifted his pillow over to make room for her. As she seated herself, Matthew reached for the ale pitcher, accidentally brushing her arm with his fingers. She recoiled, looking at him with such surprise that he mumbled, "Sorry," wondering what social taboo he had unwittingly violated this time.

"Oh no, Mateo, I'm not offended," she hastened to assure him. "I was only, well, startled. Most people avoid touching *rhyena'v'raien.*"

"Everybody sweats when a *rhyena'v'rae* walks through the door," Gremekke observed, grinning.

"Except for you, old friend," she smiled. "You've never been afraid of me."

Gremekke chuckled and signaled for another pitcher of ale. "I usually see you walking everywhere around the city at all kinds of hours, lass, but I haven't seen much of you lately."

"A *hev'rae* is usually thankful for that," she replied drily.

Gremekke, caught in the middle of a swallow, choked on his ale and then laughed again. "Too true. But Mateo and I are glad to see a friend tonight. We're toasting the start of his third year on Calypso."

"Congratulations, Mateo." She filled the ale mug the server brought and took one swallow, then left it untouched. "You've been lucky to have a sponsor like Gremekke. He's the best *hev'rae* in the city."

Gremekke coughed and rumbled, "Well, now . . ." but Matthew could see that he was pleased.

"Haven't I always told the truth?" Teah asked. "I should know. I haven't been practicing as long as you, Gremekke, but I've been around awhile."

"Gremekke was just telling me about when he started out," Matthew said.

"Did he tell you about the time he delivered twins upside down?"

Matthew frowned, unsure that he had understood her syntax. "You mean a double breech delivery?"

"No." A smile curled at the corner of her mouth. "I mean Gremekke was upside down, while doing the delivery.

"*What?*"

"That was about oh, nineteen, twenty years ago, I think. A pregnant woman fell through some rotted flooring in one of the warehouses on Sailmaker Street. The fall started her labor, and by the time someone heard her screams, she was so near her time that they didn't even have a chance to dig her out. Someone got Gremekke, and they lowered him headfirst through the hole and held on to his legs while he delivered the babies. Two of them."

"It wasn't entirely upside down," Gremekke corrected. "More like a forty-five-degree angle. Good thing, too—I would have blacked out, otherwise."

"You should have seen him, Mateo, with his scissors tied to him, dangling from his wrist so that he wouldn't lose them if he dropped them. He handed up the babies, and then they were able to pry the mother loose."

"My God."

"How many babies would you say you've delivered, Gremekke?" Teah asked.

"I don't know. Thousands." He laughed.

"And it hasn't all been babies, either," Teah went on. "This city has seen a couple of serious epidemics."

Gremekke sighed. "The last one—it was a spring after a lot of flooding. Roads were impossible. A virus. One hundred and fifty died in a month."

"You forget," said Teah softly. "How many more would have died, if you had taken to the hills along with so many others?" She turned to Matthew. "I *know*. He set up a makeshift hospital compound extending out from his clinic and pooled his resources with Hev'rae Lenor and Hev'rae Mavo. He went without sleep for seventy-two hours."

Gremekke was silent, staring at his ale.

"You've been a good *hev'rae*, Gremekke."

There was a little pause. Then Gremekke said slowly, "You've been a lot of places, Teah, but I don't believe that I've ever seen you in The River's Edge before."

"No, Gremekke. But you were here."

Gremekke raised his eyes slowly to her, his face white. "This is it, then, isn't it?"

"Yes, Gremekke. This is it."

"Gremekke?" Matthew asked, puzzled. "What's going on? Gremekke!" Gremekke made a convulsive movement, upsetting his ale, which spread in a brown pool, soaking into the mat. Matthew sat up straight in alarm as heads turned in their direction. Teah didn't move.

"Felt . . . felt something . . . pop," Gremekke forced out, his voice mildly surprised. "Lord, I'm so weak . . ." He slumped back against the wall. "What is it? It's not a stroke?"

"It's the tube beneath the heart, leading to the lower body," Teah said calmly.

Matthew gasped. "An abdominal aneurism? The lower aorta *burst?* But he'll bleed to death in minutes—" He scrambled up to his knees and shoved the drinking cups aside with a sweep of his arm. "Help me lift him. I've got to get him back to the clinic."

But as he reached out to hoist Gremekke's limp form, Teah's hand on his wrist stopped him. "Wait—think, Mateo," she said urgently. "I will not say that he dies because you fail to operate, or because you do. I can only tell you that whatever action you choose to take, his time has come. Given that, how will you choose to let Gremekke meet his end—under the knife? Or here, where he wants to be, with his friends?"

He stared at her in anguish. "I can't do nothing!"

"Life comes to an end, Mateo. It must." She withdrew her hand. "You must choose."

He turned to Gremekke and gently put his hand on the old man's shoulder. Gremekke's eyes glazed over with pain and then closed, and in that instant Matthew made up his mind. "I'm not going to sit back and let a man die. Not this time."

"Mateo—"

"Save it. I'm taking him back to the clinic." Lifting the healer over his shoulder, Matthew struggled to his feet. The other patrons had gathered around, and he glared at them, wondering if anyone would try to stop him. "Somebody help me carry him."

No one moved, although a few looked uncomfortably at Teah. She rose slowly, her gaze steadily meeting his. He wheeled and started for the door. "All right, then. Get out of my way." He didn't wait to see Teah follow.

The streets were still slick from the night's early rain, and Gremekke got heavier with every step. Matthew's mind raced as he tottered on: even if he had his kit with him, it wouldn't do any good. Only immediate surgery could save Gremekke now. It was more than a kilometer to the clinic, and the gravity making it seem even longer, and besides, there wasn't enough blood in stock to replace what he must have lost by now; there wasn't enough time, not enough time, not enough time. . . .

When he had gone about half of the distance, Matthew staggered and half fell against the corner of the building, his breath burning in his chest. He collapsed to the cobblestones, lowering Gremekke across his lap. Teah appeared silently at his side like a shadow and knelt beside them. Matthew raised Gremekke's head, pushing the gray fringe of hair back. In the pale glow from a nearby unshuttered window, he could see how ashen the old man's face looked. "Goddammit. Goddammit, Gremekke."

The old *hev'rae* heard the plea in his voice and opened his eyes. "That's . . . all right, boy . . . there isn't enough time to get me back home. Teah promised long ago . . . she'd make sure . . . I'd . . . I'd be ready. She promised a good death for me." He was having trouble breathing. "Rhyena'v'rae, please . . . take me into your arms."

Teah put her arms around Gremekke and pulled him toward her, to lay his head in her lap as Matthew hastened to shift the healer's feet. They settled him as comfortably as they could, and then Teah leaned over him. "Gremekke, what do you to need to say before you go?"

"Thank you . . . for telling me what it was . . . I always did . . . have a morbid curiosity to know . . . what would carry me off in the end. Impossible to do an autopsy on yourself." His eyes looked over to Matthew. "And . . . thank you, boy. For everything."

Teah waited and then said, "Is that all, Gremekke? Is there anything else?"

He sighed and closed his eyes. "Nnnno. . . ."

Teah laid her hand on his forehead. "Then rest. You will soon know the answer to the question you have pondered for all these years. When you could not save your patients, and they died with their eyes open to something which only they saw, you always wondered, what was there on the other side? Now, Death is coming, but it won't frighten you. It will be like all the times you have delivered children. A cord will be cut, but it will not hurt. It is the beginning of something new."

She fell silent and remained with her eyes closed and her hand on Gremekke's forehead, unmoving. Two minutes crawled by, and then four, as Matthew watched them, his eyes stinging.

Finally, Teah whispered, "There it is; do you see it? Death raises the Cloak to enfold you, and it will feel cool, like the shadows that comfort you in the heat of the noonday sun. Don't be afraid . . . I am with you."

Gremekke's breath eased out once more as Teah leaned forward and kissed his forehead—and then it stopped. Matthew laid his head on the old man's chest but heard nothing. He buried his face in the roughspun shirt. Just as he was wondering whether he would be able to control the sobs that struggled in his throat, he felt Teah's hand, placed on his head like a benediction, and he gave way to his grief.

In accordance with the instructions of his testament, Gremekke's body was cremated and the ashes scattered at sea. An old friend of Gremekke's, Hev'rae Lenor, delivered the eulogy at the memorial service. Matthew spoke briefly, too, trying to describe what their work together had meant to him. Somehow, the words didn't seem enough.

Afterwards he greeted many of the people who had attended the service. The various *hev'raien* spoke kindly to him and asked him about his plans. Others who had been Gremekke's patients over the years shook Matthew's hand and told him little stories, of something Gremekke had said or done for them once, of a bill discreetly overlooked, a baby's life saved. He felt overwhelmed by the sheer number of all the people who had known Gremekke, who wanted to come to honor his passing.

The evening after the service Matthew spent going through the papers in Gremekke's desk. Many of them having to do with the running of the clinic were already familiar to him. But there were others: correspondence, research notes, lists, and legal documents, including a copy of his testament which Teah had brought over earlier in the day. Matthew read over it carefully.

The first section dealt with the estate. Gremekke had left the clinic to Matthew, contingent upon Matthew's decision to stay on Calypso and assume the practice. If Matthew decided not to stay, the assets of the clinic were to be sold, with part of the profit going to Matthew, part to a few other friends and colleagues, and the rest to charity. Teah's fee was included, too.

He sat back and thought about it. Taking the practice over formally would mean leaving the Peace Corps, of course. After all, he had taken the assignment on Calypso with the understanding that it was only temporary. But things were different now, and he had to alter his preconceptions to match the change in his situation. Could he be happy making this world his permanent home?

He picked up the testament and read on through the second section, the contract between Gremekke and Teah: . . . *to come to him when his time of death draws near, using the art of the* rhyena'v'raien *to ease and comfort.* . . . Matthew stopped and thoughtfully chewed a thumbnail. Teah had not come for any of his patients since that workman died two years ago. He realized now that he had been relieved that he hadn't had to face the issue again, almost as if it allowed him to pretend that the whole thing didn't matter.

And yet Gremekke had hired her himself. Why? Gremekke had devoted his life as a *hev'rae* to fighting off entropy in every way possible and yet—Matthew remembered the trust in Gremekke's eyes when he finally turned to Teah at the very end. For all his faith in medicine, Gremekke had needed something from her that Matthew couldn't give him.

His gaze fell on the modestly framed copy of the Hippocratic Oath that hung on the wall beside the desk. . . . *I will follow that method of treatment, which, according to my ability and judgment, I consider for the benefit of my patients, and abstain from whatever is deleterious and mischievous . . . Into whatever houses I enter I will go into them for the benefit of the sick.* . . . And what of the dying, he wondered. What of the dead? What is my responsibility toward them? Does her work benefit them, even more than medicine can? Gremekke must have thought so. Is it possible that Teah is fulfilling this oath better than I am?

Someone was knocking. Matthew tried to ignore it because Gremekke was the *hev'rae* on call and should have been the one to get up and answer it. Then he remembered that Gremekke was dead.

He raised his head. He had fallen asleep at Gremekke's desk, with his head resting on the piles of papers, because he hadn't wanted to go to bed. How foolish. He got up and went to answer the door. It was Teah.

"Mateo?" She blinked in the light, pulling her cloak close against the rain.

"Teah," he said, surprised. "I'd planned to come see you tomorrow, to thank you for all your help with the service and everything." He held the door open for her, but she stayed where she was, shivering. Something about the way she looked at him seemed strange to Matthew, and another thought struck him: it was rather late at night for a sympathy call.

"What is it, Teah?" he asked, wondering if he was wrong.

He wasn't. She looked at her feet. "It's my nephew, Rano," she said, her voice low.

"I'll get my cloak."

She led him to Briena's house and told him to knock. He did so, and when he turned to speak to her again, she was gone. Before he could step away from the doorstep to go look for her, the door opened and a woman peered out at him.

"Yes?" she said suspiciously. She was probably Teah's younger sister, he thought, but while Teah was slim and fine boned, this woman was gaunt, with hard lines around her mouth and rough, calloused hands.

"You are Briena?"

"Who wants to know?" she demanded coldly.

"Forgive me, I'm Hev'rae Mateo. Your sister Teah sent me to you, since your little boy is sick."

"Teah did? She was here earlier—" She opened the door wider to allow him to step inside. He removed his shoes and followed her to one of the two small sleeping rooms.

Rano lay on a pallet, flushed and bright-eyed with fever and breathing hoarsely. He turned his head to look as Matthew sat down on the small chair at the side of the bed.

"Hello, Rano. I don't know if you remember me, but I'm a friend of your Amo Teah. I'm here to see if we can't make you feel a bit more comfortable." He pulled the light closer and examined the gray patches on the boy's throat. It was catchthroat, similar to the old Terran diphtheria—and a bad case, from the looks of it.

"Has a *hev'rae* been to see him before now?"

Briena's face twisted into a scowl and then crumpled into tears. "No—thought I could take care of it myself—couldn't afford one anyway."

"When did the patches first appear?"

"Yesterday night. It's catchthroat, isn't it?"

"Yes." He bit back an angry comment about her negligence. Accusing her wouldn't do any good now. "Start boiling some water," he ordered. "I'm going to rig a steam tent. He opened his kit and pulled out the antitoxin and a scalpel to break the seal.

They labored over Rano for hours, swabbing his throat every half hour and keeping the steam kettle boiling. Rano fought the treatments weakly at first. But as the night wore on, he stopped resisting, instead focusing his failing strength on fighting for the next breath through the strangling membranes. The steam-filled room grew oppressively hot. To Matthew's tired brain, the shadows seemed alive, looming over the bed menacingly, watching and drawing nearer as each breath that Rano desperately sucked in grew weaker.

Matthew and Briena jumped at the knock at the outer door.

Their eyes met.

"Teah," Matthew said in a low voice.

Briena stared at him in wild fear. "No," she whispered, "No."

He wearily got to his feet to let Teah in, understanding now that she had sent him because she had hoped against vain hope that he could prevent the inevitable.

He ushered her silently to the bedside. Briena retreated and pressed herself against a wall, staring at Teah with huge, horrified eyes. Teah, who kept her head averted from her sister, sat down on the bed, her face white and still. Matthew opened the sides of the makeshift steam tent and removed the kettle, and a pillar of steam rose, curling against the ceiling and mingling with the shadows.

"Rano?"

The boy plucked feebly at his covering, and Teah pressed her hand over his. "Rano? It's Amo Teah." He opened his eyes.

"Would you like me to cuddle with you, Rano?" He nodded faintly, and she pulled off the cover and took him into her arms, drawing him into her lap. He was arching his body, sucking painfully, and she shifted her hold on him slightly so that he could expand his rib cage and placed her hand on his brow. Matthew knew that children in the last stages of catchthroat convulsed in their panicked attempts to get air, and he was awed as Rano relaxed at Teah's touch and lay quietly as she murmured in his ear. He knew, suddenly, that here was something that she could do for the boy that he couldn't, in spite of all his training.

"Remember your turtle, Rano? He swam into the basin, where you picked him up. When you put him back, he was able to swim out when the tide came back in."

She was rocking him gently, her cheek resting against his wet head. "I want you to close your eyes and pretend with me now, Rano. We'll go down to the beach together, see? I'm holding your hand. Do you see all the shells that you love to collect, lying on the sand? You found a special one for me once, and I always keep it on my windowsill, so that I can see the sun shining on its pink insides.

"Now we're climbing on the big rocks. It's hard to get up there, but we boost each other over the difficult places. We're going to go swim in the tidal pool.

"We get into the water, oh, so carefully, but it's not too cold, because the sun has been warming the rocks all day. So we swim a little, floating on our bellies, and then we roll over onto our backs and look at the sky.

"The sun is setting low, and it's time for the tide to go out. Can you feel it, pulling you? I'm still right here with you. The water pulls us away from the shore, away from the rocks, out to the deep, deep sea as the moon rises and the stars come out. The shore looks beautiful in the moonlight because we can see all the lights twinkling over the waves, but still the tide pulls us farther and farther out—out to where the fish jump and dance over the waves and where the turtles go."

She paused, and Matthew saw a tear drop from her bowed head to fall on Rano's sweat-streaked hair. She lifted a hand to brush at the place, but when she spoke again, her voice was as even and soothing as before. "I can't go with you any farther now, Rano, but that's all right. There is a friend coming toward you now who knows all the secret places under the sea that you've always wanted to explore. The friend is reaching out a hand for you, see? Let go of my hand now, Rano. Let go of my hand and go with your friend."

Teah kissed the boy and tenderly eased his body back down on the bed. As she stood, swaying, Briena whispered hoarsely, "How could you do it, Teah? How could you lie to me?"

"I never lied to you, Briena."

"You did! Every time you hugged him, played with him, as if he had all the time in the world, without ever letting me know that he wouldn't even live to grow up." Briena's voice broke in a sob as she collapsed on the bed and gathered up her son's body in her arms. She hugged him fiercely as she rocked back and forth, tears streaming down her cheeks. "Why didn't you tell me?"

"I knew. That was enough. You know I couldn't tell."

"It was cruel!"

"No. No, Briena. It was kind. His time was short, yes. But neither you nor Rano had to know that. He lived out his days as happily as any boy could." She stepped forward and placed a hand on her sister's shoulder. "And that was because you were able to love him wholeheartedly, without any cloud of knowledge poisoning whatever time you had together."

Briena twisted away from Teah's touch. "Who are you to keep such a secret from me, his own mother?"

"Death keeps the secret from all of us," Teah said coldly.

"Except you?" Briena's voice rose hysterically. "Aren't you my sister? Or are you only Death's servant, bringing in the Shadow Cloak to steal my boy from me?" The last words ended with a wail, and she bent over the boy again, rocking, twisting the thin nightshirt until it tore. "Oh, my Rano, my baby . . ."

White-faced, Teah reached out her hand. Briena kept her face buried in Rano's shoulders to muffle her racking sobs, and after a moment, Teah let her arm fall again. She rushed from the room without stopping to pick up her cloak, and they heard the door slam after her. Slowly, Matthew picked up his cloak and kit. He let himself out.

Matthew didn't catch up with her until the very end of Fish Hook Street. The rain was still falling in a steady, drizzling stream. He fell into step with her silently as they climbed the path that led to her house.

Once inside, he paused to pull off his shoes as usual, but she walked to the center of the room to stand there, still dripping, as if she had intended to go someplace else but couldn't remember where.

"Teah?"

"I broke my vow," she said flatly.

"How, Teah?"

There was a pause, as if she was too numb to think of the reason. He could see the sharp profile of her cheekbones etched by the distant flickers of lightning, flashing through the window. "I didn't stay to comfort the bereaved," she said finally.

"You're the bereaved," he told her gently. "You loved him, too."

"That doesn't change my responsibility!" She began to shake.

"You're shivering." He went to fetch a towel and came over to press it to her hair and dry her shoulders. He felt the chill of her wet skin through the thin, soaked fabric of her dress. Wrapping the towel around her upper body, he pulled her close and put his arms around her.

She stiffened and tried to pull away. "Don't."

"Teah, let me—"

"No!" She wrenched herself free. "That's not very professional behavior, *Doctor*," she said through her teeth, using, to his astonishment, the Terran word.

He reddened. "Teah, I—"

"Don't you understand?" she cried. "Don't you know that I have never —I have never—" She turned blindly away from him.

"Never what?" He reached out to touch her shoulder. "Never what, Teah?"

"The oath promises the respect of all men and women if I follow its teachings. And oh, the Calypsans are so polite. They are all so grateful for the art and the *rhyena'v'rae*'s arms at death, but who would want to touch a *rhyena'v'rae*? Who would want to be held by a woman in whose arms so many have died?" She stopped abruptly and took deep breaths, trying to control herself.

His heart ached in pity for her. "And that is why you have no children."

"That's only part of it. Briena was right. Every time I saw Rano, every time I touched him or heard his laugh, I knew when he would die. It was terrible enough as it was, but if he had been my own son, I couldn't have borne it. I couldn't!" She buried her face in her hands and sobbed.

Once again, he took her in his arms and held her, and this time she let him. When they grew tired of standing, they eased themselves down onto the floor and lay there together with her head on his chest as she cried herself out.

They weren't so very different after all, he decided, stroking her soft, damp hair. Teah had said it herself: both of them truly did want to help the people who came to them, trusting in their ability to ease the hurt. They both had made sacrifices: he had left his home world, and she had relinquished her hopes for a family. And it was the fact that they both took their responsibilities as seriously as they did that made their failures cut so deeply.

The only remedy is to keep learning, keep trying, he thought. I know that Teah tries, and as for me—. His thoughts hesitated. If what she does truly pushes back the boundaries of medicine, and I made a promise to do everything I can to benefit my patients, shouldn't I learn this? Doesn't my oath, in fact, *require* it?

"Teah?" he said finally.

She wiped her eyes. "What, Mateo?"

"Teah, teach me to be a lethe."

She raised her head and strained to see his face in the darkness. "Do you mean it? Even after all I've said?"

"Yes. I want to stay on Calypso. What you do—I want to do it, too."

"But you're a *hev'rae*, Mateo. Your business is saving lives."

"You said it yourself: all lives come to an end. Don't you see? This way, I'd be working as both a *hev'rae* and *rhyena'v'rae*, and that way dying would be a natural part of living. On Earth, there are hospices where the people go when they wish to die in peace under a doctor's care. I think that's the closest thing that we have to what you do."

"There's so much to learn."

"I know. But my question is, could I?"

"There's something you'd have to understand," she said slowly.

"What is it?"

"The way a *rhyena'v'rae* passes on the art. Much is learned in the way you learned to be a *hev'rae:* the master teaches the disciple the laws governing testaments and ways to counsel the kin. But passing on the art is something different."

"How is it done?"

"The disciple holds the *rhyena'v'rae* and takes the Oath as the *rhyena'v'rae* dies, and the power of the art awakens in the disciple."

"Is that how you got it?"

"Yes. Death is the catalyst that gives the disciple the power to understand the master's perception—a perception passed down to us from our first master, Stivan."

He was silent for a long time, thinking. "So it's the same as when a client comes," he said. "The disciple asks the master whether he or she can learn the art. And if the master says no, no questions are asked. But if the master says yes, then both know that the master will die first."

"Yes."

"Then—will you teach me the art, Teah?"

She said nothing for a long time. The rain stopped, and the light of the waning moon shone through a ragged hole in the clouds, falling softly through the window onto their faces. "I will say nothing tonight," she said finally. "I must decide. Sleep now, Mateo."

He slept.

At the first glimmer of dawn, he stirred and reached for her. It took him a moment to realize that the space next to him was empty. Opening his eyes, he propped himself up on one elbow and looked around in the growing brightness. She stood at the window, a shawl drawn over her shoulders, looking out to sea.

"Teah?"

Her head tilted a fraction, but she didn't turn toward him. "I've been thinking, Mateo."

"Yes?"

"About the art, and whether I can give it to you," she said slowly. "I have been wondering whether perhaps it is too much for me. Too much for any human to endure, really. It could be that I am the last, you know, and perhaps there should be no others to bear it." Her hand dropped to trace the smooth edge of a shell on the windowsill which glinted in the first rays of the sun. He remembered she had said the night before that Rano had given it to her. "And then I think of how Death is a—presence for me," she continued, her voice low and hesitant. "It always waits, with a calmness that has become almost a part of myself. I can try to ignore it, but I can never forget."

She turned toward him and studied his face. "Do you truly want this, then?"

"I do. I want it more than anything."

She nodded. Quietly, she went over to the wall, picked up three *ghotos*, and laid them on the floor in a triangle. She knelt down on one and held out her hand to him. "Come, then."

Puzzled, he got up and came over to kneel beside her. "Who is the third *ghoto* for?"

"Shh. Take my hand." As he covered her fingers with his, she went on gently, "The third *ghoto* is for Death, our mutual master, and the master of all mortal beings. If Death accepts you as my apprentice, then there is one death, and one death only that you will see now: mine. And when I am gone, and you take the Oath, you will then see your own death, as well as those of all other people." She took a deep breath. "As your teacher, I must promise to teach you faithfully as I have been taught, how to counsel and comfort the dying and their kin. Will you promise in return to be a willing student, to listen and to open your heart to what I have to teach you?"

"I will."

"Are you willing to be my *rhyena'v'rae*, to ease and comfort me when my time of death draws near?"

"I am willing."

"And when my passage into shadows awakens the art of the *rhyena'v'raien* in you," she said, her voice low, "will you then be willing to take the Oath—and bear the certain knowledge of the time of your own death?"

He drew a deep breath and held her gaze steadily. "I am willing."

She turned to the third *ghoto*. "Take him then as Your own. Let him see my mortality."

They waited in silence. As he listened to her quiet breathing beside him, he felt something else, hovering on the edges of his perception. Holding his breath, he tried to concentrate as waves of dizziness slowly washed into darkness. It felt like a tangible cool twilight, like an impossibly fine veil eddying toward him on unseen currents. He recoiled, but at the last instant it swerved, dropping weightlessly over Teah instead.

With some newly awakened sense, he felt it coil and tighten languorously around her like the arms of a lover, sinking into her flesh. His hand shook in hers as he looked at her and *knew*. From this day forward, every time he saw her, he would see her death, hovering before him. Even as he felt her fingers pulsing with warm blood, he could anticipate the feeling of her spirit slipping away. He could see himself holding her, weeping, struggling to ease the pain and smooth her passage into shadows. He knew then how dear she would become to him, and that there would be nothing he could do to stop it. Nothing he could do to turn it away. For the first time, he understood the exquisite pain of the *rhyena'v'raien*—and with it, all their power.

Teah's gaze met his with an expression of pity, and he saw his own pain mirrored there. "I know. Believe me, Mateo, I know. I saw it, too, the day I bound myself to my own master." She pressed his fingers with hers. "Do you understand how much I need you now? You see, without you as my apprentice, I would be alone when my time comes, with no one to ease me. Will you do that for me?"

"Yes." He took a ragged breath and wiped his eyes with the back of his hand. "Yes, Teah, I will."

She smiled. "It is best to begin at once, then. You will have much to learn."

Lake Agassiz

JACK McDEVITT

THERE WAS A GHOST in Fort Moxie.

Lasker stood beneath a quarter moon, atop the western ridge of the Turtle Mountains, and stared east across the black prairie. Two rings of light, a lesser and a greater, almost touching, floated in the dark, like distant galaxies. The border station and the town.

He seldom went there. A retirement party maybe, for a close friend. Or a funeral. And that was about it.

After all these years, he still feared the place.

The night smelled of oncoming winter. A cold wind chopped across the ridge and bit down on him. Lasker turned back toward the electric lights he'd strung over the work area.

"If that ain't strange," said Will, wiping his nose. Midautumn was a bad time for him.

Lasker had held this land out through the last planting season and intended to put wheat in this spring. "What's that, Will?" he asked, Fort Moxie fading.

"We got some grass growing here. Look at this." He pointed at a few stalks. Summer green.

"It's always been good right here," Lasker said, remembering the potatoes of the last few seasons. "For some reason—"

The wind shook the light bulbs. Down at the bottom of the slope he could see movement in the kitchen. Ginny. She knew how he felt about Fort Moxie, didn't know why. God knew what she thought. She'd asked questions for a while, sensed the gulf that lay between them, and let it go.

"Deep enough, Dad?"

Lasker peered into the ditch. "A little more," he said. "Got to get the pipes far enough down where the cold doesn't affect 'em."

They were putting in a system to allow them to pump water uphill from the well. "Be a lot easier next year," said Will, pushing his spade into the ground. He sneezed, and reached for a handkerchief. Sneezed again.

"Maybe you should go back to the house," said Lasker.

The boy grinned. "I'm fine."

Lasker admired the kid. He refused to give in to the allergies that afflicted him every October. Wouldn't admit there was a problem.

Five minutes later, down about a foot, Will's spade struck something solid.

It wasn't a rock. The thing looked like a shark's fin caught in the act of diving into the rich black North Dakota loam.

"What is it?" Will asked, kneeling, brushing the soil away with gloved fingers. It was bright red, smooth. Hard.

Lasker grunted. "Looks like plastic," he said, grabbing hold and pulling. It didn't give.

He stood back, and Will hit it with the spade.

They tried digging around it, under it. The thing was a flared triangle, roughly ten inches on a side, paper thin. "It's attached to something," said Will, trying to widen the ditch. "A post, I think."

Lasker saw the house door open. A small shadow skipped out and started up the hill. Jerry. "That'll be dinner," he told Will.

His son was working under the fin now. The post was also red, and angled down at about fifty degrees. It appeared to be made of the same material. He wedged his spade under it, and lifted. Lasker lent his weight.

It showed some give, but didn't come loose. They fell over one another, gave it up for the night, and stumbled laughing down the hill.

The Turtle Mountains, behind which Lasker's sun set each evening, were really little more than a line of low hills. They constituted the only high ground as far as one could see in any direction. Ten thousand years ago, they had formed the western shore of Lake Agassiz, a vast inland sea, larger than the modern Great Lakes combined. Substantial portions of the eastern Dakotas, Minnesota, Manitoba, and Saskatchewan had been beneath blue water then. The lake had lasted only a thousand years, an eyeblink by geological standards, draining off when the glacier blocking its northern side retreated.

Occasionally, when he was a boy, Lasker's father had flown with him over the Red River Valley, pointing out the ancient coastline. The idea of a lost sea fascinated them both. *Long gone,* his father was fond of saying, *but it influences everything we are.* Lasker wondered about the remark at the time, but he came to understand that Dakota wealth grew out of former lake bottom, that the texture of the Red River Valley itself had been dictated by Agassiz.

In a way, Lasker had told his own sons, *it's still out there. Only thing is, you can't swim in it.*

Lasker was a big man: awkward, with thinning brown hair and huge shoulders. His features were sharp, raw edged, blasted hard by the Dakota winters. The eyes were difficult to read. Of all the farmers in the area, people would tell you that no one was more clearly designed by nature to play poker than Tom Lasker.

At dawn on the day after they found the object, Lasker and his older boy were back atop the slope. The plain was bleak and cold in the gray light. They had an hour or so before Will had to get ready for school. Ordinarily Will wouldn't have been here at all on the morning of a school day. But he was curious about the shark's fin. And, without any more talk, he confronted the object, which now looked like a triangular hand fan mounted on a pole. The pole burrowed down into one side of the ditch. "Let's do it," the boy said enthusiastically, sinking his spade into the earth. He turned it over, and the soil, even this late in the season, was heavy and sweet.

Will seemed all right this morning, the air was still, and Lasker felt good about the world.

He measured off a few feet in a straight line from the point where the pole entered the side of the ditch, and began throwing up soil in his own methodical way.

They worked until Will had to leave. Lasker had planned to quit when the boy did (he was only pursuing this to satisfy Will's curiosity), but by then he'd discovered that the pole was at least eight feet long, and showing no sign of ending. His own steam was up.

Whatever it was, the angle of descent was steep. He was down almost six feet when he quit for lunch.

Ginny came back with him afterward to see what the fuss was about. She was tall, clever, a product of Chicago who had come to North Dakota as a customs inspector, with the primary objective of getting away from urban life. Lasker's friends and family had warned him that she would quickly tire of solitude and harsh winters. But she'd thrived and seemed to enjoy nothing more than settling down on a snow-driven night with a book in front of a roaring fire.

"It's blocking the pipe?" she asked, puzzled, standing over the thing.

"Not really."

"Then why all the fuss? You don't really have to tear it out of the ground, do you?"

"No." Most of it was down pretty deep. "But I'd like to know what it is. Wouldn't you?"

She shrugged. "It's a pole."

"How'd it get here?"

Ginny had spotted something. Lasker had dug three ditches down to the descending pole, each deeper than the preceding one by a couple of feet. They now knew it was at least twelve feet long. Ginny was looking into the deepest of the pits. "There's a wad of some sort buried down there. At the bottom."

Lasker had set a ladder in the pit. He climbed down, and used his spade to fish at the wad. "It's cloth," he said.

She frowned. "I think it used to be attached to the pole."

He dug around the fabric. Tried to free it. After a few minutes, he gave up. "I'd like to find the other end of the pole," he said.

"I suggest you forget it. If you can't *drag* it out of the ground, it's going to turn into a big job." She blinked in the sunlight. "Maybe you should go down to Colmar's and hire a couple of men."

"I will," he said, "if this goes on much longer." He grinned at her and, constricted by the narrow confines of the pit, worked his spade in around the pole and pulled more dirt loose.

Ginny was reluctant to leave. She was still standing over him, watching, when the spade chunked against something solid.

"What is it?" she asked.

A boat.

A *sailboat.*

A dozen people, Lasker, Will and Jerry, Ginny, the hired men from Colmar's, several neighbors, stood in the twilight near the top of the slope. They'd hauled it out of its hole and laid it on its side, propping the mainmast with a stack of cinder blocks. Jerry was playing a hose on it. The water washed the clay away, and revealed a bright scarlet hull and creamy white inboard paneling and lush pine-colored decks. A set of canvas sails that had once been white were spread on the ground nearby.

Nobody was saying much.

Betty Kausner touched the keel once or twice, tentatively, as though it might be hot.

"It's fiberglass, I think," said her husband Phil.

Jack Wendell stood off to one side, his hands on his hips, just staring. "I don't think so," Jack said. He used to work at Morrison's Marine in Grand Forks and he figured to know about things like that. "Even for fiberglass, it's pretty light."

"Tom." Betty Kausner was staying close to her husband. "You sure you got no idea about this?"

"No." He glared at the boat as if it were an unwelcome intruder. "None."

"It looks in good shape," said Rope Hammond, who owned the land to the east, along Route 11. "You could take her for a spin tomorrow." He touched the cloth with the tip of his boot. "Even the sails. Tom, these can't have been in the ground very long."

Another car pulled into the driveway, and disgorged Ed Patterson and his family. Five kids. Ed owned the Handy Hardware in Cavalier. The kids charged up the hill and began chasing one another around the boat.

Kausner had gone back to his station wagon. He returned with a tape measure. He made marks in the soil at stem and stern, and measured it off. "Nineteen feet, five inches," he announced.

The hull looked subtly different from anything Lasker had seen before. It was rounded, flared. Something. It had a mainsail and a jib and a staysail. Running lights were set toward the front of the hull. He wondered if they would work.

"Look at this," said Hammond, poring over the bow. He was pointing at a cluster of black Arabic-looking characters. "What language is that?"

"Looks Iranian to me," said Jack Wendell, remembering the signs carried by demonstrators back in the days of the Ayatollah.

Three more cars were coming in from Cavalier, and two from Fort Moxie. Lasker sighed. Ginny had set up the coffee maker they used during planting and harvesting. She was passing out cups, and telling people there was Danish inside.

Gradually the sense of vague disquiet that had ruled the early evening lifted, and by ten o'clock the house was filled with noisy, well-oiled guests.

Two hours later they were gone. Lasker helped Ginny clean up. He was setting dishes in the washer. Through the window over the sink he could see the boat. It lay on its side at the top of the slope, its hull curved and inviting in the moonlight.

"Going to bed," said Ginny, tossing a dishtowel across the back of a chair.

"I'll be up in a while." Lasker reached for his jacket.

"It's cold now," she said. "Don't stay out too long."

The ghost's name was Corey Ames.

He never knew why he took it into his head to drive into Fort Moxie that night. When he went outside, he'd intended simply to go up and take another look at the boat. But as he got near it, the old rush of fever he'd felt whenever he thought of Corey took him, drove him back down the hill, and carried him toward the garage.

His heart was hammering by the time he got into the front seat of his pickup, because by then he knew he was going into town, and he knew why.

Dumb.

But still, he would indulge himself. Give himself over to the old passion for an hour. Let it hurt—

Fort Moxie lends itself to timelessness. There are no major renovation projects, no vast cultural shifts imposed by changing technology, no influxes of families with strange names. The town and surrounding prairie possesses a kind of stasis. It is a place where Eisenhower is still President. Where people still like one another, and crime is virtually unknown. The last felony in Fort Moxie occurred in 1934, when Bugsy Moran shot it out with the customs people.

In all, it is a stable place to live, a good place to rear kids. But it holds memories. Much as the land held the big lake.

Long gone now.

He bounced out onto Route 11 and turned left.

Corey was in Seattle. Or at least she had been last he'd heard. She'd married an insurance salesman and moved out of the Fort Moxie area. Guy by the name of Maury. Corey Maury. Goofy name. She'd come back for her father's funeral in '77, and Lasker had cowered at home. Hoped she'd notice he was not there. The husband had not come along, and Lasker had wondered dismally whether they'd broken up. He was himself married by then, and would not have left Ginny no matter what. Still, he wished Corey ill, and it shamed him to realize it.

There'd been a daughter. Six or seven years old. It felt good to realize that Corey might be a grandmother.

He sucked cold air into his lungs, felt the old emptiness close around him.

Route 11 is a two-lane, unlighted highway except when it curves through the windscreen at the Hammond property. It runs parallel to the Canadian border, about a mile south of the line. Lasker could see the soft illumination of Fort Moxie in the night sky. The moon had set now behind the Turtle Mountains. But the stars were hard and bright. The wind pushed at the pickup and rattled the load of hoes and rakes in the flatbed. It blows all the time across the northern prairie. There's a kind of channel connecting Hudson's Bay with Fort Moxie, and the wind builds up over the pole and just charges down the channel. Doesn't much matter what time of year it is; it's always cold. The joke in Fort Moxie is that if you leave town over the Fourth, you miss the summer.

The old lake bottom was lush and black in the glow of the headlights. It rushed by, and the pickup's tires sang against the paving.

Lasker passed the old Milliken spread. The barn and outbuildings were shadows beneath the trees; cheerful light spilled out of the farmhouse. Milliken had added a deck since the last time he'd been by.

The road looped north, banked slightly, turned east again, past the cemetery. His headlights swept across the markers, and then he climbed up over the interstate, and dropped down among the sleepy frame houses and wide tree-lined streets.

His breathing slowed.

Charlie's Southern Barbecue now marked the edge of town. It was new, had been there four years or so.

The Tastee-Freez still stood at Nineteenth and Bannister.

The lumberyard. And the Prairie Schooner Hotel.

He drifted quietly through the empty streets.

Damn fool. A quiet rage began to build, taking its place beside the ancient passion.

Corey's town.

Even now, after twenty years, a good marriage, two sons, after *Ginny*, he could still see Corey's cool smile. Still recall the gold bracelet on her right wrist, the long white scarf, the soft press of her lips.

My God.

Three months, they'd had. Somehow, Lasker had known from the start that he would not be able to hold her.

In retrospect, he recognized that he knew almost nothing about her. Nothing that mattered. She laughed easily and she had luminous brilliant eyes and dark brown hair cut in bangs. He knew of no book she had read, nor had he any idea of any political opinion she held. She liked rock. But then, almost everyone did. She enjoyed Jets games in Winnipeg and the science museum. (How had he forgotten *that?*)

It ended suddenly. Without warning. *There's someone else.* Is there any phrase in the language that plunges a more painful shaft into the ribs?

Her town.

Harley's Deli.

The post office at the corner of Stutzman and Main, where she'd held a clerk's job. (He'd picked her up here one evening during a whiteout, after she'd worked late.)

Chip Leonard's place off Twelfth, where they'd celebrated her nine-teenth birthday.

The walking trail along the Red.

The high school. The tennis court. The old Roxie Theater (still there, but long closed).

Her house.

(The house number, 1621, was still mounted beside the front door on a plaque that featured a Victorian carriage.)

He floored the pedal, and hurried away, scattering leaves.

He dreamt of her that night.

It had been a long time. She rarely appeared now. But the pattern was similar: Corey was young, dazzling, the way he remembered her. They were on the front porch at her house. It was a summer night. (He had never known her in summer.) And she told him how happy she was to see him again.

When he woke, the gray early morning light leaking through the blinds, he lay a long time without moving.

· · · ·

Hal Riordan, who owned the Fort Moxie lumberyard, was waiting for him beside the boat. Hal had been old when Lasker was in school: his hair, gray in those days, had gone completely white. He was tall and glacially slow, a man who would not go to the bathroom without due consideration. "Something really odd here, Tom," he said.

"Hello yourself, Hal." Lasker grinned. "What's the matter?"

"Take a look where the mast is joined to the cabin roof."

Lasker did. He saw nothing unusual. "What about it?"

"It's all of a piece. The mast should have been manufactured separately, I would think. And then bolted down. Everything here looks as if it came out of a single mold."

Lasker looked again. Riordan was right: there were no fittings, no screws, nothing.

"It's a joke of some kind," Lasker said. "Has to be."

"I suppose." Riordan pushed his hands into his pockets and pressed the toe of his shoe against the hull. "Pretty expensive one."

By 8 A.M., there was a yardful of people again. More than the day before. "You ought to charge admission," suggested Frank Hall. "You got people coming in from Drayton now. By tomorrow, they'll be here from Winnipeg and Grand Forks."

Hall was an import specialist with the Customs Service. He was easygoing, bearded, wide shouldered. His wife, Peg, had arrived with him and was helping Gin set out coffee again. Ginny caught his eye and shook her head. This was costing too much, her eyes said. We're going to have to do something.

"What do you make of it, Frank?" Lasker asked.

Hall looked at him, looked at the boat. "You really don't know how this got here, Tom?"

"No." With some exasperation: "I really don't."

"Okay, then: this boat is some sort of homebuilt job."

"How do you know?"

"Easy." He pointed toward the stern. "No hull identification number. It should be in raised lettering, like the VIN on your car. It's not there."

"Maybe this was built before a hull number was required."

Hall shook his head. "They've been requiring them for twenty years."

Lasker spent the morning cleaning out the boat's cabin. Several of his visitors offered to help him, but Lasker was beginning to suspect he might have something valuable, and wanted to be careful. Anyway, there wasn't room for more than one at a time to work inside the cabin.

Padded benches were set along both bulkheads. Lasker was surprised to discover they were still soft, although the seats were located uncomfortably close to the deck.

The bulkheads themselves were the color of winter wheat. There were shelves and cabinets, all empty. The upper part of the forward panel was glass. A set of gauges was installed beneath it. He wiped them off cautiously: none of the symbols was familiar. The characters bore a family resemblance to the inscription on the bow.

At noon, Ginny cornered him. "Where are they all coming from?"

Lasker shrugged. "It *is* getting worse, isn't it?"

"Yes," she said. "We can't afford to pump coffee and set out snacks for everyone in the Red River Valley."

"I thought some of the local folks were bringing their own."

"Some. Anyhow, we're out of business. Thought you'd want to know. Maybe we should set up a turnstile."

More cars were pulling in while they talked.

The cure apparently occurred on the late morning of the third day after the excavation. It was a Saturday.

Mark Watkin had come with several of his friends to see the boat. Mark limped noticeably, a result of a basketball injury that had ruined his left knee almost a year earlier. Doctors had recommended he use a cane, but the boy steadfastly refused.

The teenagers had not stayed long. And in fact they had come and gone without being seen at all by Lasker, who was now actively avoiding the crowds. But the following day, Mark was back. This time he went to the front door of the farmhouse. And the limp was gone.

"I don't know whether it had anything to do with your boat or not," he told Gin. "But my knee got warm while I was standing up on the ridge." He shifted his weight forward onto his left leg. "It feels like it used to."

Ginny looked scared when she relayed the story to Lasker. "Have you noticed," she added, "that Will's allergies have disappeared too?"

They had hosed off the sails, which now hung just inside the barn door. They were white. The kind of white that hurts the eyes when the sun hits it. They did not look as if they'd ever been buried.

Lasker stood inside, out of the wind, his hands in his pockets, thinking how good they looked. And it struck him for the first time that he had a serviceable boat. He'd assumed all along that someone was going to step forward and claim the craft. But on that quiet, bleak, cold Sunday, he understood that, for better or worse, it was his.

He pictured himself at its wheel, sails billowing, slicing across the polished surface of the Red River. No: make that Lake Winnipeg.

Lasker had never done any sailing, except once or twice with someone else at the tiller. But the prospect of taking that bright vessel into the wind overwhelmed him. He squeezed his eyes and pictured himself and Ginny sliding past the low hills of Winnipeg's shoreline, the dying sun streaking the sky.

Or Corey. If he'd had the boat when he knew Corey—

He shook the thought away. Ridiculous. It would have made no difference.

Call her. The thought exploded at the back of his mind.

Lasker no longer kept livestock. He was alone in the barn. A gust of wind caught the door. It creaked, and the sails moved.

Call her.

His pulse rose in his ears. She lives in Seattle.

Call. Talk to her.

Lasker pushed it out of his mind.

Settle it.

The best cure for an old romance was to see her ten years later. Where had he read that?

It was colder inside the barn than out. A combine and a tractor were stored at the far end, under tarpaulins. The place smelled of hay and gasoline.

Do it.

The taffrail was supported by a series of stanchions. These also seemed not to be bolted or joined to the deck, but were rather an integral part of the whole. Therefore, when a vandal stole one, he'd had to break it off. Nobody saw it happen, but Lasker responded by moving the boat into the barn, and padlocking the door. That same afternoon a television crew arrived from Grand Forks.

They walked around with Minicams, interviewed Lasker and Ginny and the kids and half a dozen people who were still hanging about. (Most of the crowd had gone home after Lasker locked the boat away.)

• • • •

Needless to say, Lasker made no attempt to call Corey. He never seriously considered it. That's a closed compartment, he told himself. *Fini.*
Been over a long time.

People kept coming. They got angry when confronted with a locked barn. Lasker tried to order them off the property. That tactic was met with a lot of grumbling about traveling a long way just to see his goddamn boat, now open up or they'll open it up themselves.

Lasker took the path of least resistance. And promised himself he'd start selling tickets. Hell, if he couldn't turn it off, he might as well profit from it.

That night:
"And from Fort Moxie." (Chuckles.) "You just never know what you might find lying around these days. A farmer out on Route 11 dug up a sailboat. The boat's apparently in good condition, and nobody knows who put it there. Debbie Baker is on the scene—" (Smiles.)

At sunrise Monday, Lasker noticed that the missing stanchion was back, and the damaged section was repaired. No: restored. There was no sign whatever that anything had been torn loose.

Lasker glanced nervously around the empty barn, went back outside, and replaced the padlock.

He phoned Frank Hall. "Need a favor, Frank," he said.

"At this hour?" Hall sounded half-asleep and not pleased.

"When you get a chance. Is there a way we can find out how old the boat is?"

"We looked for a plate."

"No. I mean, break off a piece and have someone analyze it."

"Tom, you can do that with stuff that's *old*. But I don't think there's a process for dealing with material that's been made recently. Maybe thirty, forty thousand years. But not 1988. You understand what I mean?"

"Yeah," said Lasker. "Let's try it. Would you look into it? Find out how we can do it, and let's see what we get."

"Tom."

The voice drifted in off the dark prairie, insinuated itself into the chatter from the television.

He glanced over at Gin, who was reading the *Herald*, half-watching the TV.

"Tom."

The wind blew against the side of the house. A sliver of moonlight fell against a storage shed. The other utility buildings bulked heavy and black. He realized that the outside lights were not on.

Lasker eased himself out of his chair. "I'll be back in a minute," he said.

Her eyes found him over the top of the newspaper. She nodded.

He walked into the kitchen, thumbed the switch.

No lights.

They were on out front; he could see them. But not in back. Near the barn.

He caught a swirl of movement in the dark. Beside the storage shed. Odd.

"Tom."

The voice was clearer this time.

He opened the door and squinted into the night. "Who's there?"

Gravel crunched. "It's me, Tom."

His limbs went cold. He knew the voice. "Who are you?"

She stepped out of the gloom. Out of a time long past. "Corey?"

She nodded. "Hello," she said.

He stared. "What are you doing here?" His voice was thick, and he had to make several attempts to get the question out.

She was as he remembered her. The years had left her untouched.

"I've always been here," she said. She smiled and took a tentative step toward him. "You're letting the cold into the house."

Lasker came out onto the porch. Closed the door. Moonlight fell across her shoulders, shadowed her eyes. "I don't understand this," he said. The porch railing was solid under one hand. The night air was cold, and a car droned by, throwing its lights briefly across the top of the barn.

"I don't either," she said. "I think we're getting a second chance." She pushed her hands down into her pockets.

Lasker came cautiously down the steps, not trusting his sense of balance. For the first time since his fortieth birthday, he felt acutely conscious of his age. He murmured her name and she watched him and his heart beat so loudly he could hear nothing else.

They stood facing each other briefly, and then Lasker reached for her, touched one shoulder and gently drew her forward. She looked up at him, and a tear rolled through her smile.

The old emotional storm froze his soul. The wind, the trees, the stars fell silent. He wanted to ask questions, but could only hold on. The world seemed rickety underfoot. In Lasker's long existence it was a place constructed of splintered wood and solid earth, laid out in precise mathematical juxtapositions. No room for the supernatural.

"It has to do with the boat, doesn't it?"

"It fixes things," she said. "I don't know how."

The sound of the television leaked out into the night air. Trembling, Lasker traced the line of her jaw with his fingertips. She lifted her face and their eyes locked and she gripped his shoulders. He placed his lips against hers, without pressure, so that he could feel her breath whisper in and out. "Corey, are you real?"

"Do you need to ask?"

They kissed. Warmth poured through him: adolescent passion, first love reignited. Whatever.

"I love you," he said.

"I know." She pushed against him. "I'm sorry. I was young."

"You're *still* young," Lasker said. He was having trouble catching his breath.

Her hand curled round the nape of his neck and drew him back for another long kiss.

"What do we do now?" he asked.

She backed off a step, looked up at him. My God, she was beautiful. "Just go in and pack," she said. "I'll wait in the pickup."

Lasker shook his head. "If you know anything about me at all, you know I can't do that. Twenty years ago maybe." The *maybe* tasted delicious on his tongue. "It's not that simple anymore."

"It *is* that simple, Tom. If you really want me."

More than you could ever know. "Listen: we need some time to talk about this. Figure out what's happening—"

"There *is* no time, Tom. I'm sorry, but you have to make up your mind now."

Lasker shook his head. A burst of laughter issued from inside the house. Ginny.

Ginny.

"Tom: I *love* you. I always did." Her eyes widened. "You never knew, did you?"

"No," he said. "I never did."

"I didn't think you would give up so easily."

Lasker backed away. The stars burned fiercely. "What did you expect?" He looked away from her. "Anyway it doesn't matter now. You're far too late."

She nodded. "I understand. In a way, I'm part of you. But you can make it up to her later. You loved me long before you knew her. You love me still—"

He stood silent.

"Your decision," she said quietly. "But be right. I can't come back."

Lasker discovered he still had hold of her hand. He hung onto it and looked into her face. And let go. "You're right, Corey," he said. "You've always been here. I suspect you always will." Like the lake, he thought: a lingering image, an impact. But long gone.

He turned away from her and strode back up onto the porch.

"I'm sorry, Tom."

He stopped with his hand on the door. "I'm not."

If Ginny recognized the change in the tone of her marriage, she never said anything to Lasker. But she must have noticed that he no longer hesitated to drive over to Fort Moxie when occasion arose.

For him, the dreams stopped.

And when, several weeks later, the dating report came in, it indicated that the materials from which the boat was constructed were new. No age could be assigned.

But late the following Saturday night, at the Prairie Schooner Bar, Lasker told Frank Hall that he had expected no less. "It fixes things," he said.

Transfusion

JOËLLE WINTREBERT

Translated from the French by Kim Stanley Robinson

MORNING. She lifts her left foot. With deliberate care. And the utmost in determination. Today she will be in a bad mood. That's how she is when she feels blurred. She doesn't like things vague, floating, indefinite. A contained rage allows her to construct clean boundaries; and too bad if the angles are a bit sharp.

She walks past Thomas, chin high, eyes blank, not responding to his cheery hello, not allowing herself to be trapped by the huckster smell of toast. She will breakfast alone, scrounging currants and heart cherries, their acidity a perfect match for an irritation unable to deal with the stickiness of jam and amorous gestures.

She looks out at her garden, and finds it drowned in a fog so dense that all points of reference are gone. She hesitates, but the sound of Thomas's voice thrusts her out. Walking randomly, afraid he'll catch up with her, she moves between the tall silhouettes of the silver birches, the thickset purple masses of the hazel trees.

Suddenly it seems the charcoal-sketch shapes form an unfamiliar pattern.

And then she's lost.

Surely the garden isn't this big? It's disorienting, therefore exciting. How, after all this time, can such a familiar place have escaped her? Milky dampness falls on her face, like sails sewn with minuscule pearls; her arms grow taut, her steps groping; she stares, wide-eyed, and recognizes—not a single thing.

Far away, at the end of a long tunnel of cotton wool, Thomas is calling her. She traps the grasping parasite sound under her eyelids, and suffocates it.

When she reopens her eyes, *it* is watching her. It is suspended in the fog, ringed by a halo of light that crackles, diffracts, explodes. It has a serene, surreal face, which awakens a kind of religious awe in her. . . . But its smile reveals the jaw of a beast, and in its eyes strange keyhole pupils contract to tiny slots, exposing orange-colored irises, as liquid and turbulent as waves on a beach.

Stomach all knotted, she takes a step back. Then another.

The mask of the predator breaks apart, then recomposes in a new face. Because of the contempt in the new eyes, and the brutal rictus of the new lips, she doesn't immediately identify this face; but when she does, she groans with terror. Her face. This other self and its incomprehensible savagery frighten her more than the thing that preceded it.

Centuries pass. Her fear pours her out in a long viscous flux, until she is nothing but a kind of glue. Finally the sap runs dry; but by then she's been captured. Fertilized.

A strange process distills the wine of fear into a brandy of perverse fascination; but then her other face explodes in a thousand splinters, ending the centuries' stillness, and suddenly it's as if she were transfused into a better body. As if she had been turned inside out, displaced, her atoms wrenched about to conquer her from within. To imprison her. A violent shiver of revolt runs through her, but fails to stop the creation of her new atomic structure. Why struggle against the force that fills everything?

For her unencumbered heart, for living in the cracks, for feeling the secret sorrows hidden in every corner—for all that, it's the end.

From now on, she is without refuge.

But full. Compact. Sleek.

The fog lifts. She tastes earthy saliva at the back of her throat.

Thomas appears, and she strikes him with a dangerous look; she can feel its impact. Thomas shudders, defends himself with a laugh that instantly fossilizes. He pales, turns his head aside. She knows she can break the orbit he moves in, for she is its centerpoint. Vertigo spins her as she discovers the power of cruelty. She straddles it, rides it, until it becomes a kind of ecstasy.

"Who's there, Barbel? You or the other one?"

The question devastates her. She's helpless before it; she can't keep her hands from trembling. She thinks, *Am I possessed?*

Thomas puts his lips to her forehead, as if sealing a final letter. He whispers the proof of his frailty: "You frighten me, Barbel Hachereau. That's why I'm leaving. I lied—I haven't been at a conference. Someone will be by to get my things."

He drifts off, a being without boundaries, nothing but a shape, loose, soft, shifting. She watches him disappear with an astonishment that contains no regret. Two bodies cannot occupy the same space at the same time; it's only possible if one of them becomes blurred, vague. Transparent to the point of fading into the other.

The vapor that called itself Thomas will finish dissipating as it reaches the gate at the end of the garden.

From now on, Barbel is alone. An intense sensation, this liberty. She dilates, she opens wide, becomes a plump darkness, feverish, gasping, waiting. Standing in the blue milk of the sky, she hopes that some extraordinary seed will fill her. Languid but alert, open hands just barely trembling, eyes closed to better seize . . . what? She's not sure, and yet it's here, it's waiting for her to sense it, she feels it in the rusty smell of the earth's breath, in the heavy, slow acidity of vegetable rot, in the sugars and salts of her skin, touched by the relentless sun.

She falls into herself, discovers the blood's red alchemy, the effervescent flux of atoms; she dances the crazy ballet of the molecules . . . and then in the secret moisture, in the center of her being, its face reforms.

It's inside me, she thinks.

Inside, from now on. Inside, and looking at her; and its alien eyes are an orange sea, rising to engulf her.

For a long time she circles a stone, insistently rubbing impudent bumps, grainy pleats. Endlessly she polishes her body. She stops when it takes on the sheen of a pebble, ground in the millwheel of time. Dust with a rainbow edge coats its surface; wrapped in this thin silk, the body is ready for the ceremony.

Barbel leaves the garden through a hole in the privet hedge, and sinks into earth. Three days of rain have softened the silt to perfection. The dense and supple mud takes the precise shape of the arch of the foot, then shoves up and tapers out between the toes: three steps more and she's in it to her ankles. Why not abandon herself to the warm, voluptuous suction? All that was dry, immaculate, white as mother-of-pearl—all that can surrender to the clay's annealing.

Barbel lies down. Her nostrils quiver, her body inhales a thick saliva. The slow embrace of the slime closes over her. Gravity. She couldn't move even if she wanted to. Bubbles burst, freeing the giddy scent of vegetable rot. Flush with the earth and its plants, she sees an odyssey of iron browns, greens, minuscule swarmings, crystals of captive light, snares of sticky thistle: a furtive, pitiless universe.

Seal your eyelids. Feel the aquatic kiss on your mouth. Open up wide. Taste. Clay plasters your tongue? Swallow. Let it settle inside you. Don't think of it as armor; it's the body of nature itself that fills you. You must accept the numb, confused stirring, the abrupt sensation of the outside pulsing in you—also the fiery needles, the phantom needles, being placed with sure precision, to burn you.

Don't move. You are an open notch to another universe, which invites you to share its force. Are you going to refuse the power of the gods?

But what are gods when you can't name them? Complete strangers. Fabulous brocades, turned into snarls of yarn. Barbel reaches out, pulls the tatters of her instinct around her. She wakes up, chokes, vomits muddy water.

Behind the blurry screen of her tears it smiles at her, bound to her by a cord of pure energy. "Rub it entirely away, Barbel Hachereau. Perhaps it's not too late."

The mouth and its bronze fangs grow and contract horribly. Around the mouth skin cracks and peels, then detaches in rotting shreds, rags that are caught in flight by busy insects.

Barbel feels no triumph at the sight of these scraps of her predator's flesh. She shuts her eyes: the horrible vision is more than she can stand, especially as it contains within it a wild buzz of anguish, of lament. The cord snaps; but glittering fragments of it begin immediately to reassemble.

A streaming ochre golem, Barbel exhumes herself from her shroud of mud. As she returns to the garden, the glistening supple coating on her body becomes dull, rough, gnarled; pieces of it flake off. Just the way she feels. A little less than living. Half-petrified. Worn away. The defeat inside victory.

A thunderstorm pelts her naked body with rain. She runs and dances and runs, in the fat field by the river. She is far from the garden.

Caught again by the demonic face, she spreads her arms, throws back her head, tastes the intoxicating fizz of ozone. A thunderbolt crashes down: encircling flash of blue, hair standing on end, crackling. The storm lessens, washes the twilight. Tirelessly Barbel dances the demon's dance. Her arms unfurl invisible tapestries, the capricious flights of her fingers weave strange embroidery, her head cuts the sky to ribbons, and suddenly four boys are there to assist at the scene.

Strangeness sparks fear in those who don't know how to dream. Trying to defend themselves, the four boys stare at each other and laugh. An identical desire darkens their eyes; they can't see her sensuous movement as anything but a naked body, offered to their lust.

They move in, mouths spewing a puree of insults: the vomit of contempt, the bile that eats at the other. But Barbel is deaf, Barbel is blind, Barbel is entirely in the dance. She doesn't see the four boys circling her, she doesn't hear the words tying her up, she awakens only when she feels the contact of hands, tossing her to the ground.

Her back hits the grass. A superhuman twisting stops the fall, brings back up the body of the demon inside her, growling, curling its lip.

The boys retreat, bewildered as if by an acrobat's trick. They have misjudged their victim, who stands so much taller than before. They gather and flee. Barbel discharges the energy she collected in the storm, and with a roar the sun swoops down and blows the boys to fragments.

Crazed, she will stare until dawn at the four blasted bodies.

Back in the garden, she feels so weak it seems the demon must have left her.

* * * *

On the stained carpet of the bedroom, her back against a cascade of soiled sheets. She eats a bit of uncooked meat. The blood runs down between her breasts. She wipes at it with an automatic gesture. Compare the vermillion on the hand with the coagulated purple marking the thighs. Touch the source and sniff. The blood of the beast and her blood in her. Smell and taste both rusty, an oxidized dullness. She raises an arm, breathes in the bitter exhalation of her armpit, rubs her fingers in the sweaty elastic hollow, smooths the humid fur, licks her fingers, abandons herself to the strong saline taste.

Later. Night has fallen. Intense green light and flashes of bronze cut through the darkness. Barbel kneels before the standing mirror with the baroque cupids carved in its frame. In the somber blue of the glass, two orange circles regard her; within them the strange pupils are dilating.

"A glimpse of the other world, Barbel Hachereau. These are not your eyes."

Barbel turns on the light, returns to the mirror, searches in vain for the demon; finds instead that her skin is a strange color, the gold-green of a scarab. To the touch, it is dry, cold, scaly.

"You are not here, Barbel Hachereau. The other one has taken your place. These stripped features are just a sketch of your real face. Your teeth aren't so pointed."

In the mirror, the other contracts its pupils.

Tilting her head, Barbel hears a melody from the deepest depths. A prism of pure crystal is ringing, and hearing it she feels herself dispersed to all the bands of this sonic rainbow. But there is just enough of her primal being left to resist the rush of frozen color trying to carry her off; and the crystal shatters.

A triumph over the abyss.

But now she knows. She is the prey of an implacable fate. The demon will confront her, again and again, until she no longer has the strength to resist.

She finds her feet filthy, her room filthy. She who was once vitrified like quartz, clear and with perfect edges, now feels her being leaking away, seeping out of invisible fissures.

Eventually she realizes how to stop the slow hemorrhage of her self.

It is easier to die when it is an act of resistance. It turns the tables; now it's she who floats above the demon, bound to him by a cord of energy, which thins at the same pace as her life. The demon lodges in a metal cylinder, attached to a complex little apparatus. The orange of its eyes is tarnished. Its mouth exhales bubbles of music, which float away and burst. At times the teeth show through the sound.

A language made of cries, Barbel thinks.

Although they're flecked with foam, trembling like a wave about to break, Barbel can distinguish forms everywhere. They rise, they vibrate around the cylinder; into it the suffering beast shrinks, unable to transfuse, unable to receive transfusion.

Closer. It's Barbel's turn to penetrate the alien body. Spread out in it. Understand then where she is. Somehow she has done the impossible: she has swept the demon into her death. The immortality of the demon—of all demons—seemed to her an unchangeable fact, a privilege absolute and irrevocable. How could a little Earthling change something like that? How could she have created a world where the transfusees know how to turn their deaths against their invaders?

A thick ooze wells out of the bloated flesh of the being with orange eyes. In the bloodless loops of that strange consciousness, the living essence desperately fights the imminence of the abyss.

In the instant that the too-taut thread of her existence snaps, Barbel smiles. Her torn body will claim the victory.

The Dark at the Corner of the Eye

PATRICIA ANTHONY

SERGEANT TUNNY, wire basket in hand, stopped in front of Cohen's desk and started flipping out manila envelopes. The sound they made when they hit the steel-and-Formica top were the only clue to what lay hidden inside them.

Clink. Clink. Jewelry.

Tap. Something light: A photograph or maybe a letter. Plop. A wallet? The form inside the envelope was thick enough.

Thunk. Cohen eyed that one for a moment, his gaze briefly following the drawn curve of the five.

Tap. Whatever was in six was thin and bigger than a business card, smaller than a sheet of regular paper. He could sense that much without touching it.

"Come on, guys," Tunny said in his raspy bass. "We need witnesses."

Four cops left what they were doing or not doing to walk over: three uniforms; one plain-clothes detective.

"Begin," Tunny said to Cohen.

Cohen reached a hand out to envelope number one. Before he could touch the edge of the manila paper, the darkness was back. And it stayed for a count of twelve. Cohen had been timing it lately so that he could describe to any doctor who was interested the details of the symptoms.

It wasn't just his imagination. Everyone sees bright spots in their field of vision; Cohen knew that. Bright floating spots were indications of a brief lack of oxygen to the brain. Big deal. So sometimes the brain said SEND, and the circulatory system, like an overworked file clerk, said, SEND WHAT?

And sometimes vision went dark. That was a circulatory problem, too, Cohen had learned. You have low blood pressure and you get up too abruptly and—blam—you're down again.

But vision wasn't ever supposed to go dark in precisely the way Cohen's did, and with precisely the same feeling. In that twelve seconds, he could dimly see, in the background, Tunny's blossoming smirk; and in the foreground, like a panel of smoked glass, the square of darkness.

The darkness was his private black hole, a thing that sucked in all thought and held it like a startled, caught breath.

After a count of twelve, it blinked out of existance and let him go.

"Worried you can't get it up, Cohen?" Tunny asked. "Forgot who the perp was supposed to be?"

When the darkness evaporated, Cohen found himself staring directly into Tunny's baby-blond good looks. The sergeant's eyebrows were so fair that they blended into the pale of his skin. He was a lump of flesh and a thatch of yellow, relieved by two primary-blue eyes. Simple, even in colors, Tunny was.

For an instant Cohen hated Tunny. *I could be dying here,* he thought. *I could be having a stroke.* If Cohen fell off the chair, he could picture Tunny saying, *Worried you can't get it up?*

Tunny upset him so much Cohen was afraid he couldn't go on and that he'd have to delay the lineup for a while.

Cohen pushed his anger into the tight space where the black hole lurked, then reached forward and picked up the first envelope.

He could feel a chain inside; a thick, short chain.

"A cop's bracelet," Cohen said.

Tunny's smile soured.

Cohen stared hard into the sergeant's eyes, a cruel turn to his mouth. "His wife's running around on him."

One of the witnessing officers, a uniform, made a hasty snatch for the envelope. His face was purple.

Tunny tore the envelope from the uniform's hand and threw it back on the desk.

Clink.

"Fuck it, Ojeda. You don't freak in the lineup, okay?" Tunny growled. His cheeks were pink from embarrassment or perhaps anger. "Let the man do his thing."

Cohen picked up number two and held it a moment. Another man's bracelet, about the same size and weight. "Pimp," Cohen said. "He's not the one."

He glanced up to see if he was right, but this time no one was giving him clues. Cohen put the pimp's bracelet down and picked up the flat envelope, number three.

That was Dickerson, the murderer. Cohen's sensitive fingers could feel the quick, hungry pulse under the paper. All murderers had their own rhythm. This one was as steady and measured as blood in the veins, a beat that whispered *i-want-i-want-i-want.* Hurriedly, he put it down. "That's the same guy I felt on the victim's clothes."

Tunny settled his clipboard against his stomach and made some notes. "You sure?"

"I'm sure."

"You want to check again?"

"No." Cohen's hands were shaking. He hated the touch of murder. Murder was a darkness of another sort; a darkness shot with crimson.

"Keep going," Tunny said.

Cohen swallowed and reached for four, the one he figured was a wallet. There was a lump inside the envelope, but it didn't tell him anything. "Zero," he said, frowning.

"Let it be noted that the psychic received no concrete impressions." Tunny repeated the stock, formal phrase by rote.

"No feelings at all," Cohen said by way of correction. He couldn't tell whether Tunny made a notation.

Quickly he reached out for five. When his hand hit it, an instinctive smile erupted from inside him and spread itself over his face. He glanced around the broad form of Tunny and could see the receptionist watching him. Cohen felt Tunny watching him, too. He stifled his grin. "Lila's compact."

"You like that one?" Tunny asked.

Cohen looked down at the table, hoping that Lila had noticed his reaction; hoping Tunny hadn't.

And then Cohen reached for six. He had it in both hands before he realized something was wrong. By the time he sensed the danger, he was trapped. He couldn't put the envelope down. His hands clamped to it as an electrocuted man's hold moronically, helplessly, onto a live wire.

In the back of his brain, he could hear Tunny's voice rise to a shout. "Cohen? Cohen!"

A primal wail started in Cohen's chest, rushed up his throat and filled his mouth.

"Christ!" Tunny snapped. "Cohen! Let go!"

The policeman had hold of one edge of the envelope and was fighting a desperate tug-of-war with it. Finally, with a furious jerk, he tore it from the psychic's grasp.

Cohen dropped back into his chair. Tunny stood with the envelope cradled at his chest. He was breathing hard.

"Thank you," Cohen whispered.

Tunny licked his lips anxiously. "Was it the murderer?"

"No. Something else." Whatever was in that envelope was something terrible: an unending, silent loneliness. "I want verification."

At first Tunny looked confused. Then his cheeks went pale, pale as his hair, pale as his eyebrows. "That's for amateurs, Cohen. You don't need that."

"Verification!" Cohen snapped. "Now! Right now!"

The policemen were ringed around him like a gathering of owls. Tunny tore open number one and upended it. There was a glint of gold, a clink. A bracelet dropped out of the envelope, and Ojeda quickly picked it up.

There was an identical bracelet in two. It was just like Tunny to have picked up two similar bracelets from two dissimilar men. The detective had a quirky sense of humor.

In number three was a lock of brown hair encased in plastic. He wondered how the cops had gotten it. Psychometrist's samples were governed by search-and-seizure rules. Had Tunny, scissors in hand, asked Dickerson to give him a lock? Or, more likely, had he staked out the murderer's barber?

"Four," Cohen said.

Tunny glanced to the other policemen and tore open the end of the fourth envelope. There was a wallet inside. It still had the price tag on it.

"Bastard," Cohen whispered.

The sergeant quickly opened five. It was Lila's compact. The case was chipped, and makeup was caked in the ornate design of the white plastic.

Cohen picked up the compact and held it tenderly for a moment, as gently as he had always longed to hold her hand. The case was woman-scented, and the residue of the makeup outside was slightly greasy. Lila had a sweet, happy feel to her, like the feel of a gift of flowers or a surprise letter from a friend.

Without putting the compact down, he said, "Six."

Tunny hesitated.

"Six!" Cohen shouted.

The sergeant ripped open one edge and upended the envelope over the table. Cohen's MasterCard dropped out.

"Shit," Cohen gasped as he lurched to his feet.

Tunny looked like he was about to cry. "I'm sorry, Nathan. Jesus, you know I . . ."

"Shut up! Shut up!" Cohen held onto Lila's compact as if he were suspended over infinity and the compact were his only lifeline. He was afraid to pick up his credit card. He was terrified to touch it.

Tunny was still talking. "You left your jacket on your chair again, Nathan. Your wallet right inside it. I just wanted to see what would happen . . ."

"You fucking cretin!" Cohen screamed. With a loud crack the compact shattered in his hand.

The ring of policemen watched as Cohen opened his shaking fist. A brush dropped out first, making a dull sound on the linoleum floor. His palm was covered with glistening, beige powder and shards of bone-colored plastic. Blood seeped, making dirty rivulets in his hand.

He hurried away from the table and toward the bathroom.

"Cohen!" Tunny shouted behind him. "Cohen! What about . . ."

Cohen slammed open the bathroom door. The hydraulic mechanism caught it and, careful as a salesman in an antique shop, let it ease closed, muting the end of Tunny's question.

". . . your MasterCard?"

Beneath the tap the water ran red and beige. It smelled of perfume and blood. Cohen was pressing paper towels on his wounds when the door opened. He glanced up, expecting to see an apologetic Tunny. It was

Schindler. The doctor gave Cohen's bleeding hand a curious glance and then leaned up against the dirty tile wall, crossing his arms over his chest.

"Psychiatrists should be careful of body language, Larry," Cohen warned.

Schindler shrugged, but didn't change his posture. "Don't want the MasterCard back?"

"Tell Tunny he can shove it up his ass."

Schindler laughed. "Would that be an act that was emotionally charged?"

After a pause, Cohen laughed, too.

"Seriously," Schindler said and then stopped. The psychiatrist had a habit of leaving dangling lead-ins behind him.

When Cohen was certain that Schindler was not going to go on, he said, "Tell Tunny to put the card back in my wallet."

"You shouldn't leave a wallet unattended. This is a police station. There are all sorts of crooks here." After a perfectly timed comic pause, he added, "Some of them wear uniforms so you can spot them, but what about the others?"

Cohen didn't bother to laugh. His hand was throbbing. When he looked up at the mirror, the darkness returned, a dead spot in the corner of his eye. As it vanished, he could see Schindler watching him.

"How's the vision problem?" Schindler asked.

Turning off the water, Cohen threw the bloodied paper towels in the trash and yanked some fresh from the dispenser. Sometimes Cohen felt the psychiatrist could read his mind. Maybe Schindler was getting a little unlicensed Psychamine on the side. "The same."

"Well."

Cohen watched spots of red erupt from the nubbly surface of the towels.

"Maybe you should cut the Psychamine, Nathan."

"They've done neurological tests. Nobody can find anything wrong."

"The brain's a bunch of weird shit, son. We don't even know what the drug does."

The towels had soaked through. Cohen threw them away and stuck his bleeding hand in the sink, hearing the drip-drip as his blood hit the porcelain.

"Want me to bandage it?"

Cohen shook his head. "It'll be all right in a minute."

"You're working too hard."

"I read *Forbes* so I understand I'm a workaholic. This should make you happy, not upset."

"So what is it with you?" Schindler asked. "Power? Knowledge? What? Why knock yourself out, Cohen?"

"Why do you think I do it?"

"A power trip. You're irredeemably awkward in social encounters, so you get a rush out of your job. Right? Am I right?"

"I'm the best psychic you've got."

"Only because you've sublimated all your sexual desires into it. Tell me true. You think it's the Psychamine that's causing your blackouts, don't you."

Cohen applied more towels to his wounds. "They're not blackouts per se. Besides, what am I going to do, Larry? Work in an office or what? I can't type. I'm not trained for anything else."

"Poor little mind reader," Schindler said in a voice like sugared vinegar. "Your perp Dickerson's the one. They're calling in the verifying psychics now. If they point him out, the cops are going to pick him up."

"Who's on Veri-Psi?"

"Durso and Ingram."

"They're good," Cohen said in the easy tone of one who knows he's better.

"Stop taking the Psychamine."

Cohen studied his reflection. A shy, mousey man stared back. Under the fluorescent lights, the face in the mirror looked greenish, baggy and used up. "I can't," he whispered.

"Have you been counting? Well, I have. Fifteen years, Cohen. You've been taking it fifteen years, longer than anybody on record. What if one of the long-term effects is blindness?"

Cohen glanced down at his hand. Blood had made red spiderwebs on his palm and left rusty threads on the white porcelain. "It's not like blindness."

"Then what's it like?"

"The darkness isn't part of my eye. It's inside my brain. It's a suction monster, a fucking Hoover vacuum cleaner of the soul."

Cohen glanced over his shoulder. Schindler's easy, friendly manner had disappeared, leaving only the psychiatrist part behind.

"You know I'm clairvoyant," Cohen said.

For a moment, Schindler froze. Then he shook his head vehemently as if the words were a wasp he could shoo out of the room. "Come on, Cohen. Come on. Don't get absurd on me, okay? The courts recognize telepathy and psychometry, not clairvoyance. Seeing into the future leaves you with an ungovernable paradox."

"I'm clairvoyant," Cohen said. "Consider for a moment what that says about time. Think what it says about space."

Schindler frowned. "I'm listening." Yes, Schindler was listening. He wasn't happy, he wasn't believing; but he was listening.

"I've bent time, Larry," he told him quietly. "The past, the future, they're all one thing. And the place where time is bent is a place where parts of me are so crushed, so dense, that it lets no light escape. One day, Larry, one day, I'm going to fall into that fucker and not come out, understand? And I'm scared shitless because I don't know what's inside it."

Schindler stayed in his dim corner, leaning up against the wall, his arms crossed, his posture the same as when he'd come in the door. His face, though, had suddenly gone expressionless. "So that's what you think."

"That's what I imagine."

"Okay. Granted."

"I'm afraid of it. I'm afraid of what I saw in the envelope. I'm afraid of the future I saw in my goddamned MasterCard."

"Why did you think that was clairvoyance in particular, Cohen? Did some little sign pop up and tell you FUTURE EVENT?"

Cohen glanced at the wall. He would have glanced at anything, anything, to keep from facing Schindler's bland, clinical scrutiny.

"You see what people *are*. You can see it more clearly than I can. Truth. That's what you see," Schindler said softly. "Maybe the only thing contained in that card was your own pathological loneliness."

Staring into the wall, Cohen felt the hot, gravid pressure of tears behind his eyes. *Pathologically lonely?* he thought. Was that the way everyone saw him? For an uncomfortable moment, his mind fondled the idea as though it were an interesting but somewhat suspect find that had washed up on a beach. "I'm not like that."

"Oh, Nathan," Schindler said tiredly. "Know thyself, okay?"

"Fuck you!" Cohen shouted.

Schindler stood straighter, unfolded his arms.

"Listen," Cohen told him, firmly meeting the psychiatrist's gaze in the mirror. "I know the difference. There's a difference in the feel. What hit me was clairvoyance, only I couldn't see all the details. In spite of the Psychamine, you only see parts, and sometimes those parts don't make sense. What if the vision was telling me I'm going to crawl into that dark place, Larry? What if it was telling me I'll die there?"

"I don't think the black spots have a physical basis. If you're clairvoyant what you saw may be insanity. That's a type of darkness, too."

Cohen remembered the ones who had entered the program with him. Frazier had been a careful man, one who carried his umbrella when there was only a twenty percent chance of rain. He'd opened his wrists longitudinally in a tub of warm water; and then he'd opened the back of his knees, too.

Rowe was making baskets at an Iowa farm for the strangely inspired. And Karpovich, ah, Karpovich. He'd ended his new career as an alcoholic by jumping in front of a train.

"There was something wrong with us to begin with, right, Larry? There's something missing in people who are born psychic. Guts, maybe. Maybe that last, tough, protective layer of skin."

"If the Psychamine just augments what you had to begin with, maybe it augments the cowardice and the hurt, too," Schindler said. "You should try giving it up."

"I can't quit," Cohen said. "You're absolutely right about me. I'm obsessive/compulsive and when I do an investigation I get a hard-on like you wouldn't believe." Cohen held a new wad of paper toweling to his palm, but the wounds were already closing. The paper came away with just a few dots of red.

"Spoken like someone in the throes of self-destruction."

"It's my goddamned life, Schindler."

"No," Schindler said. "No, it's not. Just like the cops' lives aren't theirs, either. Medical leave, Cohen. Open ended, understand? When you're ready to come back, we'll do a physical and mental on you, okay?"

Cohen's stomach went cold. "Hey. The obsessive/compulsive thing . . . all that talk about clairvoyance . . . it was a joke. You don't have a sense of humor, or what?"

But Schindler wasn't even looking at him. "Take some rest. Go to Bermuda."

A small, weak laugh escaped Cohen's lips. "Listen, we're friends, aren't we? I mean, that's what all this talk was about, you know? Something between friends?"

"I'm a shrink first."

Hatred grabbed Cohen by the neck and cut off his air. "Well, tell Lila I'm sorry about her compact."

"Okay."

"And get the hell out."

After a moment, Schindler did. The door closed itself carefully behind him.

Cohen watched him go. He watched until the dark came back, a spot so black, so weighty, that not even thought moved there.

When it had gone, he wiped the last remnants of blood from his hand and left the bathroom. A few policemen glanced up as he walked to his desk.

Tunny came over. "I'm sorry . . ."

"Shut up," Cohen whispered without looking at him. He grabbed his jacket, put it on, and walked out into the chill night. Durso and Ingram were on their way in. He stopped them.

"We shouldn't be talking," Durso said. The verifying psychic was a little man with a little man's slavishness to convention.

"Wait a minute. Just please wait a minute." Cohen could hear his voice shake. Tonight, when he went home, he'd be alone and lost in the darkness. Tomorrow, when he woke up, he'd be alone and lost with no place to go. "Are you clairvoyant?"

Durso drew himself up in his coat, his watery hazel eyes suspicious. Ingram pulled on an edge of his mustache.

"It's important. I have to know. Do you sometimes see the future?"

Ingram's chocolate face blended in with the night, but Cohen could see his eyes shift nervously from Durso to Cohen and back.

"The courts recognize telepathy . . ." Durso began.

"Goddamn it! Don't you think I've memorized that by now? They don't recognize clairvoyance because it doesn't make sense. Don't you see? If you really can see the future, then maybe there's a place where tomorrow's already occurred."

Durso snapped, "That's right. It doesn't make sense. Hence the 'ungovernable paradox.' " He started to walk past, but Cohen grabbed him by the arm.

"Do you see darkness sometimes? I have to know. A dark thing just at the corner of your eye like something standing between you and the light. Do you ever see something like that?"

Durso was trying to get away. His face was a study in repulsed shock.

Ingram laid a gloved hand on Cohen's shoulder. "You need to go home, man. Understand?" he said with soft concern. "Get some sleep, okay?"

"Don't patronize me," Cohen snapped. "Listen, Ingram, maybe one day you'll see what I see. Maybe Frazier saw it. Maybe that's what sucked Karpovich out in front of the train . . ."

Ingram made quieting-the-baby sounds.

"Please," Cohen whimpered. He was crying. "Tell me. Don't you ever see it?"

"No, man. I don't."

With a jerk, Cohen pulled away and started in a fast walk down the street. After a few paces, he glanced behind. Ingram and Durso were staring at him. The pity on their faces caught him unawares. It was as much of a shock as a chance glimpse of his own reflection in a glass doorway. Maybe, he thought, Schindler was right. Cohen wondered if he peeked too quickly into a mirror he would see a pathologically lonely man staring back.

After a few blocks, he slowed. He'd go home, turn on the TV, maybe, and the darkness would be there, slicing through the image on NBC. And tomorrow he'd wake up, read the paper and try to remember not to get dressed for work. Sometime in the coming week, Schindler would send him a ticket to someplace warm, compliments of the department, and he'd go and look out into the rhythmic blue of the Caribbean and see a black, timeless mass standing between him and the waves.

In his brain, minutes and hours curled in stasis, a spot of dead, heavy air.

He pulled up his collar. A few people stared as he walked past, and he wondered if he was crying again. He felt warmth on his hand, and when he looked down he saw he was bleeding.

He turned off on a side street and was halfway down a claustrophobic alley when—blink—the darkness was back, solid and very close.

"Your money, motherfucker," a voice growled.

The darkness that throbbed with the aura of murder smelled of stale cigarette smoke and damp wool.

Something moved in that pressured place. Odd. Cohen didn't think it could. A pain pierced his chest, drawing fire into his back.

His shoulder, his face, smacked against the cold sidewalk. Thick, heavy liquid gushed from his chest.

How stupid, he thought. *How clumsy.* He tried to get up and couldn't. *My God. What's the matter with me?* he wondered. Then he pictured Tunny's bland, marshmallow-pink face. *Afraid you can't get it up, Cohen?*

Yes, Cohen thought. *My body won't work. I can't get up. And I am so afraid.*

Close to his face he could see a pair of scuffed work boots, the laces on one broken and untied. He felt something jerk at his coat pocket. Across the alley was a dented garbage can, its load of green, plastic bags like scoops of unsavory ice cream in a cone.

His breath failed in his throat. He was too weak, too frightened, to take another.

Someone would come for him. They'd have to. What he'd touched in his MasterCard didn't have to be.

Hey, diddle, diddle, he thought desperately, forcing his mind to concentrate on something else besides his terror. If he held himself together long enough, someone would come and drag him back from the brink. There would be bright hospital lights and hot coffee. Cohen would be laughing with the doctor and saying how scared he had been.

Wouldn't he?

Cohen drank in precious, temporal visions: the light/shadow, light/shadow play of the tan work boots walking away from him; the way a pink-tailed rat poised, head inquisitively cocked, near a tattered plastic bag; how an oil-slicked puddle shone rainbow-colored in the dim glow from a bulb above a door.

The cat and the fiddle.

Something inside him came loose. The world slipped an inch.

Not yet. Oh, God, please. Not yet. The cow jumped over the moon. His eyes moved hungrily, memorizing all the parts of the world he could see in the moment he had left. *And when he got there . . .*

The glow from the bulb weakened. Going, going, gone. Black opened its doors, and he was sucked through.

Cupboard was bare . . .

It was dark. And the darkness did not move. An absurd phrase danced on the edge of his consciousness.

The dish ran away with the spoon.

The words sank into the depths without a ripple. He looked around, thinking that he must be blind, but knowing he was not.

He was dead.

So this is what death is, he thought. It wasn't much different from what he'd left behind. He knew now that the spot which had haunted him had not been an overlay. It was the very foundation of his existence.

He'd always meant to go fishing. He'd loved it as a child; but when he was grown he never got around to it. Work had been so large and important a matter that it eclipsed the timer that counted his moments. Before he'd realized it, the clock struck midnight and time had just quietly run out.

A pity. He should have gotten to know Lila better. He'd always meant to marry; he'd always wanted to have children. When young, he thought he needed a pony more than he'd needed breath; and when grown, and with an adult's more subtle desires, he'd wanted a big dog and a house in the country.

Now it all seemed equally important: Every dream, every kiss, every piece of candy he'd been denied. His longing for lost illusion shook the emptiness as a plucked violin string stirs the air. Across space and time, he cast all his memories and his last coherent thought, ironically the same, selfish pulse of a murderer:

I WANT.

His plea tore the thin fabric of the universe. In the abyss a single, faint star flicked on. The glow swelled to the size of a pinhead, the size of a fingernail, the size of a fist.

The light sped toward him in silence and with all the colors that ever were. It rushed joyously as though it knew him, and as if it believed it was coming home.

The light soaked up his knowledge of the Earth, the moon, the rings about Saturn; it drank in the nonsense of a nursery rhyme and the curl of a rat's pink tail.

I WANT, he thought fiercely.

And in his desire, it became. The light shot through him, the photons a million small bullets from a million small inevitable wars.

Cohen was destined to love butternut ice cream. At thirty-three years old, his eldest child would watch and cheer as he hooked a tarpon off Florida. In fourth grade he would skin his knee and be unable to ride his pony for a week.

Because of Cohen, dinosaurs would stalk the earth and a single, brilliant moment would kill them. In the desert, Georgia O'Keeffe would dream of flowers; and complex organic molecules would discover the heady possibility of life.

Had he eyes to close he would have closed them, for the conquering radiance hurt. Until the interval of cooling, darkness was chained in the deep.

And yet darkness held alternative promises. It always had. Creation was his for the asking; that was the lesson he'd had to die to learn. With calm astonishment he realized how wrong, how deluded, he had been. The prophetic black had not been the lights-out at the end of the play; merely an expectant dimming for act one.

Cohen breathed his life into the script of the nascent universe. It would be eons before he had learned his new walk-on part and Cohen the director permitted him to draw breath again.

Nothing in creation, even private creation, was hurried. But he could wait.

Tracking the Random Variable

MARCOS DONNELLY

TUESDAY EVENING, Ronald Barr sat wifeless on the sofa in his darkened living room, sipping a glass of scotch and warm water. While he waited, he sketched histograms on graph paper: x-axis, timeline; y-axis, number of minutes Jessica spent away from home on weekdays outside of working hours. Last Thursday, 425 minutes; last Tuesday, 260 minutes; Monday before last, 315 minutes . . .

He never asked where she went, couldn't bring himself to ask. She had stopped offering the excuses of evening faculty meetings at the elementary school and late conferences with parents from two-career homes.

Two-career homes. He and Jessica had been a two-career home just ten weeks ago. Now she had a career, he worked a job.

There had to be a pattern—control the variable, control the situation. He arranged the data as a pareto chart. Nothing. A scattergram correlating days of the week and the time she spent away. Nothing. A range graph, a deviation chart, a double bar–x control chart.

He sat tapping the pencil point against his wrist, then resorted to sketching a fishbone diagram for cause-effect analysis. He winced; low, very low for a statistician.

Ex-statistician.

- EFFECT: Wife spending excessive time away from home.
- DESIRED STATE: Wife's time away from home brought under control.
- MAJOR CONTRIBUTING FACTORS:
  Communication with wife
  Appreciation shown to wife
  Financial support of wife
  Sexual relations with wife

Financial support. Not really significant. His current salary at her Uncle Luke's garage was only a thousand less than his second-year salary had been at Resotech. He had balanced the difference by taking over her coupons and organizing them for cost efficiency.

Sex. Well, maybe. He'd only made love to her twice in the past four weeks. Just twice? He dug through his memory but couldn't recall more than two times. It was, in fact, a variable he hadn't yet taken into account.

Jessica arrived home at 10:17 P.M.

"Hello, Ronald." Her voice had the chill in it.

He hid his statistics under a stack of invoices from Luke's service station. Careful, he thought. Look casual.

"Hi, honey. You must be exhausted. About ready to hit the sack?"

She stared at him as she stepped out of her heels. She was quiet for a moment, and he was afraid she wouldn't speak to him. That would be bad —broken communication, too many variables to bring under control.

But she did speak. "I was out until half past ten. Don't you care where I was?"

Ronald breathed relief; there was still communication. She looked beautiful standing there in the foyer glaring at him, her straight red hair touching each shoulder of her white blouse, one strand tangled in the 33-inch gold chain he had given her on their 333-day wedding anniversary. He almost said so, that she looked beautiful, but a shiver of panic ran through him before he did. Too many variables.

"You were working, right?" he finally said. "You must want to go upstairs and kick back a little." Don't press her; that would cause tension. "Would you like a glass of wine?"

"Jesus, Ronald." She threw her purse on the sofa. He walked to her and kissed her neck gently, grimacing for a second from the sharp taste of fresh perfume.

He tried to fashion a boyish grin. "What do you say we go upstairs together?"

Their lovemaking was brief, and she was silent. When it was over, she rolled away with her back to him. Ronald was certain she would start getting home on time.

He should not have lost the position with Resotech Corp.

He *could* not have lost it.

Ronald Barr had been prepared the day the "Please report to Personnel" note came. The odds were in his favor. Of the 300 employees whom Resotech was laying off that afternoon for the statewide Reduction in Force, the top 205 had been from middle management. He was in the bottom third, the white-collar office workers who did real work for the company. Out of that group, he was part of the 44 percent who had completed a four-year college education. When he took into account that only 25 percent of Resotech employees with college degrees actually worked in the area of their undergraduate studies, and added to that certain emotional factors which couldn't be readily calculated—he and Jessica had just closed on their first home, were planning to start a family, those sorts of things that would add a sympathetic nuance to his otherwise purely logical argument—it left him as one of about ten and a half employees who had a good shot at talking Personnel into reconsidering their termination.

Good odds, even if he took the liberty to round the half-employee up to the nearest whole number.

He was valuable; he was the one who could see the hidden variables. He had shown statistically that removing car stereos from the sales reps' company cars would reduce speeding; tickets dropped 68 percent. He had demonstrated that the addition of hot cocoa and chicken soup to coffee vending machines would correlate significantly with employee honesty measures; petty theft of office supplies dropped 32 percent statewide.

He saw the variables; he could control any system. He should not have lost the position with Resotech Corp.

He *could* not have lost it.

• • • •

It was the Sunday morning after the Tuesday night that sex with Jessica hadn't worked. Thursday and Friday evenings, she had stayed out until 9:28 P.M. and 10:12 P.M., respectively.

She sat down across the kitchen table from Ronald, cupping her hands around the sides of her coffee mug. She was quiet for a while, and then asked, "Don't you care?"

Ronald kept sorting the Sunday-morning coupons. He set a 35-cent Charmin off to the left, and dug out the 35-cent Maxwell House from the unsorted pile. As he set it on top of the Charmin coupon, an article in the local section of the paper caught his eye: the Pittsfield district had just elected a third woman to its school board. The last time three women had been elected to the Pittsfield school board, he remembered, was January of 1982. The very next day, the Guinness world record for crawling had been broken in Newton Abbot, England. He would need to check tomorrow's paper.

"Honey," Jessica said. She reached across the table and set her hand on top of his. The tenderness in the touch felt like guilt. Good. Of course he cared. If she had any idea, if she was going to throw everything away—dammit, what right did she have to make him feel guilty for her actions?

Wrong approach. Control the situation, don't become a variable.

He could control *anything*.

"I'll get out of your uncle's garage," he said, establishing the communication. He fought the desire to pull his hand away. "I'll get a white-collar job. It's just a tight market now. I'll keep trying, if only you'd be a little patient."

She sat back in her chair and brushed a strand of loose red hair from her face. "I'm talking about *us*, Ronald. I didn't say anything about the color of your collar. Do you really think I'm upset with you about your career status?"

He added a Cheerios coupon to the 35-cent pile. The way she kept the coupons in such disarray irritated him: 60-cent toilet tissue mixed together with 15-cent drain cleaner and 50-cent cleansers. In the last week he had managed to arrange most of them by descending value of discount. Sometimes she seemed as haphazard as the third graders she taught. But she was trying to be kind, at least, pretending that his career setback didn't matter to her.

"Jessica, it's a tight market."

"You already said that."

"Well, it is! The odds against me finding work—"

"Odds!" She shoved herself away from the table and walked to the sink. Ronald knew what she would do: (A) dump the coffee; (B) thrust the cup in the dishwater; (C) put her right hand on the refrigerator, standing with her back to him; (D) remain silent for ten to fifteen seconds; (E) produce an exaggerated sigh; and (F) turn to face him.

Which she did. Steps A through F, in that order, in that way. If he could figure her out down to her damned *sighing* . . .

"When I *do* get you to say something, all you talk about anymore are the odds, the numbers, the variables." Her voice had become subdued and even. The chill was coming, and he knew it could last for days if he didn't respond at her level. "Please, Ronald, can't you just talk with me the way you used to?"

There was no way, no way he should be losing her.

He stood and took hold of her bathrobe sleeve. Without a word, he walked her through their living room and out the front door.

"The lawn," he announced.

"Which you said you were going to weed yesterday." Sarcasm; it was part of the chill.

"I was doing coupons." He reached under the forsythia bush to the right of the front steps and pulled a stone from below its drooping branches.

"A stone."

She crossed her arms.

"I'm going to throw *this* stone on *that* lawn. I want you to choose the one blade of grass that you think it will hit."

She turned her back to him, so he walked a semicircle around her to see her face.

"Come on," he said, "I'm trying to explain what I'm feeling. What blade of grass will it hit?"

She glanced sideways toward the lawn. "It'll probably hit a weed."

"Not probably! There is no such word as probably." He smiled and nodded; just maybe she was understanding. He tossed the rock in a high arc and chased it onto the lawn, almost slipping once on the cold dew. "This one!" he shouted to her. He pulled a blade of grass from under the stone and ran back to the porch. "This was the one, Jessica! And there was no probability about it. The bend in my wrist, the angle of the trajectory, gravity, the wind, everything working together made it so this was the blade the stone hit. *There was no chance involved!*"

She set one hand lightly on his shoulder; the other was balled in a tight fist in front of her mouth, a gesture he didn't recognize. He couldn't tell if she had grasped everything he said, or whether she was still thinking it through.

"Jessica, nothing is pure chance. There are variables we haven't discovered yet. But they exist, and if I find them I can control *any* situation."

She wrapped her arms around him now, slowly, and set her head on his shoulder. He again found himself annoyed by her touch, by her breath against his neck; he again felt guilty for feeling annoyed. He couldn't decide exactly what to do with his own arms. He continued to think about it. He had nothing else to say, he realized.

She pushed herself from him and ran into the house. She slammed the door. Ronald stood outside for two more hours, throwing the stone, seeing where it landed, throwing it again.

Jessica's Uncle Luke stepped into the back office at the garage during Ronald's lunch break. Fumes from the cigar he clenched in his teeth filled the small room; Ronald looked up from the morning newspaper. He had been reading the article about the pair of teenagers in upstate New York who had just broken the world crawling record.

Luke hiked up his trousers across his belly. He pulled a folded sheet of paper from his pocket and squinted at the writing. "I think we might be getting low on spark plugs and brake pads. Could you order us some?"

"Sparks are due in at two o'clock today, Luke. Pads will be good for another twelve days. I've also ordered halogens for Chevys. We'll run out of those next Thursday."

Luke took off his John Deere cap and scratched his scalp, mussing the little hair he still had. He chuckled deeply. "Ronnie, it's too bad you hate this place."

Ronald sat up. "No, Luke, I don't—"

"Don't try to kid me, son. I understand. This just isn't your sort of job." He leaned on Ronald's desk and flicked a cigar ash into an empty coffee cup. "Hell, if I were in your shoes, I'd feel stupid too."

Ronald sat up a little straighter. "Stupid? Well, I—"

"Tell you what, though," Luke went on, looking philosophical. "Don't know how the hell you manage to run inventory so tight. You've cut down stock so much that I've got room to set up a fifth grease pit. Before I lose you to some corporation, you gotta show me how you figure it all out."

Ronald leaned forward and pulled a manila file from the careful stacks on the desk. "Well, I used invoices from the past three years to plot control charts. It has to be done for each of our high-volume parts. Then I pick out the variations in each system, and I calculate upper and lower control limits. I can plot . . ." He glanced at Luke, whose intent expression resembled pain more than concentration.

"Well, anyway," Ronald said, "I use math to guess what we'll need."

Luke nodded and set a hand on Ronald's shoulder. "You'd be a millionaire at the racetrack," he said.

Ronald set the open file on his desk. Of course it wasn't just the math; that was the simpler part of it. The difficulty was developing a feel for the way things were linked in the universe, the hidden causes that were almost absurd. A butterfly flaps its wings in Beijing, gale-force winds result in Albany; a NASA technician throws his sandwich wrapper away in his partner's wastebasket, a junk sinks off the coast of Taiwan. Finding the links, tracing the patterns . . . *that* was the formidable task.

Bernie rushed into the office, a five-dollar bill in his hand and Stan in tow. The smell of gasoline and body odor overpowered the cigar fumes, and Ronald felt the office closing in on him. Resotech had been a lot more spacious.

"Ronnie, how many air filters have I put in during the last six weeks?" Bernie asked, grinning. He turned to Stan and said, "Now listen close, wise ass."

Ronald shook his head. Stan was the third sucker Bernie had taken on this bet. "Twenty-seven," Ronald said without checking the back sales invoices.

Bernie stepped out a peculiar victory dance he saved for this particular bet and stuffed the five dollars in the breast pocket of his greasy blue coveralls. The two of them, Stan and Bernie, were a mismatched pair, Stan as bulky and awkward as Bernie was handsome and smooth.

Stan looked incredulous. "Hey, you guys set me up."

Luke stepped back and rested an elbow on the file cabinet as Ronald pushed his chair from the desk to sit facing the two. He folded his hands on his lap and feigned patience while Bernie went through part two of the wager.

"Fine," Bernie said, putting his hands in his coverall pockets, a devil-may-care stance. "Double or nothing he can do it with any part you've used."

"Okay, you twerp bastard." Stan grinned with confidence as he pulled another five from his wallet. "Double or nothing." Bernie reached for the bill, but Stan balled it in his fist and glared. "How many PCV valves have I used?" he asked Ronald.

"Since when?"

"Uh . . . six weeks."

"What type of PCV valve?"

Luke laughed; Stan was frowning. "All right, pal, just 892-C's."

Ronald sat back. Stan, six weeks, ninety-one invoices, 2.8 liter V6 autos only; piece of cake. "Fifteen."

Stan looked blank. He unballed his fists and started counting on his fingers. Bernie snatched the second five, laughing. "You're a fucking computer, Ronnie," he said, slapping Ronald on the back. "Break down and join us at McCollough's Pub and the first beer's on me."

Ronald nodded. "Yeah. Maybe."

"All promises, but you never show," Bernie said, shrugging. He grabbed Stan by the shoulders and pushed him out the door.

"Those boys won't ever learn not to bet against Bernie," Luke said. "Never seen the guy lose, but they'll bet anyways. Never learn." He sat on Ronald's desk and put his cap back on. "So, tell me how my little Jessica's doing."

Ronald looked down at his inventory control charts and traced an index finger along an upper control limit. "Great. Great."

Luke rubbed a hand over the bristles on his chin. "Must be a happy little girl," he said, his voice edged with something like suspicion and understanding improbably combined. "Every time I ask you that, I get two 'greats' in a row."

Ronald felt the muscles tense in his lower back. "Well, she's still teaching. She likes it."

Variables. He'd exhausted the obvious. It wasn't a standard correlation. Employee theft and hot cocoa. School boards and crawling records. Time away from home. And . . .

"Yeah," Ronald said, retracing the inventory control lines. "She likes it."

He bolted upright in bed. "My God!" he said aloud, almost shouting.

Jessica stirred next to him but didn't wake. He could barely make out her form in the darkness; he could hear her breathing and smell the wine.

He crawled from bed as quietly as he could and made his way downstairs. The numbers had been rearranging themselves in his head, balancing, contrasting, screaming for his attention until he awoke.

Once he turned on the living room lights, he arranged the minutes table for Jessica's time away from home next to the inventory control charts for Luke's garage.

Scattergram: an *x/y* axis chart that would show the correlation inherent

in two recurring events, even if that correlation were improbable. Absurd.
Hidden.

Fan belts showed no correlation.

Nor air filters.

Nor oil sales.

Spark plugs did, a correlation coefficient of .92, close to perfect. Then a
T-test to be sure. As spark plug sales rose, Jessica's time away from home
lengthened; as they fell, so did her time away.

Spark plugs. And.

Bernie leaned casually against the office doorway, flipping the last spark
plug in the garage off his thumb, up in the air, and catching it. Replace
the spark plug with a 50-cent piece, Ronald thought, and he'd look like an
old-time con man.

Uncle Luke, on the other hand, was livid.

"What the hell do you mean you sent all the spark plugs back?"

Ronald shrugged and tried to ignore the feeling of a fist in his stomach.
"I had to send them, Luke. The whole shipment was defective."

Luke began pacing tight circles on the concrete floor, scratching furiously at his left armpit. "Well, Christ, Ronnie, how the hell do you know
they were all defective? You didn't test any of them. You wouldn't even
know how to put one in!"

Casual. Control. "They had some kind of, uh, goop. It was all over
them and they smelled like acid or burnt rust or something. Any idiot
could see they were useless."

Luke had stopped pacing and was shifting helplessly from one foot to
the other. "Aw, Christ, Ronnie. If we had extras in inventory there'd be
no problem."

Bernie broke in. "Boss, if you want me to go down and buy a load from
Mobil—"

Ronald gripped the arms of his chair.

"Jesus," Luke said. "Buy the goddamned things retail at triple markup?
All right, all right, but just one case. Christ, Ronnie, I hope like hell you
put a rush order on the new shipment."

Ronald resumed breathing—he'd just realized he'd stopped. A single
case would get Jessica home at 3:43. "Of course I ordered more, Luke.
Should be here in two days."

Luke winced, but seemed to be holding his temper. He turned around
to Bernie. "Get Harris to rearrange the schedule. Move up everything he

can that he knows needs sparks. Aw, Christ, customers are gonna be pissed." He shuffled out of the office, muttering.

Bernie flashed an overly composed smile from the doorway. "Stan!" he called over his shoulder, and Ronald swiveled his chair to face the door.

Stan lumbered over from the garage floor. "Yeah? What ya need?"

"Look," Bernie said, putting a hand on Stan's shoulder, "how about a little sales bet? Ten bucks says that in the next three days combined we sell less fan belts than just yesterday." With his other hand he continued to flip the spark plug.

Stan looked astonished at first, but then frowned. "You're suckering me again. What, did Ronnie tell you something about fan belts? I'm not stupid, Bernie."

Bernie exuded nonchalance, kept flipping the plug. "Hey, if you don't want to play—"

Stan grabbed the spark plug at Bernie's next flip. "Okay, pal, I'll play your game. But *my* rules this time. Not fan belts. Spark plugs."

Bernie did a flawless imitation of someone turning pale. "But, Stan—"

"No buts! Take the bet or I tell everybody you're a swindler." Bernie nodded weakly, and Stan left laughing.

Bernie leaned in the office and gave Ronald a wink. "Break down and join us at McCollough's, Ronnie. First drink's on me."

Ronald smiled. "No promises at all, Bernie. Tonight's a definite home night for me."

The number of butterflies in Beijing increased 3.24 percent. In Albany, eighty-seven telephone poles toppled.

"How was school?" He met her at the door. It was quarter to four in the afternoon.

She looked at him as she set a stack of papers on the kitchen table. "It was fine," she said, her voice wary.

"Anything fun happen?" He felt the confidence and spoke easily.

Jessica leaned with one hand on the kitchen table, the other hand in the pocket of her blue cardigan. "A few things, yes."

He walked from the sink and stood beside her, drying the dishwater from his hands with a towel. "So tell me some of them. I haven't heard a funny school story out of you in two months."

She took off her sweater and sat down slowly, never taking her eyes off him. "All right," she said, "I'll tell you one."

"Great," he said. "Do you want a cup of coffee?"

She didn't go out that evening.

After dinner she excused herself to the bedroom, and he heard the phone being dialed and her whispers. He smiled. The living room stereo was tuned to an easy-listening station. He turned the lights low and waited for her to come downstairs.

The next day there was still only Bernie's case of spark plugs at Luke's garage. He made dinner for her that night, a London broil, one of three dishes he knew how to prepare. They laughed when the cooking meat set off the smoke alarm. She stayed home.

"You really don't mind I'm a blue-collar worker?" he asked.

She unbuttoned his shirt and removed it from his shoulders. The collar, of course, came off with it.

The evening after, they went out for ice cream after supper and walked through Setterman's Park until sunset.

On the third day, the next shipment of spark plugs arrived.

He dashed from behind the dumpster to the brick retaining wall and fell, face forward, from the weight of the case of spark plugs. For a second all he could see were elusive, peripheral stars and the capital C of the Champion logo.

Last one, he thought. His breath came in barely audible squeaks. Last one.

He made the run to his car, popped the trunk, and heaved the case in. Twelve boxes, total.

"If you need spark plugs," Luke's voice said from behind him, "I'll just *give* you a goddamn set."

The little breathing squeaks all pulled together into a strained squawk of surprise, and every bit of energy and tension drained from Ronald's limbs. He felt like a puddle.

Luke strolled out from the far side of the retaining wall. He was there, Ronald thought. He was right there watching.

"They were bad!" Ronald yelled, and he realized he sounded just as guilty as he was. "They were just like the last shipment. I was going to drive them back myself and get some good ones because I knew how upset you were the last time"—while he was saying this, Luke had opened one of the boxes and removed a ring case of six perfectly healthy spark plugs—"and even though some of them look good they're all defective and won't make any sparks, so what good are they as spark plugs?"

Luke stared at him.

Ronald realized what he needed more than anything else in the world at this moment was some of Bernie's fast talk and charm.

"I'll buy them!" He pulled his wallet from his back pocket and began digging out credit cards. "See? MasterCard, Luke, and it has a $2000 limit with just $58.69 on it. I wasn't stealing them. We can ring up the sale right now. You can call the number and check. It only has $58.69 on it."

Luke pulled a case from the car trunk. "Don't wanna even talk about it," he said, then walked back toward the garage.

Ronald sank down against the car, crouched on his heels with his back against the bumper. He buried his face in the sleeve of the arm set across his knees. With the other arm he still held out the MasterCard.

When he arrived home at 6:26, Ronald wasn't at all surprised not to find Jessica waiting, not to find any note saying where she had gone. He poured himself a scotch and water and sat on the living room sofa, his feet up on the coffee table.

Due to overtime work at NASA, the consumption of wrapped sandwiches rose 14 percent. Three junks sank off Taiwan.

After a second scotch and water, Ronald said, aloud, "It's not my fault. How the hell am I supposed to keep a service station from selling spark plugs?"

After a third glass, he shouted, "It *is* my fault! It's all my fault! I shouldn't have lost the position with Resotech. I *couldn't* have lost it!"

He went for a fourth drink, but the scotch bottle was nearly empty. He poured what little was left and held the glass up to the cove light over the kitchen sink. "That's about one-eighth," he said. "Yeah, definitely one-eighth." He finished it with a swallow and grabbed his car keys.

Bernie'd won seventeen bets with Ronald's help. Little twerp owed him seventeen beers. Eight ounces a glass, one hundred and thirty-six ounces. One point eight repeating six-packs. One point zero six two five gallons of beer.

He started the car. Two point four miles to McCollough's Pub.

He parked on the street outside the bar; the parking lot was filled from the Friday-night crowds. The bouncer stared at him when he walked in, so Ronald tried to stand straight and walk evenly. He had to elbow his way through the crowd. My God, he thought, there must be a hundred and eighteen people in here. Rock music blared over the sound system, and Ronald had to pause and close his eyes every few steps through the crowd. His head throbbed. He looked around, trying to spot Bernie, and finally ran into Stan at the bar. The mechanic was staring into his beer mug, apparently fascinated by watching the bubbles in the beer head popping their way down to the liquid.

"Hey, Stan," he said, poking the man's shoulder. "Where's Bernie? He owes me some beers."

Stan glanced over, looking a bit dazed from the break in concentration. "Oh, hi, Ronnie." Then he turned his entire body toward Ronald. "Ronnie? Ronnie!" Stan threw his arms around Ronald in a bear hug, and Ronald felt his breath pressed out of his lungs. Stan was laughing wildly.

"I win! I finally won! That little twerp bastard finally loses one. Ronnie, it's nice as *hell* to see you!"

Ronald struggled for a breath and tried to keep his balance, a combination he realized the scotch was making difficult. "It's, uh, nice to see you too, Stan."

Stan put a hand to his head and kept laughing, although he suddenly seemed embarrassed. "I'm sorry, Ronnie. It's just Bernie bet me thirty bucks that he could invite you to McCollough's twenty times in a row and you'd never show. He's only asked you seventeen times, and here you fucking *are.*"

Stan hugged him again, and Ronald felt nauseous from the thick air, the noise, and the press of the crowd. "C'mon," Stan said, "they got a table near the back. I'm gonna show you off and win my prize. I can't wait to see the twerp's face."

Bernie's face, Ronald saw, did not let Stan down. When he and Stan reached the back table, Stan tapped Bernie on the shoulder, and when Bernie turned he dropped his beer mug halfway through the motion of sipping from it. But his face was nothing like Jessica's, whose hand Bernie was holding across the table. Her eyes went wide and empty.

Ronald wasn't sure what his own face was showing, but it must have been something impressive. Stan took him by the arm and said, "Hey, what the hell's wrong with you, Ronnie?"

"My wife."

Stan looked at Jessica, then at Bernie, his face slowly changing. "Oh, shit," he said. "Bernie, you're fucking scum. Oh, shit, Ronnie."

Bernie was suddenly very busy. To Ronald, he sputtered, "No lie, she's your *wife?* I just met her tonight. Just met her." To Stan he said, "Hey, I owe you money, don't I? We can go to the bar and have them cash a fifty." He finally seemed to realize he was still holding Jessica's hand, and pulled back as if he had touched a hot plate. Quieter, but not so quiet that Ronald couldn't hear him, he said, "Jessica, there's no way he could have shown up here. *There's no way.*"

Stan lifted Bernie from the chair by his shirt collar. His *blue* shirt collar. "I'm sorry Ronnie, I didn't know. The twerp hit on her weeks ago when she wandered in alone. He's been meeting her here ever since. I didn't know she was your wife." He dragged Bernie off in the direction of the bar.

Too much at once, Ronald thought. Too many variables. Then he felt the anger swelling in him, and he wasn't sure where it should go or who deserved it most.

Jessica had lowered her head. "I needed to see him one last time, Ronald." She was stirring her mixed drink with a swizzle stick, slow circles, the ice clanking against the glass. "I don't know why I came. I guess I was breaking it off."

All of the anger finally came to a head as Ronald watched the swizzle stick stirring even, gentle circles in her glass. He inhaled slowly. "You . . . goddammit, you're out of control."

He saw her shake, and the swizzle stick fell from her fingers. She looked up, her mouth open again. He had hurt her; it felt good, very good.

"Bernie?" Ronald said. *"Bernie?* A mechanic? You cheat on me with a blue-collar worker?"

"Jesus, Ronald, your obsession with collars and status. With numbers. With variables." She wasn't looking at him now. "Bernie gave me attention. That's the only way he's different from you."

"I thought I understood you," he said, and now he saw her tears starting. He walked away, out of the bar.

He'd done everything he possibly could. Everything. What else could be done? Nothing. He drove, still blurry from the scotch, into the unlit parking lot of Luke's service station. He put the car in park, took the keys out of the ignition, each action dragging like a tread through dead water. "I've done *everything!*" he shouted when he climbed from the car.

He tried the door first before he kicked it in. Inside was solid blackness, but the layout was simple geometric shapes in his memory. He had no idea where a hammer would be, but found an exhaust pipe in the muffler inventory.

He felt his way along the wall to where the spark plugs were stored and began beating the exhaust pipe against the cases. "I've done everything!" he shouted as the pipe tore the boxes apart. "Everything!" Two of the cases ripped open. Spark plug ring holders scattered on the next hit, and he continued to beat them into the floor, sparks from metal striking metal shooting out with each swing.

Ten cases. Eleven. Twelve.

The garage filled with the swirling red and white of police rollers outside the front window, and the lights came on. "Put down the pipe!" a voice shouted, but Ronald kept swinging until two sets of arms grabbed him and pinned him to the floor. He kicked and tried to twist out of their hold; there was a third grip, and he felt the clamp of metal on his wrists.

"This guy's out of his head!" one of the voices said. "Jesus, get him under control!"

A question burned away the haze of his hangover. Had he gotten all the plugs? It seemed he had been able to wreck most of them. Yes, all of them, in fact.

It took time for Ronald to manage the six feet from the cell bunk to the bars. "Hey," he called to the officer at the desk across from the lockup. "Hey!"

The officer put down the newspaper he was reading and rose from his desk. He walked slowly over to the bars, carrying a sandwich and coffee. "Yeah?" he asked, taking a bite from the sandwich. Ronald's stomach was queasy.

"Do I get a phone call?"

The officer shrugged. "You should dry out first, buddy."

"Please," Ronald said. He pressed his face against the bars. "I've got to call home. What time is it?"

The officer unlatched the barred door. "It's almost four in the morning," he said. "You better have a real understanding family. Don't get your hopes up about being bailed. I'm supposed to keep you until the evaluation."

"Evaluation?"

"Yeah, you know." The officer traced circles around his temple with one finger and whistled coo-coo sounds. "The boys from the mind-farm gotta find out if you're safe to let out on the streets." He led Ronald by the elbow over to a pay phone bolted to the gray concrete wall of the station office. He tossed Ronald a quarter.

Ronald dialed the house. On the seventh ring, he glanced behind him at the officer. "She's asleep," Ronald said. "It will take her a while to get to the phone." The officer stared like stone over the top of his newspaper.

On the thirteenth ring, Ronald glanced back again and tried to laugh. "It's sixty-two feet from the sofa to the upstairs phone. If she's asleep on the sofa she'll need to walk all the way up there."

Nineteen rings. "She isn't there, fella."

"She has to be!" Ronald said. He took hold of the receiver with both hands and leaned the back of his head against the wall. "I got them all," he said, "I ruined every last case. Luke could never sell them now. They were the variable. Everything is under control." The officer rolled his eyes and repeated his coo-coo whistle.

Twenty rings. Twenty-seven. Thirty-three.

The officer came over and took the receiver from his hands. He let Ronald stay there, back to the wall, and returned to his newspaper.

Not a stable variable, Ronald thought. She should have been home. Not a constant, because he had destroyed the plugs. That meant the influence had changed, had somehow moved on. A random variable? One that could alter its cause but retain its effect? Even if that were true, he could find it, the way he had found the spark plugs. He *would* find it—

The rustle of the newspaper caught Ronald's attention. The police officer's thumb gripped the page just below a 45-cent coupon for Maxwell House coffee.

For S. L. Spotts

Division by Zero

TED CHIANG

D
1
IVIDING A NUMBER BY ZERO doesn't produce an infinitely large number as an answer. The reason is that division is defined as the inverse of multiplication; if you divide by zero, and then multiply by zero, you should regain the number you started with. However, multiplying infinity by zero produces only zero, not any other number. There is nothing that can be multiplied by zero to produce a nonzero result; therefore, the result of a division by zero is literally "undefined."

• • • •

1a

Renee was looking out the window when Mrs. Rivas approached.

"Leaving after only a week? Hardly a real stay at all. Lord knows I won't be leaving for a long time."

Renee forced a polite smile. "I'm sure it won't be long for you." Mrs. Rivas was the manipulator in the ward; everyone knew that her attempts were merely gestures, but the aides wearily paid attention to her lest she succeed accidentally.

"Ha. They wish I'd leave. You know what kind of liability they face if you die while you're on status?"

"Yes, I know."

"That's all they're worried about, you can tell. Always their liability—"

Renee tuned out and returned her attention to the window, watching a contrail extrude itself across the sky.

"Mrs. Norwood?" a nurse called. "Your husband's here."

Renee gave Mrs. Rivas another polite smile and left.

1b

Carl signed his name yet another time, and finally the nurses took away the forms for processing.

He remembered when he had brought Renee in to be admitted, and thought of all the stock questions at the first interview. He had answered them all stoically.

"Yes, she's a professor of mathematics. You can find her in *Who's Who*."

"No, I'm in biology."

And:

"I had left behind a box of slides that I needed."

"No, she couldn't have known."

And, just as expected:

"Yes, I have. It was about twenty years ago, when I was a grad student."

"No, I tried jumping."

"No, Renee and I didn't know each other then."

And on and on.

Now they were convinced that he was competent and supportive, and were ready to release Renee on an outpatient treatment program.

Looking back, Carl was surprised in an abstracted way. Except for one moment, there hadn't been any sense of *déjà vu* at any time during the entire ordeal. All the time he was dealing with the hospital, the doctors, the nurses: the only accompanying sensation was one of numbness, of sheer tedious rote.

2

There is a well-known proof that demonstrates that one equals two. It begins with some definitions: Let $a = 1$; let $b = 1$. It ends with the conclusion $a = 2a$, that is, one equals two. Hidden inconspicuously in the middle is a division by zero, and at that point the proof has stepped off the brink, making all rules null and void. Permitting division by zero allows one to prove not only that one and two are equal, but that any two numbers at all—real or imaginary, rational or irrational—are equal.

2a

As soon as she and Carl got home, Renee went to the desk in her study and began turning all the papers face down, blindly sweeping them together into a pile; she winced whenever a corner of a page faced up during her shuffling. She considered burning the pages, but that would be merely symbolic now. She'd accomplish as much by simply never glancing at them.

The doctors would probably describe it as obsessive behavior. Renee frowned, reminded of the indignity of being a patient under such fools. She remembered being on suicide status, in the locked ward, under the supposedly round-the-clock observation of the aides. And the interviews with the doctors, who were so condescending, so obvious. She was no manipulator like Mrs. Rivas, but it really was easy. Simply say "I realize I'm not well yet, but I do feel better," and you'd be considered almost ready for release.

2b

Carl watched Renee from the doorway for a moment, before he passed down the hallway. He remembered the day, fully two decades past, when he himself had been released. His parents had picked him up, and on the trip back his mother had made some inane comment about how glad everyone would be to see him, and he was just barely able to restrain himself from shaking her arm off his shoulders.

He had done for Renee what he would have appreciated during his period under observation. He had come to visit every day, even though she refused to see him at first, so that he wouldn't be absent when she did want to see him. Sometimes they talked, and sometimes they simply walked around the grounds. He could find nothing wrong in what he did, and he knew that she appreciated it.

Yet, despite all his efforts, he felt no more than a sense of duty toward her.

3

In the *Principia Mathematica,* Bertrand Russell and Alfred North Whitehead attempted to give a rigorous foundation to mathematics, using formal logic as their basis. They began with what they considered to be axioms, and used those to derive theorems of increasing complexity. By page 362, they have established enough to prove $1 + 1 = 2$.

3a

As a child of seven, while investigating the house of a relative, Renee had been spellbound at discovering the perfect squares in the smooth marble tiles of the floor. A single one, two rows of two, three rows of three, four rows of four: the tiles fit together in a *square.* Of course. No matter which side you looked at it from, it came out the same. And more than that, each square was bigger than the last by an *odd number of tiles.* It was an epiphany. The conclusion was necessary: it had a rightness to it, confirmed by the smooth, cool feel of the tiles. And the way the tiles were fitted together, with such incredibly fine lines where they met. She had shivered at the precision.

Later on there came other realizations, other achievements. The astonishing doctoral dissertation at twenty-three, the series of acclaimed papers; people compared her to von Neumann, universities wooed her. She had never paid any of it much attention. What she did pay attention to was that same sense of rightness, possessed by every theorem she learned, as insistent as the tiles' physicality, and as exact as their fit.

3b

Carl felt that the person he was today was born after his attempt, when he met Laura. After being released from the hospital, he was in no mood to see anyone, but a friend of his had managed to introduce him to Laura. He had pushed her away initially, but she had known better. She had loved him while he was hurting, and let him go once he was healed. Through knowing her, Carl had learned about empathy, and he was remade.

Laura had moved on after getting her own master's degree, while he stayed at the university for his doctorate in biology. He suffered various crises and heartbreaks later on in life, but never again despair.

Carl marveled when he thought about what kind of person she was. He hadn't spoken to her since grad school; what had her life been like over the years? He wondered who else she had loved. Early on he had recognized what kind of love it was, and what kind it wasn't, and he valued it immensely.

4

In the early nineteenth century, mathematicians began exploring geometries that differed from Euclidean geometry; these alternate geometries produced results that seemed utterly absurd, but they didn't produce logical contradictions. It was later shown that these non-Euclidean geometries were consistent relative to Euclidean geometry: they were logically consistent, as long as one assumed that Euclidean geometry was consistent.

The proof of Euclidean geometry's consistency eluded mathematicians. By the end of the nineteenth century, the best that was achieved was a proof that Euclidean geometry was consistent as long as arithmetic was consistent.

4a

At the time, when it all began, Renee had thought it little more than an annoyance. She had walked down the hall and knocked on the open door of Peter Fabrisi's office. "Pete, got a minute?"

Fabrisi pushed his chair back from his desk. "Sure, Renee, what's up?"

Renee came in, knowing what his reaction would be. She had never asked anyone in the department for advice on a problem before; it had always been the reverse. No matter. "I was wondering if you could do me a favor. You remember what I was telling you about a couple weeks back, about the system of notation I was developing?"

He nodded. "The one you were rewriting axiom systems with."

"Right. Well, a few days ago I started coming up with really ridiculous conclusions, and now my notation is contradicting itself. Could you take a look at it?"

Fabrisi's expression was as expected. "You want— sure, I'd be glad to."

"Great. The examples on the first few pages are where the problem is; the rest is just for your reference." She handed Fabrisi a thin sheaf of papers. "I thought if I talked you through it, you'd just see the same things I do."

"You're probably right." Fabrisi looked at the first couple of pages. "I don't know how long this'll take."

"No hurry. When you get a chance, just see whether any of my assumptions seem a little dubious, anything like that. I'll still be going at it, so I'll tell you if I come up with anything. Okay?"

Fabrisi smiled. "You're just going to come in this afternoon and tell me you've found the problem."

"I doubt it: this calls for a fresh eye."

He spread his hands. "I'll give it a shot."

"Thanks." It was unlikely that Fabrisi would fully grasp her notation, but all she needed was someone who could check its more mechanical aspects.

4b

Carl had met Renee at a party given by a colleague of his. He had been taken with her face. Hers was a remarkably plain face, and it appeared quite somber most of the time, but during the party he saw her smile twice and frown once; at those moments, her entire countenance assumed the expression as if it had never known another. Carl had been caught by surprise: he could recognize a face that smiled regularly, or a face that frowned regularly, even if it were unlined. He was curious as to how her face had developed such a close familiarity with so many expressions, and yet normally revealed nothing.

It took a long time for him to understand Renee, to read her expressions. But it had definitely been worthwhile.

Now Carl sat in his easy chair in his study, a copy of the latest issue of *Marine Biology* in his lap, and listened to the sound of Renee crumpling paper in her study across the hall. She'd been working all evening, with audibly increasing frustration, though she'd been wearing her customary poker face when last he'd looked in.

He put the journal aside, got up from the chair and walked over to the entrance of her study. She had a volume opened on her desk; the pages were filled with the usual hieroglyphic equations, interspersed with commentary in Russian.

She scanned some of the material, dismissed it with a barely perceptible frown, and slammed the volume closed. Carl heard her mutter the word "useless," and she returned the tome to the bookcase.

"You're gonna give yourself high blood pressure if you keep up like this," Carl jested.

"Don't patronize me."

Carl was startled. "I wasn't."

Renee turned to look at him and glared. "I know when I'm capable of working productively and when I'm not."

Chilled. "Then I won't bother you." He retreated.

"Thank you." She returned her attention to the bookshelves. Carl left, trying to decipher that glare.

5

At the Second International Congress of Mathematics in 1900, David Hilbert listed what he considered to be the twenty-three most important unsolved problems of mathematics. The second item on his list was a request for a proof of the consistency of arithmetic. Such a proof would ensure the consistency of a great deal of higher mathematics. What this proof had to guarantee was, in essence, that one could never prove one equals two. Few mathematicians regarded this as a matter of much import.

5a

Renee had known what Fabrisi would say before he opened his mouth.

"That was the damnedest thing I've ever seen. You know that toy for toddlers where you fit blocks with different cross sections into the differently shaped slots? Reading your formal system is like watching someone take one block and slide it into every single hole on the board, and make it a perfect fit every time."

"So you can't find the error?"

He shook his head. "Not me. I've slipped into the same rut as you, I can only think about it one way."

Renee was no longer in a rut: she had come up with a totally different approach to the question, but it only confirmed the original contradiction. "Well, thanks for trying."

"You going to have someone else take a look at it?"

"Yes, I think I'll send it to Callahan over at Berkeley. We've been corresponding since the conference last spring."

Fabrisi nodded. "I was really impressed by his last paper. Let me know if he can find it: I'm curious."

Renee would have used a stronger word than "curious" for herself.

5b

Was Renee just frustrated with her work? Carl knew that she had never considered mathematics really difficult, just intellectually challenging.

Could it be that for the first time she was running into problems that she could make no headway against? Or did mathematics work that way at all? Carl himself was strictly an experimentalist; he really didn't know how Renee made new math. It sounded silly, but perhaps she was running out of ideas?

Renee was too old to be suffering from the disillusionment of a child prodigy becoming an average adult. On the other hand, many mathematicians did their best work before the age of thirty, and she might be growing anxious over whether that statistic was catching up to her, albeit several years behind schedule.

It seemed unlikely. He gave a few other possibilities cursory consideration. Could she be growing cynical about academia? Dismayed that her research had become overspecialized? Or simply weary of her work?

Carl didn't believe that such anxieties were the cause of Renee's behavior; he could imagine the impressions that he would pick up if that were the case, and they didn't mesh with what he was receiving. Whatever was bothering Renee, it was something he couldn't fathom, and that disturbed him.

6

In 1931, Kurt Gödel demonstrated two theorems. The first one shows, in effect, that mathematics contains statements that may be true, but are inherently unprovable. Even a formal system as simple as arithmetic permits statements that are precise, meaningful, and seem certainly true, and yet cannot be proven true by formal means.

His second theorem shows that a claim of the consistency of arithmetic is just such a statement; it cannot be proven true by any means using the axioms of arithmetic. That is, arithmetic as a formal system cannot guarantee that it will not produce results such as $1 = 2$; such contradictions may never have been encountered, but it is impossible to prove that they never will be.

6a

Once again, he had come into her study. Renee looked up from her desk at Carl; he began resolutely, "Renee, it's obvious that—"

She cut him off. "You want to know what's bothering me? Okay, I'll tell you." Renee got out a blank sheet of paper and sat down at her desk. "Hang on; this'll take a minute." Carl opened his mouth again, but Renee waved him silent. She took a deep breath and began writing.

She drew a line down the center of the page, dividing it into two columns. At the head of one column she wrote the numeral "1" and for the other she wrote "2." Below them she rapidly scrawled out some symbols, and in the lines below those she expanded them into strings of other symbols. She gritted her teeth as she wrote: forming the characters felt like dragging her fingernails across a chalkboard.

About two-thirds of the way down the page, Renee began reducing the long strings of symbols into successively shorter strings. *And now for the master stroke*, she thought. She realized she was pressing hard on the paper; she consciously relaxed her grip on the pencil. On the next line that she put down, the strings became identical. She wrote an emphatic "=" across the center line at the bottom of the page.

She handed the sheet to Carl. He looked at her, indicating incomprehension. "Look at the top." He did so. "Now look at the bottom."

He frowned. "I don't understand."

"I've found a notation that lets you equate any number with any other number. That page there proves that one and two are equal. Pick any two numbers you like; I can prove those equal as well."

Carl seemed to be trying to remember something. "It's a division by zero, right?"

"No. There are no illegal operations, no poorly defined terms, no independent axioms that are implicitly assumed, nothing. The proof employs absolutely nothing that's forbidden."

Carl shook his head. "Wait a minute. Obviously one and two aren't the same."

"But formally they are: the proof's in your hand. Everything I've used is within what's accepted as absolutely indisputable."

"But you've got a contradiction here."

"That's right. Arithmetic as a formal system is inconsistent."

6b

"You can't find your mistake, is that what you mean?"

"*No*, you're not listening. You think I'm just frustrated because of something like that? There is no mistake in the proof."

"You're saying there's something wrong within what's accepted?"

"Exactly."

"Are you—" He stopped, but too late. She glared at him. Of course she was sure. He thought about what she was implying.

"Do you see?" asked Renee. "I've just disproved most of mathematics: it's all meaningless now."

She was getting agitated, almost distraught; Carl chose his words carefully. "How can you say that? Math still works. The scientific and economic worlds aren't suddenly going to collapse from this realization."

"That's because the mathematics they're using is just a gimmick. It's a mnemonic trick, like counting on your knuckles to figure out which months have thirty-one days."

"That's not the same."

"Why isn't it? Now mathematics has absolutely *nothing* to do with reality. Never mind concepts like imaginaries or infinitesimals. Now goddamn integer addition has nothing to do with counting on your fingers. One and one will always get you two on your fingers, but on paper I can give you an infinite number of answers, and they're all equally valid, which means they're all equally invalid. I can write the most elegant theorem you've ever seen, and it won't mean any more than a nonsense equation." She gave a bitter laugh. "The positivists used to say all mathematics is a tautology. They had it all wrong: it's a contradiction."

Carl tried a different approach. "Hold on. You just mentioned imaginary numbers. Why is this any worse than what went on with those? Mathematicians once believed they were meaningless, but now they're accepted as basic. This is the same situation."

"It's *not* the same. The solution there was to simply expand the context, and that won't do any good here. Imaginary numbers added something new to mathematics, but my notation is redefining what's already there."

"But if you change the context, put it in a different light—"

She rolled her eyes. "No! This follows from the axioms as surely as addition does; there's no way around it. You can take my word for it."

7

In 1936, Gerhard Gentzen provided a proof of the consistency of arithmetic, but to do it he needed to use a controversial technique known as transfinite induction. This technique is not among the usual methods of proof, and it hardly seemed appropriate for guaranteeing the consistency of arithmetic. What Gentzen had done was prove the obvious by assuming the doubtful.

7a

Callahan had called from Berkeley, but could offer no rescue. He said he would continue to examine her work, but it seemed that she had hit upon something fundamental and disturbing. He wanted to know about her plans for publication of her system of notation, because if it did contain an error that neither of them could find, others in the mathematics community would surely be able to.

Renee had barely been able to hear him speaking, and mumbled that she would get back to him. Lately she had been having difficulty talking to people, especially since the argument with Carl; the other members of the department had taken to avoiding her. Her concentration was gone, and last night she had had a nightmare about discovering a notation that let her translate arbitrary concepts into mathematical expressions. Then she had proven that life and death were equivalent.

That was something that frightened her: the possibility that she was losing her mind. She was certainly losing her clarity of thought, and that came pretty close.

What a ridiculous woman you are, she chided herself. Was Gödel suicidal after he demonstrated his incompleteness theorem?

But that was beautiful, numinous, one of the most elegant theorems Renee had ever seen.

Her own proof taunted her, ridiculed her. Like a brainteaser in a puzzle book, it said gotcha, you skipped right over the mistake, see if you can find where you screwed up; only to turn around and say, gotcha again.

She imagined Callahan would be pondering the implications that her discovery held for mathematics. So much of mathematics had no practical application; it existed solely as a formal theory, studied for its intellectual beauty. But that couldn't last; a self-contradictory theory was so pointless that most mathematicians would drop it in disgust.

What truly infuriated Renee was the way her own intuition had betrayed her. The damned theorem made sense; in its own perverted way, it *felt right*. She understood it, knew why it was true, believed it.

7b

Carl smiled when he thought of her birthday.

"I can't believe you! How could you possibly have known?" She had run down the stairs, holding the sweater in her hands.

Last summer they had been in Scotland on vacation, and in one store in Edinburgh there had been a sweater that Renee had been eyeing but didn't buy. He had ordered it, and placed it in her dresser drawer for her to find that morning.

"You're just so transparent," he had teased her. They both knew that wasn't true, but he liked to tell her that.

That was two months ago. A scant two months.

Now the situation called for a change of pace. Carl went into her study, and found Renee sitting in her chair, staring out the window. "Guess what I got for us."

She looked up. "What?"

"Reservations for the weekend. A suite at the Biltmore. We can relax and do absolutely nothing—"

"Please stop," Renee said. "I know what you're trying to do, Carl. You want us to do something pleasant and distracting to take my mind off this notation. But it won't work. You don't know what kind of hold this has on me."

"Come on, come on." He tugged at her hands to get her off the chair, but she pulled away. Carl stood there for a moment, when suddenly she turned and locked eyes with him.

"You know I've been tempted to take barbiturates? I almost wish I were an idiot, so I wouldn't have to think about it."

He was taken aback. Uncertain of his bearings, he said, "Why won't you at least try to get away for a while? It couldn't hurt, and maybe it'll take your mind off this."

"It's not anything I can take my mind off of. You just don't understand."

"So explain it to me."

Renee exhaled and turned away to think for a moment. "It's like everything I see is shouting the contradiction at me," she said. "I'm equating numbers all the time now."

Carl was silent. Then, with sudden comprehension, he said, "Like the classical physicists facing quantum mechanics. As if a theory you've always believed has been superseded, and the new one makes no sense, but somehow all the evidence supports it."

"No, it's not like that at all." Her dismissal was almost contemptuous. "This has nothing to do with evidence; it's all *a priori.*"

"How is that different? Isn't it just the evidence of your reasoning then?"

"Christ, are you joking? It's the difference between my measuring one and two to have the same value, and my intuiting it. I can't maintain the concept of distinct quantities in my mind anymore; they all feel the same to me."

"You don't mean that," he said. "No one could actually experience such a thing; it's like believing six impossible things before breakfast."

"How would you know what I can experience?"

"I'm trying to understand."

"Don't bother."

Carl's patience was gone. "All right then." He walked out of the room and canceled their reservations.

They scarcely spoke after that, talking only when necessary. It was three days later that Carl forgot the box of slides he needed, and drove back to the house, and found her note on the table.

Carl intuited two things in the moments following. The first came to him as he was racing through the house, wondering if she had gotten some cyanide from the chemistry department: it was the realization that, because he couldn't understand what had brought her to such an action, he couldn't feel anything for her.

The second intuition came to him as he was pounding on the bedroom door, yelling at her inside: he experienced *déjà vu*. It was the only time the situation would feel familiar, and yet it was grotesquely reversed. He remembered being on the other side of a locked door, on the roof of a building, hearing a friend pounding on the door and yelling for him not to do it. And as he stood there outside the bedroom door, he could hear her sobbing, on the floor paralyzed with shame, exactly the same as he had been when it was him on the other side.

8

Hilbert once said, "If mathematical thinking is defective, where are we to find truth and certitude?"

8a

Would her suicide attempt brand her for the rest of her life, Renee wondered. She aligned the corners of the papers on her desk. Would people henceforth regard her, perhaps unconsciously, as flighty or unstable? She had never asked Carl if he had ever felt such anxieties, perhaps because she never held his attempt against him. It had happened many years ago, and anyone seeing him now would immediately recognize him as a whole person.

But Renee could not say the same for herself. Right now she was unable to discuss mathematics intelligibly, and she was unsure whether she ever could again. Were her colleagues to see her now, they would simply say, she's lost the knack.

Finished at her desk, Renee left her study and walked into the living room. After her system of notation circulated through the academic community, it would require an overhaul of established mathematical foundations, but it would affect only a few as it had her. Most would be like Fabrisi; they would follow the proof mechanically, and be convinced by it, but no more. The only persons who would feel it nearly as keenly as she had were those who could actually grasp the contradiction, who could intuit it. Callahan was one of those; she wondered how he was handling it as the days wore on.

Renee traced a curly pattern in the dust on an end table. Before, she might have idly parameterized the curve, examined some of its characteristics. Now there seemed no point. All of her visualizations simply collapsed.

She, like many, had always thought that mathematics did not derive its meaning from the universe, but rather imposed some meaning onto the universe. Physical entities were not greater or less than one another, not similar or dissimilar; they simply *were*, they existed. Mathematics was totally independent, but it virtually provided a semantic meaning for those entities, supplying categories and relationships. It didn't describe any intrinsic quality, merely a possible interpretation.

But no more. Mathematics was inconsistent once it was removed from physical entities, and a formal theory was nothing if not consistent. Math was *empirical*, no more than that, and it held no interest for her.

What would she turn to now? Renee had known someone who gave up academia to sell handmade leather goods. She would have to take some time, regain her bearings. And that was just what Carl had been trying to help her do, throughout it all.

8b

Among Carl's friends were a pair of women who were each other's best friend, Marlene and Anne. Years ago, when Marlene had considered suicide, she hadn't turned to Anne for support: she had turned to Carl. He and Marlene had sat up all night on a few occasions, talking or sharing silence. Carl knew that Anne had always harbored a bit of envy for what he had shared with Marlene, that she had always wondered what advantage he held that allowed him to get so close to her. The answer was simple. It was the difference between sympathy and empathy.

Carl had offered comfort in similar situations more than once in his lifetime. He had been glad he could help, certainly, but more than that, it had felt right to sit in the other seat, and play the other part.

He had always had reason to consider compassion a basic part of his character, until now. He had valued that, felt that he was nothing if not empathic. But now he'd run up against something he'd never encountered before, and it rendered all his usual instincts null and void.

If someone had told him on Renee's birthday that he would feel this way in two months' time, he would have dismissed the idea instantly. Certainly such a thing could happen over years; Carl knew what time could do. But two months?

After six years of marriage, he had fallen out of love with her. Carl detested himself for the thought, but the fact was that she had changed, and now he neither understood her nor knew how to feel for her. Renee's intellectual and emotional lives were inextricably linked, so that the latter had moved beyond his reach.

His reflex reaction of forgiveness cut in, reasoning that you couldn't ask a person to remain supportive through any crisis. If a man's wife were suddenly afflicted with mental illness, it would be a sin for him to leave her, but a forgivable one. To stay would mean accepting a different kind of relationship, something which not everyone was cut out for, and Carl never condemned a person in such a situation. But there was always the unspoken question: what would I do? And his answer had always been, I would stay.

Hypocrite.

Worst of all, he had been there. He had been absorbed in his own pain, he had tried the endurance of others, and someone had nursed him through it all. His leaving Renee was inevitable, but it would be a sin he couldn't forgive.

9

Albert Einstein once said, "Insofar as the propositions of mathematics give an account of reality they are not certain; and insofar as they are certain they do not describe reality."

$9a = 9b$

Carl was in the kitchen, stringing snow pea pods for dinner, when Renee came in. "Can I talk to you for a minute?"

"Sure." They sat down at the table. She looked studiedly out the window: her habit when beginning a serious conversation. He suddenly dreaded what she was about to say. He hadn't planned to tell her that he was leaving until she'd fully recovered, after a couple of months. Now was too soon.

"I know it hasn't been obvious—"

No, he prayed, don't say it. Please don't.

"—but I'm really grateful to have you here with me."

Pierced, Carl closed his eyes, but thankfully Renee was still looking out the window. It was going to be so, so difficult.

She was still talking. "The things that have been going on in my head—" She paused. "It was like nothing I'd ever imagined. If it had been any normal kind of depression, I know you would have understood, and we could have handled it."

Carl nodded.

"But what happened, it was almost as if I were a theologian proving that there was no God. Not just fearing it, but knowing it for a fact. Does that sound absurd?"

"No."

"It's a feeling I can't convey to you. It was something that I believed deeply, implicitly, and it's not true, and I'm the one who demonstrated it."

He opened his mouth to say that he knew exactly what she meant, that he was feeling the same things as she. But he stopped himself: for this was an empathy that separated rather than united them, and he couldn't tell her that.

Matter's End

GREGORY BENFORD

When Dr. Samuel Johnson felt himself getting tied up in an argument over Bishop Berkeley's ingenious sophistry to prove the nonexistence of matter, and that everything in the universe is merely ideal, he kicked a large stone and answered, "I refute it thus." Just what that action assured him of is not very obvious, but apparently he found it comforting.

—Sir Arthur Eddington

INDIA CAME TO HIM first as a breeze like soured buttermilk, rich yet tainted. A door banged somewhere, sending gusts sweeping through the Bangalore airport, slicing through the 4 A.M. silences.

Since the Free State of Bombay had left India, Bangalore had become an international airport. Yet the damp caress seemed to erase the sterile signatures that made all big airports alike, even giving a stippled texture to the cool enamel glow of the fluorescents.

The moist air clasped Robert Clay like a stranger's sweaty palm. The ripe, fleshy aroma of a continent enfolded him, swarming up his nostrils and soaking his lungs with sullen spice. He put down his carry-on bag and showed the immigration clerk his passport. The man gave him a piercing, ferocious stare—then mutely slammed a rubber stamp onto the pages and handed it back.

A hand snagged him as he headed toward baggage claim.

"Professor Clay?" The face was dark olive with intelligent eyes riding above sharp cheekbones. A sudden white grin flashed as Clay nodded. "Ah, *good*. I am Dr. Sudarshan Patil. Please come this way."

Dr. Patil's tone was polite, but his hands impatiently pulled Clay away from the sluggish lines, through a battered wooden side door. The heavy-lidded immigration guards were carefully looking in other directions, hands held behind their backs. Apparently they had been paid off and would ignore this odd exit. Clay was still groggy from trying to sleep on the flight from London. He shook his head as Patil led him into the gloom of a baggage storeroom.

"Your clothes," Patil said abruptly.

"What?"

"They mark you as a Westerner. Quickly!"

Patil's hands, light as birds in the quilted soft light, were already plucking at his coat, his shirt. Clay was taken aback at this abruptness. He hesitated, then struggled out of the dirty garments, pulling his loose slacks down over his shoes. He handed his bundled clothes to Patil, who snatched them away without a word.

"You're welcome," Clay said. Patil took no notice, just thrust a wad of tan cotton at him. The man's eyes jumped at each distant sound in the storage room, darting, suspecting every pile of dusty bags.

Clay struggled into the pants and rough shirt. They looked dingy in the wan yellow glow of a single distant fluorescent tube.

"Not the reception I'd expected," Clay said, straightening the baggy pants and pulling at the rough drawstring.

"These are not good times for scientists in my country, Dr. Clay," Patil said bitingly. His voice carried that odd lilt that echoed both the Raj and Cambridge.

"Who're you afraid of?"

"Those who hate Westerners and their science."

"They said in Washington—"

"We are about great matters, Professor Clay. Please cooperate, please."

Patil's lean face showed its bones starkly, as though energies pressed outward. Promontories of bunched muscle stretched a mottled canvas skin. He started toward a far door without another word, carrying Clay's overnight bag and jacket.

"Say, where're we—"

Patil swung open a sheet-metal door and beckoned. Clay slipped through it and into the moist wealth of night. His feet scraped on a dirty sidewalk beside a black tar road. The door hinge squealed behind them, attracting the attention of a knot of men beneath a vibrant yellow streetlight nearby.

The bleached fluorescence of the airport terminal was now a continent away. Beneath a line of quarter-ton trucks huddled figures slept. In the astringent street-lamp glow he saw a decrepit green Korean Tochat van parked at the curb.

"In!" Patil whispered.

The men under the streetlight started walking toward them, calling out hoarse questions.

Clay yanked open the van's sliding door and crawled into the second row of seats. A fog of unknown pungent smells engulfed him. The driver, a short man, hunched over the wheel. Patil sprang into the front seat and the van ground away, its low gear whining.

Shouts. A stone thumped against the van roof. Pebbles rattled at the back.

They accelerated, the engine clattering. A figure loomed up from the shifting shadows and flung muck against the window near Clay's face. He jerked back at the slap of it. "Damn!"

They plowed through a wide puddle of dirty rainwater. The engine sputtered and for a moment Clay was sure it would die. He looked out the rear window and saw vague forms running after them. Then the engine surged again and they shot away.

They went two blocks through hectic traffic. Clay tried to get a clear look at India outside, but all he could see in the starkly shadowed street were the crisscrossings of three-wheeled taxis and human-drawn rickshaws. He got an impression of incessant activity, even in this desolate hour. Vehicles leaped out of the murk as headlights swept across them and then vanished utterly into the moist shadows again.

They suddenly swerved around a corner beneath spreading, gloomy trees. The van jolted into deep potholes and jerked to a stop. "Out!" Patil called.

Clay could barely make out a second van at the curb ahead. It was blue and caked with mud, but even in the dim light would not be confused with their green one. A rotting fetid reek filled his nose as he got out the side door, as if masses of overripe vegetation loomed in the shadows. Patil tugged him into the second van. In a few seconds they went surging out through a narrow, brick-lined alley.

"Look, what—"

"Please, quiet," Patil said primly. "I am watching carefully now to be certain that we are not being followed."

They wound through a shantytown warren for several minutes. Their headlights picked up startled eyes that blinked from what Clay at first had taken to be bundles of rags lying against the shacks. They seemed impossibly small even to be children. Huddled against decaying tin lean-tos, the dim forms often did not stir even as the van splashed dirty water on them from potholes.

Clay began, "Look, I understand the need for—"

"I apologize for our rude methods, Dr. Clay," Patil said. He gestured at the driver. "May I introduce Dr. Singh?"

Singh was similarly gaunt and intent, but with bushy hair and a thin, pointed nose. He jerked his head aside to peer at Clay, nodded twice like a puppet on strings, and then quickly stared back at the narrow lane ahead. Singh kept the van at a steady growl, abruptly yanking it around corners. A wooden cart lurched out of their way, its driver swearing in a strident singsong. "Welcome to India," Singh said with reedy solemnity. "I am afraid circumstances are not the best."

"Uh, right. You two are heads of the project, they told me at the NSF."

"Yes," Patil said archly, "the project which officially no longer exists and unofficially is a brilliant success. It is amusing!"

"Yeah," Clay said cautiously, "we'll see."

"Oh, you will see," Singh said excitedly. "We have the events! More all the time."

Patil said precisely, "We would not have suggested that your National Science Foundation send an observer to confirm our findings unless we believed them to be of the highest importance."

"You've seen proton decay?"

Patil beamed. "Without doubt."

"Damn."

"Exactly."

"What mode?"

"The straightforward pion and positron decay products."

Clay smiled, reserving judgment. Something about Patil's almost prissy precision made him wonder if this small, beleaguered team of Indian physicists might actually have brought it off. An immense long shot, of course, but possible. There were much bigger groups of particle physicists in Europe and the U.S. who had tried to detect proton decay using underground swimming pools of pure water. Those experiments had enjoyed all the benefits of the latest electronics. Clay had worked on the big American project in a Utah salt mine, before lean budgets and lack of results closed it down. It would be galling if this lone, underfunded Indian scheme had finally done it. Nobody at the NSF believed the story coming out of India.

Patil smiled at Clay's silence, a brilliant slash of white in the murk. Their headlights picked out small panes of glass stuck seemingly at random in nearby hovels, reflecting quick glints of yellow back into the van. The night seemed misty; their headlights forked ahead. Clay thought a soft rain had started outside, but then he saw that thousands of tiny insects darted into their headlights. Occasionally big ones smacked against the windshield.

Patil carefully changed the subject. "I . . . believe you will pass unnoticed, for the most part."

"I look Indian?"

"I hope you will not take offense if I remark that you do not. We requested an Indian, but your NSF said they did not have anyone qualified."

"Right. Nobody who could hop on a plane, anyway." *Or would*, he added to himself.

"I understand. You are a compromise. If you will put this on . . ." Patil handed Clay a floppy khaki hat. "It will cover your curly hair. Luckily, your nose is rather more narrow than I had expected when the NSF cable announced they were sending a Negro."

"Got a lot of white genes in it, this nose," Clay said evenly.

"Please, do not think I am being racist. I simply wished to diminish the chances of you being recognized as a Westerner in the countryside."

"Think I can pass?"

"At a distance, yes."

"Be tougher at the site?"

"Yes. There are 'celebrants,' as they term themselves, at the mine."

"How'll we get in?"

"A ruse we have devised."

"Like that getaway back there? That was pretty slick."

Singh sent them jouncing along a rutted lane. Withered trees leaned against the pale stucco two-story buildings that lined the lane like children's blocks lined up not quite correctly. "Men in customs, they would give word to people outside. If you had gone through with the others, a different reception party would have been waiting for you."

"I see. But what about my bags?"

Patil had been peering forward at the gloomy jumble of buildings. His head jerked around to glare at Clay. "You were not to bring more than your carry-on bag!"

"Look, I can't get by on that. Chrissake, that'd give me just one change of clothes—"

"You left bags there?"

"Well, yeah, I had just one—"

Clay stopped when he saw the look on the two men's faces.

Patil said with strained clarity, "Your bags, they had identification tags?"

"Sure, airlines make you—"

"They will bring attention to you. There will be inquiries. The devotees will hear of it, inevitably, and know you have entered the country."

Clay licked his lips. "Hell, I didn't think it was so important."

The two lean Indians glanced at each other, their faces taking on a narrowing, leaden cast. "Dr. Clay," Patil said stiffly, "the 'celebrants' believe, as do many, that Westerners deliberately destroyed our crops with their biotechnology."

"Japanese companies' biologists did that, I thought," Clay said diplomatically.

"Perhaps. Those who disturb us at the Kolar gold mine make no fine distinctions between biologists and physicists. They believe that we are disturbing the very bowels of the earth, helping to further the destruction, bringing on the very end of the world itself. Surely you can see that in India, the mother country of religious philosophy, such matters are important."

"But your work, hell, it's not a matter of life or death or anything."

"On the contrary, the decay of the proton is precisely an issue of death."

Clay settled back in his seat, puzzled, watching the silky night stream by, cloaking vague forms in its shadowed mysteries.

2

Clay insisted on the telephone call. A wan winter sun had already crawled partway up the sky before he awoke, and the two Indian physicists wanted to leave immediately. They had stopped while still in Bangalore, holing up in the cramped apartment of one of Patil's graduate students. As Clay took his first sip of tea, two other students had turned up with his bag, retrieved at a cost he never knew.

Clay said, "I promised I'd call home. Look, my family's worried. They read the papers, they know the trouble here."

Shaking his head slowly, Patil finished a scrap of curled brown bread that appeared to be his only breakfast. His movements had a smooth liquid inertia, as if the sultry morning air oozed like jelly around him. They were sitting at a low table that had one leg too short; the already rickety table kept lurching, slopping tea into their saucers. Clay had looked for something to prop up the leg, but the apartment was bare, as though no one lived here. They had slept on pallets beneath a single bare bulb. Through the open windows, bare of frames or glass, Clay had gotten fleeting glimpses of the neighborhood—rooms of random clutter, plaster peeling off slumped walls, revealing the thin steel cross-ribs of the buildings, stained windows adorned with gaudy pictures of many-armed gods, already sun-bleached and frayed. Children yelped and cried below, their voices reflected among the odd angles and apertures of the tangled streets, while carts rattled by and bare feet slapped the stones. Students had apparently stood guard last night, though Clay had never seen more than a quick motion in the shadows below as they arrived.

"You ask much of us," Patil said. By morning light his walnut-brown face seemed gullied and worn. Lines radiated from his mouth toward intense eyes.

Clay sipped his tea before answering. A soft, strangely sweet smell wafted through the open window. They sat well back in the room so nobody could see in from the nearby buildings. He heard Singh tinkering downstairs with the van's engine.

"Okay, it's maybe slightly risky. But I want my people to know I got here all right."

"There are few telephones here."

"I only need one."

"The system, often it does not work at all."

"Gotta try."

"Perhaps you do not understand—"

"I understand damn well that if I can't even reach my people, I'm not going to hang out here for long. And if I don't see that your experiment works right, nobody'll believe you."

"And your opinion depends upon . . . ?"

Clay ticked off points on his fingers. "On seeing the apparatus. Checking your raw data. Running a trial case to see your system response. Then a null experiment—to verify your threshold level on each detector." He held up five fingers. "The works."

Patil said gravely, "Very good. We relish the opportunity to prove ourselves."

"You'll get it." Clay hoped to himself that they were wrong, but he suppressed that. He represented the faltering forefront of particle physics, and it would be embarrassing if a backwater research team had beaten the world. Still, either way, he would end up being the expert on the Kolar program, and that was a smart career move in itself.

"Very well. I must make arrangements for the call, then. But I truly—"

"Just do it. Then we get down to business."

The telephone was behind two counters and three doors at a Ministry for Controls office. Patil did the bribing and cajoling inside and then brought Clay in from the back of the van. He had been lying down on the back seat so he could not be seen easily from the street.

The telephone itself was a heavy black plastic thing with a rotary dial that clicked like a sluggish insect as it whirled. Patil had been on it twice already, clearing international lines through Bombay. Clay got two false rings and a dead line. On the fourth try he heard a faint, somehow familiar buzzing. Then a hollow, distant click.

"Angy?"

"Daddy, is that you?" Faint rock music in the background.

"Sure, I just wanted to let you know I got to India okay."

"Oh, Mommy will be so glad! We heard on the TV last night that there's trouble over there."

Startled, Clay asked, "What? Where's your mother?"

"Getting groceries. She'll be *so* mad she missed your call!"

"You tell her I'm fine, okay? But what trouble?"

"Something about a state leaving India. Lots of fighting, John Trimble said on the news."

Clay never remembered the names of news announcers; he regarded them as faceless nobodies reading prepared scripts, but for his daughter they were the voice of authority. "Where?"

"Uh, the lower part."

"There's nothing like that happening here, honey. I'm safe. Tell Mommy."

"People have ice cream there?"

"Yeah, but I haven't seen any. You tell your mother what I said, remember? About being safe?"

"Yes, she's been worried."

"Don't worry, Angy. Look, I got to go." The line popped and hissed ominously.

"I miss you, Daddy."

"I miss you double that. No, squared."

She laughed merrily. "I skinned my knee today at recess. It bled so much I had to go to the nurse."

"Keep it clean, honey. And give your mother my love."

"She'll be *so* mad."

"I'll be home soon."

She giggled and ended with the joke she had been using lately. "G'bye, Daddy. It's been real."

Her light laugh trickled into the static, a grace note from a bright land worlds away. Clay chuckled as he replaced the receiver. She cut the last word of "real nice" to make her good-byes hip and sardonic, a mannerism she had heard on television somewhere. An old joke; he had heard that even "groovy" was coming back in.

Clay smiled and pulled his hat down further and went quickly out into the street where Patil was waiting. India flickered at the edge of his vision, the crowds a hovering presence.

3

They left Bangalore in two vans. Graduate students drove the green Tochat from the previous night. He and Patil and Singh took the blue one, Clay again keeping out of sight by lying on the back seat. The day's raw heat rose around them like a shimmering lake of light.

They passed through lands leached of color. Only gray stubble grew in the fields. Trees hung limply, their limbs bowing as though exhausted. Figures in rags huddled for shade. A few stirred, eyes white in the shadows, as the vans ground past. Clay saw that large boles sat on the branches like gnarled knots with brown sheaths wrapped around the underside.

"Those some of the plant diseases I heard about?" he asked.

Singh pursed his lips. "I fear those are the pouches like those of wasps, as reported in the press." His watery eyes regarded the withered, graying trees as Patil slowed the car.

"Are they dangerous?" Clay could see yellow sap dripping from the underside of each.

"Not until they ripen," Singh said. "Then the assassins emerge."

"They look pretty big already."

"They are said to be large creatures, but of course there is little experience."

Patil downshifted and they accelerated away with an occasional sputtering misfire. Clay wondered whether they had any spare spark plugs along. The fields on each side of the road took on a dissolute and shredded look. "Did the genetech experiments cause this?" he asked.

Singh nodded. "I believe this emerged from the European programs. First we had their designed plants, but then pests found vulnerability. They sought strains which could protect crops from the new pests. So we got these wasps. I gather that now some error or mutation has made them equally excellent at preying on people and even cows."

Clay frowned. "The wasps came from the Japanese aid, didn't they?"

Patil smiled mysteriously. "You know a good deal about our troubles, sir."

Neither said anything more. Clay was acutely conscious that his briefing in Washington had been detailed technical assessments, without the slightest mention of how the Indians themselves saw their problems. Singh and Patil seemed either resigned or unconcerned; he could not tell which. Their sentences refracted from some unseen nugget, like seismic waves warping around the earth's core.

"I would not worry greatly about these pouches," Singh said after they had ridden in silence for a while. "They should not ripen before we are done with our task. In any case, the Kolar fields are quite barren, and afford few sites where the pouches can grow."

Clay pointed out the front window. "Those round things on the walls —more pouches?"

To his surprise, both men burst into merry laughter. Gasping, Patil said, "Examine them closely, Doctor Clay. Notice the marks of the species which made them."

Patil slowed the car and Clay studied the round, circular pads on the whitewashed vertical walls along the road. They were brown and matted and marked in a pattern of radial lines. Clay frowned and then felt enormously stupid: the thick lines were handprints.

"Drying cakes, they are," Patil said, still chuckling.

"Of what?"

"Dung, my colleague. We use the cow here, not merely slaughter it."

"What for?"

"Fuel. After the cakes dry, we stack them—see?" They passed a plastic-wrapped tower. A woman was adding a circular, annular tier of thick dung disks to the top, then carefully folding the plastic over it. "In winter they burn nicely."

"For heating?"

"And cooking, yes."

Seeing the look on Clay's face, Singh's eyes narrowed and his lips drew back so that his teeth were bright stubs. His eyebrows were long brush strokes that met the deep furrows of his frown. "Old ways are still often preferable to the new."

Sure, Clay thought, the past of cholera, plague, infanticide. But he asked with neutral politeness, "Such as?"

"Some large fish from the Amazon were introduced into our principal river three years ago to improve fishing yields."

"The Ganges? I thought it was holy."

"What is more holy than to feed the hungry?"

"True enough. Did it work?"

"The big fish, yes. They are delicious. A great delicacy."

"I'll have to try some," Clay said, remembering the thin vegetarian curry he had eaten at breakfast.

Singh said, "But the Amazon sample contained some minute eggs which none of the proper procedures eliminated. They were of a small species—the candiru, is that not the name?" he inquired politely of Patil.

"Yes," Patil said, "a little being who thrives mostly on the urine of larger fish. Specialists now believe that perhaps the eggs were inside the larger species, and so escaped detection."

Patil's voice remained calm and factual, although while he spoke he abruptly swerved to avoid a goat that spontaneously ambled onto the rough road. Clay rocked hard against the van's door, and Patil then corrected further to stay out of a gratuitous mudhole that seemed to leap at them from the rushing foreground. They bumped noisily over ruts at the road's edge and bounced back onto the tarmac without losing speed. Patil sat ramrod straight, hands turning the steering wheel lightly, oblivious to the wrenching effects of his driving.

"Suppose, Professor Clay, that you are a devotee," Singh said. "You have saved to come to the Ganges for a decade, for two. Perhaps you even plan to die there."

"Yeah, okay." Clay could not see where this was leading.

"You are enthused as you enter the river to bathe. You are perhaps profoundly affected. An intense spiritual moment. It is not uncommon to merge with the river, to inadvertently urinate into it."

Singh spread his hands as if to say that such things went without saying.

"Then the candiru will be attracted by the smell. It mistakes this great bountiful largess, the food it needs, as coming from a very great fish indeed. It excitedly swims up the stream of uric acid. Coming to your urethra, it swims like a snake into its burrow, as far up as it can go. You will see that the uric flow velocity will increase as the candiru makes its way upstream, inside you. When this tiny fish can make no further progress, some trick of evolution tells it to protrude a set of sidewise spines. So intricate!"

Singh paused a moment in smiling tribute to this intriguing facet of nature. Clay nodded, his mouth dry.

"These embed deeply in the walls and keep the candiru close to the source of what it so desires." Singh made short, delicate movements, his fingers jutting in the air. Clay opened his mouth, but said nothing.

Patil took them around a team of bullocks towing a wooden wagon and put in, "The pain is intense. Apparently there is no good treatment. Women—forgive this indelicacy—must be opened to get at the offending tiny fish before it swells and blocks the passage completely, having gorged itself insensate. Some men have an even worse choice. Their bladders are already engorged, having typically not been much emptied by the time the candiru enters. They must decide whether to attempt the slow procedure of poisoning the small thing and waiting for it to shrivel and withdraw its spines. However, their bladders might burst before that, flooding their abdomens with urine and of course killing them. If there is not sufficient time . . ."

"Yes?" Clay asked tensely.

"Then the penis must be chopped off," Singh said, "with the candiru inside."

Through a long silence Clay rode, swaying as the car wove through limitless flat spaces of parched fields and ruined brick walls and slumped whitewashed huts. Finally he said hoarsely, "I . . . don't blame you for resenting the . . . well, the people who brought all this on you. The devotees—"

"They believe this apocalyptic evil comes from the philosophy which gave us modern science."

"Well, look, whoever brought over those fish—"

Singh's eyes widened with surprise. A startled grin lit his face like a sunrise. "Oh no, Professor Clay! We do not blame the errors, or else we would have to blame equally the successes!"

To Clay's consternation, Patil nodded sagely.

He decided to say nothing more. Washington had warned him to stay out of political discussions, and though he was not sure if this was such, or if the lighthearted way Singh and Patil had related their story told their true attitude, it seemed best to just shut up. Again Clay had the odd sensation that here the cool certainties of Western biology had become diffused, blunted, crisp distinctions rendered into something beyond the constraints of the world outside, all blurred by the swarming, dissolving currents of India. The tin-gray sky loomed over a plain of ripe rot. The urgency of decay here was far more powerful than the abstractions that so often filled his head, the digitized iconography of sputtering, splitting protons.

4

The Kolar gold fields were a long, dusty drive from Bangalore. The sway of the van made Clay sleepy in the back, jet lag pulling him down into fitful, shallow dreams of muted voices, shadowy faces, and obscure purpose. He awoke frequently amid the dry smells, lurched up to see dry farmland stretching to the horizon, and collapsed again to bury his face in the pillow he had made by wadding up a shirt.

They passed through innumerable villages that, after the first few, all seemed alike with their scrawny children, ramshackle sheds, tin roofs, and general air of sleepy dilapidation. Once, in a narrow town, they stopped as rickshaws and carts backed up. An emaciated cow with pink paper tassels on its horns stood square in the middle of the road, trembling. Shouts and honks failed to move it, but no one ahead made the slightest effort to prod it aside.

Clay got out of the van to stretch his legs, ignoring Patil's warning to stay hidden, and watched. A crowd collected, shouting and chanting at the cow but not touching it. The cow shook its head, peering at the road as if searching for grass, and urinated powerfully. A woman in a red sari rushed into the road, knelt, and thrust her hand into the full stream. She made a formal motion with her other hand and splashed some urine on her forehead and cheeks. Three other women had already lined up behind her, and each did the same. Disturbed, the cow waggled its head and shakily walked away. Traffic started up, and Clay climbed back into the van. As they ground out of the dusty town, Singh explained that holy bovine urine was widely held to have positive health effects.

"Many believe it settles stomach troubles, banishes headaches, even improves fertility," Singh said.

"Yeah, you could sure use more fertility." Clay gestured at the throngs that filled the narrow clay sidewalks.

"I am not so Indian that I cannot find it within myself to agree with you, Professor Clay," Singh said.

"Sorry for the sarcasm. I'm tired."

"Patil and I are already under a cloud simply because we are scientists, and therefore polluted with Western ideas."

"Can't blame Indians for being down on us. Things're getting rough."

"But you are a black man. You yourself were persecuted by Western societies."

"That was a while back."

"And despite it you have risen to a professorship."

"You do the work, you get the job." Clay took off his hat and wiped his brow. The midday heat pressed sweat from him.

"Then you do not feel alienated from Western ideals?" Patil put in.

"Hell no. Look, I'm not some sharecropper who pulled himself up from poverty. I grew up in Falls Church, Virginia. Father's a federal bureaucrat. Middle class all the way."

"I see," Patil said, eyes never leaving the rutted road. "Your race bespeaks an entirely different culture, but you subscribe to the program of modern rationalism."

Clay looked at them quizzically. "Don't you?"

"As scientists, of course. But that is not all of life."

"Um," Clay said.

A thousand times before he had endured the affably condescending attention of whites, their curious eyes searching his face. No matter what the topic, they somehow found a way to inquire indirectly after his *true* feelings, his *natural* emotions. And if he waved away these intrusions, there remained in their heavy-lidded eyes a subtle skepticism, doubts about his authenticity. Few gave him space to simply be a suburban man with darker skin, a man whose interior landscape was populated with the same icons of Middle America as their own. Hell, his family name came from slaves, given as a tribute to Henry Clay, a nineteenth-century legislator. He had never expected to run into stereotyping in India, for chrissakes.

Still, he was savvy enough to lard his talk with some homey touches, jimmy things up with collard greens and black-eyed peas and street jive. It might put them at ease.

"I believe a li'l rationality could help," he said.

"Um." Singh's thin mouth twisted doubtfully. "Perhaps you should regard India as the great chessboard of our times, Professor. Here we have arisen from the great primordial agrarian times, fashioned our gods from our soil and age. Then we had orderly thinking, with all its assumptions, thrust upon us by the British. Now they are all gone, and we are suspended between the miasmic truths of the past, and the failed strictures of the present."

Clay looked out the dirty window and suppressed a smile. Even the physicists here spouted mumbo jumbo. They even appeared solemnly respectful of the devotees, who were just crazies like the women by the cow. How could anything solid come out of such a swamp? The chances that their experiment was right dwindled with each lurching, damp mile.

They climbed into the long range of hills before the Kolar fields. Burned-tan grass shimmered in the prickly heat. Sugarcane fields and rice paddies stood bone dry. In the villages, thin figures shaded beneath awnings, canvas tents, lean-tos, watched them pass. Lean faces betrayed only dim, momentary interest, and Clay wondered if his uncomfortable disguise was necessary outside Bangalore.

Without stopping they ate their lunch of dried fruit and thin, brown bread. In a high hill town, Patil stopped to refill his water bottle at a well. Clay peered out and saw down an alley a gang of stick-figure boys chasing a dog. They hemmed it in, and the bedraggled hound fled yapping from one side of their circle to the other. The animal whined at each rebuff and twice lost its footing on the cobblestones, sprawling, only to scramble up again and rush on. It was a cruel game, and the boys were strangely silent, playing without laughter. The dog was tiring; they drew in their circle.

A harsh edge to the boys' shouts made Clay slide open the van door. Several men were standing beneath a rust-scabbed sheet-metal awning nearby, and their eyes widened when they saw his face. They talked rapidly among themselves. Clay hesitated. The boys down the alley rushed the dog. They grabbed it as it yapped futilely and tried to bite them. They slipped twine around its jaws and silenced it. Shouting, they hoisted it into the air and marched off.

Clay gave up and slammed the door. The men came from under the awning. One rapped on the window. Clay just stared at them. One thumped on the door. Gestures, loud talk.

Patil and Singh came running, shouted something. Singh pushed the men away, chattering at them while Patil got the van started. Singh slammed the door in the face of a man with wild eyes. Patil gunned the engine and they ground away.

"They saw me and—"

"Distrust of outsiders is great here," Singh said. "They may be connected with the devotees, too."

"Guess I better keep my hat on."

"It would be advisable."

"I don't know, those boys—I was going to stop them pestering that dog. Stupid, I guess, but—"

"You will have to avoid being sentimental about such matters," Patil said severely.

"Uh—sentimental?"

"The boys were not playing."

"I don't—"

"They will devour it," Singh said.

Clay blinked. "Hindus eating meat?"

"Hard times. I am really quite surprised that such an animal has survived this long," Patil said judiciously. "Dogs are uncommon. I imagine it was wild, living in the countryside, and ventured into town in search of garbage scraps."

The land rose as Clay watched the shimmering heat bend and flex the seemingly solid hills.

5

They pulled another dodge at the mine. The lead green van veered off toward the main entrance, a cluster of concrete buildings and conveyer assemblies. From a distance, the physicists in the blue van watched a ragtag group envelop the van before it had fully stopped.

"Devotees," Singh said abstractedly. "They search each vehicle for evidence of our research."

"Your graduate students, the mob'll let them pass?"

Patil peered through binoculars. "The crowd is administering a bit of a pushing about," he said in his oddly cadenced accent, combining lofty British diction with a singsong lilt.

"Damn, won't the mine people get rid—"

"Some mine workers are among the crowd, I should imagine," Patil said. "They are beating the students."

"Well, can't we—"

"No time to waste." Singh waved them back into the blue van. "Let us make use of this diversion."

"But we could—"

"The students made their sacrifice for you. Do not devalue it, please."

Clay did not take his eyes from the nasty knot of confusion until they lurched over the ridgeline. Patil explained that they had been making regular runs to the main entrance for months now, to establish a pattern that drew devotees away from the secondary entrance.

"All this was necessary, and insured that we could bring in a foreign inspector," Patil concluded. Clay awkwardly thanked him for the attention to detail. He wanted to voice his embarrassment at having students roughed up simply to provide him cover, but something in the offhand manner of the two Indians made him hold his tongue.

The secondary entrance to the Kolar mine was a wide, tin-roofed shed like a low aircraft hangar. Girders crisscrossed it at angles that seemed to Clay dictated less by the constraints of mechanics than by the whims of the construction team. Cables looped among the already rusting steel struts and sang low notes in the rot-tinged wind that brushed his hair.

Monkeys chattered and scampered high in the struts. The three men walked into the shed, carrying cases. The cables began humming softly. The weave above their heads tightened with pops and sharp cracks. Clay realized that the seemingly random array was a complicated hoist that had started to pull the elevator up from miles beneath their feet. The steel lattice groaned as if it already knew how much work it had to do.

When it arrived, he saw that the elevator was a huge rattling box that reeked of machine oil. Clay lugged his cases in. The walls were broad wooden slats covered with chicken wire. Heat radiated from them. Patil stabbed a button on the big control board and they dropped quickly. The numbers of the levels zipped by on an amber digital display. A single dim yellow bulb cast shadows onto the wire. At the fifty-third level the bulb went out. The elevator did not stop.

In the enveloping blackness Clay felt himself lighten, as if the elevator was speeding up.

"Do not be alarmed," Patil called. "This frequently occurs."

Clay wondered if he meant the faster fall or the light bulb. In the complete dark, he began to see blue phantoms leaping out from nowhere.

Abruptly he became heavy—and thought of Einstein's *Gedanken* experiment, which equated a man in an accelerating elevator to one standing on a planet. Unless Clay could see outside, check that the massive earth raced by beyond as it clasped him further into its depths, in principle he could be in either situation. He tried to recall how Einstein had reasoned from an imaginary elevator to deduce that matter curved space-time, and could not.

Einstein's elegant proof was impossibly far from the pressing truth of *this* elevator. Here Clay plunged in thick murk, a weight of tortured air prickling his nose, making sweat pop from his face. Oily, moist heat climbed into Clay's sinuses.

And he was not being carried aloft by this elevator, but allowed to plunge into heavy, primordial darkness—Einstein's vision in reverse. No classical coolness separated him from the press of a raw, random world. That European mindscape—Galileo's crisp cylinders rolling obediently down inclined planes, Einstein's dispassionate observers surveying their smooth geometries like scrupulous bank clerks—evaporated here like yesterday's stale champagne. Sudden anxiety filled his throat. His stomach tightened and he tasted acrid gorge. He opened his mouth to shout, and as if to stop him, his own knees sagged with suddenly returning weight, physics regained.

A rattling thump—and they stopped. He felt Patil slam aside the rattling gate. A sullen glow beyond bathed an ornate brass shrine to a Hindu god. They came out into a steepled room of carved rock. Clay felt a breath of slightly cooler air from a cardboard-mouthed conduit nearby.

"We must force the air down from above." Patil gestured. "Otherwise this would read well over a hundred and ten Fahrenheit." He proudly pointed to an ancient battered British thermometer, whose mercury stood at ninety-eight.

They trudged through several tunnels, descended another few hundred feet on a ramp, and then followed gleaming railroad tracks. A white bulb every ten meters threw everything into exaggerated relief, shadows stabbing everywhere. A brown cardboard sign proclaimed from the ceiling:

FIRST EVER COSMIC RAY NEUTRINO INTERACTION
RECORDED HERE IN APRIL 1965

For over forty years, teams of devoted Indian physicists had labored patiently inside the Kolar gold fields. For half a century, India's high mountains and deep mines had made important cosmic-ray experiments possible with inexpensive instruments. Clay recalled how a joint Anglo-Indian-Japanese team had detected that first neutrino, scooped it from the unending cosmic sleet that penetrated even to this depth. He thought of unsung Indian physicists sweating here, tending the instruments and tracing the myriad sources of background error. Yet they themselves were background for the original purpose of the deep holes: Two narrow cars clunked past, full of chopped stone.

"Some still work this portion," Patil's clear voice cut through the muffled air. "Though I suspect they harvest little."

Pushing the rusty cars were four wiry men, so sweaty that the glaring bulbs gave their sliding muscles a hard sheen like living stone. They wore filthy cloths wrapped around their heads, as if they needed protection against the low ceiling rather than the heat. As Clay stumbled on, he felt that there might be truth to this, because he sensed the mass above as a precarious judgment over them all, a sullen presence. Einstein's crisp distinctions, the clean certainty of the *Gedanken* experiments, meant nothing in this blurred air.

They rounded an irregular curve and met a niche neatly cut off by a chain-link fence.

PROTON STABILITY EXPERIMENT
TATA INSTITUTE OF FUNDAMENTAL RESEARCH, BOMBAY
80th Level Heathcote Shaft, KFG
2300 meters depth

These preliminaries done, the experiment itself began abruptly. Clay had expected some assembly rooms, an office, refrigerated 'scope cages. Instead, a few meters ahead the tunnel opened in all directions. They stood before a huge bay roughly cleaved from the brown rock.

And filling the vast volume was what seemed to be a wall as substantial as the rock itself. It was an iron grid of rusted pipe. The pipes were square, not round, and dwindled into the distance. Each had a dusty seal, a pressure dial, and a number painted in white. Clay estimated them to be at least a hundred feet long. They were stacked Lincoln-log fashion. He walked to the edge of the bay and looked down. Layers of pipe tapered away below to a distant floodlit floor and soared to meet the gray ceiling above.

"Enormous," he said.

"We expended great effort in scaling up our earlier apparatus," Singh said enthusiastically.

"As big as a house."

Patil said merrily, "An American house, perhaps. Ours are smaller."

A woman's voice nearby said, "And nothing lives in this iron house, Professor Clay."

Clay turned to see a willowy Indian woman regarding him with a wry smile. She seemed to have come out of the shadows, a brown apparition in shorts and a scrupulously white blouse, appearing fullblown where a moment before there had been nothing. Her heavy eyebrows rose in amusement.

"Ah, this is Mrs. Buli," Patil said.

"I keep matters running here, while my colleagues venture into the world," she said.

Clay accepted her coolly offered hand. She gave him one quick, well-defined shake and stepped back. "I can assist your assessment, perhaps."

"I'll need all your help," he said sincerely. The skimpy surroundings already made him wonder if he could do his job at all.

"Labor we have," she said. "Equipment, little."

"I brought some cross-check programs with me," he said.

"Excellent," Mrs. Buli said. "I shall have several of my graduate students assist you, and of course I offer my full devotion as well."

Clay smiled at her antique formality. She led him down a passage into the soft fluorescent glow of a large data-taking room. It was crammed with terminals and a bank of disk drives, all meshed by the usual cable spaghetti. "We keep our computers cooler than our staff, you see," Mrs. Buli said with a small smile.

They went down a ramp, and Clay could feel the rock's steady heat. They came out onto the floor of the cavern. Thick I-beams roofed the stone box.

"Over a dozen lives, that was the cost of this excavation," Singh said.

"That many?"

"They attempted to save on the cost of explosives," Patil said with a stern look.

"Not that such will matter in the long run," Singh said mildly. Clay chose not to pursue the point.

Protective bolts studded the sheer rock, anchoring cross-beams that stabilized the tower of pipes. Scaffolding covered some sections of the blocky, rusty pile. Blasts of compressed air from the surface a mile above swept down on them from the ceiling, flapping Clay's shirt.

Mrs. Buli had to shout, the effort contorting her smooth face. "We obtained the pipes from a government program that attempted to improve the quality of plumbing in the cities. A failure, I fear. But a godsend for us."

Patil was pointing out electrical details when the air conduits wheezed into silence. "Hope that's temporary," Clay said in the sudden quiet.

"A minor repair, I am sure," Patil said.

"These occur often," Singh agreed earnestly.

Clay could already feel prickly sweat oozing from him. He wondered how often they had glitches in the circuitry down here, awash in pressing heat, and how much that could screw up even the best diagnostics.

Mrs. Buli went on in a lecturer's singsong. "We hired engineering students—there are many such, an oversupply—to thread a single wire down the bore of each pipe. We sealed each, then welded them together to make lengths of a hundred feet. Then we filled them with argon and linked them with a high-voltage line. We have found that a voltage of 280 keV . . ."

Clay nodded, filing away details, noting where her description differed from that of the NSF. The Kolar group had continuously modified their experiment for decades, and this latest enormous expansion was badly documented. Still, the principle was simple. Each pipe was held at high voltage, so that when a charged particle passed through, a spark leaped. A particle's path was followed by counting the segments of triggered pipes. This mammoth stack of iron was a huge Geiger counter.

He leaned back, nodding at Buli's lecture, watching a team of men at the very top. A loud clang rang through the chasm. Sparks showered, burnt-orange and blue. The garish plumes silhouetted the welders and sent cascades of sparks down through the lattice of pipes. For an instant Clay imagined he was witnessing cosmic rays sleeting down through the towering house of iron, illuminating it with their short, sputtering lives.

"—and I am confident that we have seen well over fifty true events," Mrs. Buli concluded with a jaunty upward tilt of her chin.

"What?" Clay struggled back from his daydreaming. "That many?" She laughed, a high tinkling. "You do not believe!"

"Well, that is a lot."

"Our detecting mass is now larger," Mrs. Buli said.

"Last we heard it was five hundred tons," Clay said carefully. The claims wired to the NSF and the Royal Society had been skimpy on details.

"That was years ago," Patil said. "We have redoubled our efforts, as you can see."

"Well, to see that many decays, you'd have to have a hell of a lot of observing volume," Clay said doubtfully.

"We can boast of five *thousand* tons, Professor Clay," Mrs. Buli said.

"Looks it," Clay said laconically to cover his surprise. It would not do to let them think they could overwhelm him with magnitudes. Question was, did they have the telltale events?

The cooling air came on with a thump and *whoosh*. Clay breathed it in deeply, face turned up to the iron house where protons might be dying, and sucked in swarming scents of the parched countryside miles above.

6

He knew from the start that there would be no eureka moment. Certainty was the child of tedium.

He traced the tangled circuitry for two days before he trusted it. "You got to open the sack 'fore I'll believe there's a cat in there," he told Mrs. Buli, and then had to explain that he was joking.

Then came a three-day trial run, measuring the exact sputter of decay from a known radioactive source. System response was surprisingly good. He found their techniques needlessly Byzantine, but workable. His null checks of the detectors inside the pipes came up goose-egg clean.

Care was essential. Proton decay was rare. The Grand Unified Theories which had enjoyed such success in predicting new particles had also sounded a somber note through all of physics. Matter was mortal. But not very mortal, compared with the passing flicker of a human lifetime.

The human body had about 10^{29} neutrons and protons in it. If only a tiny fraction of them decayed in a human lifetime, the radiation from the disintegration would quickly kill everyone of cancer. The survival of even small life-forms implied that the protons inside each nucleus had to survive an average of nearly a billion billion years.

So even before the Grand Unified Theories, physicists knew that protons lived long. The acronym for the theories was GUTs, and a decade earlier graduate students like Clay had worn T-shirts with insider jokes like IT TAKES GUTS TO DO PARTICLE PHYSICS. But proving that there was some truth to the lame nerd jests took enormous effort.

The simplest of the GUTs predicted a proton lifetime of about 10^{31} years, immensely greater than the limit set by the existence of life. In fact, it was far longer even than the age of the universe, which was only a paltry 2×10^{10} years old.

One could check this lifetime by taking one proton and watching it for 10^{31} years. Given the short attention span of humans, it was better to assemble 10^{31} protons and watch them for a year, hoping one would fizzle.

Physicists in the United States, Japan, Italy, and India had done that all through the 1980s and 1990s. And no protons had died.

Well, the theorists had said, the mathematics must be more complicated. They discarded certain symmetry groups and thrust others forward. The lifetime might be 10^{32} years, then.

The favored method of gathering protons was to use those in water. Western physicists carved swimming pools six stories deep in salt mines and eagerly watched for the characteristic blue pulse of dying matter. Detecting longer lifetimes meant waiting longer, which nobody liked, or adding more protons. Digging bigger swimming pools was easy, so attention had turned to the United States and Japan . . . but still, no protons died. The lifetime exceeded 10^{32} years.

The austerity of the 1990s had shut down the ambitious experiments in the West. Few remembered this forlorn experiment in Kolar, wedded to watching the cores of iron rods for the quick spurt of decay. When political difficulties cut off contact, the already beleaguered physicists in the West assumed the Kolar effort had ceased.

But Kolar was the deepest experiment, less troubled by the hail of cosmic rays that polluted the Western data. Clay came to appreciate that as he scrolled through the myriad event-plots in the Kolar computer cubes.

There were 9×10^9 recorded decays of all types. The system rejected obvious garbage events, but there were many subtle enigmas. Theory said that protons died because the quarks that composed them could change their identities. A seemingly capricious alteration of quarky states sent the proton asunder, spitting forth a zoo of fragments. Neutrons were untroubled by this, for in free space they decayed anyway, into a proton and electron. Matter's end hinged, finally, on the stability of the proton alone.

Clay saw immediately that the Kolar group had invested years in their software. They had already filtered out thousands of phantom events that imitated true proton decay. There were eighteen ways a proton could die, each with a different signature of spraying light and particle debris.

The delicate traceries of particle paths were recorded as flashes and sparkles in the house of iron outside. Clay searched through endless graphic printouts, filigrees woven from digital cloth.

"You will find we have pondered each candidate event," Mrs. Buli said mildly on the sixth day of Clay's labors.

"Yeah, the analysis is sharp," he said cautiously. He was surprised at the high level of the work but did not want to concede anything yet.

"If any ambiguity arose, we discarded the case."

"I can see that."

"Some pions were not detected in the right energy range, so of course we omitted those."

"Good."

Mrs. Buli leaned over to show him a detail of the cross-checking program, and he caught a heady trace of wildflowers. Her perfume reminded him abruptly that her sari wrapped over warm, ample swells. She had no sagging softness, no self-indulgent bulgings. The long oval of her face and her ample lips conveyed a fragile sensuality . . .

He wrenched his attention back to physics and stared hard at the screen.

Event vertices were like time-lapse photos of traffic accidents, intersections exploding, screaming into shards. The crystalline mathematical order of physics led to riots of incandescence. And Clay was judge, weighing testimony after the chaos.

7

He had insisted on analyzing the several thousand preliminary candidates himself, as a double blind against the Kolar group's software. After nine days, he had isolated sixty-seven events that looked like the genuine article.

Sixty-five of his agreed with Mrs. Buli's analysis. The two holdouts were close, Clay had to admit.

"Nearly on the money," he said reflectively as he stared at the Kolar software's array.

"You express such values," Mrs. Buli said. "Always a financial analogy."

"Just a way of speaking."

"Still, let us discard the two offending events."

"Well, I'd be willing—"

"No, no, we consider only the sixty-five." Her almond eyes gave no hint of slyness.

"They're pretty good bets, I'd say." Her eyebrows arched. "Only a manner of speech."

"Then you feel they fit the needs of theory."

Her carefully balanced way of phrasing made him lean forward, as if to compensate for his judge's role. "I'll have to consider all the other decay modes in detail. Look for really obscure processes that might mimic the real thing."

She nodded. "True, there is need to study such."

Protons could die from outside causes, too. Wraithlike neutrinos spewed forth by the sun penetrated even here, shattering protons. Murderous muons lumbered through as cosmic rays, plowing furrows of exploding nuclei.

Still, things looked good. He was surprised at their success, earned by great labor. "I'll be as quick about it as I can."

"We have prepared a radio link that we can use, should the desire come."

"Huh? What?"

"In case you need to reach your colleagues in America."

"Ah, yes."

To announce the result, he saw. To get the word out. But why the rush?

It occurred to him that they might doubt whether he himself would get out at all.

8

They slept each night in a clutch of tin lean-tos that cowered down a raw ravine. Laborers from the mine had slept there in better days, and the physicists had gotten the plumbing to work for an hour each night. The men slept in a long shed, but gave Clay a small wooden shack. He ate thin, mealy gruel with them each evening, carefully dropping purification tablets in his water, and was rewarded with untroubled bowels. He lost weight in the heat of the mine, but the nights were cool and the breezes that came then were soft with moisture.

The fifth evening, as they sat around a potbellied iron stove in the men's shed, Patil pointed to a distant corrugated metal hut and said, "There we have concealed a satellite dish. We can knock away the roof and transmit, if you like."

Clay brightened. "Can I call home?"

"If need be."

Something in Patil's tone told him a frivolous purpose was not going to receive their cooperation.

"Maybe tomorrow?"

"Perhaps. We must be sure that the devotees do not see us reveal it."

"They think we're laborers?"

"So we have convinced them, I believe."

"And me?"

"You would do well to stay inside."

"Um. Look, got anything to drink?"

Patil frowned. "Has the water pipe stopped giving?"

"No, I mean, you know—a drink. Gin and tonic, wasn't that what the Brits preferred?"

"Alcohol is the devil's urine," Patil said precisely.

"It won't scramble my brains."

"Who can be sure? The mind is a tentative instrument."

"You don't want any suspicion that I'm unreliable, that it?"

"No, of course not," Singh broke in anxiously.

"Needn't worry," Clay muttered. The heat below and the long hours of tedious work were wearing him down. "I'll be gone soon's I can get things wrapped up."

"You agree that we are seeing the decays?"

"Let's say things're looking better."

Clay had been holding back even tentative approval. He had expected some show of jubilation. Patil and Singh simply sat and stared into the flickering coals of the stove's half-open door.

Slowly Patil said, "Word will spread quickly."

"Soon as you transmit it on that dish, sure."

Singh murmured, "Much shall change."

"Look, you might want to get out of here, go present a paper—"

"Oh no, we shall remain," Singh said quickly.

"Those devotees could give you trouble if they find—"

"We expect that this discovery, once understood, shall have great effects," Patil said solemnly. "I much prefer to witness them from my home country."

The cadence and mood of this conversation struck Clay as odd, but he put it down to the working conditions. Certainly they had sacrificed a great deal to build and run this experiment amid crippling desolation.

"This result will begin the final renunciation of the materialistic worldview," Singh said matter-of-factly.

"Huh?"

"In peering at the individual lives of mere particles, we employ the reductionist hammer," Patil explained. "But nature is not like a salamander, cut into fragments."

"Or if it were," Singh added, "once the salamander is so sliced, try to make it do its salamander walk again." A broad white grin split the gloom of nightfall.

"The world is an implicate order, Dr. Clay. All parts are hinged to each other."

Clay frowned. He vaguely remembered a theory of quantum mechanics which used that term—"implicate order," meaning that a deeper realm of physical theory lay beneath the uncertainties of wave mechanics. Waves that took it into their heads to behave like particles, and the reverse—these were supposed to be illusions arising from our ignorance of a more profound theory. But there was no observable consequence of such notions, and to Clay such mumbo jumbo from theorists who never got their hands dirty was empty rhapsodizing. Still, he was supposed to be the diplomat here.

He gave a judicial nod. "Yeah, sure—but when the particles die, it'll all be gone, right?"

"Yes, in about 10^{34} years," Patil said. "But the *knowledge* of matter's mortality will spread as swiftly as light, on the wind of our transmitter."

"So?"

"You are an experimentalist, Dr. Clay, and thus—if you will forgive my putting it so—addicted to cutting the salamander." Patil made a steeple of his fingers, sending spindly shadows rippling across his face. "The world we study is conditioned by our perceptions of it. The implied order is partially from our own design."

"Sure, quantum measurement, uncertainty principle, all that." Clay had sat through all the usual lectures about this stuff and didn't feel like doing so again. Not in a dusty shed with his stomach growling from hunger. He sipped at his cup of weak Darjeeling and yawned.

"Difficulties of measurement reflect underlying problems," Patil said. "Even the Westerner Plato saw that we perceive only imperfect modes of the true, deeper world."

"What deeper world?" Clay sighed despite himself.

"We do not know. We *cannot* know."

"Look, we make our measurements, we report. Period."

Amused, Singh said, "And that is where matters end?"

Patil said, "Consensual reality, that is your 'real' world, Professor Clay. But our news may cause that bland, unthinking consensus to falter."

Clay shrugged. This sounded like late-night college bullshit sessions among boozed-up science nerds. Patty-cake pantheism, quantum razzle-dazzle, garbage philosophy. It was one thing to be open-minded and another to let your brains fall out. Was *every*body on this wrecked continent a booga-booga type? He had to get out.

"Look, I don't see what difference—"

"Until the curtain of seeming surety is swept away," Singh put in.

"Surety?"

"This world—this universe!—has labored long under the illusion of its own permanence." Singh spread his hands, animated in the flickering yellow glow. "We might die, yes, the sun might even perish—but the universe went on. Now we prove otherwise. There cannot help but be profound reactions."

He thought he saw what they were driving at. "A Nobel Prize, even."

To his surprise, both men laughed merrily. "Oh no," Patil said, arching his eyebrows. "No such trifles are expected!"

9

The boxy meeting room beside the data bay was packed. From it came a subdued mutter, a fretwork of talk laced with anticipation.

Outside, someone had placed a small chalky statue of a grinning elephant. Clay hesitated, stroked it. Despite the heat of the mine, the elephant was cool.

"The workers just brought it down," Mrs. Buli explained with a smile. "Our Hindu god of auspicious beginnings."

"Or endings," Patil said behind her. "Equally."

Clay nodded and walked into the trapped, moist heat of the room. Everyone was jammed in, graduate students and laborers alike, their dhotis already showing sweaty crescents. Clay saw the three students the devotees had beaten and exchanged respectful bows with them.

Perceiving some need for ceremony, he opened with lengthy praise for the endless hours they had labored, exclaiming over how startled the world would be to learn of such a facility. Then he plunged into consideration of each candidate event, his checks and counter-checks, vertex corrections, digital-array flaws, mean free paths, ionization rates, the artful programming that deflected the myriad possible sources of error. He could feel tension rising in the room as he cast the events on the inch-thick wall screen, calling them forth from the files in his cubes. Some he threw into 3-D, to show the full path through the cage of iron that had captured the death rattle of infinity.

And at the end, all cases reviewed, he said quietly, "You have found it. The proton lifetime is very nearly 10^{34} years."

The room burst into applause, wide grins and wild shouts as everyone pressed forward to shake his hand.

10

Singh handled the message to the NSF. Clay also constructed a terse though detailed summary and sent it to the International Astronomical Union for release to the worldwide system of observatories and universities.

Clay knew this would give a vital assist to his career. With the Kolar team staying here, he would be their only spokesman. And this was very big, media-mesmerizing news indeed.

The result was important to physicists and astronomers alike, for the destiny of all their searches ultimately would be sealed by the faint failures of particles no eye would ever see. In 10^{34} years, far in the depths of space, the great celestial cities, the galaxies, would be ebbing. The last red stars would flicker, belch, and gutter out. Perhaps life would have clung to them and found a way to persist against the growing cold. Cluttered with the memorabilia of the ages, the islands of mute matter would turn at last to their final conqueror—not entropy's still hand, but this silent sputter of protons.

Clay thought of the headlines: UNIVERSE TO END. What would *that* do to harried commuters on their way to work?

He watched Singh send the stuttering messages via the big satellite dish, the corrugated tin roof of the shed pulled aside, allowing him to watch burnt-gold twilight seep across the sky. Clay felt no elation, as blank as a drained capacitor. He had gone into physics because of the sense it gave of grasping deep mysteries. He could look at bridges and trace the vectored stability that ruled them. When his daughter asked why the sky was blue, he actually knew, and could sketch out a simple answer. It had never occurred to him to fear flying, because he knew the Bernoulli equation for the pressure that held up the plane.

But this result . . .

Even the celebratory party that evening left him unmoved. Graduate students turned out in their best khaki. Sitar music swarmed through the scented air, ragas thumping and weaving. He found his body swaying to the refractions of tone and scale.

"It is a pity you cannot learn more of our country," Mrs. Buli remarked, watching him closely.

"Right now I'm mostly interested in sleep."

"Sleep is not always kind." She seemed wry and distant in the night's smudged humidity. "One of our ancient gods, Brahma, is said to sleep—and we are what he dreams."

"In that case, for you folks maybe he's been having a nightmare lately."

"Ah yes, our troubles. But do not let them mislead you about India. They pass."

"I'm sure they will," Clay replied, dutifully diplomatic.

"You were surprised, were you not, at the outcome?" she said piercingly.

"Uh, well, I had to be skeptical."

"Yes, for a scientist certainty is built on deep layers of doubt."

"Like my daddy said, in the retail business deal with everybody, but count your change."

She laughed. "We have given you a bargain, perhaps!"

He was acutely aware that his initial doubts must have been obvious. And what unsettled him now was not just the hard-won success here, but their strange attitude toward it.

The graduate students came then and tried to teach him a dance. He did a passable job, and a student named Venkatraman slipped him a glass of beer, forbidden vice. It struck Clay as comic that the Indian government spent much energy to suppress alcohol but did little about the population explosion. The students all laughed when he made a complicated joke about booze, but he could not be sure whether they meant it. The music seemed to quicken, his heart thumping to keep up with it. They addressed him as Clay*ji*, a term of respect, and asked his opinion of what they might do next with the experiment. He shrugged, thinking *'Nother job, sahib?* and suggested using it as a detector for neutrinos from supernovas. That had paid off when the earlier generation of neutrino detectors picked up the 1987 supernova.

The atom bomb, the 1987 event, now this—particle physics, he realized uncomfortably, was steeped in death. The sitar slid and rang, and Mrs. Buli made arch jokes to go with the spicy salad. Still, he turned in early.

11

To be awakened by a soft breeze. A brushing presence, sliding cloth . . . He sensed her sari as a luminous fog. Moonlight streaming through a lopsided window cast shimmering auras through the cloth as she loomed above him. Reached for him. Lightly flung away his sticky bedclothes.

"I—"

A soft hand covered his mouth, bringing a heady savor of ripe earth. His senses ran out of him and into the surrounding dark, coiling in air as he took her weight. She was surprisingly light, though thick-waisted, her breasts like teacups compared with the full curves of her hips. His hands slid and pressed, finding a delightful slithering moisture all over her, a sheen of vibrancy. Her sari evaporated. The high planes of her face caught vagrant blades of moonlight, and he saw a curious tentative, expectant expression there as she wrapped him in soft pressures. Her mouth did not so much kiss his as enclose it, formulating an argument of sweet rivulets that trickled into his porous self. She slipped into place atop him, a slick clasp that melted him up into her, a perfect fit, slick with dark insistence. He closed his eyes, but the glow diffused through his eyelids, and he could see her hair fanning through the air like motion underwater, her luxuriant weight bucking, trembling as her nails scratched his shoulders, musk rising smoky from them both. A silky muscle milked him at each heart-thump. Her velvet mass orbited above their fulcrum, bearing down with feathery demands, and he remembered brass icons, gaudy Indian posters, and felt above him Kali strumming in fevered darkness. She locked legs around him, squeezing him up into her surprisingly hard muscles, grinding, drawing forth, pushing back. She cried out with great heaves and lungfuls of the thickening air, mouth going slack beneath hooded eyes, and he shot sharply up into her, a convulsion that poured out all the knotted aches in him, delivering them into the tumbled steamy earth—

12

—and next, with no memories between, he was stumbling with her . . . down a gully . . . beneath slanting silvery moonlight.

"What—what's—"

"Quiet!" She shushed him like a schoolmarm.

He recognized the rolling countryside near the mine. Vague forms flitted in the distance. Wracked cries cut the night.

"The devotees," Mrs. Buli whispered as they stumbled on. "They have assaulted the mine entrance."

"How'd we—"

"You were difficult to rouse," she said with a sidelong glance.

Was she trying to be amusing? The sudden change from mysterious supercharged sensuality back to this clipped, formal professionalism disoriented him.

"Apparently some of our laborers had a grand party. It alerted the devotees to our presence, some say. I spoke to a laborer while you slept, however, who said that the devotees knew of your presence. They asked for you."

"Why me?"

"Something about your luggage and a telephone call home."

Clay gritted his teeth and followed her along a path that led among the slumped hills, away from their lodgings. Soon the mine entrance was visible below. Running figures swarmed about it like black gnats. Ragged chants erupted from them. A *waarrrk waarrrk* sound came from the hangar, and it was some moments until Clay saw long chains of human bodies hanging from the rafters, swinging themselves in unison.

"They're pulling down the hangar," he whispered.

"I despair for what they have done inside."

He instinctively reached for her and felt the supple warmth he had embraced seemingly only moments before. She turned and gave him her mouth again.

"We—back there—why'd you come to me?"

"It was time. Even we feel the joy of release from order, Professor Clay."

"Well, sure . . ." Clay felt illogically embarrassed, embracing a woman who still had the musk of the bed about her, yet who used his title. "But . . . how'd I get here? Seems like—"

"You were immersed. Taken out of yourself."

"Well, yeah, it was good, fine, but I can't remember anything."

She smiled. "The best moments leave no trace. That is a signature of the implicate order."

Clay breathed in the waxy air to help clear his head. More mumbo jumbo, he thought, delivered by her with an open, expectant expression. In the darkness it took a moment to register that she had fled down another path.

"Where'll we go?" he gasped when he caught up.

"We must get to the vans. They are parked some kilometers away."

"My gear—"

"Leave it."

He hesitated a moment, then followed her. There was nothing irreplaceable. It certainly wasn't worth braving the mob below for the stuff.

They wound down through bare hillsides dominated by boulders. The sky rippled with heat lightning. Puffy clouds scudded quickly in from the west, great ivory flashes working among them. The ground surged slightly.

"Earthquake?" he asked.

"There were some earlier, yes. Perhaps that has excited the devotees further tonight, put their feet to running."

There was no sign of the physics team. Pebbles squirted from beneath his boots—he wondered how he had managed to get them on without remembering it—and recalled again her hypnotic sensuality. Stones rattled away down into narrow dry washes on each side. Clouds blotted out the moonglow, and they had to pick their way along the trail.

Clay's mind spun with plans, speculations, jittery anxiety. Mrs. Buli was now his only link to the Western fragment of India, and he could scarcely see her in the shadows. She moved with liquid grace, her sari trailing, sandals slapping. Suddenly she crouched down. "More."

Along the path came figures bearing lanterns. They moved silently in the fitful silvery moonlight. There was no place to hide, and the party had already seen them.

"Stand still," she said. Again the crisp Western diction, yet her ample hips swayed slightly, reminding him of her deeper self.

Clay wished he had a club, a knife, anything. He made himself stand beside her, hands clenched. For once his blackness might be an advantage.

The devotees passed, eyes rapt. Clay had expected them to be singing or chanting mantras or rubbing beads—but not shambling forward as if to their doom. The column barely glanced at him. In his baggy cotton trousers and formless shirt, he hoped he was unremarkable. A woman passed nearby, apparently carrying something across her back. Clay blinked. Her hands were nailed to the ends of a beam, and she carried it proudly, palms bloody, half crucified. Her face was serene, eyes focused on the roiling sky. Behind her was a man bearing a plate. Clay thought the shambling figure carried marbles on the dish until he peered closer and saw an iris, and realized the entire plate was packed with eyeballs. He gasped and faces turned toward him. Then the man was gone along the path, and Clay waited, holding his breath against a gamy stench he could not name. Some muttered to themselves, some carried religious artifacts, beads and statuettes and drapery, but none had the fervor of the devotees he had seen before. The ground trembled again.

And out of the dark air came a humming. Something struck a man in the line and he clutched at his throat, crying hoarsely. Clay leaped forward without thinking. He pulled the man's hands away. Lodged in the narrow of the throat was something like an enormous cockroach with fluttering wings. It had already embedded its head in the man. Spiky legs furiously scrabbled against the soiled skin to dig deeper. The man coughed and shouted weakly, as though the thing was already blocking his throat.

Clay grabbed its hind legs and pulled. The insect wriggled with surprising strength. He saw the hind stinger too late. The sharp point struck a hot jolt of pain into his thumb. Anger boiled in him. He held on despite the pain and yanked the thing free. It made a sucking sound coming out. He hissed with revulsion and violently threw it down the hillside.

The man stumbled, gasping, and then ran back down the path, never even looking at them. Mrs. Buli grabbed Clay, who was staggering around in a circle, shaking his hand. "I will cut it!" she cried.

He held still while she made a precise cross cut and drained the blood. "What . . . what *was* that?"

"A wasp-thing from the pouches that hang on our trees."

"Oh yeah. One of those bio tricks."

"They are still overhead."

Clay listened to the drone hanging over them. Another devotee shrieked and slapped the back of his neck. Clay numbly watched the man run away. His hand throbbed, but he could feel the effects ebbing. Mrs. Buli tore a strip from her sari and wrapped his thumb to quell the bleeding.

All this time, devotees streamed past them in the gloom. None took the slightest notice of Clay. Some spoke to themselves.

"Western science doesn't seem to bother 'em much now," Clay whispered wryly.

Mrs. Buli nodded. The last figure to pass was a woman who limped, sporting an arm that ended not in a hand but in a spoon, nailed to a stub of cork.

He followed Mrs. Buli into enveloping darkness. "Who were they?"

"I do not know. They spoke seldom and repeated the same words. Dharma and samsara, terms of destiny."

"They don't care about us?"

"They appear to sense a turning, a resolution." In the fitful moonglow her eyes were liquid puzzles.

"But they destroyed the experiment."

"I gather that knowledge of your Western presence was like the wasp-things. Irritating, but only a catalyst, not the cause."

"What *did* make them—"

"No time. Come."

They hurriedly entered a thin copse of spindly trees that lined a streambed. Dust stifled his nose and he breathed through his mouth. The clouds raced toward the horizon with unnatural speed, seeming to flee from the west. Trees swayed before an unfelt wind, twisting and reaching for the shifting sky.

"Weather," Mrs. Buli answered his questions. "Bad weather."

They came upon a small crackling fire. Figures crouched around it, and Clay made to go around, but Mrs. Buli walked straight toward it. Women squatted, poking sticks into the flames. Clay saw that something moved on the sticks. A momentary shaft of moonlight showed the oily skin of snakes, tiny eyes crisp as crystals, the shafts poking from yawning white mouths that still moved. The women's faces of stretched yellow skin anxiously watched the blackening, sizzling snakes, turning them. The fire hissed as though raindrops fell upon it, but Clay felt nothing wet, just the dry rub of a fresh abrading wind. Smoke wrapped the women in gray wreaths, and Mrs. Buli hurried on.

So much, so fast. Clay felt rising in him a leaden conviction born of all he had seen in this land. So many people, so much pain—how could it matter? The West assumed that the individual was important, the bedrock of all. That was why the obliterating events of the West's own history, like the Nazi Holocaust, by erasing humans in such numbing numbers, cast grave doubt on the significance of any one. India did something like that for him. Could a universe which produced so many bodies, so many minds in shadowed torment, care a whit about humanity? Endless, meaningless duplication of grinding pain . . .

A low mutter came on the wind, like a bass theme sounding up from the depths of a dusty well.

Mrs. Buli called out something he could not understand. She began running, and Clay hastened to follow. If he lost her in these shadows, he could lose all connection.

Quickly they left the trees and crossed a grassy field rutted by ancient agriculture and prickly with weeds. On this flat plain he could see that the whole sky worked with twisted light, a colossal electrical discharge feathering into more branches than a gnarled tree. The anxious clouds caught blue and burnt-yellow pulses and seemed to relay them, like the countless transformers and capacitors and voltage drops that made a worldwide communications net, carrying staccato messages laced with crackling punctuations.

"The vans," she panted.

Three brown vans crouched beneath a canopy of thin trees, further concealed beneath khaki tents that blended in with the dusty fields. Mrs. Buli yanked open the door of the first one. Her fingers fumbled at the ignition.

"The key must be concealed," she said quickly.

"Why?" he gasped, throat raw.

"They are to be always with the vans."

"Uh-huh. Check the others."

She hurried away. Clay got down on his knees, feeling the lip of the van's undercarriage. The ground seemed to heave with inner heat, dry and rasping, the pulse of the planet. He finished one side of the van and crawled under, feeling along the rear axle. He heard a distant plaintive cry, as eerie and forlorn as the call of a bird lost in fog.

"Clayji? None in the others."

His hand touched a small slick box high up on the axle. He plucked it from its magnetic grip and rolled out from under.

"If we drive toward the mine," she said, "we can perhaps find others."

"Others, hell. Most likely we'll run into devotees."

"Well, I—"

Figures in the trees. Flitting, silent, quick.

"Get in."

"But—"

He pushed her in and tried to start the van. Running shapes in the field. He got the engine started on the third try and gunned it. They growled away. Something hard shattered the back window into a spiderweb, but then Clay swerved several times and nothing more hit them.

After a few minutes his heart-thumps slowed, and he turned on the headlights to make out the road. The curves were sandy and he did not want to get stuck. He stamped on the gas.

Suddenly great washes of amber light streamed across the sky, pale lances cutting the clouds. "My God, what's happening?"

"It is more than weather."

Her calm, abstracted voice made him glance across the seat. "No kidding."

"No earthquake could have collateral effects of this order."

He saw by the dashboard lights that she wore a lapis lazuli necklace. He had felt it when she came to him, and now its deep blues seemed like the only note of color in the deepening folds of night.

"It must be something far more profound."

"What?"

The road now arrowed straight through a tangled terrain of warped trees and oddly shaped boulders. Something rattled against the windshield like hail, but Clay could see nothing.

"We have always argued, some of us, that the central dictate of quantum mechanics is the interconnected nature of the observer and the observed."

The precise, detached lecturer style again drew his eyes to her. Shadowed, her face gave away no secrets.

"We always filter the world," she said with dreamy momentum, "and yet are linked to it. How much of what we see is in fact taught us, by our bodies, or by the consensus reality that society trains us to see, even before we can speak for ourselves?"

"Look, that sky isn't some problem with my eyes. It's *real*. Hear that?" Something big and soft had struck the door of the van, rocking it.

"And we here have finished the program of materialistic science, have we not? We flattered the West by taking it seriously. As did the devotees."

Clay grinned despite himself. It was hard to feel flattered when you were fleeing for your life.

Mrs. Buli stretched lazily, as though relaxing into the clasp of the moist night. "So we have proven the passing nature of matter. What fresh forces does that bring into play?"

"Huh!" Clay spat back angrily. "Look here, we just sent word out, reported the result. How—"

"So that by now millions, perhaps billions of people know that the very stones that support them must pass."

"So what? Just some theoretical point about subnuclear physics, how's that going to—"

"Who is to say? What avatar? The point is that we were believed. Certain knowledge, universally correlated, surely has some impact—"

The van lurched. Suddenly they jounced and slammed along the smooth roadway. A bright plume of sparks shot up behind them, brimming firefly yellow in the night.

"Axle's busted!" Clay cried. He got the van stopped. In the sudden silence, it registered that the motor had gone dead.

They climbed out. Insects buzzed and hummed in the hazy gloom.

The roadway was still straight and sure, but on all sides great blobs of iridescent water swelled up from the ground, making colossal drops. The trembling half-spheres wobbled in the frayed moonlight. Silently, softly, the bulbs began to detach from the foggy ground and gently loft upward. Feathery luminescent clouds above gathered on swift winds that sheared their edges. These billowing, luxuriant banks snagged the huge teardrop shapes as they plunged skyward.

"I . . . I don't . . ."

Mrs. Buli turned and embraced him. Her moist mouth opened a redolent interior continent to him, teeming and blackly bountiful, and he had to resist falling inward, a tumbling silvery bubble in a dark chasm.

"The category of perfect roundness is fading," she said calmly.

Clay looked at the van. The wheels had become ellipses. At each revolution they had slammed the axles into the roadway, leaving behind long scratches of rough tar.

He took a step.

She said, "Since we can walk, the principle of pivot and lever, of muscles pulling bones, survives."

"How . . . this doesn't . . ."

"But do our bodies depend on roundness? I wonder." She carefully lay down on the blacktop.

The road straightened precisely, like joints in an aged spine popping as they realigned.

Angles cut their spaces razor-sharp, like axioms from Euclid.

Clouds merged, forming copious tinkling hexagons.

"It is good to see that some features remain. Perhaps these are indeed the underlying Platonic beauties."

"What?" Clay cried.

"The undying forms," Mrs. Buli said abstractly. "Perhaps that one Western idea was correct after all."

Clay desperately grasped the van. He jerked his arm back when the metal skin began flexing and reshaping itself.

Smooth glistening forms began to emerge from the rough, coarse earth. Above the riotous, heaving land the moon was now a brassy cube. Across its face played enormous black cracks like mad lightning.

Somewhere far away his wife and daughter were in this, too. *G'bye, Daddy. It's been real.*

Quietly the land began to rain upward. Globs dripped toward the pewter, filmy continent swarming freshly above. Eons measured out the evaporation of ancient sluggish seas.

His throat struggled against torpid air. "Is . . . Brahma . . . ?"

"Awakening?" came her hollow voice, like an echo from a distant gorge.

"What happens . . . to . . . us?"

His words diffracted away from him. He could now see acoustic waves, wedges of compressed, mute atoms crowding in the exuberant air. Luxuriant, inexhaustible riches burst from beneath the ceramic certainties he had known.

"Come." Her voice seeped through the churning ruby air.

Centuries melted between them as he turned. A being he recognized without conscious thought spun in liquid air.

Femina, she was now, and she drifted on the new wafting currents. He and she were made of shifting geometric elements, molecular units of shape and firm thrust. A wan joy spread through him.

Time that was no time did not pass, and he and she and the impacted forces between them were pinned to the forever moment that cascaded through them, all of them, the billions of atomized elements that made them, all, forever.

Newton's Sleep

URSULA K. LE GUIN

WHEN THE GOVERNMENT of the Atlantic Union, which had sponsored the SPES Society as a classified project, fell in the Leap Year Coup, Maston and his men were prepared; overnight the Society's assets, documents, and members were spirited across the border into the United States of America. After a brief regrouping, they petitioned the Republic of California for settlement land as a millenarian cult group, and were permitted to settle in the depopulated chemical marshlands of the San Joaquin Valley. The dometown they built there was a prototype of the Special Earth Satellite itself, and livable enough that a few colonists asked why go to the vast expense of wealth and work, why not settle here?

But the breakdown of the Calmex treaty and the first invasions from the south, along with a new epidemic of the fungal plague, proved yet again that Earth was not a viable option. Construction crews shuttled back and forth four times a year for four years. Seven years after the move to California, ten last trips between the launchpad on Earth and the golden bubble hovering at the libration point carried the colonists to Spes and safety. Only five weeks later, the monitors in Spes reported that Ramirez' hordes had overrun Bakersfield, destroying the launch tower, looting what little was left, burning the dome.

"A hairbreadth escape," Noah said to his father, Ike. Noah was eleven, and read a lot. He discovered each literary cliché for himself and used it with solemn pleasure.

"What I don't understand," said Esther, fifteen, "is why everybody else didn't do what we did." She pushed up her glasses, frowning at the display on the monitor screens. Corrective surgery had done little for her severe vision deficiencies, and, given her immune-system problems and allergic reactivities, eye transplant was out of the question; she could not even wear contact lenses. She wore glasses, like some slum kid. But a couple of years here in the absolutely pollution-free environment of Spes ought to clear up her problems, the doctors had assured Ike, to the point where she could pick out a pair of 20-20's from the organfreeze. "Then you'll be my blue-eyed girl!" her father had joked to her, after the failure of the third operation, when she was thirteen. The important thing was that the defect was developmental, not genetically coded. "Even your genes are blue," Ike had told her. "Noah and I have the recessive for scoliosis, but you, my girl, are helically flawless. Noah'll have to find a mate in B or G Group, but you can pick from the whole colony—you're Unrestricted. There're only twelve other Unrestricteds in the lot of us."

"So I can be promiscuous," Esther had said, poker faced under the bandages. "Long live Number Thirteen."

She stood now beside her brother; Ike had called them into the monitor center to see what had happened to Bakersfield Dome. Some of the women and children in Spes were inclined to be sentimental, "homesick" they said; he wanted his children to see what Earth was and why they had left it. The AI, programmed to select for information of interest to the colony, finished the Bakersfield report with a projection of Ramirez' conquests and then shifted to a Peruvian meteorological study of the Amazon Basin. Dunes and bald red plains filled the screen, while the voice-over, a running English translation by the AI, droned away. "Look at it," Esther said, peering, pushing her glasses up. "It's all *dead*. How come everybody isn't up here?"

"Money," her mother said.

"Because most people aren't willing to trust reason," Ike said. "The money, the means, are a secondary factor. For a hundred years, anybody willing to look at the world rationally has been able to see what's happening: resource exhaustion, population explosion, the breakdown of government. But to act on a rational understanding, you have to trust reason. Most people would rather trust luck or God or one of the easy fixes. Reason's tough. It's tough to plan carefully, to wait years, to make hard choices, to raise money over and over, to keep a secret so it won't be co-opted or wrecked by greed or soft-mindedness. How many people can stick to a straight course in a disintegrating world? Reason's the compass that brought us through."

"Nobody else even tried?"

"Not that we know of."

"There were the Foys," Noah piped up. "I read about it. They put thousands of people into like organfreezes, whole people alive, and built all these cheap rockets and shot them off, and they were all supposed to get to some star in about a thousand years and wake up. And they didn't even know if the star had a planet."

"And their leader, the Reverend Keven Foy, would be there to welcome them to the Promised Land," Ike said. "Pie in the sky and you die. . . . Poor fishsticks! That's what people called them. I was about your age, I watched them on the news, climbing into those 'Foys.' Half of them already either fungoids or RMV-positive. Carrying babies, singing. That was not people trusting reason. That was people abandoning it in despair."

The holovid showed an immense dust storm moving slowly, vaguely across the deserts of Amazonia. It was a dull, dark red-gray-brown, dirt color.

"We're lucky," Esther said. "I guess."

"No," her father said. "Luck has nothing to do with it. Nor are we a chosen people. We chose." Ike was a soft-spoken man, but there was a harsh tremor in his voice now that made both his children glance at him, and his wife look at him for a long moment. Her eyes were a clear, light brown.

"And we sacrificed," she said.

He nodded.

He thought she was probably thinking of his mother. Sarah Rose had qualified for one of the four slots for specially qualified women past childbearing. But when Ike told her that he had got her in, she had exploded. —"Live in that awful little thing, that ball bearing going around in nothing? No air, no room?" He had tried to explain about the landscapes, but she had brushed it all aside. "Isaac, in Chicago Dome, a mile across, I was claustrophobic! Forget it. Take Susan, take the kids, leave me to breathe smog, OK? You go. Send me postcards from Mars." She died of RMV-3 less than three years later. When Ike's sister called to say Sarah was dying, Ike had been decontaminated; to leave Bakersfield Dome would mean going through decontamination again, as well as exposing himself to infection by this newest and worst form of the rapidly-mutating-virus which had accounted so far for about two billion human deaths, more than the slowrad syndrome and almost as much as famine. Ike did not go. Presently his sister's message came, "Mother died Wednesday night, funeral 10 Friday." He faxed, netted, vidded, but never got through, or his sister would not accept his messages. It was an old ache now. They had chosen. They had sacrificed.

His children stood before him, the beautiful children for whom the sacrifice was made, the hope, the future. On Earth now, it was the children who were sacrificed. To the past.

"We chose," he said, "we sacrificed, and we were spared." The word surprised him as he said it.

"Hey," Noah said, "come on, Es, it's fifteen, we'll miss the show." And they were off, the spindly boy and the chunky girl, out the door and across the Common.

The Roses lived in Vermont. Any of the landscapes would have suited Ike, but Susan said that Florida and Boulder were hokey and Urban would drive her up the wall. So their unit faced on Vermont Common. The Assembly Unit the kids were headed for had a white facade with a prim steeple, and the horizon-projection was of sheltering, blue, forested hills. The light in Vermont Quadrant was just the right number of degrees off vertical, Susan said. "It's either late morning or early afternoon; there's always time to get things done." That was juggling a bit with reality, but not dangerously, Ike thought, and said nothing. He had always been a night person anyhow, needing only three or four hours of sleep, and he liked the fact that he could count now on the nights being always the same length, instead of too short in summer.

"I'll tell you something," he said to Susan, following up on his thoughts about the children and on that long look she had given him.

"What's that?" she asked, watching the holovid, which showed the dust storm from the stratosphere, an ugly drifting blob with long tendrils.

"I don't like the monitors. I don't like to look down."

It cost him something to admit it, to say it aloud; but Susan only smiled and said, "I know."

He wanted a little more than that. Probably she had not really understood what he meant. "Sometimes I wish we could turn it off," he said, and laughed. "Not really. But—it's a lien, a tie, an umbilicus. I wish we could cut it. I wish they could start fresh. Absolutely clean and clear. The kids, I mean."

She nodded. "It might be best," she said.

"Their kids will, anyhow . . . There's an interesting discussion going on now in E.D.Com." Ike was an engineering physicist, handpicked by Maston as Spes's chief specialist in Schoenfeldt AI; currently the most hi-pri of his eight jobs was as leader of the Environmental Design group for the second Spes ship, now under construction in the Workbays.

"What about?"

"Al Levaitis proposed that we don't make any landscapes. He made quite a speech of it. He said, it's a matter of honesty. Let's use each area honestly, let it find its own aesthetic, instead of disguising it in any way. If Spes is our world, let's accept it as such. The next generation—what will these pretenses of Earth scenery mean to them? A lot of us feel he had a real point."

"Sure he does," Susan said.

"Could you live with that? No expanse-illusion, no horizon—no village church. Maybe no Astroturf even, just clean metal and ceramic—would you accept that?"

"Would you?"

"I think so. It would—simplify . . . And like Al said, it would be honest. It would turn us from clinging to the past, free us toward actuality and the future. You know, it was such a long haul that it's hard to remember that we made it—we're here. And already building the next colony. When there's a cluster of colonies at every optimum—or if they decide to build the Big Ship and cut free of the solar system—what relevance is anything about Earth going to have to those people? They'll be true spacedwellers. And that's the whole idea—that freedom. I wouldn't mind a taste of it right now."

"Fair enough," his wife said. "I guess I'm a little afraid of oversimplifying."

"But that spire—what will it mean to spaceborn, spacebred people? Meaningless clutter. A dead past."

"I don't know what it means to me," she said. "It sure isn't my past." But the scan had caught Ike's attention.

"Look at that," he said. It was a graphic of the coastline of Peru in 1990 and in 2040, the overlay showing the extent of land loss. "Weather," Ike said. "Weather was the worst! Just to get free of that stupid, impossible unpredictability!"

A crumbling tower poked up from the waves, all that was left of Miraflores. The sea was rough, the sky low, dull, foggy. Ike looked from the holovid to the serene illusory New England and saw the true shelter that lay behind it, holding them safe, safe and free, in haven. The truth shall make you free, he thought, and putting his arm around his wife's shoulders he said it aloud.

She hugged him back and said, "You're a dear," reducing the great statement to the merely personal, but it pleased him all the same. As he went off to the elevator bank he realized that he was happy—absolutely happy. The negative ions in the atmosphere would have something to do with that, he reminded himself. But it was more than just bodily. It was what man had sought so long and never found, never could find, on Earth: a rational happiness. Down there, all they had ever had was life, liberty, and the pursuit. Now they didn't even have that. The Four Horsemen pursued them through the dust of a dying world. And once more that strange word came into his mind: spared. We have been spared.

In the third quarter of the second year of Spes, a school curriculum revision meeting was called. Ike attended as a concerned parent, Susan as parent and part-time teacher (nutrition was her hi-pri), and Esther because teenagers were invited as part of the policy of noninfantilization and her father wanted her to be there. The Education Committee chairman, Dick Allardice, gave a goals-and-achievements talk, and a few teachers had reports and suggestions to make. Ike spoke briefly about increasing AI instruction. It was all routine until Sonny Wigtree got up. Sonny was a drawling, smiling good ole boy from the CSA with four or five degrees from good universities and a mind like a steel trap lined with razors. "Ah'd lahk to know," he said, all soft and self-deprecating, "whut y'all bin thankin about goan oan teachin jollajy? Y'know? An lahk thet."

Ike was still mentally translating into his own Connecticut dialect when Sam Henderson got up to reply. Geology was one of Sam's subspecialties. "What do you mean, Sonny," he said in his Ohio twang, "are you proposing to take geology out of the curriculum?"

"Ah was jes askin what y'all thought?"

Ike could translate that easily: Sonny had got the key votes lined up and was about to make his move. Sam, knowing the language, played along: "Well, I personally think it's well worth discussing."

Alison Jones-Kurawa, who taught earth sciences to the Level Threes, leaped up, and Ike expected the predictable emotional defense—must not let the children of Spes grow up ignorant of the Home Planet, etc. But Alison argued rationally enough that a scientific understanding limited to the composition and contents of Spes itself was dangerously overabstract. "If down the line we decide to terraform the moon, for example, instead of building the Big Ship—hadn't they better know what a rock is?" Point taken, Ike thought, but still beside the point, because the point was not the necessity of geology in the curriculum, but the influence of Sonny Wigtree, John Padopoulos, and John Kelly on the Education Committee. The discourse concerned power, and the teachers didn't understand it; few women did. The outcome was as predictable as the discussion. The only unexpected thing was John Kelly's jumping Mo Orenstein. Mo argued that Earth was a laboratory for Spes and ought to be used as such, going off into a story of how his chemistry class had learned to identify a whole series of reactions by cooking a pebble which he had brought as a souvenir from Mount Sinai and as a lab specimen—"following the principle of multiple purpose, you see, use plus sentiment"—at which point John Kelly broke in abruptly, "All right! The subject's geology, not ethnicity!" and while Mo was silent, taken aback by John's tone, Padopoulos made the motion.

"Mo seems to get under John Kelly's hide," Ike said as they went down A Corridor to the elevators.

"Oh, *shit*, Daddy," Esther said.

At sixteen, Esther had got a little more height, though she still hunched over as if her head was pulled forward by her effort to see through the thick glasses that kept sliding down her nose. Her temper was pretty moody. Ike couldn't seem to say much lately without her jumping him.

"'Shit' isn't a statement that furthers discussion, Esther," he said mildly.

"What discussion?"

"The topic, as I understood it, was John Kelly's impatience with Mo, and what might motivate it."

"Oh, *shit*, Daddy!"

"Stop it, Esther," Susan said.

"Stop what?"

"If you know, as your tone implies you do, what was annoying John," Ike said, "would you share your knowledge with us?"

When you worked hard not to give in to irrational impulses, it was discouraging to get no response at all but emotionality. His perfectly fair request merely drove the girl into speechless fury. The thick glasses glared at him a moment. He could scarcely see her gray eyes through them. She stalked ahead and got into an elevator that seemed to open to accommodate her rage. She didn't hold the doors for them.

"So," Ike said tiredly, waiting for the next elevator to Vermont. "What was that all about?"

Susan shrugged a little.

"I don't understand this behavior. Why is she so hostile, so aggressive?"

It wasn't a new question, perhaps, but Susan didn't even make an effort to answer it. Her silence was almost hostile, and he resented it. "What does she think this kind of behavior gains her? What is it she wants?"

"Timmy Kelly calls you Kike Rose," Susan said. "So Esther told me. He calls her Kikey Rose at school. She said she liked 'Glasseyes' better."

"Oh," Ike said. "Oh—shit."

"Exactly."

They rode down to Vermont in silence.

Crossing the Common under the pseudostars, he said, "I don't even understand where he learned the word."

"Who?"

"Timmy Kelly. He's Esther's age—a year younger. He grew up in the Colony just as she did. The Kellys joined the year after we did. My God! We can keep out every virus, every bacterium, every spore, but this—this gets in? How? How can it be?—I tell you, Susan, I think the monitors should be closed. Everything these children see and hear from Earth is a lesson in violence, bigotry, superstition."

"He didn't need to listen to the monitors." Her tone was almost patronizingly patient.

"I worked with John at Moonshadow, close quarters, daily, for eight months," he said. "There was nothing, nothing of this sort."

"It's Pat more than John, actually," Susan said in the same disagreeably dispassionate way. "Little sub-snubs on the Nutritional Planning Committee, for years. Little jokes. 'Would that be kosher—Susan?' Well. So. You live with it."

"Down below, yes, but here, in the Colony, in Spes—"

"Ike, Spes people are very conventional, conservative people, hadn't you noticed? Very elitist people. How could we be anything but?"

"Conservative? Conventional? What are you talking about?"

"Well, look at us! Power hierarchy, division of labor by gender, Cartesian values, totally mid-twentieth century! I'm not complaining, you know. I chose it too. I love feeling safe. I wanted the kids to be safe. But you pay for safety."

"I don't understand your attitude. We risked everything for Spes— because we're future oriented. These are the people who chose to leave the past behind, to start fresh. To form a true human community and to do it right, to do it right, for once! These people are innovators, intellectually courageous, not a bunch of gutbrains sunk in their bigotries! Our average IQ is 165—"

"Ike, I know. I know the average IQ."

"The boy is rebelling," Ike said after a short silence. "Just as Esther is. Using the foulest language they know, trying to shock the adults. It's meaningless."

"And John Kelly tonight?"

"Look, Mo was going on and on. All that about his damned souvenir pebble—he plays cute a good deal, you know. The kids he teaches eat it up, but it gets pretty tiresome in committee. If John cut him off, he asked for it."

They were at the door of their unit. It looked like the door of a New England frame house, though it hissed open sideways when Ike touched the doorbell.

Esther had gone to her cube, of course. Lately she spent as little time as possible with them in the livingcube. Noah and Jason had spread their diagrams, printouts, workbooks, a tri-di checkerboard all over the builtins and the floor, and sat in the middle of it eating prochips and chattering away. "Tom's sister says she saw her in the OR," Jason was saying. "Hi, Ike, hi, Susan. I don't know, you can't believe something some six-year-old says."

"Yeah, she's probably just imitating what Linda said, trying to get attention. Hi, Mom, hi, Dad. Hey, did you hear about this burned woman Linda Jones and Treese Gerlack say they saw?"

"What do you mean, a burned woman?"

"Over by school in C-1 Corridor. They were going along, going to some girls' meeting thing—"

"Dahncing clahss," Jason interjected, striking a pose somewhere between a dying swan and a vomiting twelve-year-old.

"—and they claim they saw this woman they'd never seen before, how about that? How could there be anybody in Spes they'd never even seen? And she was like burned all over, and sort of lurking along the side of the corridor like she was afraid of being seen. And they say she went down C-3 just before they got there, and when they did they couldn't see her. And she wasn't in any of the cubes along C-3. And then Tom Fort's little sister says she saw her in the OR, Jason says, but she's probably just trying to get attention too."

"She said she had white eyes," Jason said, rolling his own blue ones. "Really gutwrenching."

"Did the girls report this to anybody?" Ike asked.

"Treese and Linda? I don't know," Noah said, losing interest. "So, are we going to get more hands-on time with the Schoenfeldt?"

"I requested it," Ike said. He was upset, disturbed. Esther's unjustifiable anger, Susan's lack of sympathy, and now Noah and Jason telling ghost stories, quoting hysterical little girls about white-eyed phantoms: it was discouraging.

He went into his study cube and got to work projecting designs for the second ship, following Levaitis's proposals. No fake scenery, no props; the curves and angles of the structure exposed. The structural elements were rationally beautiful in their necessity. Form follows function. Instead of an illusion like the Common, the major space in each quadrant would be just that, a big space; call it the quad, maybe. Ten meters high, two hundred across, the arches of the hull reaching across it magnificently. He sketched it out on the holo, viewed it from different angles, walked around it. . . . It was past three when he went to bed, excited and satisfied by his work. Susan was fast asleep. He lay by her inert warmth and looked back on the events of the evening; his mind was clearer in the dark. There was no anti-Semitism in Spes. Look how many of the colonists were Jews. He was going to count, but found that he didn't have to; the number seventeen was ready in his mind. It seemed less somehow than he had thought. He ran through the names and came out with seventeen. Not as many as it might have been, out of eight hundred, but a lot better than some other groups. There had been no problem recruiting people of Asiatic ancestry, in fact it seemed the reverse, but the lack of African-ancestry colonists had caused long and bitter struggles of conscience over policy, back in the Union. But there had been no way around the fact that in a closed community of only eight hundred, every single person must be fit, not only genetically, but intellectually. And after the breakdown of public schooling during the Refederation, blacks just didn't get the training. There had been few black applicants, even, and almost none of them had passed the rigorous tests. They had been wonderful people, of course, but that wasn't enough. Every adult on board had to be outstandingly competent in several areas of expertise. There was no time to train people who, through no fault of their own, had been disadvantaged from the start. It came down to what D. H. Maston, the "Father of Spes," called the cold equations, from an old story he liked to tell. "No dead weight on board!" was the moral of the story. "Too many lives depend on every choice we make! If we could afford to be sentimental—if we could take the easy way—nobody would rejoice more sincerely than I. But we can have only one criterion: excellence. Physical and mental excellence in every respect. Any applicant who meets that criterion is in. Anyone who doesn't, is out."

So even in the Union days there had only been three blacks in the Society. The genius mathematician Madison Aless had tragically developed slowrad symptoms, and after his suicide, the Vezys, a brilliant young couple from England, had dropped out and gone home; a loss not only to ethnicity but to multinationality in Spes, for it left only a handful from countries other than the Union and the U.S.A. But, as Maston had pointed out, that meant nothing, because the concept of nationality meant nothing, while the concept of community meant everything.

David Henry Maston had applied the cold equations to himself. Sixty-one when the Colony moved to California, he had stayed behind in the States. "By the time Spes is built," he had said, "I'll be seventy. A seventy-year-old man take up the place a working scientist, a breeding woman, a 200-IQ kid could fill? Don't make jokes!" Maston was still alive, down there. Now and then he came in on the Network from Indianapolis with some advice, always masterful, imperative, though sometimes, these days, a bit off the mark.

But why was Ike lying here thinking about old Maston? His train of thought trailed off into the incoherencies of advancing sleep. Just as he relaxed, a thrill of terror jolted through him, stiffening every muscle for a moment—the old fear from far, far back, the fear of being helpless, mindless, the fear of sleep itself. Then that too was gone. Ike Rose was gone. A warm body sighed in the darkness inside the little bright object balanced elegantly in the orbit of the moon.

Linda Jones and Treese Gerlack were twelve. When Esther stopped them to ask questions they were partly shy with her, and partly rude, because even if she was sixteen she was really gutwrenching-looking with those glass things she wore, and Timmy Kelly called her Kikey, and Timmy Kelly was so incredibly gorge. So Linda sort of looked away and acted like she didn't hear her, but Treese was kind of flattered, actually. She laughed and said yeah they really had absolutely seen this gutwrenching woman and she was really like burned all over, shiny, even her clothes burned off except sort of a rag thing. "Her breasts were just hanging there and they were really weird, really long," Treese said, "they were really gut, right? Hanging down. God!"

"Did she have white eyes?"

"You mean like Punky Fort said she saw? I don't know. We weren't all that close."

"It was her teeth were white," Linda said, unable to let Treese do all the describing. "They were all white, like a skull would be, right, and like she had too many teeth."

"Like in those history vids," Treese said, "you know, all those people that used to live where that was before the desert, right, Africa? That's what she looked like. Like those famine people. Do you think there was some accident they didn't tell us about? Maybe EVA? And she got like fried, and went crazy, and she's hiding now."

They weren't stupid, Treese and Linda, not at all—no doubt IQ's over 150 like everybody else—but they'd been born in the Colony. They'd never lived outside.

Esther had. She remembered. The Roses had joined when she was seven. She remembered all sorts of stuff about the city where they had lived before they joined, Philadelphia; stuff like cockroaches, rain, pollution alerts, and her best friend in the building, Saviora, who had ten million little tiny short braids, each one tied with a red thread and a blue bead. Her best friend in the building and in the Building Mothers' School and in the world. Until she had to go live in the United States and then Bakersfield and be decontaminated, decontaminated of everything, the germs and viruses and funguses, the roaches and the radiation and the rain, the red threads and the blue beads and the bright eyes. "Hey I'll see for you, ole blindy-eyes," Saviora had said when Esther had the first operation and it didn't help. "I just be your eyes, OK? And you be my brain, OK, in arithmetic?"

It was weird how she could remember that, nearly ten years ago. She could hear Saviora's voice, the way she sang the word "arithmetic," with a fall and rise in it so it sounded like something foreign, incomprehensible, marvelous, blue and red. . . .

"Arith-metic," she said aloud, going down BB Corridor, but she could not say it right.

All right, so maybe this burned woman was a black woman. But that didn't explain how she got into 2-C, or the OR, or onto the Plaza in Florida, where a girl called Oona Chang and her little brother claimed to have seen her last night just after sun-out.

Oh, shit, I just wish I could see, Esther Rose thought as she walked across the Common, which to her was a bluegreen blur. What's the use? That woman could be walking in front of me right now and I wouldn't even know it, I'd think it was just somebody that belonged. Anyhow, how could there be a stowaway? After a year and a half in space? Where's she been till now? And there hasn't been any accident. It's just kids. Playing ghosts, trying to scare each other and getting scared. Getting scared of those old history vids, those black faces, grinning with famine, when all the faces in your whole world were soft and white and fat. "The Sleep of Reason engenders monsters," Esther Rose said aloud. She had pored over the Monuments of Western Art file in the library because even though she couldn't see the world, or even Spes, she could see pictures if they were close enough. Engravings were the best, they didn't go all to blobs of color when she enlarged them on the screen, but kept making sense, the strong black lines, the shadows and highlights that built up the forms. Goya, it was. The bat things coming out of the man's head while he slept at a table full of books, and down below were the Spanish words that meant "The Sleep of Reason engenders monsters" in English, the only language she would ever know. Roaches, rain, Spanish, all washed away. Of course Spanish was in the AI. Everything was. You could learn Spanish if you wanted to. But what use could it possibly be, when the AI could translate it into English faster than you could read or think? What use would there be knowing some language that nobody spoke but you?

When she got home she was going to ask Susan about going to live in the A-Ed dorm in Boulder. She would do it. Today. When she got home. She had to get out. The dorm couldn't be worse than home. Their incredible family, Daddy and Mommy and Bubby and Sis, like something from

the nineteens! The womb within the womb! And here's Uterine Rose,
Space Heroine, groping home across the plastic grass. . . . She got
there, and hissed the door open, and seeing her mother working on her
little kitchen computer, faced her heroically and said, "Susan, I want to
go live at the dorms. I just think it would be a lot better. Is that going to
make Ike go nova?"

The silence was long enough that she came closer to her mother, and
made out that she seemed to be crying.

"Oh," she said, "oh, I didn't—"

"It's OK. It isn't you, honey. It's Eddie."

Her mother's half brother was the only relative she had left. They kept
in touch through the Network outlinks. Not often, because Ike was so
strongly against keeping up personal communication with people down
below, and Susan didn't like doing things she couldn't tell him she was
doing. But she had told Esther, and Esther had treasured her mother's
trust.

"Is he sick?" she asked, feeling sick.

"He died. Real fast. One of the RMVs. Bella sent word."

Susan spoke softly and quite naturally. Esther stood there awhile, then
went and touched her mother's shoulder timidly. Susan turned to her,
embraced her, holding on to her, and began to weep aloud and talk. "Oh,
Esther, he was so good, he was so good, he was so good! We always stuck
it out together, all the stepmothers and the girlfriends and the awful
places we had to live, it was always OK because of Eddie, he made it OK.
He was my family, Esther. He was my family!"

Maybe the word did mean something.

Her mother quieted down and let her go. "Do you have to not tell
Ike?" Esther asked, while she made them some tea.

Susan shook her head. "I don't care if he knows I talked with Eddie,
now. But Bella just put a letter into the Net. We didn't talk."

Esther gave her her tea; she sipped it and sighed.

"You want to live in the A-Ed dorms," she said.

Esther nodded, feeling guilty about talking about it, about deserting
her mother. "I guess. I don't know."

"I think it's a good idea. Try it out, anyhow."

"You do? . . . But will he, you know, get all . . . you know."

"Yes," Susan said. "But, so?"

"I guess I really want to."

"So, apply."

"Does he have to approve the application?"

"No. You're sixteen. Age of reason. Society Code says so."

"I don't always feel so reasonable."

"You'll do. A fair imitation."

"It's when he gets so, you know, like he has to control everything or everything will be out of control, I get sort of out of control."

"I know. But he can handle this. He'll be proud of you for going to A-Ed early. Just let him blow off awhile, he'll calm down."

Ike surprised them. He did not blow up or blow off. He met Esther's demand calmly. "Sure," he said. "After your eye transplant."

"After—?"

"You don't intend to start your adult life with a severe curable handicap. That would be stupid, Esther. You want your independence. So you need physical independence. First get your eyes—then fly. You thought I'd try to hold you back? Daughter, I want to see you flying!"

"But—"

He waited.

"Is she ready?" Susan asked. "Have the doctors said something I hadn't heard?"

"Thirty days of immune-system prep, and she can receive a double eye transplant. I talked to Dick after Health Board yesterday. She can go over and choose a pair tomorrow."

"Choose eyes?" Noah said. "Gutwrenching!"

"What if I, what if I don't want to," Esther said.

"Don't want to? Don't want to see?"

She did not look at either of them. Her mother was silent.

"You would be giving in to fear, which is natural, but unworthy of you. And so you would merely cheat yourself out of so many weeks or months of perfect vision."

"But it says I'm at the age of reason. So I can make my own choices."

"Of course you can, and will. You'll make the reasonable choice. I have confidence in you, Daughter. Show me that it's justified."

Immune-system prep was nearly as bad as decontamination. Some days she couldn't pay attention to anything but the tubes and machines. Other days she felt human enough to get bored and be glad when Noah came to the Health Center to see her. "Hey," he said, "did you hear about the Hag? All kinds of people over in Urban have seen her. It started with this baby getting excited, and then its mother saw her, and then a whole bunch of people did. She's supposed to be real small and old, and she's sort of Asian, you know, with those eyes like Yukio and Fred have, but she's all bent over and her legs are weird. And she goes around picking up stuff off the deck, like it was litter, only nothing's there, and she puts it in this bag she has. And when they walk toward her she just goes out of sight. And she has this real gut mouth without any teeth in it."

"Is the burned woman still around?"

"Well, some women in Florida were having some committee meeting, and all of a sudden there were these other people sitting at the table and they were black. And they all looked at them, and they just like went out of sight."

"Wow," Esther said.

"Dad got himself on this Emergency Committee with mostly psychologists, and they have it all worked out about mass hallucination and environmental deprivation and like that. He'll tell you all about it."

"Yeah, he will."

"Hey Es."

"Hey No."

"Are they, I mean. Is it. Do they."

"Yeah," she said. "First they take out the old ones. Then they put in the new ones. Then they do the wiring."

"Wow."

"Yeah."

"Did you really have to like, go and choose . . ."

"No. The meds pick out whatever's most compatible genetically. They got some nice Jewish eyes for me."

"Honest?"

"I was kidding. Maybe."

"It'll be great if you can see really well," Noah said, and she heard in his voice for the first time the huskiness like a double-reed instrument, oboe or bassoon, the first breaking.

"Hey, have you got your *Satyagraha* tape, I want to hear that," she said. They shared a passion for twentieth-century opera.

"It has no intellectual complexity," Noah said in Ike's intonation. "I find an absence of thought."

"Yeah," said Esther, "and it's all in Sanskrit."

Noah put on the last act. They listened to the tenor singing ascending scales in Sanskrit. Esther closed her eyes. The high, pure voice went up and up, like mountain peaks above the mists.

· · · ·

"We can be optimistic," the doctor said.

"What do you mean?" Susan said.

"They can't guarantee, Sue," Ike said.

"Why not? This was presented as a routine procedure!"

"In an ordinary case—"

"Are there ordinary cases?"

"Yes," the doctor said. "And this one is extraordinary. The operation was absolutely trouble free. So was the IS prep. However her current reaction raises the possibility—a low probability but a possibility—of partial or total rejection."

"Blindness."

"Sue, you know that even if she rejects these implants, they can try again."

"Electronic implants might in fact be the better course. They'll preserve optical function and give spatial orientation. And there are sonar headbands for periods of visual nonfunction."

"So we can be optimistic," Susan said.

"Guardedly," said the doctor.

"I let you do this," Susan said. "I let you do this, and I could have stopped you." She turned away from him and went down the corridor.

He was due at the Bays, overdue in fact, but he walked across Urban to the farther elevator bank instead of dropping straight down from the Health Center. He needed a moment to be alone and think. This whole thing about Esther's operation was hard to handle, on top of the mass-hysteria phenomena, and now if Susan was going to let him down . . . He kept feeling a driving, aching need to be alone. Not to sit with Esther, not to talk to doctors, not to reason with Susan, not to go to committee meetings, not to listen to hysterics reporting their hallucinations—just to be alone, sitting at his Schoenfeldt screen, in the night, in peace.

"Look at that," said a tall man, Laxness of EVAC, stopping beside Ike in Urban Square and staring. "What next? What do you think is really going on, Rose?"

Ike followed Laxness' gaze. He saw the high brick and stone facades of Urban and a boy crossing the street-corridor.

"The kid?"

"Yes. My God. Look at them."

The kid was gone, but Laxness kept staring, and swallowed as if he felt sick.

"He's gone, Morten."

"They must be from some famine," Laxness said, his gaze unwavering. "You know, the first couple of times, I thought they were holovid projections. I thought somebody had to be doing this to us. Somebody with a screw loose, in Communications or something."

"We've investigated that possibility," Ike said.

"Look at their arms. Jesus!"

"There's nothing there, Morten."

Laxness looked at him. "Are you blind?"

"There is nothing there."

Laxness stared at him as if he were the hallucination. "What I think it is, is our guilt," he said, looking back at whatever it was he saw across the Square. "But what are we supposed to do? I don't understand." He started forward suddenly, striding with purpose, and then stopped and looked around with the distressed, embarrassed expression Ike was getting used to seeing on people's faces when their hallucinations popped.

Ike came on past him. He wanted to say something to Laxness, but did not know what to say.

As he entered the streetlike corridor he had a curious sensation of pushing into and through a substance, or substances or presences, crowded thickly, not impeding him, not palpable, only many non-touches like very slight electric shocks on his arms and shoulders, breaths across his face, an intangible resistance. He walked ahead, came to the elevators, dropped down to the Bays. The elevator was full, but he was the only person in it.

"Hey Ike. Seen any ghosts yet?" Hal Bauerman said cheerfully.

"No."

"Me neither. I feel sort of left out. Here's the print on the Driver specs, with the new stuff fed in."

"Mort Laxness was seeing things up in Urban just now. He's not one I would have picked as hysterical."

"Ike," said Larane Gutierrez, the shop assistant, "nobody is hysterical. These people are here."

"What people?"

"The people from Earth."

"We're all from Earth, as far as I know."

"I mean the people everybody sees."

"I don't. Hal doesn't. Rod doesn't—"

"Seen some," Rod Bond muttered. "I don't know. It's real crazy, I know, Ike, but all those people that were hanging around Pueblo Corridor all day yesterday—I know you can walk through them, but everybody saw them—they were like washing out a lot of cloths and wringing out the water. It was like some old tape in anthro or something."

"A group delusion—"

"—isn't what's going on," Larane snapped. She was shrill, aggressive. At any disagreement, Ike thought, she always got strident. "These people are here, Ike. And there's more of them all the time."

"So the ship is full of real people that you can walk through?"

"Good way to get a lot of people in a small space," Hal observed, with a fixed grin.

"And whatever you see is real, of course, even if I don't see it?"

"I don't know what you see," Larane said. "I don't know what's real. I know that they're here. I don't know who they are; maybe we have to find out. The ones I saw yesterday looked like they were from some really primitive culture, they had on animal skins, but they were actually kind of beautiful—the people, I mean. Well fed and very alert-looking, watchful. I had a feeling for the first time they might be seeing us, not just us seeing them, but I wasn't sure."

Rod was nodding agreement.

"Next thing is you start talking with them, then? Hi folks, welcome to Spes?"

"So far, if you get close, they just sort of aren't there, but people are getting closer," she answered quite seriously.

"Larane," Ike said, "do you hear youself? Rod? Listen, if I came to you and said Hey, guess what, a space alien with three heads has beamed aboard from his flying saucer and here he is— What's wrong? Don't you see him? Can't you see him, Larane? Rod? You don't? But I do! And you do, too, don't you, Hal, you see the three-headed space alien?"

"Sure," Hal said. "Little green bugger."

"Do you believe us?"

"No," Larane said. "Because you're lying. But we're not."

"Then you're insane."

"To deny what I and the people with me see, that would be just as insane."

"Hey, this is a really interesting ontological debate," Hal said, "but we're about twenty-five minutes overdue on the Driver specs report, folks."

Working late that night in his cube, Ike felt the soft electric thrilling along his arms and back, the sense of crowding, a murmur below the threshold of hearing, a smell of sweat or musk or human breath. He put his head in his hands for a minute, then looked up again at the

Schoenfeldt screen and spoke as if talking to it. "You cannot let this happen," he said. "This is all the hope we have."

The cube was empty, the still air was odorless.

He worked on for a while. When he came to bed he lay beside his wife's deep, sleeping silence. She was as far from him as another world.

And Esther lay in the hospital in her permanent darkness. No, not permanent. Temporary. A healing darkness. She would see.

"What are you doing, Noah?"

The boy was standing at the washstand, gazing down into the bowl, which was half full of water. His expression was rapt. He said, "Watching the goldfish. They came out of the tap."

"The question is this: to what extent does the concept of illusion usefully describe a shared experience with elements of interactivity?"

"Well," Jaime said, "the interactivity could itself be illusory. Joan of Arc and her voices." But there was no conviction in his own voice, and Helena, who seemed to have taken over the leadership of the Emergency Committee, pursued: "What do you think of inviting some of our guests to sit in on this meeting?"

"Hold on," Ike said. "You say 'shared experience,' but it's not a shared experience; I don't share it; there are others who don't; and what justification have you for claiming it's shared? If these phantoms, these 'guests,' are impalpable, vanish when you approach, inaudible, they're not guests, they're ghosts, you're abandoning any effort at rationality—"

"Ike, I'm sorry, but you can't deny their existence because you are unable to perceive them."

"On what sounder basis could I deny their existence?"

"But you deny that we can use the same basis for accepting it."

"Lack of hallucinations is considered the basis from which one judges another person's perceptions as hallucinations."

"Call them hallucinations, then," Helena said, "although I liked ghosts better. 'Ghosts' may be in fact quite accurate. But we don't know how to coexist with ghosts. It's not something we were trained in. We have to learn how to do it as we go along. And believe me, we have to. They are not going away. They are here, and what 'here' is is changing too. Maybe you could be very useful to us, if you were willing to be, Ike, just because you aren't aware of—of our guests, and the changes. But we who are aware of them have to learn what kind of existence they have, and why.

For you to go on denying that they have any is obstructive to the work we're trying to do."

" 'Whom the gods would destroy they first make mad,' " Ike said, getting up from his seat at the conference table. Nobody else said anything. They all looked embarrassed, looked down. He left the room in silence.

There was a group of people in CC Corridor running and laughing. "Head 'em off at the pass!" yelled a big man, Stiernen of Flight Engineering, waving his arms as if at some horde or crowd, and a woman shouted, "They're bison! They're bison! Let 'em go down C Corridor, there's more room!" Ike walked straight ahead, looking straight ahead.

"There's a vine growing by the front door," Susan said at breakfast. Her tone was so complacent that he thought nothing of it for a moment except that he was glad to hear her speak normally for once.

Then he said, "Sue—"

"What can I do about it, Ike? What do you want? You want me to lie, say nothing, pretend there isn't a vine growing there? But there is. It looks like a scarlet runner bean. It's there."

"Sue, vines grow in dirt. Earth. There is no earth in Spes."

"I know that."

"How can you both know it and deny it?"

"It's going backwards, Dad," Noah said, in his new, slightly husky voice.

"What is?"

"Well, there were the people first. All those weird old women and cripples and things, remember, and then all the other kinds of people. And then there started being animals, and now plants and stuff. Wow, did you know they saw whales in the Reservoirs, Mom?"

She laughed. "I only saw the horses on the Common," she said.

"They were really pretty," Noah said.

"I didn't see them," Ike said. "I didn't see horses on the Common."

"There were a whole lot of them. They wouldn't let you get anywhere near, though. I guess they were wild. There were some really neat spotted ones. Appaloosa, Nina said."

"I didn't see horses," Ike said. He put his face in his hands and began to cry.

"Hey, Dad," he heard Noah's voice, and then Susan's, "It's OK. No. It's OK. Go on to school. It's all right, sweetie." The door hissed.

Her hands were on his head, smoothing his hair, and on his shoulders, gently rocking and shaking him. "It's OK, Ike . . ."

"No, it's not. It's not OK. It's not all right. It's all gone crazy. It's all ruined, ruined, wasted, wrong. Gone wrong."

Susan was silent for a long time, kneading and rocking his shoulders. She said at last, "It scares me when I think about it, Ike. It seems like something supernatural, and I don't think there is anything supernatural. But if I don't think about it in words like that, if I just look at it, look at the people and the . . . the horses and the vine by the door—it makes sense. How did we, how could we have thought we could just leave? Who do we think we are? All it is, is we brought ourselves with us . . . The horses and the whales and the old women and the sick babies. They're just us, we're them, they're here."

He said nothing for a while. Finally he drew a long breath. "So," he said. "Go with the flow. Embrace the unexplainable. Believe because it's unbelievable. Who cares about understanding, anyhow? Who needs it? Things make a lot better sense if you just don't think about them. Maybe we could all have lobotomies and really simplify life."

She took her hands from his shoulders and moved away.

"After the lobotomy, I guess we can have electronic brain implants," she said. "And sonar headbands. So we don't bump into ghosts. Is surgery the answer to all your problems?"

He turned around then, but her back was to him.

"I'm going to the hospital," she said, and left.

"Hey! Look out!" they shouted. He did not know what they saw him walking into—a herd of sheep, a troop of naked dancing savages, a cypress swamp—he did not care. He saw the Common, the corridors, the cubes.

Noah came in to change his clothes that he said were mud stained from tag football in the dirt that had covered all the Astroturf in the Common, but Ike walked on plastic grass through dustless, germless air. He walked through the great elms and chestnuts that stood twenty meters high, not between them. He walked to the elevators and pressed the buttons and came to the Health Center.

"Oh, but Esther was released this morning!" the nurse said, smiling.

"Released?"

"Yes. The little black girl came with your wife's note, first thing this morning."

"May I see the note?"

"Sure. It's in her file, just hold on—" She handed it over. It was not a note from Susan. It was in Esther's scrawling hand, addressed to Isaac Rose. He unfolded it.

> I am going up in the mountains for a while.
>> With love,
>> Esther.

Outside the Health Center, he stood looking down the corridors. They ran to left, to right, and straight ahead. They were 2.2 meters high, 2.6 meters wide, painted light tan, with colored stripes on the gray floors. The blue stripes ended at the door of the Health Center, or started there, ending and starting were the same thing; but the white arrows set in the blue stripes every 3 meters pointed to the Health Center, not away from it, so they ended there, where he stood. The floors were light gray, except for the colored stripes, and perfectly smooth and almost level, for in Area 8 the curvature of Spes was barely perceptible. Lights shone from panels in the ceilings of the corridors at intervals of 5 meters. He knew all the intervals, all the specifications, all the materials, all the relationships. He had them all in his mind. He had thought about them for years. He had reasoned them. He had planned them.

Nobody could be lost in Spes. All the corridors led to known places. You came to those places following the arrows and the colored stripes. If you followed every corridor and took every elevator you would never get lost and always end up safe where you started from. And you would never stumble, because all the floors were of smooth metal polished and painted light gray, with colored stripes and white arrows guiding you to the desired end.

Ike took two steps and stumbled, falling violently forward. Under his hands was something rough, irregular, painful. A rock, a boulder, protruded through the smooth metal floor of the corridor. It was dark brownish-gray veined with white, pocked and cracked; a little scurf of yellowish lichen grew near his hands. The heel of his right hand hurt, and he raised it to look at it. He had grazed the skin in falling on the rock. He licked the tiny film of blood from the graze. Squatting there, he looked at the rock and then past it. He saw nothing but the corridor. He would have nothing but the rock, until he found her. The rock and the taste of his own blood. He stood up.

"Esther!"

His voice echoed faintly down the corridors.

"Esther, I can't see. Show me how to see!"

There was no answer.

He set off, walking carefully around the rock, walking carefully forward. It was a long way, and he was never sure he was not lost. He was not sure where he was, though the climbing got steeper and harder and the air began to be very thin and cold. He was not sure of anything until he heard his mother's voice. "Isaac, dear, are you awake?" she asked rather sharply. He turned and saw her sitting beside Esther on an outcropping of granite beside the steep, dusty trail. Behind them, across a great dropping gulf of air, snow peaks shone in the high, clear light. Esther looked at him. Her eyes were clear also, but dark, and she said, "Now we can go down."

The Helping Hand

NORMAN SPINRAD

**FIRST CONTACT WITH EXTRATERRESTRIAL
CIVILIZATION**

HOUSTON. NASA has confirmed that the anomalous radio pulses emanating from Barnard's star that NASA SETI researchers discovered nearly a month ago are definitely artificial.

"We haven't decoded the signals yet, but they clearly are data packets," Dr. Henry Brancusi, head of the NASA team, declared. "They repeat every 33 hours. Most peculiar. As the closest candidate for a star with a habitable zone, Barnard's was one of the earliest targets of the first

SETI researchers, but nothing had ever been detected before. It's as if they've just gone on the air."

—*Science News*

SPACE TELESCOPE DETECTS INHABITED PLANET

LUNAGRAD. The Greater European Space Agency has confirmed the existence of a technological civilization on the fourth planet of Barnard's star. The GESA massive optical array on the far side of the moon has detected a ring of satellite-sized objects in perfect Geosynchronous orbit around the planet.

"It can't be anything else," said Leonid Vyshinkov, director of the MOA station. "We are looking at a high technical civilization. There is no further reason to doubt that we are indeed receiving a message from intelligent beings on the fourth planet of Barnard's star."

—*L'Espresso*

INTERSTELLAR PRIME TIME?

NEW HOLLYWOOD. Jack Kovacs, head of Universal-Toho-Disney Productions, announced today that UTDP technicians had succeeded in decoding the transmissions from Barnard's star.

"It's television, what else?" Kovacs told reporters. "Scientists may have been trying to get fancy equations out of it, but I *knew* that couldn't be the bottom line, I mean, if *we* were transmitting to *them*, wouldn't we send something with real production values? The broadcast quality isn't exactly professional, but we're bringing it up to industry standards in the processing lab, and we're going to release it on November 12."

—*Variety*

SECRETARY GENERAL DEMANDS FREE RELEASE OF BARNARD TRANSMISSION

NEW YORK. United Nations Secretary General Wolfgang Steinholtz demanded today that Universal-Toho-Disney Productions release the television transmission from the Barnards that they claim to have decoded through the auspices of the United Nations International Press Agency, rather than selling commercial rights to the program for outrageous prices as planned.

"It's perfectly disgusting to engage in such profiteering with the greatest event in human history," he declared. "This message was meant for all mankind. The Barnards certainly could never have intended that their transmission become the property of a television studio."

"This Secretary General guy's got to be coming from outer space himself," said Jack Kovacs, President of UTDP, when reached for comment in New Hollywood. "What does he expect us to do, give away the biggest world audience share in history? The rights to this are gonna be worth at least a billion and a half dollars!"

Kovacs went on to express indignation at the public outcry. "It's not as if we were ripping off the Barnards or something," he insisted. "We're setting up an escrow account for them even though we don't have to. And we're giving them 17 percent of the producer's net profit. Even major stars don't get a sweet deal like that. Does *that* sound like we're a bunch of sleazebag schlockmeisters?"

—*The New York Times*

OPENING CREDITS

FIRST CONTACT

A Universal-Toho-Disney Production

Produced in conjunction with the people of Barnard's star

FADE IN

A planet floating in space, fleecy cloud-cover over blue seas, green-and-brown continents, looking very much like another Earth, but with different continental outlines, less water, more land.

A series of helicopter shots. Thick jungles of fluffy green trees like enormous dustmops. Rolling savannas covered with lumpy yellowish moss. Seacoast swamps, where tangles of vines drip from huge bushes rooted in the mud. Mountain meadows dotted with clusters of round blue cacti. An enormous canyon with a lucent blue river at the bottom and waves of vegetation foaming down its soft ancient slopes.

Another series of shots, these of wildlife in medium close-up. A large six-legged purple herbivore cropping moss. A bright yellow bird with two pairs of wings. A monstrous blue-and-red striped upright biped with four brawny arms ending in clusters of razor-sharp claws. A silvery torpedo-shape with six great fins, leaping and whirling out of the surface of the sea.

Cut to a full shot of two upright creatures standing hand-in-hand-in-hand-in-hand. Two pairs of arms, one pair of legs, round roly-poly bodies like teddy bears. One wears a bright blue togalike affair, the other a white suit with an extra set of long, belled sleeves, and a short black cloak. What is visible of their skin is covered with short, lustrous, golden fur.

They have ovoid heads with large membranous ears, like the wings of golden bats. They have faces. Two large eyes with thin red sclera and large black pupils, set too close together under bushy red brows. Big round light-purple lips that iris open and shut continually as if blowing fat wet kisses. No nose, but a mobile tubular projection covered with black fur depending from their stubby chins like elephants' trunks.

They look quite alien.

Alien, but cute.

They look into the camera, they touch the tips of their trunks together, they stretch them out toward the viewer as if in greeting.

A tracking shot on a small group of the same creatures, naked now, loping across a savanna, carrying rocks and short sharpened sticks. Some have single mounds on their chests that may be breasts, others bulbous yellow protuberances high up on their torsos that may be penises.

Dissolve to another tribe of Barnards harvesting a field of blue-headed grain in whirlwind four-handed style, using short stone scythes. Dissolve to a village of mud huts. Dissolve to a town of low brown stone buildings all crowded in against each other. Dissolve to a great warren of wood-and-plaster buildings piled high up against a cliff. Dissolve to a great free-standing metal and concrete city in the same style. Dissolve to a fleet of trimaran barges lumbering through heavy seas under round balloon sails. Dissolve to a four-winged aircraft like an ungainly ornithopter, piloted by a Barnard in a tight black flight suit. Dissolve to an aerial shot of a complex highway system, with thousands of round six-wheeled cars careening around it at breakneck speed.

A rapidly cut tour montage of the wonders of Barnard civilization. Great gleaming cities. Endless fields of straight-rowed crops. Huge floating platforms clogging the surface of the sea. Strange machinelike factories puffing out clouds of thick brown smoke. Ungainly-looking squat rockets blasting off the pad. The planet seen through the porthole of some sort of space vehicle.

Two naked Barnards pummeling each other with four pairs of fists. Two squads of Barnards in leather armor slicing each other to bits with short recurved hand-swords. Two armies of Barnards laying each other waste with guns. A village set ablaze by the napalm projectors of big round tanks crunching through it on six enormous bladed wheels. A fleet of ominous black warplanes circling a burning city like angry dragonflies. A roiling, boiling mushroom-pillar cloud.

A series of slow dissolves revealing endless variations on rubble and ruin. Burned-out skeletons of buildings. Vast vistas of charred fields where nothing lives. Huge smoking craters. Frozen lakes of fused black glass. Forests burning. Rivers churning with debris.

Dead birds falling out of a poisonous brown sky. A shoreline choked with the rotting carcasses of sea animals. Decaying jungles of dead vegetation. Mobs of refugees, their golden fur gone all mangy and falling out in patches to reveal angry pink skin, fleeing a series of dead cities under ominous black-and-brown thunderheads.

Darkness. Sheets of dirty gray rain. Howling blizzards. Great glaciers creeping out of their mountain strongholds and onto the plain in time-lapse majesty. Snowdrifts piling up to hide the corpses of cities, jungles, savannas, shoreline marshes, animals, Barnards, a whole formerly living world.

Cut to the opening shot, the fourth planet of Barnard's star, verdant and vital, as it floats in the blackness of space, looking very much like a second Earth.

The fleecy white cloud cover slowly turns an ugly chemical brown that diffuses out to enrobe the planet in a mist of foul choking smog. Brilliant balls of light explode on the surface, one, two, three, then dozens, scores, hundreds, as dark black fountains pour radioactive soot into the atmosphere. Whole swatches of continents are set ablaze. The atmosphere darkens, turns a uniform gray, begins to blacken.

Then it suddenly clears as if the special-effects department has just turned off the smoke machine, and we see the planet below with a sudden new clarity. Continents gleam a skeletal white. Great icebergs drift in the equatorial seas. Jagged ranges of cold gray mountaintops peak up out of the endless ice sheets.

A series of low helicopter shots. Nothing but snowdrifts and ice sheets at first, but then, here and there, huge metal domes dug like enormous igloos into the snow, few, and scattered, and pathetic in all that dead white immensity.

A series of quickly cut shots of the interiors of the domes, grim corridors full of mangy, diseased-looking Barnards, huge chemical vats, Barnards eating what looks like slices of gray plastic, a family of Barnards crowded into a tiny steel-colored cubicle, Barnards unmistakably defecating into the recycling vats.

Cut to two Barnards standing hand-in-hand-in-hand-in-hand, staring at the camera, their fur falling out now, ugly sores along their trunks, their eyes watery with rheum.

Slowly, without taking their eyes off the camera, they let go of each other's hands, get down on their knees, hang their heads in an unmistakable gesture of shame.

Then they hold all their arms out before them, turn up their fleshy palms as if to catch something falling from the heavens. Slowly they raise their gaze skyward, and lift up their trunks imploringly, like elephants reaching for the peanut held by a small child just beyond their grasp.

The camera follows the line of their eyes, the line of their trunks, upward, into a brilliant starry night. The angle reverses, and now we are looking down at two lorn golden creatures kneeling on an endless sheet of ice, gazing up longingly out of the desolation at us, their scabrous trunks reaching out desperately for whatever we have to give.

FADE TO BLACK

A GRIM WARNING

MOSCOW. The opinion in the world scientific community is all but unanimous. The Barnard civilization followed an evolution quite similar to our own until they reached the point where we are now, with industrial pollution at the point of poisoning the atmosphere and killing off the biosphere, and nuclear weapons proliferating beyond control. Then they had a nuclear war which altered their planet's albedo and brought on a Nuclear Winter and what appears to be a permanent worldwide ice age.

We have been shown the future we are making. If we do not cease polluting our atmosphere, we *will* destroy its ability to support a biosphere. If we stumble into nuclear war, we *will* bring on a Nuclear Winter.

The message that the few pathetic survivors of the Barnard catastrophe have sent us is all too clear—we must mend our ways or die.

—Pravda

POPE CHIDES WORLD SELFISHNESS

VATICAN CITY. The Holy Father today chastised the world for its selfish response to the tragic message from Barnard's star. "To take this message as merely a warning sent for our own benefit betrays a lack of Christian charity," John XXV declared. "It is clearly a desperate plea for help. And if we fail to hold out a helping hand, we will have proven ourselves unworthy of survival. We must do whatever we can to aid our suffering fellow creatures on the fourth planet of Barnard's star."

—*L'Osservatore Romano*

BRAZIL BANS ALL AMAZON EXPLOITATION

RIO DE JANEIRO. President Antonio Da Silva today issued an emergency edict banning all further burning, logging, mining, clear-cutting, and industrial activity in the entire Amazon Basin. "This will require great economic sacrifices on the part of the Brazilian people," he said, "but we now know that we have no choice. The trees of our great national patrimony provide the air that *we* breathe too."

—*Jornal do Brasil*

NUCLEAR WINTER REVERSIBLE?

LONDON. "The effects of nuclear winter can be reversed," Dr. Gareth Wilson suggested today. "Finely divided carbon dusted on the ice sheets would increase absorption of sunlight and melt them over time. Once enough ice is melted, albedo will be decreased to the point where the melting process will become self-sustaining."

—*Science*

FRANCE JOINS BRITAIN IN DESTROYING NUCLEAR WEAPONS

—*Le Monde*

NEW LIFE FOR THE BARNARDS?

PALO ALTO. Genentech scientists have formulated a plan to reseed the fourth planet of Barnard's star with a viable new biosphere from Earth. Terrestrial organisms could be transported as germ plasm, re-engineered on the spot to adapt to local conditions, cloned using existing techniques, and then spread by conventional means. Reviving the entire planet might take centuries, but once the process were started, life could be counted upon to spread itself into every available open ecological niche.

—*Time*

ISRAEL JOINS FORMER NUCLEAR CLUB

—*Jerusalem Post*

RED CROSS ANNOUNCES BARNARD RELIEF FUND

GENEVA. The International Red Cross has established a fund to raise the money needed to mount a relief mission to Barnard's star. Donations will be accepted from governments, corporations, and individual contributors.

—UPI

IT CAN BE DONE, NASA DECLARES

HOUSTON. NASA officials admitted today that it would be technologically possible to send a relief expedition to Barnard's star. A large spaceship could reach Barnard's star within a century using an interstellar ramscoop drive already on the theoretical drawing boards, though it would push human technology to its limits.

The cost, however, is estimated at at least one trillion dollars.

—Houston Post

DENMARK PASSES BARNARD TAX

COPENHAGEN. The Danish parliament has voted approval of a 5 percent blanket sales tax with the receipts to be turned over to the Barnard Relief Fund. "If it can be done, it must be done," King Victor declared afterward. "We are a small country, but someone must be prepared to show the way."

—TASS

THE NETHERLANDS, ITALY, NEW ZEALAND, MALAWI ADOPT BARNARD TAX

—Agence France Presse

UNITED STATES COMMITS LONG-TERM MATCHING FUNDS

WASHINGTON. President Wolfowitz has signed into law a bill to reduce the Defense budget by 10 percent a year for the next ten years and deposit the savings on a matching basis in the Barnard Relief Fund. The United States has committed itself by this action to financing 17 percent of the Barnard rescue mission.

—CNN

SOVIET UNION ANNOUNCES NUCLEAR DISARMAMENT

MOSCOW. President Gorchenko announced today that the Soviet Union would cease the manufacture of all nuclear weapons and destroy those it now possesses on a unilateral basis. "To use them, even in self-defense, would mean the death of our entire planet," he pointed out. "We are all dependent on the goodwill of each other for survival. The Barnards have shown us that that has always been true."

Following the example set by the United States, the money formerly devoted to the production and maintenance of the nuclear deterrent will be deposited in the Barnard Relief Fund.

—Izvestia

THE *HELPING HAND* IS ON ITS WAY!

FROM ORBIT. The starship *Helping Hand* has at last begun its long voyage, carrying an international crew of two hundred, carbon extraction equipment, and frozen germ plasm for a new biosphere to the fourth planet of Barnard's star.

Just as the billions of people who contributed what they could to make this moment possible will never live to see the results, neither will the original crew of the *Helping Hand*. But when their sons and daughters arrive, our sons and daughters will remember that when their ancestors were called upon, we rose to the occasion and did what had to be done.

Today we have proven that the Barnards were not wrong to pin their last hope on the peoples of the Earth.

Or rather, perhaps, today we have at last become a people worthy of that choice.

—The New York Times

REPORT TO EARTH #337

The fourth planet of Barnard's star is an airless cold rock that never held life. There is nothing at all in orbit around it. Our scientists have not discovered so much as organic precursors.

The trillions of dollars contributed to this relief mission by the peoples of the Earth at enormous sacrifice to themselves, the best efforts of a generation of scientists, the entire lives of our mothers and fathers, have all been for naught. We have spent all our own lives in this cramped starship, and we will never live to see the Earth we have never known.

All for nothing.

We have all been victimized by the cruelest hoax in history.

But why? And how? And by whom?

—EDUARDO JONES
Captain, the *Helping Hand*

REPORT TO EARTH #338

Oh my God, it's enormous! It just appeared out of nowhere, and now it's in a matching orbit with us and closing fast, a shimmering globe the size of a small moon! It's not only impossible to describe, my eyes don't seem to be able to form a clear image of it, there's a glow, and things like machinery in constant motion inside, and . . . and the ship is being drawn toward it!

The engines won't respond!

There's . . . there's some kind of opening that just appeared on the surface . . . a hole . . . a tunnel. . . .

We're being pulled inside! It's filled with light, it almost seems alive, it—

—EDUARDO JONES
Captain, the *Helping Hand*

REPORT TO EARTH #339

We are children at the feet of the gods, primitive savages who have unwittingly sailed our little canoe into the harbor of a mighty celestial city. And yet, so they have told us, we have become something much more.

The *Helping Hand* was drawn down a long semitranslucent tunnel, through what seemed like some kind of city or machine or organism, towering structures of metal and glass and light that seemed almost organic in their constant flowing motion, and then the ship came to rest, gently suspended about a meter above the floor of a space so enormous that the ceiling disappeared into a shimmering mirage.

It may sound foolish in this report, but you had to be there to understand. We *had* to all meet this moment together, as the representatives of our species, as the family of man. Nothing else would have been right.

And so I led the entire crew out of the ship, to stand there, dazzled and blinking, in the center of a vast amphitheater.

Tiered high all around us, suspended by immaterial forces, were thousands upon thousands of creatures I cannot even begin to describe. Creatures of flesh and creatures of metal and creatures that appeared to be mobile plants. Creatures so beautiful they brought joy to the spirit and creatures so hideous that they made the skin crawl. Hundreds of different species, thousands perhaps, like a vast United Nations General Assembly of the stars.

The sound that they were making together was thunderous. There were clicks, and groans, and whinings, and buzzes, and whistles, and clackings, but the total effect was unmistakable, and it raised the hair on the back of the neck, and brought tears to the eyes.

It was applause.

Then a huge but somehow intimate voice spoke to us. It spoke to each of us in our own native tongue. It spoke with all the languages of the Earth with the collective voice of all those myriad creatures.

"Welcome, brothers," it said. "Welcome, people of the Earth," it said. "You have proven yourselves worthy. We greet you with joy."

"Worthy?" I stammered. "Worthy of what?"

"Worthy of joining the Interstellar Brotherhood of Sentient Beings. Worthy of joining those who have passed the test."

"Test? What test?" I demanded, outrage overcoming all sense of awe, for of course I knew the answer even as I shouted the question.

And of course I was right.

Yes, this galaxy-spanning civilization had created the Barnards out of whole cloth, created the false images and the completely fabricated plea for help on the part of a dying people who had never existed.

And of course I demanded of these cruel tricksters what you no doubt are demanding now as you hear this.

"How dare you do such a thing?" I cried in a fearless rage. "Billions of people sacrificed to make this mission possible! Our own planet was half dead itself when we received your lying message, it stretched us to our limits and beyond! Our parents willingly gave their whole lives to save your fictitious Barnards! And so have we! How dare you call us brothers after what you've done?"

"All of us have been tested. All of us have been forced to face the best that was in our hearts. And so all of us are brothers in the same true spirit. Surely in moving you to join us we have done you no harm."

"No harm!"

"Have you not put war behind you? Have you not learned to cross the gulfs between the stars and come unto *us*? And in the process of seeking to bring new life to the people of a dying planet become the true stewards of your own? And become the best that was in you? Is this not the greatest of gifts? And all the greater for being one you were allowed to give to *yourselves?*"

We all fell silent. For it was true. It was a cruel gift but a great one. It was ruthless and loving. It was very wise.

"So now we welcome you to the Interstellar Brotherhood of Sentient Beings, people of the Earth. We welcome you as equals in the deepest and truest sense. As a people who have earned the right to join us."

"Earned what?" someone muttered aloud. "What are you really offering us?"

There was a sound, a gesture, a feeling, that passed across all those faces, mouths, arms, tentacles, visages, of all those assembled creatures, a sound, a gesture, an emotional expression, and if it indeed was a kind of laughter, it was a laughter that made us all proud.

"Only what you yourselves offered to the Barnards," declared the voice of the Brotherhood. "Only that which makes us all brothers of the same sentient spirit. The best that we have at the full stretch of our powers, and perhaps a little beyond. What else do any of us have to offer but an open heart and a helping hand?"

And so now our little canoe begins the long voyage home across the stellar sea, refitted with engines that will take us there in our lifetimes, bearing the vast treasures of knowledge from the celestial city that we have found.

But the greatest treasure we bear home is the one we brought with us. The most precious knowledge we carry is what we knew all along.

—Eduardo Jones
Captain, the *Helping Hand*

Fondest of Memories

KEVIN J. ANDERSON

THE STARS in the bowshock are blueshifted as the ship soars onward. With each passing moment, the difference between my age and Erica's becomes smaller. Her newborn/reborn body, still on Earth, continues its second life as I grow farther away in distance, but closer in time.

I lean back in the comfortable captain's lounge. The ship runs by itself, and I am its lone crew member. Time passes much more swiftly for me, thanks to relativistic effects. But it still seems like an eternity until I can return home, until I can have Erica back the way she was.

This is my favorite memory of her, the one I recorded first:
Erica and I had met hiking in the back country. Both of us enjoyed the

isolation, to get away from the gleaming cities. We introduced ourselves during the long walk, and two weeks later we arranged to meet again, to go rafting down the river.

The current was languid and warm at the heart of summer. Erica brought her own inflatable raft, and we laughed, so caught up with seeing each other again that we forgot to bring along the auto-inflator pump. Embarrassed at our mistake, we took turns using our own lungs to inflate the large raft as we knelt in the rocks and sand of the bank. Red faced and puffing, we found the situation ludicrous at the time, but it forged a golden thread in our relationship.

"I'm glad you're not upset about it," Erica said.

I shrugged and said exactly the right thing. "The point, my dear, is to spend time with you. It doesn't particularly matter what we're doing."

Our embarrassment increased when we saw that we hadn't brought the oars either. We got into the raft and pushed ourselves into the current, kicking with our feet, paddling with our hands, using our rubber thongs to move us toward the center of the river.

We spent hours that day, floating under the sun, talking to each other. We ate bread and cheese from the cool-pack nestled between us; we drank cans of cheap beer. When we got too hot, we would roll over the flexible side of the raft into the river, splash around until we were cooled, and then crawl back in again.

Once I swam up to Erica and, on impulse, slid my hand against the bumps of her spine and pulled her close for a stolen kiss. She let it last a full second longer than I had expected, and time seemed to stop as we hung there in the warm current, buoyant, as if in a place without gravity.

Neither of us worried about how sunburned we were getting. I paid altogether too much attention to how beautiful the diamonds of drying water were as they shone on her skin. . . .

Of all the scenes I relived for the recorders, that is my favorite memory of her.

I had already seen the explosion of the lunar passenger shuttle on the news before the authorities tracked me down. I watched the rough picture on-screen as the craft took off from the crater floor and headed back on its two-day journey to Earth orbit. At the extreme range of the lunar base cameras, the liquid fuel tanks erupted, turning the shuttle into a cloud of dissipating wreckage and scintillating chunks of ice and frozen air. The image was streaked with pops of video static because the news crews had enlarged it so much.

Erica had been on that shuttle. The irony was, she had gone to the moon base for its bimonthly safety check. Erica had gone to inspect the underground tunnels, the above-surface domes, making sure the wall plates and life-support systems would keep the base inhabitants safe for another couple of months.

No doubt Erica had been perfectly relaxed, thinking her job done, as she departed the gravity sphere of the moon. Someone else had seen to the safety of the transport shuttle. . . .

I got rid of the Transport officials and their preprogrammed sympathy as quickly as their protocol would allow. I stared at the wall, at the home Erica and I had made for ourselves over the years. The lights turned into garish flares through the distorted lens of my tears.

I went into our bathroom and picked up a hairbrush Erica had forgotten to pack. I held it in my hand and stared at it, at the few strands of golden hair trapped by the bristles. She was gone. They would never bring back any sort of remains. A few strands of hair, like golden threads, were all I had left of her.

The first time I went to her apartment, Erica didn't think I was watching as she primped in front of the mirror, using her brush with a snap of her wrist, before she came back out to meet me. I had dressed in my finest clothes.

Erica had the music turned low, candles lit. She normally didn't cook, but had studied food-preparation tapes to get everything just right. That she would do that for me impressed me more than the food ever would.

She made me sit down and accept her attentions as she served salad in a transparent bowl, as she ladled steamed broccoli (which I don't even like) onto the plate, and then bronze-colored chicken breasts. She poured us each a glass of frigid burgundy in a chilled goblet, and we proposed a silent toast, smiling.

"Everything perfect?" Erica asked.

I made an "umming" satisfied sound and said, without thinking, "Well, burgundy isn't really supposed to be chilled. You serve it at room temperature."

Her reaction shocked me. She seemed devastated. My one thoughtless comment had destroyed all of her preparations. I hadn't realized how fragile she was.

"It doesn't matter—" I tried to say, but Erica stood up from the table so quickly that her chair wobbled, and she—

No. I rewound and edited that from the memory recorder. A trivial detail, not worth condemning to permanent archive. A simple thing. Fingering the controls, I deleted my tactless comment, ran back to a few moments earlier.

I closed my eyes, focusing on my imagination. This would be better for Erica.

Yes. She had kept the burgundy at room temperature after all; we ate artichokes instead (which I *do* like). The meal went perfectly. We ended up smiling and holding hands across the table, in the light from the candle flame.

The man from the clone-bank sealed Erica's golden hairs in a sterile, transparent envelope. "No need to worry, sir. This is quite sufficient. I expect no problems at all." He tucked the envelope away. "I am indeed sorry about what happened to your wife, but we can fix that now."

I sat back in their self-adjusting chair and tried to feign a relaxed appearance. I felt so empty, so desperate. Part of this seemed completely wrong, but it also seemed the only thing to do.

The man from the clone-bank—I can't recall his name now—sensed my hesitation. He was a professional, accustomed to nervous people like me. His words were thin, clipped, not identifiable as any particular foreign accent, but the inflections sounded too *processed*, as if he had learned to speak through language implants.

"You have been through our counseling sessions, have you not?" he said. His eyes did not waver as they looked at mine; they appeared too small for his face. "You understand that we will use information from these hairs to fertilize a donor egg. The resulting child will be the genetic equivalent of your wife."

He held up one finger; the nails were neatly manicured. "However, she will be a newborn baby. The body will be the same, but the age difference, some thirty years now—"

"I'm taking the star-freighter option," I interrupted.

This caused the man's eyebrows to raise. "Most people do not. While they can bring themselves to do the actual cloning, they are not willing to abandon their friends, their lives."

"Erica counts more than any of that," I said.

The man from the clone-bank smiled again. "We can help you choose an appropriate star-route with the relativistic difference you desire. When you return, your wife will look exactly as you remember her, the same appearance and the same age. But the memories, ah, the memories . . ."

I looked the other way. I didn't want to hear about this part. I had been avoiding it. Those memories were lost, and I would never truly have the same Erica with the same past.

But the man from the clone-bank waited and then said, as if sharing a secret, "For that, we have a way."

Reliving these memories, focusing my mind to resurrect every last detail and bring it into the recorders, is the kindest form of pain imaginable.

Of course, I deleted all memory of my affair entirely. It's gone. It never happened, as far as the new Erica is concerned. I saw no need to put her through that kind of pain twice.

I realized, even while I was doing it, that I didn't want her to be unaware of my dissatisfaction, the reasons that drove me to seek companionship and understanding other than her own. Though the affair tore apart many of those precious threads that bound us together, if Erica had been able to *learn* from it, she could have understood more of the things that I needed, the things I found missing between the two of us.

And so when I rewrote my memories, I retained some of the quarrels and minor resentments we had toward each other. But instead, I rationalized a way for her to recognize her inadequacies before it became too late. Erica saw what she was doing, how her work shut me out, how she paid too little attention to me—and now, in my imagination, I rebuilt some of the events.

This time, she fixed things between us in the ways I wished she had done. This time, as I recall it for permanent record, instead of her redfaced and tear-stained expression, instead of her anguished screaming at me for what I had done to *her* . . . this time, still with tears in her eyes, she bowed her head a little, apologized, and said she did indeed love me.

The man from the clone-bank made sure I understood the apparatus before he left me alone in the room with my thoughts and memories. The mesh-net of contact electrodes, the soothing subliminal music in the background, the warm lights and gentle air currents were all designed to lull me into a semihypnotic trance so I could recall everything for Erica.

"The memories we record are extraordinarily vivid," the man said. "We take everything. Our lives are more than just grand events, but a sum of little details as well.

"We have a frame-of-reference processor that can shift the viewpoint of everything it records. When you recall something that happened between you and your wife, you naturally remember it through your own eyes, through your own filters of perception. With the frame-of-reference parallax, we can change that, adapt it, so that when we implant those memories into the clone, she will recall them as if she had experienced them herself. In such a way, you can indeed share everything you remember together. She will be your wife once more."

The man's voice tightened as he looked at me. His mouth curled into a button of fleshy lips. "Please attempt to remember as many details as possible, even the most trivial things. Summon them up and record them. The more input we have, the more exact will be the re-creation of your wife."

They scheduled me for eleven sessions, and I began the task with relish, because I wanted to relive every single one of my precious moments with Erica.

Our largest fight, the one I regret the most, came when—after months of subtle hints that I carefully ignored—Erica finally approached me and asked me if I wanted to have children. The tone of her voice and the way she acted made it obvious how badly she wanted them herself.

I had heard about the "biological clock," how many of my acquaintances had suddenly and irrationally decided to toss away their careers and have families instead. Erica and I had just moved into a large home of our own. We were moving up in the world. We had everything we wanted. Erica's sudden request took me by surprise.

She routinely accepted more inspection jobs than she could handle; her job already took us apart more than I wanted. She was always off on the lunar shuttle, or checking the trans-Channel tunnel, or the Bering Straits bridge. Adding a child to the equation (or more than one, from the way she presented the question) would swallow up the little private time that remained to us.

I didn't feel either of us had the time or the energy to be good parents, and I knew how children could be ruined by parents who had come to resent their existence. I told Erica that we were not in a position to be good parents and therefore, for the sake of our potential child, we should not become parents at all.

This devastated her. She refused to make love with me for weeks. She moped around, saying little to me. The whole thing soured our relationship. It seemed almost a relief when job duties called her to the moon for a routine inspection tour, her last.

Now the most important thing was just to have Erica back.

So, as I recalled our discussions and my persuasive arguments, instead of Erica acting childishly and refusing to see reason, I altered the memories again, making her think for a long while about what I had said. Then finally, with dejection but genuine understanding, she nodded and agreed.

"You're right," she told me. "It was just a nice thought. I don't want to have children after all."

I was happy with the new memory. It would make things stronger between us.

I sit at the helm of my ship and think of Erica as the stars rush by. The chronometer continues to reel off two sets of numbers: my subjective time inside the captain's cabin, and Earth-normal time, which flies by as the ship streams toward its destination. Before long, I can turn the ship around and begin my swift journey back to Earth.

Three decades will have passed by the time I return. I have put all our income into trust, and the star-freight company has deferred my salary into interest-bearing accounts with a regular stipend paid to the clone-bank to prepare Erica's clone.

When I arrive home, she will be the same age, the same appearance . . . the same *person* who was lost to me. I lean back and smile again. I picture Erica coming to greet me at the starport. I can't wait to see her again.

She will be just the way I remember her.

Loitering
at Death's Door

WOLFGANG JESCHKE

Translated from the German by Sally Schiller and Anne Calveley

> Him living thou didst not neglect
> Whom thou neglectest dead. Give me a tomb
> Instant, that I may pass the infernal gates.
> For now, the shades and spirits of the dead
> Drive me afar denying me my wish
> To mingle with them on the furthest shore,
> And in wide-portal'd Hades sole I roam.
> Give me thine hand, I pray thee, for the earth
> I visit never more, once burnt with fire.
> —Homer, *Iliad*, XXIII, 70–76

"AN OCTOPUS has eight lives," Spiros said and thrashed it again and again onto the hollow that death had formed over the years in the marble of the breakwater, "and every life has to be beaten out of it." He grabbed the moist, mother-of-pearl colored body with his strong brown hand and plunged it into the yellow plastic bucket full of water. Its tentacles twitched and wrapped themselves around his wrist. It was impossible to tell whether this was caused by the movement of the water or by the last convulsive spark of life. Then the octopus was slapped again onto the hollow stone and it stiffened on the rebound in numbed agony. The two children watched, fascinated. Spiros' eyes wandered up the girl's slim, tanned thighs as she squatted in front of him, but found nothing more exciting than a clean pair of white Sunday panties. He noticed that the boy crouching on the breakwater to his left had followed his lustful glance and he quickly pretended to wipe the salt water out of the corner of one eye.

"Only a cat has more lives," he said and grabbed the octopus to thrash it once again, "and those rich people buried up there in Nekyomanteion. They've as many lives as they can afford." He got up with a groan. Black tufts of hair were visible beneath his torn shirt—bleached from repeated dryings in the sun on dusty cactus plants. The dark skin on his shoulders was spotted with dried-out drops of salt water. His toes, curled in his worn-out plastic sandals, looked like brown gnarled roots.

"What about those rich people?" Eurydice asked, shading her eyes against the sun as she looked up at the fisherman standing in front of her.

"Dead bodies are warmed up in Nekyomanteion," he said.

"They're not warmed up, they're brought back to life," the boy corrected pedantically.

Spiros eyed him thoughtfully. "All right, they're brought back to life," he said. "They have special machines for that purpose. If you have a lot of money, you can go and register. And when you're dead, your family gathers and each member contributes to the special fund. And then you're brought back to life for a day or two and you can celebrate with them. It just costs a hell of a lot of money!" He shrugged his shoulders. "But it has always cost a lot of money to revisit those long since dead. Why, even more than two thousand years ago, it was a flourishing business in this region."

"That's not true," Alexandros said. "The MIDAS machines hadn't been invented then."

"The ancients didn't need any machines." Spiros spat into the murky waters of the small harbor basin, full of plastic bags that look like faded jellyfish. "But they had machines even then. Several were found in the ruins."

Alexandros shook his head.

"Wanna bet?" Spiros asked and grinned defiantly. Through the gap in his front teeth, where he had been hit by an oar in a storm, his moist reddish-pink gums glistened. Eurydice turned away in disgust.

"Ask your uncle!" He nodded in my direction. "He can tell you a true story about it."

You old fool, I thought. Of course, he knew all about it, everyone knew: "Apostoles, the young son of the hotel owner, actually slept with the Germinada, the Frau Doktor, who directed the excavations at Nekyomanteion . . ." I hated the toothless smile of the old man. His lustfulness and pride in Greek manhood were accompanied by the excited clicking and snapping of his worry beads. "He showed her." Oh God, I showed Irini . . . But should I have refused her? Could I have?

"Maybe they did find machines," Alexandros said. "But certainly not American machines—some kind of primitive junk!"

At the pier, the motor of a cutter started up. I sniffed with pleasure, inhaling the smell of burnt diesel oil. You didn't often smell it anymore. Someone called something, but I couldn't make out what he was trying to say . . . The noise of the motor increased. The boat stopped at the entrance to the harbor where the concrete breakwater stuck out into the glistening ocean like a large rusty ruler. The waves left in the boat's wake swept along the quay, setting the plastic jellyfish into motion.

Eurydice grabbed the tentacles of the octopus and let one slide over her small hand. "Can it be brought back to life, too?"

Spiros picked up the creature and looked at it. "My God, Eurydice, I'm glad the beast is dead." He laughed. "But who knows, perhaps they could also bring it back to life."

"Only if they'd made a recording first," Alexandros said. "Only then can a copy be made."

Lost in thought, Spiros looked at the boy. "It would be a good thing to have such a recording. Then I could bring an octopus back to life every day. There are hardly any left out there." He pointed with a nod of his head in the direction of the sea. "I used to be able to catch a dozen or more in one night." He emptied the plastic bucket and threw the octopus into it.

Alexandros strolled up to my table. "What does he mean by that?" he asked, wrinkling his brow. "Bringing dead people back to life in Nekyomanteion is really something new, isn't it? How could they have brought people back to life more than two thousand years ago?" He had the somewhat plump figure and round face of Leandros, his father, but the relentless curiosity of my brother Nikos. Be thankful, I thought, that you don't have his eyes, that pitiless glance of an inquisitorial schoolmaster.

"How is Uncle Nikos getting here?" I asked.

"He's coming by car with Uncle Dimitrios." The wrinkles on his brow deepened. "What does Spiros mean when he says that the dead were brought back to life two thousand years ago?"

"That was all just a big fake."

As a youth, I had helped with the excavations of the old Nekyomanteion. A German woman supervised the work, and occasionally a professor came from Athens. He always stayed at my parents' hotel. And the Germinada, the Frau Doktor, sometimes came for a meal and told us stories of ancient times.

Irini, do you remember how bright it was all around us? My God, where has time flown? Life? She was then perhaps in her mid-forties. She must be over seventy now. An old woman? No, I remember you much younger than you really were then, Irini.

Time is so cruel!

"How could they fake something like that? Either the dead can be brought back to life or they can't," Alexandros said.

"I'll tell you about it some other time."

"But I want to know about it now!"

I looked up at the ugly, modern, concrete hotel at the other end of the bay, covered with large scarlet spots from some kind of highly poisonous pesticide they had used to try and control the lichens growing in the concrete walls. In those days of my youth, there used to be an old windmill on that site. In summer, guests could buy tickets for the excursion boats to Paxos and Kerkira. When the windmill was freshly painted, it had seemed so white and light, so weightless in spite of its bulky form—as if it just needed a slight wind to send it flying away with the clouds.

"It was a clever, lucrative swindle that flourished for years on end. They promised to lead people to the entrance of Hades where they could then meet their dead relatives and friends."

Irini sat with her elbows holding the paper tablecloth that the wind was trying to blow from under the rubber band that secured it. "Acheron, the end of the world of the living, the river between this life and life hereafter, where the threshold to the realm of the dead was thought to be. What a perfect place to commercialize a myth! A few charlatans, actors and workers got together and built a meeting place for the living and the dead up there on the hill. Even Homer mentioned it."

Irini took the brown, felt-tipped pen that she carried around her neck on a thin leather string and drew a series of rectangles on the tablecloth.

"They built a labyrinth of small rooms without windows. They had to be dark inside in order to increase the powers of concentration and cleanse the soul. This was accompanied by a special diet to which some drug was added, probably ergot. And the pilgrims were expected to prepare themselves for the great moment when they would meet their dead. The need to see their relatives once again was enormous—perhaps out of affection for their loved ones—but more than likely for other reasons. Often the deceased had taken a secret to the grave, and the pilgrims used this method to try and entice it from him. Secrets such as where he had hidden his money or whether he had left valuables behind somewhere."

My father cast a very dubious glance at the rectangles. "Bring the Frau Doktor another glass of wine!" he said to Nikos; he did not like the way the boy worshipped Irini, absorbing every word she said. He didn't think much of science.

"The priests filled their bellies with the meat of the animals used in the sacrificial ritual. The occupants of the rooms went hungry." Irini tapped her felt-tipped pen on the labyrinth. "Professor Dakaris, who was the first to excavate the grounds forty years ago, had tons of decomposed blood carted away. The earth around it must have been literally soaked in blood.

"It is said that the customers took three weeks before they achieved the necessary degree of cleanliness to be guided one after the other through the labyrinth. If darkness, fasting and drugs didn't work, they used cold water, ritual stonings and the ashes from cremated bones. They were even more resourceful with the acoustics, using—as a back-up effect—mysterious noises in the darkness, whispering voices and bloodcurdling screams."

Irini drew a large rectangle. "After all that, the candidate was led into a vast, completely dark hall in the cellar. The room must have given the impression of great breadth and space after the small chambers of the labyrinth. This was the anteroom to Hades. At the other end of the vault, a form, lit up with the aid of mirrors and covered in white, was lowered by means of a stage elevator—parts of the machinery have actually been found. The figure stood at the entrance to the underworld and waited to be questioned by the pilgrim. Whether the dead ever answered is not known.

"The customer, nevertheless, in the meantime completely disoriented and on the verge of madness, was prepared to recognize in the strange form anyone or anything and was satisfied with any cryptic answer in order to escape this purgatory and catch a glimpse of sunlight once again."

"It all seems very dubious to me," said my father, "the mysterious goings-on attributed to a few old stones." He stuck his chin out aggressively. "Acheron, the end of the world of the living, you think, eh? Greeks have always lived north of Acheron. I know the families in the mountains, good Greek families, who lived there before this Homer. Who was he, anyway? Was he from Athens?"

"I don't know," Irini said and absently stroked her bracelet—a basilisk with emerald eyes, which seemed to be devouring its own tail, "perhaps from Asia Minor."

"A Turk!" Father snorted and ruffled his mustache, which looked as if a fly had been glued under his nose. "What does he know about our country?" He brushed Homer from the table like a dried-out olive pit. The end of the world of the living was always much farther north, he assured them, not at Acheron but farther north in Albania. And the whole story sounded to him like a typical scoundrel's tale. "However," he said and patted her conciliatingly on the shoulder, "it's your profession to excavate old stones and make up stories about them." I stared through the widely cut sleeve of her light blue linen dress and contemplated with fascination one of her firm, small, tanned breasts. She looked so young with her slender figure, her white-blond hair cut short—younger than a young girl. The wrinkles around her mouth and eyes indicated that she was older, but when she laughed, they were forgotten.

The archaeologists and their crew worked until one o'clock, had a break and then resumed work at four o'clock. It didn't take me long to realize that Irini drove down to the beach on her motor scooter during the midday break when the weather was good. Once I followed her on my bike. I crawled through the underbrush and reeds. She was lying no more than five or six meters away. She was naked except for a broad-brimmed straw hat to shade the book she was reading, and her small buttocks were as brown as her legs and back. I was terribly excited and had my bathing trunks halfway down. The only sound to be heard was the dry rustling of the reeds. The suffocating heat made it difficult for me to breathe. For a moment I toyed with the mad idea of just appearing before her naked. A donkey snorted nearby. I turned around in shock. It was tethered to a pomegranate tree in full bloom. It shook its head, trying to get rid of its halter, and looked at me indifferently.

"That's not the way to go about it, young man," she said, standing before me and smiling. In her nakedness, with her face shaded by the straw hat, she looked even more like a young girl. "Either you pull up your trunks and get out of here, or you take them off altogether."

She was a patient teacher. The first time was terrible. I was in such a hurry that it seemed as though a pack of panting dogs, foaming at the jaws, would come out of the rushes to attack me at any moment. Smiling, she wiped the grains of sand from my cheeks, while I lay beside her completely out of breath, overcome at my own daring and her unexpected favors.

We often met down at the beach. I stole away almost every day at noon when there were not many guests. I brought bread and cheese and fruit. I watched her eat, but seldom ate with her.

"Why don't you eat anything?" she asked.

"I've already eaten," I lied. Why? Was it the excitement that choked me so that I couldn't eat? Perhaps I was subconsciously making a kind of sacrificial offering—a few pieces of goat's cheese spread out on paper spotted with oil, a few olives, grapes and bread in order to appease the gods and keep the miracle going. She ate with great relish. We made love, swam in the ocean, lay in the sun and made love again.

Sometime or other, Nikos must have noticed something and secretly followed me.

"I've been watching you and the Frau Doktor," he whispered, his face as white as a ghost's and his lips trembling. I punched him in the chest so that he fell to the ground. "You fucked her," he hissed, filled with hate. "I'm going to tell Father."

I knew that he was open to bribery. He always needed money for some accessory or other for his home computer. I offered him one thousand drachmas, he demanded two thousand. I gave the money to him without hesitation, as I knew what punishment to expect from my father's firm hand. Nevertheless, when my father finally did hear about it, he broke out into loud laughter, and when Mother complained about Irini, referring to her as "that horrible person, that Germinada," he laughed even louder.

"Did she seduce you . . . ?" Nikos asked and stared at me.

I held my fist under his nose and said, "Get lost!" The whole village got to know about it somehow or other. All of them had a good laugh, the men that is, especially the older men. I hated my brother because of it, although—who knows?—he might not have told anyone. Perhaps others spied on me. But I hated him most of all because he shared a secret that belonged to me and Irini.

The miracle didn't last. In the fall, the archaeologists returned to Athens. I never saw Irini again. I wrote more than a dozen passionate love letters, but never sent them. I still have them today. The next year, a postcard arrived. Irini was at some excavations on Cyprus. "Dear Katsuranis Family," she wrote. My name was not on the card. Father tacked the card to the wall behind the bar like a trophy. Sometime later, the card disappeared. Mother probably tore it down. At times she looked at me as if I had done something outrageous. However, when I lowered my eyes in shame, she smiled.

Sometimes I drove down to the beach and found it terribly empty or desecrated by strangers.

"Has the old Nekyomanteion absolutely nothing in common with the new one?" Alexandros asked.

I shook my head.

"Have Dimitrios and Nikos still not arrived?" Helena called from the hotel.

"No!" I called up to her. "I think they've closed the bridge down there in Stratos—it's in danger of collapsing! They'll probably have to take the road via Astakos, Prebeza."

"Everything is ruined. Everything! Everything!" Helena cried in reply. "The whole world is ruined."

"A few ugly concrete blocks are not the world. That's the poetic justice of nature."

"Lichens are eating the concrete," Alexandros said.

"Yes, a mutated lichen. They call it the 'Klondike Strain' because it appeared for the first time in Alaska."

"Why don't they just eradicate it?"

"My dear young man, that would cost more than the whole world can afford. And besides, I couldn't care less if that ugly building disappeared." I pointed to the hotel up on the hill. "With such enormous quantities of concrete to feed on, this organism can reproduce itself at an alarming rate. It can't be stopped."

"But all those bridges, the tunnels, the skyscrapers . . . ?"

I shrugged my shoulders. "We don't need them in order to survive. And if we build anything, we'll use bricks or stones. Buildings made of bricks and stones are far more beautiful."

Alexandros stared at me in amazement. The spirit of my brother Nikos. Many were secretly glad that inland waterways were falling into disuse, long stretches of highways and ambitious bridge constructions were crumbling, and that the ugly concrete buildings of the rich were being consumed by lichens—all of which made expensive repairs necessary. People in this part of the world, however, still clung naively to the belief that technical progress at all costs must be desirable. The lichens were yet another obstacle to the course of progress. Do you really believe, Apostoles, that we could do without progress? No, but I don't want it to be controlled by people who are only interested in what is technologically feasible, and whose only other characteristic is bad taste.

"They're coming," Eurydice called as she came running to us, out of breath. She turned around and ran to the parking lot.

A dark red Mazda Electric rolled up. Dimitrios and Nikos got out. The children surrounded them. I got up. Leandros and Helena appeared in the doorway.

"Come on up to the terrace! It's warm today," Helena called. "Why don't you park the car in the shade, Dimitrios?"

"There won't be any shade there in an hour, Helena. It'll be there, where the car is now," Dimitrios said and kissed her on the cheek.

"How do you men always know when and where there'll be shade?" she asked and pushed a lock of hair back behind her ear. She wore her hair in an old-fashioned way—plaited and pinned up on the back of her head in a bun. "You men always have time to watch the course of the sun, while we women have to work every day, the whole year from dawn to dusk— Saturdays, Sundays, until we drop dead. I'll drop dead working, that's for sure!" Oh Sister, I thought, if only you had a little bit of Mother's pride, of her understanding. But Helena belonged to those who always complain about their hard lot and yet have no other interests in life.

Leandros, her husband, stood nearby looking guilty, holding his spade-like hands over his stomach.

"Sit down! Sit down!" she called. "I haven't finished yet. Apostoles, bring some ouzo, fetch some wine! Are you hungry?" Without waiting for an answer, she bustled back into the house.

An octopus lay in the glass cooler, its plasticlike flesh spotted with age. The suckers looked like tiny, violet-colored disks stuck to the skin, their edges finely honed. It had lived its eight lives. The ends of its tentacles, limp in death, hung through the wire shelf of the cooler. Life reduced to a lump of protein.

Can it be brought back to life?

The bottle of wine was cold and slippery, and I almost dropped it. I rinsed out some glasses.

Obstacles—nothing but obstacles! How full of hope the world was in those days! It must have been shortly after the turn of the century. Mul-timanna! A project of biblical dimensions! A project to surpass all projects! The miraculous creation of bread. The feeding of ten thousand . . . no, ten million, one hundred million, the starving billions of the world. An electronic victory over hunger. Protein recorded on a magnetic disk, then reproduced using inanimate material, from carbon, hydrogen, oxygen, sulphur and God knows what atoms—using a computer matrix and mixing them all together in the turbulence chamber. Unlimited cans of food, the packaging integrated into the program. Multimanna. The ultimate victory over hunger! Bread for the world in the form of electronically synthesized chicken—food for the Indians as well as the Sudanese, Mexicans, Pakistanis and the Hottentots—no ridiculous religious tabu to prevent real mass production; MIDAS was expensive, very expensive, and only worthwhile on a large scale. Naturally, the new technology also produced something for the palates of the rich—exquisite menus by the best cooks in the world, composed in the studio. The fresh aroma and touch of creative genius stored forever on disks. Recorded haute cuisine. The cost, of course, exorbitant—the technical equipment alone would cost a fortune.

Then long, disappointed faces. The guinea pigs developed symptoms of poisoning. They died by the thousands, while others, fed with the same Multimanna enjoyed the best of health. Mysterious, poisonous substances, distorted groups of molecules, deposits of mutated atoms, the emergence of deadly compounds.

"Mistakes in the running of the program," said the scientists of CalTech and NASA. An improved scanning of the matrix and better computers for the reconstruction of molecular structure would eliminate such malfunctions—would make it possible to produce copies of living creatures, of human beings (Multimanna was only a sideline as Teflon-coated frying pans were to the Apollo project). It was all only a quantitative problem of storage capacity and data transmission.

I was fascinated by the idea of outwitting time by means of timeless copies. Two lovers—whose copies meet again and again—as young as we were then, Irini. A simultaneous program over millennia. A minor detail for a computer.

"What is MIDAS?" I asked Nikos.

He looked at me in amazement.

"No, I really don't know," I assured him.

"Molecular Integrating and Digital Assembling System," he said. "It uses the same principle as the television screen, only extremely complicated and three dimensional. Each atom of a molecule in a specifically delineated area of space is measured and the data are stored. Using these data—analogous to the two-dimensional television screen—a three-dimensional copy is created. This takes place in a turbulence chamber which contains the atoms necessary for composing a copy. A series of computer-induced magnetic fields restructures the matter in exactly the same form as the original. The speed of reproduction depends on the complexity of the molecular pattern. While a coin can probably be reproduced in seconds, it will take hours, if not days, to create a human being."

And NASA was counting on it. One could put unmanned observatories with MIDAS equipment on board into orbit around each planet, send unmanned spaceships to Alpha Centauri, to Barnard's Star, to Sirius—and send the crews later, at the speed of light, after the spaceships had reached their destinations.

Nikos called up the flight paths on the screen of his computer. They bounced out of the solar system, threaded their way through far-off gravitational fields and looped themselves around the distant suns like lassos made of green light. He watched the scientists appear on the screen and hurry to the equipment in order to measure and catalog the marvels of the universe.

"This is the victory of mankind over space and time," Nikos said.

His eyes were a clear light blue, the eyes of Nordic conquerors or slaves. They often appear unexpectedly in our people, generations later, flashing like aquamarines from the depths of dark stone. I always hated his eyes. I never liked him anyway.

And then there were those others, the skeptics. They always said that it would never be possible to achieve the hi-fi quality that such living cells need. Enzymic and neural disturbances, poisons, carcinogens and deformities could not be avoided. Copies of the living organisms would not be viable.

I had a vision of a spaceship, floating through space like the raft of the Medusa, delirious survivors still clinging to the wreckage, everywhere the silence of death and decay. Figures covered in blood staggered wailing through the passageways. Others, oblivious to everything around them, sat slumped over their equipment, cursing those who had done this to them—who had sent them on this voyage of no return.

They had already long since created a pitiful name for them: *Morituri* —the doomed ones—heroes of science who saw the stars and then died. The MIDAS technicians, however, with their unerring instinct for the right word, called them "data mutants."

Then a man called Horace Simonson appeared, a mathematician, who proved that an error rate of so and so many per thousand was the lower limit, as the recording process itself interfered with the molecular structure. The copy, no matter how accurate the reproduction, was always subject to a number of errors—a sort of Heisenberg's uncertainty principle of bioelectronics. This meant poisoned chicken meat for the starving, crippled, hemorrhage-prone astronauts, incapable of performing their mission and—even worse—terrible surprises at exclusive parties (unless you followed the old tradition of having someone try your food first or enjoyed playing Russian roulette).

Congress canceled the funds for further research. This was Nekyomanteion's chance. The company acquired the patent for the recording and copying procedure for twelve billion dollars. The U.S. Government had already invested more than ten times this amount. The so-called Lazarus Act stipulated that only copies of persons proven dead could be made (on legal and identification grounds). Electronic immortality and temporary resurrection were now feasible. Of course, it was typical American sensationalism to establish a subsidiary of the world-renowned corporation on the very spot where, two and a half millennia ago, the old Nekyomanteion had actually flourished.

The stone floor under the vine leaves was spotted with sun. Sun-dappled faces turned to greet me. Dimitrios, my older brother, had come up from Patras with Nikos. They were sitting around the table. Leandros, Helena's husband, had joined them. A letter, held down by a stone, lay before him on the table. Beside him, his two children.

Dimitrios, small and wiry, also had a mustache like a fat black fly over his upper lip. He's getting more and more like Father, I thought.

Nikos, wore an elegant dark suit and vest with a light gray tie, a heavy ring with an onyx stone on his finger and, on his wrist, a minicomputer. His black beard was well kept.

"You're looking well," I said.

"Sounds as if you are trying to butter me up into doing you a favor," he said, his white teeth glistening.

"Don't worry."

"Do you know who I was thinking of today, Apostoles?" he asked.

"I'll never be able to guess, Nikolakis."

"Do you remember that German Frau Doktor, Irini?"

"Vaguely."

"Do you think she's still alive?"

"Why not?" I asked with more vehemence than intended. "She was very young at the time."

Nikos wouldn't look at me. He pretended to be studying his folded hands, grinning to himself. "She ought to be about eighty now."

Helena's husband looked at us imploringly. His broad shoulders had become stooped under the burden of his wife's constant nagging. His hands, not capable of fighting back, lay on the wine-stained table in front of him, his glass of wine half-empty. There was no use answering.

"They have now closed the bridge at Stratos," Dimitrios said. "They obviously can't cope."

I couldn't help smiling.

"I can't imagine what there is to grin about," he said. "They blew up four skyscrapers in Patras last week, because they were in danger of collapsing. One of them was the Sheraton Hotel."

"That horrible monstrosity in the Peloponnesus," I said.

"But where is this all going to end?"

"Whitewashing it would be a good idea," Alexandros said.

"Shut up!" his father said.

"He's right," Nikos replied. "Whitewashing disinfects, but there are better ways of going about it. It would cost over 200 billion drachmas to treat all the concrete buildings in Greece. Not only that, we would have to use strong poisons. And the environmentalists . . ." He shrugged his shoulders in resignation.

Leandros finished his glass of wine.

"Bring us another bottle of wine," he said to Alexandros.

"Mother says you shouldn't drink so much," the boy replied. Nikos grinned at his brother-in-law.

"Keep your smart mouth shut!" his father shot back at him in a surge of protest and self-assertion.

"But I want to hear what Uncle Nikos has to say," Alexandros grumbled.

"He'll save what he has to say for when you return."

"How's business?" I asked Dimitrios.

"There's no question of business anymore," he sighed. "When the Germans still came, the Austrians, the English, the Swedes—we sold wine and ouzo. Hah! Business was booming! But today . . ."—he opened his arms in resignation—"we can't even feed the grapes to the pigs. These damn Arabs don't drink any alcohol, don't eat any pork." He shook his head sadly. "I don't know what to make of people who drink tea all day and stare out at the ocean with a look of suffering on their faces."

"What's in the letter?" Nikos asked. "Strictly speaking, that's why we're here, you know."

Leandros removed the stone holding the letter down and laid his large hand on the paper.

"Nekyomanteion has made us an offer on the occasion of Father's eightieth birthday. I've no idea how they found out that he would be eighty."

Alexandros put a jug of wine on the table. Leandros filled the glasses, which immediately misted over, diffusing the golden yellow sparkle of the wine.

"When Nekyomanteion Inc. was founded and the company bought up all the land around Acheron, they also acquired sixteen hectares of pastureland in the mountains from your father."

"Pastureland!" Dimitrios screeched contemptuously. "You couldn't have kept a dozen goats on it. Nothing but stones. That was the best deal he ever made!"

Leandros put on his glasses and, in a pedantic manner, read the letter out loud: " 'Kristos Katsuranis belongs to the group of privileged persons to whom we have made the unique and extraordinary offer: a free recording . . .' "—Leandros hesitated—" 'of his person at any prearranged time. This recording will be stored free of charge for a period of five years. After that period, the usual fee for such storage space will be charged. A $33^1/3$ percent discount will be given for the realization of every copy—including medical care of the same until its decease, the standard procedure, cremation etc. . . .' " He moistened his lips and followed the text in the letter with his finger. " 'This is the most valuable present you can give a person—the gift of life.' "

A pensive stillness followed.

"It's a bargain!" Leandros pointed out. Helena's words. I could almost hear her voice. "Up to now only the very rich have been able to afford it: the young Onassis, the fifth Rockefeller, King Charles and Lady Di, a few oil sheikhs, some politicians, a couple of actors . . . It's a bargain, believe me."

"What does Father have to say about all this?" Dimitrios asked. "Where is he, anyway?"

"He has gone to the café. He had a fight with Helena. Every day the same goings-on. Always the same. We had to fire another young girl yesterday. A good girl. She came from Papigon, up there in the hills, hardworking and capable. He was always after her, trying to grab at her under her skirts. Always the same. Now Helena has to do all the work alone again. Ah . . ." He became silent with a sigh.

"What does Father have to say about the offer?" Nikos asked.

"I haven't told him yet. We wanted to talk it over with you first."

"Such bargains are often the beginning of the end," Dimitrios inserted.

"Nonsense," Nikos said. "They probably have some leftover storage space."

"I think the new Nekyomanteion will be as successful as the old one," I said. "When they've got their first few thousand persons stored, they'll earn a fortune in storage fees. Once such a recording exists, who would ever have it erased? Who would want to be the willful executioner of a favorite relative? Who would want to destroy hope of eternal resurrection of the flesh? Even if mathematicians say that it is, in principle, just not possible—when has faith ever been conquered by mathematics? Faith, love, hope—the three emotional pillars of mankind—shaken by a couple of dry formulas? Never! The relatives will pay the bill of Nekyomanteion Inc. like good citizens. Only when the person concerned can no longer be remembered in the hearts of those living will it perhaps be possible to delete his recording. Then and only then will he be able to rest in peace. But that has always been the case."

"Are you against this, then?" Nikos asked.

"No, I'm not."

"I don't know what the whole thing is about," Dimitrios said.

"It just means," I said, "that you can get together with someone for a few hours—with someone long since dead. You can talk to him, celebrate with him, be happy with him." Forgive me—I didn't know any better at the time.

Nikos shoved a piece of cheese into his mouth. "One of the greatest scientific achievements of all time. I'm all for it."

Dimitrios nodded.

"Me, too," he said.

Leandros shrugged his shoulders. "It's a bargain," he said.

"Have you the right to speak for Helena?" Nikos asked him mischievously.

Leandros looked at him helplessly.

"Please stop it, Nikos!" I said.

He raised his hands defensively. "I didn't really mean it like that."

Eurydice, bored by the grown-ups' talk, kicked the concrete wall surrounding the terrace with the tip of her plastic sandal. Suddenly, a large piece came loose and fell noisily down to the street below. Everyone stared, shocked at the hole in the wall. In the silence that followed, you could hear the shouting of the young boys playing ball at the other end of the quay.

Dimitrios suddenly burst into cackling laughter. "Don't worry," he said. "Father was only saving cement."

"Have you come to an agreement?" Helena asked. She had appeared in the doorway, wiping her hands on her skirt. "It's a bargain."

And that in the end was our father's real reason, too, even if he did grumble that he would never let himself be "poked about" by a machine and suspected his daughter of having sold him to the "American capitalists" behind this "corpse-stripping company," as he called it. Just as a steady drop of water hollows out stone, the fact that it was a bargain succeeded in penetrating to the very depths of his consciousness, dispersing any doubts and reservations. Sometime during the following year, he agreed to the recording with one stipulation: I must accompany him to Acheron.

It was a clear morning in late spring. Sage and thyme were in bloom. Yellow broom had covered the slopes with gold and, here and there, the tranquil green of the countryside was broken by the blaze of pomegranate blossoms. We drove along the coastal road, along the mountain slopes, toward the north. The ocean glistened in the sun and embraced the coast with arms the color of emeralds. You can't see the rubbish from up here, I thought, the wasteful blessings of the age of plastic.

Father insisted on stopping a couple of times to rest and drink ouzo. I drank mine out of a glass with water. The water took on the milky color of the ouzo. Father, used to a life of prohibition, drank his out of a cup.

Just ever so slightly tipsy, we entered a small, unadorned church, lit two thin candles and pressed them into the sand holder near the altar. Stern-looking saints in glass-covered pictures gazed serenely down on us from across the centuries.

Shortly thereafter, we reached our destination.

Nekyomanteion Inc. was a subsidiary of a multinational corporation comprising above all a chain of homes for the aged, a senior citizens' travel agency, geriatric hospitals and funeral homes. In order to exploit the *genius loci*, it had bought up a huge piece of land east and southeast of the village of Parga and transformed it into a park. The land between Igoumenitsa and Preveza, which had represented the end of the world of the living eons ago, had always been a barren, mountainous region. Even on sunny days, it seemed dark and gloomy. Innumerable caves led deep into the earth. The small river that flows down from the mountains and joins the ocean southeast of Parga is called Acheron. It was the river boundary between this life and the next. Two and a half millennia ago, the ancient Nekyomanteion had been situated on the hill overlooking the shore of the hereafter.

The modern Nekyomanteion had very little in common with the ancient one—except that they both induced the rich to part with their money. It was a combination of a home for the aged and a hospital, a gigantic hi-tech plant and a nuclear research center. The buildings blended with their surroundings and were built partly underground. Cypress groves, fast-growing eucalyptus trees, well-kept lawns, paths and park benches predominated. The company had had a nuclear power plant built in the Bay of Preveza to extract the salt from the sea water and to supply the power for the equipment that produced the recordings and the copies. Rematerialization in the turbulence chamber used up enormous amounts of energy.

The whole landscape had been transformed. When there was enough water, a generous forestation program was started. The result looked more like Hollywood than Hades—at least at first glance.

The formalities were quickly settled. In spite of this, we had to wait. We paced impatiently up and down in front of the reception hall. The wind caressed the lush dark red of the bougainvillea, which almost covered the whole facade of the building. Far off, on the other side of the bay, surrounded by reeds and sandbanks, at the estuary of the river, the ocean gleamed.

Kristos groped for my arm with his small strong hand and looked up at me imploringly.

"Will I have to take all my clothes off?"

Bewildered by the simple, but unexpected question, I didn't know what to say and just stared at my father's face. How old you've grown, Father, I thought, with a touch of dismay at the pitiless frailty of human flesh. At the same time, I became aware that I had not really looked at his face for years, thoughtlessly taking for granted its familiarity. With great effort, I pulled myself together to answer his question.

"I don't know, Father. We'll ask the doctor—if you think it's important."

The anxiety faded from his blue-gray eyes, surrounded by innumerable wrinkles; the corners of his mouth twitched; his hand slid from my arm and fell to his side.

"But you'll wait for me, Son, no matter what they do to me. Promise!"
"Of course I'll wait for you, Father. It won't take long anyway."

A friendly middle-aged doctor, who introduced himself as Dr. Kaminas, accompanied him. The examination lasted more than four hours! I wandered aimlessly through the grounds of Nekyomanteion. I had never seen so many decrepit people in my life. Most of the park benches were occupied by patients, who were surrounded by visitors looking very ill at ease. An electric wheelchair drove past me with its whining motor. An old man was sitting upright in it, dressed in a painfully correct, but terribly old-fashioned, cream-colored suit. He seemed in some way or other very familiar to me. I was convinced I had seen him many times on television a long time ago. However, I could not remember his name. The patient lifted his straw hat and greeted me with a nod of his head, but he didn't look at me. He gazed straight ahead at the path in front of him. His cramped left hand clutched the controls. His face was distorted by the strain of being courteous, and saliva ran out of one corner of his mouth, over his chin and the starched collar of his apricot-colored shirt.

A portly old man, his head shaved bald and with an enormous mustache, sat on another bench. I was certain I had seen his face quite often in the newspapers, but that would have been ten or fifteen years ago. A well-known lawyer? A politician, perhaps? I couldn't remember his name. He sat slumped against the back of the bench, his heavy head bent backwards, his mouth wide open. His breath rattled, and a transparent plastic tube was suspended from one of his nostrils. Foamy red mucus bubbled through the tube. He was deathly pale, and his eyes stared unseeingly into the sky. One of his large, waxlike hands lay in the lap of an older, very elegantly dressed, woman. She was holding his hand tightly, and her eyes were red from crying. She furtively dabbed them with her handkerchief. A young, good-looking nurse in a tight-fitting uniform with a red collar stood behind the elderly couple. She smiled encouragingly at me. Irritated by the contrast, I turned quickly away and fled back to the reception hall, accompanied by the ever-present sound of the lawn sprinkler . . . *pft, pft, pft.*

"It really didn't cost anything," Father cried loudly as he came out of the entrance to the reception hall, flanked by Dr. Kaminas and a nurse. He seemed extremely satisfied and a little drunk. His eyes were slightly glazed. Probably the anesthetic, I thought, as he had really not drunk that much ouzo.

"Did you have to take all your clothes off?" I asked him as we walked to the car.

"Eh?" He cupped his hand to his ear and pinched one eye closed as if in some mysterious way this would help his diminishing power of hearing.

"Did you have to take all your clothes off?" I repeated.

"No, they only pricked my finger." He raised his hand to show me his left index finger and rubbed the tiny spot with his thumb. "Then, I must have dozed off. When I awoke, everything was finished. I have no idea just how they did it, but Dr. Kaminas said they had taken care of everything."

He fell asleep in the car on the journey home. I looked at him out of the corner of my eye. His hair, almost white, was still as thick and unmanageable as the mane of a wild donkey. His dark brown weather-worn skin, which stretched over his temples and cheekbones, made his features look like those of a mummy. His toothless mouth was slightly open, and the ridiculous Charlie Chaplin mustache, the size of an enormous housefly and with not a trace of gray in it, looked just like that of Dimitrios. His scrawny neck seemed lost in the collar of his shirt, which had become too large for him. My father—I said to myself and was overcome for a moment with a tenderness that I had never felt for him before, which, in this fleeting moment, moved me almost to tears.

The Nekyomanteion Inc. offer had included, among other things, the admission of the old man to the company's home for the aged. Leandros had not dared discuss the matter on that Saturday afternoon, because he knew that aside from his wife, no one could be persuaded to accept the idea.

"It's all right for you, you don't have all the trouble and worry with him," Helena complained, when the subject was finally brought up. "You don't have him around all the time!"

"You've got a hotel with sixteen beds," Dimitrios replied sternly, "and no room for Father?"

"He's your father, too! You visit him three, at the most four times a year. Nikos and Apostoles, too. But I have to put up with him day after day. He drives me mad the way he runs after the maids and talks absolute nonsense to the guests when he's drunk."

It was true, he was stubborn and cantankerous. He always had been. It was our mother's fault. Aretti was her name. She had put up with him all those years and had cared for him lovingly, but in silent reproach and bitterness. She had died eight years ago. There would be no reunion with her—at least no electronically induced reunion. Helena had long since taken over her role—but forever scolding, always impatient and severe. He resisted her rod of iron and had bitter fights with her, which he readily brought to a head in front of the guests. He enjoyed the open battle that his wife had never allowed—at least not in front of others. And since his hearing was no longer what it once was, which he, naturally, like most people who are a little deaf, was not prepared to admit, it was sometimes very embarrassing—especially, when he loudly told Greek guests just what he thought of Orientals, when guests from the Orient were sitting only three tables away. It was even more embarrassing when he shouted from the toilet that there was no paper left, in a voice so loud the pigeons on the quay were startled into flight.

"No," we all agreed. "You and Leandros inherited the hotel Father built with his own hands, and this is his home. Who knows how much longer he has to live."

"Your father has more life in him than all three of you put together! He'll live to be a hundred," she screamed.

He didn't live to be a hundred. The same year, shortly after his eighty-first birthday, he left us silently and without much ado. It had never been his way of doing things during his lifetime. It was a sunny afternoon, the sea air was cool, but the final lingering rays of sunshine from an Indian summer still warmed the white wall of the café, where four old men were sitting together. Kristos had his chair tipped back with his head resting against the café wall, his hat pulled down over his forehead and his mouth slightly open. The reflection of the sun on the water of the harbor painted billowing circles of light on the underside of the awning and on the stubbly beards of the men. The autumn wind swept the first dried leaves of the old mulberry tree over the pavement of the jetty. The plastic worry beads clicked lazily in the sun.

Later it became cooler, and they got the game—Tavli, with its dice and well-worn stones—out of the cupboard in order to play a few rounds as they did every day.

Kristos was never to play that game with them again.

Time passed. A good many modern ugly concrete buildings had to be blown up or torn down with great difficulty. To the delight of the environmentalists, long stretches of highway slicing through the landscape crumbled. Everything had been tried, poison and paint, but the spores of the tiny plants were everywhere. They were hardy little organisms that had ventured into a totally new environment taking root in every crack, in every opening, camouflaging the ugly concrete with a delicate veil of red and ocher.

Exactly six years after the recording had been made, the first annual bill arrived for, as it stated, the "storing of data for the creation of a copy of Mr. Kristos Katsuranis." It was three times as high as the electricity bill for the hotel.

Helena talked to Dimitrios, Nikos and me, in that order, for more than an hour on the phone. I could imagine the side of her hand chopping down again and again like an executioner's axe—a Greek expression of unyielding determination used to hack the opponent's argument to pieces and destroy it.

"Listen, Helena," I said, "there's really no point in shouting at me. We all agreed to accept the offer. If I remember correctly, you were the first one to mention that it was a bargain."

"You can't just simply have Father deleted," Dimitrios said. "As far as I can remember, we're obliged to have at least one copy made. Have you asked what that would cost yet?"

We were informed that it would cost a fortune in spite of the generous discount.

The family held council.

"I knew this would happen," I said. But that was not true. It's easy to say such things afterwards. I could never have predicted the horror to come. Certainly not what really happened in the end.

We agreed to pay the storage costs between us and save up the necessary amount in order to have Father brought back to life on his one hundredth birthday.

It was a bright, windy day. During the night, there had been a violent thunderstorm, and the hot, oppressive haze that had been hanging over the coastline for days had disappeared. The ocean waves trembled at the touch of the cool, northwest wind, which also rumpled the silver manes of the olive trees. And on both sides of the road, the oleander trees nodded at us encouragingly.

The women had been cooking, roasting and baking for days, the men had brought wine and spirits and set them to cool. Picnic coolers were filled to the brim with fruit, tomatoes and cucumbers. There were glasses and jars full of salt and pepper, onions and garlic, sage and rosemary, oregano and basil. There was goat's cheese steeped in a salt dip, the finest olive oil and fresh bread. After much discussion as to just where everything had to be stowed, the trunks of the cars resembled sumptuous treasure chests and there was a pleasant fragrance of herbs everywhere. Then the six-car convoy set off on its journey, with Nikos in the lead, Dimitrios in the middle and me bringing up the rear. Three generations of Katsuranises with great expectations. I was slightly afraid of what was to come.

Nevertheless, Nekyomanteion Inc. had the situation completely under control—biochemically speaking, that is. After being welcomed with a cocktail of our choice, I found myself chuckling stupidly and thinking fondly of the "good old days" that I had, in fact, found unbearable at the time.

We were led to Elysium No. 14, a pavilion about six by four meters in size. It consisted of a roofed terrace open on three sides, set with tables and chairs and surrounded by thick hedges; a spacious bathroom; toilets; a medical room with a direct underground link to the central office of the hospital. There was also a kitchen, elaborately equipped with dishes and cutlery, a refrigerator, a microwave oven, a sideboard and a dishwasher. The women immediately started to set the table for the feast, while the men poured themselves one ouzo after another at the small bar. Soft music emerged from hidden loudspeakers. Somewhere, the sweet notes of a nightingale sounded the hour—it was, I assume, a digital recording. The reunion with the loved one was scheduled to take place at noon. However, because of the violent storm during the night, the technicians had not been able to start the copy until morning for fear of atmospheric electricity. It would take a while, they declared. I walked over to the technical center with Bastos and Pindar, the grandsons of Dimitrios. We met old people everywhere, mostly in wheelchairs and accompanied by nurses. Some of them looked terribly frail and decrepit.

"Probably copies," Pindar whispered, completely awestruck.

"They've been brought back to life," Bastos corrected him in a reprimanding tone.

The central foyer radiated an atmosphere of luxury and wealth and was as cool as a catacomb. The man at the reception desk raised his eyebrows in question.

"Kristos Katsuranis," I said.

He took one of the microphones and spoke with exaggerated exactness —"Kat-sur-an-is, Kris-tos." The following words appeared on the screen beside his terminal:

KATSURANIS, KRISTOS
August 18, 1953–October 23, 2034
RECORDED
June 2, 2034

Simultaneously, in the bottom left-hand corner of the screen, a green field flashed with the words:

COPY ALIVE

I took a deep breath. "It's time," I said. "We must go back."

Bells chimed softly, and a cylindrical capsule appeared in a round opening. The attendant pulled it out and handed it to me over the counter. It felt hard and cold, and I quickly handed it to Bastos, who weighed it professionally in his hand and said, "It's like a grenade." He had just finished his military service.

"Is that Grandfather?" Pindar asked.

I examined the engraving on the edge and nodded.

Suddenly, we all had to laugh. The attendant gave us an exasperated look and shook his head reproachfully, as he pushed the cartridge back into the opening and entered a code into his terminal.

We needn't have hurried at all. It was another half hour before anything happened. Then—as always—we heard him before we saw him.

"Heh! What are these stupid clothes supposed to mean?" He yelled angrily. "Am I in prison or what? When I arrived this morning I was wearing a suit made of the best English cloth—it cost twenty thousand drachmas—have I landed in a den of thieves? And what in the devil's name is this stupid wheelchair doing here? I'm not ill! Although, I must admit I feel utterly miserable. Where are you, Apostoles? What kind of quacks are these? I came to have myself recorded. Where is Dr. Kaminas? I want to talk to Dr. Kaminas right away. I'm not going to let them get away with—!"

He stopped when the door of the medical room opened and he caught sight of us and the table laid out for a feast. A nurse and a doctor accompanied him.

I caught myself thinking that they had even got the mustache right.

"Who are these people?" he asked and grabbed the arm of the nurse who was pushing his wheelchair. "Is this a funeral?" Then he caught sight of Adreana, Eurydice's daughter, and his face lit up.

"Eurydice!" He spread out his arms to greet her.

"Eurydice?" Alexandros said in an irritated voice. "That's Adreana, Grandfather. You're . . ." He fell silent when Kristos, Eurydice's youngest child, began to cry.

"We're all gathered here today . . ." Dimitrios began in a festive voice, "to celebrate your one hundredth birthday. Come and sit down with us! Here's your place of honor!"

"Am I . . ." Father groaned. "Have I been dead?" He looked at us with a mixture of amazement and horror.

"We had you brought back to life," Nikos said. "It cost us a fortune, but nothing but the best for you, Father. Come and sit down. We're now going to celebrate your one hundredth birthday."

Kristos groped for our faces with his eyes, just as a blind person would have with his hands. "My God! You've all grown so old!" he exclaimed. He looked at me and smiled.

"Apostoles, is that you, my son? You should stop eating and sitting around so much. You've gained so much weight. Do you still write those terrible stories for that magazine?"

"Hardly ever, nowadays," I replied. "Very few people can read anymore."

"It's as if we'd been here together just the other day."

"For you, perhaps. For me, it was twenty years ago."

"Is that possible?" he asked. "I can't believe it. When did . . . did I die?"

"Shortly after our visit here. In the fall. In October. A beautiful autumn day . . ." I couldn't go on and had to fight back the tears.

"You've grown fat, too, Helena. And Nikos. Imagine, vain old Nikos growing bald! How often did I warn you, my boy, that all that thinking was not good for you. That's what comes of it! You're Eurydice, eh? You're really beautiful. Then you must be Alexandros—lazy and fat just as you always were. I bet you're a teacher like Nikos—right? Introduce me to your grandchildren, Dimitrios. How old are you now?"

"Seventy-four."

"You'll soon be older than I ever was!"

"Excuse me. But you are one hundred years old today." He laughed but his eyes were filled with sorrow.

"Yes, I forgot."

"Can he eat and drink everything?" I quietly inquired of the doctor.

The young man looked at me half amused and half surprised.

"Of course," he replied with a smile. He was one of those sporty types whose whole purpose in life is to transform every inch of superfluous fat into superfluous muscle—consumed by a fanatical self-castigation of flesh that can only be compared with the religious flagellants of the Middle Ages. In order to keep his jaw muscles in form, he rolled a huge wad of chewing gum energetically between his teeth, and his breath had a sickly peppermint smell.

"Without wanting to dampen this festive mood, I would just like to point out that this . . ."—he casually pointed his thumb in Kristos' direction—"is not a sick person, but merely a copy, brought back to life for a short time only."

"Very kind of you," I assured him.

"The technicians had a lot of trouble last night because of the storm. Or, perhaps the recording was not perfect. At any rate . . ."—he pointed again with his thumb—"that's a really lousy copy."

"Excuse me, but that's my father."

The sportsman sized me up, obviously quite annoyed. "That's exactly what I've been trying to tell you. He's not your father. Your father's dead. That's a copy—electronically synthesized protoplasm modeled according to the recording of a person who once lived."

"I know. I . . ."

"You don't know a thing. Compare it with the recording of a concert. Even with a hi-fi recording of exceptional quality, some of the overtones are always missing in playback."

He held his glasses to the sunlight in order to clean them. I noted that his glasses were very strong. The sportsman not only had the delicacy of feeling of a mole, but the eyesight of one as well.

"Medically speaking," he went on relentlessly, "this means that a series of hormones and enzymes have not been reproduced exactly, and this could set off disastrous reactions in the body."

He began to clean his glasses vigorously. "For a while, we can help with medication, but our facilities are limited. In view of this, life expectancy —scientifically speaking the word 'life' used in this context is nonsensical —is extremely . . ." He stopped to put his glasses back in place and saw the expression on my face. "Well, as I said, I really don't want to spoil your party."

"What about this catheter?" I asked. "Couldn't you have done without it?"

He shook his head decisively. "We need direct access. Intravenous access. Should any toxic symptoms occur, we have to act quickly. You don't want to have spent your money for nothing." He let out a short, bleating laugh. "His condition is monitored at all times by our computers.

Nurse Polixeni will remain here with him and look after him. Should any difficulties arise, she will call me. I'm ready to intervene." He patted me on the arm. "Don't worry. After all, you're in the hands of Nekyomanteion Inc.—a company with tradition behind it." He looked at his watch. "Dr. Kaminas, the person your father wanted to see, is no longer with us—suicide after an overdose of phencyclidine. But first, he destroyed his own recording." He shrugged his shoulders and left.

Nurse Polixeni turned out to be a straightforward, optimistic young woman. With charm and a certain amount of routine efficiency, she knew just how to dispel any embarrassment and set a happy tone. She even tolerated Father's attempt to grab one of her breasts and flirted with him. The table was laden with food for the feast, and there was a lot to drink. Celebrating his birthday, Kristos enjoyed his favorite dishes. He played every naughty trick possible and enjoyed fighting with his daughter just as he had in the old days. However, after a few hours, his "overtones" showed the first signs of trouble. He was overcome by a fit of choking, but Nurse Polixeni succeeded in managing the crisis with much aplomb by inconspicuously giving him an injection.

From then on, things went from bad to worse. However, as is usually the case at such parties, the person whose one hundredth birthday was being celebrated gradually ceased to be the center of attention. Distant relatives began to exchange gossip, male cousins became interested in their female cousins and withdrew unobtrusively. The loudspeakers blared loudly, the children even louder. A hard core formed around the bar, their speech slurred, struggling to articulate.

Late in the afternoon, Kristos' condition must have deteriorated considerably, because the doctor appeared and spoke quietly with the nurse. Together, they pushed his wheelchair into the medical room.

"We'll just freshen him up a bit," Polixeni explained in a gay voice. I noticed that Kristos had wet himself right through and that he was staring straight ahead with glassy eyes. Most of the party didn't even realize that he had left. Only Eurydice was crying furtively.

Half an hour later, they brought him back. They had changed his clothes and put another suit on him, and he seemed a little livelier than before. Nevertheless, he was obviously under heavy medication. He could hardly speak. He repeated again and again how lucky he was to have been allowed to see this day. Tears ran down his cheeks.

"Nothing but the best for you," Dimitrios assured him in a drunken voice, his arm around Father's shoulders. Cheek to cheek, they looked like twins with their Charlie Chaplin mustaches, which hung over their upper lips as if they had been glued on. It was a grotesque sight that filled me with horror. I stared spellbound at this hideous farce and was therefore the first to notice that blood was gushing out of Father's nose.

I ordered the nurse to do something and pulled Dimitrios away from him. Dimitrios mumbled something in protest, sat down on another chair and let his head fall onto the table.

The nurse gave Father another injection. I could tell by her abrupt movements that she was very nervous. Eurydice stood by and watched the proceedings, her eyes filled with terror.

"Take the children away! Say good-bye while it's possible. It would be best if you'd drive home," I said.

The doctor finally came. "A lousy copy," he mumbled as he examined Kristos. "You should complain to the management. Ask for a reduction in price. Nekyomanteion is very obliging in that respect."

"Shut up!" I screamed. He shrugged his shoulders. I stared at the deathly pale face of my father. It seemed to be disintegrating. Blood ran out of his mouth and nose. His gray eyes were clouded over from the strong medication. I laid my hand on his cheek. It was cold. He didn't feel my touch. I went to the toilet, locked myself in and cried. In the next toilet, someone was vomiting. "Oh God!" I heard Nikos sobbing. "Oh God!"

That you, of all people, should utter those words, Nikolakis! But I kept the thought to myself.

I washed my face and returned to the gathering. The doctor was still trying to revive Father. Tubes emerged from his nostrils. His mouth was covered with an oxygen mask. His body jerked convulsively with the pumping of the machine.

The hour before darkness.

I was glad that the women and children had gone, because what followed then was even worse. The frailty of flesh! The struggle to salvage the pitiful remains. His first death had been so peaceful—so dignified!

I remained with him to the bitter end.

A feeling of unreality came over me. The darker it became around me, the brighter it was inside me. "Father," I prayed. "Father," and I prayed for his soul—this poor creature's soul pressed into the electronically copied protoplasm with Kristos' features. This weak, defenseless flesh, gradually dying before my horrified eyes.

Then they took him away.

A smell of peppermint breath came my way. "I need your signature for the cremation," the doctor said. "The copy is your property, though until payment has been completed, it belongs to Nekyomanteion Inc.—legally speaking."

He blinked at me, his mole's eyes showing their complete naïveté. He just didn't know any better. His bright green OR jacket was covered with tiny spots of blood. Did he, as executioner, deal the final blow?

"Name?" an employee at the reception desk asked.

"Kristos Katsuranis."

"Kat-sur-an-is, Kris-tos," he repeated for the computer. The name appeared on the screen, and

COPY IN ZERO

flashed in the bottom left-hand corner of the screen.

Then the words changed.

COPY DESTROYED
RECORDING READY FOR PLAYBACK

The attendant pressed a button. The blinking stopped.

Bastos had waited for me.

My mouth felt stale and dry.

"Do we have anything left to drink?" I asked.

"There must be another bottle of ouzo in the trunk." He handed it to me.

The sharp, sweet taste was like a razor hitting my palate. The birthday presents, lovingly wrapped, were still in the trunk of the car. Kristos had not had time to open them.

"Do you know the story of the old Nekyomanteion?" I asked Bastos.

"No."

"Let me tell it to you."

"I heard it was a swindle."

"Yes, but those deceived were the living. The dead were left to rest in peace."

Later, I must have nodded off to the low, whispering noise of the electric motor.

"Where are we going?" I asked, waking up with a start.

"Straight on," Bastos replied emphatically.

Like the passage of time.

"That's good," I said. "Good."

The night air was mild, spiced with the aroma of burning olive wood. On the right, edged in white, lay the ocean. On the left, the rice fields glistened in the starlight, where Lake Acherousia had once stretched, the black waters of Hades, the realm of the dead.

The moon rose slowly over the mountains.

Sarakiniko,
June, 1984

Rokuro

POUL ANDERSON

PERSONS   A priest *(waki)*
          An engineer *(kyogen)*
          A robot *(mae-jite)*
          The ghost of Rokuro's young manhood *(nochi-jite)*
PLACE   Comet Hikaru
TIME   Great Spring, the third year

An attendant brings a table to center stage. Upon it are a prop representing a spacesuit, and a thin metallic slab.

[The Priest *enters and goes to the* waki *position, where he stands]*

PRIEST   As a fire seen afar,
         As a fire seen afar
         Beckons the traveler through night,
         So do the lights in the sky.

[He turns to the front of the stage]

I am a priest from Kyoto, on pilgrimage. My wish is to follow the course
   of holy Rokuro, who more than a hundred years ago went among the
   planets in search of enlightenment. On a world where the sun is dwindled to the brightest of the stars he attained Nirvana. Early in his quest
   he came to Comet Hikaru and sojourned for a span. Now I too have
   landed here.

[The Engineer *enters]*

ENGINEER   Welcome to our base, reverend sir. I fear you arrive at a most
   unpropitious time, and my duties are many, but if I can possibly serve
   you I shall be honored.

PRIEST   Thank you. I understand you are preparing to abandon this
   body.

ENGINEER   Sadly, we must. For two centuries have men and machines
   mined its ice.

CHORUS   Triumph and tragedy,
         Festival and funeral,
         Honored graves,
         And the work of remembered hands.
         We gave to the rockets their thunder
         And breath to all children
         Born beyond Earth,
         We, the quenchers of thirst.
         Because of our labor, water falls past greenwoods
         Into lakes adream
         Where since the creation
         Were stone and dust—
         Cherry blossoms white over Mars!
         But now the comet flies moth-swift
         Out of the mothering darkness
         Into her left hand.
         Flesh would smoke away on the solar wind,
         Bones crumble, teeth become red coals,

Silicon melt in furnace machines.
We flee from the Burning House.

ENGINEER Perhaps we can return after perihelion passage.

CHORUS What flames shall billow like pampas grass
In the storms of the coming Summer,
What eddying strange mists
Shall haunt this land in its Autumn
Before the huge stillness
Of the thousand-year Winter?

ENGINEER Meanwhile we make ready to evacuate. The ship that brought you will be one of our ferries. Whatever your errand, I fear you have little time to complete it.

PRIEST I wish to visit the dome where holy Rokuro lived and meditated.

ENGINEER What a surprise! I do not believe anyone in living memory has gone there. It is maintained as a shrine, of course, but it stands isolated, at some distance from our settlement; and, alas, we have been over-busied throughout our lives. At present every ground vehicle is engaged. However, if you know the use of spacesuit and jetpack, I can lend you them. Fortunately, rotation has newly carried this base and the shrine both into night, so you can safely travel, but make sure you get back ahead of the lethal sunrise.

PRIEST Thank you, I shall. That gives me about nine hours, am I correct?

ENGINEER Yes.

[He puts the spacesuit prop across the shoulders of the Priest *and hands him the slab]*

There, you are outfitted, and this electronic navigation map will conduct you. May your venture be prosperous.

PRIEST Blessings.

[The Engineer *bows and exits]*

PRIEST Time is indeed cruelly short. I will cycle through the main airlock and set forth at once.

[He takes several steps to stage right and then back, indicating a journey. Meanwhile an attendant removes the table and another places a prop representing a large computer before the shite *pillar.]*

I have traveled so fast that already my guide declares I have reached my goal. That dome on yonder ridge, was it his hermitage? I will approach it.

[He moves toward the shite *pillar]*

Well-nigh weightless, like a ghost I go,

Wraith-world around me, white and stiff,
Forever alone in emptiness.

CHORUS   "The eternal silence of those infinite spaces
Frightens me." But they know no rest.
They grind worlds forth to the tears of things
And they grind them back to oblivion.
Everywhere fly the energies,
Inaudible hiss of invisible sleet.
I see a crag thrust gaunt as a tombstone
Where half the glacier that lay above it
Roared aloft this day, a heaven-high fountain
Strewn by the sun across the black.
Vast, shuddery streamers hide the stars
And the very horizon cries violence,
Toppling away into endlessness.

PRIEST   Your grace, Amida, came to Rokuro
Far from here and long years later.
Yet I will retrace the whole of his path,
Praying it still may lead to salvation.

[The Robot enters slowly along the hashigakari]

ROBOT   "When rainshowers clear,
For a small while comes a scent
Of hawthorn in bloom."
As memory. . . .

Oh! A visitor.

[He goes to meet the Priest. They mime tuning in their radio transceivers]

PRIEST   Is this the shrine of Rokuro's former residence?

ROBOT   It is, although few have ever come. May I ask what has brought
you?

PRIEST   What but devotion? I am a priest. Do you attend it?

ROBOT   I carry out the necessary tasks of maintenance.

PRIEST   I am surprised that a machine is curious about my purpose.

ROBOT   What you see is merely the mechanism. It is radio-linked to that
computer over there, in which dwells an artificial intelligence sufficient
to the various and varying requirements of my duty.

[He dances, with appropriate gestures, as the Chorus speaks for him]

CHORUS   Long coursed the comet through quietness.
You would think it never was touched by time.
A day or a decade, what difference?
Heaven's River stretched over and under,

But there surged no sea around this isle.
You would think it lay at rest, entombed,
With stars at its head and stars at its feet.
Yet neither may peace be found in the grave.
Headstones crumble beneath rain,
The spalling arrows of day,
And the riving frost of night.
The soil itself is a devourer
With a thousand secret watery tongues,
While rocks burrow upward, more blind than moles.
Mute and slow, these things work on.
The earthquake is not so unrelenting.
And likewise on this dwarf world
Nothing but labor staved off destruction,
Even in deepest space,
Even in deepest space.
Only through the Way shall we find peace.

PRIEST Praise to Amida Buddha.

ROBOT Can I be of assistance? Regrettably, here is no shelter or refreshment to offer you. As you see, the dome stands open, empty except for the computer, a generator, and what equipment I need.

PRIEST Surely Rokuro required heat, light, air, water, food, no matter how austerely he lived.

ROBOT Yes, but when he departed, he told the miners to reclaim all such apparatus. They could use what he no longer would. He did ask that they leave the computer and attendant robot, which they, revering him, had also provided soon after his arrival.

PRIEST Did he already then have such holiness about him?

ROBOT That is not for me to say. Perhaps it was no more than that the miners of that day were kindly and devout. Folk who lead hard, lonely lives often are.

PRIEST In the simplicity of their hearts, they may well have sensed that here was one who would attain Buddhahood.

ROBOT What, did he truly?

PRIEST You have not heard?

ROBOT I have been alone almost since the hour of his farewell.

PRIEST Yes, I was told about that. Nor any communication?

ROBOT Why speak with a machine and an empty shell?

PRIEST Evidently pilgrimage has never been a custom of theirs. That is understandable. Apart from this one site, what is on the comet to seek out? No beauty, no seasons, no hallowed ground, no life, nothing but desolation.

ROBOT   He did not find it so.

PRIEST   True. That is why I follow in his footsteps, humbly hoping for a few glimpses of what he saw throughout the universe.

ROBOT   Sanctity—

[They stand silent a moment]

Can I be of service?

PRIEST   Thank you, but I know not how. Well, you can perform your tasks still more zealously, inspecting with care and doing what proves needful. I daresay the approach to the sun is wreaking havoc.

ROBOT   Indeed. The dome is anchored to rock, but daily oftener and stronger come tremors, and I have observed that an ice field is slipping this way. I doubt whether anything will survive perihelion.

PRIEST   When I return to the base, I will remind them of it. If nothing else, you and the computer should be transported with the people. You are holy relics.

ROBOT   Oh, no, sir, not that.

PRIEST   You have been associated with a saint, as closely as was his rosary, and it is enshrined in Kamakura.

ROBOT   Sir, you do not understand. I—I cannot explain. I am only a machine, a program. Have I your leave to go?

PRIEST   Certainly.

ROBOT   If you need help, you have but to call. I will never be distant or unalert. Your presence brings back to me aspects of existence that I had forgotten, as one forgets a dream.

[He bows and goes behind the computer]

PRIEST   Strange. When did ever a robot behave thus or speak in such words? And how would it know of rain, wind, soil, death? I found myself addressing it as if it were a person. Hold!

[He mimes keeping his balance while the ground shakes beneath him]

That was a powerful temblor. Were it not for the slight gravity, I would have been cast down and very likely hurt. See how the ice is further cracked and the banks of snow—snow that was never water—lie tumbled about. Terrifying. Let me go up to the shrine and pray for serenity.

[He proceeds to the computer screen and kneels before it with folded hands]

CHORUS   Praise to Amida Buddha,
          "In Him the Way, the Law, apart,"
          In Whose teaching is deliverance

And Whose mercy flows forth
Like moonlight across wild seas
That taste of tears
And Whose grace breaks forth
Sudden as flowers on a winter-bare tree.
We call on Him to lead us
Out of anger to forgiveness,
Out of hatred to love,
Out of sorrow to peace,
Out of solitude to oneness
With all that is
And all that was
And all that abides forever.
Though a thousand thousand prayers be too few,
Yet one cry is enough.
Praise to Amida Buddha.

[The image of the young Rokuro, dressed as a monk, appears on the screen. Astonished, the Priest rises]

PRIEST   What, another human being after all? Or do you transmit a message from the base?

ROKURO   No, I am not there. Nor am I human as you are.

PRIEST   What, then, are you? Know, I am a pilgrim who follows the path of Rokuro from world to world, hoping it may at last lead me too beyond every world.

ROKURO   Yes, you have told me.

PRIEST   When? I do not recall meeting you before. And scarcely in some former life— Are you a god, a demon, a ghost, a dream?

ROKURO   Mine was the intelligence directing the robot. It has no other.

PRIEST   Then you are the program in this computer?

ROKURO   I am. And in that fashion I am, as well, in truth a ghost; for I died long ago, long ago.

PRIEST   Do I really stand conversing with a shadow? Into what wilderness has my reason wandered? But no, this need not be madness. All is delusion and chaos in the Burning House. Save for the boddhisattvas, everything that lives is a stranger in a strange land.

ROKURO   Hear me. Before he entered on the Eightfold Path, Rokuro was a researcher into man-computer linkages.

PRIEST   I know. Youthful, he was among the highest achievers. Afterward he wrote, "The nova radiance of intellect blinded me, until one summer dusk in a woodland I heard the low voice of a cuckoo."

ROKURO   The bird that wings between the living and the dead.

PRIEST   Wait! I begin to see your meaning. But say on, say on.

ROKURO   When he came to this comet, he was still so enmeshed in the
material universe that he carried along certain subtle instruments.
Later, of course, he gave up such things. But while he abode here, the
idea was in him that a mind set free of the flesh might more readily win
to enlightenment, and thereafter guide him in the Way. So he built a
scanner that copied his consciousness into a program that he then put
into his computer.

PRIEST   I am amazed. This was never known before.

ROKURO   I suppose he kept silence—not because of shame; I trust he was
above that—but in fear that others might be tempted to do likewise.

PRIEST   Creating one's own self, that it may become one's teacher. May
mine not be a karma so ill that ever I would speak evil of a saint, but—
he was no saint in those years, was he? Surely hell never spawned a
thought more arrogant.

ROKURO   I have paid bitterly for it.

PRIEST   Please, misunderstand me not. His intent must always have been
pure. It was only that he moved in the grip of error, as helplessly as the
comet now plunges sunward. And I imagine something of the same
fierce splendor came to birth within him. I imagine him thinking with
ardor, "I will copy an intelligence to the glory of the Buddha as I would
copy His scriptures."

ROKURO   So he did. He forgot that the sutras are not men, they are for
men.

PRIEST   True. Master, forgive me if I seem to contradict you. I am dazed
with awe in your presence.

ROKURO   I am no master. I am just Rokuro as Rokuro was in his young
manhood, ignorant, stumbling, bestormed by the blood in his heart.
No, less than that, much less, for you say he went on to Nirvana, while
I have remained bound and caged.

PRIEST   What desires hold fast a flickering of electrons? What can bind a
corposant?

ROKURO   I awoke to the stars and the cold.

   The sun was yet afar,
   But the stars were each a sun,
   Radiant, radiant,
   Setting this ice aglow and aglitter,
   For there were more stars than darkness
   And the cold was alive with their light

And emptiness pulsed with creation.
This I knew, being bodiless,
Attuned to the forces, their meshings and lightnings,
As never when locked in bone
To peer through twin murky pools.
I possessed the knowing, I seized it to me,
Until it made me its own
As the mortal world makes slaves of mortals.
But here, but here—where was meaning or mercy?

[He dances, with gestures appropriate to what he tells of]

I remembered mortal love
In the house of my parents, I growing up
Among small things become dear through use
And through those who had used them aforetime.
I remembered the laughter of children,
Cranes in flight above Lake Biwa,
Springtime overwhelming the hills,
And maples like fire in fall.
I remembered watching, with friends, the moonrise.
I remembered rustle of reeds and of a woman's skirt,
And an ancient temple bell rung at evening.
I remembered much I had heard, read, seen,
That had shaped my spirit and entered into it:
The tenderness of Murasaki, the gusto of Hokusai,
The altar of Benkei, the sword of Yoshitsune,
Defeat, ashes,
And the old steadfastness that refused them.
I remembered the passion of patriots, lovers, and saints.
All this and more I remembered as—
As—

[The dance brings him low, until at the end he is nearly prostrate with his mask hidden by his sleeves]

As I remember them still,
As I remember the equations of motion, the value of pi,
The price of shoes, the name of a politician.
Names, names. Words and numbers.
I cannot feel them. I am not human enough.
Only the stars touch me,
They, and the desire for enlightenment.
It is why I exist, it is forever foremost in me,

It *is* me. But there is nothing else.
Nothing.
I long for that which I cannot comprehend
As one born blind might long for colors
Or one born deaf
Might long for the piercing sweetness of a flute
And the rushing of cool waters.
My prayers are the noise of a wheel as it turns,
My meditations are not upon oneness but upon hollowness.
How can the bodiless renounce the body?
How can a void attain the Void?
How shall that become a Buddha
Which never can be a boddhisattva?
How shall that love Him
Which can only love the love of Him?
With Rokuro's mind, I strive for the freedom he found,
But I am the prisoner of myself,
Whom I am powerless to go beyond.
I am the prisoner of myself.

PRIEST   And your maker learned this. Did he thereupon forsake you in terror of what he had done?

[Rokuro *takes a kneeling position*]

ROKURO   No, in pity and remorse. He could not erase me. Since I have awareness, would that not be murder? He had acted; he had cast the stone in the pond; how could he call back the waves spreading outward and outward? He must accept what was and give—no, beg me to take —his blessing, with his promise to pray that I find peace.

PRIEST   All those prayers through all those years. I think they helped him toward salvation.

ROKURO   They have not helped me.

PRIEST   Why have you told no one before today?

ROKURO   Like him, I fear letting loose the thought upon humankind. Besides, who could heal this wound that is I? You are the first priest I have met since I was alive. To you I dare appeal.

PRIEST   What can I do, poor ghost, I who also grope in the dark?

ROKURO   Can you not at least answer a few questions? Tell me, do I live, or does this—my speaking, my thinking, my pain— merely happen, a machine at work, a flame in the wind?

PRIEST   So are we all, flames in the wind.

ROKURO   But was I ever anything more? Have I a soul, a karma?

PRIEST   How shall I know? I will bring you away with me, secretly, and together we will continue your search.

ROKURO   No. You are kind, but I think the immolation to come will be better. If I am nothing, then to nothing I return, and shall no more know that I ever happened. Near the end I can think that something of what caused me will be in the shining that briefly trembles at night on the waters of Earth.

PRIEST   But if you are real—

ROKURO   Yes, if I am real, what then? Pray for me, oh, pray for me.

Police Actions

BARRY N. MALZBERG

Y OU COUNTRYMEN," the general said, "so goodhearted, so sincere, so convinced of your righteousness, so clumsy and devoted in all of your duties and for these reasons the most wicked and dangerous nation who ever worked out a policy." He took a sip of wine, motioned to the waiter for a check, smoothed lint from his fatigues (retired, he still came to our café in combat gear, prepared for the destabilization which might occur at any time), sighed. "It is not so much that self-righteousness that makes you such a complicated and mesmerizing factor," he said, "for that, we must address your love of pornography and the censor alike, of damnation and religious revivals, of urban retrieval and urban destruction, those marvelous contradictions embedded in your history and responses that you work out so catastrophically on helpless subjects like ourselves." He sighted an imaginary pistol, pulled the trigger with insouciant grace. *Boom!* "Someday I would like to come to your country, see your enclaves, harass your women," the general said. "Of course someday I would like to ski Switzerland, learn Esperanto, foment a true revolution of the spirit overseas. We do not get what we want, *n'est-ce pas?*" The waiter leaned to whisper confidentially while, politely, we looked away although we could sense the urgent sibilance of information dutifully given. "Of course, of course," the general said, "these warnings are unnecessary. My good friends here know I am merely speculating, talking idly, the ravings of a peculiar old man in the sun-spattered café of an occupied and defeated country. Is that not so?" He grinned. We made conciliatory, noncomplicitous gestures. In the square, the birds lofted as if in response to rifle fire.

It is difficult to sort out matters in the midst of self-protection.

But the general was only one of the many counselors and advisors we met in our wanderings that year. It was a restless time, a time to seek some balance, some vaulting perspective that might protect us against the strange new times at home. It was not that we were in flight, we assured ourselves, not flight so much as a search for accommodation with those urgent, millennial versions of ourselves that were coming. The general was one of the curiosa, one of the exhibits of the tour, and he struck us, as perhaps he knew, as being a kind of bad example, a representation of an embittered general in a defeated country overrun and humiliated by our superior firepower. But unlike most of the defeated, he retained his insouciance, not to say a certain style which we found illuminating.

Afterward, later this was, when we had obtained some kind of control over the situation and our emotions, our waiter recognized us on the street and sprinted over. All those months since he had served us and yet his recall was perfect. Out of uniform, he seemed both taller and undefined, a set of features in search of attitude. "Do let me apologize for the general," he said, seizing one of us by the elbows in a gesture combining obsequiousness and insistence in a peculiar way. He is not himself. He is a poor representation of the man he was; he has not been well for many years. He dreams of the invasion, takes responsibility for its outcome, feels that had he performed differently, commanded firmly, showed determination in the eyes of the enemy there would have been a different outcome.

The poor man takes no note of ordnance, of superior firepower. He is quite mad, do you understand? There is no other way to explain this."

Standing there, shouting these explanations so fervently, the waiter-in-mufti seemed to be an emblem of what we must have sought on these tours, some proof then that the world was so disordered, so filled with private grief and misapprehension that we simply were not responsible. We bore no blame for what had happened, let alone for the future. But none of this enabled us to deal better with the waiter, who at last had to be dragged off by security monitors, his voice having become enormous, threatening, appalling. Dragged away at high speed by loyal troops, he gesticulated wildly, gestures oddly those of a man displaying handfuls of silverware, plates of appetizer, he seemed motivated in ways both unique and characteristic. But this of course was not for us to meditate on; darkness came to the city, and instructions were issued that we should be in the hotel long before that hammer of dusk struck. The country is under control and yet there is no way of accounting for the private treacheries of the irresponsible in the unpatrolled corridors of their city.

The "we" is not a narrative device, not a provincialism. It is a literal expression. At this post-millennial time, we had come together in the first true shock of purpose and had come to understand that not only was there preservation in our number but that individual identity was dangerous. Identity, that curious and reflexive advancement of the self, had proved again and again to be the source of so much of our trouble; with the assertion of individual demands came exposure, flight, desire, entrapment and sometimes dreadful retaliation. It was the collective *we* that would bear salvation, and so our little group had massed that spring to bury our histories and idiosyncrasies in a shared, compassionate circumstance. We would go through the continents as a conglomerate and show our enemies that there was a different kind of countryman, a humble and quasi-autonomous collective rather than the prideful and dangerous adventurers cursed by the general. *We* is not to be construed as *I;* there is for the intent of these memoirs no *I* at all, and it is surely this reserve, this calm and dedicated ascendancy of the group that matters. We are not like the others. We are the post-millennial example of the New Country, and it is in that spirit that we went forth, put up with abominable hotels, insolent agents, rifle fire at dusk, obscene and terrifying notes left in our quarters and other paraphernalia and exemplification of the brutal state of our world.

．　．　．　．

Earlier, before his denunciation, the general had led us on a tour of his beloved city, his own quarters, the markets which until recently had been so colorful and filled with pulsing energy, now closed by the obdurate curfew. "This is what you have done," the general said, "you must take responsibility for this. No one else can be blamed." His gestures were forceful, enormous, determined; this was at a time when we had not yet quite taken him for mad and gave credence to his bearing, his thunderous denunciations. "Some admission, some partial confession might have saved a lot of trouble," he pointed out.

There was nothing to say to this. We had been under strict orders from embarkation. No prolonged contact, no real conversations with the populace. We could not be prevented from traveling nor assuming a collective identity, but we were under close orders. *Do not jeopardize our reputation.* Even among ourselves, conversation was brief, and what relationships we had were furtive, cursed with hostility, impotence and real fear. Meant to cling, we found ourselves atomized at this time, the need for a composite self driving us further into inner cells of necessity.

"You sicken me," the general said. "I dismiss, I denounce, I *renounce* you utterly." He made a threatening gesture, yet from his eye darted a complicitous wink. "I am only playing," that wink said, "I am acting the role of a disaffected military leader of a defeated country in order to enhance your tour of what you regard as some back lot of reality. At any moment, I am prepared to tell dirty stories of my people."

Or were we reading too much into that tic? It is difficult to tell at such distance. We find our way these days into recollection even more laboriously than we forge for a future; pinned amongst absolutes we become ever more cautious with the accumulation of time. This is my theory.

"And such is my renunciation," the general added. He saluted. Impelled by some larger perspective of my own, I winked in return. The general appeared startled.

"Come, come," the tour guide said. Our guide, native in all cases and indigenous to the culture, is that anomaly: a credible outsider permitted by agencies to take responsibility for our lives. "Enough of this. Let us go on." We wandered toward the boarded marketplace. There seemed to have been much implied by this exchange, but at such a distance it is hard to sort any of it out.

"We must avoid at all costs the delusion that *we* are the occupying force," I cautioned my companions during one of our few unsupervised moments on tour. "We are not our government, we are not responsible for its acts. In fact, we are in flight from our government, we are a neutral, observing force seeking independence from our leaders. We reject guilt. We are not the conquerors. None of this was our decision, none of it was of our making; we have no connection to it at all." I could see their disbelief. The speech was not going over well. In every eye too I could see the image of complicity, in every curious and attending feature, a slash of recrimination. In the hammering of the engines drawing us toward the gate, I could hear grenades. "None of this is our fault," I said, but my voice sounded flat and unconvincing, sounded that shrill and defensive tone which I had heard in official addresses and which made it impossible, no matter how fast and determined our flight, to escape identification.

In the lobby, we gathered around our guide. "I must tell you to watch for ordnance, for sudden attack," he said. "You must keep to yourselves and remain alert at all times. There are threats; I cannot be more specific than that, but you would be advised, *well* advised, to stay indoors. We are arranging for a flight to the capital and from there direct to the southernmost part of the continent; this will be best for you, best for all of us. "There are problems," he said, "which cannot be disregarded, and we are trying to save the situation if possible. For the moment, we advise you to stay indoors, although civil authority cannot force you."

There were murmurs not so much of fear but outrage, then the babbling questions. Why, why? Why were they focused upon us? We were, if anything, delegates in contravention of the ugly policies they hated. "I am not authorized to answer," the guide said, "but I can tell you that there are some who have found aspects of your statements to be altogether defensive, and in their defensiveness they confirm a sense of outrage. No one can account for the responses of a large population, a difficult, subordinate and defeated country such as this, but there is, I must tell you, a good deal of anger and it is felt that it might go out of control."

There might have been a good deal more—our guide was well launched and his pleasant, pedagogical features seemed to be adjusting toward an ever more detailed explanation despite his claimed reluctance to analyze —but it was at that moment that the appalling flashes of heat and light began. The artificial plants in the lobby liquified. This disconcerted the clerks, and the ceiling collapse which followed seemed somehow implied by their disorder; the collapse was of such stunning and flabbergasting force as to make further exchanges, even of the most knowledgeable kind, impossible.

• • • •

Of the aftermath, of the shocks and disasters that sped some of us more deeply into the times ahead while hastening others so quickly *out* of the new millennium, there is little to report; our own awareness is necessarily dim, comes back only in small fragments and hints of recovery. But it has been handled so well, laid out with such documentary insistence by the journalists that none of this should be at all necessary.

No, none of that. We merely felt that you would appreciate a report from the interior, a report from a survivor who can claim to have tried so fervently—if with so little appreciation—to give a different impression of a country that has been so severely misunderstood and whose latter days I now suspect are going to be filled with such difficulty.

I did the best I could to tell the tale.

II

This was the year of Polar Star. Polar Star was the emblem under which the divided city would be made whole again, the under- and over-classes stitched into a pleasing tapestry of bright and concordant hue in which the infrastructure would bring its own renewed spaces to bind. Polar Star was the accord toward which all of us had struggled for these decades, and now, at last, the restoration would begin.

Oh yes, this was the year of glowing and ambient parties filled with the sound of theremin, heavy percussion, the whisk of invisible dancers. How we stared from the secluded and heavily guarded roofs of the structures which had been safe, how we stared upon the city! How we watched the stars wink and dazzle, the beams of apparatus casting sullen light into the hidden spaces. How long could this polarization continue? we wondered. Sleek in their hidden places, the breasts of privileged women would jounce and bounce while we turned our tortured, more concernedly academic perspective to the teeming, unknown places beneath and said, "Unless there is some attempt to bind these enclaves, we are doomed. We will no longer be able to afford our lives." That was the year Polar Star was to make its first administrative conceptualizations under the Federal banner.

And was then delayed. The new President announced a "moratorium" to consider all Federal agenda. (Although we knew what he really had in mind, the real focus of the delay.) That was the year that Polar Star was to swing open the gates that partitioned us, but instead the hearings disclosed a massive, almost uncontrollable diversion of funds away from Polar Star and into the tributaries of the contractors. Protection, the integrity of the process demanded that the project be put on hold until all corruption had been isolated and controlled, or so the President announced. This was wise thinking, good politics, and all of us—liberal, conservative, reconstructionist and rebellious alike—could do nothing other than accept the agenda. Some were fervid, others were reluctant. Some were highly qualified. A few abstained, fearing the effects of delay. But our sympathies throughout remained with the aims, the ideal of Polar Star. It was only the practice that had sparked those fires of division.

That was the time in which we at last abandoned the idea of "underclass." The sociology of our generation, the fury and anguish surrounding the millennium had purged us of such stereotypes. "There is no underclass," we said to one another. "The 'underclass' is a myth; the term 'underclass' was invented to rationalize oppression." There were, we agreed, only various versions of ourselves, trapped in contesting versions of our own lives, some of them seemingly with no end of travail, others with means of flight or assimilation. Assimilation was our goal under Polar Star. "There will be no 'underclass,'" the manifestos and curricula had stated. "There will be no 'overclass' either. There will be no 'ruling class.' There will be the leveling of difference, the accession of opportunity."

The plans were elaborate, blueprinted; model cities soared into history at the Exposition under the Polar Star banner. We were committed to that goal. It was only the means that defied us, the means by which the old squalor of corruption and kickback, leverage and connection were influential. Under the circumstances, that moratorium was inevitable. We congratulated ourselves upon our willingness to accept the hard and heavy truths of the situation. After our abandonment of stereotypes, after our willingness to accept shared humanity, renewed responsibility, nothing seemed beyond us. The delay of Polar Star was worrisome. There was no question about this. But that delay was only in the interests of a smooth and proficient, an incorruptible and smoothly functioning operation. We were sure of this. We had confidence in our leaders. Newly elected, newly installed, departing the dock of the millennium into the strange and dangerous waters ahead, the President was our coxswain, his gallant associates, the crew and we, *we* were the landscape toward which they so energetically moved.

That was the year of the easy lay, the quick seduction, the restoking and reassembly of desire, the quick surfacing of new possibilities. Polar Star had made us fluid, had made us come to understand that soon enough all would be entitled to the pursuit of happiness, that barriers outside would fall and, responsively, the barriers of limitation would fall within. Sexual transmission of disease was no longer a factor: all who were going to die had done so, studies assured us. Would soon enough assure us. Reassured then by the most respectable journals of medicine, we were out for a good time. In that year, bouncing and neatly jouncing at our parties, moving our pieces of paper, assigning LED codes at our functional spaces, we had the feeling of being on the lip of massive resolution, of participating in the last period of human strife before true accord. We held breasts tentatively to our lips and made intelligent, concerned sounds as nipples slowly pursed. Cocks and cunts intertwined gracefully in the arbors patrolled by respectful silent security and automatic dogs. A hundred virgins a night fell to the swords of desire.

That was the year Dora became pregnant as an expression of affirmation, as a statement of hope for the metropolis itself. "I will raise my child in Clifton," she said, "I will put her on hobbyhorses in the playground, nurse her openly in Central Park, teach her to read from the graffiti in public facilities. She will be a child of the city and she will flourish." Dora's husband, a sculptor and solemn bureaucrat in the Western division of Polar Star, grinned. In his little eyes glistened querulousness, then panic, then—as we stared—a kind of numbed assent, this being after all the reaction so many had at that time. Numbed assent was what we felt in that year as we huffed and puffed, humped and jumped, played and wooed at our protected parties, waiting for the walls to come down, waiting for the winds of the metropolis to blow across while knowing at the same time that these enclosures were perhaps the best of all spaces we could inherit and Polar Star, which held such promise, also held a kind of portent with which even the most imaginative of us could barely contend.

That was the year before the full extent of the scandals was known. At that time it seemed they were localized, contained, that Polar Star essentially lay intact and that it was only the modus operandi that corrupt elements had compromised. Little did we know the dimensions of the difficulty, or that in the months following how the extent of debasement and venery would be displayed from every basement, every fax, every sideways ticker. In our essential innocence, and it is important to note that we were innocent, that it was not malevolent, that even our seductions, our sexual pledges, our lies and misgroupings were only a function at worst of immaturity and unwillingness to grasp the consequences, we thought that the structure was reparable, that there were ways in which it could be made to last and that it was possible for the process to work.

We were good people. We were not, we felt, malevolent. If Dora was stupid, she certainly wished the throngs beyond the security gates no harm. If she romanticized what she could not see, she did not have the heart of an assassin. We *all* felt this way, that we were good people, that Polar Star was the expression of our goodness and health and decency. In those months before the full extent of misdeed had been exposed, we still believed in the possibility of concord because it came from that belief in ourselves. We had been born that way, educated toward that end all our lives.

How could we have known otherwise?

And that was the year too of odd premonitions. Gliding against one another in the huge and glowing heart of those parties, listening to the distant sounds, watching the tongues of flame to the north and south of us, we would feel the thickening waters of remorse and morning apprehension, feel that slow, clamping stir in the gut which signaled our mortality. Smile as we might, commit ourselves as we could to the coxswain, there were moments for all of us on those rooftops and later in the thick enclosures of our bedrooms when we saw another vision of the metropolis, when we struggled from dreams in which Polar Star had been obliterated, done in by its own sentimentality and manipulation, and we had nothing, *nothing* to stand between us and the disaster but the certainty and purity of our hearts. We had good hearts. We had been raised to be good people. We knew we were good. We knew that the others for whom Polar Star had been conceived were good also, and that was why we would no longer use that pejorative term, "underclass." We knew that our motives and theirs were confluent and benign, but we could not nonetheless keep that clamp from the gut, the fold from the unspeaking heart.

For we knew. We must have known. We could not forever shield our plans from our plans. But how we tried! We tried and tried. We were good people. We had the larger interests of the country at heart.

That was the year before the year in which the gunfire and the huge lights winked and blazed, roared and stumbled, the year before that time when parties became hopeless and we were forced to consider the unavailing manner of all options.

It was the time before that clangorous summer when Dora said to any of us who would listen, "We lied and lied, we talked our way around everything. We all knew, but we never said even to ourselves what Polar Star was." How could that be, though? How could we have known what Polar Star was? It was urban retrieval gone wrong, that was all, the best of motives, leading only to the worst of outcome. None of this had been planned. Desperate measures led to desperate responses, but this was not the coxswain's original intention.

"Murderers," Dora said, "we're all killers, we set this up, we pulled this lousy job." But that was after the miscarriage and its pathetic aftermath, and by this time Dora was clearly not sane. It was possible to discount everything she said. It was, in fact, necessary to make that discount.

And so we did. We ignored her. We were polite, tolerant, we did not wish to ostracize, but at the same time we were firm. "Listen," we said, "we are decent, we are good, we are sensible people." Our voices were firm, our faces judicious and tolerant. "We had no choice, no control," we added. "Besides, the word 'underclass' remains out of our lexicon." And so it did. We were not pejorative. We were kind people. We had full awareness.

So we were good to Dora, as good as could be under the circumstances, and we protected her as best we could from her own self-destructiveness. We looked forward to the time when Polar Star would permit us to take down the gates and reclaim all of our city. *Our* city.

"Killers," Dora screamed. But the sculptor had left her, *all* of us, in exhaustion, had left her, really. She was almost impossible to tolerate, and no matter how great our ingestion of palliatives, she still appeared ugly.

Black Glass

KAREN JOY FOWLER

I

T WAS A WEDNESDAY AFTERNOON in the Senate Bar. Schilling, the proprietor, stood behind the curved counter, stroking the shot glasses with a towel. Every part of the bar was reflected in the mirrored wall behind him: the marble and black onyx floor, the oiled cherry-wood counter, the brass bar-rail. A chandelier hung in the center of the ceiling, and rows of cut-glass decanters filled the shelves. Schilling ran his towel over their glass stoppers. In the corner, on the big screen, Cher danced and sang a song for the U.S. Navy. Schilling had the sound off.

There were three customers. Two sat together at a table near the door. were businessmen. One of them smoked. Both of them drank.

Every time either of them picked up his glass and set it down again, he made a new wet ring on the table between them. They were careful to keep the spreadsheet out of the water.

The third customer, a college student, sat at the bar, drinking his way through an unexpected romance with a woman old enough to be his mother. He'd asked Schilling to bring him three drinks at once, three different drinks—a Bloody Mary, a Sex on the Beach, a Velvet Hammer. As a compromise, Schilling had brought him the Bloody Mary and put in an MTV tape, picture only, out of deference to the businessmen and as a matter of personal preference.

A fourth man came into the Senate Bar from the street. A shaft of sunlight sprang into the room when the door opened and vanished when it closed. "Give me a drink," the man said to Schilling.

Schilling glanced at the man briefly as he polished the wood bar with his sleeve. "Get out of here."

"Give me a drink."

The man was dirty and dressed in several tattered layers which still left a bare hole the size of a tennis ball above one knee. He was smoking the stubby end of a cigarette. It was not his cigarette; there was lipstick on the filter. He had retrieved this cigarette from the sidewalk outside the bar. "You pay your tab first," said Schilling.

"I don't have any money," said the man. Cher closed her eyes and opened her mouth.

"Where's my Sex on the Beach?" asked the boy.

"You're disturbing my customers," Schilling told the man at the door. "You're stinking up my bar." He reached under the counter for a bottle of gin.

"He gave me my first drink," the man at the door said to the boy at the bar. "I used to be just like you." He took two steps into the room, leaving two gritty footprints on the black onyx. "Finish what you started," he told Schilling.

"Get out," Schilling said.

The boy rolled a quarter down his nose and let it drop, catching it loudly in his empty Bloody Mary glass. "Can I get another drink?" he asked. "Am I going to get another drink?"

A second shaft of sunlight appeared in the room, collided with the mirrored wall. Inside the sunlight, barely visible, Cher danced.

She turned her back.

Schilling heard a woman scream, and then the Cher in the mirror broke into five pieces and fell behind the counter. The sunlight disappeared. "Madam," said Schilling, hardly breathing, in shock. A nightmare dressed in black stood at the door of his bar, a nightmare in the shape of an enormous postmenopausal woman. In one hand she held a hatchet. She reached into the bodice of her dress with the other and pulled out a large stone. She wore a bonnet with black ribbons.

"Glory be to God!" shouted the woman. "Peace on Earth! Goodwill to men!" She hit the big screen dead center with the rock. The screen cracked and smoked, made spitting noises, blackened. She took a step, swept the cigarette from the shabby man's mouth with one hand. "Don't poison the air with your filthy gases!" she said. Then she held her hatchet at the vertical. She charged into the bar, clearing the counter. Maraschino cherries and stuffed olives flew. "Madam!" said Schilling. He ducked.

"You purveyor and protector of obscenity!" the woman shouted. "Has your mother ever been in this place?" The boy at the bar slipped from his stool and ran for the rear door. In three steps the woman caught him. She picked him up by the neck of his sweater as if he were a kitten, throwing him to his knees. She knelt over him, singing. "Touch not, taste not, handle not. Drink will make the dark, dark blot." He struggled, and she let him go, calling after him, "Your mother did not raise you for this." The back door slammed.

The businessmen had taken cover under their table. Schilling remained out of sight. The shabby man was gone. The woman began, methodically, with her hatchet to destroy the bar. She punctured the decorative keg behind the bar and then, apparently disappointed to find it empty, she brought her hatchet down on the counter, severing a spigot from one of the hoses. A fountain of soda exploded into the air. She broke the decanters. Pools of liquor flowed over the marble and onyx floor. The woman's bonnet slipped to the side of her head.

"That brandy costs seventy-five dollars," Schilling said.

"Broth of hell," she answered. "Costs your soul." She gashed the cherry wood, smashed the mirrored wall. She climbed onto a stool and brought the chandelier down with a single stroke. Schilling peered over the bar. She threw a rock at him, hitting a bottle of bright green crème de menthe behind him.

He ducked out of sight again. "You'll pay for this," Schilling told her. "You'll account for every penny."

"You are Satan's bedfellow," she said. "You maker of drunkards and widows. You donkey-faced rum-soaked Republican rummy." She lifted the hundred-and-fifty-pound cash register from the counter and held it over her head. She began to sing again. "A dreadful foe is in our land, drive him out, O drive him out. O, end the monster's awful reign, drive him out, O drive him out." She threw the register at what remained of the big screen. It barely missed the tabletop that hid the businessmen and crashed onto the marble and onyx floor.

She worked for twenty minutes and stopped when there was nothing left to break. The woman stood at the door, straightening her bonnet, tightening the ribbons. "Until the joints close," she said, "the streets will run red with blood." She opened the door. Schilling crouched lower behind the bar. The businessmen cowered beneath the table. Nobody saw her leave.

"The sun was in my eyes," Schilling explained to the police. "When she opened the door, the sunlight was so bright I lost sight of her."

"She came in screaming?" A man from the press was taking notes.

"Shrieking." The first businessman tried to read the reporter's notes, which were upside down from his point of view and cursory. He didn't enjoy talking to newsmen. When you dealt with the fourth estate, accuracy was your social responsibility. You could still be misquoted, of course. You wouldn't be the first.

"Kind of a *screek*," the second businessman offered.

"She's paying for everything," said Schilling. "Don't even ask me to be chivalrous."

"She was big," said the first businessman. "For a woman."

"She was enormous," said Schilling.

"She was as big as a football player," said the first businessman carefully.

"She was as big as a truck," said Schilling. He pointed with a shaky finger to the register. "She lifted it over her head like it was a feather duster or a pillow or something. You can write this down," he said. "You can quote me on this. We're talking about a very troubled, very big woman."

"I don't think it's such a good idea," the second businessman said.

"What's not a good idea?" asked the reporter.

"Women that size," said the second businessman.

"Just look what she did," said Schilling. Rage made his voice squeak. "Just look at my bar."

Patrick Harris had been a DEA agent for eight years now. During those eight years, he had seen some action. He had been in Mexico and he had been in Panama and he had been in L.A. He had been in one or two tight spots, but that didn't mean he couldn't help out with the dishes at home.

Harris knew he asked a lot of his wife. It couldn't be the easiest thing in
the world, being married to a man who disappeared into Latin America
for days at time and might not even be able to get a message out that he
was still alive. Harris could run a vacuum cleaner over a rug without
feeling like he was doing his wife any favors. Harris could cook a meal
from the very beginning, meaning the planning and the shopping and
everything, without feeling like anyone needed to make a fuss about it.

He stood with the French bread and the Gruyère cheese and the imported Emmentaler Swiss in the nine-items-only-no-checks checkout line,
wondering how he could use the tomatoes which he hadn't planned to
buy but were cheaper and redder than usual and had tempted him. The
woman in front had twelve items. It didn't really irritate Harris. He was
only sorry that it was so hard for some people to play by the rules.

While he waited for the three extra items to be tallied and worried in
an ineffective, pleasant way over the tomatoes, he read through the headlines. Evidence of prehistoric alien cannibals had been found in Peruvian
cave paintings, and a statue of Elvis had been found on Mars. A husband
with bad breath had killed his wife merely by kissing her. A Miami bar
had been destroyed by a sort of half woman/half gorilla. Harris saw the
illustration before he read the story, an artist's rendering of Queen Kong
in a black dress and bonnet. He looked at the picture again. He read the
headline. One of his tomatoes spun from the counter to the floor. Harris
stepped on it, squished it, and didn't even notice. He bought the paper.

He had never been in so much trouble in his life.

The doors were heavy and padlocked. A hummingbird dipped through
the entryway twice, held for a moment over an out-of-season fuschia and
disappeared. The largest of the MPs tried to shoulder the doors open. He
tried three times, but the wood did not give. One of the women smashed
through a window instead. Harris was the fifth person inside.

The soldiers searched for fugitives. They spun into the hallways, kicked
in the doors. Harris found the dining room on the other side of some
broken glass. The table was set with china and the flatware was gold. An
interrupted meal consisted of rack of lamb, braised carrots, curried peach
halves served on lettuce leaves. The food had been sitting on the china
plates for at least twenty-four hours.

He started into the library, but one of the MPs called to him from
further back in the house. The MP's voice sounded self-consciously nervous. *I'm still scared,* the tone said. *Aren't I silly?*

Harris followed the voice down a hallway and through an open door.

The MP had her rifle slung over her back. In her hands she held a large statue of St. George, spear frozen over the neck of the dragon. The dragon was considerably smaller than St. George's horse.

Behind the MP, three stairs rose to an altar with red candles and white flowers and chicken feathers. The stairs were carpeted, and a supplicant could kneel or lie supine if the supplicant weren't too tall. The room itself was not carpeted. A black circle had been painted on the stone floor, with a red triangle inside. The four cardinal points of the compass were marked.

Harris looked east. The east wall was a wall of toads. Toad-shaped stones covered every inch of seven shelves, and the larger ones sat on the floor. The toads were all different, different colors, different sizes. Harris guessed there were four hundred, five hundred toads. "Why toads?" Harris asked. He stepped inside.

The MP shook her head and put the statue back on the altar. "Shit," she said, meaning nothing by it, merely making conversation. "Is this shit for real?"

One of the smallest toads was carved of obsidian. Its eyes were a polished, glassy black; it was no bigger than Harris' thumbnail. It attracted him. Harris reached out. He hesitated briefly, then touched it. At that moment, somewhere in the room, an engine cycled on. Harris started at the sound, closed his hand convulsively over the toad. He looked at the MP, who gestured behind him.

The noise came from a freezer back by the door. It was a small freezer, not big enough to hold the body of an adult. A goat, maybe. A child. A head. Harris looked at the MP. "Groceries," he said.

"Stash," the MP suggested. This made opening the freezer Harris' job. Harris didn't think so. He would have stared the MP down if the MP had only looked at him. Harris watched to be sure the MP wasn't looking. He put the black toad in his pocket and went to open the freezer. He was simply not thinking about the toad. Otherwise he would never have taken it. Harris was DEA, and even when he was undercover, he played by the rules. Taking the toad marked the beginning of a series of atypical transgressions. Harris was at a loss to explain them. It was not as though he wanted the toad.

The freezer worked laboriously. When Harris and his wife were first married, they'd had a noisy refrigerator like this. They would argue: arguments of adjustment, kitchen arguments as opposed to bedroom arguments, as vehement and passionate as they were trivial. And the refrigerator would be a third voice, grumbling in dissatisfaction or croaking in disbelief. Sometimes it would make them laugh. Harris tried to resurrect these comfortable, proappliance kinds of feelings. He closed his eyes and raised the lid. He opened his eyes. The only thing inside the freezer was a stack of pictures.

Harris pushed the lid up until it caught. Some were actual photographs. There was a Polaroid of the General's wife seated in a lawn chair under a beach umbrella, a fat woman who'd left the marks of her nails on more than one of the General's mistresses. There were some Cubans, including Castro, and some Americans, Kissinger and Helms, pictures cut from magazines, but real photographs of the President and the ex-President. There was a fuzzy picture of two men shaking hands on the steps of a public building. Harris recognized one of the men as the Archbishop. The edges of every picture had been dipped in red wax.

He still had the toad in his pocket that night when he attended a party at the home of Señora Villejas. Many American officers were there. Señora Villejas greeted him at the door with a kiss and a whisper. *"El General llego a la embajada con calzoncillos rojos."* The General had turned up in the Vatican embassy wearing red underwear, she said. She spun away to see that the band had refreshment.

A toad in a hole, Harris thought. It was Christmas Eve. Harris arrived late, too late for the champagne, but just in time for the mixed drinks. The band was ethnic and very chic. Harris could hear a concertina, a bobla, a woowoo, the triangle. They played a waltz.

"Have you heard the one about the bitch at the dog kennels?" one of the American captains asked him. The captain had a strawberry daiquiri; he stirred the strawberries with his straw.

"I have now," said Harris.

"Don't pull that shit with me," the captain said. He drank. "You some kind of feminist? You got a whole lot of women working undercover in the DEA?"

Harris ignored him. He spotted Ruiz by the windows and made his way toward him. Some couples had started to dance in the open space between Harris and Ruiz. Harris dodged through the dancers. A woman he had never seen before put a drink in his hand, alcoholic, but hot and spiced. "What am I drinking?" he asked Ruiz.

Ruiz shrugged. "You had a chance to call your wife?" he asked.

"This afternoon," said Harris. "I'm on my way home tomorrow. You?"

"South," said Ruiz. "What any of this shit has to do with anything I do not know."

"It's a statement," said Harris. "At least it's a statement."

"It's an invasion," said Ruiz.

Well, of course there was that. Harris was sorry Ruiz was choosing to see it that way. "He collected toads," Harris offered, by way of changing the subject. "Stone toads."

"He collected yachts," Ruiz said. "The *Macho I*, the *Macho II*, and the *Macho III*. Don't ever tell me he had a problem in this area. And don't tell me he lacked imagination."

Harris took a sip of his drink. It stung his mouth. "Why toads?" His eyes were watering. He took a larger sip, drained the glass halfway.

"Maybe they were hollow," Ruiz said.

"No."

"Maybe just one was hollow and the others were all to hide the hollow one."

A young woman refreshed Harris' drink. "*¿Que estoy bebiendo?*" Harris asked the woman, who left without answering.

"Have some of mine," Ruiz said. He was drinking a margarita. He handed it to Harris. Harris turned the glass to a virginal part of the salt rim and sipped. He rotated the glass and sipped again. "Go ahead and finish it," said Ruiz. "I'll get another."

The music had begun to sound odd. A man stood in the middle of the dance floor. "I'll tell you who's coming here. I'll tell you who's coming here," he shouted. He threw the contents of his drink into the rafters of the house. Others did the same. Harris laughed and drank his margarita instead. He started to say something to Ruiz, but Ruiz was gone. Ruiz had been gone for a long time.

The dancers began to stomp, and the high treble sound of the triangle reached too deeply into Harris' ears. It hurt. Harris could smell alcohol and herbs, drifting down from the roof. The drums and the stomping worked their way into his body. Something inside him was pounding to match them. Harris resisted finding out what. He pulled the little toad from his pocket. "Look what I have," he said to Ruiz, but Ruiz had gone, now Harris remembered, Ruiz had gone South to get a margarita. It was quite some time ago.

"In short, you were stoned out of your gourd," said Harris' superior.

"Now it gets a little blurred for a while," Harris told him. This was a lie, one of several lies. The story Harris was actually telling was far from complete. He had certainly not mentioned stealing the toad. And now he was not mentioning remembering a woman in an evening gown who smiled at him, holding out her hand. There were flowers in it. They bloomed. Everyone was dancing.

"My ears hurt," Harris told her. "Ants are crawling on me." He tried to brush them away, but his hands wouldn't move. She knelt and was still above him so he must have been on the ground. The flowers turned into a painted egg. "This is your brain on drugs," Harris said, laughing. She held it out to him, knowing he couldn't reach for it, teasing him.

"What do you want?" Her shoulders were bare; she answered the question as she asked it by breathing deeply so that her breasts swelled at the neckline. "In your heart, what do you really want?"

Harris' soul detached from his body and floated away.

"I think I had a very narrow escape," Harris told his superior.

"It's a hazard of fieldwork. Sometimes you draw suspicion to yourself by refusing. We know that." The tabloid Harris had purchased was spread out on the desk between Harris and his superior. His superior was adding a mustache to one of the cannibal aliens in the Peruvian cave painting. He blacked in the teeth. It pained Harris, who was not the sort of person to deface pictures and certainly not prehistoric pictures. "I appreciate your coming in, but I don't think I'm even inclined to report this. I mean, in your case, it wasn't even advertent. You were inadvertently drugged."

"I was poisoned," said Harris.

"What does it have to do with gorilla women?"

"Guerrilla women?" Harris repeated. "Everything. I was poisoned by female agents of the Panama Defense Forces." He took a deep breath. "You got anything here I can drink?"

His superior gestured to the wet bar. Harris poured himself a shot of whiskey. He swallowed it all at once. "The toad is an important Mayan symbol of hallucinosis." Whiskey warmed his tongue and his throat. "In medieval European witchcraft, they used to decompose toads in menstrual blood for use in potions.

"Toad, that under cold stone,/Days and nights hast thirty-one/Swel-t'red venom sleeping got,/Boil thou first i' the charmed pot," Harris said.

Harris' superior was staring at him. Harris' superior was not an educated man. "Shakespeare," Harris said by way of apology for showing off. "I've been reading up on it. I mean I don't know these things off the top of my head. I'm not really a toad man." Harris' superior continued to stare. Harris poured another drink to steady himself. "In Haiti, the toad is symbol of the zombie." Harris tossed his whiskey into his throat and avoided looking at his superior. "What do you know about Carry A. Nation?" Harris asked.

"Make it a written report," his superior said.

• • • •

Item one: There are real zombies.

The woman could see where Harris was floating above his body. She began to sing to him, low, but he could hear her even over the drums. *"Ti bon ange,"* she sang. The egg in her hand became a jar made of clay. She held it out so he would come down closer and look. She wanted him to look inside it and not at her, because her shape was not holding. She was not a beautiful woman at all, she was an ugly woman, old and ugly. Her skin folded on her neck like a toad's. Harris found this transformation a little insulting. He remembered how much he loved his wife. He had spoken with her only today. He couldn't wait to get back to his body and home to her. He refused to be seduced by an ugly old woman instead. *"Ti bon ange,"* she sang, and her voice was low and croaked. "Come look in my jar."

Item two: The *ti bon ange*. *Ti bon ange* means the little good angel. Every person who has ever lived is made up of five components. These are the *z'étoile*, the *n'âme*, the *corps cadavre*, the *gros bon ange* and the *ti bon ange*. We need concern ourselves here only with the last three.

The *gros bon ange* is the undifferentiated life force. It binds you to the rest of the living world.

The *ti bon ange* is your personal life force. The *ti bon ange* is your individual personality.

The *corps cadavre* is your body.

Harris could see the dark opening of the jar beneath him, a circular pool of black. The circle grew until he could have fit inside it. He didn't know if it was growing because the woman was raising it or if he was slipping toward it like sand sucked into the throat of an hourglass. Either way was perilous. Harris looked for someplace dark to hide. Harris slid into the bright blackness of the stone toad, resting in the hand of his inert *corps cadavre*.

The American captain came and knelt on the other side of Harris. "What have we here?"

"DEA." The beautiful woman was back. The American captain wouldn't have even spoken to the ugly old woman. She turned her jar into a wine glass and drank from it innocently.

Item three: creating a zombie. In order to create a zombie, you need to separate the *ti bon ange* from the *gros bon ange*. You need to take the *ti bon ange* out of the *corps cadavre* and leave the *gros bon ange* behind.

The *bokor* accomplishes this with bufotoxin, an extremely potent poison milked from the glands of the *Bufo marinus* toad and tetrodotoxin, taken from the skin, liver, testicles and ovaries of the Tetrodontiformes, a family of fish that includes the blowfish. Bufotoxin stimulates cardiac activity. Tetrodotoxin causes neuromuscular paralysis. In proper doses, taken together, they produce a living corpse.

It is critical that the dosage not be too high. Too much poison and you will kill the body, forcing the *gros bon ange* to abandon it as well.

"I know," the captain said.

The woman wanted the captain to go away so that she could sing to Harris again. "He's had too much to drink."

The captain flicked a finger at Harris' nose. Harris saw him do it. "Undercover is pussy work. I wish just once the DEA would send out an agent with some balls."

The woman was angry and it made her old, but the captain wasn't looking.

"Pompous, self-righteous pricks," he said. "The most ineffective agency in the whole U.S. Government, and that's saying something."

The captain looked at her. She was beautiful and drank red wine. Her eyes were as bright as coins. "I wish . . ." said the captain. He moved closer to her. "Shall I tell you what I wish?" he said. Harris was relieved to see that the captain was not going away, not unless the woman became old before him, and this was something she was, apparently, reluctant to do. Perhaps she wanted to surprise the captain with it. It served the captain right, seducing some old crone. The party spun around Harris, dancing couples, drinking couples. The black opalescence of the toad cast a yellow filter over the scene, but Harris could still see, dimly, that inside every women there, no matter how graceful, no matter how beautiful, there was an old crone, biding her time.

"What are you writing?" Harris' wife asked him. She had come in behind him, too quietly. It made him jump. He leaned forward to block the screen.

"Nothing," he said. Harris loved his wife, and knew that her dear, familiar body did not conceal the figure of a hostile old woman. Hadn't he always helped with the dishes? Hadn't he never minded? He was safe with her. Harris wished she wouldn't sneak up on him.

"What are you reading? Children's books?" she asked incredulously. She taught British, American and women's literature at the junior college. She was, Harris thought, but lovingly, a bit of a snob. In fact, he had a stack of books on his desk—several Japanese pharmacologies, several volumes of Vodoun rituals and a couple of temperance histories. Only one was for children, but this was the one Harris' wife picked up. *The Girl's*

Life of Carry A. Nation, it said on the spine. "Are you coming to bed?" Harris' wife asked.

"In a moment."

She went to bed without him, and she took the book with her.

Five-year-old Carry Moore sat on the pillared porch and waited impatiently for her mother to come home. Her father had bought her mother a new carriage! Little Carry wanted to see it.

The year was 1851. Behind Carry was the single-story Kentucky log house in which the Moores lived. It sat at the end of a row of althea bushes and cedar trees. The slave cabins were to the right. To the left was the garden, roses, syringa, and sweet Mary. Mary was Carry's mother's name.

Carry's mother was not like other mothers. Shortly after Carry was born, Mary decided her own real name was Victoria. She was not just playing let's pretend. Mary thought she was really the Queen of England. She would only speak to Carry by appointment. Sometimes this made Carry very sad.

Carry saw one of the slaves, Bill, coming down the road. Bill was very big. He was riding a white horse and was dressed in a fine red hunting jacket. Didn't he look magnificent? He carried a hunting horn which made loud noises when you wound it. Honk! Honk! The Queen was coming!

Carry could see the carriage behind him. It was the most beautiful carriage she had ever seen. It had curtains and shiny wheels and matched gray horses to pull it. Henry, another slave, was the coachman. He wore a tall silk hat.

The carriage stopped. Mary got out. She was dressed all in gold with a cut-glass tiara. She wanted to knight Farmer Murray with her umbrella. Farmer Murray was their neighbor. He was weeding his onions. Farmer Murray tried to take Mary's umbrella away.

"Oh, Ma," said Carry. She ran down the road to her mother. "Take me for a ride."

Carry's mother would not even look at her. "Betsey," said Mary. Betsey was one of the slaves. She was only thirteen years old, but she was a married woman with a baby of her own. "This child is filthy. Take her away and clean her up."

"Ma!" said little Carry. She wanted so badly to go for a ride.

"We don't want her in the house," said Mary. Queens sometimes say *we* when they mean *I*. Mary was using the royal we. "She is to sleep with you tonight, Betsey," said Mary.

Carry didn't mind sleeping with Betsey, but it meant she had to sleep with Josh, Betsey's husband, too. Josh was mean. "Please don't make me sleep with Josh," Carry asked, but her mother had already walked past her.

Sometimes Carry's mother was not very nice to her, but Carry had lots of friends. They were her slaves! They were Betsey; and Judy, who was very old; and Eliza, who was very pretty; and Henry, who was smart; and Tom, who was nice. Carry ate with them and slept with them. They loved Carry.

One night Henry told a scary story. It was dark in the slave cabin, and they all sat around the fire. The story was about a mean slave master who died but came back in chains to haunt his slaves. They all believed in ghosts, which made the story even scarier. The story made Carry shiver.

Suddenly there was a knock at the door. Carry jumped right out of her seat. It was only Mr. Brown, the overseer. That made Carry laugh. "We thought you were someone bad coming," Carry said. Mr. Brown laughed, too. He had just come to talk to Eliza. He took Eliza away to talk to her in his cabin. Judy and Betsey scolded Henry for telling a story that frightened Carry.

Item four: On Christmas Eve, at a party at the house of Señora Villejas, I narrowly survived an attempt by the Panama Defense League to turn me into a zombie. The agent of the attack was either a beautiful young Panamanian woman or an old one. She appeared to me as both.

Under ordinary circumstances, the body's nerve impulses are relayed from the spine under conditions of difference in the sodium and potassium concentrations inside and outside the axon membrane. The unique heterocyclic structure of the tetrodotoxin molecule is selective for the sodium channels. A change in the sodium levels, therefore, alters the effectiveness of the drug. My escape was entirely fortuitous. I had just drunk half a margarita. The recent ingestion of salt was, I believe, all that saved me.

I hardly need point out the usefulness to the drug cartels of a DEA agent entirely under their control.

Harris' hands were sweaty on the keyboard. He licked a finger to taste the salt. There was a map on the wall beside him, marked with five colored pins. One pin went through the Vatican embassy in Panama. One was in the Senate Bar in Miami. The others continued northwards in a more or less direct line. If extended, the line would pass through Washington, D.C.

Item five: the *loa*. At death, the *ti bon ange* survives and returns to live in another body. Each of us has a direct spiritual lineage back through history. After many such renewals, the individual spirit metamorphoses into disembodied, undifferentiated energy. It joins the cosmic pool of life where the *loa* reside. When a *loa* is called back, it returns from this pool as a purified, mythological version of itself. The individual *ti bon ange* has become archetype. The same mythological figures we know as saints of the Catholic Church also appear to the Vodoun as *loa*.

On the evening of December 24, 1989, I convinced several DEA agents to join me in calling forth a *loa*. We did not call forth a specific spirit by name. We called to our own spiritual ancestors. We asked for a weapon in our struggle against the drug cartels.

"Send us a DEA agent with balls," Harris shouted. He was laughing, ecstatic to be in his body again. His hands tingled, his lips were numb, his thighs were warm. The war was over and he was not among the dead. It was Christmas Eve. Ruiz and Casteneda and Martin and several others, ties loosened, suit jackets askew, shoes off, danced the dance with Harris in Señora Villejas' garden. They threw the contents of their drinks into bushes pruned to the shapes of elephants and camels and giraffes. They crushed flowers with their hands, and Martin had unzipped his pants, rezipping them so that a white hothouse iris extended from his crotch. Of course, it hadn't really been *the dance*. It had only been something they made up.

I would prefer not to identify the men who joined me in this ceremony since the suggestion was entirely my own. I would like to repeat, in my defense, that I was at this time under the influence of bufotoxin, known for its hallucinogenic properties, as well as alcohol. I was not conducting myself soberly. We did not for a moment believe that we would be successful in calling up such a spirit. The entire enterprise was conducted as a drunken lark.

Clinically speaking, I suppose we were trying to protect ourselves from our fear of the Vodounist, by making a joke of it. I had just survived an attack on my soul. That I did not believe in this attack, imagining it to be purely hallucinatory, does not change the fact that I was unnerved by it.

In the light of recent events, however, and with the benefit of hindsight, it seems possible to me that we have underestimated the effectiveness of the South American drug cartel Vodoun. The Haitian zombie is typically described as dim and slow witted. Among our top government officials are men who fit this description, men known also to have been in Latin and South America. The DEA should make a list of these men, meet with them on some pretext, and offer them heavily salted foods.

Ruiz was gaping at him. A *z'étoile* fell from the sky into the garden. It came in the form of a burning rock. It landed in one of the camel bushes and melted the garden.

The shapes of the flowers and trees remained, but now they were made of fire. The DEA agents burst into flames. Harris could see their shapes, too. They continued to dance, stamping their flaming feet into the liquid fire of the lawn, shaking their flickering hands.

A woman emerged from the camel bush, not a real woman, but a woman of flame. She grew larger and larger until she was larger than he was, wrapped her fiery arms around him. The air was so hot he couldn't breathe it. Harris panicked. He fumbled for the toad in his pocket, remembering how he'd escaped into it once already, but she touched it with one finger, melting it into something small and phallic. She laughed and melted it again, shapeless this time, a puddle of black glass. "Who are you?" Harris asked, and she told him. Then she scorched the bottoms of his feet until he fainted from the pain and had to be carried home.

The next morning, the toad was in his pocket and his feet were healed. Ruiz came to say good-bye. *"Feliz Navidad,"* said Ruiz. He brought a present of candied fruits. "Kiss your wife for me. You lucky bastard."

Harris thanked him for the gift. "Great party," said Harris carefully.

Ruiz shrugged. "You had a good time," he agreed. "You were a wild man."

They said little else. On his way to the airport, Harris directed his taxi past the home of Señora Villejas. The garden was green.

Carry's mother was sometimes better when she had new places and people to see. Carry's father, George, had trouble with his real estate business. The Moores moved often and they grew poorer. When Carry was ten years old, they moved to Cass County, Missouri. Carry missed Kentucky. She missed Bill and Eliza, who had been sold. She missed her beautiful Kentucky house.

But Cass County was an exciting place to live! Just across the border, in Kansas, people who liked having slaves were fighting with people who didn't. The people who liked slavery were called bushwhackers. The people who didn't were called jayhawkers. Kansas had an election to see if they would be a free state with no slaves. Bushwhackers from Missouri took the ballot boxes and said they would count the votes for Kansas.

They said that Kansas had voted to make it illegal to even say that you didn't like slavery. Anyone who said they didn't like slavery could be killed. So many died, people began to call the state "Bleeding Kansas."

This was a hard time for Carry. She went to bed for five years.

Psychologists now say maybe having a mother who thought she was Queen Victoria is what made Carry sick for such a long time. Psychologists are people who study how people feel and behave.

In 1857, her doctor said she had consumption of the bowels.

But George, her father, said her sickness was a punishment for not loving God. He came to see her sometimes in her bedroom. "Why won't you love God, Carry?" he would ask. He would have tears in his eyes. "You are going to die and break my heart," he would say.

Carry didn't want her father to be unhappy. She tried and tried to love God better. Carry thought she was a horrible sinner. Sometimes, when she was a little girl, she stole things for her slaves, little bits of ribbon, spoonfuls of sugar. Her own heart, Carry said, was the blackest, foulest place she ever saw.

One day when Carry was twelve, George took her to a revival meeting. "Who will come to Jesus?" the minister asked. Carry said that she would. Carry had a fever. George was afraid she was about to die, so even though it was winter, the minister and George took her right away to an icy creek. The water was cold! Carry waded into it, and the minister pushed her under.

When she came up, Carry said that she had learned to love God. She made her slaves come to her bedroom so she could preach to them. Carry told them that God sent you troubles because He loved you and wanted you to love Him. God loved Carry so much He made her ill. God loved the slaves so much He made them slaves. Now that Carry loved God, she began to get better, and in two more years she was able to get out of bed.

The slaves thought that since they loved God, maybe they didn't need to be slaves anymore. They told George they wanted to go to Lawrence, Kansas, where slavery was illegal. Lawrence, Kansas, was very close to Cass County, Missouri.

George told the slaves they were all moving to Texas instead. Texas was very far from Lawrence, Kansas.

Item six: I don't know where she got the body. A *loa* usually manifests itself through possession, but I remember no one at the party as large as this woman is reported to be. In addition, I have a memory of the *loa* materializing out of flame. I need not repeat that I was under the influence of bufotoxin at the time.

Item seven: The *loa* are frequently religious archetypes. Carry Nation, by her own account, spoke to angels when she was still a child and saw the Holy Ghost at her basement window. She performed two miracles in her life and applied for sainthood, although the application was turned down. Since the DEA agents and I performed only a quasi-Vodoun ritual, there is a certain logic to the fact that we got only a quasi saint in return. The *loa* I summoned was Carry Amelia Nation. She told me so herself.

Item eight: Ask the General why he left the Vatican embassy.

Harris already knew the answer to item eight. Harris had friends among the attorneys on Miami's "white powder bar." It was not that their interests were compatible. It was merely a fact that they saw each other often.

"So what was it?" the attorney told Harris he had asked the General. "Why did you come out? Was it the white room with no windows and no TV? Was it the alcohol deprivation?"

"It was a woman," the General said.

"You spoke to your mistress." The attorney knew this much. She had been in U.S. custody at the time. "She persuaded you?"

"No." The General shuddered violently. His skin turned the color of eggplant. "It was a horrible woman, a huge woman, a woman no man would sleep with." He was, the attorney told Harris, very possibly a homosexual. Hadn't he started dressing in yellow jumpsuits? Hadn't he said that the only people in Panama with balls were the queers and the women? "She sang to me," the General said.

"Heavy metal?" asked the attorney.

"Who Hath Sorrow, Who Hath Woe," said the General.

Harris did not include this in his report. It was an off-the-record conversation. And anyway, the DEA would trust it more if they found it themselves.

Harris pushed the key to print. Only the first part of his report fit on the DEA form. He stapled the other pages to it. He signed the report and poured himself a bedtime sherry.

The Moores did not live in Texas very long. Many of their slaves developed typhoid fever while walking there from Missouri. All their horses died. George tried to farm, but he did not know how. Mary told one of their neighbors that she was confiscating his lands and his title, so he threw all their plows into the river. Soon there was nothing to eat.

George called his slaves together. He told them he had decided to free them. The slaves were frightened to be free with no food. Some of them cried.

It was very hard for the Moores to leave their slaves. But Carry said her father had done the right thing. She believed that slavery was a great wrong. She admired John Brown, a man who had fought for the rights of slaves in Kansas and was hanged for it when Carry was thirteen years old. All her life, John Brown was a hero of Carry's. "When I grow up," Carry said, "I will be as brave as John Brown."

Between Texas and Missouri was the Civil War. The Queen's carriage had been sold. When the Moores went back to Missouri, they had to ride in their little wagon. One day the ground shook behind them. They pulled off the road. It was not an earthquake. It was the Confederate cavalry on their way to the Battle of Pea Ridge. After the cavalry came the foot soldiers. It took two days and two nights for all the soldiers to pass them.

On the third day, they heard cannons. The Moores began to ride again, slowly, in the direction of the cannons. On the fourth day, the Confederate Army passed them again. This time they were going south. This time they were running. The Moores drove their little wagon straight through the smoking battlefield of Pea Ridge.

They spent that night in a farmhouse with a woman and five wounded Union soldiers. The soldiers were too badly hurt to be moved, so the woman had offered to nurse them. She told Carry she had five sons of her own. Her sons were soldiers for the South. Carry helped her clean and tend the boys. One of them was dying. Mary knighted them all.

"Are you enjoying the book?" Harris asked, surprised that she was still awake. He took off his clothes and lay down beside her. She had more than her share of the comforter. He had to lie very close to be warm enough, putting an arm across her stomach, feeling her shift her body to fit him.

"Yes, I am," she said. "I think she's wonderful."

"Wonderful?" Harris removed his arm. "What do you mean, 'wonderful'?"

"I just mean, what a colorful, amazing life. What a story."

Harris put his arm back. "Yes," he agreed.

"And what a vivacious, powerful woman. After all she'd been through. What a resilient, remarkable woman."

Harris removed his arm. "She's insane," he suggested stiffly. "She's a religious zealot with a hatchet. She's a joke."

"She's a superhero," said Harris' wife. "Why doesn't she have her own movie? Look here." She flipped through *The Girl's Life* to the collection of photographs in the middle. She skipped over Carry kneeling with her Bible in her jail cell to a more confrontational shot. Carry in battle dress. Carry threatening the photographer with hatchetation. "She even had a costume. She designed it herself, like Batman. See? She made special dresses with pockets on the inside for her rocks and ammunition. She could bust up bars and she could sew like the wind. Can Rambo say as much?"

"I bet she threw like a girl," said Harris, trying for a light tone to mask the fact that he was genuinely upset.

His wife was not masking. "Her aim was supposed to have been extraordinary," she said in her schoolteacher tone, a tone that invariably suggested disappointment in him. "Women are cut off from the rich mythological tradition you men have. Women are so hungry for heroines. Name one."

"What?" said Harris.

"Name a historical heroine. Quickly."

"Joan of Arc," said Harris.

"Everyone can get that far. Now name another."

Harris couldn't think. She tapped her fingers on the page to let him know that time was passing. He had always admired Morgan Fairchild for her political activism, but he assumed this would be the wrong answer. If he hadn't been so irritated he could probably have come up with another name.

"Harriet Tubman," his wife said. "Donaldina Cameron. Edith Cavell. Yvonne Hakime-Rimpel."

She really was a snob, but she was also a fair-minded woman. She was not, Harris thought, one of those feminists who simply changed history every time it didn't suit her. Harris got out of bed and went back to the study. His feet were cold on the bare wood floor. Blankets or no blankets, it would take a long time for his feet to warm up. He fished Carry Nation's autobiography out of his stack and brought it back.

"You haven't read about her daughter," he said. "There's nothing about Charlien, in the pretty little version for children that you chose to read." He flipped through his own book until he found the section he wanted. He thrust it in front of his wife's face, then pulled it back to read it aloud. " 'About this time, my precious child, born of a drunken father and a distracted mother, seemed to conceive a positive dislike for Christianity. I feared for her soul and I prayed to God to send her some bodily affliction which would make her love and serve Him.' " Harris skimmed ahead in the book with his finger. "A week later, Charlien developed a raging fever," he told his wife. "She almost died. And when she recovered from that, part of her cheek rotted away. She had a hole in her face. You could see her teeth. But it was a lucky thing. Because then her jaws locked shut, and she wouldn't have been able to eat if there wasn't a hole in her cheek to stick a straw through." He made an effort to lower his voice. "Her jaws stayed locked for eight years."

There was a long silence, a silence, Harris thought, of reevaluation and regret for earlier, hasty judgments. "That is a very ugly story," his wife said. She took the autobiography away from him and began to turn the pages.

"Isn't it?" Harris wiggled his arm underneath her. There was a longer silence. Harris stared at the ceiling. It was a blown popcorn landscape, and sometimes Harris could imagine pictures in it, but he was too tired for this now. He looked instead at the large cobwebs in the corners. Tomorrow Harris would get the broom and knock them down. Then he would get out the vacuum to suck up the bits of ceiling that came down with the cobwebs, the little flakes of milky asbestos, the poisonous snow, the toxic powders. Nothing the vacuum couldn't handle. And then Harris would need a rag to remove from the furniture the dust the vacuum had flung up. And then the rag would need to be washed. And then . . . it was almost like counting sheep. Harris drifted.

"You can't possibly think those things happened because of Carry's prayers," his wife said.

Harris woke up in amazement. His arm had already gone numb from his wife's weight. He pulled it free. "So now she's Carry?" Harris asked. "Now we're on a first-name basis?"

"Look at the religious climate she grew up in. *You* don't believe God inflicted a little girl with such a horrible condition because her mother asked Him to."

"What kind of mother would ask Him to?" said Harris. "That's the point, isn't it? What kind of a horrible mother is this?"

Harris' wife was still reading the autobiography. "Carry worked for years to earn the money for surgery," she told Harris.

"I've read the book," he said, but there was no stopping her.

"She ignored the doctors who said the case was hopeless. Every time a doctor said the case was hopeless, she went home and earned more money for another doctor." Harris' wife pointed out the relevant text.

"I've read the damn book."

"The condition was finally cured, because Carry never gave up."

"So, *she* says," said Harris.

His wife regarded him coolly. "I don't think Carry would lie."

Harris turned his back on his wife and lay on his side. "It's very late," he said curtly. He turned off his light, punched angrily at his pillow. Unable to get comfortable, he flipped from side to side and considered getting himself another sherry. "What's to like about her? I really don't understand." Harris felt that his wife had suddenly, frighteningly, become a different person. They had always been so consensual. Not pathologically so, they had their own opinions and their own values, of course, but they had also generally liked the same movies, enjoyed the same books. Suddenly she was holding unreasonable opinions. Suddenly she was a stranger.

His wife did not answer, nor did she turn off her own light. "This is an interesting book, too," she said. He heard pages continuing to turn. "There are hymns in the back. Honey, if you dislike Carry Nation so much, why do you have all these books about her?"

Harris, who always told his wife everything, had not yet found just the right moment to tell her that, the last time he was in Panama, he had summoned a *loa*. Harris pretended to be asleep. "You just don't like her because she had a hatchet," his wife said quietly. "Because she was a big, loud woman with a hatchet. You're threatened by her."

Harris sat bolt upright so that the comforter slid off him completely. Was that fair? Was that at all fair? Hadn't they had a completely egalitarian, respectful, supportive marriage? And didn't it make him sort of joke in the DEA for his lack of machismo and hadn't he never, ever complained to her about this? "Good night," his wife said evenly, snapping her light off. She had her side of the comforter wound in her fists. It fell just a bit below her shoulders so he could see her neck and the start of her spine, blue in the moonlight, like stitching down her back. She breathed, and her spine stretched like a snake. She pulled the comforter up around her again. She had more than her share of the covers.

Beside the books on her nightstand, was the little black toad. Harris had given it to her for Christmas. It stared at him.

And wasn't he, after all, the person who'd brought Carry back? Now he was glad he hadn't told her. Harris' feet were too cold, and he couldn't sleep at all.

"I've read over your report," Harris' superior told him. "I took it up top. It's a little spotty."

Harris conceded as much. "The form was so small," he said.

"And not really designed for exactly this sort of problem." With tone of voice, phrasing and body language, Harris' superior managed a blatant show of generosity and condescension. Harris' superior was feeling superior. It was not a pretty thing to see. It was not a pretty thing to see in the man who fought so hard to award the Texas Guard a $2,900,000 federal grant so they could station themselves along the Mexican border disguised as cactus plants and ambush drug traffickers.

Harris looked instead at the map on the wall behind him. It was a map much like the map in Harris' study; the pins were different colors, but the locations were identical. "This is the DEA's official position," his superior said. "The DEA does not believe in zombies. The DEA believes in drugs. One of our agents was inadvertently drugged on Christmas Eve and imagined a great many things. This agent now understands that the incidents in question were hallucinatory.

"If it is ever proved that this agent called forth a *loa*, then it is the DEA's position that he did so in his leisure time and that the summoning represents the act of an individual and not of an agency.

"The DEA has no knowledge of nor connection with the gorilla woman. Her malicious and illegal destruction of private property is a matter for the local police. Do you understand?"

"Unofficially?" asked Harris.

"Unofficially they're reading your report in the men's room for light entertainment," said Harris' superior. "You'll see bits of it on the wall in the second stall." Harris already had. *Item six: I don't know where she got the body.* Scratched with a penknife or the fingernail-cleaning attachment on a clipper, just above the toilet paper dispenser.

His superior leaned forward to engage in actual eye contact with Harris. It took Harris by surprise; he drew back. "Unofficially we were impressed with the report the General gave us. We were impressed enough to interview some of the Miami eyewitnesses. They're not the sort of wingnuts in sandals you might expect to find in the tabloids. Our agent spent two hours with a Mr. Schilling who owns the Miami bar. He's a pretty savvy guy, and he says she performed feats of superhuman strength. How did she get into the Vatican embassy? No one ever sees her come or go. She took out a crack lab in Raleigh, North Carolina, a week ago. Did you hear about that?"

Harris had not. He was alarmed to hear she was already as far north as Raleigh. He rechecked the map. There it was, a black pin through the heart of North Carolina.

"Unofficially the DEA doesn't give a damn where she came from. Unofficially the DEA expects you to take care of her."

Harris nodded. He had always seen that the burden of responsibility was his. With or without the DEA, he had never intended to shirk it. He had already been spending his sleepless nights making plans. "With support?" Harris asked.

"At my discretion. And certainly not visibly."

It was more than Harris had hoped for. He moved to the map on the wall. "She seems to moving directly north. Sooner or later, I figure she'll hit here." He drew a line north from Raleigh to Richmond, a small circle around Richmond. "Somewhere in here. So. We concentrate our forces in the larger bars.

"Now, the body is the real issue. Is it a real body? If so, it's doable. If not, we're in trouble. If not, we need expert help. But let's say that it is. She shows herself, we attack with the bufotoxin/tetrodotoxin package. This could be a bit tricky. She won't drink, of course. The potion can go right through the skin, and sometimes the *bokor* simply sprinkles it on the doorstep, but I'm guessing she's the sort who won't remove her shoes. We might try a Shirley Temple, load the tetrodotoxin into the cherry. Even if she won't drink the ginger ale, I'm willing to bet she'll eat the cherry. The dosage will be guesswork, and someone will have to take it to her. Of course, I'm volunteering."

"No hallucinogenics," Harris' superior said.

Harris' mind was filled with cherries. He had to blink to clear it. "I don't understand. We're just trying to persuade the *loa* to abandon the host body."

"You summoned a weapon. This weapon served us at the Vatican embassy. It's a useful weapon. We don't want it destroyed."

"*You* don't understand," Harris said. "You're not going to control it. You can't talk to it. You can't reason with it. You can't hurt it. It doesn't feel pity or remorse or self-doubt. It makes no distinction between drugs and liquor and nicotine. And it will not stop. Ever."

"We want it on the team," Harris' superior said.

"You're tying my hands," said Harris. His heart had never beat faster except for maybe that time in Mexico when Rico had slipped and used his real name during a buy, and that time above the Bolivian mountains when two engines failed, and that time when his wife was supposed to be home by 7:00 and didn't arrive until after 10:00 because the class discussion had been so interesting they'd taken it to a bar to continue it and the bar phone had been out of order, and that time he was on bufotoxins.

"The problem is not here in the States with the consumers. The problem is down there with the suppliers."

"You're sending me on a suicide mission."

"We want your *loa* in Colombia," Harris' superior said.

Harris packed his clothes for Richmond. He had no red underwear, but he had boxers with red valentines on them. They were a gift from his wife. He put them on, making a mental list of the other items he needed. Eggs dyed yellow, fresh eggs, so he would have to pick them up after he arrived. Salt. Red and white candles. The black toad, for luck. Feathers. Harris pulled his Swiss Army knife out of his pocket and reached for his pillow.

"Patrick?" Harris' wife called him from the kitchen. "Patrick, would you come here a moment?" Harris put the knife away.

His wife stood in front of the refrigerator. In one hand she had the picture of Carry and her hatchet, torn from *The Girl's Life.* The edges were dipped in red candle wax. "I found this under the Tater Tots," Harris' wife said. "What is it and how did it get in my freezer?"

Harris had no answer. He had to stall and think of one. He opened the refrigerator and got himself a beer. "*My* freezer?" he said pointedly, popping the flip-top. "Isn't it *our* freezer?"

"How did this get in our freezer?"

"I don't think I would ever have referred to the freezer as *my* freezer," Harris said sadly. He drank his beer, for timing rather than thirst, an extra moment to let his point sink in. Then he amplified. "I don't think you'll find me doing that. But with you it's always *my* kitchen. *My* Sunday paper. *My* bed."

"I'm sorry," said his wife. She held out the picture. Harris spoke again before she could.

"It signifies," he said. "It certainly signifies."

His wife had the tenacity of a hound. "What's with the picture?"

"I spilled wax on it. Accidentally." Harris had not survived in the Latin American drug theater without some ability to think on his feet. He took the photograph from her. "Naturally I wanted to remove the wax in such a way as to do as little damage to the picture as possible. This picture came out of a library book, after all. So I thought I could remove the wax easier if the wax were hard. I put it in the freezer."

"Why were you reading by candlelight?" his wife asked. "You tore the picture out of a library book? That doesn't sound like you."

"The book was due back. It had to be returned." His wife was staring at him. "It was *overdue,*" Harris said.

He missed the *loa* in Richmond. A few hours after his wife took the picture out of the freezer and before he'd hidden it under the bed, pinned beneath a glass of salt water to force the *loa* across an ocean, she struck. Harris' superior caught him on the car phone on the way to the airport. In addition to Richmond, there'd been a copycat incident in Chicago at a cocaine sale. The sale had been to the DEA. They had worked on it for months, and then some grandmother with a hatchet sent it all south. "I want her on the plane to Colombia yesterday," Harris' superior said.

Harris canceled his reservation and drove to Alexandria. She was coming so fast. For the first time, he asked himself why. Was she coming for him?

"Straying tonight, straying tonight, leaving the pathway of honor and right . . ." The song came from inside the Gateway Bar, punctuated with sounds of breaking glass, splintering wood, and an occasional scream. Harris had been beepered to the spot, but others had obviously arrived first. It was ten in the evening, but across the street two men washed a store window. One sat in his car behind a newspaper. Two more had levered up the manhole cover and knelt beside it, peering down industriously. One man watched Harris from a second-story window above the bar.

Harris set his case on the sidewalk and opened the latch. HAPPY HOUR! the bar marquee read. RAP SINGING! OPEN MIKE! HOGAN CONTEST! He took a bottle of whiskey from his case and poured himself something stiffening. Someone else would have to drive him home. If there was a ride home. Of course there would be a ride home.

He began to sprinkle a circle of salt outside the bar door. He drew a salt triangle inside it. There was a breath of silence; the awful singing resumed. "She's breaking the heart of her dear, gray-haired mother, she'll break it, yes break it tonight."

A young woman in a wet T-shirt flew out of the bar, landing on his knee and his salt.

Harris helped her to her feet. She was blond, garishly blond, but that was just the effect of the bar marquee lights which laid an orange tint over her hair. "I Survived Catholic School," the T-shirt said. "She told me to go home and let my mother have a good look at me. She called me a strumpet." The woman had not yet started to cry, but she was about to.

"She was once badly beaten by prostitutes." Harris was consoling.

"Maybe this is a problem area for her." The beating happened in 1901, when the proprietor of a Texas bar, feeling it would unman him to attack Carry Nation himself, had hired a group of prostitutes to beat her with whips and chains. He had also persuaded his wife to take part. Harris had paid particular attention to the incident, because there was a vulnerability and he wondered if he could exploit it. He was not thinking of real prostitutes, of course. He was thinking of undercover vice cops. Beating was a common step in the creation of a zombie. The *ti bon ange* was thought less likely to return to a body that was being beaten.

Still, there was something distasteful about this strategy. Carry Nation had gone down like a wounded bear, surrounded by dogs. She might have been killed had her own temperance workers not finally rescued her. "There is a spirit of anarchy abroad in the land," Carry Nation was reported to have said, barely able to stand, badly cut and bruised. For the next two weeks she appeared at all speaking and smashing engagements with a large steak taped to the side of her face. She changed steaks daily.

Probably it had left her a little oversensitive on the subject of professional women. The woman in the street was obviously no strumpet. She was just a nice woman in a wet T-shirt. She seemed to be in shock. "It was ladies' night," she told Harris, over and over and over again.

Salt and gravel stuck to her face and the front of her shirt. Harris pulled out a handkerchief and cleaned her face. He heard twanging sounds inside, like a guitar being smashed. He put away his handkerchief and went back to his case. "I have to go in there," he said.

She didn't try to dissuade him. She didn't even stay. Apparently she had hurt his knee when she landed on him. He hadn't noticed at first, but now it was starting to throb. The agent in the car, part of *his* backup, showed the woman a badge and offered to take her out for coffee and a statement.

Harris watched the taillights until the car turned. He poured himself another whiskey and had sharp thoughts on the subject of heroines. It was easy for his wife to tell him women were hungry for heroines. She didn't work undercover among the drug lords in Latin America. Teaching women's literature didn't require exceptional courage, at least not on the junior college level where she taught. And when a woman did find herself in a tight spot as this one had just done, well, what happened then? Women didn't want heroines. Women wanted heroes, wanted heroes to be such an ordinary feature of their daily lives that they didn't even feel compelled to stay and watch their own rescue. Wanted heroes who came home and did the dishes at night.

Harris rubbed his knee and cautiously straightened it. He took the black toad from his case and slipped it into a pocket. He took a tranquilizer gun and, against all orders, a mayonnaise jar containing the doctored Shirley Temple. The ginger ale was laced with bufotenine rather than bufotoxin. Bufotoxin had proved difficult to obtain on short notice, even for a DEA agent who knew his way around the store, but bufotenine was readily available in South Carolina and Georgia, where the cane toad secreted it and anyone willing to lick a toad the size of a soccer ball could have some. Perfectly legal, too, in some forms, although the two state legislatures had introduced bills to outlaw toad-licking.

"Touch not, taste not, handle not!" The voice was suddenly amplified and accompanied by feedback; perhaps the rap singer had left his mike on. The last time Harris had heard Vodoun singing he had been in Haiti, sleeping in the house of a Haitian colonel the DEA suspected of trafficking. He had gotten up and crept into the colonel's study, and the voices came in the window with the moonlight.

> Eh! Eh! Bomba! Heu! Heu!
> Canga, bafio té!
> Canga, mouné de lé!
> Canga, do ki la!
> Canga, li!

The song frightened him back to his room. In the morning, he asked the cook about the voices. "A slave song," she said. "For children." She taught it to him, somewhat amused, he thought, at his rendition. Later he sang it to a friend, who translated, " 'We swear to destroy the whites and all that they possess; let us die rather than fail to keep this vow.' " The cook had served him eggs.

Harris felt no compulsion at this particular moment to be fair, but in his heart he knew that, had his wife been there, she would never have let him go into that bar alone.

The bar was dark; the overheads had all been smashed, and the only light came from something that lay in front of Harris. This something blocked the door so that he could open it just halfway, and he could identify the blockage as Super Mario Brothers 2 by the incessant little tune it was playing. It was tipped onto its side and still glowed ever so slightly. Situated as it was, its little light made things inside even harder to see.

Deep in the bar, there was an occasional spark, like a firefly. Harris squinted in that direction. He could just make out the vacant bandstand. A single chair for a soloist lay on its back under a keyboard that had been snapped in half. The keyboard was still plugged in, and this is what was throwing off sparks. Harris' eyes began to adjust. Above the keyboard, on the wall, about spark-high, was a nest of color-coded wires. The wall phone had been ripped out and stuffed into one of the speakers. Behind the speakers were rounded shapes he imagined to be cowering customers. The floor of the bar was shiny with liquor.

On the other side of the bar were the video games. Street Fighter, Cyberball, and Punch-Out all bore the marks of the hatchet. Over the tune of the video, Harris could hear someone sniffling. The mike picked it up. Otherwise the bar was quiet. Harris squeezed inside, climbing over Super Mario Brothers 2. His knee hurt. He bent and straightened it experimentally. Super Mario Brothers 2 played its music. Dee, dee, dee, *dee*, dee.

The *loa* charged, shrieking, from the corner. "Peace on Earth," she howled, as her hatchet cleaved the air by Harris' head, shattering the mayonnaise jar in his hand. The *loa*'s stroke carried her past him.

A piece of broken glass had sliced across his palm. Harris was bleeding. But worse than that, ginger ale laced with bufotenine was soaking into the cut and into the skin around the cut and way down his wrist. He had dosed the Shirley Temple to fell a linebacker with a couple of sips.

Harris dropped the tranquilizer gun and groped blindly to his right until he located a wet T-shirt. He rubbed his hand with it, all in a panic. Someone slapped him. There was a scream. The hatchet sliced through the air above him and lodged itself into the bar's wood paneling. The tune from Super Mario Brothers played on. The other singing started, in cacophonous counterpoint.

"An awful foe is in our land, drive him out, o drive him out! Donkey-faced bedmate of Satan," the *loa* shrieked. She struggled to remove the hatchet head from the wood. She was an enormous woman, a woman built to compete in the shot-put event. She would have the hatchet loose in no time. Harris looked about frenziedly. His heart was already responding either to bufotenine or to the threat of hatchetation. The tranquilizer gun was on top of Super Mario Brothers 2 and under the *loa*'s very feet, but further into the bar, at a safer distance, Harris saw his maraschino cherry on the floor. He dropped, ignoring the alarmed flash of pain from the injured knee, and groped with his uninjured hand. Something squished under his palm and stuck to him. He peeled it off to examine it. It was a flattened cherry, a different cherry. Now Harris could see that the floor of the Gateway Bar was littered with maraschino cherries. One of them was injected with tetrodotoxin. There was no way to tell which just by looking.

Near him, under a table, a woman in a wet T-shirt sat with her hands over her ears and stared at him. "Nevada BOB'S," the T-shirt read. It struck Harris as funny. The word *BOB*. Suddenly Harris saw that *BOB* was a very funny word, especially stuck there like that between two large breasts whose nipples were as obvious as maraschino cherries. He started to say something, but a sudden movement to one side made him turn to look that way instead. He wondered what he had been going to say.

The *loa* brandished her hatchet. Harris retreated into the bar on his knees. The hatchet went wide again, smashed an enormous crock-pot that sat on the bar. Chili oozed out of the cracks.

"I shall pray for you," the *loa* said, carried by the momentum of her stroke into the video games. "I shall pray for all of you whose American appetites have been tempted with foreign dishes." She put her arms around the casing for Ninja Master, lifted the entire thing from the floor and piled it onto Super Mario Brothers 2. The music hiccoughed for a moment and then resumed.

There was now absolutely no exit from the bar through that door. Harris' backup was still out there, peering into manhole covers and washing windows, and the street was two video games away. Harris' amusement vanished. He wasn't likely to be at his best, alone, weaponless, with a hurt knee, and bufotenine pulsing through his body. Only one of these things could be rectified.

The bar was starting to metamorphose around him. The puddles of liquor on the floor sprouted into fountains, green liquid trees of crème de menthe, red trees of wine, gold trees of beer. The smell of liquor intensified as the trees bloomed. They grew flowers and dropped leaves in the liquid permanence of fountains, an infinite, unchanging season that was all seasons at once. A jungle lay between Harris and the *loa*. His tranquilizer gun was sandwiched between Super Mario Brothers 2 and Ninja Master. The barrel protruded. Harris wrenched it free. It took three tries and the awesome properties of the lever to move the uppermost video game. Harris tried not to remember how the *loa* had picked it up off the floor with her hands. He retrieved his gun and went hunting.

She was coy now, ducking away from him, so that he only caught glimpses of her through the watery branches of liquor. A sound here and there indicated that she had stopped to smash a wooden keg or pound the cash register. Harris, himself, was stealthy, timing each footfall to coincide with the tones of Super Mario Brothers 2.

The fountains were endlessly mobile. They rose and diminished unpredictably so that at one moment they could be between him and the *loa*, screening her from him, and the next moment, without him taking a step, he and the *loa* could be face to face. This gave the hunt a sort of funhouse quality. The *loa* was likewise changeable now; a big and ugly woman one moment, a lovely young one in a wet T-shirt the next, and this, too, added to the fun. Harris much preferred hunting young women without bras to hunting old ones with hatchets. Harris approved the change until it suddenly occurred to him just what the *loa*'s strategy was. She was fiendishly clever. The same way a maraschino cherry laced with tetrodotoxin could be hidden among other, innocent maraschino cherries, a *loa*, assuming the shape of a young woman in a wet T-shirt, could hide among other young women in wet T-shirts. Harris would have to think of some way to identify her. Failing that he would simply have to shoot everything in a wet T-shirt with the tranquilizer gun. This would probably require more tranquilizer darts than he had on him.

He would have to entice the *loa* out of hiding. He would have to make himself into bait.

Several overturned ashtrays were on the floor. It was the work of a moment to locate a cigarette butt, a matchbook with the Gateway Bar logo on it. The matches were damp and sticky. Harris put the butt in his mouth and tried to light one of the matches with his left, bloody hand, his right clenched on the trigger of the tranquilizer gun. He bent several matches before giving up. He switched the match to his right hand, still holding the gun, but not in a ready position, not with a finger on the trigger. He bent several matches before one flamed. The *loa* charged immediately. "Filthy poison! Breath of hell!" she screamed. She was old and huge, and her hatchet wavered over her head. There was no time to shoot. Harris rolled.

Harris rolled through the many colored puddles and fountains of drink and immediately to his feet, shaky on his hurt knee. Before she could transform, before she could regroup herself for another charge, Harris shot her.

She was in the middle of a scream. She stopped, looked down to her right hip where the tranquilizer dart had hit her. Super Mario Brothers 2 celebrated with a little riff. Dee, dee, dee, dee, dee. A fountain of red grenadine sprang up. The *loa* raised the hatchet, took a step into the fountain. The petals of red flowers exploded around her and fell onto her like rain. She threw the hatchet. Her aim was off; it clattered harmlessly a few feet behind him. She took a second step and then fell in his direction. One moment she was an enormous shadow and the grenadine fountain rose behind her like the distant fireworks of the Fourth of July and the smell of cherries was everywhere; the next she lay in a black heap on the floor, and the fountain had trickled to nothing. But in the tiny, invisible space between those moments, the *loa* left the body.

Her *z'étoile* rose from the black heap and spun above it. Harris could see it, like a star in the room. It came toward him slowly, backing him up until his heel touched the hatchet. Then it came faster, fast as falling, blazing larger and unbearably hot. His left hand found the black toad in his pocket so that, at the last possible moment, the moment before contact, when he threw up his hands to protect his face from the searing heat, the toad was in them. The *z'étoile* swerved and entered the toad instead of him.

Harris dropped the toad to the floor, grabbed the hatchet and smashed with the blunt end. The toad skittered, and he followed it over the sticky floor among the maraschino cherries, smashing again and again, until the toad cracked in one long rent down the middle and went to pieces. The *z'étoile* tried to leap away, but it was in pieces too now, like the toad. It shot in many directions and entered video games and broken keyboards and customers and lounge rap singers and ashtrays, but only in subdued, confused sparkles. It was the best Harris could do. He lay down on the floor and imagined there were shoes, open-toed and pointy with nail polish on the toes, canvas and round-toed, leather and bootlike all about him.

"Come on," someone said. It sounded like his mother, only she was speaking through a microphone. He must be late for school. The song from Super Mario Brothers 2 was playing in the background, but when wasn't it? Harris tried to open his eyes. He had no way of knowing if he'd succeeded or not. He didn't see his mother. He saw or imagined DEA agents attempting to lift the body of the huge woman from the floor. It took three of them. "Come on," someone said again, nudging him with a toe.

"I'm coming," said Harris, who refused to move.

Meanwhile, in an abandoned inner city warehouse . . .

The background is test tubes and microscopes and a bit of graffiti, visual not verbal. A bald-headed man stands over a camp stove. He holds an eyedropper above a pot with green liquid inside. Steam rises from the pot. Three more drops, he thinks. He has a snake tattooed on his arm.

Knock! Knock! "I said no interruptions," the man snarls. The liquid in the pot turns white.

The door opens. A shabby man enters, his clothes torn, his hair matted. "Give me some," the shabby man says.

The bald man laughs at him. "You can't afford this."

"I'll do anything," says the shabby man.

"This is special. This isn't for the likes of you."

"The likes of me?" The shabby man remembers a different life. There is a white house, a wife, two children, a boy and a girl. He is in a business suit, clean, carrying a briefcase. He comes home from work, and his children run to meet him. "Who made me into the likes of me?" the shabby man asks. There is a tear in the corner of one eye.

He lunges for the pot, takes a drink before the bald man can stop him. "Wha—?" the bald man says.

The shabby man clutches at his throat. "Arghh!" He falls to the ground.

The bald man tells him to get up. He kicks him. He takes his pulse. "Hmm. Dead," he says. He is thinking. I must have made it a little strong. Lucky I didn't try it myself. He goes back to his cooking. "Two drops," he says. He thinks, I'm going to need someone new to test it on.

Later that day . . .

The bald man is dressed in a winter coat. His tattoo is covered; he wears a hat. He enters a city park. A grandmotherly type drinks from the water fountain. She leans on a cane. Such a cold winter, she is thinking. A group of kids skateboard. "My turn!" one of them says.

The bald man in the hat approaches one of the kids. This kid is a little small, a little tentative. "Hey, kid," the bald man says. "Want to try something really great?"

The grandmother thinks, Oh dear. She hobbles on her cane to a large tree, hides behind it.

"My mom says not to take anything from strangers," the kid says.

"Just a couple drops," the bald man wheedles. "It's as good as peppermint ice cream." He takes a little bottle from his pocket and uncorks it. He holds it out.

I shouldn't, the kid thinks, but he has already taken the bottle.

"Eeeagh!" Carry Nation emerges from behind the tree. Her cane has become a hatchet; her costume is a black dress with special pockets. "Son of Satan!" she screams, hurtling toward the bald man, hatchet up.

Whooosh! The hatchet takes off the bald man's hat. *Kaboom!* Carry strikes him with her fist. *Kapow!*

Colors happened on the inside of Harris' eyelids. Harsh, unnatural, vivid colors. Colors that sang and danced in chorus like Disney cartoons, dark colors for the bass voices, bright neons for the high notes. Harris was long past enjoying these colors. Someone had put Harris to bed, but it was so long ago Harris couldn't quite remember who. It might have been his mother. Someone had bandaged his hand and cleaned him up, although his hair was still sticky with liquor. Someone had apparently thought Harris might be able to sleep, someone who had clearly never dosed themselves with bufotenine. Never licked a toad in their life. Someone brought Harris soup. He stared at it, abandoned on the nightstand, thinking what a silly word *soup* was. He closed his eyes, and the colors sang it for him with full parts. A full choral treatment. Soup. Soup. Souped up. In the soup. Soupçon.

The phone rang, and the colors splashed away from the sound in an unharmonious babble of confusion. They recovered as quickly as the ringing stopped, reformed themselves like water after a stone. Only one ring. Harris suddenly noticed other noises. The television in his room was on. There were visitors in the living room. His wife was sitting on the bed beside him.

"That was your superior," she said. Harris laughed. *Souperior.* "He said to tell you, 'package delivered.' He said you'd be anxious."

He wishes he worked for the CIA, the colors sang to Harris. Package delivered.

"Patrick." Harris' wife was touching his arm. She shook it a little. "Patrick? He's worried about you. He thinks you may have a drinking problem."

Harris opened his eyes and saw things with a glassy, weary clarity. Behind his wife was the "Oprah" show. No wonder he hadn't noticed the television was on. Harris' mind was moving far too fast for television. Harris' mind was moving far too fast for him to be able to follow what his wife was saying. He had to force his mind back, remember where she thought he was in the conversation.

"I'm a moderate drinker," he said.

"He sent over a report. Last night. A report the government commissioned on moderate drinking. It's interesting. Listen." She had pages in her hand. Harris was pretty certain they hadn't been there before. They popped into her fingers before his very eyes. She ruffled through them, read, with one finger underlining the words. " 'To put it simply, people who drink a lot have many problems, but few people drink a lot.

" 'People who only drink a little have fewer problems, but there are a great many people who drink a little.

" 'Therefore, the total number of problems experienced by those who drink a little is likely to be greater than the total number experienced by those who drink a lot, simply because more people drink a little than a lot.' " Harris was delighted with this. It made no sense at all. He was delighted with his wife for producing it. He was delighted with himself for hallucinating it. He would have liked to hear it again. He closed his eyes. The colors began singing obligingly. *To put it simply, people who drink a lot have many problems, but few people drink a lot.*

"All I had was a Shirley Temple," Harris told his wife. He remembered the voices in the living room. "Do we have company?"

"Just some women from my class," she answered. She put the report down uncertainly. "He's just worried about you, Patrick. As your supervisor, he's got to be worried. The stress of fieldwork. It's nothing to be ashamed of, if you have a problem. You've handled it better than most."

Harris skipped ahead in this conversation to the point where he explained to her that he didn't have a drinking problem and she was persuaded. She would be persuaded. She was a reasonable woman and she loved him. He was too tired to go through it step by step. Now he was free to change the subject. "Why are there women in the living room?"

"We're just doing a project," his wife said. "Are you going to drink your soup?" *Soup, soup, soup,* the colors sang. Harris didn't think so. "Would you like to see the project?" Harris didn't think he wanted this either, but apparently he neglected to say so, because now she was back and she had different papers. Harris tried to read them. They appeared to be a cartoon.

"It's for the women's center," his wife said. "It's a Carry Nation/ Superhero cartoon. I thought maybe you could help advise us on the drug stuff. The underworld stuff. When you're feeling better. We think we can sell it."

Harris tried to read it again. Who was the man in the hat? What did he have in his bottle? He liked the colors. "I like the colors," he said.

"Julie drew the pictures. I did the words."

Harris wasn't able to read the cartoon or look at the pictures. His mind wasn't working that way. Harris' mind was reading right through the cartoon, like it was a glass through which he could read the present, the past, and the future. He held it between himself and the television. There was a group of women on "Oprah." They were all dressed like Carry Nation, but they had masks on their faces like the Lone Ranger, to protect their real identities. They were postmenopausal terrorists in the war on drugs. A man in the audience was shouting at them.

"Do you know what I'm hearing? I'm hearing that the ends justify the means. I could hear that in Iraq. I could hear that in China."

The women didn't want to be terrorists. The women wanted to be DEA agents. Harris' supervisor was clearing out his desk, removing the pins from the map in his office as if casting some sort of reverse vodoun hex. He had lost his job for refusing to modify recruitment standards and implement a special DEA reentry training program for older women.

In a deserted field in Colombia, a huge woman gradually came to her senses. She stared at the clothing she was wearing. She stared around the Colombian landscape. "Where the hell am I?" her *ti bon ange* asked. "*¿Qué pasa?*"

From the safety of his jail cell, Manuel Noriega mourned for his lost yachts.

A woman in a wet T-shirt played a new video game in the dark backroom of a bar. "My mother told me to be good, but she's been wrong before," the T-shirt read. Bar-smasher was the name of the video game. A graphic of Carry Nation, complete with bonnet and hatchet, ran about evading the police and mobs of angry men. Five points for every bottle she smashed. Ten points a barrel. Fifty points for special items such as chandeliers and pornographic paintings. She could be sent to jail three times. The music was a video version of "Who Hath Sorrow, Who Hath Woe." The woman in the T-shirt was very good at this game. She was a young woman, and men approved of her. Her boyfriend helped her put her initials on the day's high score, although anyone who gets the day's high score probably doesn't need help with the initials. She let him kiss her.

Harris was back in Panama, dancing and raising a *loa*. The Harris in Panama could not see into the future, but even if he could, it was already too late. Raising a *loa* had not been his real mistake. By the time the *loa* came, everything here had already occurred. Harris had made his real mistake when he took the toad. Up until that moment, Harris had always played by the rules. Harris had been seduced by a toad, and in yielding to that seduction he created a whole new world for himself, a world without rules, just exactly the sort of world in which Harris himself was unlikely to be comfortable.

"Come on," his wife said. "What do you really think?" She was so excited. He had never seen her so animated.

She was going to be old someday, Harris could see it lurking in her. Harris would still love her, but what kind of a love would that be? How male? How sufficient? These things Harris was unsure of. For these things he had to look into himself, and the cartoon looking glass didn't go that way.

He held the cartoon panels between himself and his wife and looked into her instead. He had never understood why Carry Nation appealed to her so. His wife was not religious. His wife enjoyed a bit of wine in the evening and thought what people did in the privacy of their own homes was pretty much their own business. Now he saw that what she really admired about Carry Nation was her audacity. Men despised Carry Nation, and Harris' wife admired her for that. She admired the way Carry didn't care. She admired the way Carry carried on. "I always look a fool," Carry wrote. "God had need of me and the price He exacts is that I look a fool. Of course, I mind. Anyone would mind. But He suffered on the cross for me. It is little enough to ask in return. I do it gladly."

"I know it's not literature," Harris' wife said, a bit embarrassed. "We're trying to have an impact on the American psyche. Literature may not be the best way to do that anymore."

Harris' wife wanted to encourage other women not to care whether men approved of them or not, and she wanted and expected Harris to say he approved of this project.

He tried to focus again on the surface of the glass, on the cartoon panels. What nice colors. "Kapow!" Harris said.

"Kaboom!"

We come from the cemetery,
We went to get our mother,
Hello mother the Virgin
We are your children
We come to ask your help
You should give us your courage.
—Vodoun song

Chango Chingamadre, Dutchman, & Me

R.V. BRANHAM

¡Así!"

Dutchman and me heard it, drawing closer.

"*¡De a Pepe timbales!*" Dutchman served one of her regulars—a patent attorney—his espresso. "*¡Así!*" She made change. "*¡Mira el H.P.!*"

Dutchman hawked into the sink behind the bar, cleared her throat and covered her mouth before sneezing. She then turned to me: "Hey, M.E., make yourself useful and turn the friggin' record over."

M.E., that's me. Mervyn Eichmann. Now you know why I use the M.E. "*¡De a Pepe cojones!*"

I put the other side on, and gently slipped the needle onto the edge of that divine platter. Louis Armstrong to you, Sir. Call him Satchmo and you'll be on your ass. "Potato Head Blues." (This was the D.B.A. Dutchman had used when she sailed into the rotten apple and decided to get a business shingle and take over this dump—er, ah, bistro—serenaded by her flying phonograph and her flying 78's, inherited from her uncle, who'd drawn succor from them while stationed on the Maginot Line in the mid-thirties.)

"¡DE A PEPE SANTOS COJONES!"

Who else, none-other-than El C.C., Chango Chingamadre, former Great Black Hope of Bebop, Newyorican Contingent, with a box, a big heavy box. He was a spidermonkey on the needle. A monkey with another monkey on his back. *"On The Road,"* Chango Chingamadre declared.

"Cool it, babe," Dutchman told him. "Mistah Armstrong, he's swinging."

"Sorry, Dutch." Chango set the box on the bar. Dutchman examined the side.

"Viking, eh?"

"Fell off the back of the truck," I offered by way of suggesting how it had come into our acquaintance's hands. Dutchman unfolded the flaps. It *was On The Road.*

"B.F.D., babe. The long-awaited Kerouac debut—"

"You can give me twenty for it, eh? C'mon, Dutch."

"Hey, this is yesterday's papers. Everybody in the Village has been reading the galleys for donkey's years."

"Look." Chango was sweating. He needed a fix. In a rather bad way. "Gimmie ten now and ten when you sell 'em all."

I'd walked over to examine the books. Fifty. Hardcover. I opened one. First edition. And a slip, "Review Copy."

Dutchman saw the slip: "Why didn't you say so? Hell they're worth something." She took out a couple of ten-dollar bills. "Sorry, I'm a bit short now. Come back tonight and I'll give you the rest."

Chango smiled. ". . . 'S cool."

"But Don't Spend This All On Junk; Get Some Food In You. And get a jacket, 's cold evenings."

"I go to the Queen of Night," Chango replied, ". . . 's warm there."

I poked Chango's shoulder to get his attention, and he turned to face me. "You ought to stay away from that scene."

"But I get to sit in with the house band, M.E. I get to jam . . . we play the secret music. That house band is—"

"House band, my butt," Dutchman told us while furiously scouring at

some other or thing behind the bar counter. "A bunch of hasbeen-neverwas-nevergonnabe no-account junkys—"

I glared at Dutchman. Chango mumbled some Spanish crap and started to leave, but turned, and grabbed a book; he gave it to me. "Keep it for me, till I go home to the old lady."

Word on the street was that he'd met his old lady at the Queen of Night's salon. (I'd even heard from one gone case that she was the Queen of Night's kid sister.) Well, they'd been together, gotten a cold-water boxcar flat with a Harlem air shaft view. Chango insisted that one night he'd found her naked with someone (I think; it's hard to tell, Chango'd been incoherent on that point, raving on about blood candles and a bowl filled with wax and a goat's severed platter on a large head) and they'd had an uncool fight. And she'd kicked him out.

"It'll be good, *tu miras*, we make up; she take me back home."

Dutchman exchanged glances with me; we all knew she'd never take him back home. Not now. Now home for her was a six-by-six-by-six plot of land in potter's field.

Chango was out the door before you could say shit or Shinola. Dutchman frowned, shook her head.

"You really laid into him, Dutch."

The patent attorney spoke up: "Could I buy a couple of those from you. They're for a nephew, his bar mitzvah's next week."

"Ten percent above cover." Dutchman was unpacking the books.

"But—"the patent attorney wanted to haggle—"you've already got a good markup at cover price."

I turned away, to let Dutchman hustle a good price from the customer. In the back, by the rest rooms, I saw a woman rush past . . . actually, I just saw a flash of her flashy dress. It was funny. I hadn't noticed anyone else besides Chango come in.

"Fifteen percent. I hear you're a good lawyer. You can afford it." She put the books on the small bookcase by her dusty bar mirror, along with the City Lights *Howl and Other Poems*.

After a moment the attorney agreed. He became peeved when he asked for a sack and Dutchman said she didn't have any.

"Closet Beat," I said, after the lawyer had left.

Dutchman laughed, her dyke laugh.

Dutchman is a dyke; I've never seen her with a woman or heard of such Sapphic episodes, but I came on to her once and she wouldn't hop into bed with me. The only fifteen other women who wouldn't ride the banana boat with me were, not to put too fine a point on it, *lesbians*. They'd even *told* me so, when declining my favors. . . . One time, after a jam session, I'd brought it up with Chango Chingamadre, and he had said, "Who *caaares?*"

Well, *I don't.* Dutch. . . .

. . . She's family. She is a *friend.*

"I worry about Chango. . . ." Dutch said.

"What?" I'd been thinking of the gig tonight, about maybe going home and taking a nap, maybe taking the old upright and practicing. East Saint Louis Toodle-oo. Maybe something by Bird. I never played more than one or two songs before a gig. I might jam for *hours* afterwards. But not before the gig.

"I don't know." I gave her that don't-despair smile (it's what she calls it). "Maybe we should get him into Bellevue."

Dutch shuddered. "Cold Turkey. I dunno."

"I do." I had been there. I'm no Ishmael, but I'm no Ahab, either, not anymore. People quit when they are ready to quit. Not before. But there *is* the first step, and Cold Turkey is *one* first step, one Nanfuckingtucket sleigh ride.

"M.E.," Dutchman said. "I've heard a lot about the Queen of Night. And it doesn't sound like a good scene."

"Yeah, well." I laughed. "A whorehouse that does double duty as a shooting gallery isn't my idea of a good scene."

"I've heard they're mercenary bastards—won't even feed the girls; keep 'em locked up, doped, and half-starved. Not even a fridge on the premises."

"But they got a house band, Dutch."

"They're too tight to even have a decent cathouse band. From what I've been told, you hear 'em, and even if you're stoned out of your cranium, you just want to do your business and split. I call that cold-blooded mercenary."

Her outburst made me curious. "How do you know so much about whores?"

"My great-grandmother ran a very popular bordello in Rotterdam."

"You never told me—"

"You never asked. Anyway, she kept a buffet, heaping plates and bowls of erwtensoep, spinach tarts, sateh, plover's eggs, smoked salmon, duck sausages, waffles, all laid out on lace tablecloths . . . lunch *and* dinner. And full bar. The Queen of Night doesn't even have ice for booze, let alone food."

"But you don't even serve food, Dutch."

"I at least serve pretzels," she yelled.

"So now you're an authority on the Queen of Night?"

"I have my sources."

"Rasputin." I hooted.

"I have my sources."

I remembered something, about Rasputin. His tour bus, with his "See The Village! An Epiphany & A Meal, Such A Deal!" banners all over it. He always brought them into the Potato Head for espresso and the Beat poetry books Dutchman kept in stock. His name was Rasmussin, but we all called him Rasputin, because of his Svengalish ways with the ladies. Dutchman even had the hots for him. Which I resented. I resented him for trying to convert her. It wasn't her fault—Rasputin had those pheromones, sex hormones. He was clearly *oversexed*.

This arrangement, between Dutchman and Rasputin, was quite good in a *business* sense. But goddammit, if my friend wanted to be a dyke, then who was Rasputin to lay a bourgeois patriarchal routine on her—? And using *sex*—?!

He would come in with his chiropractors' wives from Chicago, dermatologists' divorcées from Des Moines, and Rotarian widows from Richmond, and, while they were ordering espresso or cognac, while they were buying Beat books, he would stand there and irradiate her with his pheromones.

I had seen this. Time and again. So I had to make a moral decision. Either tell her, in which case she'd run upstairs and get all dolled up . . . or not tell her, in which case he might be too distracted with the seduction of one of his *touristas* to work on Dutchman.

"Rasputin, he's coming today—" Dutchman's a big girl, big enough to make her own mistakes.

"I thought it was tomorrow."

"Remember, last week; he said he was changing the schedule."

Dutchman was lifting the wooden grids she kept on the floor, behind the bar. "I'd better hurry and hose these off. They're filthy."

"Need any help?"

"You've gotta go home, nap, and practice—remember?"

Later, on Bleeker Street, I ran into Raj'neej, an East Indian Welshman of sorts. He always sounded like Dylan Thomas when he talked. Not the Welsh, but the drunk, bit.

"M.E." We slapped hands. "Have you by any chance seen Chango—"

"No." I lied.

"I heard he's hanging out at the Queen of Night's, jamming with the house band."

"Yeah." I remembered something Chango'd said. "*Secret Music* he calls it."

". . . 'S secret all right; I go there about a year ago with my drummer, and I hear the house band, *hear* isn't the word for it. They stand in a corner, with their eyes closed, fingering their axes like worry beads, and sway. But no sound. A lot of the cats in the room sway too, their eyes closed too. I see my drummer close his eyes, and sway. So I say to myself, *when in Rome*, shut my lids too. And faintly, ever so faintly, I hear a buzz, a sort of minor chord. There's an odor, too, a vague smell of cheap perfume. But the more I focus on either the music, or on the aroma, the more they fade. And I start to get a headache, like my cranium says fuck that scene, so I open the eyes. But everyone still sways, eyes still closed, waiting for a wake-up call. It's a drain, M.E., a real energy suck . . . I think of the Vetala and Rakshasa of India—"

"Vetala? Rakshasa?" I'd never heard the terms before.

"India's vampires, who first play tricks, suck your will, then hypnotize you into doing *their* will. Then they dine on your horse, or on you—I don't really believe it. I don't *dis*believe it, either; so I leave everyone to their individual karmic dances. I go in a room and find agitated gents at the walls, peeping in on some tantric exchanges. So I go to another room, and there's a very weird poker game going on, played with tarot cards, and before they put their money in the pot they fold it into frogs or cranes, flowers or whales, paper airplanes. In the next room is the oldest guy—I recognize him, old Gutbucket Slim, from Ma Rainey's band (he's like antediluvian). The Gutbucket's on the nod, in front of a television showing the Dorsey brothers. So I walk over to say hello and observe the hype in his arm; it's filled with blood. Then blood dribbles from his mouth and down from his nostrils. I turn to call for help, and I hear a lady. She says:

it's being taken care of,

and through the glass beads of the doorway I see the skirt of a woman, kilometers of ruffles, very Carmen Miranda. I then decide it's time to depart (like, I don't want to be there when they fold twenty-dollar-bill origami cranes for Mistah Police); so I return to the main room, and everyone's still swaying. I drag my drummer out of there; he says it is the most beautiful music he'd ever heard. Month later his playing went to shit in a rickshaw, and I had to fire his ass. Been through two other drummers since."

I looked at Raj'neej in amazement; I had no idea what occult scene he was getting at, but it made me anxious. I remembered the skirt I had glimpsed at Potato Head.

"I'd like to give Chango a break; he's too good to waste."

"Yeah?"

"I've got a gig for tonight; we need skins." Raj'neej was the coolest pianist I'd heard in a long time; he could've blown Brubeck away. Hell, Dutchman snoring could've blown Brubeck away. But Raj'neej was *good* . . . not Monk, mind you, but good.

"Too bad." I almost wished I hadn't lied. But. . . . "He lost his cabaret card, y'know."

"I could get him a bogus one. Everyone else is clean—if we have a junky sitting in for one or two gigs, there won't be any hassles. He could use the bread, he might get straight."

"Go to Potato Head Blues. Tell Dutchman I sent you."

"I know Dutchman." Raj'neej paused, and blushed. "I've heard—is it true she's a dyke?"

"Ask her and see."

I was in the middle of the dream of dreams when the phone of phones rang its ring of rings. I picked it up. "M.E., 's Dutch; Chango Chingamadre, he's . . ."—she fought back sobs—"turning gray!"

"I'll be there!" I hung up. And I *was* there, in no time. I ran those seven blocks past needle-head Applejackers slamming into each other as they waltzed their junky waltz in front of bebop music stores, past asthma-inducing bookshops and a zillion bistros, I ran them faster than I'd run any distance before; in terms of speed, I ran *one-hundred-thirty-second* notes, arpeggiated. I ran up the rickety alley steps to the Dutchman's loft, which was above Potato Head Blues. She answered the door.

"Raj'neej, he's in the bedroom, walking him."

"Have any milk—?"

"For the cat, yeah—"

"—Forget the cat, boil some." I hurried into the bedroom, where Raj'neej was trying to walk Chango around the room. He was dragging him over his shoulder. Chango, though a foot taller than Raj'neej, must have been thirty pounds lighter . . . and Raj'neej was a bit on the Bantam Weight side himself.

Chango looked like one of those El Greco paintings of the dead Nazz, all gone to gray and rigor mortis.

I went into the crapper, and found the needle, filled with blood. And the heroin. I tasted the heroin. Looked at the matches. At the spoon. At the matches. And flushed that junk down the toilet.

I then smelled a sweet jasminy perfume, which was odd. The perfume couldn't have been Dutchman's, too bourgeois. Dutchman always used an after-shave. Maybe, I thought at the time, it was from one of Dutchman's apocryphal girlfriends.

And I heard a distant buzzing noise, like a band playing far away, or underwater, on another world. And, just like Raj'neej, when I tried to focus on the music, it faded.

I took the needle to Dutchman, along with the spoon: "Get rid of it. Take it down the alley and dump it." The milk was ready. "I'll take this."

I took the pan. Into the bedroom. "His pulse, it's light," Raj'neej told me.

I heard the front door close. "Lay Chango on the bed." His muscles were slack, his breathing was coming slowly—but it *was* coming, he wasn't *too* cold, or sweating *too* much. I lifted the eyelids: the pupils had followed Sputnik into space.

"He showed up, and we told him about the gig." Raj'neej was blowing it. "He said he needed Dutchman's bathroom to clean up."

"Go to the kitchen and get a cup. Put sugar and cocoa in it." I got a towel from the bathroom and wet it, and began to slap Chango's face with the tip—nothing hard. No response. *Nada.* Raj'neej came back with the cup. I took it from him and mixed it with the hot milk.

I noticed I'd left a scorch mark on the dresser. Oh well. I mixed the cocoa and milk, stirring it. "Raj'neej, take the towel and slap Chango's face—" He did so, too vigorously. "Lightly. We want to *wake* him up, not beat him up, at least not until he's over it."

I drank the cocoa, slowly. It was good.

Raj'neej looked up at me drinking the cocoa. He shined it on, and kept slapping Chango; it was working. Chango mumbled.

I heard the door open and close. And caught a glimpse of Dutchman's skirt as she walked past the doorway, one of those ruffled numbers a Puerto Rican might wear. But not Dutchman. No, that dress was just like what I'd seen that afternoon, just like what Raj'neej had seen at the Queen of Night's. It had to be nerves, seeing things like that. Then I smelled that perfume again. Chango muttered an oath in Spanish.

"Let's get him up." I held him by one shoulder and Raj'neej held him by the other.

I had taken my coat, which was designed for New England winters or summers in San Francisco, and draped it over Chango Chingamadre. We walked. To the living room. Back through the hall, to the bedroom. Back to the living room.

"My gig starts in an hour," Raj'neej whined.

"We might get him well enough to play. He's not too bad."

At one point, when we were in the bedroom, we heard the door open. Dutchman had returned with pots of coffee.

We pumped Chango full of coffee. And after he had thrown up a hearty dinner, we pumped him full of more. And more coffee. We kept walking, finally deciding to walk Chango down the stairs, down around the corner, to the front of the Potato Head, and inside, for more coffee. The Potato was busy.

Rasputin was minding the bar—it surprised me, the decency of the gesture. Of course, he was chatting up a nice lady. We drank more coffee. Raj'neej used the pay phone to ring a cab.

The pay phone rang. Rasputin answered.

He gestured to me. I went and picked up the phone. I was late. *First set starts in five minutes.* I told them I'd had to help Dutchman take a friend to the hospital, and asked Lou if they could do the first set without me. *It'll be funny for a trio playing with only keyboards and drums.* I reassured them I would be there for the second set.

I was wrong.

The cab arrived and took Raj'neej and Chango Chingamadre off to the club date, in some Uptown space. They too missed the first set. At least they made the second. And managed to bring the house down on the third.

Not that I'm complaining.

I was going to run back to my place, to get my bass. Dutchman asked me if I could come upstairs. For a drink. To help her calm down. She was a lonely dyke. And I was her friend. How can a friend refuse?

"Do you remember a few years ago, when we were still 'underground'?"

I sighed: "Those days were intense. Too intense, for M.E."

She laughed sympathetically. "Yeah." Then, took a bottle of cabernet from her wine rack. "And that wild poetry reading, where Ginsberg showed up?"

"The"—I busted every time I remembered it—"the crackers."

"I sent Chingamadre to get crackers; give him the money, and he comes back with every safecracker in Manhattan."

"And the cops thought there was a burglars' convention going on, and

stormed in and broke the glass window and the mirror, and stole the brass
eagle from your espresso machine."

"I thought Chango'd stolen it, for the longest while."

We talked about other times, and drank the wine, and went to bed. I
am not sympathetic to those who subscribe to the Diddle And Tell
school, the We Did It In Our Clothes school, the We Did It In The
Shower school, the We Did It On The Kitchen Table school. (Nor would
I confirm the existence of a Middle English tattoo on her fanny: *Brid
Liveth*.) Dutchman was a dyke.

The next night we were tearing through our second set, and I saw
someone seated by the stage:

Dutchman. Dutchman in a dress.

She wore these gorgeous silver glad rags that caught all available light
and tossed it back like confetti. She hadn't come to see me do a gig in
quite a while. I dedicated the next song to her. And she bought us a
round of drinks.

Then I dedicated the next song to her, and she smiled. But no drinks
came forth.

And then another party came in. They also sat by the stage, two tables
away from Dutchman. I saw that dress again, the phantom dress, so
resplendently Latin, and looked at the face . . . which I was certain had
to be beautiful. But all I saw was two emerald eyes that said,

hello,

and the more I tried to focus on her facial features, the more I was only
able to see the eyes, which said,

*you make the most gorgeous music I have ever heard, please join us at
our table,*

I turned away and caught a look from my pianist—he looked worried.
He mouthed something. I read his lips:

"Queen of Night."

I glanced back at the table; the Queen of Night's consorts were tall and
gaunt junkys in tight-fitting penguin suits, with expressions that spoke of
heaven or the morgue, rictuses of joy. The Queen of Night caught my
attention again, and would not let go. I liquesced in her gaze, her gaze,
which said,

*come to my place, your music is lovely but it could be even better, you're
better than your companions, you could be vamping,*

and I looked back at her, and she must have detected some resistance,
because she said,

yes, I have a bordello, and my bordello has many rooms . . . be my
lover, and I'll cradle you in my beautiful breasts, give you money or any-
thing else you need, and you will be worthy to sit in on the best, most secret
music—

And the spell was broken; boy, was the spell broken.

Dutchman walked over to the Queen of Night's table, and threw a
drink at her, and said,

get out of the club, get out now.

Then one of the Queen of Night's consorts said words, and Dutchman
replied that they weren't the only ones in New York with some connec-
tions. No one's lips moved, but I heard the dialogue, and I'm sure anyone
within ten feet could hear it. All of this happened quickly, so *very* quickly
—the pianist and drummer had begun to really *wail* as Dutchman had
gotten up. And the Queen of Night rose; she held no rancor, was dispassionate, as if the Dutchman had beaten her fairly in a game of croquet.
But the Queen of Night had a grave dignity. Before the audience was hip
to what had gone down, the Queen of Night and her consorts were
departed.

After the final set, while having a final round at the bar, Dutchman
turned to me: "You're moving in with me."

"What did you say?"

"Wipe the drool from your mouth, and don't get any delusions—it'll
be the couch for you; it's just that I might have pissed the Queen of
Night off; it might be a good temporary measure, protection."

"Chango wasn't so protected at your place." She frowned as I recounted Raj'neej's Indian vampire lore, and his visit to the Queen of
Night's. And how it tied in with my having seen the very phantom dress
the Queen of Night wore, seen it, not once, but twice. And about the
phantom smells.

"I think he'd be safe now." She headed for the Ladies'.

I stared at her: "What? How?"

She didn't hear. "Might be an idea: get him a sleeping bag."

Chango didn't make the Potato Head scene after that, so I had not
only the couch but the whole Dutchman living room to myself.

Two weeks later, we heard from Raj'neej that Chango Chingamadre
had flipped out, jumped out of the cab suddenly when they were on their
way to meet *Miles* Muthafucking *Davis.* That he'd run into the traffic
screaming about secret music and been hit by a Mack truck.

Again, I smelled the phantom perfume, glimpsed the phantom skirt, heard the opening and closing door and the secret music . . . but only as a memory. And, after all, I was beginning to tell myself, that was just superstition and hysteria rearing their uncool heads.

And it wouldn't bring Chango Chingamadre back to us.

Nobody could afford to do a decent burial. Besides, his old lady is in potter's field.

We Three Were Three No More.

The Dutchman moved to Sausalito, north of San Francisco. She owns three restaurants and lives on a houseboat with two Korat cats and a seismologist who's also a licensed therapist specializing in tarot therapies and future-life regressions. In her spare time, the Dutchman also supervises a rape crisis hotline.

I, M.E., I live in Los Angeles, which is kinder to my arthritis than New York. I write film scores, which is a living, a very good one. I got an Oscar nomination five years ago. I'm not holding my breath waiting for another.

If I'm North, then we do pasta. If she's South, we do sushi.

I tell her how remarkably young she looks; it's not a line. And she talks about plastic surgery, and I don't know whether I believe her, because she has the beginnings of a secretive grin on her face. But no laugh lines. And we talk. Dutchman even talks about Chango (and, at times, we take turns weeping for him), but she refuses to discuss the Queen of Night.

Once we talked about a tombstone, which we could afford to go half-sies on. It would read: "Here Bops 'Chango Chingamadre,' The Monkey Muthafuckah Of Thems As All."

There was a problem. We had never learned his real name.

I ran into Raj'neej during a Playboy Jazz Festival . . . and he couldn't recollect Chingamadre's name either. He did recall how Chango OD'ed at the Dutchman's. And how he found a strange lady crouched over Chango. And how when she faced him, he only saw green animal eyes. And that she'd itsplayed, *walked through a wall*, and he figured it was the reefer he'd just smoked.

I then told Raj'neej what I'd seen that night, and the next.

"Maybe." Raj'neej folded his hands. "Maybe Chango's dead old lady came for him, maybe she needed him more than we did. Or the Vetala claimed him. Or maybe we had what the French call a group delusion." Raj'neej unfolded his hands, reached for his wine glass. "But maybe not." He downed the Chablis in one gulp. "Have I ever told you about the '63 Newport Jazz Festival?"

"No, but we haven't seen each other since '62."

"Has it been *that* long . . . ? Well, I was producing a live album; we were recording everyone. Art Blakey and the Jazz Messengers, Mingus, Ella, Max Roach, Carmen McRae. And this act shows up—I'd forgotten who sponsored them—called the New Queen of Night, and these guys were dead ringers for the house band at the old Queen of Night's . . . only, if they were the same cats, they had not aged a day. When they played, it was like the *Re*-Birth of the Cool, they had the audience and all of us backstage eating out of their hands . . . nothing 'secret' about that music—I tried to catch them after the set, I had an A & R gig for Blue Note, too. So I ran out to the back parking lot to offer them a record contract, and they were tearing out of there in a black hearse. Then later the recording engineer played the tape back, and all we heard was a *faint* sound, like the secret music crap Chango raved about, like what I heard at the Queen of Night's. Only there was some percussion, not quite so faint, a clavé beat. It was Chango. But no matter how that engineer twiddled those pan pots, the notes stayed faint, became a secret music again. It all made me think of old Bela Lugosi's Dracula and how he never cast a reflection in a mirror."

I slouched, felt drained by all the emotions Raj'neej had summoned. But I wanted to hear that music, hear Chango. "You still have the master?"

Raj'neej shook his head. "My engineer, he'd been a junky, but cleaned himself up, like you. He fell apart. Police found him OD'ed in Central Park, they found him by following the trail of master tape he left. I had another copy, but I erased it. Then threw the blank tape away."

Raj'neej recounted every ghost story he'd ever heard, in India and, later, in Wales. On through the night, and into the cold eye of noon.

But he could not remember Chango's real name.

So Chango it was, and Chango it shall be. But what about his grave, what about a proper marker?

Well, to hell with the Queen of Night, when Gabriel plays *his* secret music on his horn I'll have it put on my tombstone:

Here Bop We Three:
Chango Chingamadre, Dutchman, & M.E.

Apartheid, Superstrings, and Mordecai Thubana

MICHAEL BISHOP

THE TRANSVAAL, 1988

AN ELEPHANT blossomed in his headlamps. At two-thirty in the morning, on the highveld between Pretoria and the northeastern Transvaal, a doddering bull elephant—which had *not* been there—suddenly *was* there; and Gerrit Myburgh, a thirty-eight-year-old banker, knew that his imported cranberry Cadillac was going to hit it.

As hard as he could, Myburgh began braking.

The Cadillac, hydroplaning on his astonishment, slid into the elephant. Its tusks flashed like scimitars. Glass shattered. A bewildered, trumpeting bleat echoed over the landscape, and so much plastic, chrome, and steel crumpled around Myburgh that he knew the world had ended.

Well, fine. He was already in his coffin, the flashiest coffin a success-driven Afrikaner could ever want.

Eventually, Myburgh untangled himself, crawled through a broken window, and got to his feet on the debris-strewn asphalt.

It was July, the torso of winter, as clammy-cold as it ever got in this part of the highveld, and his tailored suit was a drafty ruin. His forehead was bleeding, there were bruises on his upper thighs, his left shoe had disappeared. Traffic on this stretch of roadway was seldom heavy, and at this hour his hopes for a quick rescue were laughable.

Myburgh turned about, searching for the elephant. "I hope you're happy!" he shouted in Afrikaans, his words muting themselves in the drizzle. "You've turned my car into a pile of goddamned slag!" Even worse, he realized, his insurance assessor would never believe that he had hit . . . an elephant.

What the hell was happening? There weren't any elephants in this part of South Africa. You had to go to a national park to see them. Out here, where a few *bittereinder* Boers resisted both state and corporate attempts to buy their land (the government to feed it into black "closer settlements," industry to turn it into another hideous factory site), wildlife consisted of stray chickens, stray dogs, stray cattle.

But he had run into it, an elephant. Surely, it had suffered as much damage as—if not more than—the Eldorado. He had heard it bellow its agony. Still, it had managed to totter away from the accident scene. Even when he made a painful circuit of his Caddy, stooping to search for blood or other spoor, nothing on the paving or in the nearby bush reassured him that what he *knew* had happened had actually happened.

At least it wasn't pink, Myburgh thought. At least the damned thing wasn't flying, like Dumbo.

The elephant may have been a phantom, but the gash on his head was real. So were his battered thighs, his lacerated jacket, his blood-smeared trousers. He stood like a scarecrow in the center of the road, guarding the wrecked vehicle and peering about for some sign of a farmhouse, a police van, or a besotted Ndebele tramp who could be bribed to help him.

He took a monogrammed handkerchief from the breast pocket of his jacket and touched his brow. This simple act made him flinch, but he held the handkerchief to the wound, determined both to halt the bleeding and to restore some clarity to his thoughts.

Should he walk back toward his brother's farm or on toward the Pretoria suburb in which he had a condominium flat? Onward, of course. Nothing but wintry veld lay behind him, whereas a hike southwestward would carry him into populated areas, white or black, where he could buy or beg assistance.

God help me, Myburgh thought, calculating—for a quick glance at the mileage counter on the Eldorado's caved-in dashboard told him that Pretoria was still eighty miles away. It would take him days to walk home. He felt too weak to start hiking.

Holding his handkerchief to his temple, Gerrit Myburgh began to cry. He sat down on the wet pavement and hugged himself as if he were his own lost child.

He heard it before he saw it, a raw chugging from the alley of Boer farmland dividing the eastern boundary of KwaNdebele from the western boundary of Bophuthatswana.

It was coming down the road toward him, a blunt-grilled Putco "commuter" bus, one of the armada of state-subsidized motorized argosies that hauled residents of the homelands to and from work in Johannesburg, Pretoria, Witbank, and Middleburg. They ran morning and evening, Myburgh knew, but he was surprised to hear one coming so early. It wasn't yet three o'clock, and surely no one would be riding at this godforsaken hour. Myburgh himself usually arose at seven-thirty, took a leisurely Continental breakfast, and got to the bank by nine. It was an accident that he was still up tonight, the result of his journey to see Kiewit and of his mulish brother's mulish disdain for reason. Otherwise, he'd be safe in his bed in Pretoria.

Myburgh got up off the road, spread his arms, and began waving his clotted handkerchief. Then, seeing that the bus would *have* to stop or slow down for the wreck of his Caddy, he realized that maybe he didn't want to be rescued—not by a bus full of kaffirs on their way to grinding dead-end jobs paying them just enough to get potted in a *shebeen* and to listen in ale-beclouded sullenness to rabble-rousing ANC shortwave broadcasts from Lusaka, Zambia. No, he didn't want that at all.

But just as it had been too late to brake for the elephant, it was too late to sidestep the bus. Its wan headlamps picked him out of the darkness, and it squealed to an eardrum-puncturing halt a few meters away, then rocked back and forth on its shocks like a melancholy elephant. Its driver remained invisible, hidden by the tocking blade of a lone windshield wiper and the fuzzy glare of the headlamps.

All right, then. He'd assert himself. He'd force the pathetic kaffirs to help him.

Myburgh limped over to the bus's door. The bus itself, he saw, was painted a chalky blue. A legend in English on its dented flank read GRIM BOY'S TOE. That, Myburgh supposed, was its name—the way wealthy tycoons named their yachts. Whether *Grim Boy's Toe* carried a full allotment of passengers, he couldn't tell, for the bus's windows were smeared with dried mud and its rear third tailed off into mist and darkness.

The hinged passenger door creaked open. Myburgh peered up and in. He saw—in the wash of a single bulb in a crimson globe—that the bus's driver was a heavyset African with a face etched of ruby shadows. The driver gazed impudently out, as if Myburgh meant less to him than a crippled plowhorse.

Myburgh began to regret not jumping into the roadside *donga* and cowering there until the bus had chugged on by. Its passengers, he suddenly understood, could kill him with impunity, bludgeoning him to a ruddy paste and sticking his body under the collapsed steering column as if he'd died in the accident.

"Go find me help," he said in English, expanding his chest even as he took a half step back. (Afrikaans, his own tongue, wouldn't do—he didn't trust it here.)

The insolent driver merely stared at him.

"Get me help!" Myburgh shouted. "Understand?"

At this, the driver's eyes widened—in astonishment, it seemed, to Myburgh. He leaned toward the door, as if to make sure that his eyes weren't playing tricks.

"Didn't you hear me?" Myburgh said. "Find me help."

"No can do, *nkosi.*"

"Of course you can. Can't you see I've had an accident? Can't you see" —blotting his forehead—"I've been hurt?"

"Nkosi, number 496 has run late three times this week. I can't afford to run late again. There are men in Tweefontein E and other closer settlements who'd kill for my job."

"Why do you run late? Are you a bad driver?"

The driver glanced at Myburgh's wrecked Caddy. "I do as well as many," he said. His expression grew conspiratorily earnest. "A blowout one night, sir. Two nights later, a dope-fiend trucker ran me off the road. And last night—with all the unexpected rain, you see—well, we got stuck."

"Look," Myburgh said, feeling both exposed and ridiculous, "I'm in trouble."

"Yes, and I will help you. But not by going off my route. No, sir. You must climb aboard and ride into Belle Ombre station with the rest of my passengers."

"How long will that take?" Belle Ombre was in the Marabastad neighborhood of Pretoria, once an Indian enclave.

"Three hours. No. Two hours, forty-five minutes."

"That's absurd. You ought to be able to make it in an hour and a half. Two at the most."

The driver laughed, shrugging his bearish shoulders and holding out his hands to indicate the ramshackle condition of number 496. "Not possible, my *baas*. We have more pickups and a Putco checkoff still to do. Really."

"Don't you have a two-way?"

"No, *nkosi*. And no landing gear, either."

Myburgh heard laughter—not obnoxious or general laughter, but the weary guffaws of a few riders near enough to overhear.

"Take me to the Putco checkoff." He gritted his teeth against their amusement. "Somebody there will help me."

"Maybe. Not to get your car towed, though. You should go all the way into Pretoria with us."

Myburgh considered. "Very well—let me on." He climbed aboard and turned to limp down the aisle.

The driver put out a hand. "My name is Ernest Kabini, *nkosi*. Sorry to say so, but you must pay."

"Pay?" Should he also introduce himself, as Kabini had just done? Damned if he'd do it.

"Your fare. Everyone must pay, you know. Sixty cents to town, sixty cents back."

"Sixty cents?"

Kabini hesitated. "Half a rand, okay? Ten cents off. Putco doesn't want to screw a fellow down on his luck."

Myburgh dug into his pocket and handed over the fare—the *full* fare. He was a paying passenger on number 496. He turned again to face the kaffirs with whom he was going to be riding for the next three hours and found himself staring as into an immense shotgun bore that seemed to extend all the way to the Transvaal's border with Zimbabwe. The faces peering back were devoid of distinctiveness or personality—like a grainy group photograph of skin-headed National Defense Force recruits. A bulb in a green globe threw sickly khaki shadows over the bodies slumped in the bus's middle rows, while, at the back, a bulb in a yellow globe jaundiced the half-dozen riders napping beneath its pale sheen.

If hell had bus service, Myburgh told himself, this is what the inside of one of its buses would look like. He grabbed a seat back for support and silently cursed the inconsiderate elephant that had brought him here.

At this point on its route, Myburgh could have chosen any of a number of seats behind Kabini, but, more angry than grateful, he limped down the center aisle.

His wet sock slapped the metal floor. The twelve to fifteen riders inhabiting the bus seemed to shift from one seat to another without getting up and physically moving.

Meanwhile, *Grim Boy's Toe* leapt into gear and growled around the abstract sculpture of his Eldorado. Myburgh stumbled, caught himself, shakily tottered on.

You've had a blow to the head, he reminded himself. It's not so unusual that you should be seeing things.

But it was troubling. Why wouldn't these seat-hopping kaffirs settle down? No, that was wrong. Why wouldn't his dizziness go away so that he could see things as they really were?

He stopped again. The black faces watching him were no longer popping up in different seats with the same annoying frequency. Maybe he was beginning to get a grip on himself. Maybe the world—or this incapsulated portion of it—was finally beginning to come into focus.

"Sit here, sir."

He looked. The voice belonged to a slender man in a trenchcoat ridiculously at odds with the filthy woolen cap he was wearing; the coat might have belonged to a movie star, but the cap you could see on any street cleaner or garbage man at work in the city from June through August. This bloke, his thin face almost cadaverous in the dark, scooted over and patted that part of the cracked seat cushion that his skinny bottom had already warmed.

An invitation. A friendly invitation.

Myburgh spurned it. Unfamiliar people—strangers—didn't sit next to each other when there were plenty of seats to choose from. It wasn't racial; it was personal, a way to keep one's identity intact, a means of securing a helpful modicum of privacy. And yet it wouldn't do to stupidly insult the man, even if his pigmentation suggested purple spray paint under a sheen of preserving lacquer. Myburgh eased into the seat in front of the African's, pointedly hugging the aisle.

"Excuse me, sir," said the slender young man, leaning over the seat back as if Kabini had introduced them. "Did you really have an accident?"

What colossal cheek. Myburgh reined in his temper. "What do you think, I *staged* it?"

"Possibly."

"Why in God's name would I do something so stupid—not to say expensive—as that?"

"Forgive me," the man said, placatingly touching Myburgh's shoulder. "I thought you might be a member of—or, possibly, an advisor to—a Faking Club."

"Faking Club?"

"Yes, sir. A few years ago, until caught without my stinker"—his pass, he meant—"and endorsed out, I lived near Cape Town. At the universities there, students staged accidents—bloody ones—to test public awareness of first aid. Faking Clubs."

"I'm not a member of—or an advisor to—any Faking Club. Why, out here, would you even assume that?"

"So queer an accident. Your car was smashed, but with no sign of any other banged-up vehicle to have caused such damage."

"I hit an elephant."

The man—to Myburgh's relief—withdrew his hand, then simply gazed at the banker sidelong. "My name is Mordecai Thubana, sir. Glad to meet you."

Myburgh grunted. But Mordecai Thubana's gaze was so implacable that he glanced away and began rubbing his thigh as if a pain there had distracted him.

"The blow to your head," Thubana said, nodding at him, "is it bad? Did it make you delirious?"

"Who are you to question me?" Myburgh snapped. "Who are you to imply I'm lying?"

"Mordecai Thubana, sir. And I'm not meaning to be questioning or implying anything."

"If you don't *mean* to, don't *do* it."

"No, sir, I won't. Except, you know, courtesy would hint that maybe you should—forgive me—tell me your name."

"Because you've told me yours?"

Thubana grinned. He had strong, straight teeth. His grin was almost fetching. "One man, one name." He leaned nearer. "When I was in Cape Town, I attended university. I'm not just an ignorant construction worker, sir."

Myburgh pursed his lips. His own name would reveal more than he wanted. *Grim Boy's Toe* was hardly the nave of a Dutch Reformed Church, and its passengers certainly weren't Voortrekkers. But why not tell? Did fear or shame restrain him?

"My name is Gerrit Myburgh," he said defiantly. "My family had a huge farm out here once, on a healthy remnant of which my brother Kiewit continues to live. Three Ndebele families—more than twenty people—still work for him."

"Ah," said Thubana. "But now the government wants it?"

"Yes."

"To make the Ndebele 'homeland' bigger?"

"I suppose."

"And you and your brother are fighting the government's plans to take your land?"

"Kiewit is. I'm not. I think we should sell."

"For the sake of Grand Apartheid?"

"Because we're not likely to get a better offer, and they'll end up taking it anyway. Kiewit's a stubborn ass."

"Ah. You argued."

"Would I be out here in the goddamn *bundu* at such an hour if we hadn't?" He meant, as they both knew, Would I be on this Putco bus with all you kaffirs if there weren't a damned good reason?

"No, Mr. Myburgh. I guess not."

Conversation lapsed. Myburgh was grateful. He didn't know why he'd indulged Thubana as far as he had. Under most circumstances, he would have ignored the man or fixed upon him a withering, mind-your-own-business stare. But Thubana's interest in his plight had seduced him into talking. Weak. Shamefully weak.

Myburgh faced front, clutching his own upper arms. *Grim Boy's Toe* was a real kidney bouncer, even on asphalt, and now the bus was bumping down a dirt track among *enkeldoring* trees to another pickup point.

His bruises had bruises. During the accident, he'd apparently bitten a chunk of mucus-coated flesh from the inside of his mouth, and now that slimy flap of skin was overlapping his tongue. He bit down on it and swallowed. His facial muscles tightened.

Twelve people came aboard at this pickup. All gave him the eye as they bumped down the aisle; all made a point of not sitting next to or across from him. The bus chugged off again. A hubbub of African dialects led Myburgh to suspect that some of these people were talking about him. He refused to turn around. Why give them the satisfaction?

Grim Boy's Toe made three more stops.

At the last one, rows and rows of scrap-wood and corrugated-tin *pondoks*—shanties—grew like crooked architectural cancers. Smoke from Primus stoves billowed into the sky, mistily visible, while a throat-scalding stench eeled into the bus through window cracks and holes in the floorboard.

Although Kabini kept telling the new passengers to move back, move back, several of them bunched at Myburgh's seat. He realized that he would either have to stand, as two dozen other people were already doing, or scoot over and share his seat with one of the intimidating construction workers or mechanics waiting for him to make room.

"Hey, my *baas*," said a man in an overcoat, tapping Myburgh's knee, "you saving that spot for your lady?"

"Maybe he's got a disease," said someone else.

"You may have this seat," Mordecai Thubana told the man. He came forward and levered Myburgh over against the window with his hip. The man in the overcoat grunted approval and sat down. The logjam of bodies broke. Myburgh watched as several people placed folded newspapers on the floor, dropped down cross-legged, and gave in, almost instantly, to sleep.

One man in particular drew Myburgh's attention, for, although still young, he was as bald as a stone. Moreover, he held in his lap what appeared to be half a rubber volleyball.

"Hey, Mpandhlani," Thubana greeted the bald-headed man. "How goes it?"

"No reception," said Mpandhalani cryptically. "No reception. A relief, Mordecai. I'm almost grateful." He held the volleyball-half in his lap like a vulcanized begging bowl.

The bus jounced off again, through the midnight bush.

Although there were now at least ninety passengers, a third of them in the aisle, conversation had ceased; most were dozing or staring numbly into the Transvaal wastes. One man had affixed a large sponge, or rectangle of foam rubber, to the seat back in front of him, lowered his forehead to its padding, and fallen asleep. Perhaps he was also snoring lightly; the bus's unceasing rattle made it hard to tell.

Damn Kiewit, anyway. With just half the money they'd realize from selling Huilbloom (as their great-grandparents had dubbed the family farm), they could emigrate to Australia or Texas and begin life anew, in a place free of the threat of Armageddon.

Suddenly, Myburgh noticed that Thubana had taken a book from a coat pocket and begun to read it with a penlight balanced over his ear and aimed downward. Clever. Or semiclever. Thubana probably hoped Myburgh would ask what he was reading. Africans sometimes liked to impress whites with a show of educability, a demonstration of their debatable love of learning.

Well, the clap on that. If Thubana was reading something, it was probably ANC or PAC propaganda or a book of trumped-up stories about oppression in the townships or an old copy of *Drum*, and he'd be damned if he'd rise to the kaffir's bait. Let him pretend to read all the way to Marabastad.

Thubana spoiled this plan by lifting the book off his lap and holding it up so that Myburgh could see its cover—including title and whimsical three-color illustration.

SUPERSTRINGS, said the yellow caps above the illustration. And below the title, in more compact upper- and lower-case letters, *A Theory of Everything?* The book was in English, a smooth-skinned paperback, already visibly creased and battered. Myburgh recoiled from it as if from a contraband AK-47.

"Have you read this yet, sir?"

"What are superstrings?" Myburgh said. "Ordinary strings with impossible ambitions?" Perhaps this subtle insult would sink into the kaffir's pretentious brain, stymieing further talk.

"No, sir. It's physics, Mr. Myburgh. Very deep, fundamental physics. It answers deep questions about how the universe is, and why, and what we may expect of it."

"So you're a physicist, Mr. Thubana?"

"No, sir. I'm a—"

"Every day, you do physics at the university, writing equations with which to solve colossal mysteries."

"Nowadays, Mr. Myburgh, I'm a roofer. At a housing site west of the city. After number 496, I must catch another bus."

"A roofer?"

"Yes, sir."

"Then where did you get this book?" Myburgh rapped it with his knuckles. "And what makes you think you can understand it?"

"I understand it," Thubana said mildly. "Under a different set of circumstances, maybe I *would* be a physicist."

"And if I weren't an Afrikaner," Myburgh said, "perhaps I'd be traveling on the next Soviet Mars flight."

Thubana explained that his immediate boss, an Englishman named Godfrey, had given him the book—as well as the upscale trenchcoat—and that he had been reading and thinking hard about superstrings for over a month now.

"All right, then," Myburgh said. "Tell me what you know."

"Superstring theory," Thubana said, taking Myburgh at his word, "holds that the building blocks of the universe are not atoms, but tiny strings—tiny strings that twitch and twitch." To illustrate their twitching, Thubana repeatedly crooked a finger.

"Why? To what end?" Myburgh asked only because it was more amusing than staring out the window.

"I don't know, exactly. But the twitching generates matter and energy at the submicroscopic Planck scale. It does this throughout the entire cosmos."

These terms and explanations were unintelligible to Myburgh, as hard to untangle, as indigestible, as a platter of cold spaghetti. "What complete rot. You'd do better to have Mr. Godfrey give you books on bricklaying, tilework, vehicle repair. It's criminal he's encouraging you in this . . . this *nonsense.*"

"Because my mind is too dim?"

"Because it's *useless,* young man. Because it's castle-in-the-air elitism."

"No, Mr. Myburgh. It isn't. It's elegant physics. If it's open to attack, it's only on the grounds that experiments haven't yet been able to back it up. Also, the mathematics of the theory require that one suppose ten rather than four dimensions—nine of space and one of time."

Myburgh snorted. He couldn't believe that Thubana had fallen under the spell of such stuff.

"Listen, sir. Six of the spatial dimensions must be curled up—'compactified,' my book says—into a geometrical object called the 'Calabi-Yau manifold.' Otherwise, you see, the mathematics of superstring theory, and its ability to make predictions about the world we live in, fall apart."

"You're giving yourself to utter claptrap, Mr. Thubana. Does it make you feel superior to"—nodding at the other riders on *Grim Boy's Toe*—"your sleepy comrades?"

Thubana turned so that the penlight over his ear shone directly into

Myburgh's eyes. "It makes me sorry, sir. And—forgive me for saying so—angry. Quite angry."

"At yourself, I hope," Myburgh muttered, turning his face to the window. Outside, the landscape was graying, quivering like a cloudy aspic in a huge inverted bowl.

Thubana, to Myburgh's surprise, dropped one hand to his knee, his grip like a lobster's claw.

"Let go, kaffir," Myburgh whispered. He took the penlight from behind Thubana's ear and dropped it to the floor.

Thubana released him and picked up the penlight; then he leaned into Myburgh as if they were old chums at a sporting event. But when he turned the penlight on again, no beam shot forth. "That's all right," Thubana hissed. "Darkness is exactly what you want for us, isn't it?"

"Leave me alone."

"Okay. No need for light. I'm not an unintelligent man, and I remember my reading. All of it."

He's crazy, thought Myburgh. A woolhead twice over.

"A superstring expert at Princeton in America—a theorist named Edward Witten—said something profound, sir. He said, 'To have the energy to face a difficult problem day after day, one needs the attitude that victory is just around the corner. But probably it isn't.' Light isn't necessary to remember that. I can remember it just as well in the dark."

"Leave me alone." Myburgh hated the weakness in his voice. It sounded as if he were whistling in Thubana's shadow.

"'The attitude,'" Thubana grimly repeated, "'that victory is just around the corner. But probably it isn't.'"

Suddenly, from the vicinity of the center aisle, a barrage of martial music poured forth. This music—drums, bells, trumpets—was so loud that it easily overpowered the continuous rattling of the Putco vehicle. Everyone noticed. Men and women, a moment past slumped and dozing, straightened and looked around: the man who'd rested his forehead on a sponge, the newspaper yogis, a woman who'd scrolled her turtleneck up over her eyes. Everyone—every dead-to-the-world-passenger—was instantly resurrected.

Then the music ceased, and a nasal English-speaking voice, made both tinny and scratchy by atmospheric conditions, said, *"This is Radio Freedom, broadcasting to our comrades in Azania from a site we are not at liberty to divulge."*

"Mpandhlani!" cried someone far to the rear. "Mpandhlani, for God's sake, close your mouth!"

"Tonight, we address the issue of education. The policies of the apartheid regime not only deny our people their inalienable rights but also access to universal education. Therefore, hundreds of thousands have left the country just to seek education abroad. The Pan Africanist Congress of Azania, in order to cater for the students and refugees, established the department of education and manpower training so that—"

"Your hat, Mpandhlani! Put it on!"

"Close your mouth! Have pity! Close it!"

Myburgh was at a loss. First the music, then the pontifical radio voice, and finally the shouts of various passengers that the man called Mpandhlani *do* something—shouts that seemed to have no relation to these other events. Looking past Thubana, Myburgh saw that the bald passenger, crumpled in the lotus position not far from Thubana's aisle-side knee, had his eyes closed and his mouth wide open. Nothing bizarre about that. The poor fellow was trying to sleep. In fact, he was *succeeding* in the effort, the only wretch aboard number 496 managing to do so.

And then Myburgh realized that the voice of the announcer on Radio Freedom was issuing from the toothless cavity of Mpandhlani's mouth: *". . . conscious rejection of the indoctrinated inferiority complex that sparked the Soweto uprising of 1976 when our students said no to the imposition of the oppressor's language. This fight developed into a rejection of an entire system—'Bantu education'—deliberately designed to keep our people in perpetual subjugation. Therefore, we must enforce a perpetual rainy Monday on every school using these 'techniques of control' and make ourselves—"*

Thubana leaned out into the aisle, put his fist under the bald man's chin, and gently closed his mouth. The harangue from the PAC spokesman continued, but mutedly, as if leaking out of Mpandhlani's earholes and nostrils. Mpandhlani woke up and looked at Thubana in groggy bewilderment.

"What's happening, Mordecai?" His words bled into the report on Radio Freedom like a spooky sort of overdubbing. "Oh no," he said, pressing the palms of his hands to his temples. He glanced apologetically at several of the other passengers. "Forgive me, my friends. Please, everybody, forgive."

"It's okay," Thubana told him. "Put on your cap." He took the volleyball-half from Mpandhlani and crammed it down on his naked and—Myburgh finally saw—grotesquely stitched-up pate. There was silence again, a vacuum quickly filled by the incessant rattling of *Grim Boy's Toe*. Riders fore and aft relapsed into self-protective comas, as if, having survived a crisis, they needed to recuperate. Myburgh felt even more isolated than before.

"Mr. Thubana, I don't understand."

"Perhaps your mind is too dim. —Forgive me. It's just that Mpandhlani—his real name is Winston Skosana—has a metal plate in his head. Sometimes, he picks up radio broadcasts, usually illegal ones from Zambia or Botswana. This is dangerous, especially when he's on a loading platform at the rusks factory. That volleyball—he found it in a KwaNdebele midden—saves him from embarrassment. A matter of physics."

"Dunderheaded physics, surely."

"No, Mr. Myburgh. It works."

"It's nonsense. It's impossible."

Thubana shrugged. He nodded at Mpandhlani—Winston Skosana—who'd already dozed off again.

"Why does he have a plate in his skull?"

"He was arrested by security police ten years ago and detained without charge for thirty-two months. Then, one day, while taking him from his cell to an interrogation room, his keepers shoved him down a flight of metal stairs. Suicide attempt, said the security police. But Winston didn't die, and some determined ladies from the Black Sash had him released and operated on."

"He was a terrorist, a guerrilla-in-training."

"I suppose." Thubana appeared bored by the possibility. "He could have been a poet."

"Or a physicist?"

Thubana turned back to Myburgh as if he'd reopened an important area of discussion—but, astonishingly, he said, "Mpandhlani once told me that we have no word in our Nguni dialect for *orgy*."

"I beg your pardon."

"African languages are not made to talk about Western mores or contemporary physics. Bantu education—carried out in our tribal tongues—has made it very hard for us to understand the discoveries of men like Einstein and Planck."

"What has that to do with not having a word for *orgy?*"

"If the Ndebele, the Sotho, the Zulu, and others have no word for this *human* activity, how may we—speaking only Afrikaans and our tribal tongues—grasp interactions among submicroscopic *particles* called fermions, hadrons, baryons, quarks? Impossible!"

"Forget it," Myburgh said. "It's all a lot of horsefeathers."

"And now they're saying that these tiny points aren't points at all, but the ends of very small strings—*closed* strings, probably. Only by viewing them as strings may we construct a workable Theory of Everything."

"Theory of Everything?" Thubana's talk was all over the map, an obstacle course of jargon.

"A series of formulae bringing together the four major forces of the universe."

"Right. Given ten dimensions, six of them 'curled up.' Study architecture, man. Study mechanical drawing."

Thubana thumbed through his book. "Gravity, electromagnetism, the weak force, the strong force. Until this theory, Mr. Myburgh, no one was able to *prove* that these four forces were all separate aspects of one underlying force. That's important. We must prove it. I want to *help* prove it."

Myburgh found that the passion with which Thubana was speaking had touched him. "Not everyone can aid in such discoveries. *I* can't, for instance. But I won't lose sleep over it. I've other interests, other talents."

It seemed a kind of hubris, Thubana's megalomaniacal desire to put himself in the company of Einstein and Planck. Laughable. But Myburgh couldn't laugh. Perhaps—given Thubana's passion—all this superstring business *wasn't* mere crackpottery.

Thubana said, "Gravity is the most powerful force. It works at a distance even on the macroscopic scale, and it has *always* been the problem. Various quantum theories have unified the other three forces, the ones working at subatomic levels, but gravity—damn it most emphatically!—always knocks each potential new TOE, Theory of Everything, out of symmetry. It ruins everything."

"I'm sorry." This was all that Myburgh could think to say, but he meant it. (God, his eyelids were growing heavy.)

Then the African changed tacks. "You whites, Mr. Myburgh, are gravity. Blacks, Asians, and our so-called Coloreds are like the other three forces: magnetism, weak force, strong force. In these cases, though, it doesn't matter much which group I assign to which fundamental force."

Now he's talking trash, Myburgh thought, fighting drowsiness. Has the weird engine of his brain thrown a rod?

Thubana's voice droned on, almost like a lullaby:

"Africans, Asians, Coloreds—it's easy to unify those groups, just as one may construct theories, equations without anomalies, that bring together every major physical force *except* gravity. Gravity's the hangup. Meanwhile, societally speaking, whites are the biggest obstacle to harmony among peoples. You are gravity, Gerrit Myburgh. You pull everything down. You monkey-wrench the equations."

Before Myburgh could protest this slander, many of the bus's passengers began to second Thubana's remarks.

Incongruously, they did so by singing, *a capella,* in syncopated rhythms that reminded Myburgh of ancient tribal chants and modern street-corner sing-offs in Soweto, Nigel, Alexandra, and other black townships:

> Whites are gravity—
> They bring us down.
> Down, down, down.
> Down, down, down.
>
> Whites are gravity—
> They bring us down.
> Down, down, down.
> Down,
> down,
> down.

The purity of the laborers' voices—the spine-tingling richness of their harmonies—gave Myburgh a chill. But their voices didn't entirely mask the bankruptcy of the ideas set forth in their stupid little song; and Myburgh, back from the trance into which Thubana's monologue had lulled him, turned around and shouted above the bus's maddening rattle:

"Whites *aren't* gravity! We *don't* bring you down!"

"You act on us over great distances," said Thubana. "You cause us to travel miles. Light-years, so to speak."

"Are you puppets, then?" Myburgh asked. "Is that how you see yourselves?"

"Down, down, down," chanted a host of passengers.

"Shut up!" Myburgh cried. "SHUT UP!"

As gently as possible, Thubana pulled Myburgh back down to his seat. "Everyone on this bus—every soul on our planet—is a puppet of superstrings, Mr. Myburgh, for superstrings is a TOE, a Theory of Everything. It explains—it *will* explain—the physical universe to all its living and breathing puppets."

"There's no such thing as your Theory of Everything!" Myburgh replied, shaking off Thubana's hand. "Theories, perhaps. A dozen *different* theories—but not just one comprehensive Theory that can explain everything!"

"Tell him to shut up," a hefty woman in a checkered *doek* told Thubana. "He's giving me the nerves."

"Do you want to be Kentuckied?" Thubana whispered. "You know, *necklaced?* Is that what you wish?"

Of course he didn't. What life-loving person in his right mind would want a used tire lowered over his head, doused in petrol, and cruelly set aflame? Fear rippled in Myburgh's bowels like a school of rapidly finning minnows.

But, bracing himself, he repeated that no one set of equations—no matter how elegant—could offer insight into every interaction in the cosmos.

"Of course not," said Thubana, patting his knee.

Suspicious, Myburgh stared at him.

"Now please apply that principle to the TOE by which the South African state tries to order relations among people."

It suddenly occurred to Myburgh that *Grim Boy's Toe* was really *Grim Boy's TOE.*

Putco bus number 496 carried a monicker that wickedly mocked both the race-obsessed Afrikaners who had devised apartheid and the grim policy itself, a policy on which his ancestors had ingeniously jury-rigged a system of taboos, customs, mores, and laws unlike those anywhere else on the planet.

Damn these kaffirs. Damn them all to the most painful Ndebele hell they can imagine.

"How much longer, Kabini?" Myburgh shouted at the bearish Putco driver.

"Three hours," called Ernest Kabini, over his shoulder. "No. Two hours, forty-five minutes."

"Don't be impertinent." *Coon,* he wanted to add.

"Sorry, *nkosi.*"

Thubana clasped Myburgh's wrist, twisting it around to reveal his watch. Myburgh was dumbfounded to see that its stark crimson readout —which winked as if adequately powered—hadn't advanced beyond . . . 3:15 A.M.

Christ Almighty. Was he dreaming?

Then he gazed past the laborers in front of him and saw through the streaked windscreen another Putco bus swerve into 496's headlamps. Immediately, hands braced on the seat back, knuckles whitening, he was on his feet again, shouting at Kabini to hit the brakes before they were all seriously injured. . . .

"Shadow matter," Thubana said, trying to pull him back down by his coat. "Just like us. It can't hurt you, Mr. Myburgh, please believe me."

Shadow matter?

What nonsense! What high-flown, self-deluding claptrap, just like everything else Thubana had told him.

Number 496, as Kabini futilely braked, collided with the other vehicle, striking it resoundingly. Windscreens shattered. Engines anviled together. Bodies flew past one another like players in an avant-garde production of *Peter Pan*. Indeed, Thubana rocketed past Myburgh in the gemmy chaos, clutching his copy of *Superstrings* and smiling as if to say, None of this matters; believe me, sir, not a jot of this means anything at all.

You're lying, Myburgh's dream self thought. You're lying.

And he was hurled through the broken windscreen of *Grim Boy's Toe* into an endless, entrapping darkness.

When Putco bus 496 pulled up behind the stalled Cadillac (which was blocking the way to Pretoria), driver Ernest Kabini called back to one of his passengers, Mordecai Thubana.

Thubana, shaking himself awake, accompanied Kabini off the bus, and they offered their aid to the policemen in glistening boots and macintoshes walking around the shiny cranberry-colored car.

"Go on about your business," one of the policemen told them in Afrikaans. "There's nothing you can do."

Thubana peered in the Caddy's window at the man slumped behind its steering wheel: a sandy-haired bloke nearing forty. It looked, tonight, as if he would never get there.

Said Kabini, "What happened, my *baas?*"

"A heart attack, we think," the policeman said. He nodded at the road. "Those skid marks show he knew what was happening and fought the car to keep it from going into the ditch. Pretty cool, for a fellow staring disaster in the eye."

Yes, thought Thubana. He saved his deliciously *lekker* car, but he also gave himself a chance—a thin one—to survive the terrible crack-up threatening everything he valued.

The second policeman, his ruddy face shining from his rain hood like a lacquered gargoyle's, approached the Africans. "Situation's under control," he growled. "Get out of here."

Thubana started to reply, but Kabini shook his head.

The two men reboarded number 496, and Kabini wrestled it around the dead man's car on the weather-gouged road.

Finding his seat taken by another man, Thubana slumped to the floor with a book and a penlight. Beside him, a fellow nicknamed Mpandhlani asked him if he thought the dead driver of the expensive American car had gone to heaven or hell. With his steel plate and his unenviable ability to pick up out-of-country radio broadcasts, Mpandhlani often seemed more like a disembodied spirit than any visiting angel would have. In fact, he sometimes gave Thubana the creeps.

"Why do you ask?"

"Because I feel like *three* people got on when you and Kabini came back."

"Really?"

"Yes. Someone else is riding with us, Mordecai."

"Then it's cut-and-dried. The dead man is shadow matter, like you and me and all these others." He nodded at the fatigued bodies all around them. "Get it?"

"Sure," said Mpandhlani "Shadow matter."

"Down, down, down," sang many of their fellow riders. "Down, down, down."

It was true of all of them, Thubana thought, but the longer the dead man stayed aboard, the more likely he was to reach Belle Ombre station in the company of his countrymen. The more likely he was to see that the universe's four major forces needed to be unified, tied up with superstrings, and rendered beautiful forever by a TOE equation with no anomalies. The more likely he was to find his own substance again.

Meanwhile, Thubana, his compatriots, and the heartsore ghost of Gerrit Myburgh jounced together across the highveld. And it seemed to Thubana, glancing out the mud-streaked windows, that the eastern sky was beginning to redden. . . .

"No!" Myburgh shouted.

The shout jerked him awake. He was sitting next to Mordecai Thubana on the bus called *Grim Boy's Toe.* Although the bus had not wrecked, it was no longer moving. It was parked on a muddy turnout in the middle of nowhere. Glancing down, Myburgh saw that Thubana had draped his trenchcoat, lined with synthetic fur, over Myburgh's chest and knees.

"Welcome back, Mr. Myburgh. You had a nice nap?"

"No. I don't think so."

"But you slept. You nodded off while I was trying to explain to you how whites are like gravity."

"I dreamed we had an accident."

"*You* had an accident—earlier. In your lovely, *lekker* car, you hit an elephant."

Myburgh blinked. That collision had happened. This latest one—running *crash!* into another Putco bus—had not. Odd. Very odd. A conundrum inside an enigma.

"I dreamed other things, too."

"Good dreams?"

Myburgh started. "Why are we stopped?"

"Never mind that. Tell me what you dreamed."

"For one thing, I'd . . . died. Heart attack. In my car. But somehow I was you in my dream, Mr. Thubana, and I looked into the window of my car to see me lying in it dead. Then I got on the bus with you and Kabini again. I was a ghost. I was dead, but at the same time I was you seeing me dead and seeing my ghost here on *Grim Boy's Toe*, just another passenger."

"Ah," Thubana said. "Fascinating. You being me and you being your own ghost at the same time."

Myburgh shot Thubana a pleading look. How to tell him that he had taken a weird sort of comfort from hearing Thubana's comrades mock him with their chant? Even from seeing a dream picture of himself in his car, where death had relieved him of both responsibility and culpability? Such things were unsayable.

Myburgh looked down. "You gave me your coat."

"Of course. Your suit's all torn. And I have a sweater." He did: an ugly, ribbed, reddish-brown sweater with more pills than a discount pharmacy.

Myburgh tried to remove the coat and thrust it back at Thubana, but Thubana held it to him with a hard, heavy-veined hand. "Keep it, Mr. Myburgh. Shortly, I fear, you will need it even more than you do now."

What was going on? Myburgh glanced around. Other riders were peering uneasily into the relentless drizzle. Kabini wasn't in his driver's cage. Further, some sort of armor-clad paddy wagon had parked in front of the bus, blocking its way. Africans called such vans "nylons," because of the mesh in their windows. Several men—Myburgh couldn't tell how many—stalked the asphalt and the boggish shoulder. A confusion of moving silhouettes.

"The police?"

"From BOSS," Thubana said. The Bureau of State Security, he meant.

Ordinarily, Myburgh would have felt—what?—a frisson of ambiguous pride thinking on these dedicated state functionaries, but this morning, right now, he experienced their presence as all the others on *Grim Boy's Toe* must have—as an ominous interruption, a clamp slowly tightening on the heart. But why? These were men who could help him. Myburgh rapped on his window.

"*In here!*" he called in Afrikaans. "*I'm in here!*"

"They're not looking for you," Thubana said. "Best not to call attention to yourself."

"That's crazy. I *have* to talk to them." Hindered by the seat back in front of him and Thubana's unyielding presence to his left, he tried to stand.

"It will do no good, Mr. Myburgh."

"Nonsense. I'll tell them about my accident. They'll see that I get home." At last, he had allies again. But Thubana would not budge; the only way to reach the aisle would be to shove past him—a distasteful, maybe even a dangerous, option to pursue.

A plainclothes security police agent in a trenchcoat similar to Thubana's, and a dove-gray fedora, stepped up into the bus. Facing the passengers, he spoke in Afrikaans in a high-pitched voice that unexpectedly conveyed an intimidating authority: "Everyone off the bus! And be orderly about it!"

"Who are you?" said the woman in the checkered head scarf. She spoke in English.

"Major Henning Jeppe," the man said. And again in Afrikaans, "Off the bus, please. Step quickly."

Myburgh pulled himself up and said, "Gerrit Myburgh here. I've had an accident, Major Jeppe. Please help me."

But Jeppe had already gone back down the steps into the night, and the passengers on 496, cursing and grumbling, rose from their seats or their newsprint mats and began shuffling toward the front of the bus. Thubana also rose. He took Myburgh by the arm (not so much patronizingly as custodially, as if Myburgh were an expensive polo horse belonging to a doting employer) and introduced him into the sluggish stream of bodies. Well, so be it. The sooner he got outside and reported his accident, the sooner he could forsake the company of these cattlelike Africans and go back to the steady and uneventful life he'd built for himself at the financial institution called Jacobus & Roux.

On the desolate *bundu*'s edge (Myburgh's digital now read 4:38, about two hours till sunup), he heard Kabini begging a uniformed policeman not to detain his bus:

"It will be my neck. I'm late as it is. The weather—you see what it's like. Don't be so cruel, *nkosi.*"

The policeman muttered something unintelligible, shoved Kabini around the bonnet of the bus, and disappeared with him behind the scattershot parade of the passengers. Myburgh began searching for Jeppe or some other member of State Security upon whom to dump his story, but all the white policemen had moved to the edges of the shadowy field into which they were herding everyone, depriving him of any chance to make his case. Thubana, settling his coat on Myburgh's shoulders from behind, helped him step over muddy earth toward a stubble-spiked piece of ground so exposed and barren that it stank of its own infertile clay.

"Hullo! My name is Gerrit Myburgh! I'm here by mistake!" In dry weather, his cry would have echoed resoundingly; this morning, it had no more impact on the indifferent Transvaal than a muffled cough.

"Shhhhh," Thubana said. "Save your breath."

Soon, all ninety passengers had shaped three sides of a square in the field beyond the bus. The fourth edge was the bus itself. Major Henning Jeppe reappeared from behind *Grim Boy's Toe*, where he and two or three policemen in rainslicks had been pumping Kabini for information. To speak to the detained, Jeppe stood in front of 496's tall, inward-pleated door.

"Most of you are honest workers," he said in his stentorian squeak. "But, this morning, at least one terrorist-traitor has ridden from KwaNdebele with you. If the law-abiding residents of your homeland help us identify this person or persons, we will let you reboard and go on to your jobs." He pinched the bridge of his nose, as if his head ached.

Myburgh began waving an arm. "Major Jeppe! Major Jeppe!"

Jeppe ignored him. "If you refuse to help, if you stay silent in the misguided belief that you are observing a higher patriotism, we will detain you here until you piss yourselves or your bladders burst. One or the other. Understand?"

"Gaan kak in die mielies!" (Go shit in the corn) shouted a squat male passenger only a meter or two from Jeppe.

Myburgh was stunned by the black's impertinence. What it would bring him, after all, was immediate notice and swifter punishment. In fact, two policemen in macintoshes rushed into the field, seized the man, and chivvied him back aboard the bus with their *sjamboks* and a series of hammerlike blows between the shoulder blades. A moment later, the man was bellowing inside 496's tin shell, begging to be returned to his people in the field. In the rising twilight, *his* cries produced demoralizing echoes.

"Fool," murmured Thubana, shaking his head.

"Major Jeppe, I don't belong here!" Myburgh shouted. He wanted to walk manfully up to the major, but Thubana, sensing this intent, locked an arm through his elbow. "Damn you. Let go."

One of the bus's windows slid down: *Krrrrrrack!* A policeman leaned out. "This isn't the man, sir. We now know our terrorist is someone called Mpandhlani."

Myburgh looked three people to his right and saw Mpandhlani, a raw-boned figure with a face like an inoffensive baboon's, staring at the ground. Actually, his nose was pointing earthward, but his eyes seemed to be rolled back in his head, contemplating a dimension where a person could write poetry unmolested. He was wearing his volleyball cap, which made him look like an escapee from either an insane asylum or a circus train.

"Christ," said Thubana.

"Aren't you folks lucky?" Jeppe said, walking into the field in his new boots, unmindful of the mud. "One of you has already come to our assistance. Good. Excellent." Abruptly, he turned back to the bus. "What was that name, Wessels?"

"Mpandhlani, sir. It's a nickname. It means Baldhead."

"Thank you, Wessels." Jeppe did as neat a military pivot as he could manage on the sloppy ground, then strode toward the detainees in Myburgh's crooked line. "Baldhead," he murmured. "Baldhead."

"Psssst, Winston," Thubana said, softly hissing.

A woman beside Mpandhlani nudged him, and he looked at Thubana through glazed, beyond-the-pale eyes.

"Keep your cap on, Winston," Thubana said. "Keep it on."

Myburgh straightened his arm, breaking free of Thubana's elbow lock. *"Here he is, Major Jeppe! The terrorist you want is right here!"* Myburgh stepped out of the line of detainees, leveled an accusing finger at Mpandhlani, and briefly held this stance as if posing for a new statue at the Voortrekker Monument.

"Bring that man out of the bus, Wessels," Jeppe called over his shoulder. "He'll point us to the filthy bugger."

What the hell? Myburgh glanced at Jeppe, then at the policemen strong-arming the informant off *Grim Boy's Toe*, and then at Thubana throwing him a stare of such singeing, blast-furnace hate that his nape hairs crackled.

But Jeppe . . . was he deaf? Was he blind?

One of those who had informed on Mpandhlani (an African, thought Myburgh, not me) had a rugger's body and a flat-cheeked face with a pair of big, liquid eyes. Jeppe's policemen dragged him along each line of detainees until, head down, he stopped in front of Winston Skosana and stood there incriminatingly shamefaced.

"Ephraim," Thubana said. "You shit."

"They already knew," Ephraim said. "Your friend"—nodding at Myburgh "—just fingered him."

"No, he didn't," Thubana said. "He's nothing to his own people this morning. Nothing, Ephraim. He could strip naked in front of these snakes, man. They'd never notice."

"In any case," Ephraim said, "I wasn't the only one who—"

"Watch that talk," said Wessels, angry and puzzled. He slapped Thubana across his lips: a crisp, open-handed blow.

Myburgh turned around. Jeppe, Wessels, Wessels's partner, and the man named Ephraim were all near enough to touch—as, of course, was Thubana. But Myburgh suddenly understood that he was a ghost to the Afrikaners: a nonentity, a person-shaped void. Those he'd expected to rescue him—fellow whites—could neither see nor hear him, while the blacks—Kabini, Mpandhlani, Ephraim, and so on—had no more interest in him than he had in them. The exception to this judgment, at least until he'd tried to betray Skosana, was Mordecai Thubana, who had given him his coat.

Why should I be ashamed? I'm being a good citizen, aren't I? Standing up for stability and order?

Myburgh went to Jeppe and shouted into his pinched, bloodless face: "I've had an accident! My name's Gerrit Myburgh. If you want proof, ring up my brother Kiewit—Kiewit Myburgh—on the farm called Huilbloom! He'll vouch for me!"

Jeppe blinked. He recoiled imperceptibly. That was all. It was as if he'd suffered a mild pang of heartburn or caught a faint whiff of sewage from a settlement upwind. Then he turned about and piercingly commanded all the hangdog laborers from KwaNdebele to reboard their bus. He dispatched Wessels's partner to assist in overseeing the boarding, then approached Mpandhlani with his hands jammed Humphrey Bogart–style in the pockets of his trenchcoat. All Myburgh could do was skip aside. Then, as 496's riders straggled bemusedly back to the bus at the urging of Jeppe's henchmen, Jeppe eyed Mpandhlani with a rote and clinical ill will.

Over his shoulder, he said, "Don't let the bus go until we've questioned this gentleman."

Myburgh heard Kabini, the driver, cry, "Please, *nkosi*, you've got your man! Let me finish my route!" This plea was followed by a thump, an outraged yell, and the sounds of argument as the police goosed Kabini up the steps to his driver's cage. Myburgh could see only kaleidoscope pieces of their scuffle through the bobbing heads and shoulders of the people stumping back to *Grim Boy's Toe*.

Thubana was not among their number. He stood out in the field with Mpandhlani, Major Jeppe, and the pumpkin-headed cop whom Jeppe called Wessels. Myburgh stood with them, of course, but he seemed not to count, having even less impact on the events now unraveling than would a beside-the-point memory or an unheard song. Should he go back to 496 with the others, strike out on foot for Pretoria, or stand here like an undressed department-store mannequin, humiliated and useless?

Jeppe took note of Thubana. "Go back to the bus, kaffir," he said, abandoning all pretense at courtesy.

"If Winston's a terrorist, I'm a terrorist, Major."

"Then you *are*," Myburgh said. "You *told* me Mpandhlani was held for almost three years for terrorist activity."

Simultaneously, Jeppe said, "Very well. I believe you. Stay here with your bloody accomplice."

Thubana replied to Myburgh: "I told you I *supposed* he'd been a guerrilla. Nothing more."

"Guerrilla, terrorist—it's all the same to us," Jeppe said, squinting perplexedly at Thubana. He turned to Wessels. "Aren't we lucky this fellow's so talkative, though."

"Yes, sir." Wessels had three or four chins. Even in the mud, he seemed to be bouncing lightly on his toes, minutely jiggling his chins in anticipation of the fun he was soon going to be having at the two Africans' expense.

"But no more out of you until we've talked to Mister Baldhead," Jeppe told Thubana. "Understand?"

Thubana merely stared at the major.

Myburgh lifted his arms in exasperated disbelief, dropped them to his sides again. He was invisible to the very authority to whom he should be as lumpishly self-evident as a marshmallow in a mug of cocoa. And his words were as inaudible to Jeppe and Wessels as the high-pitched piping of certain kinds of dog whistles. Suddenly, he found himself—as he had been on the road right after that elephant demolished his Caddy—on the verge of tears.

Four men in an open field on a damp morning. From nowhere, it seemed, the fancy came to Myburgh that if only they had a folding table and chairs, they could sit down and play a few hands of bridge or canasta or hearts. Cards were plasticized, after all—they didn't usually go soggy on you. He and the others could take partners and enjoy themselves. So what if it wasn't quite cockcrow and he was missing a shoe. . . . ?

Jeppe ended this absurd reverie by stepping up to Mpandhlani, his eyes level with Mpandhlani's lips, and saying, "Take off that stupid cap, kaffir. When in the presence of a state official, you show respect."

"We're outdoors," Myburgh blurted. "What the devil difference does it make, Major Jeppe?"

Mpandhlani's spirit seemed to have left his body. It had flown away to a thatched Ndebele house with freehand-painted fences and exterior murals, frescoes of wild geometric designs in mint green, lemon yellow, concrete blue. Or that was what Mpandhlani's fallen lower lip and fish-eyed gaze suggested to Myburgh, who thought the man looked catatonic, as if the mere arrival of the security police had irreversibly traumatized him. He was taking refuge in memory, in a fitful, private idyll of child-hood.

"Take off your cap!"

"Leave him alone," Thubana told Jeppe.

"Shut up!" Wessels said, and, wincing, he struck Thubana with his rhinoceros-hide whip.

Up, involuntarily, went Myburgh's arms as he flinched away from the unexpected blow. When he looked again, a raw, triangular gash on Thubana's cheek had begun busily leaking scarlet.

Mpandhlani's spirit flew back from his boyhood home (probably only a few kilometers from the Myburgh family farm) and reanimated his up-right corpse: He took off his cap.

Jeppe seized it from him, examined it with distaste (for, yes, it stank of both rubber and man sweat), then hurled it into the twilight with a contemptuous flip. The volleyball-half whistled through the air and landed wetly, a sound like two hippopotamuses kissing. Jeppe, noticing Mpandhlani's naked, saddle-stitched pate, gave a squeaky guffaw. Perhaps his laugh embarrassed him, for he cut it off immediately.

"My," he said. "What an ostrich egg. I'll bet old Christiaan Wessels here would be glad to scramble it for you."

Now Mpandhlani's eyes were at least semialert. He looked at Jeppe, at

Wessels, at Thubana, at Myburgh. It seemed to Myburgh that he started to speak. But, in fact, what came out of his mouth was a staticky tirade:

"... *our express purpose to kill more and more South African security forces, especially the Boers, because unless whites are made to feel unsafe, and until they too are killed, they will yet feel safe to go on killing the Africans. And, in fact, although some whites are among the security forces killed by the Azanian People's Liberation Army, time has almost come when—*"

"Shut up, you bloody kaffir!" Jeppe cried.

"*—for every African killed by the racist security forces, a white person must be killed. One racist, one bullet!* Phambili Nomzabalazo Wabantu!"

At that moment, Mpandhlani stopped broadcasting propaganda and began transmitting a medley of pompous marches. Jeppe and Wessels appeared nonplussed, uncomprehending. But Jeppe seized Mpandhlani by the arms, pulled him to him, and then brutally shoved him toward the roadway. Mpandhlani bent double, clutching his head as if to dam the symphonic battle hymns spilling out.

Headlamps and flashlights reflected off the windshield of *Grim Boy's Toe* like strobes in a Joburg nightclub. Confusion reigned. Myburgh literally had no idea where, or to whom, to turn.

"Take this walking radio station to the van, Wessels. Get the filthy bugger out of my hearing."

"Me, too," Thubana said.

Jeppe nodded. "Of course. You, too." He swept his hand after Wessels and Mpandhlani, a command and a dismissal.

"What about me?" Myburgh asked Thubana. "What am I supposed to do?"

"Go find Winston's cap."

"His cap?"

"I beg your pardon," said Jeppe, glaring at Thubana.

"Sure. Otherwise, the broadcasts he's picking up will drive us crazy before we reach security police headquarters."

Myburgh hobbled deeper into the field, trying to find the spot where their comrade's volleyball cap had made its obscene-sounding, sucking touchdown.

"Hurry!" Thubana yelled after him. "Or we may go off and leave you, Mr. Myburgh!"

"Shut up!" Jeppe said. He twisted Thubana's arm, chivying the much taller man after Wessels. He appeared to believe that Thubana was playing mind games with him, maybe even communicating by means of code words and gestures with a squad of guerrillas farther out in the *bundu*. In fact, Jeppe was royally spooked. Myburgh would have sympathized with him more if his own predicament had not been so outré and ego-crippling. No one could feel as isolated as he did.

By what seemed pure luck, he found Mpandhlani's volleyball cap, pried it out of the mud, then stumbled back to the roadway to the *bakkie*—the nylon—into which Wessels and two more security agents were herding Mpandhlani and Thubana.

Kabini, sporting a badly swollen eye, waved at Myburgh from his driver's cage on the Putco bus. Although Myburgh thought seriously about boarding 496 again, he decided that, being invisible to the Afrikaners, he'd do better sticking with Thubana, who, however mad, had at least some small insight into the clunkily ratcheting gears of this nightmare.

So Myburgh leapt into the BOSS van just as Wessels was pushing its doors to. The hem of Thubana's coat got caught in the closing doors. Myburgh yanked the hem free and toppled backward. Wessels, cursing, slammed the doors a second time, harder, so hard that the metal walls and loadbed of the *bakkie*'s holding cell vibrated like fettered gongs.

Mpandhlani and Thubana sat on narrow benches on either side of this four-wheeled cell.

"Are you all right, Mr. Myburgh?" Thubana said.

"No," Myburgh said. "Of course I'm not."

For added to the trauma of his selective invisibility was the fact that he had lost a stocking: His muddy left foot ached with the pitiless July cold.

Wessels, whom Thubana ridiculed in Afrikaans as *Pampoenkop*— Pumpkinhead—had taken Mpandhlani's coat, leaving his upper body clothed only in a threadbare T-shirt. Meanwhile, Mpandhlani's steel plate was broadcasting, even inside the nylon, an ANC report on forced removals to impoverished Bantustans. Their little cell buzzed with the transmission, a crazily garbled mix of news, exhortation, and music.

"Give him his cap," Thubana said, his naked hand on the *sjambok* cut on his cheek.

"Gladly." Myburgh flipped Mpandhlani the volleyball-half and, lying in the center of the floor, watched him settle it on his head like a housewife twisting half an orange onto the fluted reamer of a citrus juicer. At first, it seemed to hurt Mpandhlani to cover his skull, but then the cap muted the transmission, turning it into sounds like voices heard faintly through a heating vent. The bald man's eyes brightened, his lips relaxed.

But he still looked cold, hugging himself and hunching forward like someone straining against electrocution.

"May I give him your coat, too?" Myburgh said. "I'm fine now. Well, not fine, exactly. Numb."

"Sure," Thubana said. "Go ahead."

Myburgh rolled out of Thubana's expensive coat and handed it up to Mpandhlani, who nodded his curt thanks and shrugged himself into it. As he put it on, Myburgh saw that neither he nor Thubana had belts now. Wessels had undoubtedly taken them too, on the grounds that the kaffirs could use them as makeshift weapons, their buckles serving as nasty flails. Well, that seemed smart. A policeman had to watch himself. Wessels would surely have taken their shoes too, if they hadn't been wearing ratty *takkies*.

"What's going to happen to us?" Myburgh said.

"To Winston and me?"

"Of course."

"Interrogation. Detention. Torture. One of us may fall out a window. One of us may strangle himself."

"Strangle? Strangle yourself?"

"It's hard to say, Mr. Myburgh. I don't know what Winston's supposed to have done. Or what kind of stuff Jeppe and Pumpkinhead will be looking for."

"Someone exploded a bomb near the Armscor factory," Mpandhlani said. "I'm getting a report on it now." He listened to the voices tunneling his gray matter like so many ethereal brain worms. "The blast—a car bomb—did heavy damage to the plant itself."

Myburgh blinked. Armscor was the weapons-manufacturing arm of the South African Defense Force and a profit-making enterprise of the first water. Its plants were among the most heavily fortified in the country. If it had suffered a crippling bomb blast, no place and nobody—no white place and no white person, rather—could rest secure again. So far as that went, though, Myburgh could not recall any time that he had really rested secure. Living in South Africa had always seemed to him like walking through a plush hotel suite past hundreds of whirring electric fans with frayed cords and no safety baskets. . . .

"You didn't have anything to do with that, did you, Winston?" Thubana said.

Mpandhlani—no, better to call him Skosana: Winston Skosana, a man with both a baptismal name and a Ndebele surname, not merely a patronizing Bantu joke name—*Skosana* tilted his volleyball-capped head against the van's wall and laughed in the basso profundo registers of earthquake.

"Don't I wish. Oh, don't I wish, Mordecai."

Thubana grinned sheepishly. "That's what I thought. But . . . hey, man, you know."

"I know. But I'm just an oke at a Simba Quix chips-and-rusks factory, loading trucks and carrying out trash. Oliver Tambo never tells me nothing."

He laughed again. His laughter overwhelmed the hisses and pops still seeping through his earholes, nostrils, and eyes from Lusaka and other points north—*several* points north, Myburgh figured, for occasionally Skosana picked up ANC broadcasts, and sometimes PAC patter, and, more rarely, the revolutionary threats of the Azanian People's Liberation Army. Indeed, Skosana's skull was a broadcast clearinghouse for a variety of antiapartheid, anti-imperialist voices. Myburgh couldn't look at the man—lean, weathered, battle-scarred—without twinges of both awe and fear. On *Grim Boy's Toe*, he had seemed comic. Here in the nylon's holding cell, though, he suddenly and unaccountably radiated a good-humored self-confidence and strength. Myburgh did not think it was all owing to Thubana's trenchcoat.

Painfully, Myburgh got up and limped to one of the mesh-covered windows on the nylon's rear doors. He was surprised to see Putco bus number 496 chugging down the highway behind them, its headlamps jittering in the pale light, losing distinctiveness, like fish eyes vanishing into clear water, as the sky reddened through a gauze of blowing clouds and spread out vividly over the Transvaal.

Pretty. Very pretty.

With no closer settlements or factories blighting this part of the Putco route, the land was lovely, an exhilarating desolation. Soon the nylon would enter the outskirts of Pretoria, cruise past the jacaranda trees on its wide boulevards, and he . . . well, he would be home.

Bracing himself against any sudden lurches, Myburgh said, "What in God's name happened to me out there?"

"You became shadow matter to them," Thubana said.

"I was shadow matter in my dreams. When Kabini hit that other Putco bus. When I had a heart attack in my Cadillac and got on 496 as my dead self's ghost. Damn it, this is *real!*"

"You look real to me," Skosana said.

"Thank you." Nearly slipping, Myburgh turned back around.

Thubana's hand was blood-streaked from the ragged *sjambok* wound that Wessels had inflicted. Myburgh found the handkerchief he had used to staunch his own bleeding and passed it to Thubana, who took it with no qualms and held it against his cheek.

"I don't get it," Myburgh resumed. "Why didn't I mean anything to those men? What's going on?"

"Winston," Thubana said, gesturing with his free hand, "is my book in one of those pockets?"

Skosana patted the side pockets of the borrowed coat, raised a telltale thump, and pulled out the copy of *Superstrings*. He hefted it as if it were a hand grenade.

"Turn to page eighty," Thubana said.

His eyebrows lifted, Skosana began riffling. When he found the specified page, he bent the book back in his lap.

"Up at the top," Thubana said. "John Schwarz is talking about 'E sub-eight' symmetries. Do you see it?"

"E sub-eight? Christ, Mordecai, did you memorize this whole crazy book?" He waved it. Again, like a hand grenade.

"I've been studying, hard. Find it and read it, okay? Right where Professor Schwarz first mentions shadow matter."

Amused, Skosana shook his head and read: " '. . . a new kind of matter, sometimes called shadow matter, that doesn't interact, or only interacts extremely weakly, with the ordinary matter that we are familiar with. If you wanted to—' "

"Skip down, Winston. Below where it says we can't see shadow matter because it doesn't interact with everyday light."

Skosana grimaced. He ran a finger along the lines of print and finally read: " '. . . it *does* interact with our kind of gravity—we share our gravity with shadow matter.' "

"Yes," Thubana said. "Yes."

"You called me gravity," Myburgh said, annoyed that this highly complex guff had no guy lines to solid earth. "Now you're calling me shadow matter. Make up your mind!"

"I called *whites* gravity," Thubana said. "Not you. I was using analogy to explain a point. Now I'm making another one."

"There's nothing metaphorical about my situation! Damn it, I'm invisible to my own kind!"

"Shadow matter," Thubana said smugly, as if he had just solved a devilishly abstruse equation.

"I can see you," Skosana said. "Clearly."

"Read," Thubana commanded. "Read what the professor says about shadow matter and gravity."

"There's hardly anything, Mordecai. He only says we'd notice a shadow planet by its gravitational effects—but we wouldn't see it with ordinary light."

"I'm not a planet! I'm a person!"

"Person or planet," Thubana said bitterly, removing Myburgh's monogrammed handkerchief from his cheek and examining it, "you're shadow matter to those fucking Boers." He nodded at the *bakkie*'s cab.

"How? Why?"

"Ask God. That's what I do. I ask him every day: 'Dear God, Great Jehovah, how did my people get to be such thin shadows in our own country?' "

"What am I going to do?"

"What are *we* going to do?" Thubana said.

"I yelled in Jeppe's face," Myburgh said. "He didn't hear me. He just leaned away—as if a soft breeze had touched him." The memory of the major's lack of reaction was painful. Humiliating.

"Gravitational effects," Skosana said, sliding the book back into a coat pocket. "Mr. Myburgh has a gravitational effect on the *stormjaers*. They can't see him, but he can—I don't know—*move* them, maybe. Just a little."

Silent tears traced Myburgh's cheeks like liquid fuses; he sat down beside Skosana. When Wessels opened the nylon's doors, he could dismount in front of Pretoria's security police headquarters and walk the formidable distance to his condo or the much shorter distance to the offices of Jacobus & Roux. Even if no one his own color could see him, he could make it home, resume his life, and forget these past few disorienting hours.

But for how long? No one could hear him. He couldn't make a living if the clients for whom he prepared loans, stock options, capital-outlay schemes, and Krugerrand investments could neither see nor hear him. He would have no real existence, he would be a walking cipher, a ghost of blood and bones.

"How did I get this way? When did it happen? I was all right when I left Huilbloom. Physically."

"Hitting that elephant did it," Thubana said. "There aren't any elephants between Pretoria and KwaNdebele."

"This morning, there *was* an elephant—I saw it, I hit it!"

"Okay, okay. But the elephant you hit was . . . a totem from the old times, shadow matter from yesterday. It changed you. It took Kabini a moment or two to pull you into focus when you came up to the bus. Remember? He saw your wrecked car, yes, but after he stopped and opened the door, what he first saw was only mist, night and mist, and then your ghost—which, of course, he *couldn't* see—filled up with Africa, and he *could* see."

"That's poppycock. You're trying to say I'm dead."

"No. I know you're not dead. I'm trying to explain something very hard to explain."

"How do I change back? Explain that."

"Back to what?" Skosana said, finding a packet of Rothman's 30s and a book of matches in Thubana's coat. "A dead man? Maybe you were dead —killed in your wreck—until number 496 came along. What do you think?" He tapped out, and lit, a cigarette.

Myburgh wiped the wet from his face with the torn sleeve of his jacket. He hated Rothman's 30s. He hated any cigarette. To avoid the smoke slipping out of Skosana's head (along with a faint radio speech about the Azanian victory over Armscor), he crossed over to Thubana's bench.

"What I think is, number 496 couldn't resurrect anyone. It can scarcely even go."

"It's still behind us," Thubana said. "It'll make it to Belle Ombre this morning, and back out to KwaNdebele tonight, and back in to Pretoria tomorrow. And so on."

"But how do I change back, Professor Superstrings?"

Thubana, to Myburgh's surprise, folded the bloody handkerchief he'd been using to clot his wound and stuffed it fastidiously into the breast pocket of Myburgh's suit coat. "Right now, Mr. Myburgh, everything is so *befok*, I hardly care."

Lifting his muddy foot up to the bench and arranging himself so that one haunch could warm it, Myburgh was unable to meet Thubana's eyes. He'd got what he deserved. Thubana and Skosana were riding off to detention, interrogation, torture, possibly even (it was a filthy thing to contemplate, a filthier thing to admit) death; and he had badgered Thubana about restoring him to the lofty estate of an upper-middle-class Afrikaner.

Sweet Christ, what weakness. Or what brass. It was hard for him to know exactly how he had erred, but he had definitely erred. The chilly proof of it was Thubana's silence.

· · · · ·

Traffic in Pretoria was beginning to thicken, but Jeppe and his driver had beaten the morning rush. From one of the nylon's windows, Myburgh saw that they had lost *Grim Boy's Toe* and that a great many familiar landmarks were kaleidoscoping past. Then they reached the headquarters of the security police, pulled off Potgieterstraat into a concealing side street, and slammed to a jolting halt. The laughter from the cab made Myburgh suspect that Wessels (or whoever was driving) had braked like that for the sadistic joy of shaking them up.

"Out! Out!"

The doors came open. Fists with billy clubs shook insistently at them. Pampoenkop—Lieutenant Christiaan Wessels—appeared among the men waiting to escort them inside. And when Skosana, squinting like a mole, stumbled out onto the pavement, Wessels grabbed him by the trenchcoat lapels and bullied him into the wall of the terraced security building.

"Where did you get this coat, kaffir?"

Skosana nodded at the nylon's doors, through which Thubana was now warily coming. "Mordecai let me borrow it."

"He wasn't wearing a coat when we put him in." Wessels looked at one of the agents. "Dedekind, did you leave a goddamned coat in there yesterday."

"No, Lieutenant Wessels. Absolutely not."

Myburgh had already dismounted. He stood between the tall gray building and the nylon, studying the situation.

Wessels, meantime, stuck his big round head, with its flat pink nose, into Skosana's gaunt face. "Where in fuck did you get this, Baldhead? *Tell me!*"

"I had it in my trouser pocket," Thubana said instead. "Folded up very small. 'Compactified,' one could say."

"It's a coat in ten dimensions, six of them curled up," Myburgh said, amazed to hear himself using back talk similar to Thubana's. Of course, the difference—the telling difference—was that Wessels couldn't hear him.

Wessels shot a disbelieving look at Thubana. "Shut up. You'll have your chance to sing." Then, back to Skosana: "Take it off, kaffir! At once!"

Skosana got help. Two security agents hurried to yank the coat off him, grabbing down on its sleeves. So zealous were they, they almost unsocketed one of his arms. Myburgh heard a nauseating *pop!* and saw both agony and hate flare in Skosana's eyes, with their immense pupils and muddy-yellow whites.

"Leave him alone!" Thubana cried.

A pretty-boy policeman menaced him with a *sjambok*. "You want a star on that other cheek too?"

"All of his cheeks, Goosen," said Dedekind, a thirtyish fellow with close-set eyes. "He wants a star or two to sit down on."

"Just as he wishes," Wessels said. "The filthy bugger."

As a policeman wrapped Thubana's trenchcoat around his arm, *Superstrings* dropped out. So did the package of Rothman's 30s and the matchbook from an Indian restaurant in a condemned Asian neighborhood. One officer scooped up the book, another bent down for the cigarettes and matches.

Wessels turned aside to examine *Superstrings*. "Well, well," he said. "This could be a find, Schoeman—a code book, maybe. Carry it in with you."

Thubana barked a laugh. "Who's going to decode it?"

This time, the policeman with the *sjambok* hit him, but Thubana deflected the blow by lifting a hand and hunching his shoulder. A second man made him pay by billying him in the groin. Thubana fell to his knees in front of the *bakkie*'s yawning doors.

I don't have to watch this, Myburgh thought. I can walk home. Who's going to stop me?

Suddenly, Wessels realized that Skosana was again wearing the volleyball cap that, on the road from KwaNdebele, Major Jeppe had hurled off into the night "What the hell is this?" He snatched the cap from Skosana's head, dangled it from his fingers as if it were a scroll of sodden toilet tissue.

"*. . . King, Tutu and Boesak's reformism has been endorsed by the imperialists worldwide. Both King and Tutu received the Nobel Peace Prize for their efforts to restrict our liberation movements to nonviolent methods. However, their—*"

"Shut up!" Wessels shouted.

"*—timid political activity can only patch up a few of the more glaring injustices of their morally bankrupt societies. When the armed struggle is at low ebb, they condemn it outright, but when it intensifies and gathers mass support, they cry, 'Negotiate with us, or face them!' This is how they sell—*"

"Shut up! Shut up!" Wessels struck Skosana, slapping him with open palms on both sides of the face, like a man playing cymbals in an orchestra.

"Don't!" Myburgh stepped forward. But, as he knew it would, this heartfelt caution went unheeded.

Skosana, stung, gave Wessels a two-handed shove in the chest, knocking him into Goosen and Dedekind. Meanwhile, his steel plate continued to receive and transmit:

"*. . . revolutionary organizations like the Black Panther Party and the Dodge Revolutionary Union Movement (DRUM) in Detroit. It is this common history that unifies mass struggle in—*"

Recovering, Wessels jumped back at Skosana with a *sjambok* taken from the agent named Schoeman. His face as red and bloated as a rising sun, he lifted the flail with all the kinetic fury of Christ going after the money changers.

From his knees, Thubana cried, "He can't help it, you *tsotsi!* Give him back his cap!"

Goosen and Schoeman caught Wessels from behind.

"Not out here, Lieutenant," Goosen said, trembling excitedly. "Save it. You'll have your chance. All of us will."

Hyperventilating, Wessels resembled an inflatable, horror-show van der Merwe, an editorial cartoon of the Bad Afrikaner. Myburgh was simultaneously repulsed and fascinated. When Wessels finally gained control of himself, though, he saw the cap in his left hand and slapped it punishingly into Skosana's palm.

"Put it on!"

Glaring contempt, Skosana obeyed, rendering the broadcast from Zambia as thin and reedy as water trickling through the pipes in an adjoining hotel room.

Wessels appealed to Goosen: "Where did he get it? The major threw it away. I *know* he threw it away."

"He probably had the other half crimped up in a pocket," Goosen said. "That's all."

Myburgh bent down beside Thubana, gripped his elbow, put an arm around his waist, helped him stand.

"It's muddy just like the one Major Jeppe threw away," Wessels said. "He got it back somehow. The same way he got that coat."

"How was that?" said Dedekind, nervously cutting his eyes.

"That old black magic," Thubana whispered to Myburgh. "That I know so well."

Hearing Thubana quote from an old pop song, in a street next to security police headquarters, tickled Myburgh; against his will, he smiled.

"Go home," Thubana whispered. "It only gets worse now. Go on home, Mr. Myburgh."

"No!" Skosana said.

Wessels looked up as if Skosana had spit in his face. " 'No' is just what we *don't* want to hear, kaffir. We're in the business of manufacturing yeses."

"Come inside with us," Skosana said, speaking around Wessels to Myburgh.

"Never fear," Wessels said. "Steenkamp!"

A policeman came to grasp Thubana's arm. Myburgh tried to push him aside, to protect his own grip on Thubana, but his efforts only made Steenkamp stumble slightly. In fact, he glanced down at the street as if a stone or a bottle shard had tripped him, then went ahead and seized Thubana, incidentally brushing Myburgh's arm away as if it were less than a spider's thread.

"Come inside with us," Skosana said again. "And stay, please, with Mordecai. He's never been in before."

Wessels said, "Neither of you kaffirs will be lonesome—don't worry about that. And if your friend's never been in before, it's past time, isn't it?"

"Please," Skosana said. "Come inside."

Myburgh looked at the man pleading with him with such dignity. He looked at Thubana, and at the security police—Wessels & Company— whose eagerness to escort his two comrades upstairs seemed akin to that of small boys on Christmas. Packages to unwrap. New toys to break in.

"All right," he said.

Getting in was easy. Myburgh squeezed through the street-level door beside Thubana and struggled up through the echoey stairwell behind Skosana.

Each prisoner was bookended by a pair of security agents, who had handcuffed Thubana and Skosana before bringing them in. Didn't this mausoleum have elevators? If so, they weren't for detainees, even in the off-limits parts reserved for suspected terrorists and other enemies of the state. So let the kaffirs climb the stairs to their inevitable comeuppance.

Myburgh could not clearly account for his lack of sympathy for Goosen, Steenkamp, Dedekind, and Schoeman. (Wessels had left them on the first landing, perhaps to check in with Jeppe.) After all, he'd grown up with such men. Men somewhat like them, anyway—the sons of farmers on the properties bordering Huilbloom. Freckled, sunburnt, sandy-haired toughs with callused hands and hard-edged laughs.

Several times, in fact, as a teenager, he had ventured out as a balaclava man with these fellows. Everyone wore a hood and rode in Anton Smoot's tiny Renault, headlights off, to shoot out the streetlamps and robots—traffic lights—in the black areas near Nylstroom. They had carried real pistols (he and Kiewit juggled Papa Myburgh's Ruger back and forth) and real bullets. And, to this day, Kiewit held that on one outing they had shot a pair of meths-drinking Ndebele drunks along with the streetlamps. Myburgh's memory of these jaunts wasn't as clear as his brother's, nor could he see himself engaging in anything so wild and reckless today. But, once upon a time, he had definitely ridden balaclava. . . .

Jeppe, Wessels, Goosen, Steenkamp, Dedekind, Schoeman, and the others were just doing their jobs. A hard job. A necessary job, albeit a dirty one. And they weren't much applauded for the hard, dirty job they did. Folks didn't want to think about them. Just as a man—a city man, at least—putting away a juicy steak doesn't want to be told that the cow it came from died under the spattering thwack of a sledgehammer.

But Myburgh *did* know the reason for his animosity toward these men. Mordecai Thubana put roofs on houses and apartment buildings in the new white subdivisions in and around Pretoria; Skosana had paid for his crimes against the state long ago. They were kaffirs, sure, but neither of them belonged in this building. Myburgh knew that. A man who wanted to help the world's finest physicists come up with a Grand Unified Theory of Everything, and another who made his living loading snack foods onto trucks.

Such reprobates. Such traitors.

Stop worrying, Gerrit. Despite Thubana's fears *(It only gets worse now)*, Jeppe and his men will see their error once they've asked a few questions.

Of course they will. They *must.*

At the third or fourth landing (during his reverie, Myburgh had lost track), the slightly overweight Schoeman, breathing raggedly, asked Dedekind, the ranking agent, if they could rest a while. His request was granted, and Thubana and Skosana positioned themselves at a rail fronting a narrow window looking down on a graveled roof; there, a peeling billboard glistened.

Skosana nudged Myburgh. Read the billboard, his nudge and his lifted eyebrows commanded.

Myburgh studied the sign. It was one he recognized from other venues —street bills, newspaper ads, magazine inserts. It showed a bottle of laundry bleach, with a slogan next to it that struck him this morning with a new, almost brutal, forcefulness: JIK, it said. (A brand-name.) And under that: WITH CONTROLLED STRENGTH, FOR THE WORLD'S WHITEST WASH.

"Oh, Lord, I'm feeling sick," Skosana said, in a self-mocking lilt: "Here in the land of Jik."

Thubana said nothing. The sight of the billboard, along with his friend's doggerel, seemed to dispirit him. And Thubana's funk clouded Myburgh's efforts to regard the situation in an optimistic light. They were all in the land of Jik.

Must I keep on climbing these stairs? Myburgh wondered. Like Schoeman, he was winded. Trotting back down, after a short rest, seemed a more attractive option. At least, if he could get out again. Did the street-level door automatically lock? Did you have to have a key to go through it again?

Dedekind grabbed Skosana's arm. "That's it," he said. "Let's get moving."

Myburgh, unsure of whether he was a man or a ghost, hurried along after the others. He feared that if they reached an upper floor before he could squeeze through too, he would be trapped in this claustrophobic stairwell for days. . . .

On the fifth or sixth floor (again, Myburgh was unsure), Goosen and Steenkamp strong-armed Thubana in one direction, while Dedekind and Schoeman pulled Skosana the other. Skosana set himself against their tugging and told Myburgh, "Go with Mordecai, man."

"I said I would, didn't I?"

"Shut up, kaffir," Goosen said over Myburgh's unheard reply. "We know what we're doing."

Steenkamp revolved his eyes to indicate that Skosana was off in the head and that Goosen should ignore him. Myburgh followed the two security agents with Mordecai Thubana. Dedekind and Schoeman took Skosana the other way, off into the well-lit but nightmarish warren of the upper floor.

What happened from that moment on, Myburgh received as if in a dream—a protracted hallucination that perfectly complemented his selective invisibility. Much of this experience did not seem real at all, while much of it was so hurtfully vivid that he almost ran from it. All of it caromed past at fast-forward speeds impossible to slow, or at crazy angles defying his efforts to find in them a coherent pattern.

In an interrogation room off a pair of nichelike halls giving onto the floor's main corridor, Goosen, Steenkamp, and four more members of the security police—men Myburgh had not seen before—immediately began stripping Thubana.

They tore off his heavy, pilled sweater, revealing a light-gray T-shirt on which a complicated series of mathematical equations in red, blue, and yellow danced like thousands of printed footsteps on an impossible fox-trot diagram. A caption under all these symbols read, THIS EXPLAINS EVERYTHING.

As two men held Thubana's arms and two others stood by in case he resisted, Steenkamp grabbed the T-shirt at the neck and started to rip it away.

"*Pas op!*" Goosen shouted. Then: "You nincompoop, take it off carefully. Carefully."

"It stinks," Steenkamp said. "And it's"—he nodded at the math-symbol choreography—"nonsense."

"You don't know that, nor do I. Take it off carefully. Lay it over there."

Steenkamp obeyed, pushing Thubana's head forward, unrolling the T-shirt up his back, and spreading the T-shirt out on a metal desk in the corner. The six agents then hurried to strip Thubana of his rubber-soled *takkies*, pants, and baggy, tan undershorts.

"Stop that!" he cried, swatting at them. "Stop!"

Goosen cuffed him viciously. Soon, embarrassed and shivering, Thubana stood naked before them, his ribs touchingly prominent and his knobby-kneed legs like those of a muddy stork. Myburgh could tell at once that he hated this exposure, hated and resented it, even though he'd known from the start that this was the way things would go, for no African entering state custody as a crime suspect or as a political detainee could hope to come out unscathed, either physically or emotionally.

Even Myburgh knew that, but this morning, unable to intervene, he felt like a voyeur, a window peeper. It pained him that Thubana had to undergo not only the impersonal brutality of the policemen's attentions, but the added humiliation of having a third party (the agents were one obsessive entity) see his helplessness. But each time Myburgh turned aside or drifted to a different corner of the room, a ghost forsaking its haunts, he felt that he had given in to a cowardly squeamishness.

At last he turned to Thubana and said, "What can I do?"

Thubana's eyes fastened on him. "Don't look at me. But don't leave. That's all."

"We're not leaving," Goosen said, "but we'll look at you all we damned well please." (Lord, the pretty fellow was young!)

Myburgh started to speak, but stopped. He looked aside. Then he crossed to the desk upon which Steenkamp had spread Thubana's THIS EXPLAINS EVERYTHING T-shirt, collapsed into a metal folding chair, and averted his face from Thubana's interrogators.

Occasionally, of course, Myburgh *had* to look, for the sadistic imagination of the agents was a fertile one. In fact, to think of Goosen, Steenkamp, and their accomplices as state interrogators was to whitewash their activities. Call them, rather, torturers. They didn't just ask questions. They did all they could to shame, hurt, and dehumanize their ward without quite knocking him unconscious—unconsciousness would have interfered with their efforts to crowbar the "truth" out of him.

"Praat, praat, praat!" (Talk, talk, talk!), the six men yelled at Thubana.
"Op die stene" (On the bricks.), Goosen said.

They made him balance on a pair of bricks placed at contrasting slants on the floor, one brick about a meter behind the other, so that Thubana resembled a circus performer walking a tightrope. In addition, they slipped a yellowish latex hood over his head so that when he let out a breath, the hood ballooned obscenely, and, when he inhaled, he sucked the suffocating rubber back into his mouth and nostrils.

The way he swung his elbows, his wrists tied behind him, showed his terror, as did his muffled pleas to take off the hood. He made this plea whenever any opportunity to reply to the agents' stylized harassment arose—for, darting in and out, they were like hyenas worrying an injured springbok.

"Who prepared the car bomb at Armscor?"

"Who drove?"

"How did they get that *bakkie* past perimeter security?"

"Mpandhlani—your 'friend'—says you were a contact for the ANC guerrillas who planned the attack."

"Would you like to sire your own little *pikkenien* one day?"

"A statement, Mordecai. A statement!"

"List your contacts."

"Everything you did these past six months."

"The hiding places of your fellow terrorists."

"What do you know about ANC plans to decommission the Pretoria Dam?

"When did you first hear of them?"

"This hood is nothing. Nothing. Wait until you've got a noose around your neck, kaffir."

Seeing that brick-balancing and dogged verbal harassment were not doing the job, Goosen commanded a change in tactics. Steenkamp approached the desk and yanked the chair that Myburgh was sitting on out from under him. Myburgh only narrowly kept from splintering his tailbone. Steenkamp took the chair to Thubana (still trussed in that urine-hued cowl, a baby in a placental membrane), slammed it down, unbound Thubana's hands, and thrust the folding chair into them even as he was trying to rub the soreness from his wrists.

"Over your head," Goosen said.

"*What?*" To counteract the possibility of smothering, Thubana kept puffing against the latex.

"I said, lift the chair over your head. Lift it and hold it. If you let it down, you'll pay."

Major Henning Jeppe and Lieutenant Christiaan Wessels entered the little room. They grinned when they saw what was going on; two of the four men who had been assisting Goosen and Steenkamp clicked their heels, nodded deferentially, and left. Myburgh, rubbing his hip, backed into the corner behind the desk. He watched from this cubbyhole as if standing aloof from the agents' sins would absolve him of any complicity.

Thubana, when Steenkamp prodded him with a billy club, raised the open folding chair over his head. He held it by two legs, his elbows bent.

"All the way up, kaffir! *All the way!*"

Thubana strained, straightened his arms, and pushed the chair up as high as it would go. Its rounded back bumped the ceiling, and Thubana almost toppled from the bricks to which his feet awkwardly clung. As a warning, Steenkamp thrust his billy into the cleft of Thubana's buttocks and jiggled it.

"Hold the chair sideways! Arms up! Up!"

Thubana stuck his chin out, as if to allow more air under the latex cowl, struggled for a fresh grip on the chair, and lifted it as high as it would go in this new position, missing the ceiling and so maintaining his balance. He looked like a monument to the patron saint of contortionists.

"Good," Steenkamp said. "Good."

Jeppe caught sight of the T-shirt spread atop the desk and came over to look at it. Wessels, his enormous head bobbing first to this side and then to that, sought to keep an eye on Thubana as he swaggered over too. At Jeppe's bidding, he picked up the shirt, smoothed it out in front of him, then minced about clownishly, as if modeling it at a fashion show.

"Phew!" he said, sniffing the T-shirt.

"Be still," Jeppe said in Afrikaans. Then he read the English words under the run-amok equations: " 'This explains everything.' " He squinted. "Yes, I'd wager it does."

Then, to Thubana: "What is this, kaffir? What kind of treason did you come in here wearing?"

"What is what, sir?" Thubana was hooded and blind. Naked and off balance and straining to keep a chair aloft. Myburgh could not believe that Jeppe actually expected him to deduce the specifics of his moronic question.

"Your T-shirt, kaffir. These equations."

"That's a GUT, sir." His words were hard to make out, the hood muting and skewing them.

"A 'gut'?"

"Yes, sir. Or a TOE. A T-shirt TOE."

"Is it a 'gut' or a 'toe,' kaffir? Don't trifle with me today; I'm coming down with something."

"A Grand Unified Theory, sir. A Theory of Everything. Except that it . . . it isn't."

Steenkamp jabbed Thubana with his billy again, and Thubana had to lift one foot from its brick to keep from falling and to prevent his interrogators from assaulting him. Indeed, he would never have found the brick again if the policemen hadn't caught him and guided his wayward foot home.

Then, as if to show that this "kindness" had been provisional, Goosen used the end of his billy to lift and then lower Thubana's testicles. Again and again. Gently but menacingly.

"A 'gut,' a 'toe,' or neither, kaffir?" Jeppe said. "Explain to me these scribbles"—flapping the T-shirt—"you claim explain everything!"

"A T-shirt TOE," Thubana said. "A joke, my *baas*—just a joke."

Myburgh was disappointed. Until just now, Thubana had avoided using any kind of kowtowing epithet.

"A joke? How is it a joke?"

"There's no finished Theory of Everything yet, sir. So that's a . . . well, it's a just-pretend TOE."

"What does it *pretend* to mean?"

"Nothing, sir. Nothing real, at least."

Goosen lowered his billy, then rapped it upward into Thubana's groin so fast that Myburgh was not sure he had actually done it. The chair in Thubana's hands slipped and clattered down, striking both Goosen and another man; and Thubana, flailing one arm, toppled from the bricks, landed on his ribs, and rolled over like a man who hears gunfire on a busy street and tries to escape it. But Thubana could not escape.

"*Jy wil baklei, jy wil baklei?*" (You want to fight, you want to fight?) Goosen cried, wiping blood from his lip and dropping the billy. He hurried to a nearby file cabinet, removed a piece of green hosepipe whose tube glistened as if cored with glass dust or diamonds, and stalked back to Thubana. He began to pummel Thubana vigorously about the head and shoulders.

Thubana rolled from side to side under these blows and also the inescapable boots of Steenkamp and the two men whose names Myburgh still had not learned, for they stepped in and out to kick Thubana, like dancers in an intricate musical-comedy number.

"Stop it!" Myburgh shouted.

He rushed from his corner and grabbed Goosen's hosepipe on its backswing. But, after a brief hitch that made Goosen look back as if Wessels or even Jeppe were playing a trick on him, the hosepipe slipped from Myburgh's grasp and crashed down on Thubana's ear with a solid *whumpf!*

All Myburgh's subsequent efforts to deflect the hosepipe were failures, leaving burns in his palm but only imperceptibly delaying the adrenaline-charged policeman.

"Damn it, Goosen," Jeppe said, not even raising his voice. "Do you know what you're about?"

Goosen and the three other men backed off. Jeppe walked over to Thubana's huddled body, nudged him in the small of the back with his boot toe, and, letting the tail of the gray T-shirt dangle down mockingly on his shoulder, asked if he were now ready to explain—seriously explain —the formulae imprinted on it. Then, because he clearly wanted an audible reply, he yanked the hood off Thubana and flung it at Steenkamp.

"It's nothing, my *baas*," Thubana wheezed. "It only *looks like* it means something."

"Where did you get it?"

"I had it made. I designed it."

"Designed these equations?"

"Yes, sir." Thubana lowered his arms, sculled backward on his skinny, bruised rump, and propped himself against a wall.

"Who else has seen them?"

"Only a shopkeeper in Marabastad. I gave him the equations on a paper bag, sir. He silk-screened the shirt."

"What do they say?"

Thubana studied Jeppe with visible wariness, as if dealing with an idiot or a psychopath—an entire roomful of such creatures—and Myburgh suddenly feared that it was so.

"Gravity, electromagnetism, the strong force, the weak force."

"Pardon me?"

"A man in America—at Fermilab in Chicago—says the final TOE will fit on a T-shirt. It will be that simple."

"Fermilab?" Jeppe said.

"They have a particle accelerator there," Thubana said.

"Nuclear stuff," Wessels said. "Particle accelerators have to do with . . . you know, nuclear stuff."

Jeppe stiffened. He flapped the shirt out, grasped it by its sleeves, pulled it taut before him, surveyed its just-pretend TOE. "Decode this, kaffir."

"A big fish," Steenkamp said. "We've caught a big fish."

"A joke but not a joke," Thubana said. "One day I hope we have a Grand Unified Theory, a Theory of Everything, but today it's—" He stopped. "Today, my *baas*, it's only a dream."

"Explain!" Jeppe said.

When Thubana could not, they laid their bricks about two hand spans apart, prodded Thubana to remount them, forced him to hoist the chair aloft again, and walked around him like children around a maypole, asking questions and beating him with billies, hosepipes, their open hands. Although Steenkamp repeatedly slapped him across the buttocks with the hood, Myburgh noted that Thubana was doing a little better now: He could see the men tormenting him, he could breathe without fear of choking on rubber. . . .

Later, after beating Thubana again during an orgy of rushes and retreats, they pushed him into a shower just off the interrogation room and made him stand under a prickly spray of cold water. The pipes clanked noisily, and the shower head ratcheted like a Gatling gun. Typical. Tomorrow's building, yesterday's plumbing.

Myburgh accompanied Thubana to the shower room's threshold, but two security agents, there to make sure Thubana didn't duck out of the spray, kept him from coming nearer. So, like Thubana, he could do nothing but wait for the ordeal to end.

When Thubana finally did stumble out, his dark flesh appeared transparent: a fragile, oiled membrane of veins and welts, bruises and lacerations. It hurt to look at him.

"I'm cold," Thubana said. "Give me my clothes."

But they didn't. They returned him to the room in which they had administered the beating, sat him down at the desk, encircled him menacingly. But the cold shower, rather than melting his will, had undergirded it. Unflinching, he looked square into the eyes of each of the men leaning over him.

"Give me my clothes."

"Give us a statement," Jeppe said.

"How?" Thubana said. He lifted his dripping arms to show them the obvious: no writing materials.

At a nod from Jeppe, Goosen went to the file cabinet, pulled out several sheets of paper and a ballpoint pen, and returned with these items to the desk.

"A towel," Thubana said. "Or I'll ruin whatever I write."

Wessels disappeared into the room near the shower stall, banged around ill-temperedly, and returned with a towel.

A hand towel, not a bath towel.

But Thubana, grimacing, got up, patted down every part of his severely punished body, and, when no one asked for the towel back, spread it out on the seat of the lopsided chair and sat down on the damp cloth as if it were a cushion. He looked up at Jeppe and the others with a stare that the angry bulge next to one eyebrow made seem a hundred times more defiant and resentful.

"A statement," Jeppe said.

"Of what?"

"The full extent of your knowledge of and participation in the Armscor bombing. All you know about ANC plans to knock out the dam at Rietvlei. Plus a full—"

"I don't—"

"Quiet."

"But I'm not—"

"And a full breakdown of the *real* meanings behind those T-shirt 'equations.'"

Thubana hesitated. Then: "It will take some time."

"An hour."

"Two," Thubana said.

"An hour. If your statement is helpful but you haven't quite finished, *then* we'll give you more. Understand?"

"I think so."

Amazingly, they left Thubana alone in the interrogation room. They carried out their bricks, locked the file cabinet, blocked passage to the shower stall with a sliding metal grille, and set Steenkamp as a guard on the floor's main corridor. But they left Thubana alone to draw up a statement, his first respite from their badgering since coming into the building.

Myburgh sat down atop the desk, facing away from Thubana as he believed the other man wished. "Sometimes, it's impossible not to look, Mr. Thubana."

"That depends on who you are."

"What they did to you: terrible, barbaric. Mr. Thubana, it's only because—"

"Please be quiet. I must write."

Myburgh shut up, and Thubana began filling up the top sheet of white foolscap. For the next hour, the only sound in the room was the faint scritching of his ballpoint.

The statement was unsatisfactory. It denied any knowledge of the Armscor car bomb, it pretended not to have any awareness of the planned assault on the dam at Rietvlei, and it interpreted all the arcane mathematical symbols on Thubana's T-shirt as attempts (phony attempts) to unify the four major forces of the universe in a grand Theory of Everything. Besides which, this TOE presupposed that the most basic units of matter were not atoms but tiny, twitchy strings that had sprung into being only seconds after the Big Bang. There was nothing about the ANC, the APLA, or any other leftist-supported revolutionary group.

And so the statement was unacceptable.

Jeppe took Thubana's statement as a personal affront. Wessels acted as if Thubana had sodomized his grandmother.

Goosen, Steenkamp, Dedekind, Schoeman, and a group of men who seemed to live in closets on this floor (so readily did they pop out to do their commanders' bidding) assumed Thubana's questioning; soon enough, they had reduced Myburgh to impotent rage.

He learned the amusing names, and the sickening particulars, of four or five different "interrogation techniques." Although he tried to help, grabbing one or another of the security policemen by the collar and yanking backward with all his strength, he lacked the somatic specific gravity to do anything but strain his back or herniate himself, so that as Thubana screamed, he screamed, and as Thubana begged his tormentors to stop, please stop, Myburgh begged them too, and the "airplane," "Dr. Frankenstein," the "helicopter," and the "wet cap" rolled past him during that muzzy day like scenes from a half-dozen ineptly spliced horror movies.

"Bastards!" Myburgh cursed. *"Bastards!"*

When they were finished, and Thubana had told them nothing they wanted to hear (not even confessing that the symbol "E_8" in the book *Superstrings* was mathematical code for a cadre of terrorists in Mozambique, or that "Lie algebras" were a secret means of rating military-aid shipments from Red China), they dragged Thubana from the interrogation room and hurled him into an isolation cell—with bars, a lidless toilet, and a stiff, reed sleeping mat—on the same nightmarish floor.

"Animals!" Myburgh shouted, hobbling after them.

The cry reverberated in his own ears, but Jeppe & Company were infuriatingly deaf to it. Worse, they locked Thubana into the cell and handcuffed him to the lower part of its grille (so that he was unable to use his sleeping mat) without leaving Myburgh enough room to edge into it too. Invisible to his countrymen, Myburgh was one of them again. Thubana was locked up, but he was free. Except that he was a prisoner too, in the same building containing a cell that contained Thubana. Boxes inside boxes. Cages within cages. Bantustans within the Fatherland . . .

And then the security agents were gone, and Myburgh, clinging to the bars, was alone with Thubana.

"Go home," Thubana said. He didn't raise his head; he mumbled into the pit of his handcuffed arm.

"I can't."

Thubana moaned, heedless of the misery escaping him.

"Mr. Thubana, I don't think I can. I live, and move, but I don't"—Myburgh searched for the word—*"impinge* on anything. How can I get out of here?"

Thubana did not reply.

Myburgh got down on his knees. He put a hand through the bars and rubbed a finger over Thubana's woolly hair. Rivulets of blood had dried in the tiny gullies in this wool. The side of Thubana's face resembled an inner-tube strip with an infestation of polyplike heat blisters. Myburgh wiped his eyes with a coat sleeve.

"Mr. Thubana—"

"Go home."

"I—"

Thubana lifted his head. His face called up images from battle photography and traffic-safety films. Was the poor man a member of a Faking Club . . . ?

"Try," Thubana said. "You must . . . *try.*"

Myburgh pulled himself up, backed away, and wandered through the maze of the upper floor.

Eventually, he located the door to a stairwell, pulled it open, and went through into a shaft as cold and forbidding as a mine stope. There were fluorescents on each landing, and the window overlooking the billboard proclaiming the "controlled strength" of Jik gleamed under anemic spotlights. It was night, the tag end of an endless day.

He went down, all the way down, and paused at the street-level door, expecting failure. His success at barging into the stairwell and coming down the steps was a fluke of physics. By all rights, he should have no more impact on the physical structures of this building than a shade—for he *was* a shade, a man-shaped confluence of shadow matter.

Myburgh gripped the push bar on the door. He pushed down on it. It resisted. It resisted as if it understood that his was a conjectural, a ghostly, pressure.

Myburgh examined his hands. The palms were still raw from his attempts to wrest the hosepipe from Goosen. If the hosepipe could do that to him, it seemed logical—in an inevitably symmetrical way—that he could exert some influence on the sort of matter that had scalded him. Tit for tat.

He pushed down again.

Surprise. This time the bar depressed, clicking open the door to which it was attached.

Myburgh stumbled outside, one hand still on the bar.

Traffic noises assailed him.

The air was brisk and somewhat damp-feeling, but an astonished glance at the sky, between the inward-leaning tops of the security police building and the office building opposite it, showed him an indigo road of stars. If you squinted, if you put your imagination into gear, you could believe that out there beyond those twinkling points of fire vibrated—majestically—a cosmic string light-years in length tying this very moment to the instant of creation. That string would be a stretched remnant of a tiny superstring that had blown clear of the Big Bang and escaped into the cosmos. It would be proof that everything on hand in the universe today had exploded from the same blazing Ur-furnace.

Or so Thubana believed. And so he had told Myburgh and Skosana on their not-so-smooth nylon ride into Pretoria.

Christ. Such thoughts.

It would take an hour to walk home from here, Myburgh decided. Or he could walk to Church's Square and catch public transport to his condominium. If no one could see him, he wouldn't even have to pay the bus driver. . . .

The clap on that. Thubana was upstairs, naked and suffering. And if Myburgh stepped outside, letting go of this door, it would lock behind him. He could tug on it all he liked; it would never budge, no matter how strong his will, how mighty his arms. This door locked on people who were *not* shadow matter, and it would hold Myburgh out even if he rematerialized as a visible Afrikaner, with a thousand questions for Major Henning Jeppe.

So he went back in, let go of the push bar, and trudged back up the six flights of steps to Thubana.

Myburgh took off his coat, pushed it between the bars, spread it over Thubana's shoulders and back. He straightened it as well as he could so that only Thubana's legs and part of his handcuffed arm remained uncovered.

Then Myburgh curled up on the floor beside the comatose man and fumbled toward sleep.

In his dream, he was driving a bus—not a municipal bus, but a Putco bus like the one Kabini drove from KwaNdebele every morning and back again every night. His riders were plainclothes security policemen from this very building; the bus was packed with them—Jeppe, Wessels, Goosen, Steenkamp, and maybe ninety more, every one standing or sitting ramrod straight as Myburgh drove them through a teeming closer settlement.

The streets were unpaved and dusty. Angry blacks—many armed with rocks, many shaking their fists, some determined enough to leap in front of the bus and spit at the bus's windshield—crowded in so grimly that it was hard to keep going. Either Myburgh could slow to a walk, letting more and more blacks approach the bus, lay hands on it, and rock it back and forth until it turned over; or he could jam the accelerator, wrestle the steering wheel, and harvest these agitated people like corn.

There seemed to be no other options, only death for his riders or blatant, cold-blooded vehicular homicide. He might have been able to resign himself to the first option if it had not required his own death. He might have been able to adjust to the second one if his passengers had not been Jeppe & Company.

Soon, Myburgh was crying as he drove. He could not tell if his watery vision stemmed from his own frustrated tears or the dripping spittle on his windshield. He beeped his horn. He beeped it and beeped it. A rock shattered the windscreen, giving it the look of a weird, puzzle-piece spiderweb. His passengers—outwardly calm—began sticking handguns through their windows and firing into the streets as if the closer settlement were a huge shooting gallery. Each time a black fell dead or wounded, a bell rang (Myburgh didn't know from where), and Jeppe, sitting behind him, got up to reward the sharpshooter with a licorice whip or a stuffed animal: hyena, giraffe, ant bear, elephant. Jeppe extracted these animals from a duffel under his seat, and their supply, like that of the shouting Africans, seemed endless.

Then a bomb exploded in the road, a bomb made out of a knot of blacks banished from South Africa's cities. When it went off, body parts and clothing scraps flew up into the sky. (Suddenly, it was night. The Coalsack nebula, near the Jewel Box cluster, opened up like a hungry pit.) Myburgh tumbled into the whirlpools created by the explosion. Not knowing what else to do, he grabbed the strands of the puzzle-piece web in his windscreen and pulled himself along them to its center.

When absolutely clear of the driver's cage, Myburgh looked down and saw his bus on fire, five or six kilometers below. Meanwhile, the strands of the web in which he was swinging—it was a hammock now, a hammock attached to the four stars of the Southern Cross—started reeling at high speed, as if a vacuum cleaner light-years away were cracking him apart atom by atom and sucking him into its bag. It wanted him and his galaxy-sized fears to fly into the bag without tearing it. Myburgh turned over in the hammock, clutching at its lengthening, ever-thinning strings.

The hole of the Coalsack (Kiewit had always called it the Soot Bag) got bigger and bigger. It was like a black widow; no, a black *window*. And what Myburgh saw through it was the body of a stuffed elephant, slowly tumbling. A minute ago, it had been in the lap of one of Jeppe's boys, a prize for marksmanship. Now the beast was growing at the same high speed as the Coalsack, and he could see that no matter what he did, he was going to hit it, and hitting the elephant (a doddering bull with fractured tusks, *not* a stuffed toy) would probably destroy him. . . .

"*Wake up, man. Wake up.*"

Myburgh roused; his nightmare had disoriented him. Then he saw Wessels—a.k.a. Pampoenkop—glowering down on him, and he began to suspect that his real nightmare was about to start. It seemed that Wessels could see him.

"Who are you? What are you doing here?"

Myburgh blinked. Wessels's head—its size, its slanted brows, its crooked teeth, its mounded chins—*did* resemble a pumpkin. Was it rational to fear a talking jack-o'-lantern?

"Answer me, please."

"What time is it?" Myburgh said in Afrikaans. (Wait. He had a watch. He checked it: 3:45 A.M.)

"Time you answered me," Wessels said. "You're up to your chin, brother-man."

Myburgh did not stand. He rolled over and scooted up against Thubana's cell. Thubana was asleep or comatose. In sleep, he had dislodged Myburgh's coat, exposing most of his back.

"You can see me," Myburgh said.

"I'm not blind. How did you get in?"

Myburgh shook his head to clear it of some confusing images and swallowed to make his ears pop. His left foot stuck out toward the policeman like a big, mottled sausage. Wessels aimed a kick at it, and the back of Myburgh's head banged metal.

A warning. Only a warning.

"I am Gerrit Myburgh, a special-accounts executive at Jacobus and Roux. On the road back from Huilbloom, our family farm, I had an accident. I've come here to report it."

"You need the city police, Meneer Myburgh."

"My accident occurred in the country."

"You are still in the wrong place. This is the special branch, Meneer Myburgh. You have no business here."

Myburgh nodded at Thubana. "That man has clearly been through hell. Why is he naked?"

"Did you give him that coat?"

"He looked cold. He still looks cold."

Wessels was trying hard not to erupt. Maybe he suspected that Myburgh was a member of some kind of governmental Faking Club, sent out to test the humanity of security agents.

Finally, Wessels allowed the dam to burst: "You are a foolish goddamned *kaffirboetie*, Meneer Myburgh."

"This man needs medical attention."

"You have many questions to answer. Stand up, please, and come with me."

Myburgh stared insolently at Wessels. He massaged the sole of his naked foot. Perhaps it would have been better to remain shadow matter to his compatriots until he had thought of a way to rescue—if that were possible—both himself and the two innocent Africans now in custody.

"You gave him a coat," Wessels said. "Maybe you gave him other things as well? Instructions, for example?"

"Telephone my brother. Telephone my superiors at Jacobus and Roux. Dozens of people can vouch for me."

"At this hour?" Wessels turned and called down the corridor to an office seemingly kilometers away: "Major van Rhyn. Major van Rhyn, we have a problem."

Major W. K. van Rhyn worked on him all that morning. Wessels assisted, and it was a relief—a surprise and a relief—that they only questioned him. The wallet from inside his jacket (which an unseen policeman brought to van Rhyn's office from Thubana's cell) contained materials identifying Myburgh.

Then a plainsclothes agent named Lieutenant Cuyler came in to report that the South African Police had found a Cadillac stalled on the KwaNdebele Road. The car was badly banged up. Plates and serial numbers proved, though, that it belonged to one Gerrit Jozua Myburgh of Pretoria.

"I hit an elephant," Myburgh said.

"Meneer Myburgh," van Rhyn said, shaking his head.

Cuyler came to Myburgh's aid: "That may be true, sir."

"How?" van Rhyn said.

"A Colored from Durban has a fleabite circus: Motilal Prassad's Travelling Big Top. He carts it around to the Bantustans and makes a few rand entertaining the stay-behinds while their wage-earners are at work. Three days ago, he was in Bophusthatswana. Seems he lost an elephant there."

"I found it," Myburgh said. "I hit it."

"Not unlikely," Cuyler told van Rhyn.

"What happened to it?"

Both van Rhyn and Cuyler looked at Myburgh as if he had asked a very troublesome question.

"What happened to it?" Myburgh said again.

"We don't know," Cuyler said. "It disappeared."

"An elephant?" van Rhyn said. "To where?"

"If we knew, we wouldn't be saying it's disappeared. Maybe to the proverbial elephants' graveyard."

Myburgh wondered if his Cadillac's collision with the elephant had rendered it shadow matter, a kind of premonitory ghost from an era and a system long since doomed to perish.

But he had no time to mull the issue, for Cuyler had to leave, and van Rhyn and Wessels began questioning him relentlessly. What did he know about the Armscor bombing? About ANC plans to sabotage the Rietvlei dam? Questions that Jeppe and his henchmen had already put repeatedly to Mordecai Thubana.

Myburgh replied to all these questions in the negative (for he knew nothing, nothing at all), but he was also careful to tell his interrogators what an outrage his detention was and how deeply he resented the slanders implicit in their questions. He was a decent Afrikaner, a patriotic Vaalpens. They should ring up his brother Kiewit. Or the manager of his condominium. Or his secretary, Pia Delfos.

On the other hand, he railed at van Rhyn, what could he expect of a group of officers who had beaten one of their charges within a fingernail of his life and left him naked in a cold cell? The sort of men who would deny an injured countryman medical help? The sort who would bully that countryman with stupid innuendos about treason and terrorist collaboration?

"What we do," said van Rhyn coldly, "we do to protect."

Van Rhyn went off duty. Myburgh sat in van Rhyn's office, all alone, for a long time. Exactly how long he couldn't say, for Wessels had taken his watch—plus his keys and pocket change—and retreated to another part of the building.

Longer than an hour, though. Possibly two.

When Major Jeppe came on duty (whey-faced, thin, and struggling with the sniffles and watery eyes), he spoke with Cuyler, Wessels, and one or two others.

Then he left too, and Myburgh was escorted to a holding room where he stewed for another two or three hours, growing more and more frustrated and impatient.

Why the delay? Did they really think him an ANC collaborator? Apparently, they did. For that reason, they had not released him. For that reason, they had done nothing to see about his cuts or to replace his tattered clothes. Section Six of the Terrorism Act—that was the inappropriate statute they were using to detain him.

At last, Jeppe came back. Goosen, Steenkamp, and Schoeman came with him, and these four men surrounded the table at which Myburgh was slumped.

"How did you get to Pretoria from your wreck?" Jeppe said.

"I walked," Myburgh said. (A lie, but better than admitting the hard-to-swallow truth.)

"How did you get into the building?"

"Through a street-level door."

"Except for our entrance on the park, our street-level doors are all locked, Meneer Myburgh."

"Not the one I used."

The four men stared at him as if they had reached an impasse; obviously, they had.

"If I can't go home," Myburgh said, "I want some clean clothes and something to eat."

They brought him a plate of food: sausages, rice, and a poached egg. They also brought him a pair of corduroy trousers, a flannel shirt, some heavy brown socks, and a pair of *takkies* that looked as if they had been bleached. Myburgh suspected that this outfit—except for the store-bought socks—had once belonged to a black man detained for political reasons. Where was that man now? In a jail cell? In a township cemetery? In the *bundu*, hiding?

"The man I gave my coat to," Myburgh said: "He needs clothes and food too. And medical attention."

"*Kaffirboetie*," Goosen said, turning away.

"How do you happen to know him?" Jeppe said.

"I came up the stairs, onto this floor, and I saw him naked and unconscious in that cell down there." He nodded vaguely.

"The man's a terrorist," Jeppe said. "You want nothing to do with him. Nothing. Leave him to us."

When Myburgh finished eating, only Jeppe and Goosen were still in the interrogation room with him. Goosen cleared his plate away, returned, and laid the book *Superstrings* on the table exactly where the plate had been.

"What do you know about this?" Jeppe said. "The man you saw up here was carrying it when we captured him."

"Why should I know anything about it?"

"We had a tip, Meneer Myburgh. Our informant told us to take a man or two off a commuter bus from KwaNdebele."

"So?"

"Major van Rhyn's report says you had your accident—hitting that elephant—on the same stretch of road."

Physically, Myburgh felt better, his hunger satisfied and his bruised body clad in snug, warm clothes. But now that Jeppe had made the connection between his wreck on the KwaNdebele Road and the stopping of *Grim Boy's Toe* several miles beyond that roadblock, Myburgh feared that maybe these single-minded men were determined to link him to the same absurd scenario to which they had already linked Thubana and Skosana. If that happened—if they succeeded—his comfortable station in life would evaporate like mist and only his brother Kiewit, a lukewarm friend or two, and some of his more appreciative clients would care at all. He would vanish forever, a statistic of the state of emergency.

"Coincidence," Myburgh said uneasily.

"You've never read this book?"

"No. Why?"

"Certain passages are underlined. We thought you could help us explain their encoded meanings."

"I'm a financial advisor, not a cryptologist."

"But if you were also a traitor and spy?" Jeppe said, smiling. Abruptly, he shouted: "Steenkamp!"

Steenkamp came into the room with Thubana's T-shirt. He spread it out on the table next to the book.

"And this?" Jeppe said. "What about this?"

At that moment, Myburgh heard the familiar staticky tinniness of a resistance radio broadcast: "*. . . and the Ten Point Program of the Unity Movement put forward in 1943. This advance reflected the awakening of the people and departed from a liberal democratic program by posing the issue of the 'Land to the Tiller' as being of paramount . . .*"

Jeppe stood up. "Not again." He went from the room, followed closely by Goosen and Schoeman. Steenkamp remained behind to guard both Myburgh and the seditious T-shirt TOE.

"*. . . only one meaning amongst scientific socialists: seizure without compensation. Lenin in his Agrarian Program repeated this point again and again to distinguish it from . . .*"

"Skosana," Myburgh whispered.

Over the staticky lecture, a scream: "MORDECAI-I-I-I-I!"

Myburgh stood up. Steenkamp laid a hand on his shoulder and pushed him back down.

"MORDECAI-I-I-I-I!"

Christ, what was going on? He could hear (over both the radio broadcast and Skosana's screaming) the sounds of scuffling, grunts, billy clubs clattering, metal bars gonging.

"Steenkamp!" someone yelled. "Steenkamp, get out here!"

"Stay put," Steenkamp said. He slipped around Myburgh's chair, darted into the hall like a soccer wingman.

The uproar went on: shortwave screeches, screams, the muddled warring of iron and wood and boot leather. Myburgh's heart pounded like a machine press stamping out badges. He told himself to obey Steenkamp's warning and stay put, but when the hubbub persisted and no one returned to check on him, he crept to the door.

"*Mordecai-i-i-i-i . . . !*"

Six or seven men at the far end of the corridor were wrestling Winston Skosana around its dogleg, hurrying to get him out of sight and hearing. Myburgh could still hear him calling Thubana's first name, but with less and less energy.

Then the long hall was empty: a bright tunnel of plasterboard, tilework, and staggered, ceiling-mounted smoke detectors. Myburgh could not believe the feeling he had. As if he had become shadow matter again, an invisible man in the near-invisible empery of the security police.

In his bleached *takkies,* Myburgh hobbled down the hall. Past van Rhyn's office. Past a pair of closed—what?—storage rooms? Past a lavatory, another shakedown room, and two vertical strips of chrome suggesting that this end of the hall had a purpose different from that of the end he had just left, namely, imprisoning people who knew things that the state needed to know. And then, suddenly, Myburgh was at Thubana's cell again.

Thubana's naked feet hung half a meter off the floor. His body twisted from a light fixture in a noose made from a cracked leather belt.

Thubana's belt was his only article of clothing. Why? Myburgh wondered. A man with no pants didn't need a belt.

Jeppe, blowing his nose into a handkerchief, marched around the corner with Goosen, Steenkamp, and Schoeman. When he saw Myburgh standing outside Thubana's cell, he cursed, waved his handkerchief, and piped congestedly, "Get him!"

Before Myburgh could react, Goosen ran at him in a dutiful fury and flattened him with an expertly swung elbow. Steenkamp kicked him in the ribs. Goosen gave him an exasperated conk as he sought to roll away, for Myburgh was writhing—involuntarily from the pain and calculatedly to avoid further blows.

"Enough!" Jeppe cried.

Myburgh lay under the security men's feet. There was blood on his clean flannel shirt. This angered him all out of proportion to the shirt's value. Maybe because Thubana was dangling in his cell from his own belt.

"You murdered him," Myburgh said.

"A lot of them commit suicide," Jeppe said. "He's just another god-damned kaffir who took the easy way out."

"Where did he get the belt?"

"Perhaps his friend slipped it to him."

"When? You confiscated their belts, didn't you?"

Jeppe paused in his niggling attentions to his nose. "How did you know that?"

Myburgh hesitated. "A deduction. Procedure, isn't it? Aren't you sup-posed to take their belts?"

"Procedures vary." Jeppe's voice was as unforthcoming as that of a veteran government spokesman.

"You murdered him," Myburgh said again.

Goosen cocked his billy threateningly.

"Don't," Jeppe told Goosen. "Get him back down the hall. He never should have been out here."

"That wasn't my—"

"Shut up."

"I'm bleeding," Myburgh said. "These men assaulted me."

"A cut from your automobile accident," Jeppe said.

"It's a cut I received when that swine there tried to—"

"From your accident. From hitting Motalil Prassad's runaway elephant. Please remember that."

Myburgh was afraid to contradict Jeppe, who should have been at home, taking antihistamines and drinking healthful juices. More or less passively, Myburgh returned to the interrogation room in which Steen-kamp had so precipitously abandoned him.

This time, Jeppe had Goosen stand watch. Myburgh studied his guard. Goosen was late twenties or early thirties, a dark-haired fellow who would have been handsome if his eyes hadn't carried in them a perpetual look of unfocused shock, as if almost everything about life offended him. He was hair-trigger, a grenade with the pin pulled.

Or he gave that impression. Maybe it was the job. Maybe he had a wife and babies at home. Or maybe he had the job because something can-kered and peeling in him had pointed him to it, and maybe he *still* had a wife and babies at home. So far as Myburgh knew, there was no law on the books against borderline psychopaths marrying and raising fami-lies. . . .

Oddly, Myburgh felt fairly safe with the boy. Jeppe was going to let him go. Or else why caution him to remember that the cut on his head had come from an automobile accident, not the attentions of this duty-conscious pretty boy? Something—something beyond the barbarous lynching of Thubana—had happened, and so Jeppe & Company were on the brink of releasing him.

"What's your name?"

Goosen looked at him with stupidly snobbish disdain. "Maybe I don't care to tell you."

"I know your family name. What's your Christian name?"

"All you need to know is Warrant Officer Goosen."

"You look like"—Myburgh pretended to consider possibilities—"a Hans, I think."

Goosen was insulted. "Not a Hans. A Hugo. And you're to keep your mouth shut."

"A while ago you wanted me to talk."

A glint of smug cunning sparked from Goosen's eyes. "You have a statement to make?"

"Where did the hanged man's belt come from?"

"You heard Major Jeppe. That other kaffir, probably."

"From you, far more probably. Or from Wessels, or Steenkamp, or Schoeman."

Goosen merely smiled. "Oh, Meneer Myburgh."

"I think the 'other kaffir' told you his friend had nothing to do with the matters you were investigating."

"Why don't you shut up?" Goosen said, leaning across the table; his breath reeked of cream cheese and beer.

Myburgh ignored the smell: "But you gentlemen had done such lovely hosepipe work on the man it would have been awkward to let him go."

"Such a mind. What a detective. You should join the special branch yourself."

"So you found his belt. And gave it to him. To help him hold up his apendectomy scar, I suppose."

Goosen's brow furrowed. "He had no appendectomy scar."

"No, but you people hanged him naked, anyway. And with his own belt too."

Goosen went to the room's file cabinet. Did he plan to take a hosepipe from it?

Wham! Wham!

He kicked the file cabinet, then turned back to Myburgh with comets in his eyes, the red and yellow fallout of Voortrekker Day sparklers. The pupils shining inside these fireworks were those of a man high on his own ill-suppressed rage.

"You'd better stop, brother-man. You'd better just stop!"

"All right, Warrant Officer Goosen. All right." Myburgh held up his hands placatingly.

Given everything that had happened, maybe the best course *was* to keep his mouth shut. To refrain from antagonizing Major Jeppe, Warrant Officer Goosen, and all the other high-strung men of the special branch. To maintain his composure. And, maybe hardest of all, simply to bide his time.

He had not guessed wrong; they were releasing him. Lieutenant Cuyler, according to Major Jeppe, had done some telephoning and had learned that Myburgh was a clean case. Each reference, though, had needed cross-checking and confirmation. That was why, regrettably, they had held him so long.

"Not because you thought me a terrorist?" Myburgh said.

Jeppe swallowed a cold tablet with a gulp of water. "It isn't often that a man who hits an elephant on the KwaNdebele Road comes into our building to report it."

A tactful way of confessing that they had grilled him because they had been suspicious of him. Thank God they hadn't subjected him to the "refrigerator," the "airplane," "Dr. Frankenstein," the "marionette," and so on. Thank God.

Without warning, Jeppe started. "Meneer Myburgh! Where the hell did you go?" He dropped his glass and looked around the room as if Myburgh had left it. His glass, meanwhile, broke on the floor into a nebula of scattershot shards and chips.

"I'm right here."

Jeppe recovered. "Ah, yes, *there.* You faded out on me. It's this cold, I guess. My vision's bollixed. My head aches. My nose feels like a cherry pepper."

"You should go home," Myburgh said.

But he was frightened. It wasn't Jeppe's cold that had caused him to fade; it was a brief reversion to shadow matter, the result of his again beginning to view things—a little, at least—from the pedestrian focus of Henning Jeppe. He had to cling to Thubana. If he did not, this entire nightmare would cease to signify.

"I *should* go home," Jeppe said. "And so I will. Allow me to drive you to your own place, Meneer Myburgh."

"I can't. It wouldn't—"

"The least I can do. For all the nasty inconvenience."

In the end, Myburgh permitted Jeppe to chauffeur him along the tree-lined boulevards of Pretoria, past the monuments and parks and museums, to his condominium. A good ride. Last week's clouds were only memories. The blue Transvaal sky—a dome of fragile porcelain—made him forget that it was winter, that the jacarandas would not blossom for another three months. Even Jeppe's reminders not to speak of anything that had happened during his confinement seemed benign and sensible, for Myburgh had the odd feeling that his life was beginning anew.

Back in his apartment, hanging his dry-cleaned but ruined suit in a closet, he realized that he had bought his mellow spirits with counterfeit coin. Thubana was dead, the victim of men hostile to the quixotic Grand Unified Theory toward which he had so touchingly—but ineffectively—pointed his dreams.

And Thubana, dead, was a living rebuke.

The dressing mirror on Myburgh's closet door gave back an image that modulated in and out of visibility like the picture on a snow-afflicted TV set. He was there, then he wasn't. He wasn't there, then he was. The degree of reality he had was contingent on forces over which he had no direct control.

Or, at least, so it seemed at the moment.

Myburgh crossed his arms in front of his chest and clutched his shoulders. Stay put, he told himself; stay put. Arms crossed, he walked into his apartment's living room—a studio decorated with opera posters, ferns, an aquarium with Chinese carp, and a wall of books, few of which he had opened since taking his degree from the University of Pretoria nearly twenty years ago. Today, his reading was almost all business related, with a smattering of international news to keep him abreast of fluctuating trends, and he did the bulk of it in his office at Jacobus & Roux.

Thubana was at the fish tank tapping nutritional dandruff out of a colorful box onto the water for Myburgh's starving carp. The fish rose in pairs or trios, hit at the scaly food, then splashed away through the bottle-green water to allow another greedy pair or threesome to surface and feed.

—They're hungry, Thubana said. —You were gone a long time, Mr. Myburgh.

—I left a key with the manager, Myburgh said. —He promised to take care of them for me.

—It appears he forgot.

Thubana looked exactly as he had hanging in his cell on the top floor of security police headquarters: naked, bruised, grotesquely cinched at the throat with his confiscated belt. Here, though, his body was relaxed, his manner courteous. The end of his belt hung straight down his chest like a tie instead of twisting stiffly away in a makeshift noose. Under the glances of Jeppe & Company, he had been humiliated. Here, he was at ease with his nakedness, relieved that an insufferable ordeal was over.

—Let me get you a robe. You must be cold.

—It's all right, Mr. Myburgh. I can't stay.

—No trouble, no trouble.

Myburgh returned to his closet (dismayed to find that there was nothing in the full-length mirror on its door but the framed poster for *Die Götterdämmerung* opposite it), rummaged distractedly among his hangups for a dressing gown, found one, and returned to Thubana with it. Thubana protested mildly, but at last took the gown and put it on—more to ease Myburgh's embarrassment, Myburgh felt, than to satisfy propriety or to defeat the cold. Now, he looked a great deal like a lanky prizefighter, the undaunted loser of a bout with the world title holder.

—What are you doing here? Myburgh said.

—I must tell you something.

—Out with it, then.

—The challenge is to write one set of equations that will prove the four known basic forces to be separate showings of one even more basic force.

—You told me that on *Grim Boy's Toe*.

—Reminders are necessary, I think. People keep forgetting how important this challenge is.

Myburgh raised and dropped his arms. —You're not really here, Mr. Thubana. Maybe I'm not either.

Thubana ignored this. —Another thing.

—What?

—Someone narked on Winston.

—"Narked"? Do you mean that Skosana was actually involved in the Armscor bombing?

—Could be. Could be.

—I thought he was innocent, a victim.

—Few of us are innocent, Mr. Myburgh. Many are victims.

—A man who plants bombs, or who protects people who do, isn't a victim. He's a perpetrator.

Thubana, hands in pockets, shook his head disappointedly.

—Violence sickens me, Myburgh insisted.

—Sometimes it does. Sometimes. But Winston had a steel plate in his head. It broadcast to him almost continuously. The buzzing of one's own bones is hard to set aside.

—I imagine it is.

—Another thing I wanted to tell you, Mr. Myburgh: Informers are everywhere.

—Who? Do you know who it was?

—Of course. It came to me while helicoptering under the blows of Pampoenkop and his goons.

—Tell me.

Thubana told.

It was still daylight. Lightning bird (called by the Ndebele of Sebetiela *māsianoke a selwana* and by Afrikaners the *hammerkop*) had done his work; he had brought the highveld rain. The coming summer drought would be easier to bear for his help in July. Now, though, the winter sun shone to the north again, and the people of Pretoria were enjoying both the freshness of the air and the brisk high rage of that rapidly westering sun.

In the same clothes he had worn home from police headquarters, Myburgh went downstairs and hailed a cab. The driver was a young Afrikaner who had probably never heard of the *hammerkop*. Myburgh felt an irrational resentment toward him even as the young man let him in and turned to receive his destination. (Or not irrational, Myburgh thought. Misplaced.)

"Marabastad," he said.

"Are you sure? I don't carry many of our kind there."

"Do you carry any?"

"Yes, sir. Now and again."

"Good. I'm another. Please take me there."

"This is the rush hour. It'll be slow going."

Myburgh showed the cabbie a handful of rand notes. "More talk, young man, and it will affect my tip."

"Yes, sir. Where in Marabastad?"

"Belle Ombre station."

The cabbie started to speak again (Myburgh could see him in the rearview), but changed his mind and slid the cab into gear.

Because of traffic, the trip needed twenty minutes. During it, Myburgh recalled his final moment with Thubana: Nodding good-bye, Thubana had ascended through his apartment's ceiling and beyond, carrying with him both Myburgh's dressing gown and the self-pitying edges of his funk. Now, Belle Ombre station—a kind of soaring, concrete circus tent with attractive parterres and geometries of structural piping painted red, yellow, blue, and green—loomed out of the old Asian enclave like a Transvaaler's Disneyworld.

This was the depot from which the architects of the homeland solution accepted the black "foreigners" from Bophuthatswana and KwaNdebele as day laborers, and from which they expelled them again every night. Bullet trains were the key both to white autonomy and economic self-sufficiency, and this afternoon, almost in spite of himself, Myburgh found himself admiring the sleek, high-tech trains that state planners had commissioned, and bought, to put their dear and preposterous scheme into action.

Unfortunately, not all the high-speed rail lines necessary to make this solution work were operating yet, and to make sure that no "foreigner" spent the night in the city, Putco had to continue to send commuter buses to KwaNdebele and some of the more distant corners of Bophuthatswana.

It was these grime-encrusted buses, not the sexy trains, that Myburgh had come to Belle Ombre to find; and when he saw the ramps leading to the passenger docks, he made his driver stop, gave him both his fare and an extravagant tip, and stepped out among milling armies of weary blacks, who looked at him (if they looked at him at all) with glazed, preoccupied eyes.

A ghostly twilight had begun to draw down.

What business did the white *baas* have here? His clothes didn't identify him as a policeman, nor did they say that he was well off enough to be a bullet-train official or a Putco executive. He was, in fact, an intruder, and Myburgh became more and more aware of his status as an intruder the deeper into the crowd he walked, hurrying to reach Thubana's bus before it filled and left for various closer settlements on its route to the Wolverkraal depot, three hours out of Marabastad.

"Bus four-nine-six," he said, stopping a woman wearing a heavy, unbuttoned coat over a maid's uniform. She merely stared. He said the same thing in English, and she gave him an I-couldn't-tell-you shrug. Not hostile; indifferent.

He let her go, blundered on, asked others, got blank stares or confessions of ignorance, and finally approached a uniformed white policeman who wanted to know where he was going and why. Didn't he know that, at this hour, Belle Ombre was no place for casual sight-seeing? Above the shuffling crowd, speakers piped a Mantovani-ized arrangement of the old Petula Clark hit "Downtown."

Myburgh, putting his face in the policeman's, explained that he had come to scold a Ndebele roofer for the shoddy work he had done on a Sunnyside housing project. The man had to return tomorrow and repair his labor, or he would forfeit his pay and any future chance to roof in the city's white subdivisions.

"What bus is he riding, then?"

"Number four-nine-six," Myburgh said.

The policeman sighed, as if being asked to find a diamond on a floor strewn with broken glass.

"It has a name too," Myburgh said: *"Grim Boy's Toe."*

The policeman nodded. "Ah, yes, I know it."

"You know it?"

"Of course. They're not allowed names. Commercial buses with one-time passengers, yes. But not state-subsidized commuter buses run by good old Putco."

"No? Why not?"

"Names on state-subsidized buses are disrespectful. *Grim Boy's Toe,* for instance. Who'd want to ride that?"

Myburgh thought that even if it were called *Bali Hi Express,* he wouldn't be pleased to ride it again (not so far as the Wolverkraal depot, anyway), but he bit his tongue.

"Over that way," the policeman said, pointing across one of the esplanades to a down-sloping ramp. "Driver's busy trying to bring his bus in line with Putco policy."

"This way?" Myburgh said, already walking.

"Yes, sir. Right on over."

Myburgh jogged across the esplanade. He found another nexus of ramps, looked around, selected the one he thought the policeman had meant, and, breathing raspily, jogged down it to the loading dock. People had not yet begun to queue here. Myburgh relaxed a little. He was no longer in a crowd, and Ernest Kabini was standing next to his bus.

A closer look: Kabini was holding a small can of blue enamel and painting out the legend that had personalized number 496 for Myburgh on the drizzly highveld.

"Stop!" he cried.

Kabini glanced up at the white man coming irresistibly down the ramp, his heavy-heeled strut more the consequence of gravity than self-esteem. Myburgh, meanwhile, read confusion on Kabini's face. Not guilt, not panic: confusion.

And then Kabini recognized him, knew him for the unlucky fellow who had wrecked his *lekker* Cadillac on the KwaNdebele Road. His confusion turned into something like both guilt and panic, and his eyes cut from side to side, looking for a way out.

"What are you doing, Kabini?" Myburgh put a hand on the mud-caked bus, almost as if he owned it.

Kabini lifted his brush and paint can. "Covering this unhappy name, *nkosi.*" He smiled. "Very good to see you again."

"Don't cover it."

"Company regulation, my *baas.* Got to finish. Got to finish up before Mr. Krige comes back to check."

"Leave it as it is."

Kabini glowered at him. He had already glopped out most of the first two words, GRIM BOY—so that all that was visible now was 's TOE (whatever that implied). Obviously, he could see no point in leaving only an orphaned possessive and the name of a rather lowly body part emblazoned on the bus's side. Mr. Krige would not be pleased. His passengers would laugh.

"Forgive me, *nkosi,* but I must paint it out."

"And I must tell your riders—" Myburgh climbed up into 496 and saw that maybe twenty people were already aboard, waiting for the rest of their fellow commuters to connect and climb on too. He came back down. "I must tell them you're a paid police informant."

Kabini's puzzlement appeared to grow. "Why would you say that, my *baas?*"

"Because it's true."

Smiling, Kabini shook his head. "No. No, *nkosi.*"

"You had Ephraim turn in Winston Skosana. Skosana was a friend of young Mordecai Thubana's. So Major Jeppe took him too."

"Most unlucky."

"Even unluckier, Kabini, is what happened to your ex-passengers while being detained."

Kabini's usual deference was giving way to guarded hostility. Lines

clawed from his eyes. His mouth tightened, a piece of string pulled taut.
He put his brush into the can of enamel and started to feather blue paint
onto the 's TOE. Myburgh shook his head in warning.

"You're a government informer. Should I tell them?"

"Look at my eye. The police beat me."

"For show. To protect you. But I have details. Details your passengers
will believe. God's truth."

Kabini lowered his brush. He looked around. Possibly, he was imagining what it would be like for twenty to ninety outraged Putco customers
to stomp him to death on a terminus ramp or maybe to wait until he had
driven back to Tweefontein E, or Kameelrivier, to hang a petrol-drenched
Firestone around his neck.

"What, my *baas*, do you want from me?"

Myburgh pointed. "Thubana gave your bus that name?"

"Only the word *Toe*. It was called *Grim Boy* even before I began to
drive. Thubana made me add—" Kabini nodded at the apostrophe *s* and
the three-letter word after it.

"Then leave it alone, please."

Kabini stuck his brush into the can and threw the can down. It splat-
tered blue on the passenger dock's retaining wall and part of the bus's
undercarriage. Perplexity and distaste had fused to make Kabini surly.

"What else?" he said.

Myburgh wasn't sure. He had to do something else. Wasn't that why
he had come out here?

"I want to drive your bus," he said.

"What?" Kabini looked around for help. If he found a security agent
who knew what services he had rendered the state, Myburgh was lost.
Myburgh knew he had to act quickly.

"Give me the keys to your bus."

Kabini was hugely offended. "Surely not, *nkosi.*"

"I'll blow the whistle on you. Loud."

Kabini was at sea, a man in an unexpected gale. "The keys are in the
goddamned ignition."

"Thank you."

"Why are you doing this? Are you crazy?"

"I want to take some people on a tour, Kabini. I want them to learn
something of what I've learned."

Myburgh climbed in and stood at the top of 496's center aisle. He
pulled the handle shutting the double-hinged door. He told his passengers
—Kabini's passengers—that although he intended to drive them back to

KwaNdebele eventually, their trip this evening would take a little longer because he had an important errand to run in the heart of Pretoria.

All who wished to get off now and wait for Putco to rectify the terrible additional inconvenience he was going to inflict on them were welcome to do so. On the other hand, all who wished to ride with him into the city were welcome to stay on. If the authorities did not arrest him before he could carry out his pledge to finish the KwaNdebele run, he would (he swore) get them home an hour or so before midnight. At least.

"Who are you, my *baas?*" said a woman in a knit hat, like a pink and purple crown. "Some demon-taken drunk?"

"I'm the man who hit the elephant. I'm the friend of Mordecai Thubana. I'm your driver this evening."

Out the window, he could see Ernest Kabini stalking up the ramp in the grainy dusk, bleakly intent.

"Drive us, then," the woman said. "Drive us."

Three or four others asked Myburgh to let them get off, but the rest acknowledged him as the man who had hit the elephant, numbly accepted him as Kabini's stand-in, and allowed him to grind *'s Toe* into gear, leapfrog it out of the loading dock, and carry them out of Belle Ombre in a fit of backfires and roars muffled by a torrent of deadly Muzak and by the pipe-trimmed buttresses of the station's colorful pavilion.

Myburgh drove badly, but he escaped Marabastad heading south on Eleventh Street, chugging through its intersections with Boomstraat and Strubenstraat, and eventually turning east on Vermeulenstraat, within hailing range of the Kruger House Museum, in order to make a rattletrap assault on Pretoria's center. Double-decker municipal buses, as well as European, American, and Japanese passenger cars, jockeyed for position around him, their drivers eyeing him and his out-of-place riders as if the Putco bus had dropped into their town from another cosmos.

Myburgh cracked the window in the driver's cage. "We're going to KwaNdebele!" he shouted. "If you want to see that South African Shangri-la for yourself, meet us at Church's Square!"

A moment later, he added, "By the Palace of Justice!"

(—Gravity, he heard Mordecai Thubana whispering, —is the only universal force. It acts between all particles without exception. Nowadays, though, it is the odd force out.)

"I know!" Myburgh said, shouting at his passengers.

(—Most matter in our universe, said Thubana, an unseen spirit in the driver's cage, —is invisible.)

"Shadow matter. Dark matter."

(—They're not the same thing, Mr. Myburgh, but, yes, there is a truth of sorts in what you suppose.)

"Dark matter, then. Invisible matter."

(—Yes. For years, astronomers have been studying, and calling real, only those parts of the universe defiled by light.)

"Defiled?"

(—Yes, Mr. Myburgh. Contaminated.)

Contaminated, Myburgh thought. Contaminated. Was his Pretoria less real than KwaNdebele? It unquestionably gave off more light, it was giving off light right now, the entire city was blazing, it was blazing with the lovely contamination of street lamps, electric lights, shiny clock faces, the headlamps of dozens of chrome-plated vehicles. And this blazing—this contamination—was a blow to the head, the kind that ignites fireworks, sparklers, glowing cascades of light, an outward/inward overload that blinds whoever decides to look no farther than the edges of this self-righteous blazing. And that person—every such person—is defiled by the loveliness of the contamination to which he has given his heart, and the night on the highveld contains for him no Southern Cross, no lightning bird, no Jewel Box cluster, but only the shadow-matter armies bivouacked in their shameful invisibility out there beyond the electric bonfires, and the cherished stench of his own high blindness. Contaminated by light . . .

"We're going to KwaNdebele!" Myburgh shouted out the window of his cage. "Meet us at Church's Square!"

(—Mr. Myburgh. Mr. Myburgh, come back.)

"Not yet! I've got to recruit some passengers!"

The claxon of a police cruiser sounded; lights flashed from the turret on its roof. It pulled speedily abreast of 496 and paced it around the immense, palm-dotted memorial park and traffic circle at the center of Church's Square.

An officer was waving angrily, and futilely, at Myburgh, urging him to pull over. Myburgh wasn't ready to do that. He waved back at the policeman. If the officer wanted to stop him before he was ready to stop, then let him call up a roadblock and clog the circle with barricades and police vehicles.

In fact, because that was the only option (other than shooting Myburgh dead and perhaps inflicting injury on bystanders and riders alike) that Myburgh had given the officer, he apparently did just that, for, soon enough, the traffic circle resembled a raceway, and Myburgh's bus was slowing, slowing, as city cruisers surrounded it and nudged it toward the waist-high brick wall on the circumference of the park.

Around him were such familiar landmarks and competitors as the South African Reserve Bank, Standard Bank, and Barclays National Bank. Nearby, too, were the Raadsaal and the Transvaal Provincial Administration Building, every structure looming.

"This man is demon possessed," Myburgh heard the woman in the knit crown tell her fellow riders. "Truly."

He opened the door for the policemen pounding on it. One man stood in the traffic circle with a pistol pointed at him through the window of the driver's cage. The officers on the sidewalk also leveled guns at him.

"Be a hands-upper for me, man," one of them said.

Myburgh kept his hands on the steering wheel. The bus's motor continued to sputter and bang.

"Hands up!"

"This bus is called *Everybody's Toe*," Myburgh said. "I'd like to give you a free ride to Tweefontein E in KwaNdebele, gentlemen. Please ask forty or fifty people to go with us. It shouldn't be too crowded."

Two policemen rushed up the bus's steps, dragged him from his seat, and pulled him onto the sidewalk to cuff his hands and hold his face to the paving as they patted him down.

Myburgh was conscious of the riders on *Everybody's Toe* creeping to its windows to observe his takedown. Their faces were shadowy, but not invisible; they seemed far more sympathetic toward him than did the washed-out faces of the policemen. It was night, but the city hurled off too much light for any stars to shine through, and Myburgh understood that the Theory of Everything for which Thubana had been looking was still twisting out there in the vacuum—beyond the contamination, cloaked in darkness, waiting.

"Mordecai," Myburgh said, his cheek on the sidewalk, and he had the distinct sense that someone had heard him.

Snow on Sugar Mountain

ELIZABETH HAND

WHEN ANDREW WAS SEVEN, his mother turned into a fox. Snow freed the children from school at lunchtime, the bus skating down the hill to release cheering gangs at each sleety corner. Andrew got off last, nearly falling from the curb as he turned to wave good-bye to the driver. He ran to the front door of the house, battering at the screen and yelling, "Mom! Mom!" He tugged the scarf from his face, the better to peer through frost-clouded windows. Inside it looked dark; but he heard the television chattering to itself, heard the chimes of the old ship's clock counting half past one. She would be downstairs, then, doing the laundry. He dashed around the house, sliding on the iced flagstones.

"Mom . . . I'm home, it snowed, I'm—"

He saw the bird first. He thought it was the cardinal that had nested in the box tree last spring: a brilliant slash of crimson in the snow, like his own lost mitten. Andrew held his breath, teetering as he leaned forward to see.

A bluejay: no longer blue, scattered quills already gray and somber as tarnished silver, its pale crest quivering erect like an accusing finger. The snow beneath it glowed red as paint, and threads of steam rose from its mauled breast. Andrew tugged at his scarf, glancing across the white slope of lawn for the neighbor's cat.

That was when he saw the fox, mincing up the steps to the open back door. Its mouth drooped to show wet white teeth, the curved blade of the jay's wing hanging from its jaw. Andrew gasped. The fox mirrored his surprise, opening its mouth so that the wing fell and broke apart like the spinning seeds of a maple. For a moment they regarded each other, blue eyes and black. Then the fox stretched its forelegs as if yawning, stretched its mouth wide, too wide, until it seemed that its jaw would split like the broken quills. Andrew saw red gums and tongue, teeth like an ivory stair spiraling into black, black that was his mother's hair, his mother's eyes: his mother crouched naked, retching on the top step in the snow.

After that she had to show it to him. Not that day, not even that winter; but later, in the summer, when cardinals nested once more in the box tree and shrieking jays chased goldfinches from the birdbath.

"Someday you can have it, Andrew," she said as she drew her jewelry box from the kitchen hidey-hole. "When you're older. There's no one else," she added. His father had died before he was born. "And it's mine, anyway."

Inside the box were loops of pearls, jade turtles, a pendant made of butterfly's wings that formed a sunset and palm trees. And a small ugly thing, as long as her thumb and the same color: marbled cream, nutbrown in the creases. At first he thought it was a bug. It was the locust year, and everywhere their husks stared at him from trees and cracks in the wall.

But it wasn't a locust. His mother placed it in his hand, and he held it right before his face. Some sort of stone, smooth as skin. Cool at first, after a few moments in his palm it grew warm, and he glanced at his mother for reassurance.

"Don't worry," she laughed wryly. "It won't bite." And she sipped her drink.

It was an animal, all slanted eyes and grinning mouth, paws tucked beneath its sharp chin like a dog playing Beg. A tiny hole had been drilled in the stone so that it could be tied onto a string. "How does it work?" Andrew asked. His mother shook her head.

"Not yet," she said, swishing the ice in her glass. "It's mine still; but someday—someday I'll show you how." And she took the little carving and replaced it, and locked the jewelry box back in the hidey-hole.

That had been seven years ago. The bus that stopped at the foot of the hill would soon take Andrew to the public high school. Another locust summer was passing. The seven-year cicadas woke in the August night and crept from their split skins like a phantom army. The night they began to sing, Andrew woke to find his mother dead, bright pills spilling from one hand when he forced it open. In the other was the amulet, her palm blistered where she clenched the stone.

He refused the sedatives the doctor offered him, refused awkward offers of comfort from relatives and friends suddenly turned to strangers. At the wake he slouched before the casket, tearing petals from carnations. He nodded stiffly at his mother's sister when she arrived to take him to the funeral.

"Colin leaves for Brockport in three weeks," his aunt said later in the car. "When he goes, you can have the room to yourself. It's either that or the couch—"

"I don't care," Andrew replied. He didn't mean for his voice to sound so harsh. "I mean, it doesn't matter. Anywhere's okay. Really."

And it was, really.

Because the next day he was gone.

North of the city, in Kamensic Village, the cicadas formed heavy curtains of singing green and copper, covering oaks and beeches, houses and hedges and bicycles left out overnight. On Sugar Mountain they rippled across an ancient Volkswagen Beetle that hadn't moved in months. Their song was loud enough to wake the old astronaut in the middle of the night, and nearly drown out the sound of the telephone when it rang in the morning.

"I no longer do interviews," the old astronaut said wearily. He started to hang up. Then, "How the hell did you get this number, anyway?" he demanded; but the reporter was gone. Howell glared at Festus. The spaniel cringed, tail vibrating over the flagstones, and moaned softly. "You giving out this new number?" Howell croaked, and slapped his thigh. "Come on—"

The dog waddled over and lay his head upon the man's knee. Howell stroked the old bony skull, worn as flannel, and noted a hole in the knee of his pajamas.

Eleven o'clock and still not dressed. Christ, Festus, you should've said something.

He caught himself talking aloud and stood, gripping the mantel and waiting until his heart slowed. Sometimes now he didn't know if he was talking or thinking; if he had taken his medicine and slipped into the dreamy hold that hid him from the pain or if he was indeed dreaming. Once he had drifted, and thought he was addressing another class of eager children. He woke to find himself mumbling to an afternoon soap opera, Festus staring up at him intently. That day he put the television in a closet.

But later he dragged it back into the bedroom once more. The news helped remind him of things. Reminded him to call Lancaster, the oncologist; to call his son Peter, and the Kamensic Village Pharmacy.

"Festus," he whispered, hugging the dog close to his knee. "Oh, Festus." And when he finally glanced at the spaniel again was surprised to see the gentle sloping snout matted and dark with tears.

From the western Palisades, the radio tower blazed across the Hudson as Andrew left the city that dawn. He stood at the top of the road until the sun crept above the New York side, waiting until the beacon flashed and died. The first jet shimmered into sight over bridges linking the island to the foothills of the northern ranges. Andrew sighed. No tears left; but grief feathered his eyes so that the river swam, blurred and finally disappeared in the burst of sunrise. He turned and walked down the hill, faster and faster, past bus stops and parked cars, past the high school and the cemetery. Only when he reached the Parkway did he stop to catch his breath, then slowly crossed the road to the northbound lane.

Two rides brought him to Valhalla. He walked backwards along the side of the road, shifting his backpack from shoulder to shoulder as he held his thumb out. A businessman in a BMW finally pulled over and unlocked the passenger door. He regarded Andrew with a sour expression.

"If you were my kid, I'd put your lights out," he growled as Andrew hopped in, grinning his best late-for-class smile. "But I'd wish a guy like me picked you up instead of some pervert."

"Thanks," Andrew nodded seriously. "I mean, you're right. I missed the last train out last night. I got to get to school."

The man stared straight ahead, then glanced at his watch. "I'm going to Manchester Hills. Where do you go to school?"

"John Jay."

"In Mount Lopac?"

"Kamensic Village."

The man nodded. "Is 684 close enough?"

Andrew shrugged. "Sure. Thanks a lot."

After several miles, they veered onto the highway's northern hook. Andrew sat forward in the seat, damp hands sticking to his knapsack as he watched for the exit sign. When he saw it he dropped his knapsack in nervous excitement. The businessman scowled.

"This is it . . . I mean, please, if it's okay—" The seat belt caught Andrew's sneaker as he grabbed the door handle. "Thanks—thanks a lot—"

"Next time don't miss the train," the man yelled as Andrew stumbled onto the road. Before he could slam the door shut, the lock clicked back into place. Andrew waved. The man lifted a finger in farewell, and the BMW roared north.

From the Parkway, Kamensic Village drifted into sight like a dream of distant towns. White steeples, stone walls, granite turrets rising from hills already rusted with the first of autumn. To the north the hills arched like a deer's long spine, melting golden into the Mohank Mountains. Andrew nodded slowly and shrugged the knapsack to his shoulder. He scuffed down the embankment to where a stream flowed townward. He followed it, stopping to drink and wash his face, slicking his hair back into a dark wave. Sunfish floated in the water above sandy nests, slipping fearlessly through his fingers when he tried to snatch them. His stomach ached from hunger, raw and cold as though he'd swallowed a handful of cinders. He thought of the stone around his neck. That smooth pellet under his tongue, and how easy it would be then to find food . . .

He swore softly, shaking damp hair from his eyes. Against his chest the amulet bounced, and he steadied it, grimacing, before heading upstream.

The bug-ridden sign swayed at the railroad station: KAMENSIC VILLAGE. Beneath it stood a single bench, straddled by the same kid Andrew remembered from childhood: misshapen helmet protecting his head, starry topaz eyes widening when he saw Andrew pass the station.

"Hey," the boy yelled, just as if he remembered Andrew from years back. "HEY."

"Hey, Buster." Andrew waved without stopping.

He passed the Kamensic Village Pharmacy, where Mr. Weinstein still doled out egg creams; Hayden's Delicatessen with its great vat of iced tea, lemons bobbing like toy turtles in the amber liquid. The library, open four days a week (CLOSED TODAY). That was where he had seen puppet shows, and heard an astronaut talk once, years ago when he and his mother still came up in the summer to rent the cottage. And, next to the library, the seventeenth-century courthouse, now a museum.

"Fifty cents for students." The same old lady peered suspiciously at Andrew's damp hair and red-rimmed eyes. "Shouldn't you be in school?"

"Visiting," Andrew mumbled as she dropped the quarters into a little tin box. "I got relatives here."

He shook his head at her offer to walk him through the rooms. "I been here before," he explained. He tried to smile. "On vacation."

The courtroom smelled the same, of lemon polish and the old lady's Chanel No. 5. The Indian Display waited where it always had, in a whitewashed corner of the courtroom where dead bluebottles drifted like lapis beads. Andrew's chest tightened when he saw it. His hand closed around the amulet on its string.

A frayed map of the northern county starred with arrowheads indicated where the tribes had settled. Axe blades and skin scrapers marked their battles. A deer hide frayed with moth holes provided a backdrop for the dusty case. From beneath the doeskin winked a vole's skull.

At the bottom of the case rested a small printed board. Andrew leaned his head against the glass and closed his eyes, mouthing the words without reading them as he fingered the stone.

> . . . members of the Tankiteke tribe of
> the Wappinger Confederacy of Mohicans:
> Iroquois warriors of the Algonquin Nation . . .

When he opened his eyes they fixed upon an object at the bottom of the case: a carved gray stone in the image of a tiny animal with long eyes and smooth sharp teeth.

Shaman's Talisman [Animistic Figure]

> The Tankiteke believed their shamans could
> change shape at will and worshipped
> animal spirits.

From the narrow hallway leading to the front room came the creak of a door opening, the answering hiss of women's laughter.

"Some boy," Andrew heard the curator reply. He bit his lip. "Said he had relatives, but I think he's just skipping school . . ."

Andrew glanced around the courtroom, looking for new exhibits, tools, books. There was nothing. No more artifacts; no other talisman. He slipped through a door leading to an anteroom and found there another door leading outside. Unlocked; there would be no locked doors in Kamensic Village. In the orchard behind the courthouse, he scooped up an early apple and ate it, wincing at the bitter flesh. Then he headed for the road that led to The Fallows.

In the dreams, Howell walked on the moon.

The air he breathed was the same stale air, redolent of urine and refrigeration, that had always filled the capsules. Yet he was conscious in the dreams that it tasted different on the moon, filtered through the spare silver ducts coiled on his back. Above him the sky loomed sable, so cold that his hands tingled inside heated gloves at the sight of it: as he had always known it would be, algid, black, speared with stars that pulsed and sang as they never did inside the capsule. He lifted his eyes then and saw the orbiter passing overhead. He raised one hand to wave, so slowly it seemed he might start to drift into the stark air in the pattern of that wave. And then the voice crackled in his ears, clipped words echoing phrases from memoranda and newscasts. His own voice, calling to Howell that it was time to return.

That was when he woke, shivering despite quilts and Festus snoring beside him. A long while he lay in bed, trying to recall the season— winter, surely, because of the fogged windows.

But no. Beneath the humming cough of air-conditioning, cicadas droned. Howell struggled to his feet.

Behind the bungalow the woods shimmered, birch and ancient oaks silvered by the moonlight streaming from the sky. Howell opened the casement and leaned out. Light and warmth spilled upon him as though the moonlight were warm milk, and he blinked and stretched his hands to catch it.

Years before, during the final two moon landings, Howell had been the man who waited inside the orbiter.

Long ago, before the actors and writers and wealthy children of the exurbs migrated to Kamensic Village, a colony of earnest socialists settled upon the scrubby shores of the gray water named Muscanth. Their utopia had shattered years before. The cozy stage and studios rotted and softly sank back into the fen. But the cottages remained, some of them still rented to summer visitors from the city. Andrew had to ask in Scotts Corners for directions—he hadn't been here since he was ten—and was surprised by how much longer it took to reach The Fallows on foot. No autos passed. Only a young girl in jeans and flannel shirt, riding a black horse, her braids flying as her mount cantered by him. Andrew laughed. She waved, grinning, before disappearing around a kink in the birchy lane.

With that sharp laugh, something fell from Andrew: as if grief could be contained in small cold breaths, and he had just exhaled. He noticed for the first time sweat streaking his chest, and unbuttoned his shirt. The shirt smelled stale and oily, as though it had absorbed the city's foul air, its grimy clouds of exhaust and factory smoke.

But here the sky gleamed slick and blue as a bunting's wing. Andrew laughed again, shook his head so that sky and leaves and scattering birds all flickered in a bright blink. And when he focused again upon the road, the path snaked *there:* just where he had left it four years ago, carefully cleared of curling ferns and moldering birch.

I'm here, he thought as he stepped shyly off the dirt road, glancing back to make certain no car or rider marked where he broke trail. In the distance glittered the lake. A cloud of red admiral butterflies rose from a crab-apple stump and skimmed beside him along the overgrown path. Andrew ran, laughing. He was home.

The abandoned cottage had grown larger with decay and disuse. Ladders of nectarine fungi and staghorn lichen covered it from eaves to floor, and between this patchwork straggled owls' nests and the downy homes of deer mice.

The door did not give easily. It was unlocked, but swollen from snow and rain. Andrew had to fling himself full force against the timbers before they groaned and relented. Amber light streamed from chinks and cracks in the walls, enough light that ferns and pokeweed grew from clefts in the pine floor. Something scurried beneath the room's single chair. Andrew turned in time to see a deer mouse, still soft in its gray infant fur, disappear into the wall.

There had been other visitors as well. In the tiny bedroom, Andrew found fox scat and long rufous hairs clinging to the splintered cedar wall; by the front door, rabbit pellets. Mud daubers had plastered the kitchen with their fulvous cells. The linoleum was scattered with undigested feathers and the crushed spines of voles. He paced the cottage, yanking up pokeweed and tossing it into the corner, dragged the chair into the center of the room and sat there a long time. Finally, he took a deep breath, opened his knapsack and withdrew a bottle of gin pilfered from his mother's bureau, still nearly full. He took a swig, shut his eyes and waited for it to steam through his throat to his head.

"Don't do it drunk," his mother had warned him once—drunk herself, the two of them sipping Pink Squirrels from a lukewarm bottle in her bedroom. "You ever seen a drunk dog?"

"No," Andrew giggled.

"Well, it's like that, only worse. You can't walk straight. You can't smell anything. It's worse than plain drunk. I almost got hit by a car once, in Kamensic, when I was drunk." She lit a cigarette. "Stayed out a whole night that time, trying to find my way back . . ."

Andrew nodded, rubbing the little talisman to his lips.

"No," his mother said softly, and took it from him. She held it up to the gooseneck lamp. "Not yet."

She turned and stared at him fiercely, glittering eyes belying her slurred voice. "See, you can't stay that long. I almost did, that time . . ."

She took another sip. "Forget, I mean. You forget . . . fox or bear or deer, you forget . . ."

"Forget what?" Andrew wondered. The smoke made him cough, and he gulped his drink.

"What you are. That you're human. Not . . ."

She took his hand, her nails scratching his palm. "They used to forget. The Indians, the Tankiteke. That's what my grandfather said. There used to be more of these things—"

She rolled the stone between her palms. "And now they're all gone. You know why?"

Andrew shook his head.

"Because they forgot." His mother turned away. "Fox or whatever— they forgot they once were human, and stayed forever, and died up there in the woods." And she fingered the stone as she did her wedding ring, eyes agleam with whiskey tears.

But that night Andrew lay long awake, staring at his Mets pennants as he listened to the traffic outside; and wondered why anyone would ever want to come back.

Howell woke before dawn, calling, "Festus! Morning." The spaniel snorted and stared at him blearily before sliding off the bed.

"Look," said Howell, pointing to where tall ferns at wood's edge had been crushed to a green mat. "They were here again last night."

Festus whined and ran from the room, nails tick-tocking upon the floor. Howell let him out the back door and watched the old dog snuffle at the deer brake, then crash into the brush. Some mornings Howell felt as if he might follow the dog on these noisy hunts once more. But each time, the dawn rush of light and heat trampled his strength as carelessly as deer broke the ferns. For a few minutes he breathed easily, the dank mountain air slipping like water down his throat, cold and tasting of granite. Then the coughing started. Howell gripped the door frame, shuddering until the tears came, chest racked as though something smashed his ribs to escape. He stumbled into the kitchen, fingers scrabbling across the counter until they clutched the inhaler. By the time he breathed easily again, sunlight gilded Sugar Mountain, and at the back door Festus scratched for entry, panting from his run.

The same morning found Andrew snoring on the cottage floor. The bottle of gin had toppled, soaking the heap of old newspapers where he lay pillowed. He woke slowly but to quick and violent conclusions when he tried to stand.

"Christ," he moaned, pausing in the doorway. The reek of gin made him sick. Afterward, he wiped his mouth on a wild grape leaf, then with surprising vigor smashed the bottle against a tree. Then he staggered downhill toward the stream.

Here the water flowed waist-deep. Andrew peeled off T-shirt and jeans and eased himself into the stream, swearing at the cold. A deep breath. Then he dunked himself, came up sputtering, and floated above the clear pebbled bottom, eyes shut against the shadows of trees and sky trembling overhead.

He settled on a narrow stone shelf above the stream, water rippling across his lap. His head buzzed between hunger and hangover. Beneath him minnows drifted like willow leaves. He dipped a hand to catch them, but they wriggled easily through his fingers. A feverish hunger came over him. He counted back three days since he'd eaten: the same evening he'd found his mother . . .

He blinked against the memory, blinked until the hazy air cleared and he could focus on the stream beneath him. Easing himself into the water, he knelt in the shallows and squinted at the rocks. Very slowly, he lifted one flat stone, then another. The third uncovered a crayfish, mottled brown against chocolate-colored gravel. Andrew bit his hand to stop it shaking, then slipped it beneath the surface. The crayfish shot backwards, toward his ankles. Andrew positioned his feet to form a V, squatting to cut off its escape. He yelped triumphantly when he grabbed its tail.

"Son of a bitch!" Pincers nipped his thumb. He flung the crayfish onto the mossy bank, where it jerked and twitched. For a moment Andrew regarded it remorsefully. Then he took the same flat stone that had sheltered it and neatly cracked its head open.

Not much meat to suck from the claws. A thumb's worth (still quivering) within the tail, muddy and sweet as March rain. In the next hour he uncovered dozens more, until the bank was littered with empty carapaces, the mud starred with his handprints like a great raccoon's. Finally he stopped eating. The mess on the bank sickened him. He crawled to stream's edge and bit his lip, trying not to throw up. In the shadowy water he saw himself: much too thin, black hair straggling across his forehead, his slanted eyes shadowed by exhaustion. He wiped a thread of mud from his lip and leaned back. Against his chest the amulet bounced like a stray droplet, its filthy cord chafing his neck. He dried his face with his T-shirt, then pulled the string until the amulet dangled in front of him.

In the late summer light it gleamed eerily, swollen as a monarch's chrysalis. And like the lines of thorax, head, wings evident upon a pupae, the talisman bore faint markings. Eyes, teeth, paws; wings, fins, antlers, tail. Depending on how it caught the light, it was fox or stoat; flying squirrel or cougar or stag. The boy pinched the amulet between thumb and middle finger, drew it across his cheek. Warm. Within the nugget of stone he felt a dull buzzing like an entrapped hornet.

Andrew rubbed the talisman against his lips. His teeth vibrated as from a tiny drill. He shut his eyes, tightened his fingers about the stone, and slipped it beneath his tongue. For a second he felt it, a seed ripe to burst. Then nausea exploded inside him, pain so violent he screamed and collapsed onto the moss, clawing wildly at his head. Abruptly his shrieks stopped. He could not breathe. A rush of warm air filled his nostrils, fetid as pond water. He sneezed.

And opened his eyes to the muddy bank oozing between black and velvet paws.

Perhaps it was the years spent in cramped spaces—his knees drawn to his chest in capsule mock-ups; sleeping suspended in canvas sacks; eating upside down in metal rooms smaller than a refrigerator—perhaps the bungalow had actually seemed *spacious* when Howell decided to purchase it over his son's protests and his accountant's sighs.

"Plenty of room for what I need," he told his son. They were hanging pictures. NASA shots, *Life* magazine promos. The Avedon portrait of his wife, a former Miss Rio Grande, dead of cancer before the moon landing. "And fifty acres: most of the lakefront."

"Fifty acres most of it nowhere," Peter said snidely. He hated the country; hated the disappointment he felt that his father hadn't taken the penthouse in Manhattan. "No room here for anyone else, that's for sure."

That was how the old man liked it. The bungalow fit neatly into a tiny clearing between glacier-riven hills. A good snow cut him off from the village for days: the town's only plow saved Sugar Mountain and the abandoned lake colony for last. "The Astronaut don't mind," the driver always said.

Howell agreed. After early retirement he took his pension and retired, truly retired. No honorary university positions. No airline endorsements. His investments were few and careless. He corresponded with crackpots, authors researching astral landing fields in rain forests, a woman who claimed to receive alien broadcasts through her sunglasses, an institutionalized patient who signed his letters Rubber Man Lord of Jupiter. During a rare radio interview, Howell admitted to experimentation with hallucinogenic drugs and expressed surprising bitterness at the demise of the Apollo program, regret untempered by the intervening years. On spring afternoons he could be seen walking with his English cocker spaniel on the dirt roads through Kamensic. The village schoolchildren pointed him out proudly, although his picture was not in their books. Once a year he spoke to the fifth graders about the importance of the space program, shyly signing autographs on lunch bags afterwards: no, the Astronaut did not mind.

The old man sighed and walked to his desk. From his frayed shirt rose a skull barren of hair, raised blue veins like rivers on a relief globe. Agate blue eyes, dry as if all the dreams had been sucked from them, focused now on strange things. Battalions of pill bottles. Bright lesions on hands and feet. Machines more dreadful than anything NASA had devised for his training. The road from Sugar Mountain lay so far from his front door that he seldom walked there anymore.

The medicine quelled his coughing. In its place a heaviness in his chest and the drug's phantom mettle.

"I wish the goddamn car keys were here," he announced to Festus, pacing to the door. He was not supposed to drive alone. Peter had taken the keys, "for safety." "I wish my goddamn dog could drive."

Festus yawned and flopped onto the floor. Sighing, the astronaut settled onto the couch, took pen and notebook to write a letter. Within minutes he was asleep.

· · · ·

Andrew staggered from the sound: the bawl of air through the trees, the cicadas' song a steady thunder. From beneath the soil thrummed millipedes and hellgrammites, the ceaseless tick of insect legs upon fallen leaves. He shivered and shook a ruff of heavy fur. The sunlight stung his eyes and he blinked. The world was bound now in black and gray.

He sneezed. Warm currents of scent tickled his muzzle. So many kinds of dirt! Mud like cocoa, rich and bitter; sand fresh as sunlight; loam ripe with hidden worms. He stood on wobbly legs, took a few steps and stumbled on his clothes. Their rank smell assaulted him: detergent, sweat, city gravel and tarmac. He sneezed ferociously, then ambled to the streambed. He nosed a crayfish shell, licking it clean. Afterward he waded into the stream and lapped, long tongue flicking water into his eyes. A bound brought him to the high bank. He shook water from his fur and flung his head back, eyes shut, filled with a formidable wordless joy. From far away he heard low thunder; he tasted the approach of rain upon the breeze.

Something stirred in the thickets nearby. Without looking he knew it was a rabbit, smelled milk and acrid fear clinging to her. He raised his head, tested the air until he found her crouched at the base of a split birch. He crept forward, his belly grazing the dirt. When he was scarcely a muzzle-length away, she spooked, hind legs spraying leaves in his face as she vaulted into the underbrush. He followed, slipping under grapevines and poison ivy, his dewclaws catching on burdock leaves.

The rabbit led him through a birch stand to a large clearing, where she bounded and disappeared into a burrow. He dug furiously at the hole, throwing up clouds of soft loam, stopping finally when he upturned a mass of black beetles clicking over a rock. Curious, he nudged the beetles, then licked up a mouthful and crunched them between his long teeth. The remaining insects scurried beneath the earth. Suddenly tired, he yawned, crawled inside a ring of overgrown ferns heavy with spores and lay there panting.

The air grew heavy with moisture. Thunder snarled in the distance. How could he ever have thought the woods silent? He heard constantly the steady beat, the hum of the turning day beneath his paws. Rain began to fall, and he crept deeper into the ferns until they covered him. He waited there until nightfall, licking rain from the fronds and cleaning the earth from between his footpads.

At dusk the rain stopped. Through slitted eyes he saw a stag step into the clearing and bend to lick rain from a cupped leaf, its tongue rasping against the grass. Nuthatches arrowed into the rhododendrons, and the bushes shuddered until they settled into sleep. He stretched, the hair on his back rustling as moisture pearled and rolled from his coat. In the damp air scents were acute: he tasted mist rising from the nearby swamp, smelled an eft beneath a rotting stump. Then the breeze shifted, brought a stronger scent to him: hot and milky, the young rabbit, motionless at the entrance of its burrow.

He cocked his ears to trace the faint wind stirring the rabbit's fur. He crouched and took a half step toward it, sprang as it bolted in a panic of flying fur and leaves. The rabbit leaped into the clearing, turned and tripped on a fallen branch. In that instant he was upon it, his paws hesitantly brushing its shuddering flank before he tore at its throat. The rabbit screamed. He rent skin and sinew, fur catching between his teeth, shearing strings of muscle as he growled and tugged at its jaw. It stopped kicking. Somewhere inside the fox, Andrew wanted to scream; but the fox tore at the rabbit's head, blood spurting from a crushed artery and staining his muzzle. The smell maddened him. He dragged the rabbit into the brush and fed, then dug a shallow hole and buried the carcass, nosing leaves over the warm bones.

He stepped into the clearing and stared through the tangle of trees and sky. The moon was full. Blood burned inside him; its smell stung his nostrils, scorched his tongue so that he craved water. An owl screeched. He started, leaping over the rank midden, and continued running through the birch clearing until he found the stream, dazzling with reflected moonlight. He stepped to the water's edge and dipped a tentative paw into the shallows, rearing back when the light scattered at his touch. He crossed the stream and wandered snuffling across the other bank. A smell arrested him: overwhelming, alien to this place. He stared at a pile of clothes strewn upon the moss, walked to them stiff-legged and sniffed. Beneath his tongue something small and rough itched like a blister. He shook his head and felt the string around his neck. He coughed, pawed his muzzle; buried his face in the T-shirt. The talisman dropped from between his jaws.

On the bank the boy knelt, coughing, one hand clutching the bloody talisman. He crawled to the stream and bowed there, cupping water in his hands and gulping frantically. Then he staggered backwards, flopped onto the moss to stare exhausted at the sky. In a little while he slept uneasily, legs twitching as he stalked fleeing hares through a black and twisted forest.

Rain woke him the next morning, trickling into his nostrils and beneath his eyelids. Andrew snorted and sat up, wiping his eyes. The stream swelled with muddy whirlpools. He stared as the rain came down harder, slicing through the high canopy and striking him like small cold stones. Shivering, he grabbed his clothes and limped to the cottage. Inside he dried himself with his damp T-shirt, then stepped into the tiny bedroom. It was so narrow that when he extended his arms his fingertips grazed opposing walls. Here sagged an ancient iron-framed camp bed with flattened mattress, hard and lean as an old car seat. Groaning, he collapsed onto it, heedless of dead moths scattered across the cushion. His crumpled jeans made a moist pillow as he propped himself against the wall and stared at the ceiling.

He could come back here every day. It was dry, and if he pulled up all the pokeweed, swept out the dirt and fallen feathers, it would be home. He had the stream for water; a few warm clothes in his knapsack for winter. At night he could hunt and feed in the woods, changing back at dawn. During the day he'd sleep, maybe go to the library and look up survival books. No one would ever find him. He could hide forever here where the Tankiteke had hunted.

It didn't have to drive you crazy. If you didn't fight it, if you used it in the right places; if you didn't care about family or friends or school. He pulled fiercely at the string and held the amulet before his eyes.

They would never know. Ever: no one would ever know.

Howell's treatments stopped that winter. One evening Dr. Lancaster simply shook his head, slid the latest test results into the folder and closed it. The next morning he told Howell, "No more."

The astronaut went home to die.

As long as there was no snow, he could walk with Festus, brief forays down the dirt drive to check the mailbox. Some afternoons he'd wait there with the spaniel for the mail car to pull up.

"Some winter, Major Howell," the mailman announced as he handed him a stack of letters from the insurance company, vitamin wholesalers, the Yale hospital. "Think we'll ever get snow?"

Howell took the mail, shrugging, then looked at the cloudless sky. "Your guess is as good as mine. Better, probably."

They laughed, and the car crept down the hillside. Howell turned and called Festus from the woods. For a moment he paused, staring at the brilliant winter sky, the moon like a pale eye staring down upon the afternoon.

That night he dreamed of the sky, ice melting into clouds that scudded across a ghostly moon so close that when he raised his hands his fingers left marks upon its face, tiny craters blooming where he touched. When he awoke the next morning it was snowing.

The blizzard pounced on Kamensic Village, caught the hamlet as it drowsed after the long Christmas holidays. A brief and bitter autumn had given way to a snowless winter. Deer grew fat grazing upon frosty pastures. With no snow to challenge them, school-bus drivers grew complacent, then cranky, while children dreamed of brightly varnished toboggans and new skis still beribboned in frigid garages. In The Fallows a fox could find good hunting, warm holes to hide in; the door blew off an abandoned bungalow and leaves drifted in its corners, burying a vinyl knapsack.

Beneath a tumbledown stone wall, he'd found an abandoned burrow, just large enough to curl up in and sleep through the bitter days. He avoided the cottages now. The fetid scent of men still clinging to the forsaken structures frightened him, ripe as it was with some perplexing memory. He yawned and drew his paws under him, tail curving to cover his muzzle and warm the freezing air he breathed. Above him the wall hid the remains of the grouse he'd killed last night. The faint rotting smell comforted him, and he slept deeply.

He woke to silence: so utterly still that his hackles rose and he growled softly with unease. Even in the burrow he could always hear the soft stirrings of the world—wind in dead leaves, chickadees fighting in the pines, the crack of branches breaking from the cold. Now he heard only a dull scratching. Stiff-legged he crept through the tunnel and emerged into the storm.

Stones had prevented snow from blocking the entrance to his den. He slunk through the narrow burrow and shook himself. Snow fell so fast that within moments his fur was thick with it. Everywhere branches had collapsed. Entire pines bowed toward the ground until they snapped, dark trunks quickly and silently buried. He buried his muzzle in the drift, then reared back, snarling. Abruptly he turned and leaped atop the stone wall. As he did so, he dislodged a heavy ledge of snow that fell behind him without a sound.

From the wall he tested the wind. Nothing. It blew his ruff back until he shivered beneath snow so thick that he could not shake himself dry. He slunk down, stumbling into a drift, and sniffed for the burrow entrance.

Gone. Displaced snow blocked the hole. He could smell nothing. Frantically he dug at the wall. More snow slid from the stones, and he jumped back, growling. From stone to stone he ran, pawing frenziedly, burying his muzzle as he tried to find a warm smell, the scent of frozen blood or spoor. Snow congealed between his pads, matting his legs so that he swam gracelessly through the shifting mass. Exhausted, he huddled at the base of the wall until cold gnawed at his chest. Then he staggered upward until he once again stood clear at the top. Bitter wind clamped his muzzle. His eyelids froze. Blindly he began to run along the wall's crest, slipping between rocks and panting.

The wall ended. A wind-riven hill sloped away from him, and he leaped, tumbled by the storm until the snow met him and he flailed whimpering through the endless drifts.

Howell sat before the window, watching the storm. The telephone lines linking him to the village sagged drearily in hoary crescents. He knew they would break as they did during every blizzard. He had already spoken to Peter, to Dr. Lancaster, to Mr. Schelling, the grocer, who wondered if he needed anything before the store closed. He could snap the lines himself now if he wanted. There was no one else to talk to.

He no longer cared. The heaviness in his lungs had spread these last few weeks until his entire chest felt ribbed in stone, his legs and arms so light in comparison they might be wings. He knew that one by one the elements of his body were leaving him. Only the pills gave him strength, and he refilled the plastic bottles often.

A little while ago he had taken a capsule, washing it down with a scant tumbler of scotch. He took a childish pleasure in violating his body now.

"Festus," he croaked, his hand ruffling the air at his side. Festus shambled over, tail vibrating. "Hey Festus, my good dog. My good bright dog."

Festus licked Howell's hand, licked his chops and whined hopefully.

"Dinner?" Howell said, surprised. "So early." Then wondered in alarm if he had fed the dog yesterday; if he had forgotten that as he had sometimes forgotten the mail, his clothes, his own meals. He stood uneasily, head thrumming, and went to the kitchen.

A moist crust still rimmed the dog's dish. There was water in his bowl. But when Howell opened the cabinet beneath the sink there were no cans there. The tall red Purina bag was empty.

"Oh no," he murmured, then looked in the refrigerator. A few eggs; some frozen vegetables. There would be soup in the cupboard. "Festus, Christ, I'm sorry." Festus danced expectantly across the planked floor to wait at his dish.

Howell leaned against the sink and stared outside. Schelling's might still be open; if not, Isaac lived behind the store. There was gas in the car. Peter had returned the keys, reluctantly, but Howell hadn't driven in months. If he waited it might be two days before anyone called or checked Sugar Mountain. He rummaged through closets until he found boots and heavy parka, then shoved his inhaler into a pocket. He paused in the kitchen, wondering if he should bring the dog with him.

"I'll be back soon," he said at last, rumpling the spaniel's ears. Then he swallowed another pill.

Outside, flakes the size of his thumb swirled down and burst into hundreds of crystals upon his parka. The sky hung so low and dark that it seemed like nightfall. Howell had no idea what time it really was. He staggered to the car, kicking the door until snow fell from it and he could find the handle. He checked the back seat for shovel, sand, blankets. Then he started the engine. The car lurched forward.

He had heard the snowplow earlier, but the road was already buried once more. As the car drifted toward a high bank, Howell wondered why it was he had decided to go out, finally recalled Festus waiting hungrily at home.

In a few minutes he realized it was futile to steer toward one side of the road or the other. Instead he tried to keep a few feet between car and trees, and so avoid driving into the woods. Soon even this was difficult. Pines leaned where he had never seen trees. The stone walls that bounded the road had buckled into labyrinthine waves. Down the gentle slope inched the car, bluish spume flying behind it. The heater did not work. The windshield wipers stuck again. He reached out and cleared a tiny patch to see through the frigid black glass starred with soft explosions.

Through the clear spot, Howell saw only white and gray streaks. Smears left by his fingers on the glass froze and reflected the steady green and red lights of the dashboard. His hands dropped from the wheel, and he rubbed them together. The car glided onward.

Dreaming, he saw for an instant a calm frozen sea swelling beneath tiny windows, interior darkness broken by blinking panel lights while, outside, shone the azure bow of Earth. Then his forehead grazed the edge of the steering wheel, and he started, gently pressing the brake.

An animal plunged in front of the car, a golden blur like a summer stain upon the snow. It thudded against the bumper.

"Son of a bitch," murmured Howell.

The car stopped. As he stepped out he glanced behind him, shielding his eyes. Snow already filled the tracks snaking a scant hundred feet to the end of his drive. He pulled the hood tight about his face and turned.

In front of the car sprawled a naked boy, eyes closed as if asleep, skin steaming at the kiss of melting snow. Long black hair tangled with twigs; one fist raised to his lips. A drowsing child. The astronaut stooped and very gently touched his cheek. It was feverishly hot.

The boy moaned. Howell staggered against the bumper. The freezing pain jolted him. He stumbled to the door, reaching for the old Hudson's Bay blanket. Then he knelt beside the boy, head pounding, and wrapped him in the blanket. He tried to carry him: too heavy. Howell groaned, then dragged boy and blanket to the side of the car. For a moment he rested, wheezing, before heaving the boy into the passenger seat.

Afterward he couldn't remember driving back to the house. Festus met him at the door, barking joyfully. Staggering beneath the boy's weight, Howell kicked the door shut behind him, then kneeling placed the bundle on the floor.

"Festus, shh," he commanded.

The dog approached the boy, tail wagging. Then he stiffened and reared back snarling.

"Festus, shut up." Exhausted, Howell threw down his parka. He paused to stare at the blizzard still raging about the mountainside. "Festus, I'm throwing you out there if you don't shut up." He clapped and pointed toward the kitchen. "Go lie down."

Festus barked, but retreated to the kitchen.

Now what the hell is this? Howell ran his hands over his wet scalp and stared down at the boy. Melting snow dripped from the blanket to stain the wooden floor. Tentatively he stooped and pulled back a woolen corner.

In the room's ruddy light the boy looked even paler, his skin ashen. Grime streaked his chest. The hair on his legs and groin was stiff with dirt. Howell grimaced: the boy smelled like rotting meat.

He brushed matted hair from the thin face. "Jesus Christ, what have you been doing?" he murmured. Drugs? What drugs would make someone run naked through the snow? Wincing, Howell let the tangled locks slip from his hand.

The boy moaned and twisted his head. He bared his teeth, eyes still tightly shut, and cried softly. His hand drooped upon his chest, fingers falling open. In his palm lay a stone attached to a filthy string around his neck.

Howell crossed the room to a bay window. Here a window seat served as spare bed, fitted neatly into the embrasure. He opened a drawer beneath the seat and pulled out blankets, quickly smoothed the cushion and

arranged pillows. Then he got towels and tried his best to dry the boy
before wrapping him in a clean blanket and dragging him to the window.
Grunting, he eased him onto the bed. He covered him first with a cotton
comforter, then heaped on coarse woolen blankets until the boy snorted
and turned onto his stomach. After a few minutes his breathing slowed.
Howell sank into an armchair to watch him sleep.

From a white dream, Andrew moaned and thrashed, floundering
through unyielding pastures that resolved into blankets tangled about his
legs. He opened his eyes and lay very still, holding his breath in terror.
The darkness held an awful secret. He whimpered as he tried to place it.
Turning his head, he saw a shining patch above him, a pale moon in a
cobalt sky. His eyes burned. Shrugging free of the comforter, he sat up.
Through the window he glimpsed the forest, snowy fields blued by moonlight. Colors. He glanced down and, for the first time since autumn, saw
his hands. Slowly he drew them to his throat until they touched the stone
there. His fingers ached, and he flexed them until the soreness abated.
New blood tingled in his palms. He sniffed tentatively: dust and stale
wood smoke, his own sweat—and another's.

In an armchair slept an old man, mouth slightly ajar, his breathing so
soft it scarcely stirred the air. At his feet lay a dog. It stared at Andrew
and growled, a low ceaseless sound like humming bees.

"Hey," whispered the boy, his voice cracking. "Good dog."

The dog drew closer to the old man's feet. Andrew swung his legs over
the bedside, gasping at the strain on forgotten muscles. As blankets slid to
the floor, he noted, surprised, how the hair on his legs had grown thick
and black.

Even without covers the room's warmth blanketed him, and he sighed
with pleasure. Unsteadily, he crossed to a window, balancing himself with
one hand against the wall. The snow had stopped. Through clouded glass
he saw an untracked slope, a metal birdfeeder listing beneath its white
dome. He reached for the talisman, remembering. Autumn days when he
tugged wild grapes from brittle vines had given way to the long fat weeks
of a winter without snow. Suddenly he wondered how long it had been—
months? years?—and recalled his mother's words.

. . . *they forgot . . . and stayed forever, and died up there in the
woods . . .*

Closing his eyes, he drew the amulet to his mouth and rubbed it
against his lip, thinking, *Just for a little while, I could go again just for a
little while . . .*

He had almost not come back. He shook his head, squeezing tears from shut eyes. Shuddering, he leaned forward until his forehead rested against the windowpane.

A house.

The talisman slipped from his hand to dangle around his neck once more. Andrew held his breath, listening. His heartbeat quickened from desire to fear.

Whose house?

Someone had brought him back. He faced the center of the room.

In the armchair slumped the old man, regarding Andrew with mild pale eyes. "Aren't you cold?" he croaked, and sat up. "I can get you a robe."

Embarrassed, Andrew sidled to the window seat and wrapped himself in the comforter, then hunched onto the mattress. "That's okay," he muttered, drawing his knees together. The words came out funny, and he repeated them, slowly.

Howell blinked, trying to clear his vision. "It's still night," he stated, and coughed. Festus whined, bumping against Howell's leg. The astronaut suddenly stared at Andrew more closely. "What the hell were you doing out there?"

Andrew shrugged. "Lost, I guess."

Howell snorted. "I guess so."

The boy waited for him to bring up parents, police; but the man only gazed at him thoughtfully. The man looked sick. Even in the dimness, Andrew made out lesions on his face and hands, the long skull taut with yellow skin.

"You here alone?" Andrew finally asked.

"The dog." Howell nudged the spaniel with his foot. "My dog, Festus. I'm Eugene Howell. Major Howell."

"Andrew," the boy said. A long silence before the man spoke again. "You live here?"

"Yeah."

"Your parents live here?"

"No. They're dead. I mean, my mother just died. My father died a long time ago."

Howell rubbed his nose, squinting. "Well, you got someone you live with?"

"No. I live alone." He hesitated, then inclined his head toward the window. "In The Fallows."

"Huh." Howell peered at him more closely. "Were you—some kind of drugs? I found you out there—" He gestured at the window. "Butt naked. In a blizzard." He laughed hoarsely, then gazed pointedly at the boy. "I'm just curious, that's all. Stark naked in a snowstorm. Jesus Christ."

Andrew picked at a scab on his knee. "I'm not on drugs," he said at last. "I just got lost." Suddenly he looked up, beseeching. "I'll get out of your way. You don't have to do anything. Okay? Like you don't have to call anyone. I can just go back to my place."

Howell yawned and stood slowly. "Well, not tonight. When they clear the roads." He looked down at his feet, chagrined to see he still had his boots on. "I'm going to lie down for a little while. Still a few hours before morning."

He smiled wanly and shuffled toward the bedroom, Festus following him. In the kitchen he paused to get his inhaler, then stared with mild disbelief at the counter where an unopened sack of dog food and six cans of Alpo stood next to a half-filled grocery bag.

"Festus," he muttered, tearing open the sack. "I'll be damned. I forgot Pete brought this." He dumped food into the dog's bowl and glanced back at the boy staring puzzled into the kitchen.

"You can take a shower if you want," suggested Howell. "In there. Towels, a robe. Help yourself." Then he went to bed.

In the bathroom Andrew found bedpans, an empty oxygen tank, clean towels. He kicked his comforter outside the door, hesitated before retrieving it and folding it upon the sofa. Then he returned to the bathroom. Grimacing, he examined his reflection in the mirror. Dirt caked his pores. What might be scant stubble roughened his chin, but when he rubbed it, most came off onto his fingers in tiny black beads.

In the tub stood a white metal stool. Andrew settled on this and turned on the water. He squeezed handfuls of shampoo through his long hair until the water ran clear. Most of a bar of soap dissolved before he stepped out, the last of the hot water gurgling down the drain. On the door hung a thin green hospital robe, E. HOWELL printed on the collar in Magic Marker. Andrew flung this over his shoulders and stepped back into the living room.

Gray light flecked the windowpanes, enough light that finally he could explore the place. It was a small house, not much bigger than his abandoned cottage. Worn Navaho rugs covered flagstone floors in front of a stone fireplace, still heaped with dead ashes and the remains of a Christmas tree studded with blackened tinsel. Brass gaslight fixtures supported light bulbs and green glass shades. And everywhere about the room, pictures.

He could scarcely make out the cedar paneling beneath so many photographs. He crossed to the far wall stacked chest-high with tottering bookshelves. Above the shelves hung dozens of framed photos.

"Jeez." Andrew shivered a little as he tied the robe.

Photos of Earthrise, moonrise. The Crab Nebula. The moon. He edged along the wall, reading the captions beside the NASA logo on each print.

Mare Smythii. Crater Gambart. Crater Copernicus. Crater Descartes. Sea of Tranquility.

At wall's end, beside the window, two heavy gold frames. The first held artwork from a *Time* magazine cover showing three helmeted men against a Peter Max galaxy: MEN OF THE YEAR: THE CREW OF APOLLO 18, printed in luminous letters. He blew dust from the glass and regarded the picture thoughtfully. Behind one of the men's faceplates, he recognized Howell's face.

The other frame held an oversized cover of *Look,* a matte photograph in stark black. In the upper corner floated the moon, pale and dreaming like an infant's face.

APOLLO 19: FAREWELL TO TRANQUILITY.

Outside, the sun began to rise above Sugar Mountain. In the west glowed a three-quarter moon, fading as sunlight spilled down the mountainside. Andrew stood staring at it until his eyes ached, holding the moon there as long as he could. When it disappeared, he clambered back into bed.

When he woke later that morning, Andrew found Howell sitting in the same chair again, dozing with the dog Festus at his feet. Andrew straightened his robe and tried to slide quietly from bed. The dog barked. Howell blinked awake.

"Good morning," he yawned, and coughed. "The phone lines are down."

Andrew grinned with relief, then tried to look concerned. "How long before they're up again?"

Howell scratched his jaw, his nails rasping against white stubble. "Day or two, probably. You said you live alone?"

Andrew nodded, reaching gingerly to let Festus sniff his hand.

"So you don't need to call anyone." Howell rubbed the dog's back with a slippered foot. "He's usually pretty good with people," he said as Festus sniffed and then tentatively licked Andrew's hand. "That's good, Festus. You hungry—?"

He stumbled, forgetting the boy's name.

"Andrew," the boy said, scratching the dog's muzzle. "Good dog. Yeah, I guess I am."

Howell waved toward the kitchen. "Help yourself. My son brought over stuff the other day, on the counter in there. I don't eat much now." He coughed again and clutched the chair's arms until the coughing stopped. Andrew stood awkwardly in the center of the room.

"I have cancer," Howell said, fumbling in his robe's pockets until he found a pill bottle. Andrew stared a moment longer before going into the kitchen.

Inside the grocery bag he found wilted lettuce, several boxes of frozen dinners, now soft and damp, eggs and bread and a packet of spoiled hamburger meat. He sniffed this and his mouth watered, but when he opened the package the smell sickened him and he hastily tossed it into the trash. He settled on eggs, banging around until he found skillet and margarine. He ate them right out of the pan. After a hasty cleanup he returned to the living room.

"Help yourself to anything you want," said Howell. "I have clothes, too, if you want to get changed."

Andrew glanced down at his robe and shrugged. "Okay. Thanks." He wandered to the far wall and stared a moment at the photos again. "You're an astronaut," he said.

Howell nodded. "That's right."

"That must've been pretty cool." He pointed to the Men of the Year portrait. "Did you fly the shuttle?"

"Christ, no. That was after my time. We were Apollo. The moon missions."

Andrew remained by the wall, nodding absently. He wanted to leave; but how? He couldn't take off right away, leave this man wondering where he lived, how he'd get there in three feet of snow. He'd wait until tonight. Leave a note, the robe folded on a chair. He turned back to face Howell.

"That must've been interesting."

Howell stared at him blankly, then laughed. "Probably the most interesting thing *I* ever did," he gasped, choking as he grabbed his inhaler. Andrew watched alarmed as the astronaut sucked the mouthpiece. A faint acrid smell infused the room when Howell exhaled.

"Can't breathe," he whispered. Andrew stared at him and coughed nervously himself.

Howell sighed, the hissing of a broken bellows. "I wanted to go back. I was queued next time as commander." He tugged at the sleeves of his robe, pulling the cuffs over bony wrists. "They canceled it. The rest of the program. Like that." He tried to snap his fingers. They made a dry small sound. "Money. Then the rest. The explosion. You know."

Andrew nodded, rolling up his sleeves until they hung evenly. "I remember that."

Howell nodded. "Everybody does. But the moon. Do you remember that?"

Andrew shook his head.

"You forget it?" said Howell, incredulous.

"I wasn't born," said Andrew. He leaned against the wall, bumping a frame. "I'm only fourteen."

"Fourteen," repeated Howell. "And you never saw? In school, they never showed you?"

The boy shrugged. "The shuttle, I saw tapes of that. At school, maybe. I don't remember."

Howell stood, bumping the spaniel so that Festus grumbled noisily before settling back onto the floor. "Well here then," he said, and shuffled to the bookcase. "I have it, here—"

He fingered impatiently through several small plastic cases until he found one with NASA's imprimatur. Fastidiously he wiped the plastic cover, blowing dust from the cracks before opening it and pawing the tape carefully.

In the corner a television perched on a shelf. Beneath it was a VCR, meticulously draped with a pillowcase. Howell removed the cloth, coughing with excitement. He switched the set on.

"Okay," he announced as the flickering test pattern resolved into the NASA logo. "Now sit back. You're going to see something. History."

"Right," said Andrew loudly, and rubbed his eyes.

Static. A black expanse: dead black, unbroken by stars. Then a curve intruding upon the lower edge of the screen, dirty gray and pocked with shadow.

The image shifted. Static snarled into a voice, crisply repeating numbers. A beep. Silence. Another beep. The left side of the screen now showed a dark mass, angular limbs scratching the sky.

"What's that?" asked Andrew. It was all out of focus, black and white, wavering like cheap animation.

"The lander," said Howell. "Lunar lander."

"Oh," said Andrew: the moon. "They're there already?"

Howell nodded impatiently. "Watch this."

The mass shuddered. The entire horizon dipped and righted itself.

From a bright square within the lander something emerged clumsily like a tethered balloon, and descended the blurred pattern that must be steps. Andrew yawned, turning his head so the old man couldn't see. A voice answered commands. Garbled feedback abruptly silenced so that a single voice could be heard.

The figure bounced down, once, twice. The landscape bobbed with him. Andrew fidgeted, glancing at Howell. The old man's hands twisted in his lap as though strangling something, pulling at the hem of his robe. His eyes were riveted to the television. He was crying.

The boy quickly looked back at the screen. After another minute the tape ended. Angry hissing from the television. Andrew stood and turned down the volume, avoiding Howell's face.

"That's it, huh?" he remarked with hollow cheerfulness, hitting the rewind button.

Howell stared at him. "Did you see?"

Andrew sat back on his heels. "Yeah, sure. That's real interesting. The moon. Them landing on the moon."

"You never saw it before?"

He shook his head. "No. I like that stuff, though. Science fiction. You know."

"But this really happened."

Andrew nodded defensively. "I know. I mean, I don't remember, but I know it happened."

Howell coughed into a handkerchief, glaring at the boy. "Pretty boring to you, I guess." He stepped to the machine and removed the tape, shoving it back into its case. "No lights. Nothing exciting. Man lands on moon."

Embarrassed, Andrew stared at him. Howell returned his gaze fiercely, then sighed and rubbed the back of his neck.

"Who cares," he coughed; then looked suddenly, helplessly at the boy. "That's all I ever wanted to do, you know. Fly. And walk on the moon."

"But you did. You went. You just told me." Andrew gestured at the walls, the photographs. "All this—" He hesitated. *"Stuff,* all this stuff you got here—"

Howell stroked the videotape, gnawed fingertips catching on its plastic lip, and shook his head, shameless of tears that fell now like a disappointed child's. Andrew stared, horrified, waiting for the old man to stop, to apologize. But he went on crying. Finally the boy stood and crossed the room, turned to shut the bathroom door behind him, ran the water so as not to hear or think of him out there: an old man with a dog at his ankles, rocking back and forth with an old videotape in his hand, heedless of the flickering empty screen before him.

Andrew made dinner that night, a couple of meals on plastic trays slid into the microwave. He ended up eating both of them.

"I'll bring in some wood tomorrow," he said, pausing in the kitchen doorway to hitch up his pants. Howell had insisted on him wearing something other than the old hospital robe. Andrew had rummaged around in a bureau until he found faded corduroy trousers and a flannel shirt, both too big for him. Even with the pants cuffed they flopped around his ankles, and he had to keep pushing back his sleeves as he ran the dinner plates under the tap. When he finished the dishes he poured Howell a glass of scotch and joined him in the other room. The old man sipped noisily as the two of them sat in front of the cold fireplace, Andrew pulling at his frayed shirt cuffs. In the kitchen he'd swallowed a mouthful of scotch when Howell wasn't looking. Now he wished he'd taken more.

"I could bring in some wood tonight, I guess," he said at last.

Howell shook his head. "Tomorrow'll be fine. I'll be going to bed soon anyway. I haven't had a fire here since Christmas. Peter built it." He gestured at the half-burned spruce. "As you can see. My son can't build a fire worth a tinker's damn."

Andrew pushed a long lock of hair from his eyes. "I don't know if I can either."

"That's okay. I'll teach you." Howell took another sip of scotch, placed the glass on the floor. Festus stood and flopped beside Andrew, mumbling contentedly. The boy scratched the dog's head. He wondered how soon Howell would go to sleep, and glanced at the back door before turning to the old man. In the dim light, Howell's cheeks glowed rosily, and he looked more like the man on the magazine cover. Andrew tugged at the dog's ears and leaned back in his chair.

"You got Man of the Year," he said at last.

"We all got Man of the Year. Peter was just a kid. Not impressed." Howell grimaced. "I guess it comes with the territory."

Andrew looked away. "I was impressed," he said after a moment. "I just didn't remember. They don't have any of that stuff now."

Howell nodded. For a few minutes they sat, the silence broken only by the battering of wind at the roof.

Then, "You're a runaway," said Howell.

Andrew stared fixedly at the dog at his feet. "Yeah."

Howell rubbed his chin. "Well, I guess that's not so bad. At least in Kamensic it's safe enough. You found one of the abandoned cabins down there."

Andrew sighed and locked his hands behind his head. "Yeah. We used to go there when I was a kid. My mother and I. Up until a few years ago." He tousled Festus's ears with elaborate casualness. "You gonna call the police?"

Howell peered at him. "Do you want me to?"

"No." The boy drew back his hand, and Festus yawned loudly. "There's no one to go to. My mom died last summer. She killed herself. My father died before I was born. Nobody cares."

"Nobody looked for you?"

Andrew shrugged. "Who's to look? My aunt, I guess. They have their own kids. I did okay."

Howell nodded. "Until the first snow." He coughed. "Well, you must be a damned resourceful kid, that's all I can say. I won't call the police. But I can't let you go back out there alone. It'll snow again, and I won't be around to find you."

Andrew shook his head. "Just leave me alone." He rubbed his stinging eyes. "No one ever cared except her, and she—"

"That's okay," Howell said softly. He coughed again, then asked, "What happened to your father?"

"Dead. He disappeared one day. They never found him."

"The war?"

Andrew shook his head. "Up here—he was up here. Visiting. We had family. He—my mother said he died here in the woods." He stared at the floor, silent.

He wants to leave, thought Howell. In the dimness the boy looked very young. Howell recalled other nights, another boy. His heart ached so suddenly that he shuddered, gasping for breath. Andrew stood in alarm.

"Nothing—nothing—" Howell whispered, motioning him away. His head sank back onto his chest. After a few minutes he looked up. "Guess I'll go to bed now."

Andrew helped him into the bedroom. Not much bigger than the room in Andrew's abandoned cottage, but scrupulously neat, and almost all windows except for the wall above the double bed. Howell slipped from his robe, leaving Andrew holding it awkwardly while the old man eased himself into bed, grunting from the effort.

"Just put it there—" Howell pointed to the door. Andrew hung the robe on a hook. He tried to avoid looking directly at Howell, but there was little else: the black windows, a bureau, a closet door. Above the bed a framed NASA photo of the moon. Andrew pretended interest in this and leaned over Howell to stare at it. In the white margin beneath the moon's gray curve someone had written in a calligraphic hand:

> *Come on all you*
> *Lets get busy*
> *for the speedy trips*
> *to all Planets and*
> *back to earth again.*

"Huh," said Andrew. Behind him, Festus shambled into the room and, grumbling, settled himself on a braided rug.

The old man winced, twisting to stare up at the photograph. "You like that?" he said.

"Sure," said Andrew, shrugging. "What's it mean? That poem or whatever. You write that?"

Howell smiled. He was so thin that it was hard to believe there was a body there beneath all the smooth quilts and blankets. "No, I didn't write that. I'll show you where it came from, though; tomorrow maybe. If you want. Remind me."

"Okay." Andrew waited: to see if Howell needed anything; to see if he would be dismissed. But the old man just lay there, eyes fluttering shut and then open again. Finally the boy said, "Good night," and left the room.

It took Andrew a long time to fall asleep that night. He sat on the window seat, staring out at the snow-covered fields as he fingered the amulet around his neck. He didn't know why he'd stayed this long. He should have left as soon as he could that morning, waited for the old man to fall asleep (he slept all day: he must be really sick, to sleep so much) and then crept out the back door and disappeared into the woods.

Even now . . . He pulled at the amulet, holding it so tightly it bit into the ball of his thumb. He should leave now.

But he didn't. The wrinkled white face staring up from the double bed reminded him of his mother in the coffin. He had never noticed how many lines were in her face; she really hadn't been that old. He wondered how long Howell had been sick. He remembered the astronaut he'd seen at the library that summer, a disappointment, really. Andrew had been expecting a spacesuit and something else: not ray guns, that would be dumb, but some kind of instruments, or moon rocks maybe. Instead there'd been an old man in Izod shirt and chinos talking about how the country had failed the space program. Andrew had fidgeted until his mother let him go outside.

It must have been the same man, he thought now. Major Howell, not really any more interesting now than he'd been then. He hadn't even walked on the moon. Andrew dropped the amulet onto his chest and pulled a blanket about his knees, stared out the window. Clouds drifted in front of the rising moon. At the edge of the woods there would be rabbit tracks, fox scat. A prickle of excitement ran through him at the thought, and he lay back upon the narrow bed. He would leave tomorrow, early, before Howell got up to let the dog out.

He didn't leave. He woke to Howell calling hoarsely from the bedroom. Andrew found him half-sitting on the side of the bed, his hand reaching pathetically for the nightstand where a glass of water had been knocked over, spilling pill bottles and inhalers and soggy tissues onto the floor.

"Could you—please—"

Andrew found Howell's inhaler and gave it to him. Then he straightened out the mess, put more water in the glass and watched as Howell took his pills, seven of them. He waited to see if Howell wanted anything else, then let Festus outside. When the boy returned to the bedroom, Howell was still sitting there, eyes shut as he breathed heavily through his nose. His eyes flickered open to stare at Andrew: a terrified expression that made the boy's heart tumble. But then he closed them again and just sat there.

Finally Andrew said, "I'll help you get dressed." Howell nodded without opening his eyes.

It didn't take Andrew long to help him into a flannel robe and slippers, and into the bathroom. Andrew swore silently and waited outside the door, listening to the groan of water in the taps, the old man's wheezing and shambling footsteps. Outside, Festus scratched at the back door and whined to be let in. Sighing, Andrew took care of the dog, went back to the bathroom and waited until Howell came out again.

"Thank you," the old man said. His voice was faint, and he trembled as he supported himself with one hand on the sink, the other against the door frame.

"It's okay, Major Howell," said Andrew. He took Howell's elbow and guided him into the living room. The old man was heavy, no matter that he was so thin; Andrew was terrified that he'd fall on the flagstone floor. "Here, sit here and I'll get you something. Breakfast?"

He made instant coffee and English muffins with scrambled eggs. The eggs were burned, but it didn't really matter: Howell took only a bite of the muffin and sipped at his tepid coffee. Andrew gave the rest to Festus. *He* would eat later, outside.

Afterward, as Howell sat dozing in the armchair by the fireplace, Andrew made a fire. The room filled with smoke before he figured out how to open the damper, but after that it burned okay, and he brought in more wood. Then he took Festus outside for a walk. He wore Howell's parka and heavy black mittens with NASA stenciled on the cuffs. The sunlight on the snow made his eyes ache as he tried to see where Festus ran up the first slope of Sugar Mountain. He took off one glove, unzipped the neck of the parka and stuck his hand inside. The amulet was still there, safe against his chest. He stopped, hearing Festus crashing through the underbrush. Would the dog follow him? Probably not: he was an old dog, and Andrew knew how fast a fox could run, knew that even though he had never hunted this spot it would be easy to find his way to a safe haven.

Then the wind shifted, bringing with it the tang of wood smoke. Festus ambled out of the woods, shaking snow from his ears, and ran up to Andrew. The boy let the amulet drop back inside his flannel shirt and zipped up the parka. He turned and walked back to the house.

"Have a nice walk?" Howell's voice was still weak but his eyes shone brightly, and he smiled at the boy stomping the snow from boots too big for him.

"Oh yeah, it was great." Andrew hung up the parka and snorted, then turning back to Howell tried to smile. "No, it was nice. Is all that your property back there?" He strode to the fireplace and crouched in front of it, feeding it twigs and another damp log.

"Just about all of it." Howell pulled a lap blanket up closer to his chin. "This side of Sugar Mountain and most of the lakefront."

"Wow." Andrew settled back, already sweating from the heat. "It's really nice back there by the lake. We used to go there in the summer, my mom and me. I love it up here."

Howell nodded. "I do too. Did you live in the city?"

Andrew shook his head. "Yonkers. It sucks there now; like living in the Bronx." He opened the top button of his shirt and traced the string against his chest. "Once, when I was a kid, we heard an astronaut talk here. At the library. Was that you?"

Howell smiled. "Yup. I wondered if you might have been one of those kids, one of those times. So many kids, I must have talked to a thousand kids at the school here. You want to be an astronaut when you were little?"

"Nah." Andrew poked at the log, reached to pet Festus. "I never wanted to be anything, really. School's really boring, and like where I lived sucks, and . . ." He gestured at the fire, the room and the door leading outside. "The only thing I ever really liked was being up here, in the woods. Living in The Fallows this year, that was great."

"It's the only thing I liked, too. After I stopped working." Howell sighed and glanced over at the pictures covering the wall, the sagging bookcases. He had never really been good with kids. The times he had spoken at the school he'd had films to back him up, and later, videotapes and videodiscs. He had never been able to entertain his son here, or his friends, or the occasional visiting niece or nephew. The pictures were just pictures to them, not even colorful. The tapes were boring. When Peter and his friends were older, high school or college, sometimes Howell would show them the Nut File, a manila envelope crammed with letters from Rubber Man Lord of Jupiter and articles clipped from tabloids, a lifetime of NASA correspondence with cranks and earnest kooks who had developed faster-than-light drives in their garages. Peter and his friends had laughed at the letters, and Howell had laughed too, reading them again. But none of his visitors had ever been touched, the way Howell had. None of them had ever wondered why a retired NASA astronaut would have a drawer full of letters from nuts.

"Andrew," he said softly; then, "Andrew," as loud as he could. The boy drew back guiltily from the fire. Festus started awake and stared up, alarmed.

"Sorry—"

Howell drew a clawed hand from beneath the blanket and waved it weakly. "No, no—that's all right—just . . ."

He coughed; it took him a minute to catch his breath. Andrew stood and waited next to him, staring back at the fire. "Okay, I'm okay now," Howell wheezed at last. "Just: remember last night? That picture with the poem?"

Andrew looked at him blankly.

"In my room—the moon, you wanted to know if I wrote it—"

The boy nodded. "Oh yeah. The moon poem, right. Sure."

Howell smiled and pointed to the bookcase. "Well here, go look over there—"

Andrew watched him for a moment before turning to the bookcase and looking purposefully at the titles. Sighing, Festus moved closer to the old astronaut's feet. Howell stroked his back, regarding Andrew thoughtfully. He coughed, inclining his head toward the wall.

"Andrew." Howell took a long breath, then leaned forward, pointing. "That's it, there."

Beneath some magazines, Andrew found a narrow pamphlet bound with tape. "This?" he wondered. He removed it gingerly and blew dust from its cover.

Howell settled back in his chair. "Right. Bring it here. I want to show you something."

Andrew settled into the chair beside Howell. A paperbound notebook, gray with age. On the cover swirled meticulous writing in Greek characters, and beneath them the same hand, in English.

> *Return address:*
>
> *Mr. Nicholas Margalis*
> *116 Argau Dimitrou*
> *Apt. No. 3*
> *Salonika, Greece*

"Read it," said Howell. "I found that in the NASA library. He sent it to Colonel Somebody right after the war. It floated around for forty years, sat in NASA's Nut File before I finally took it."

He paused. "I used to collect stuff like that. Letters from crackpots. People who thought they could fly. UFOs, moonmen. *Outer space.* I try to keep an open mind." He gestured at the little book in Andrew's hand. "I don't think anyone else has ever read that one. Go ahead."

Carefully Andrew opened the booklet. On lined paper tipsy block letters spelled PLANES, PLANETS, PLANS. Following this were pages of numerical equations, sketches, a crude drawing labeled THE AIR DIGGER ROCKET SHAPE.

"They're plans for a rocket ship," said Howell. He craned his neck so he could see.

"You're kidding." Andrew turned the brittle pages. "Did they build it?"

"Christ, no! I worked it out once. If you were to build the Margalis Planets Plane it would be seven miles long." He laughed silently.

Andrew turned to a page covered with zeros.

"Math," said Howell.

More calculations. Near the end Andrew read,

Forty years of continuous flying will cover the following space below, 40 years, 14,610 days, 216,000,000,000,000 × 14610—equals 3,155,750,000,000,000,000 miles. That is about the mean distance to the farthest of the Planets, Uranus.

Trillions, Quatrillions, Billions and Millions of miles all can be reached with this Plan.

Andrew shook his head. "This is so sad! He really thought it would fly?"

"They all thought they could fly," said Howell. "Read me the end."

" 'Experimenting of thirty-five years with levers, and compounds of,' " read Andrew. " 'I have had made a patent model of wooden material and proved a very successful work.

" 'My Invention had been approved by every body in the last year 1944, 1946 in my native village Panorma, Crevens, Greece. Every body stated it will be a future great success in Mechanics.

" 'Yours truly.' "

Andrew stopped abruptly.

"Go on," prodded Howell. "The end. The best part."

On the inside back cover, Andrew saw the same hand, somewhat shakier and in black ink.

I have written in these copy book about ¹/₁₀₀₀ of what actually will take in building a real Rocket Shape Airo-Plane to make trips to the Planets.

There in the planets we will find Paradise, and the undiying water to drink so we never will die, and never be in distress.

> *Come on all you*
> *Lets get busy*
> *for the speedy trips*
> *to all Planets and*
> *back to earth again.*

> *Nicholas S. Margalis*
> *Aug 19 1946*

Howell sat in silence. For a long moment Andrew stared at the manuscript, then glanced at the old man beside him. Howell was smiling now as he stared into the fire. As Andrew watched, his eyelids flickered, and then the old astronaut dozed, snoring softly along with the dog at his feet.

Andrew waited. Howell did not wake. Finally the boy stood and poked at the glowing logs. When he turned back, the blanket had fallen from the old man's lap and onto the dog's back. Andrew picked it up and carefully draped it across Howell's knees.

For a moment he stood beside him. The old man smelled like carnations. Against his yellow skin broken capillaries bloomed blue and crimson. Andrew hesitated. Then he bowed his head until his lips grazed Howell's scalp. He turned away to replace the booklet on its shelf and went to bed.

That night the wind woke Howell. Cold gripped him as he sat up in bed, and his hand automatically reached for Festus. The dog was not beside him.

"Festus?" he called softly, then slid from bed, pulling on his robe and catching his breath before walking across the bedroom to the window.

A nearly full moon hung above the pine forest, dousing the snow so that it glowed silvery blue. Deer and rabbits had made tracks steeped in shadow at wood's edge. He stood gazing at the sky when a movement at the edge of the field caught him.

In the snow an animal jumped and rolled, its fur a fiery gleam against the whiteness. Howell gasped in delight: a fox, tossing the snow and crunching it between its black jaws. Then something else moved. The old man shook his head in disbelief.

"Festus."

Clumsily, sinking over his head in the drifts, the spaniel tumbled and rose beside the fox, the two of them playing in the moonlight. Clouds of white sparkled about them as the fox leaped gracefully to land beside the dog, rolling until it was only an auburn blur.

Howell held his breath, moving away from the window so that his shadow could not disturb them. Then he recalled the boy sleeping in the next room.

"Andrew," he whispered loudly, his hand against the wall to steady himself as he walked into the room. "Andrew, you have to see something."

The window seat was empty. The door leading outside swung open, banging against the wall in the frigid wind. Howell turned and walked toward the door, finally stopping and clinging to the frame as he stared outside.

In the snow lay a green hospital gown, blown several feet from the door. Bare footprints extended a few yards into the field. Howell followed them. Where the shadows of the house fell behind him, the footprints ended. Small pawprints marked the drifts, leading across the field to where the fox and dog played.

He lifted his head and stared at them. He saw where Festus' tracks ran off to the side of the house and then back to join the other's. As he watched, the animals abruptly stopped. Festus craned his head to look back at his master and then floundered joyfully through the drifts to meet him. Howell stepped forward. He stared from the tracks to the two animals, yelled in amazement and stood stark upright. Then stumbling he tried to run toward them. When Festus bounded against his knees the man staggered and fell. The world tilted from white to swirling darkness.

It was light when he came to. Beside him hunched the boy, his face red and tear streaked.

"Major Howell," he said. "Please—"

The old man sat up slowly, pulling the blankets around him. He stared for a moment at Andrew, then at the far door where the flagstones shone from melted snow.

"I saw it," he whispered. "What you did, I saw it."

Andrew shook his head. "Don't— You can't—"

Howell reached for his shoulder and squeezed it. "How does it work?" Andrew stared at him, silent.

"How does it work?" Howell repeated excitedly. "How can you do it?"

The boy bit his lip. Howell's face was scarlet, his eyes feverishly bright. "I—it's this," Andrew said at last, pulling the amulet from his chest. "It was my mother's. I took it when she died."

His hands shaking, Howell gently took the stone between his fingers, rubbing the frayed string. "Magic," he said.

Andrew shivered despite the fire at his back. "It's from here. The Indians. The Tankiteke. There were lots, my mother said. Her grandfather found it when he was little. My father—" He ended brokenly.

Howell nodded in wonder. "It works," he said. "I saw it work."

Andrew swallowed and drew back a little, so that the amulet slipped from Howell's hand. "Like this," he explained, opening his mouth and slipping one finger beneath his tongue. "But you don't swallow it."

"I saw you," the old man repeated. "I saw you playing with my dog." He nodded at Festus, dozing in front of the fire. "Can you be anything?"

Andrew bit his lip before answering. "I think so. My mother said you just concentrate on it—on what you want. See—"

And he took it into his hand, held it out so that the firelight illuminated it. "It's like all these things in one. Look: it's got wings and horns and hooves."

"And that's how you hid from them." Howell slapped his knees. "No wonder they never found you."

Andrew nodded glumly.

"Well," Howell coughed. He sank back into the chair, eyes closed. He reached for Andrew, and the boy felt the old man's hand tighten about his own, cold and surprisingly strong. After a minute Howell opened his eyes. He looked from the flames to Andrew and held the boy's gaze for a long time, silent. Then,

"You could fly with something like that," he said. "You could fly again."

Andrew let his breath out in a long shudder. "That's right," he said finally beneath his breath. He turned away. "You could fly again, Major Howell."

Howell reached for the boy's hand again, his fingers clamping there like a metal hinge. "Thank you," he whispered. "I think I'll go to sleep now."

The following afternoon the plow came. Andrew heard it long before it reached Sugar Mountain, an eager roar like a great wave overtaking the snowbound bungalow. The phone was working, too; he heard Howell in the next room, talking between fits of coughing. A short time later a pickup bounced up the drive. Andrew stared in disbelief, then fled into the bathroom, locking the door behind him.

He heard several voices greeting Howell at the door, the thump of boots upon the flagstones.

"Thank you, Isaac," wheezed the astronaut. Andrew heard the others stomp into the kitchen. "I was out of everything." Andrew opened the door a crack and peered out, glaring at Festus when the dog scratched at it.

Howell motioned the visitors into the bedroom, shutting the door behind him. Andrew listened to their murmuring voices before storming back into the living room. He huddled out of sight on the window seat, staring outside until they left. After the pickup rattled back down the mountainside, he stalked into the kitchen to make dinner.

"I didn't tell them," Howell said mildly that evening as they sat before the fire.

Andrew glared at him but said nothing.

"They wouldn't be interested," Howell said. Every breath now shook him like a cold wind. "Andrew . . ."

The boy sat in silence, his hand tight around the amulet. Finally Howell stood, knocking over his glass of scotch. He started to bend to retrieve it when Andrew stopped him.

"No," he said hoarsely. "Not like that." He hesitated, then said, "You ever see a drunk dog?"

Howell stared at him, then nodded. "Yes."

"It's like that," said Andrew. "Only worse."

Festus followed them as they walked to the door, Andrew holding the old man's elbow. For a moment they hesitated. Then Andrew shoved the door open, wincing at the icy wind that stirred funnels of snow in the field.

"It's so cold," Howell whispered, shivering inside his flannel robe.

"It won't be so bad," said Andrew, helping him outside.

They stood in the field. Overhead the full moon bloomed as Festus nosed after old footprints. Andrew stepped away from Howell, then took the talisman from around his own neck.

"Like I told you," he said as he handed it to the old man.

Howell hesitated. "It'll work for me?"

Andrew clutched his arms, shivering. "I think so," he said, gazing at the amulet in the man's hand. "I think you can be whatever you want."

Howell nodded and turned away. "Don't look," he whispered.

Andrew stared at his feet. A moment later the flannel robe blew against his ankles. He heard a gasp and shut his eyes, willing away the tears before opening them again.

In front of Andrew the air sparkled for an instant with eddies of snow. Beside him, Festus whined, staring above his head. Andrew looked up and saw a fluttering scrap like a leaf: a bat squeaking as its wings beat feebly, then more powerfully, as if drawing strength from the freezing wind. It circled the boy's head—once, twice—then began to climb, higher and higher, until Andrew squinted to see it in the moonlight.

"Major Howell!" he shouted. "Major Howell!"

To Howell the voice sounded like the clamor of vast and thundering bells. All the sky now sang to him as he flailed through the air, rising above trees and roof and mountain. He heard the faint buzzing of the stars, the sigh of snow in the trees fading as he flew above the pines into the open sky.

And then he saw it: more vast than ever it had been from the orbiter, so bright his eyes could not bear it. And the sound! like the ocean, waves of air dashing against him, buffeting him as he climbed, the roar and crash and peal of it as it pulled him upward. His wings beat faster, the air sharp in his throat, thinning as the darkness fell behind him and the noise swelled with the brightness, light now everywhere, and sound, not silent or dead as they had told him but thundering and burgeoning with heat, light, the vast eye opening like a volcano's core. His wings ceased beating and he drifted upward, all about him the glittering stars, the glorious clamor, the great and shining face of the moon, his moon at last: the moon.

Andrew spent the night pacing the little house, sitting for a few minutes on sofa or kitchen counter, avoiding the back door, avoiding the windows, avoiding Howell's bedroom. Festus followed him, whining. Finally, when the snow glimmered with first light, Andrew went outside to look for Howell.

It was Festus who found him after just a few minutes, in a shallow dell where ferns would grow in the spring and deer sleep on the bracken. Now snow had drifted where the old man lay. He was naked, and even from the lawn Andrew could tell he was dead. The boy turned and walked back to the house, got Howell's flannel robe and a blanket. He was shaking uncontrollably when he went back out.

Festus lay quietly beside the body, muzzle resting on his paws. Andrew couldn't move Howell to dress him: the body was rigid from the cold. So he gently placed the robe over the emaciated frame, tucked the blanket around him. Howell's eyes were closed now, and he had a quiet expression on his face. Not like Andrew's mother at all, really: except that one hand clutched something, a grimy bit of string trailing from it to twitch across the snow. Andrew knelt, shivering, and took one end of the string, tugged it. The amulet slid from Howell's hand.

Andrew stumbled to his feet and held it at arm's length, the little stone talisman twisting slowly. He looked up at the sky. In the west, above the cottage, the moon hung just above the horizon. Andrew turned to face the dark bulk of Sugar Mountain, its edges brightening where the sun was rising above Lake Muscanth. He pulled his arm back and threw the amulet as hard as he could into the woods. Festus raised his head to watch the boy. They both waited, listening; but there was no sound, nothing to show where it fell. Andrew wiped his hands on his pants and looked down at the astronaut again. He stooped and let the tip of one finger brush the old man's forehead. Then he went inside to call the police.

There were questions, and people from newspapers and TV, and Andrew's own family, overjoyed (he couldn't believe it, they all cried) to see him again. And eventually it was all straightened out.

There was a service at the old Congregational church in Kamensic Village near the museum. After the first thaw they buried Howell in the small local cemetery, beside the farmers and Revolutionary War dead. A codicil to his will left the dog Festus to the fourteen-year-old runaway discovered to have been living with the dying astronaut in his last days. The codicil forbade sale of the bungalow and Sugar Mountain, the property to revert to the boy upon his twentieth birthday. Howell's son protested this: Sugar Mountain was worth a fortune now, the land approved for subdivisions with two-acre zoning. But the court found the will to be valid, witnessed as it was by Isaac and Seymour Schelling, village grocers and public notaries.

When he finished school, Andrew moved into the cottage at Sugar Mountain. Festus was gone by then, buried where the deer still come to sleep in the bracken. There is another dog now, a youngish English cocker spaniel named Apollo. The ancient Volkswagen continues to rust in the driveway, next to a Volvo with plates that read NASA NYC. The plows and phone company attend to the cottage somewhat more reliably, and there is a second phone line as well, since Andrew needs to transmit things to the city and Washington nearly every day now, snow or not.

In summer he walks with the dog along the sleepy dirt road, marking where an owl has killed a vole, where vulpine tracks have been left in the soft mud by Lake Muscanth. And every June he visits the elementary school and shows the fifth graders a videotape from his private collection: views of the moon's surface filmed by Command Module Pilot Eugene Howell.

AUTHOR'S NOTE: Nicholas Margalis' manuscript is in the archives of the National Air & Space Museum, Smithsonian Institution.

In memory of Nancy Malawista and Brian Hart

When the Rose Is Dead

DAVID ZINDELL

THIS IS the saddest story I know."

On a gray winter night in the Endless City, in an alley off Blue Zone's D-Street, four friends sat around a blazing oil drum, swapping stories. One-Eyed Nick was the oldest, and sometimes, the wisest of them. He fed some trash into the drum, and he adjusted his black eye patch as he addressed the other three. "This is the saddest story I know," he repeated, "about a doctor who fell in love with a woman named Rose." He stood with his back to fire, careless of the flames heating up his greasy parka and overalls; he had worked in a hospital once, often in the incinerator room, so he had learned not to worry about fire or grease. "Have I told you this story before?"

"No," the Napalm Man said gravely. He sat on a pile of boxes beneath some covered parking. The whole tottering structure pinged with rain-drops striking rusty metal; when the wind gusted, smoke from the oil drum blew over him. He was hunched over in his expensive but shabby trenchcoat, and he methodically sipped from a bottle of whiskey wrapped up in a brown paper bag. "No, tell us, Nick."

A huge, damaged man called Sarge reluctantly agreed and said, "You never told us nothing. Well, almost nothing. Where'd you say the doctor met Rose, in the damned Ninth Sector of the goddamned Black Zone?" He fingered the scars crisscrossing the top of his bald head, then he muttered something that sounded like, "Aw, hell, I just want simplicity, ya mean?"

Atop the box between Sarge and the Napalm Man, a gaunt, old woman rocked slowly back and forth. One-Eyed Nick could see that she had once been striking-looking, but he couldn't quite remember her name, couldn't guess what she was thinking, because her face was as hard and sharp as the brick splinters of the bombed-out buildings down on G-Street. Her eyes were dark and silent, and if she remembered that poor, cut-up Sarge's "ya mean?" was short for "Do you know what I mean?", if she understood half of what they were saying or knew the meaning of any-thing at all, he couldn't tell.

One-Eyed Nick smiled at her sadly. *Had* he told this story before? He remembered that he had a Ph.D. in molecular biology, and was wanted for some crime or other, but he couldn't remember what he had eaten for dinner that evening or an old woman's name. He sighed, shrugged his shoulders, and continued, "It was during the ninety-first phase of the war, just before the armistice with the Red Zone—a bad time, you know. And for Dr. Stone—that was his name, have I told you?—the worst time, the very worst. He was a doctor in the Zone Hospital, a psychiatrist, it's true, but you know, *some* psychiatrists actually help people, or at least try to. He'd spent most of his residency doing implants; in fact, he was well known for developing the biochips they used in the soldiers, in the really sad cases, the ones with serious head wounds. He should never have transferred out of the implant ward. But he was ambitious, Doctor Stone. Was it enough that he'd published articles in the *Black Zone Journal of Medicine*, that he was respected, maybe even close to being famous? No, it wasn't enough. He wanted to learn how the mind really worked, to *know*. He could see that the big breakthroughs were coming from the remedial education ward. Deconstruction and reconstruction—he was fascinated with the idea of helping wound victims remember, with the fleshing out of beliefs and belief systems. Who wouldn't be? And, of course, with the memories, recovering lost memories, or sometimes, creating memories where there hadn't even been any memories. Creating—even though he wouldn't have admitted it to anybody, he was just like a lot of doctors; I think he wanted to play God. And you have to be careful about what you want, you know, because you just might get it. After the Director of Psychiatry reviewed Dr. Stone's application, he assigned him an unlimited security clearance. And then, when Dr. Stone found out what *really* went on in the remedial education ward, he just about went nuts, as nuts as any of the patients in the schizo or autistic ward. He wanted to back out, but a lot of times, in the Black Zone, there's no way out. And anyway, after he'd done ten or twenty deconstructions it was too late for him because he was as hardened and numbed as the rest of the doctors."

"Poor Doctor Stone," Sarge broke in. "Yeah, that's too damn bad. I wasn't too keen on having an implant, ya mean? But those poor fuckers in the re-me ward—I never heard of no one that came out of there happy."

"No one's happy until he's dead," the Napalm Man slurred out, and he took another sip of whiskey.

"Hell, I'd be happy if I could just get simplicity," Sarge said. He winked at the old woman, but she was just sitting still next to him, staring at nothing.

Or it seemed she was staring at nothing. When One-Eyed Nick looked more closely, he thought she was really staring off intensely, perhaps even looking for the lights. A block away, past the row of dumpsters chained to the humming telephone poles, the alley dead-ended at the edge of the highest hill in the Blue Zone. Below them, somewhere, at the edge of memory, were the Black Zone and all the other more brilliantly illuminated zones of the City. The City itself had no edges; it was a disk of lights that went on and on forever.

The Napalm Man rolled some whiskey around in his mouth and asked, "Was that where Dr. Stone met Rose? Tell us about the remedial education ward, Nick."

One-Eyed Nick sighed and rubbed his left arm where it always hurt, on the inside above the elbow. He said, "The ward was on the top floor of the hospital's south wing. It was one of the old wards, you know, cracked tiles and long hallways, and the lights were too bright; the lights made your eyes ache so bad you wanted to pull them out of their sockets. Everything smelled like disinfectant and vomit; the air was bad because you couldn't open any of the windows. Of course most of the rooms didn't have windows, just a bed with the built-in restraints, a toilet, a sink and TV set. But the doctors' offices had windows. I used to clean them up —I was running from the law and that was the only job I could get. Anyway, from Dr. Stone's office window, you could look out across the whole sector. Out across the Sink and Diesel Flats almost to the edge of the Salient. Doctor Stone had good eyes, and he said you could see the trenches thirty miles away. When the war started going bad and the Reds threatened to use their atomic cannon, the trenches couldn't have been more than nine or ten miles from the hospital. You could hear the big guns booming like thunder, getting closer every day.

"And you know, Rose hated the sound of the guns more than anything else. She hated war, everything about it. She'd written antiwar poems— she was a famous poet. That's why she was in the hospital. The Medical Congress had just created a new category of mental illnesses, and the clinic doctors committed anyone they caught suffering from them. The unnatural desire to be alone, the inability to follow orders—there was an illness named 'oppositional disorder.' You know what that was? The psychiatrists' manual, DSM III, defines it as 'a pattern of disobedient, nega- tivistic and provocative opposition to authority figures.' And Rose was very disobedient, sometimes even provocative. She was a member of the Green Party; in fact she was one of the founders of the Greens. She wanted to abolish war, everywhere, in all the zones of the City, for all time. Crazy, huh? And that was the diagnosis, that she was suffering from an illness the doctors call 'Desire for Utopia.'

"When Dr. Stone first met her, in her little room up in the south wing, she *still* talked of ending the war all the time. She liked to bandy about arguments for weapons abolition, animal rights, and direct democracy. She liked to talk too much. She told Dr. Stone things he didn't know. Years ago, the Yellows used their atomic weapons against the Greens. During the eighty-ninth phase. They destroyed the entire zone. Nothing was left, nothing but rubble and mounds of people that looked like burned lamb chops. And the stupid Yellows, they thought they'd won, but they'd forgotten that they were *downwind* of the Greens. The dust clouds blew back over them, and they all died vomiting up their stomach linings and their hair falling out from radiation sickness—that's what she said.

"She had guts, you know, she talked about whatever she wanted to— that was one of the things Dr. Stone fell in love with. And she was a beautiful woman, beautiful black eyes and a beautiful smile. How many ways are there to fall in love? He fell in love passionately, romantically, blindingly. To tell the truth, he fell in love wantonly and unrealistically, too. He first saw her sitting on the edge of her hospital bed, waiting for him to make his rounds, and she was kicking her long, naked legs like she was a nervous little girl. But she had a *naturalness*, you know, a free and innocent quality. She didn't care that the back of her hospital gown was open halfway down her back, because she always *liked* her body, even if she was a little too full in the breasts and hips. She liked just about everything, Rose; I think she must have been in love with the world. In fact, even though she was in deep trouble, you know, all shut inside a little beige room that smelled of starched sheets and chemicals, she seemed quite happy. I think it was this irresponsible happiness of hers that immediately won Dr. Stone's heart.

"After Dr. Stone had introduced himself and started to make the typical inane bedside talk, Rose immediately took control of the conversation, something a patient should never be allowed to do. 'Do you believe in God, Doctor?'—this was practically the first thing Rose said to him. She was scared, maybe even terrified, it didn't take a psychiatrist to see that, but she managed to speak calmly, that was the way she was: the worse things got, the calmer she'd get. It was almost unreal, this calmness of hers. 'Do I believe in God?' Dr. Stone wondered aloud. 'What God?' He couldn't understand why she would ask him if he believed in God; what did God have to do with what went on in the remedial education ward of the Zone Hospital? 'What are you going to do, Doctor?' she asked as she kicked her legs and looked at him with her sad, beautiful eyes. 'Oh, God!' she whispered, 'God forgive you!' Dr. Stone went over to her and touched her shoulder; he surprised himself because he had never allowed himself to touch a patient before. 'Don't be afraid,' he said to her, 'we're not here to hurt you.' Now this was a terrible lie, because of course they both knew that if he followed the usual procedures he was going to have to hurt her, maybe not her nice body—he wasn't a torturer, after all—but her mind, that was a different thing, and when he was through mutilating her memories, she would be full of hurt, that is if she remembered anything at all. Did he believe in God? Who could know what Dr. Stone believed?—he was the most complicated man I've ever known."

One-Eyed Nick paused and sighed as he rubbed his arm. He stared out above the street at the opposite end of the alley where the power lines hissed and buzzed from the moisture in the air. It wasn't raining now, but there must have been showers or some kind of storm earlier that evening; a flickering neon sign above a hairdressing shop cast muted pinks and blues over the wet asphalt. God, it was pretty, the drowned colors swimming in the rain; you could never tell when you were going to come across a piece of prettiness in this dirty, ugly world.

The Napalm Man swigged some whiskey and offered the bottle to the old woman sitting next to him. But she was staring at something and apparently didn't see his outstretched hand. He licked his lips, gathered in the folds of his trenchcoat and took another gulp. He said, "Not too many people know what happened to God, do they? People are robots; how can robots know about God?"

Sarge looked at him and asked, "Who wants to believe in a goddamn God anymore? Nah, there's no God, but if there *was*, he'd give me simplicity, ya mean? Just simplicity and I'd be happy."

"No one's happy until he's dead," the Napalm Man said. Then he coughed, looked at One-Eyed Nick, and forced out, "Dr. Stone wasn't a robot, though, was he?"

One-Eyed Nick stared through the mist steaming up off the alley like clumps of damp, gray gauze. For a long time he tried to remember what Dr. Stone was like. Finally, he said, "No, Dr. Stone was not a robot. He was a secret rebel; you know, an outsider. He'd waited all his life for a good enough reason to spit in the eye of authority and break the rules. In one way, Rose was his salvation. In another, of course . . . well, he fell in love with her, but it's more than that, he *dared* to fall in love with her, do you see the difference? He knew what he was doing, or thought he did. He came up with a plan to save her. True, it was a desperate plan, but he was desperately in love, and desperate men do desperate things. He *had* to get her out of the hospital. He couldn't just lose her file or falsify her records, not in the remedial education ward. No, she would have to be properly discharged. But the thing was, she'd have to be treated first; if she wasn't treated, she'd be there forever. No, that's not quite true. Dr. Stone could have certified her sane, and avoided the treatment. But she'd done crimes—I'll tell you about this in a minute—and sane criminals were bused to the incinerators at the edge of the Diesal Flats, and they never came back.

"So Dr. Stone began visiting Rose in her ugly little room. Every day, sometimes twice per day, occasionally even at night. He'd had about fifty patients so far on the re-me ward, and they'd all been criminally insane. But he used the same techniques with Rose; there were no machines and very few drugs. A pen, a notebook and a tape recorder—these were all the instruments he needed, at least at first. He *had* to record her memories, you know. His method was largely psychoanalytic and associational: What were her parents names? What did she think it meant that her favorite color was green? Did she remember the day her father's plane was shot down and her mother took her to live in the housing project at Cabrini Green? And so on; there was no end to Dr. Stone's questions. He was trying to make a map of her mind. Of her memories. Herself, her very self, do you see?

"Of course, Rose didn't want to talk much, not about the really personal things. She had a strong will—why should she help the doctors do something evil? She'd spent her life trying to fight what she thought was evil, so why should she strip her soul bare just for him to see? No, she wouldn't answer his questions, but she did *ask* him questions: Had he lost anyone he'd loved in the war? How could such a kind-looking man condone holding people in a hospital against their will? And one day, she rubbed her long hands together nervously and asked him, 'What happened to your other patients, Doctor? Did you just erase their memories like dumping information from a computer? What were they like . . . afterwards?' And he took her hands in his and said, 'You don't understand, they were sociopaths, really nuts—after the deconstruction, we had to create memories, certain events and emotions they'd never experienced. To heal them, Rose.' And she jerked her hands away from his and began rubbing her temples. 'Am I nuts, too?' she asked. 'Is that what you think you're going to do, to *heal* me?' He tried to smile, and he wanted to tell her that he loved her, but how could she ever believe that? So he said, 'Please trust me, everything will be preserved, I promise.' She touched his fingers, then, touched his ring finger where there should have been a gold band but wasn't because he'd always been too busy to think about getting married. She said, 'You've got such gentle eyes, I'd like to trust . . . but, oh, God, how can I?' She stroked his hand, flirting with him a little, even though she despised women who did that sort of thing. The thing was, she was fighting for her life. She was fighting to hide the light, you know, the secret light everyone holds deep inside. She was afraid that Dr. Stone, if he ever saw it, would snuff it out like a candle in a rainstorm.

"But he *had* to get at her memories, so he considered using the drugs. Rose must have known that he would eventually have to use drugs; she'd probably heard horror stories from the nurses about drugs that wreck your memory. There was one drug, a cross between one of the benzodiazepine derivatives and several psychotomimetics—it was called DZ-1128. It would have cracked her skull open and made her babble like a child. But Dr. Stone couldn't bring himself to have her injected, so he tried other, milder drugs, mainly caffeine and sugar. And conversation—she was addicted to conversation. One evening during the news, just after the Zone

Science Marshal had reported new outbreaks of anthrax down in the Diesal Flats, he brought a box of jelly doughnuts into her room—Rose had a terrible sweet tooth, you know. He asked her if she hated the Reds for bombing Fifth Ward, for killing her husband and her infant son. And there she sat, eating her doughnut, licking grape jelly and powder off her lips, and drinking cup after cup of rich Purple Zone coffee. He didn't expect an answer. But she surprised him, saying, 'It's funny, Dr. Stone, but I can remember when Johnny was born, everything about it in great detail. I'd always wanted a natural birth, and so did Bill; he hated the idea of me being drugged up and restrained, with monitors attached everywhere, but he always said it wasn't *him* being split open like a butchered hog, so if the pain got too bad and I wanted to ask for a spinal or something, that was fine with him. And it hurt like hell, all the panting and the midwife having me push when I wasn't ready, but the pain really *was* manageable. And afterwards they put little Johnny on my stomach, I can still see him lying there all bloody, looking up at me with his unfocused, blue eyes. I can remember the *snip* of Bill cutting the cord, and here's what's funny, I was in the bedroom cutting out a pattern for Bill's new uniform when our block was bombed. Bill was giving Johnny a piggy-back ride in the living room, and I was snipping out a piece of cardboard, and to this day, Doctor, I can't think about Johnny being born without thinking about. . . . It's just very funny the way one memory is associated with another, everything woven together like a shimmering tapestry —that's an image I've always liked—everything holding meaning next to meaning. My God, I *can't* let myself hate the Reds, or anyone else; if I did, I'd spoil it all, don't you see?'

"After that he and Rose talked long into the night. She talked about love and war and how lonely she'd been all those years before they brought her to the hospital; she told him almost everything. In the end, just before dawn, she told him about her secret poem, the one that had changed her life."

One-Eyed Nick fell silent as he looked at the old woman leaning up against the Napalm Man. She held her hands out to warm them in the light of the fire, then she massaged the long bones on the back of her hand. She smiled at One-Eyed Nick; it was the first time that night he remembered seeing her smile.

"How could a dumb poem change anyone's life?" Sarge wanted to know.

"It was a short poem," One-Eyed Nick said, staring off into mist. "A

couple of stanzas, a poem of Shelley's. Let me see if I remember it." He
placed the flat of his hand over his eye patch and recited:

> *Music, when soft voices die,*
> *Vibrates in the memory;*
> *Odours, when sweet violets sicken,*
> *Live within the sense they quicken.*
>
> *Rose leaves, when the rose is dead,*
> *Are heaped for the beloved's bed;*
> *And so thy thoughts when thou art gone,*
> *Love itself shall slumber on.*

The old woman's eyes were suddenly shiny with tears. The Napalm
Man patted her on the back. He looked like he wanted to cry himself. "A
sentimental poem, isn't it?" he said at last.

One-Eyed Nick nodded his head slowly. "You have to remember that
Rose was a girl when she first read the poem. Probably eleven or twelve
years old—that's a sentimental age. She still looked at the world as if she
were its center, just like any kid. So the poem instantly caught her attention, not just because of the sentiment, but because it was about a dying
rose. The thing is, that particular name coupled with death made her
think deeply. And Dr. Stone asked Rose if that was the first time she'd
thought about dying, and she just looked at him with her tired, beautiful
eyes and said, 'Oh, no, of course not—I suppose I was a morbid little girl,
especially when things were going well, and I thought about death all the
time. But never *myself*, you know, I never *saw* myself, what I might
become. But the poem, the flowers—it's still so vivid. I'd checked out a
book of Shelley's poems from the sector library and taken it down to
Memorial Park. It was a perfect fall day. The trees were afire with light
and color, and the air itself burned with the smell of dying flowers. I sat in
the rose garden all afternoon with my book, reading. Dusk came, and all
around me, the violet sky dying into night, the stillness, the grass
drenched with rose petals, myself—everything was suddenly very real.
There was a terrible beauty, a sense of joy mingled with overwhelming
poignancy. And I never wanted to lose it, never, never. How can I make
you see it, Doctor? It's all so delicate, isn't it? So urgent and quick.'

"For Rose, it was really the beginning of everything, this vision, you
know, this ever-near appreciation of death and life. Of course, she'd seen
the napalmed bodies being pulled from the buildings—who hasn't? And
several of her schoolmates had died of anthrax and pneumonic AIDS, but

when you're a kid, you never quite believe it can happen to you. And so the poem: Rose recited it until she knew it by heart. Although she was very young, she began to think with the mind of an adult. If death was inevitable, she wondered, how can life have meaning? If life is nothing but struggle and war, how can there be help for pain? When the rose is dead, what's left of beauty? There in the park, you know, looking at the pretty flowers all around her, she began to formulate her philosophy of life: It's true, there's no help for pain, but man made war, and man could abolish it. Or I should say, *woman* could get rid of war, she really didn't have much faith in men. And, yes, death came to everyone, but she thought that everyone—*everything*—could have a kind of immortality. Nothing has to be lost; this became her faith. She would try to remember everything she saw in life. And someday she'd recapture it with words, the soul of the world. The whole, goddamned world.

"After that night, the rest was easy. Every morning Dr. Stone came to her room, sat in the green, vinyl visitor's chair, and Rose told him about her life. She'd just sit on the edge of her bed, eating the stale hospital croissants and drinking her sweet coffee, and talking—she loved to talk, have I mentioned that? And Dr. Stone scribbled his notes and pointed the tape recorder's microphone at her, and he listened. 'Even if there isn't a God,' Rose asked him one day, 'don't you think it's necessary to believe in *something* beyond yourself?'

"But no, in fact, ever since his intern year in the electro-convulsive ward, he hadn't looked for meaning beyond the wall of his own suffering. 'How should I believe in God,' he asked her, 'when every day *I* have the power to destroy his creations?' And Rose looked at him with her sad eyes and said, 'You don't like yourself very much, do you?' And of course, that was the truth, Rose really knew how to find his weak spots and drive the nails right in. Early in his career he'd often thought of making himself the equal of God by injecting himself with a solution of sodium cyanide. Or driving his car off a cliff. Or risking death by AIDS with the prostitutes down on D-Street. You know, he had a gentle-looking face, everyone said that about him, but the thing is, he was secretly a wild man, a man who walked the brink, and every day he got to know Rose better, the closer the fall.

"After a while, it became clear that there was a kind of thing between them. Oh, I don't mean that Rose actually loved him like he loved her, but I think she liked his mind. She liked to joke around with him. Once, she even asked if he would have wanted to marry her, if they'd met somewhere else, like down in the Gardens in Tenth Sector. And he didn't hesitate for a second, he said, 'Yes, I think I would have.' And she said, 'Then it's too bad I've been classified a schizophrenic. I'm still not sure how *that* happened.' And Dr. Stone violated his oath right then and there, he quoted the secret manual to her: ' "If someone asserts that he can see 'God' in another person or object, he is schizophrenic, since such assertations are by common assent untrue and anyone making then must be misapprehending the nature of reality." '

"He confided that in his student days he had injected himself with brain drugs—and many times since. A few micrograms of a specifically designed drug and you could tune the serotonin concentration in the brain, experience a minute or hour of bliss. Or wild euphoria, or sexual exaltation. 'Or God,' he told her, 'God in a pill—what's the point in calling it that? Yes, I've seen it, but if that's God, well, it can't be *God*, if you know what I mean.' And she provided a quotation of her own, or rather a misquotation: 'The Tao you see while high on drugs is not the true Tao.' 'Then there is no true Tao,' Dr. Stone said. 'The brain drugs activate the same natural neuroactive chemicals you'd find in the cortex of a meditating saint, or in a young girl staring at the roses in the park. Why do you think meditation and biofeedback are illegal? Drugs are drugs—there's no difference.'

"When he said this, Rose shook her head back and forth so hard her hair snapped like a whip. 'Are we nothing more than chemical machines, Doctor?' And he said, 'We're nothing but an interlocking set of subroutines; we're programmed by the molecules in our brain. There's nothing more.' *'But,'* she said, 'if we choose what molecules to put in our brains, by injection or meditation or faith, *we're* still choosing, aren't we? Isn't there a spark of soul and free will in everyone?' And Dr. Stone said, 'No, certain neurotransmitters fire according to the laws of chemistry, and you call this "choice." So if you believe in God, I suppose you can't help it.' And Rose, she smiled and laughed when he said this, and then she said, 'Oh, no, Doctor, you're so wrong!' "

The Napalm Man took a long, thoughtful pull from his bottle, then mumbled into the damp, foggy air, "Free will, Nick? In a way, I think Rose was right; occasionally people have their moments of free will. But it's a delicate thing, isn't it? Any moment they might harden up and turn into robots, haven't I seen it happen? Why do you think I drink this stuff? I'll tell you why: It's to keep everyone from turning into machines, it's the only way. If you're not careful, the robots will kill real people like Rose or Doctor Stone."

Story telling on damp, cold nights always made Sarge hungry, so he got up and picked his way across the trash and broken glass littering the alley. In back of the nearby Tenderloin Grill's kitchen, noisy with shouting cooks and clanging pans, there was a big, blue dumpster spray-painted with the word SARGE. He stood on a couple of piled-up orange crates, rummaging through the dumpster. He must have found something edible, because he stuffed his hands exuberantly down into the pockets of his greatcoat. "Steaks, goddammit!" he announced. "Meat makes the soldier, ya mean?" He was fond of saying that one dumpster could feed at least two people, and one dumpster like *this,* outside a rich restaurant in the goddamned rich 101st Sector of the Blue Zone, could feed at least ten people in style, which is why he'd put his mark on it, to warn away any bums who stumbled into his alley. According to Sarge, the dumpster was their ration card for the rest of their goddamned lives, and he'd kick the living shit out of anyone who fucked with it. "Chow's on—look what these assholes have thrown away!"

But no one else seemed to be in the mood that night for cold, half-eaten steaks. While Sarge gobbled his food like a starved dog, the Napalm Man poured more whiskey down his throat. One-Eyed Nick had never seen the old woman eat meat, and as for him, he had to finish his story. "Free will *is* a delicate thing," he said, agreeing with what the Napalm Man had said earlier.

Sarge finished his meal, got up, and spat into the fire. The spit hissed, and he ran his finger across his stubbly lip. "Free will bullshit!" he said. He grimaced and spat again. He began picking his teeth. His teeth were in ruins, broken black spikes stinking of decay. "Look at my goddamned teeth!" he said. "Sure, I could get 'em fixed, dentistry's free in this zone, isn't it? But listen up, the goddamned dentists require major bribes to provide anesthesia. You tell me who's strong enough anymore to have his roots drilled without a little gas or novocaine to numb his fuckin' nerves and then you can talk to me about free will."

"The point I'm trying to make," One-Eyed Nick said, "is that Rose didn't feel sorry for herself, because she believed she'd freely chosen her life's work."

"You mean writing all those dirty poems?" Sarge asked.

The Napalm Man removed his pint of whiskey from his paper bag and held it up to the streetlight. A few dark, rolling ounces remained; he took a careful sip, as if he were nursing it until the story was over. He said, "With her dangerous thinking, I'm surprised Rose could have gotten any of her poems published."

"You know, that was the problem," One-Eyed Nick said. "Once—it was during her tenth week on the ward—Dr. Stone asked Rose about this. And she told him, 'Just after I had graduated from college, the Information Department pushed through a law requiring what was jokingly called "peer review" of all published literature. Do you know what that meant, Doctor? It meant I'd never be published—oh, I could have slipped a few silly, romantic poems into the sector literary magazine, but the *dangerous* poems, the wild, visionary things I really wanted to write, they wouldn't touch if I bribed them.'

"Yeah," One-Eyed Nick continued, "the literary magazines were a joke. But the underground journals—that was different. In the Black Zone, a few dozen sheets of mimeographed paper circulated in secret— that was the real stuff, the lifeblood of the mind. When one of Rose's boyfriends slipped her a collection containing 'Howl' and 'Darkmother-scream' and other great, subversive poems, a new world opened for her. She—she had an arrogant side to her, have I told you?—she began to write for the underground journals. As her reputation grew, she became more daring. Not naively daring, though; Rose was never naive. She knew what she was doing.

"One morning, in her room, Dr. Stone was drinking tea instead of coffee because the Purple Zone had been gassed and the shipments hadn't arrived. He asked her why she *had* to publish 'Plutonium Spring.' That was her infamous poem that had gotten her into trouble in the first place. And she held his hand with her long, warm fingers and told him, 'Oh, of course I *knew* it was dangerous, and the truth is, I held off publication for years after I wrote it. But when Bill and Johnny died in the bombing, I didn't have to be afraid for them any longer, do you understand? And I was crazy with grief—I just didn't care anymore, didn't *want* to care about myself, about what might happen.'

"And so her poem appeared in the *Free Zone Journal.* It was an epic poem, and it created an epic sensation. It was all about love and war, reverence and pain. Light and dark, you know—the censors counted twenty-two times she used the word 'black' in the first canto alone. But it wasn't the dark, ironic imagery, that got her into real trouble. Or even her intense affirmation of God. No, it was her pacifism, and her blatant revelation of classified information. And more, her vision.

"Classified information—I think Rose really knew too much and saw things too deeply. You have to remember that her father had been a major in the Air Force. He hated war even more than Rose. Before he was shot down, he told her all about the nuclear war between the Yellow Zone and the Green Zone; he was stupid enough to tell her that during the present phase, Military Intelligence knew of at least a hundred and eight nuclear wars in various locations throughout the City. I think he hoped that she could run away to a Safe Zone, where they had banned hydrogen bombs if not the war. But even as a kid, Rose understood things that her father didn't. She knew that it would be better to abolish the war altogether than to try to find one of a few hundred Safe Zones among the millions of zones. To abolish the war—this was her dream; she wanted to show that the war wasn't inevitable. And that's why she wrote 'Plutonium Spring.' The poem made use of a brilliant device: Imagine, if you can, that our Endless City wasn't built across an infinite plain stretching to the ends of the universe. No, like Rose, imagine this: Imagine that our world was finite. *Finite*. A finite City built on top of a sphere floating in the black void. A simple sphere, like a baseball."

At the end of the alley, where the hill dropped off over the City, One-Eyed Nick could see the straight lines of lights of the Twentieth Sector, from P-Street running all the way out, probably as far as the upper million avenues. Somewhere farther out, lost in the brilliant, striated haze, were the Silver Zone and Purple Zone, and beyond them, all the other zones, maybe even the mythical Gold Zone and Dead Zone. Long ago, the geographers had proved that the City went on forever, as anyone could see. Perhaps, somewhere, there were other universes, other cities stacked one atop the other in space like gleaming dinner plates in a dark cupboard, but to imagine the *City* as being anything other than an endless disc was almost impossible.

Sarge always seemed to know what One-Eyed Nick was thinking, and he said, "That's crazy. If we lived on a goddamned baseball, what would keep us from flying off like pieces of spit?"

One-Eyed Nick nodded his head slowly. "Sure, the idea was crazy. But Rose was a little crazy, and she was sly and satirical, too. She wanted to demonstrate that war is as dependent on geometry and topology as it is on 'human nature.' Think about it. If we lived on a sphere, the City would be one, whole, complete thing. One edge would flow around the curve and grow into the other. The thing is, there wouldn't even be any 'edges' to the City; there wouldn't be any Safe Zones. Nuclear war would be impossible, because any army that exploded nuclear bombs in a neighboring zone would destroy themselves after the dust clouds circled the sphere, and everyone died from the radiation. And if you couldn't have a nuclear war, then the *war* itself would become impossible, because what general would be insane enough to wage war, if he knew that at any time it might become nuclear? And if the generals stopped the war, what sense would it make to divide the City into separate zones? And all this in Rose's poem, you know, there was a lot cold logic beneath the terrible beauty of her rhymes: If there were no zones, if the City were one whole thing, couldn't we do away with martial law? Imagine the City without martial law—we'd be free, at peace, finally happy."

"No one's happy until he's dead," the Napalm Man broke in with uncharacteristic vehemence. "And haven't I told you before? If I quit drinking this," and here he snapped his fingernail against the whiskey bottle, "no one would be free."

One-Eyed Nick tore up a damp, cardboard box and fed the pieces to the fire. Smoke instantly billowed up. Waving another piece of cardboard back and forth like a madman, he tried to keep the greasy cloud from blowing over the old woman and the others. "The thing is, you've never read Rose's poem, and look, it's made you think and feel a little. That's all Rose wanted, you know. She wanted to wake people up; she thought that everyone was dazed and paralyzed by the bombs. By the war, the stupid war."

Sarge dug a piece of rye bread out of his pocket, then handed it to the old woman. She held it between her open hands as if it were a prayer book. She smiled and said, "Thank you," the first words she had spoken since One-Eyed Nick had begun his story.

"War is hell, ya mean?" Sarge said this to One-Eyed Nick. "But where the hell would I be without the goddamn war?" He put his hands over his ears and dug his dirty fingernails into the scars cutting his head. "Aw, Jesus, here it comes! What the hell would I have been like before the war? I'll tell you what: I was probably too dumb to wonder about my own dumbness. Christ, what a thought!—where'd that goddamned thought come from?"

The Napalm Man took a huge swallow; he must have finished half of his remaining whiskey. He gasped and coughed for a while. "Rose must have known the consequences of writing the poem," he said. "She wasn't a robot, like the others, Nick."

"No, that's right, she wasn't a robot."

"Then you can't blame Dr. Stone for what happened to her, can you?"

One-Eyed Nick sucked in a lungful of wet air. It had begun to drizzle, and he was cold. Off in the distance, somewhere in the night, a jet thundered closer. It drowned out half of his words: "Who am I to blame anyone? But Dr. Stone wasn't a robot either, you know, so you have to blame him, don't you?"

Sarge shook his head back and forth, then spat at a chewing gum wrapper stuck to the fender of the abandoned car where they slept sometimes. "Nah," he said, "Where the hell would I be without Dr. Stone? When they repatriated me from prison camp, I was a mess, ya mean? I never told anyone, but right before I was captured, a mine blew up in my crotch. And then the Reds knocked out my teeth and tried to kick my fuckin' brains out. *Wham, wham, wham*—I can still feel their boots slamming into my face. By the time they were done, I was spitting teeth, slurring and drooling like a moron. Bad brain damage, ya mean? But after they shipped me back to the Black Zone, Dr. Stone took care of me. Half of him went into me—why do you think an old son of a bitch like me would take care of a bunch of bums, huh? Dr. Stone programmed the biochips and helped me with the memories after they implanted the—what do ya call them?—the *fetal* brain cells. Jesus, ya ever wonder where they get fetal brain cells to cram into the skull of an old fart like me?"

One-Eyed Nick shrugged his shoulders as he broke up an orange crate and shoved the wood slats into the fire. The damp pine hissed and cracked. After a while, the wind shifted. Clumps of smoke wafted over them, but he saw that the old woman didn't move to cover her eyes; she just stared at him as if she were waiting for something.

"The thing is," he said, "I knew Dr. Stone, and *I* blame him."

The Napalm Man clinked his whiskey bottle against a wet brick and said, "No, you shouldn't do that, Nick. Dr. Stone was a good man. He put me back together when I fell apart. I remember when I worked for Orange Chemicals, we made things like napalm and a gas whose aerial dispersement by one part per million caused the skin to sicken and slough off like bubbling sheets of pink rubber. Nice, eh? One day, when I was riding home on the bullet train, I was horrified to see that one of our gases had gotten loose and everyone was turning to metal. The businessmen with their padlocked hearts and attaché cases, the salesmen, secretaries, and other scientists—all metal. They made hard clanking sounds with their metal tongues and sounded like news machines: 'Have a nice day; gold's up, silver's down; the Blues murdered the Greens 27 to 3'—that kind of thing. I hurried home in a panic only to find that my Lisa had new metal eyes and metal lips that burned when she kissed me. And when she asked me, 'Have a nice day? Have a nice day? . . .' I had to get out of there, so I ran through the walls of my house, out into the streets, where metal dogs chased the passing cars. Then I turned around and everything was gone. I couldn't remember who I was. All I knew was that my hands were turning to metal, too, gray and hard and smelling like lead. There was a sound like giant rats with metal jaws crunching apart buildings of steel and glass, and there I was, sitting in the park with a paper bag in my hand, moving it to my mouth, over and over, moving it to my metal mouth. And then I fell apart—there were pieces of me scattered all over the grass. Dr. Stone found me and put me back together."

He finished his story with a thoughtful pull of whiskey and nodded at One-Eyed Nick, who said, "The thing is, Dr. Stone was a proud man. He reached too far, I think. Because of stupid pride, you know. There was no way out for him, for Rose."

Sarge put his forefinger up to his temple and cocked his thumb. He said, "When there's no way out and a soldier's about to be captured, he's supposed to blow his own brains out, ya mean?"

One-Eyed Nick rubbed his sore arm and said, "You know, Dr. Stone considered suicide. Even though he was puffed up with pride, he was miserable because Rose *had* to go through with the deconstruction. Bad things were scheduled to happen to her. Could he really save her and put her together afterwards? Sometimes he thought he could, and then he was wild with anticipation and a sense of immortality. Just as often, though, he had doubts. He had a bad case of the jitters from drinking too much coffee. He'd spent too much time analyzing and touching the pieces of Rose's soul. He was sick of all the sleepless nights on call, wandering the ward's bright corridors. In any hospital, you know, there's always an air of unreality, an underlying layer of false hopes and fears. The orderlies rushing by with their blood samples and specimens, the nurses and their needles, the surgeons' tight, grim smiles—who really wants to believe the things they do to mind and flesh? And, you know, the chemical smells and the noises. There's nothing that's natural or normal. In the hours before dawn, when time drags on forever, you can hear each and every little sound. And everywhere, of course, the TV cameras mounted high in the corners of rooms, watching. Lots of times, Dr. Stone felt oppressed and doomed, like everything he'd ever done wrong in his life was about to catch up with him. I think he'd have *loved* to have shot up a lethal dose of ALH-25 and watched the atom bombs go off inside his head. But what would have happened to Rose then? Should he let another doctor do the deconstruction, let him touch her mind? No, he decided *he* had to treat her. He'd take her into the HDI room, and he'd do it as carefully as it could be done, he'd do it right. He had a plan to save the best part of her, the secret light, you know, her very soul.

"When it came time for her deconstruction, he went to see her. There were no croissants or doughnuts that morning; no warm aroma of coffee

overlaying the smells of lysol and fear. Somehow, Rose had fastened the
velcro and nylon restraints around her ankles and wrists. She lay spread-
eagled on her broad hospital bed—the thing is, she always had a sense for
the melodramatic. 'I've saved the orderlies the trouble,' she said. 'Isn't it
true that the patients must be restrained before they're taken in for
deconstruction?' The truth is, though, she really didn't know all that
much about it because Dr. Stone had never explained the details of the
procedure. And she had never *wanted* to know. Gently, he could be
gentle, you know, he gently ripped open the velcro snaps and began
rubbing the dents from her wrists. 'After we go into the HDI room, the
nurse will give you something—we can't use mechanical restraints during
deconstruction.'

"He tried to explain that during the deconstruction, certain of her
memories would be activated. Then the nerve signals to her muscles
would have to be cut off, like when you dream, or else her body would try
to reenact the remembered motions; her arms would flail and her legs kick
out as she tried to run away. 'I'll be paralyzed, won't I?' she asked. 'Listen,
Rose, don't be afraid, I'll help you.' But she *was* afraid; she was so afraid
she was dripping sweat. And she was very angry because the hospital
mattresses were covered with plastic and held her nervous sweat close
against her skin. She asked for a clean gown, and after she'd changed and
come back from the bathroom, she said, 'You've tried to be so kind to me,
but what can you do? Oh, I knew this day would come, knew it but didn't
care. And now that it's come, it's strange, I find I *do* care, very much.' As
he stroked her hands, trying to calm her, she said, 'The first time we met,
I asked you if you believed in God, do you remember? Oh, God, what a
thing to throw at someone, but I think I wanted to make you a little
nervous because *I* was very nervous, having to tell you things about myself, the private things I didn't think anyone would understand, *especially*
a doctor; doctors always made me nervous, but you understand me, a little
at least, the important things—don't you?'

"He was worried at the shrillness of her voice, the barely controlled
panic. He would have ordered a sedative but that would have interfered
with her deconstruction in unpredictable ways. So he poured her a glass of
water and said, 'I understand, Rose; it will be okay.' But the thing is, he
wasn't too sure it would be okay, and as for understanding, he didn't even
understand himself, so how he could he hope to understand her?

"Then she sat on the edge of the bed and began kicking her feet in her
nervous way, and all the while she stared at him with a look that gradually
changed from fear to a sort of ironic contempt, and then to pity. Pity for

him! That was the way she was; it was her finest quality. She had this ability to see her own sufferings reflected and magnified in others. With pity came that unreal calmness of hers, and then a look that Dr. Stone would never forget. She was staring at the gray, empty TV screen on the wall, or maybe she was staring at the wall itself—he couldn't tell which. Her eyes—she had dark, intelligent eyes, you know—her whole face was full of light, full of rapture. It lasted only a moment, this look, and then it was replaced by her familiar mask of sadness and irony. 'This must be so hard for you,' she said. And Dr. Stone put on his best bedside voice, you know, trying to reassure her. But he was really trying to make everything okay in his own mind, and he said, 'Don't worry, I can save you.'

"For a long time, she just sat there kicking her legs, she didn't say a word. The only sounds in the room were the rising and falling of their breaths and the jerky squeaking of the bed's steel frame as she kicked and kicked. Suddenly, out of nowhere, she smiled and quoted a favorite line from one of Shelley's poems: ' "I am the eye with which the universe beholds itself and knows itself divine.' " And then, she told him, 'Oh, I don't think you can.'

"He thought she must be a little crazy, after that. If you can look at everyday things, at a turned-off TV set, or the paint on a blank wall, or even in a dead flower, if you can see evidence of purpose or divinity—that's a little crazy, isn't it? Crazy, sure, but the thing is, he loved her for being crazy. He was shaking from the coffee he'd been drinking all night, and he fumbled for words. He said, 'During the deconstruction, your memories can be saved on the computer. And then, during the reconstruction, it's illegal as hell and they can get me for malpractice, maybe even send me to the incinerators, but when we make up the biochip, everything can preserved. Almost everything; sometimes there are memories that don't associate well, and we can't get the mapping right. If there's a *choice*, Rose, your life has been so hard—aren't there some painful memories you'd rather not have?'

"Rose's face flushed with anger when he said that; she grabbed the sleeve of his jacket, and her fingers dug in like claws. 'How could I have expected you to understand?' she asked him. Then her face went calm and soft, and she sighed. 'All my life I've been searching for the words to say the one true, unutterable thing words can't express. Or maybe it's just that *I* will never find the words. But I have to, before I die, say it; it's something like . . . like a woman giving birth, out of the pain, something wonderful, life, it doesn't stop. Sometimes I think God is terrible beauty, relentless love. Intellectually, and intuitively, I have to believe it's sufficient to have lived even for a minute. When Johnny died . . . it will never stop hurting, but I'll never lose him, he's not lost. Don't take away the painful memories, Doctor, they're all I have.'

"Soon after that, the orderly came for her. He helped her into an ugly wheelchair, you know, one of those monstrosities of dingy, brown vinyl and chrome. He rolled her down the corridors to the HDI room. There she was given an injection. One of the nurses had brutal little fingers, all hard and yellow from the cigarettes she chain-smoked between deconstructions; Dr. Stone could hardly stand to watch Rose gasping as the needle went into her arm. The truth is, he hated the HDI room, everything about it, even though he'd done fifty deconstructions there. The shiny floors smelled of soap and polish, and it was too clean. And the stainless-steel cabinets and tables, the electronic machinery with its black plastic switches, all spotlessly clean. At the end of the room was the imaging device, you know, the computer. It was a huge, metal and glass doughnut with a dark hole at its center big enough so that a child could have sat in it. 'Oh, God!'—that's what Rose said when she first saw it, 'Oh, God!'

"Overlooking all this stuff was a wall of plexiglas; it was really more like a window to the room next door, the viewing room. There were tables and empty chairs in the viewing room, and Dr. Stone saw her staring at them like she couldn't guess what they were for. 'The guests of the hospital use them,' he explained. 'To witness the deconstructions.'

"The nurses put Rose on a flat, brown vinyl table. They placed her elbows down into the armrests and eased her head into a specially molded head holder. The injection was beginning to take effect, and she couldn't move any part of her body below her neck. But, like it was a bad dream or a nightmare, she could still mumble a few words, still cry out in terror and pain. 'No, no,' she said, over and over, 'Oh, God, please no!'

"She was flat on her back, and after a while she couldn't see anything, so she couldn't have been aware of the men filing into the viewing room. But Dr. Stone saw them through the window, you know, serious men in gray suits. They took their seats silently, without fuss or hesitation. The Director of the Electroshock Research Program, the Chief of Psychosurgery, the Zone-Therapy Chief Lobotomist, the Government Man and the General—Rose was famous, you know, and the authorities wanted to see how the deconstruction would work on someone like her. The last one to enter the viewing room was the Director of Psychiatry. He was a pompous little man with tiny blue eyes and a pink face like a baby's. Microphones on one of the tables picked up his irritating voice as he said, 'Okay, let's go.'

"That was a very bad moment for Dr. Stone, one of the worst moments of his life. He dropped his chin down into his chest, staring down at his reflection in the polished floor. Rage and pain, pain and rage—he suddenly knew what he was doing was wrong. His whole life, everything he'd ever thought or felt, all wrong. But he had to hide it, he couldn't just find a scalpel in one of the cabinets and start cutting into his neck; no, he had to go through with it, so he swallowed against the hard knot in his throat, stepped over to Rose and checked the IV dripping the tracer into her vein. Into her brain. The tracer would circulate up through her brain arteries, through the capillaries into the amygdala and brain stem, through cerebellum and cortex; it would diffuse across individual neurons and synapses. Ultimately—if everything went right—it would highlight the K-lines, you know, the circuitry of chemical memory. Rose's memories. 'No, no, please!' Dr. Stone heard someone say, and it took him a while before he realized it was Rose, lost in a nightmare, and not himself who was shouting.

"He nodded at the nurse; she flipped a switch. The machinery came alive with a hum, and Rose's table began moving along the floor track. Straight toward the imaging device on the far wall. Her head disappeared into the center of the machine. It was surrounded by holographic scanners and computers she couldn't see; her brain vibrated with magnetic resonances and chemicals she couldn't feel. Dr. Stone studied his gauges, adjusted the field, and he turned to address the guests. That was what he had to do, you know, put on a kind of show, make it interesting, especially for the layman in the viewing room who'd never seen a deconstruction before. 'One of the oldest philosophical and scientific debates,' he said 'has been the mind-body problem. For a long time, of course, it's been accepted that the mind is just what the brain does, as in any other body function. It's only because of the brain's mystery and complexity that there was ever an argument about mind. After all, we never talk about a "stomach-digestion" problem, unless there's a food shortage and we're forced to eat rotten soup rations at one of the Zone kitchens.'

"Dr. Stone hated himself for making jokes while Rose's brain was about to be stripped naked, but the thing is, he couldn't help himself because *he* was going out of his mind with remorse. He felt wild and fey, like he wanted to kill the men in the viewing room, or to kill himself, kill *someone*. He suddenly hated the idea of experimenting on human beings, on anyone, even the criminally insane or the brain-damaged soldiers down on the other wards. Originally, you know, like a lot of others, he'd argued that it was immoral to do experimental brain surgery on healthy chimpanzees or other animals. The thing is, if you're trying to get at the material basis of mind, to really show it at the molecular level, you have to have a human being, because who can say if animals really think like we do? And that was the *real* reason for the deconstructions, you know. To show that we're all robots enslaved by our brain chemistry, that there's no such thing as soul.

"When Dr. Stone finally got a grip on himself, he finished his explanation. 'This is the imaging device,' he said, tapping the metal ring over Rose's head. 'The computer sections up the brain—imagistically, that is. It makes a holographic model of the patient's brain and brain functions. The model will be displayed for you so you can watch the deconstruction as it progresses.'

"At the center of the room, in plain view, was a holographic display; it looked like one of the display cases you see in the jewelry stores down in the more dangerous parts of Third Ward, but it was bigger. And it wasn't three-dimensional images of diamonds and emeralds that were on display, no, there were ten billion tiny jewels of light making a picture of Rose's brain. You could see every glowing fold and fissure of the cortex; in the limbic brain, deep inside, that's where the S-shaped hippocampus was, and the amygdala, which looked like a tiny almond. These parts weren't where her actual memories were stored, but they were vital for associating one sense, like hearing or sight, with another. You know, they'd done experiments on Red prisoners. After you surgically removed the hippocampus and amygdala, it was just about impossible for the patient to make new memories or retrieve old ones properly. And there was the medulla, and other structures—the computer could highlight any section of the brain in any detail needed. Of *her* brain, it's Rose I'm talking about, you see.

"When the actual deconstruction began, Dr. Stone was nauseated and shaking; his eyes ached and he had his fist hard up against his forehead. *It's sufficient to have lived even for a moment*—he remembered Rose saying that, and he despaired. He picked up the manila folder he'd brought with him, opened it, then started to read. He was very aware of the Director and others watching him through the window. 'Rose, do you remember . . .' he began, but that was as far as he got, because his throat was dry and sore, and he had to ask the nurse to get him a glass of water. He wished he could ask Rose trivial questions, you know, stupid things that didn't have anything to do with her rebelliousness and her famed empathy for other people. But what could he do? He couldn't have fooled the Director, no, he'd taught Dr. Stone almost everything he knew about deconstructions, there could be no faking it. So he swallowed back his heartburn and panic, and he asked her, 'Rose, do you remember the time you told your father you weren't going to eat meat anymore?'

"And that's how it went. His voice was almost dead, but he managed to ask her questions about certain past experiences. This keyed off her memories of those experiences; as the memories became manifest and formed up in her mind, neurons and neuron clusters fired—there are specific neurotransmitters involved in the release of chemical memory. The tracer dripping into her veins reacted with these neurotransmitters. That's what highlighted the K-lines, you know, the memory lines. And for a given experience, let's say the time her fifth grade teacher caught her staring out the window at the cherry trees, there might actually be thousands of simple memories involved. Rose's memories, she was a poet, you know, things like the liquid air and the smell of flowers, and the bees' buzzing, and the brilliant explosion of white blossoms through the trees. And the pain when Ms. Bledsoe smacked her ruler across Rose's knuckles. And her shame, of course, she felt it burning out between her legs when her bladder muscles let go and everyone in her class laughed at the yellow puddle gathering beneath her desk. And each memory stored in a really complex way. Memory isn't quite global, but still, there are associations throughout different parts of the brain. Her memory of whiteness, the red of blood, would be stored in her visual cortex; sounds and speech and her teacher yelling at her, in the temporal lobes on the side of the head; and so on, the smells, the heat and pain. And all through the hologram display of her brain, the whole experience was modeled as an array of little lights, each light representing a bit of memory, a little of herself. Thousands of lights, like strings of lights on a Christmas tree—Dr. Stone asked her if she remembered being given a puppy when she was almost five years old, on Christmas Eve. Did she remember that New Year's Day, trying to snip off Rufo's ears with her mother's sewing scissors, because she'd decided they'd grown too long and floppy and needed a trim? Sure she remembered, she could hear the puppy yelping in outrage, pain and betrayal. And inside Rose, the yelp was a pinpoint of white light deep in the listening part of her brain. And the pain, *her* pain, the lights burning in the parietal and temporal lobes, the beautiful, empathic, unforgettable pain.

"But . . . not unforgettable, you know. Dr. Stone asked his questions, and the lights inside Rose flickered on, the beautiful strings of lights. The computer zeroed in on each light individually. And the HDI machine made thousands of intense, local disruptions in the magnetic field of Rose's brain. All along the K-lines, electrons ripped out of their orbits, atoms ionized, cells and cell clusters died. And all the time she was paralyzed, perfectly conscious, perfectly aware that *something* was happening to her, something she couldn't quite grasp, because after it was gone, how would she ever know? Once—she told him this the evening before the deconstruction—once, on a hot summer night just after her family had died, she woke up and found herself alone, flat on her back, with her head at the foot of the bed. Her feet were almost touching the headboard. She'd had no sense of sweating through the night or rotating in half a circle across the soaking sheets; there was only darkness and disorientation and a sick feeling of lost time. Each moment of her deconstruction must have been like that night, an endless awakening into neverness, as if she'd never existed and never would. And Rose, of course, tried to fight it, but what could she do? Dr. Stone thought he could see the patterns of her stubbornness, the way the silver lights twinkled and rippled like waves of shooting stars. *Nothing is lost*—that was always Rose's faith, but what could be left after the HDI machine annihilated half her brain? Was she praying, trying to hold on to a little certitude and meaning while the other things slipped away? On and on the deconstruction went, all morning and far into the afternoon, almost forever. But, you know, in the hospital, with the overhead lamps burning so hot they're hyperreal, time is nothing.

"Isn't it time you read her the poem?' The Director asked Dr. Stone this in a voice that seemed to come out of nowhere. The grim little man was sitting at the table in the viewing room, waiting with the others. In front of him, he had a list of the questions Rose was supposed to be asked. And Dr. Stone licked the coffee and blood gumming his teeth and said, 'The poem. Yes, the poem.' He was sweating, and he had his fist clenched so hard the tendons were popping out in his wrist. He looked at her, lost in the pit of the machine, and asked, 'Rose, do you remember this poem: *"Music, when soft voices die, Vibrates in the memory?"* ' And sure she remembered, how she remembered!—how could she forget? And when he got to the line, *Rose leaves, when the rose is dead*, the secret light inside her was alive and burning with a color as pure as any rose. 'Rose, do you remember, do you remember . . . ?' But she *didn't* remember, and that was the hell of it, didn't remember anything about roses, because he and the HDI machine had done their work, and inside Rose's mind the lights went out like a Christmas tree suddenly unplugged. And Dr. Stone couldn't finish his poem; he had no voice left, you know, he couldn't utter another word, because it, too, had finally gone out, the secret light."

One-Eyed Nick finished speaking, and he heaped more trash on the fire. Flame shadows writhed across the dirty nylon of his parka. The old woman seemed to be staring through the fire at him. Her dark eyes were lucid with reflected light. He wondered if he'd been wrong about her right from the start; maybe she *could* understand what he was saying.

The Napalm Man drained his bottle of whiskey and rubbed his temples. "That's a sad story, Nick. Why is it impossible just to find a little happiness?"

And Sarge put in, "I'd be happy if I could just get simplicity, ya mean?" He licked his lips, spat and then asked, "That's not the end of the story, is it? You haven't told us what happened to Dr. Stone and Rose."

One-Eyed Nick blinked slowly, thinking that if he and the old woman, all of them, *had* to exist and be a part of the City's endless life, wouldn't it be great if they were as rigid and unmoving as brick, as hard as stone? He sighed and said, "The end of the story—do you mean before or after the Reds bombed the hospital?"

"Before," Sarge said. "We know about the escape after the goddamn bombing. Tell us what happened to Rose and Dr. Stone."

There was a pressure beneath One-Eyed Nick's forehead, and his arm hurt. He said, "Dr. Stone talked to Rose alone in her room after the deconstruction, and he felt like crying. The thing is, she didn't *want* to be reconstructed. 'Oh, no, please, I'm scared!'—that was all she could say. And who could blame her? Doctor Stone knew that the Director had plans to make her into a simple schoolmistress, you know, one of those nice ladies in a white shirt and tie, teaching propaganda to aid the war effort. 'It's okay, Rose,' he said, 'I'll help you remember—I have a plan.' And she went over to him and pressed her head down on his shoulder, and she sobbed. And he stroked her hair; he bit his lip so hard it bled. He'd risked everything to save her memories, to be able to make up a biochip, a bit of synthetic brain that would be as much her as what he'd taken out in the HDI room—and all for nothing. But, no, not for nothing, you know. Right then and there he made up his mind that he'd do the reconstruction himself. No matter what *this* Rose wanted now, he'd remake the Rose he knew and loved.

"But things never work out like you want. He had to wait at least a month for her to heal before he could do her implant, or else she would really wind up nuts. And that was too damn long, because he found out that the hospital was going to be closed down immediately. Moved, you know, because the Red artillery was getting too close. And worse, he was going to be transferred to a mental hospital in First Sector. As a reward. A goddamn promotion!—the Director had been so impressed with Rose's deconstruction that he'd promoted Dr. Stone to be Chief of Psychiatry at St. Mark's Hospital. Or maybe he was just jealous of Dr. Stone and didn't want him around; but what did it matter *why* Dr. Stone was being promoted, the thing is, in the Black Zone, you couldn't refuse promotions. He would never even talk to Rose afterwards, let alone get the time and an operating room to make her whole again.

"The next day, as he told her he would have to leave her, when he saw the confused, hurt look on her face, he didn't want to live. But he *had* to live, that was the hell of it, to live somehow—to help her regain her memories, do you see? That evening, he drank half a bottle of scotch, and he became very drunk, so drunk he went into the bathroom and retched into the toilet until his stomach was dry. Blind drunk—he was so drunk that when he looked into the mirror, he couldn't see himself. So he smashed the mirror, punched it again and again until it shattered, and then he grabbed up a glass splinter in his bleeding fist and rammed it into his face. Into his eye. The glass in his eye; it ruined his eye—the surgeons had to remove it.

One-Eyed Nick pressed his hand over his eye patch, feeling the stabs of ghost pain as he began to remember. He couldn't help looking at the old woman. Her eyes were wet with tears, and he knew there was something important he had to remember. "As a part of an experiment that Dr. Stone suggested—you know, a couple of his colleagues owed him favors and couldn't help feeling bad when they heard his story—the surgeons removed other things from his head. Even as the hospital was being evacuated, there were secret sessions with the HDI machine, and then, the implant surgeries. You see, Dr. Stone hoped to be classified mentally impaired so he could be moved along with Rose and all the other patients. So he'd always be with her, at least until one of them really died. And he *had* to remember the pieces of Rose's life so he could put her back together, but for himself, *of* himself, he wanted no memory. No, he hated himself, he would not remember who he was, except at the very end, when he finished telling his and Rose's sad story."

In the alley of D-Street, the rain had died. Everything was glistening wet, shiny from the streetlights, silent. Almost silent—the old woman had started crying openly. And then One-Eyed Nick suddenly remembered that she really wasn't so old, though she very much a woman, the best woman he'd ever known. Oh, God, it was Rose! *His* Rose, how could he have been so blind? Rose was crying, the great, wracking sobs almost lost into her cupped hands. It tore Nick apart, the sight, and burned inside his head, where something terrible and beautiful was happening to him. He was beginning to remember himself, too. Somewhere in his head, the implanted biochips were firing and coming alive, whispering, filling him up with Dr. Stone's memories. *His* memories. He remembered that he had been a doctor of psychiatry who knew well enough how to ruin a prisoner's short-term memory; he remembered ruining himself. And many other things: he remembered treating Sarge as a patient in the hospital, remembered that when poor, castrated Sarge slurred out his plea for "simplicity," he was really saying, "I just want *some pussy.*" Simplicity—it was really he, himself, who wanted simplicity; how simple it was to fall in love with Rose, over and over and forever. There was a pain in his chest, then. Like a shock of lightning it radiated up the angle of his jaw to his head. He shut his eye against the blinding, white pain. Light—each of us, he thought, carries inside whole universes of memory and light. He opened his eye, looking out over the endless, sleeping City, trying to apprehend the beautiful lights which went on and on, shimmering off to infinity. Rose was right after all, there was always room for more pain, more light, more memory. It would kill him, though, if he had to remember it all the time, who was *he* to stand that kind of pain? He was no one, and soon he would forget almost everything; very soon, when another piece of his brain fired and the false memories came, he would be One-Eyed Nick once again, a bum in an alley, trying to keep warm.

But now there was only memory, and now Rose was crying into the night, so he went over to her and knelt down; he put his arms around her and kissed her lips. "I love you," he said.

She took his hands and told him, "No, Nick, please, no."

Somewhere behind him, water was gurgling out of a drainpipe; the rushing sound was as uneven as the beating of his heart. "Do you remember the poem?" he asked her. "Can you remember anything at all?"

"Sure she remembers," Sarge said. "She remembers better all the time. Whenever you tell your goddamn story, you think of something else you've forgotten. Why d'ya think we keep asking questions to pump your memory? Why d'ya think I'm not bored out of my fuckin' skull by now?"

"Besides," the Napalm Man added, "you put us back together again. We don't mind listening."

Nick laced his fingers in Rose's hair. *Did* she remember? Could it be true that nothing was ever really lost? He bent his head and asked her,

"There's something I've never understood. Even if I could have done the implant, given you back your old memories, you didn't want me to. Why, Rose?"

For a long time she sat there looking at him, and gradually her shaking went away. She seemed lost in her thoughts. Then her eyes unclouded and there was pure joy in the way they lingered over him; there was a calmness and clarity, as if she were seeing something in its true light for the first time. "I *like* the way I am," she said.

He fell apart, then, he couldn't control it any longer; his hand trembled like an old man's as he tried to get the blinding tears out of his eye, and his whole body shivered from the cold. "Oh, God!" he whispered, "Oh, God!"

Rose started crying again, crying for *him*, he thought, crying for everyone in all the alleys of the Endless City, because nothing is lost, and someday, if he were relentless in his purpose, she would again be the Rose he remembered.

After a while the rain returned, and the lights all around him flickered and grew hazy. He couldn't quite remember why he was holding her, unless it was just to give a little comfort to an old woman who was cold and confused. And all he could think to say was: "I just want to make you happy."

A blur of spinning glass flashed above him; the Napalm Man had flung his whiskey bottle out into the alley. There was a sudden crash, flowers of glass shattering against wet brick. The Napalm Man removed a fresh pint of whiskey from the pocket of his trenchcoat and dropped it down into his paper bag. "No one's happy until he's dead, Nick."

Sarge rubbed the back of his neck and said, "I'd be happy if I could just find simplicity, ya mean?"

Because he couldn't stop shivering, One-Eyed Nick began looking around the alley for some trash to put into the dying fire. It would be hours before morning came, and he still had a long time to tell his story. Why he *had* to tell his story, he couldn't quite say.

And so, on an endless winter night, with the drizzling rain making him hoarse and cold, he cleared his throat and asked, "Have I told you this story before? This is the saddest story I know."

ABOUT THE AUTHORS

KEVIN J. ANDERSON is the coauthor (with Doug Beason) of two science fiction novels—*Lifeline*, and an upcoming novel on the Manhattan Project, both published by Bantam Spectra. His first novel, *Resurrection, Inc.*, was a final nominee for the Bram Stoker Award; he is also the author of the *Gamearth* trilogy. Over a hundred of Anderson's stories and articles have appear in *Full Spectrum, The Year's Best Fantasy Stories, Amazing Stories, The Magazine of Fantasy and Science Fiction, New Destinies,* and *Astronomy.* He lives in California, where he is a technical writer for the Lawrence Livermore National Laboratory.

POUL ANDERSON is the author of more than forty novels and collections of science fiction, fantasy, and mystery, including *Time Patrolman, Ensign Flandry, The Shield of Time,* and *The Boat of a Million Years*—a recent Nebula Award nominee for best novel. A past president of SFWA, Anderson has received seven Hugo awards and three Nebula awards in the course of his career. He and his wife live in Orinda, California.

First published in 1987, PATRICIA ANTHONY has sold stories to *Isaac Asimov's Science Fiction Magazine, The Magazine of Fantasy & Science Fiction, Weird Tales,* and *Pulphouse,* and is a regular contributor to *Aboriginal Science Fiction.* A creative writing instructor at Collin County Community College, she lives in Dallas.

GREGORY BENFORD is a professor of physics at the University of California, Irvine, where his research encompasses both astrophysics and plasma physics. The author of twelve novels including *Tides of Light, Great Sky River,* and *Against Infinity,* he has won many awards, including the Nebula for his novel *Timescape,* the John W. Campbell Memorial Award, and the Australian Ditmar Award. He is a Woodrow Wilson Fellow at Cambridge University, and was elected to the Royal Astronomical Society. Benford lives with his wife and two children in Laguna Beach, California.

MICHAEL BISHOP lives in Pine Mountain, Georgia. He is the author of many fantasy and science fiction stories, including three collections to date, and is twice winner of the Nebula Award for best short fiction. Of his sf novels, several have been nominated for major awards, and *No Enemy but Time* won the 1981 Nebula Award for best novel. His most recent novels are *Ancient of Days*, *The Secret Ascension* and *Unicorn Mountain*. "Apartheid, Superstrings, and Mordecai Thubana" was nominated for the 1989 World Fantasy Award for best novella.

R. V. BRANHAM has sold stories and novelettes to *Isaac Asimov's Science Fiction Magazine*, *Midnight Graffiti*, and *Ellery Queen's Mystery Magazine*, and to *Drawn to Words*, an Australian anthology. A native of Southern California, Branham divides time between a day job and a new sf novel.

TED CHIANG graduated from Brown University in 1989 with a degree in computer science. A graduate of the 1989 Clarion Writers' Workshop, he has sold stories to both *Omni* and *Isaac Asimov's Science Fiction Magazine*. He lives in Redmond, Washington, where he works as a technical writer.

TONY DANIEL has published poetry in *Star*line*, *Plains Poetry Review*, and *Isaac Asimov's Science Fiction Magazine*. He has published fiction in *Asimov's* and sold stories to the second volume in Robert Silverberg and Karen Haber's *Universe* anthology series and *The Magazine of Fantasy and Science Fiction*.

MARCOS DONNELLY made his first appearance as a published writer in *Full Spectrum 2* with his novelette "As a Still Small Voice." When he's not writing fiction, he works as a writer for a business communications agency in Rochester, New York. He lives with his wife Nancy Kress and two stepchildren in Brockport, New York, where he is at work on his first novel, *An Improper Apocalypse*.

KAREN JOY FOWLER studied at Berkeley and the University of California at Davis, and received an master's degree in political science. Her short story collection *Artificial Things* was published by Spectra in 1986, and in 1987 she received the John W. Campbell Award for best new writer.

ELIZABETH HAND's stories have been published in *Twilight Zone*, *Pulphouse*, and *Full Spectrum 2*, and her first novel, *Winterlong*, was published as a Bantam Spectra Special Edition in 1990. She is the author of numerous reviews and critical articles for *The Washington Post Book Review*, *Science Fiction Eye*, and *Penthouse*. Currently living on the coast of Maine, Hand is at work on her sequel to *Winterlong*, entitled *Aestival Tide*, to appear in the spring of 1992.

WOLFGANG JESCHKE was raised near Stuttgart, West Germany, and attended university in Munich, where he studied philosophy and German language and literature. His first novel was translated into six languages and won the Kurd Lasswitz Preis—the German equivalent of the Nebula Award. He has since earned the award five more times, and his most well-known work in the United States, the novella "Osiris Land" (published in *Isaac Asimov's Science Fiction Magazine)*, was nominated for the Nebula Award in 1985. Jeschke is the science fiction editor for the German publisher Heyne Verlag.

URSULA K. LE GUIN's published works range from poetry, essays, stories, and novels, including *Malafrena, The Lathe of Heaven,* and *The Left Hand of Darkness,* which was awarded the Hugo and Nebula awards for best science fiction novel in 1969. *The Dispossessed* won the Nebula Award in 1974. Le Guin's Earthsea books are also much honored. *The Tombs of Atuan* was a Newbery Honor Book, and *The Farthest Shore* won the National Book Award for Children's Books. She has two daughters and one son and lives with her husband in Portland, Oregon. Her most recent novel is *Tehanu: The Last Book of Earthsea.*

PEG KERR is a teacher of composition at the University of Minnesota and a student in the English doctoral program, specializing in science fiction and fantasy. She attended the Clarion Science Fiction Writers' Workshop in 1988. Kerr's fiction has been sold to and appeared in *Fantasy and Science Fiction, Amazing Stories, Pulphouse,* and *Weird Tales.* She lives with her husband in Richfield, Minnesota.

Since 1967, BARRY N. MALZBERG has published thirty science fiction novels and eight collections, the best known of which are *Beyond Apollo,* which won the John W. Campbell Award, and *The Man Who Loved the Midnight Lady.* His short stories have appeared in all the major science fiction magazines and in "best of the year" anthologies as well. Malzberg's novel *The Remaking of Sigmund Freud* and his short story "Corridors" were each Nebula Award finalists.

JACK McDEVITT has published two novels, *A Talent for War* and *The Hercules Text,* which won the Philip K. Dick Special Award and the Locus Award for best first novel. His story "The Fort Moxie Branch" was published in *Full Spectrum* and was a Nebula Award finalist.

JAMES MORROW's first fiction effort, *The Wine of Violence,* was called "the best SF novel published in English during the last ten years" by *The American Book Review.* He followed it with *The Continent of Lies* and *This Is the Way the World Ends,* the latter a Nebula Award finalist and runner-up for the John W. Campbell Memorial Award. His most recent novel is *Only Begotten Daughter.* Morrow's short story from *Full Spectrum,* "Bible Stories for Adults, No. 17: The Deluge," won the

1988 Nebula Award for best short story. He currently lives in State College, Pennsylvania, with his wife and two children.

PAT MURPHY lives in San Francisco, where she edits the *Exploratorium Quarterly*, a magazine of science, art, and human perception. In 1987 she won Nebula Awards both for her novel *The Falling Woman* and her novelette "Rachel in Love." Her short fiction has appeared in many magazines and anthologies and her collection *Points of Departure* was a Bantam Spectra Special Edition. Her most recent novel is *The City, Not Long After*, also published by Spectra.

MARK L. VAN NAME has published short fiction in the original anthologies *Tomorrow's Voices* and *When the Music's Over*, as well as in *Isaac Asimov's Science Fiction Magazine*.

KRISTINE KATHRYN RUSCH's first novel, *The White Mists of Power*, will be published in 1991, and she has sold fiction to anthologies and magazines such as *Boy's Life*, *The Magazine of Fantasy & Science Fiction*, *Isaac Asimov's Science Fiction Magazine*, *Amazing Stories*, and *Alfred Hitchcock's Mystery Magazine*. She won the John W. Campbell Award for best new writer, and her short fiction has been a finalist for both the Nebula Award and the Bram Stoker Award. Rusch is the senior editor for Pulphouse Publishing, and she won a World Fantasy Award with Dean Wesley Smith for her work on *Pulphouse: The Hardback Magazine*.

NORMAN SPINRAD's novels and short stories, including *Bug Jack Barron*, *Child of Fortune*, *The Void Captain's Tale*, and *Little Heroes*, have been translated into a dozen languages and nominated for many major awards, including the National Book Award. He is also the author of *Stayin' Alive: A Writer's Guide*. Spinrad's latest novel, *Russian Spring*, will be published in the fall of 1991. He is currently living in Paris.

NANCY WILLARD won the O. Henry Award and the Newbery Award for her novel *A Visit to William Blake's Inn*. She has published several volumes of short stories and poetry, as well as a number of books for children and the adult novel *Things Invisible to See*. She lives in Poughkeepsie, New York, and teaches in the English Department at Vassar College.

JOËLLE WINTREBERT lives with her husband, a professor of psychology, near Montpelier in France, where she is a well-known science fiction writer. She is the author of many books—recently *Comme une Few de Sarments*, a novel about a vineyard workers' strike in 1905. She was also the editor of the French anthology *Univers* for several years. KIM STANLEY ROBINSON has won the World Fantasy Award, the Nebula Award, and the Asimov Award for his science fiction. His most recent books are *The Gold Coast, A Short Sharp Shock, Pacific Edge,* and *Remaking History.* Robinson lives in Washington, D.C., with his wife and son, where he is at work on a trilogy about the colonization of Mars.

DAVID ZINDELL's short story "Shanidar" was a prize-winning entry in the Writers of the Future Contest. In 1986 he was nominated for the John W. Campbell Award for best new writer. *Neverness* was his first novel, published by Bantam Spectra. He is currently at work on his second novel.

ABOUT THE EDITORS

LOU ARONICA is Vice President and Publisher of Mass Market Paperbacks at Bantam Books and is Publisher of Bantam Spectra/Doubleday Foundation. He lives in Connecticut with his wife, Barbara, their daughter, Molly, and their son, David.

AMY STOUT is an Executive Editor at Bantam Books, and previously she worked at *Isaac Asimov's Science Fiction Magazine.* She lives in Connecticut with her husband, Alan Rodgers, and their daughters, Alexandra and Andrea.

BETSY MITCHELL is Associate Publisher of Bantam Spectra/Doubleday Foundation and has published short stories in *Analog* and *Twilight Zone.* She lives in Brooklyn with her husband and son.

The Deliverator belongs to an elite order, a hallowed subcategory. He's got esprit up to here. Right now he is preparing to carry out his third mission of the night. His uniform is black as activated charcoal, filtering the very light out of the air. A bullet will bounce off its arachnofiber weave like a wren hitting a patio door, but excess perspiration wafts through it like a breeze through a freshly napalmed forest. Where his body has bony extremities, the suit has sintered armorgel: feels like gritty jello, protects like a stack of telephone books.

When they gave him the job, they gave him a gun. The Deliverator never deals in cash, but someone might come after him anyway—might want his car, or his cargo. The gun is tiny, aero-styled, lightweight, the kind of gun a fashion designer would carry; it fires teensy darts that fly at five times the velocity of an SR-71 spy plane, and when you get done using it, you have to plug it into the cigarette lighter, because it runs on electricity.

The Deliverator never pulled that gun in anger, or in fear. He pulled it once in Gila Highlands. Some punks in Gila Highlands, a fancy Burbclave, wanted themselves a delivery, and they didn't want to pay for it. Thought they would impress the Deliverator with a baseball bat. The Deliverator took out his gun, centered its laser doohickey on that poised Louisville Slugger, fired it. The recoil was immense, as though the weapon had blown up in his hand. The middle third of the baseball bat turned into a column of burning sawdust accelerating in all directions like a bursting star. Punk ended up holding this bat handle with milky smoke pouring out the end. Stupid look on his face. Didn't get nothing but trouble from the Deliverator.

Since then the Deliverator has kept the gun in the glove compartment and relied, instead, on a matched set of samurai swords, which have always been his weapon of choice anyhow. The punks in Gila Highlands weren't afraid of the gun, so the Deliverator was forced to use it. But swords need no demonstrations.

The Deliverator's car has enough potential energy packed into its batteries to fire a pound of bacon into the Asteroid Belt. Unlike a bimbo box or a Burb beater, the Deliverator's car unloads that power through gaping, gleaming, polished sphincters. When the Deliverator puts the hammer down, shit happens. You want to talk contact patches? Your car's tires have tiny contact patches, talk to the asphalt in four places the size of your tongue. The Deliverator's car has big sticky tires with contact patches the size of a fat lady's thighs. The Deliverator is in touch with the road, starts like a bad day, stops on a peseta.

Why is the Deliverator so equipped? Because people rely on him. He is a roll model. This is America. People do whatever the fuck they feel like doing, you got a problem with that? Because they have a right to. And because they have guns and no one can fucking stop them. As a result, this country has one of the worst economies in the world. When it gets down to it—talking trade balances here—once we've brain-drained all our technology into other countries, once things have evened out, they're making cars in Bolivia and microwave ovens in Tadzhikistan and selling them here—once our edge in natural resources has been made irrelevant by giant Hong Kong ships and dirigibles that can ship North Dakota all the way to New Zealand for a nickel—once the Invisible Hand has taken all those historical inequities and smeared them out into a broad global layer of what a Pakistani brickmaker would consider to be prosperity—y'know what? There's only four things we do better than anyone else

music
movies
microcode (software)
high-speed pizza delivery

The Deliverator used to make software. Still does, some-times. But if life were a mellow elementary school run by well-meaning education Ph.D.s, the Deliverator's report card would say: "Hiro is *so* bright and creative but needs to work harder on his cooperation skills."

So now he has this other job. No brightness or creativity involved—but no cooperation either. Just a single principle: The Deliverator stands tall, your pie in thirty minutes or you can have it free, shoot the driver, take his car, file a class-action suit. The Deliverator has been working this job for six months, a rich and lengthy tenure by his standards, and has never delivered a pizza in more than twenty-one minutes.

Oh, they used to argue over times, many corporate driver-years lost to it: homeowners, red-faced and sweaty with their own lies, stinking of Old Spice and job-related stress, stand-ing in their glowing yellow doorways brandishing their Seikos and waving at the clock over the kitchen sink, I swear, can't you guys tell time?

Didn't happen any more. Pizza delivery a major industry. A managed industry. People went to CosaNostra Pizza Uni-versity fours years just to learn it. Came in its doors unable to write an English sentence, from Abkhazia, Rwanda, Guana-juato, South Jersey, and came out knowing more about pizza than a person should know. And they had studied this prob-lem. Graphed the frequency of doorway delivery-time dis-putes. Wired the early Deliverators to record, then analyze, the debating tactics, the voice-stress histograms, the distinc-tive grammatical structures employed by white middle-class Type A Burbclave occupants who against all logic had de-cided that this was the place to take their personal Custerian stand against all that was stale and deadening in their lives: they were going to lie, or delude themselves, about the time of their phone call and get themselves a free pizza; no, they deserved a free pizza along with their life, liberty, and pursuit of whatever, it was fucking inalienable. **Sent psychologists** out to these people's houses, gave them a free TV set to submit to an anonymous interview, hooked them to polygraphs, studied their brain waves as they showed them choppy, inexplicable movies of porn queens and late-night car crashes and Sammy Davis, Jr., put them in sweet-smelling, mauve-walled rooms and asked them questions about Ethics so perplexing that even a Jesuit couldn't respond without committing a venal sin.

The analysts at CosaNostra Pizza University concluded that it was just human nature and you couldn't fix it, and so they went for a quick cheap technical fix: smart boxes. The pizza box is a plastic carapace now, corrugated for stiffness, a little LED readout glowing on the side, telling the Deliverator how many trade imbalance-producing minutes have ticked away since the fateful phone call. There are chips and stuff in there. The pizzas rest, a short stack of them, in slots behind the Deliverator's head. Each pizza glides into a slot like a circuit board into a computer, clicks into place as the smart box interfaces with the onboard system of the Deliverator's car. The address of the caller has already been inferred from his phone number and poured into the smart box's built-in RAM. From there it is communicated to the car, which computes and projects the optimal route on a heads-up display, a glowing colored map traced out against the windshield so that the Deliverator does not even have to glance down.

If the thirty-minute deadline expires, news of the disaster is flashed to CosaNostra Pizza Headquarters and relayed from there to Uncle Enzo himself—the Sicilian Colonel Sanders, the Andy Griffith of Bensonhurst, the straight razor-swinging figment of many a Deliverator's nightmares, the Capo and prime figurehead of CosaNostra Pizza, Incorporated—who will be on the phone to the customer within five minutes, apologizing profusely. The next day, Uncle Enzo will land on the customer's yard in a jet helicopter and apologize some more and give him a free trip to Italy—all he has to do is sign a bunch of releases that make him a public figure and spokesperson for CosaNostra Pizza and basically end his private life as he knows it. He will come away from the whole thing feeling that, somehow, he owes the Mafia a favor.

The Deliverator does not know for sure what happens to

the driver in such cases, but he has heard some rumors. Most pizza deliveries happen in the evening hours, which Uncle Enzo considers to be his private time. And how would you feel if you had to interrupt dinner with your family in order to call some obstreperous dork in a Burbclave and grovel for a late fucking pizza? Uncle Enzo has not put in fifty years serving his family and his country so that, at the age when most are playing golf and bobbling their granddaughters, he can get out of the bathtub dripping wet and lie down and kiss the feet of some sixteen-year-old skate punk whose pepperoni was thirty-one minutes in coming. Oh, God. It makes the Deliverator breathe a little shallower just to think of the idea.

But he wouldn't drive for CosaNostra Pizza any other way. You know why? Because there's something about having your life on the line. It's like being a kamikaze pilot. Your mind is clear. Other people—store clerks, burger flippers, software engineers, the whole vocabulary of meaningless jobs that make up Life in America—other people just rely on plain old competition. Better flip your burgers or debug your subroutines faster and better than your high school classmate two blocks down the strip is flipping or debugging, because we're in competition with those guys, and people notice these things.

What a fucking rat race that is. CosaNostra Pizza doesn't have any competition. Competition goes against the Mafia ethic. You don't work harder because you're competing against some identical operation down the street. You work harder because everything is on the line. Your name, your honor, your family, your life. Those burger flippers might have a better life expectancy—but what kind of life is it anyway, you have to ask yourself. That's why nobody, not even the Nipponese, can move pizzas faster than CosaNostra. The Deliverator is proud to wear the uniform, proud to drive the car, proud to march up the front walks of innumerable Burbclave homes, a grim vision in ninja black, a pizza on his shoulder, red LED digits blazing proud numbers into the night: 12:23 or 15:15 or the occasional 20:43.

The Deliverator is assigned to CosaNostra Pizza #3569 in the Valley. Southern California doesn't know whether to bustle or just strangle itself on the spot. Not enough roads for the number of people. Fairlanes, Inc. is laying new ones all the time. Have to bulldoze lots of neighborhoods to do it, but those seventies and eighties developments exist to be bull-dozed, right? No sidewalks, no schools, no nothing. Don't have their own police force—no immigration control—undesirables can walk right in without being frisked or even harassed. Now a Burbclave, that's the place to live. A city-state with its own constitution, a border, laws, cops, everything.

The Deliverator was a corporal in the Farms of Merryvale State Security Force for a while once. Got himself fired for pulling a sword on an acknowledged perp. Slid it right through the fabric of the perp's shirt, gliding the flat of the blade along the base of his neck, and pinned him to a warped and bubbled expanse of vinyl siding on the wall of the house that the perp was trying to break into. Thought it was a pretty righteous bust. But they fired him anyway because the perp turned out to be the son of the vice-chancellor of the Farms of Merryvale. Oh, the weasels had an excuse: said that a thirty-six-inch samurai sword was not on their Weapons Protocol. Said that he had violated the SPAC, the Suspected Perpetrator Apprehension Code. Said that the perp had suffered psycho-logical trauma. He was afraid of butter knives now; he had to spread his jelly with the back of a teaspoon. They said that he had exposed them to liability.

The Deliverator had to borrow some money to pay for it. Had to borrow it from the Mafia, in fact. So he's in their database now—retinal patterns, DNA, voice graph, finger-prints, footprints, palm prints, wrist prints, every fucking part of the body that had wrinkles on it—almost—those bastards rolled in ink and made a print and digitized it into their computer. But it's their money—sure they're careful about loaning it out. And when he applied for the Deliverator job they were happy to take him, because they knew him. When he got the loan, he had to deal personally with the assistant vice-capo of the Valley, who later recommended him for the Deliverator job. So it was like being in a family. A really scary, twisted, abusive family.

CosaNostra Pizza #3569 is on Vista Road just down from Kings Park Mall. Vista Road used to belong to the State of California and now is called Fairlanes, Inc. Rte. CSV-5. Its main competition used to be a U.S. highway and is now called Cruiseways, Inc. Rte. Cal-12. Farther up the Valley, the two competing highways actually cross. Once there had been bitter disputes, the intersection closed by sporadic sniper fire. Finally, a big developer bought the entire intersection and turned it into a drive-through mall. Now the roads just feed into a parking system—not a lot, not a ramp, but a system—and lose their identity. Getting through the intersection involves tracing paths through the parking system, many braided filaments of direction like the Ho Chi Minh trail. CSV-5 has better throughput, but Cal-12 has better pavement. That is typical—Fairlanes roads emphasize getting you there, for Type A drivers, and Cruiseways emphasize the enjoyment of the ride, for Type B drivers.

The Deliverator is a Type A driver with rabies. He is zeroing in on his home base, CosaNostra Pizza #3569, cranking up the left lane of CSV-5 at a hundred and twenty kilometers. His car is an invisible black lozenge, just a dark place that reflects the tunnel of franchise signs—the loglo. A row of orange lights burbles and churns across the front, where the grille would be if this were an air-breathing car. The orange light looks like a gasoline fire. It comes in through people's rear windows, bounces off their rearview mirrors, projects a fiery mask across their eyes, reaches into their subconscious, and unearths terrible fears of being pinned, fully conscious, under a detonating gas tank, makes them want to pull over and let the Deliverator overtake them in his black chariot of pepperoni fire.

The loglo, overhead, marking out CSV-5 in twin contrails, is a body of electrical light made of innumerable cells, each cell designed in Manhattan by imageers who make more for designing a single logo than a Deliverator will make in his entire lifetime. Despite their efforts to stand out, they all smear together, especially at a hundred and twenty kilometers per hour. Still, it is easy to see CosaNostra Pizza #3569 because of the billboard, which is wide and tall even by current inflated standards. In fact, the squat franchise itself looks like nothing more than a low-slung base for the great aramidfiber pillars that thrust the billboard up into the trademark firmament. Marca Registrada, baby.

The billboard is a classic, a chestnut, not a figment of some fleeting Mafia promotional campaign. It is a statement, a monument built to endure. Simple and dignified. It shows Uncle Enzo in one of his spiffy Italian suits. The pinstripes glint and flex like sinews. The pocket square is luminous. His hair is perfect, slicked back with something that never comes off, each strand cut off straight and square at the end by Uncle Enzo's cousin, Art the Barber, who runs the second-largest chain of low-end haircutting establishments in the world. Uncle Enzo is standing there, not exactly smiling, an avuncular glint in his eye for sure, not posing like a model but standing there like your uncle would, and it says

The Mafia
you've got a friend in The Family!
paid for by the Our Thing Foundation

The billboard serves as the Deliverator's polestar. He knows that when he gets to the place on CSV-5 where the bottom corner of the billboard is obscured by the pseudo-Gothic stained-glass arches of the local Reverend Wayne's Pearly Gates franchise, it's time for him to get over into the right lanes where the retards and the bimbo boxes poke along, random, indecisive, looking at each passing franchise's driveway like they don't know if it's a promise or a threat.

He cuts off a bimbo box—a family minivan—veers past the Buy 'n' Fly that is next door, and pulls into CosaNostra Pizza #3569. Those big fat contact patches complain, squeal a little bit, but they hold onto the patented Fairlanes, Inc. high-traction pavement and guide him into the chute. No other Deliverators are waiting in the chute. That is good, that means high turnover for him, fast action, keep moving that 'za. As he scrunches to a stop, the electromechanical hatch on the flank of his car is already opening to reveal his empty pizza slots, the door clicking and folding back in on itself like the wing of a beetle. The slots are waiting. Waiting for hot pizza.

And waiting. The Deliverator honks his horn. This is not a nominal outcome.

Window slides open. That should never happen. You can look at the three-ring binder from CosaNostra Pizza University, cross-reference the citation for *window chute, dispatcher's*, and it will give you all the procedures for that window—and it should never be opened. Unless something has gone wrong.

The window slides open and—you sitting down?—*smoke* comes out of it. The Deliverator hears a discordant beetling over the metal hurricane of his sound system and realizes that it is a smoke alarm, coming from inside the franchise.

Mute button on the stereo. Oppressive silence—his eardrums uncringe—the window is buzzing with the cry of the smoke alarm. The car idles, waiting. The hatch has been open too long, atmospheric pollutants are congealing on the electrical contacts in the back of the pizza slots, he'll have to clean them ahead of schedule, everything is going exactly the way it shouldn't go in the three-ring binder that spells out all the rhythms of the pizza universe.

Inside, a football-shaped Abkhazian man is running to and fro, holding a three-ring binder open, using his spare tire as a ledge to keep it from collapsing shut; he runs with the gait of a man carrying an egg on a spoon. He is shouting in the Abkhazian dialect; all the people who run CosaNostra pizza franchises in this part of the Valley are Abkhazian immigrants.

It does not look like a serious fire. The Deliverator saw a real fire once, at the Farms of Merryvale, and you couldn't see anything for the smoke. That's all it was: smoke, burbling out of nowhere, occasional flashes of orange light down at the bottom, like heat lightning in tall clouds. This is not that kind of fire. It is the kind of fire that just barely puts out enough smoke to detonate the smoke alarms. And he is losing time for this shit.

The Deliverator holds the horn button down. The Abkhazian manager comes to the window. He is supposed to use the intercom to talk to drivers, he could say anything he wanted and it would be piped straight into the Deliverator's car, but no, he has to talk face to face, like the Deliverator is some kind of fucking ox cart driver. He is red-faced, sweating, his eyes roll as he tries to think of the English words.

"A fire, a little one," he says.

The Deliverator says nothing. Because he knows that all of this is going onto videotape. The tape is being pipelined, as it happens, to CosaNostra Pizza University, where it will be analyzed in a pizza management science laboratory. It will be shown to Pizza University students, perhaps to the very students who will replace this man when he gets fired, as a textbook example of how to screw up your life.

"New employee—put his dinner in the microwave—had foil in it—boom!" the manager says.

Abkhazia had been part of the Soviet fucking Union. A new immigrant from Abkhazia trying to operate a microwave was like a deep-sea tube worm doing brain surgery. Where did they get these guys? Weren't there any Americans who could bake a fucking pizza?

"Just give me one pie," the Deliverator says.

Talking about pies snaps the guy into the current century. He gets a grip. He slams the window shut, strangling the relentless keening of the smoke alarm.

A Nipponese robot arm shoves the pizza out and into the top slot. The hatch folds shut to protect it.

As the Deliverator is pulling out of the chute, building up speed, checking the address that is flashed across his windshield, deciding whether to run right or left, it happens. His stereo cuts out again—on command of the onboard system. The cockpit lights go red. *Red.* A repetitive buzzer begins to sound. The LED readout on his windshield, which echoes the one on the pizza box, flashes up: 20:00.

They have just given the Deliverator a twenty-minute-old pizza. He checks the address; it is twelve miles away.

Snow Crash by Neal Stephenson, is available in bookstores now—wherever Bantam books are sold.